For Frank

The Bookers:

San Francisco Memories

Warm regards,

Don Becker
June 17, 2007

The Bookers:
San Francisco Memories

A Novel

Don C. Becker

iUniverse, Inc.
New York Lincoln Shanghai

The Bookers: *San Francisco Memories*
A Novel

iUniverse books may be ordered through booksellers or by contacting:

iUniverse
2021 Pine Lake Road, Suite 100
Lincoln, NE 68512
www.iuniverse.com
1-800-Authors (1-800-288-4677)

This is a work of fiction. All of the characters, names, incidents, organizations, and dialogue in this novel are either the products of the author's imagination or are used fictitiously.

ISBN: 978-0-595-41267-9 (pbk)
ISBN: 978-0-595-85623-7 (ebk)

Printed in the United States of America

We were passing through Utopia and didn't know it.

—H. L. Mencken

Fact and fiction are so intermingled in my work that now, looking back on it, I can hardly distinguish one from the other.

—W. Somerset Maugham

Prologue

I can't believe I am really going to start this project. I don't have to be here hunched over my laptop. It's another beautiful sunny January morning. The temperature is in the low seventies. There are no clouds. I could be watching the surfers at Zipper's or humbling myself on the fairways of the nearby Jack Nicklaus—designed Palmilla Golf Club, of which I am a member. I could be on the beach down the steps from our house walking in the gentle shore break. A few hundred yards away, near the Palmilla Hotel, I might arrange for a fishing trip with one of the local boatmen. Or I could be shopping for organic fruits and vegetables with my wife at a farm just outside the nearby town of San Jose del Cabo, perhaps taking a break later over a strong cup of Mexican-style coffee.

Usually, at this time of morning, I am reading on our balcony overlooking the Sea of Cortez, caressed by cool breezes. But instead, I am finally starting something I promised I would tackle nearly two years ago, doing something I have never tried before: writing a book about my family, the Bookers.

I've been wintering here in the beautiful Los Cabos area of Mexico for four years. I have played a lot of golf, caught plenty of fish, and stayed healthy by hiking on the beach and swimming parallel to the shore in the ocean. I've enjoyed my share of food and drink. Now I want to do something more lasting.

I am not sure if this will ever become a book for general publication. Rather, I begin with the modest aspiration that I am writing this story for present and future adult generations of the

Booker family. Of course, I want to write in such a way that it will be of interest to anyone who may chance to read it in 2007, or in 2107. Part of my motivation is to relive a great life with a great family. At age seventy, I am still not sure what motivates me. Surely this effort will lead to the discovery of new insights. Will this be a morality tale? Will I be lacing this book with advice for the new generation of Bookers by way of examples, good and bad, of how the older generation lived, reflecting on what is clearly a bygone era?

My plan is to write two or three chapters a week and cover, chronologically, events over eight decades that I think are important or interesting. I will try not to get bogged down in trivia. Still, there is much to tell, some of which will require a bit of literary license. So if I become an all-seeing narrator from time to time, be assured that I am basing what I say on some solid reporting and that I am not being loose with the facts.

Let us begin.

CHAPTER 1

I have on my desk a wonderful black-and-white photo, a headshot of my mother that I had copied from a snapshot onto glossy eight-by-ten paper quite a few years ago. It was taken in Hawaii in 1932 when my mother was eighteen, a year before she was put into a family way by a young second lieutenant, a recent graduate from the West Point Military Academy on temporary assignment in Hawaii. She is smiling, showing even white teeth. A garland of tropical flowers is around her neck. I don't know what the occasion was. Although the blowup is fuzzy, there is no mistaking her beauty—not classical beauty so much as youthful beauty and energy and a mirthful look in her eyes. Oh, those big round eyes. The whites are brilliantly white and the irises (which were a lustrous blue-gray in real life) show up pale and delicate in the photo. Her eyelashes appear surprisingly thick and her curly hair is naturally blonde and frames her face in the custom of that post-flapper period. Her skin is clear and slightly tanned. If she ever had a blemish or pimple on her face, there is no evidence of it. Her mouth may be a bit wide and her nose smallish, in comparison with her broad forehead.

I don't pretend to know a lot about my mother's family background, only what she told me, a lot of which I have forgotten.

I do know she was born in Honolulu, the only daughter of the Rev. Pardon Crandall Connors and his wife, Mary Teresa Cosgrove, who came to the islands in 1900 from Boston to run a small church and school near Honolulu. Pardon, a tall, slightly corpulent man with kindly features, was a third-generation Episcopalian minister. He had been an associate at St. Paul's in Boston and director of the church choir when he met Mary Teresa, who had joined the choir just after her fifteenth birthday. My mother told me that when young, my grandmother, Mary Teresa, had the face of an angel on a body just five feet tall. Mary Teresa's equally diminutive father, Patrick Cosgrove, had driven a horse-drawn beer wagon in suburban Boston and apparently loved to drink and was seldom home. Mary Teresa's mother, my great-grandmother, was an Irish immigrant named Cathleen O'Toole, whose only surviving description is that she was deeply religious.

The Rev. Pardon Connors, at twenty-nine, was nearly twice Mary Teresa's age when they first met, but he fell hopelessly in love with her. She found him to be a commanding father figure, and herself being full of the teachings of Christ (thanks to her mother), she fell in love with him for his virtue, godliness, and, perhaps most importantly, his devotion to her. Two years later, Pardon Crandall Connors, thirty-one, and Mary Teresa Cosgrove, seventeen, married and subsequently accepted an appointment in Hawaii, where the church needed young couples capable of handling difficult times and willing to set the example of virtuous Christian living. Rev. Pardon Crandall Connors, according to my mother, converted many souls and lived an exemplary life. Mary Teresa was well regarded for her sweetness and devotion to her husband and his works.

My mother, the first and only child, did not come along until fourteen years into the Connors' marriage. She was named Constance Elizabeth Connors, born on March 21, 1914. She was indulged from the moment she emerged from her mother's womb, showcased as a gift from God to the long-barren marriage. My mother told me that in her early years, she was surrounded by all kinds of people, including many native Hawaiians who attended her father's church. Constance had her mother's angelic face, sparkling eyes, very blonde hair, and a wide and ready smile. But my mother said that as she grew up, she realized she was different. To begin with, by the time she was thirteen, Constance was five feet seven inches tall, gangling, flat-chested, and full of fun, but only average at school, despite stern admonishments from her father. Second, my mother was not interested in religion nearly as much as her parents expected. Oh, she attended church and said her prayers, but by her own admission, she was just going through the motions. Her main interest as a teenager was boys, and she had a flock of admirers in all shapes and sizes. She loved the attention. As she filled out into womanhood, she became stunningly attractive. She loved the beach and sports and had native Hawaiian boyfriends as well as boyfriends from Honolulu's wealthiest classes. She did not discriminate. She had her pick. They were either fun, or they weren't. She had the good sense to hold onto her virginity ("I never went all the way until I met your father," she told me many years later), but I suspect there were a few close calls. Of course, the Rev. Connors disapproved of the undisciplined lifestyle his daughter had fashioned. Much to his dismay, she had no interest in going to college. My mother told me that although her father would get angry with her, she knew he loved her very much. She could always bring him around to her way of thinking, which my mother said was probably made easier by the fact he was forty-five years older than she was. And my mother had a way about her, a smile that could melt the resistance of any man susceptible to the charms of radiant beauty. Even so, my mother admitted years later that her father had more than once said that though she had inherited his height and his wife's loveliness, she had also inherited the undisciplined and unredeemed spirit of the Cosgrove family, none of whom, he said, had ever amounted to anything. But such an accusation seemed abstract to my mother, because she had never even met a member of the Cosgrove family other than her mother, who herself was amazingly without blemish in her daughter's eyes.

I wish I knew more about my mother's childhood and life in Hawaii and about my grandparents. I suspect that my mother's rebelliousness was mostly natural but also probably was fed by the wide generation gap and the very conservative lifestyle of her parents. Even so, she always said she dearly loved her mom and dad and had the highest respect for them both. As I begin to write this memoir, I am kicking myself that I did not ask my mother a lot more questions about her family. I can't believe my own lack of curiosity. But then, like my mother, I was never good in school and never tried to be, and I didn't like it. Mother said I might have inherited a few too many of those much maligned Cosgrove genes.

CHAPTER 2

I have another blown-up snapshot of my mother on her wedding day, November 15, 1933. She's wearing a loose-fitting, long white dress that was flowing in the ever-present Hawaiian breezes. Smiling and looking radiant, she's holding onto her white, wide-brimmed hat. Next to her, in his military dress whites, is Second Lieutenant Joseph Holt Booker. He has his arm around my mother's waist, and he too is smiling broadly. They make a very handsome couple, and there is no sign of my brother, who at the time of the photo was to emerge from my mother's lithe nineteen-year-old figure in just six months. Also in the photo, which appears to have been taken on the steps of a small church, are the Rev. Pardon Crandall Connors and his wife, Mary Teresa. The Rev. Connors appears to be smiling through a state of shock, and there is a vacant, slightly distraught look on Mary Teresa's face. Maybe I am reading too much of my own imagination into this. But when the photo was taken, Constance, their beloved only daughter, was about to leave for the mainland, for Fort Riley, Kansas, where her husband, my father, was to undertake his second assignment as an officer in the U.S. Army.

Those early days of my family's life were always hazy to me until after my mother died. Although Constance Connors was not a good student, she kept a sporadic and sometimes detailed diary. In fact, she kept eight diaries in her life, or at least that is what I found among her possessions in a storeroom of her San Francisco condo. It is safe to say that without those diaries, I could not have envisioned writing this book.

"Joe has found us a wonderful honeymoon cottage on the beach not far from Hilo," my mother had written on November 17, 1933, continuing,

> We went swimming and walking when we arrived yesterday. It was lovely to just be together and alone. I don't know what got into me, but last night after dinner I began crying and I could

> not stop. Joe held me in his arms and said how much he loved me and how sorry he was that we had to get married. He said he wanted to marry me from the first time he saw me, but he never thought it would happen, because I was so young, and he was only on temporary duty in Hawaii. Maybe it was God's will, he said. That made me cry even more. Joe, patient man that he is, held me for almost the whole night, repeating over and over how much he loved me, how happy he was, how lucky he was, and how much he wanted to make me happy. When I finally stopped crying, he kissed me for a long time. He has such sweet lips and his mouth tasted good. We made love, and for the first time, I realized how wonderful that could be. Maybe Joe is right—he is such a handsome and thoughtful person. Maybe it is God's will.

In her diary entries for the next eight days, my mother employed certain code signs and numbers. I think the code related to the number of times they had sex. If I am right, my parents got off to a very active and healthy start in their marriage. One entry said,

> Joe told me tonight that holding me in his arms was the most wonderful and beautiful thing that had ever happened to him. He said he could not describe how wonderful it made him feel and that every night he thanked God for bringing me into his life. I really never expected to get married this early, but no matter how long I waited I don't think I would ever find a better person than Joe. I get a thrill when I see him come into the room, and when he touches me I almost shiver with excitement.

Joe Booker, my father, was born in Tupelo, Mississippi, on December 11, 1909. He came from a prominent family that had its origins in Virginia in the late seventeenth century. Both tall and attractive with a square-cut face and well-proportioned features, he was a good student and a good athlete and seemed to have everything. When he was fourteen, both of his parents were killed when the car they were riding in during a heavy rainstorm slid off the road into a raging river. Joe grieved for a year, drifted, and lost his focus. He was passed from one relative to another before moving in with his uncle, Colonel Jeremiah Holt, a retired army officer who had served in France in World War I and who had also fought in the Philippines during the Spanish-American war. Jeremiah, a widower, gave his full attention to getting his nephew back on track. He loved to regale the youngster with war stories. My father told me once when I was very young that living for four years with Jeremiah changed his life, because it made him realize the importance of service and character and that life was really all about overcoming difficulties. I think the subject arose when I had come home crying with a black eye, having been pulverized by a neighborhood bully.

It was living with Jeremiah that led my father to be interested in the military. When Jeremiah asked my father if he would like to apply to West Point, my father said he definitely would. Jeremiah apparently had the connections, and my dad had the scholastic credentials. He was accepted. Dad told me that except for his freshman year in high school, he was always at or near the top of his class. He also played on the football and baseball teams, both of which he captained in his senior year. Although several girls let Dad know how much they liked him during his years in school, he told me that he really never had time for serious relationships. He said the first and only time he ever fell in love was with my mother, when he met her at a military ball in Hawaii. They had both gone with friends and without dates, and at some point in the evening, Dad had asked my mother to dance.

"That was it," he told me while on his last home leave before being shipped back to Europe during World War II. "We were married five months later. I felt like the luckiest man who ever lived. And I still feel that way. Your mother is the most beautiful person I have ever met, on the inside and the outside. I hope you and your brothers appreciate what you have in your mother."

I don't recall saying it, but in my heart I knew I had the best possible parents in the world.

CHAPTER 3

The winter of 1934 was a trying time for my mother, who had only known the verdant, tropical climate of Hawaii. The landscape surrounding Fort Riley, Kansas, was barren, flat, and bleak. The winds howled across the dry plains, making the cold days even colder. In February of that year, Mother wrote in her diary that more than thirty inches of snow had fallen in just one day. Constance felt trapped in the family's small quarters. Her morning sickness drained her energy as the infant inside her grew larger. She realized how mightily her life had changed, all by an interlude created by alcohol and bad judgment that had lasted only a few minutes. Oh, how she was being punished, alone most of the time in a horrible place with horrible weather. Oh, how she missed her life of fun and laughter in Hawaii, the magnificent weather that she had taken for granted, and the lovely lush landscape, so different from Kansas, where in winter, almost everything was dead or dormant.

"Joe is putting in long hours training, and next week he is going to be gone the entire week for a field exercise," my mother wrote in her diary, dated March 6, 1934, fifteen days before her twentieth birthday. She continued,

> I can't believe they are going to be living in tents in this weather. But Joe says it is a good thing to do, because he will be getting close to the men in his platoon, and they will be doing long marches and war exercises. He says his uncle, Jeremiah, always said that training is crucial and has to be taken seriously if everyone is to be ready for the next war. My mother said in a letter today that she and Daddy miss me very much and understand how lonely I must feel. I wrote back and said that we were doing very well but that I missed Hawaii and them especially. I didn't say how miserable I felt. The only time I am happy is when Joe is around. I have met most of the officers' wives, and they are nice and seem to want to help me. Most of them are older, and we don't have a lot in common. But I am looking forward to May and having the baby. If it is a boy, we are going to call him Joe Jr.

In a diary entry dated March 10, 1934, my mother wrote,

> Alice Combs, whose husband Tim was at West Point with Joe, invited me to stay with her while our husbands are away. I offered to pay my share of the expenses for the week, and she accepted. Alice is a very nice person, though she is rather plain looking and looks older than 22. She is also pregnant, and her baby is expected almost the same time as mine. Alice went to two years of college in Connecticut, which she said was just across the Hudson River from West Point, where she met Tim. Alice says that Joe and I are the best-looking couple at Ft. Riley and that Joe has a very good reputation and that he finished in

> the top third of his class at West Point, something he never told me. Joe never likes to brag. She also said it was very hard for someone from Tupelo, Mississippi to ever get into West Point because of ill will created by the Civil War. She says she thinks that is why Joe does not have such a strong southern accent, that he is unconsciously trying to blend in. Alice can be very frank and sometimes she shocks me with what she says. She reads a lot, and she says her favorite author is Edith Wharton, who she says I have to read. I'm going to start as soon as I get the chance. I am very grateful to have a friend like Alice.

The friendship between Alice and Constance grew during their week living together. On March 12, my mother wrote,

> Alice is a very interesting person to be with, not like any woman I have ever known. Today she told me about Ft. Riley and said it had been a very important and historic place ever since its opening in 1852. She said the horse soldiers were stationed here to protect the pioneers heading west from the Indians. Later they helped protect the workers who were building the trans-continental railroad. I asked her how she knew that, and she said she read about it in the library. She also told me about the life of Gen. George Custer, who she said was quite a handsome and dashing figure who came to Ft. Riley in 1866 after the Civil War and was in charge of the 7th Cavalry fighting the Indians. She said there were many books written about him but that the big thing was the Battle of Little Bighorn in Montana, when Custer and his men were annihilated by the Indians in 1876. She had many interesting details about Custer's life, and she showed me a book with his picture. He was quite handsome. I will have to ask Joe if he knows about Custer.

On March 15, my mother wrote,

> Alice asked me if I knew what horrible disaster the month of March was known for at Ft. Riley, and of course, I didn't. She said it was the month a lot of people thought the flu epidemic of 1918 began, which killed some 600,000 Americans. She said it started right here in Ft. Riley. Back then, she said, there were 26,000 men stationed at Ft. Riley, and there were many thousands of horses, all of whom created a lot of manure, tons of it, which they got rid of by burning. Alice said that she had read that on March 9, 1918, a severe dust storm occurred, and it combined with the smoke from the manure fires to darken the sun and caused everyone's eyes to sting and got a lot of people coughing. Within a week there were more than 100 cases of flu, and a number of soldiers died. Those were the first cases of flu reported, and it spread from Ft. Riley and Kansas all around the states, but also to Europe when the soldiers from here were shipped to fight in France. Alice said I should go with her to the library and she would show me lots of books I would find interesting. Alice certainly has a great deal of curiosity, and she loves to tell me things. If I had met someone like Alice earlier, I might have wanted to go to college.

My mother clearly grew as a person during that dreary winter in Kansas. She also grew in her respect for her husband.

"I asked Joe if he knew anything about Gen. George Custer," she wrote in her diary, dated March 20, 1934.

> He said that Custer was one of the most intriguing and misunderstood soldiers who ever lived. He said that all most people remember about him was that he lost his life and all of the men under his direct command at Little Bighorn. Joe said

> Custer had 650 soldiers in his regiment but divided them into three groups. He had no idea that the Indian encampment numbered between 10,000 and 15,000 and that the number of warriors was an estimated 2,500. Custer and his cavalry unit numbered 197 men, all of whom were massacred in just under an hour by a charge led by Crazy Horse. Joe said the commander was ultimately responsible but that it was faulty intelligence that cost him the battle. He said Custer never would have divided his forces if he knew there were so many Indian warriors at Little Bighorn. Joe said what people forgot about Custer was that he was one of the most successful commanders in the Civil War, never having lost a battle. Joe said that he was fearless, was always at the front of his men, and eleven times he had his horse shot out from under him. Joe said that unlike most officers, he did not drink, did not smoke, and was a devout believer in God. He was an acting general by the time he was twenty-three and he spent fourteen years of his thirty-seven years on this earth fighting either Indians or the soldiers from the South. Joe said his uncle Jeremiah believed Custer to be one of the greatest, most daring soldiers who ever lived, and he proved it in battle after battle. When I hear about people like Gen. Custer or the great flu epidemic, it makes me feel how insignificant my discomforts are. I love learning about history, especially when you are at the place where things happened.

Entries in my mother's diary show that she and Alice spent an increasing amount of time together, and subsequently, their little group of pregnant women was expanded to five—all of which had the effect of reducing my mother's loneliness and her apprehensions about pending motherhood and of helping her accept the fact that even though she had only just turned twenty, she was a very married woman and, I would infer, a happy person. That was true about my mother all of her life. No matter how severe the problem, no matter how tragic the event, she would, after a time, overcome it completely. But it helped her to be around the right kind of people, and Alice Combs played an important role in my mother's maturation.

"We had the most wonderful time at the Officer's Club Spring Dance last night," my mother wrote in mid-April.

> We were at a table with five couples, including Alice and Tim, and there was a live orchestra with terrific male and female singers. I must have danced every dance even though the baby is due in less than a month. I have never had so many compliments in all of my life, and Tim told me that everyone thought I was the most beautiful woman at Ft. Riley. I know that is not true, because there were a lot of women at the dance who looked beautiful, but it was nice to hear it. The singer sounded a lot like Russ Colombo, and when he sang "I'm Just a Prisoner of Love," Joe danced with me and said he was a prisoner of love. He said, "I'm so proud of you. I love you more than I can put into words." Joe always says the right thing, especially when he has had a couple of drinks. I love him too, and I am proud to say it. I thank God he is my husband. He was very understanding after the dance when he wanted to make love, and I said I did not think it was such a good idea with the baby due. Actually, Alice was the one who told me that it was best to avoid sex during the last two months, and I can understand that it is probably a good thing not to have someone poking around inside you so close to the baby.

CHAPTER 4

Spring of 1934 arrived at Fort Riley a bit later than usual, and my mother could not have been more pleased at the passing of the most miserable weather she could imagine.

"I don't think I ever really appreciated flowers or greenery until being forced to live without them," she wrote on April 21.

> I cannot for the life of me understand why anyone would choose to live in a place like this. Thank goodness Joe is in the army, and we won't have to stay here for much more than three years. He says there is a good chance that we might be sent to the Philippines after our time is up here. Some of the West Point graduates from his class are already there with their wives. He said everyone has servants, and life is supposed to be pretty good except for the hot weather, which he said is also very humid. Today the weather was perfect, about 70 degrees with a soft wind. Alice Combs and I went for a long walk around the post, which she told me covers 20,000 acres. Alice knows everything. She is due to have her baby in a week or so, and she looks it. I was amazed at how fast she can still walk. I was sort of lagging behind her after awhile, even though my baby isn't due until the middle of May. Yesterday we went to a meeting of the Officers' Wives Club. Alice said all the wives of the second lieutenants are at the bottom of the ladder and are not expected to say anything, but we will get to do a lot of the work. She explained that the club is always headed by the wife of the commanding officer, speaking of whom, we are invited to a dinner at his house in two weeks. I feel a bit nervous, but Alice says to just smile and say thank you and laugh if someone tells a joke. I hope I am feeling okay. Ethel Crumbine is going to join us for a walk tomorrow. Her baby is not due until September.

On May 2, my mother wrote,

> I was so proud of Joe at the general's dinner last night. There were only four couples there, and it was quite an honor to be invited. I was seated next to the general, and he asked me about life in Hawaii and what it was like growing up there. He laughed when I said it was wonderful, but it had not prepared me for Kansas. I asked the general where he had been in his army career, and that took care of the conversation for the next thirty minutes, anyway. At the end, everyone was listening to the general, but he seemed to be directing his comments to me. The general said many interesting things and said his worst experience was being gassed in France during the war. He said it took months to fully recover. What made me proud of Joe was what he had to say after we finished eating and the general went around the table, asking the men what they felt was the most important issue facing the army. He said to keep it short so the ladies would not be bored. One of the other two officers, a major, said he felt that development of the Air Corps was the most important. The captain said he agreed and said there would never be another trench war like World War I. Joe said he agreed on both points. But he said he felt the men on the ground would always be crucial and their needs could not be forgotten. He said, from what he understood, that the army was not ready for any serious combat and that it lacked tanks and weapons. He said that infantrymen badly needed modern rifles and should not be forced to use the thirty-three-year-old Springfield models. The general nodded his head as Joe was talking. He said that all three of his guests were right and that the trouble was that the people in Washington really believed that World War I was the war to end all wars. He said, in addition, the American people would never agree to go back to Europe. But then he said anyone who thinks there won't be

> another war has forgotten his history. I certainly hope the general is wrong. I would hate to think of Joe off fighting. It is bad enough when he goes on those field exercises. After dinner we walked back home and Joe put his arm around me and said "Honey, you really wowed them tonight. You had the general eating out of your hand." I laughed and said I thought the general was going to promote Joe on the spot. Joe said that in peacetime, army promotions come very slowly and that he probably would not make first lieutenant until another three years. He also said the army had not raised its pay scale since 1920. Well, at least we have money coming in, enough to live on. That's more than can be said for millions of Americans who don't even have a job.

Joseph Holt Booker, Jr., was born on May 17, 1934. He weighed seven pounds and six ounces and, in the words of his mother, was "perfect in every way, a perfect example of God's will." Constance Connors Booker, two months into her twentieth year, was in labor for four hours and said afterward that the experience was not nearly as bad as she expected. Earlier, Mother had written about Alice's nine hours of labor in giving birth to her child, who weighed nine pounds and had a slightly misshapen head, though the doctors said that it would straighten out over time.

"Little Joe is nursing with a lot of energy, and I must say that giving him milk is one of the most satisfying things I have ever done," my mother wrote on June 23, continuing,

> I don't care if it causes my breasts to sag a little. Thank goodness they aren't as big as Alice's. Hers are practically down to her waist. I don't know why men get so excited about breasts. Joe says mine are the perfect size. Joe says he is dying to make love but won't force himself on me until I feel ready. Right now I

don't feel like it. I feel content nursing the baby and taking care of the house and visiting with my friends. Alice and I and our babies get together every morning about 10:00 and often stay together until after lunch. Some of the other mothers sometimes join us, and Ethel Crumbine usually comes, even though she is still pregnant. Ethel's father was a colonel in the army, and she knows just about everything there is to know about being an officer's wife. She and Alice get into some fascinating conversations. For the past couple of days, they have been talking about the ghosts of Ft. Riley. There are all kinds of stories, and Gen. Custer's old house is supposed to be haunted. My father always said that ghosts were the figment of people's imagination. But he believes there is a devil and evil spirits. Ethel says the ghosts just appear but never harm anyone. You can't say that about the devil or evil spirits. I have to say I worry about the devil. I sometimes have the worst thoughts, things that I would not even write in this diary. My father said everyone has evil thoughts and that the trick is to not give in to them.

CHAPTER 5

The summer of 1934 in Kansas was sweltering. From June 20 until September 8, the temperature rose into the nineties virtually every day, sometimes the high nineties. Between the heat and the physical strain of nursing, my mother never felt so listless, she said in her diary. Of course, no one had air-conditioning back then. If it hadn't been for Alice and Ethel and her other friends, my mother's life would have been much worse. Adding to her unhappiness was that Joe had to be away at nearby Fort Leavenworth three times during the summer, each time for a week, to attend training seminars. Still, there were many moments of delight with Joe Jr., who she said was obviously a very intelligent child because of the way he stared at her and at the things around him. He also learned to smile a lot, and he slept all through the night starting in his third month.

My parents got into their first disagreement in the middle of July, just after Dad returned from his first week at Fort Leavenworth.

"I told Joe that I thought he was smoking too much and that he also had gotten into the habit of drinking more than he should," she wrote in her diary on July 17.

> He just laughed and said there was not a single officer on the post who did not smoke and that while sure he drank like everyone else, he never got drunk. I told him my father said that cigarettes were "coffin nails" and said they were the cause of him coughing all of the time. He said it was the dust that he inhaled every day in the field that caused the cough. One thing about Joe, he is hard to argue with. He said he had gotten used to smoking and it soothed his nerves and that it was almost impossible not to smoke when everyone else was. I said I managed to survive without smoking even though all of my friends except Alice smoked. Joe smiled and said everyone in the movies smoked and that if it was good enough for Cary Grant it was okay for him. Then, he said, "Honey, I don't want to make you unhappy. I'll stop smoking here in the house and I won't have a drink when I come home." I said I thought the drink was okay, because that is when we do a lot of our talking. Joe always makes it very hard to get mad at him.

Actually, reading my mother's diary revealed to me that the summer of 1934 was not quite as bad as she sometimes made it out to be. She and the girls spent a lot of time at the officer's club swimming pool. They even played some tennis, though the heat was a big problem. She wrote about the wonderful summer evenings when they and other couples pooled their food for cookouts. They were a young crowd, and Mother wrote that there was a lot of laughter and witty joking with each other. Mother was quickly getting her figure back, and she liked to record compliments from Joe's friends.

"Ethel's husband, Robert, told me I look like a younger Carole Lombard," she wrote on August 13. "I told him I thought he was more handsome than any movie star except for the chimpanzee in the Tarzan movies. He laughed and said the trouble with me was that I could not take a serious compliment without making a joke out of it. Actually, I love the compliments but I don't want people to know it."

It was on September 18 that the big surprise came in the form of a registered letter from Tupelo, Mississippi.

"A very important looking letter was delivered this morning," my mother wrote.

> I had to sign for it even though it was addressed to Joe. I started to open it but then I decided not to. When Joe came home I immediately showed it to him and he looked at it and said he wanted to fix a drink before he opened it. That just added to the suspense. He said he thought the letter might contain some good news since it was from his uncle, Robert, from whom he had not heard in more than a year. He said Robert had taken over the family furniture business after his parents died. Joe had never spoken much about the family business, even though he said he was still a part owner—but he said that did not mean much, because since 1930, the company had not been profitable. "How about that," said Joe after he opened the letter. He handed me a check. It was made out to him for $1,844.19.

> He said the money was his share of the profits for 1933. I said that it was almost as much money as we make in a year and that we were rich. He said he was not going to spend the money, not now, anyway, and that he was going to seek advice for a smart way to invest it. I had hoped maybe we could buy a car but Joe said that would have to wait, though he did not rule it out. I could tell the money made Joe very relaxed and happy. We made love that night and he was quite the animal!"

Maybe that was the night I was conceived. If not, it was close. I was born on June 14, 1935, and they named me Daniel Pardon Booker. I never, ever used that middle name. Mother wrote in her diary how disappointed she was in not having a girl. She also noted that I seemed quite healthy but was not as pretty as Joe, who by that time had already learned to walk; his achievements continued to be a major focus of her diary. Mother had pretty much settled into life at Fort Riley, where she had lots of girlfriends and more than a few male admirers who found her fascinating. Obviously, her good looks and ready smile were widely appreciated by both sexes. She stopped nursing me after three months, saying I was too hard on her.

One of the big topics of discussion among Joe Sr. and his friends in 1935 was the Great Depression that was then in its sixth year. Mother wrote that Dad was losing confidence in President Roosevelt's ability to make things better, despite all of the people going on the government payroll. He said that the depression was now worldwide, and with high tariffs, American companies could not sell things such as furniture overseas. There was no check from Tupelo in 1935, only a letter from Robert saying that 1934 was not profitable.

My mother kept up her weekly letters to her parents in Hawaii, and they exchanged snapshots. Mary Teresa knitted things for my brother and me and said they were probably going to retire in a few years and likely would head back to Boston to be near their relatives; they would hopefully come to see the grandchildren on the way, they said.

"I told Mom that we expected to be leaving Ft. Riley by 1937 and that I thought there was a good chance we would be sent to the Philippines," my mother wrote on January 3, 1936. "That is why I have decided to get pregnant again. I really hope it is a girl this time. If it is not, I quit. Having a baby every year is tough on the body. I have stretch marks on my stomach and my figure is not quite as good as before. But I guess that is a small price to pay for two wonderful children, especially Joe Jr."

My mother's diary entries fell off in their frequency over the next six months. She said Dad still had his cough and that she was worried about it. Otherwise, she seemed happy, and considering the code markings in her diary, I think they were having a lot of sex. And why not? My mother was twenty-two, and Dad was twenty-seven. Both Mom and Dad seemed to be making the most of their life at Fort Riley, despite its numerous drawbacks.

James Crandall Booker was born on September 2, 1936. Mom wrote that she was very disappointed not to have a girl, but she was happy that the baby looked a lot like Joe Jr. I have seen pictures taken of all three of us as young children, and it is quite true I was the ugly duckling—not that I was really ugly, but both of my brothers were better-looking.

"Joe was promoted to First Lieutenant today," my mother wrote on October 20, 1936. "I was told by Ethel that he is one of the first of the West Point class of 1932 to get his silver bar. Joe never tells me, but Ethel says that Joe is regarded as one of the best tactical minds at Ft. Riley, and that his views on tank warfare are very respected. We celebrated Saturday night. We had a table of 12 at the officers club. Everyone at the club came up to congratulate Joe and I was pleased that a lot of men asked me to dance."

One of my first memories in life came in April of 1937, when I was twenty-two months old. I was standing by my parents' bed, and my dad was sick, with the covers pulled up over his ears; he seemed to be shivering. I can visualize that scene as if it happened yesterday. I remember standing there, not knowing what to make of it. My mother came in and quickly shooed me away, saying she did not want me to get sick. The next day (although I don't remember this), my father was taken to the hospital with pneumonia. According to my mother's diary, he was there eight days and was very drained and weak when he came out. Several weeks went by, and he still was not ready to go back to duty, because in the aftermath of the pneumonia, he had somehow contracted a virulent form of arthritis. My mother said in her diary that the second day he was out of the hospital, they went out to dinner at a Chinese restaurant in nearby Manhattan. When he got home, Dad was violently ill, alternately throwing up and experiencing horrible diarrhea. Mom wrote that it was probably food poisoning. The arthritis began to show up slowly over the next week, during which time Dad had a low-grade fever and an elevated pulse. The doctors prescribed aspirin, and that made Dad feel better. Young as I was, I can remember that he was up and around the house, but he wore his bathrobe all day. He spent most of his time reading. Over the next two months, his arthritis grew worse, and the pain and swelling would move from day to day to different parts of the body. Mom wrote that the pain was awful. Mom's mother wrote to them and suggested that Dad take cod-liver oil mixed with orange juice three times a day and stay in bed and rest—because that was what his body needed. He followed that advice, and it seemed to help, my mother wrote.

The upshot of all this was that we did not go to the Philippines. Dad was officially put on sick leave. My mother wrote that she had been looking forward to having full-time servants to take care of her increasingly rowdy band of boys. Baby Jim, it seemed, woke up crying two or three times a night demanding attention. And I apparently would not mind and would wander out of the house whenever Mom was not looking. Often, it was Joe Jr. who would find me. My mother must have been exhausted from taking care of three very young children and an ailing husband.

"I am getting dark circles under my eyes," she wrote on October 20, 1937.

> Joe is a little stronger, and his fever has gone but the arthritis is still there. His left knee is badly swollen and so is his left middle finger. His neck is so stiff looking, he reminds me of Frankenstein. His hip has an inflamed nerve, and he limps when he walks, and sometimes I can see him wince from the pain. Oh, I feel so badly for him. I think he is worried that his military career may be over, yet I never hear him complain. He says it is just a matter of time before he has a complete recovery. He is always quoting his uncle Jeremiah about how everyone's job in life is to overcome the numerous obstacles that are put before us. We certainly have our share. I just wish Alice was still here. I am

> surprised she hasn't written. She should be in the Philippines by now. I sure wish we were with them.

But she could not have wished for that for long. On November 2, it was decided that the Booker family would transfer to the plum of all military bases, the Presidio of San Francisco. There, Dad would help work on a defense plan for the West Coast and also be treated for his arthritis at the army's Letterman General Hospital. It was a great break, and my mother was elated. She would be that much closer to her beloved Hawaii.

"Ft. Riley has been a very good experience for us and while I am happy we are leaving I do so with many fond memories," my mother wrote on December 2, 1937.

> I came here a very young and inexperienced person, and I leave having learned a lot about life and the army. I have made a lot of wonderful friends, and most important of all, I have had three sons who make Joe and me especially grateful to God. I feel very fortunate to have a husband like Joe, and I think I love and appreciate him even more now than when we were just married, and I am glad he has quit smoking. I don't know what lies ahead. There is talk of war in Europe because of Hitler, and Joe says that the invasion of China by Japan has what he calls potentially ominous consequences. I am more worried about Joe's arthritis and the pain it causes him. I hope the climate in San Francisco agrees with him. I understand it never gets either too hot or too cold there.

CHAPTER 6

As I write this, I'm looking at another one of my favorite photos. It is a blowup of a snapshot taken on January 3, 1938, and in it are the five members of the Joseph Booker family. We are aboard a ferry crossing San Francisco Bay, and visible in the background are part of the newly constructed Bay Bridge and the prominent clock tower of the Ferry Building. We are outdoors at the bow of the ferry, and the sun is shining in our faces, so the crossing from Oakland must have taken place midmorning. The sky is clear. Everyone is bundled up. Dad is in uniform and wearing an overcoat, and he has one arm around Mom and the other on Joe Jr.'s shoulder. Mom is holding fourteen-month-old Jimmy in her right arm and has her left arm on my shoulder. Although Joe, at three and a half, is only a year older than I am in this photo, he appears at least five inches taller. All five of us look happy and excited. I can vaguely remember that crossing. It was the first great experience of my life, and I do remember the enormous size of the Bay Bridge and the look of the San Francisco skyline.

It had taken three or four days to come by train to Oakland from Fort Riley, with all five of us sleeping in a two-bed compartment. Joe and I investigated every inch of the train, with Joe in the lead. Sometimes, Jimmy would toddle along. I remember Joe talking with just about all of our fellow passengers. I spent a lot of time looking out the window, and I can still picture going through the snowy mountains. We spent New Year's Eve on the train, and I remember that the dining car was specially decorated, and a lot of people were in a good mood.

"Joe told me he hadn't seen me look so happy in a long time," my mother wrote in her diary on January 1, 1938, while aboard the train for San Francisco.

> To tell the truth, I could not be happier. I know the boys are going to love their new life and the Letterman Hospital is the army's best, and I feel that Joe is finally going to throw off whatever is causing the arthritis. Despite all his pain, Joe is so good with the kids. He is very patient but he can be stern when they misbehave. He is much tougher on them than I am but they love him very much. Joe is getting more handsome with each year. Quitting smoking has helped and I notice his skin is clearer and smoother, and his cough is gone. He rarely takes a drink now, though both of us had several to celebrate the New Year last night in the bar car after we put the kids to bed.
>
> Just before midnight, Joe Jr. came into the bar car and wanted to know when we were coming to bed. Everyone laughed at the sight of Joe Jr. in his pajamas, with that earnest little face of his. I took him back to our compartment and said Dad and I would be there shortly. When midnight came, Joe gave me a big kiss and said he thought 1938 was going to be a good year for the Booker family. May God grant that it be thus.

Mother subsequently wrote in her diary that she really liked the house that the army had assigned to us at the Presidio. Located amid a cluster of other houses on a hillside near a heavily wooded area, it was spacious and nicely furnished. She wrote that it was much better than the triplex we had at Fort Riley.

"Previously, our house was reserved for captains and majors and their families, but the number of officers at the Presidio is well below the peak numbers during World War I so we got lucky," she wrote.

Following army custom, my mother had tea with all of the ladies in our neighborhood, and she and Dad attended a series of evening cocktail gatherings and dinners. Though army etiquette for officers and their wives was through long tradition formal and exacting, it helped newcomers quickly meet everyone, which was important, because assignments seldom lasted more than three years, and people came and went constantly. That Mother was tall and very attractive and full of energy no doubt helped her introduction. Somehow Mother rarely made other people jealous. I think it was because of her friendly, open nature and because she seemed unaware of her own beauty. She liked people and accepted them on their terms rather than her own.

Mom and Dad and us kids loved being in San Francisco. In 1938, the city was coming of age, taking on the appeal that today marks it as one of the most beautiful cities in the world. Three important landmarks were created in the mid-1930s. First was Coit Tower, the 210-foot tower at the top of Telegraph Hill, the money for which ($100,000) was bequeathed by Lillie Hancock Coit, a wealthy philanthropist whose life was saved by a fireman when she was a child. From that point on, she strongly supported and cared about firemen, rallying to their causes throughout her life. The tower, opened to the public in 1934, was said to resemble the nozzle of a fire hose, notwithstanding its rather phallic appearance. Next on the scene was the San Francisco-Oakland Bay Bridge, which was completed in 1936 at a cost of $77.6 million with financing from Washington, thanks to strong support from President Herbert Hoover, a native Californian who had attended nearby Stanford University. Some would argue that his critical support of the Bay Bridge project was one of his most important contributions.

Of course, the jewel in the crown was the Golden Gate Bridge, one of the most famous landmarks in the world. Located at the entrance to San Francisco Bay, the Golden Gate Bridge was finished in 1937 at a cost of $35 million, which was financed by a bond issue ultimately paid off by tolls. When the bridge opened, the toll was a rather hefty fifty cents for a car, but it stayed at that level until the 1950s.

Another San Francisco landmark, Alcatraz Island, was turned into a federal prison in 1933. It had been an army installation and fort before that.

Treasure Island was a frenzy of construction in 1938, because preparations were underway for the 1939 opening of the San Francisco International Exposition, which rivaled in scope and size the New York World's Fair of that same period.

And for true San Franciscans, and I count myself as one, it would be impossible to overestimate the importance of a transplanted Sacramento newspaperman, Herb Caen, who began writing a daily column for the *San Francisco Chronicle* in 1938; he would write his last fifty-nine years later. Caen had fallen in love with the city (who wouldn't after Sacramento?), and over the decades, he wrote about its many moods and myriad inhabitants with a skill and style seldom achieved by anyone anyplace. In time, the first thing most *Chronicle* readers did when they picked up the paper was turn to Caen's column, located on the first page of the second section. When Caen switched over to the rival *San Francisco Examiner* in 1950, he took 40,000 readers with him. But the sensitive Caen returned to the *Chronicle* in 1958, saying that he did not like the Hearst-owned *Examiner,* because no one there ever said "nice column." What Caen did for San Francisco was create an excitement over life in the city. His romantic descriptions of wandering through fog-bound streets at three in the morning or watching the moon come up from behind the Bay Bridge, and thousands of other romantic images were among reader favorites. But his staple was the unending and clever anecdotes fed to him by publicists and fans. Caen wrote about all kinds of people, important and not. In those years, many people's notion of being a San Franciscan was defined by what they read in Herb Caen's column.

My mother had learned from Alice Combs the value of reading about her place of residence, and Mother's diary is chock-full of facts gleaned from the post library about both San Francisco and the Presidio. My mother read Herb Caen's columns regularly, and later in life, she met him and was subsequently mentioned numerous times in his column.

My mother wrote on January 28, 1938,

> I was surprised to learn that San Francisco Bay was not discovered until 1769. And the Spanish did not begin colonizing until 1776 with the establishment of a fort here at the Presidio and a church, Mission Dolores, the sixth of 21 built by the Franciscan monks. Oh, I sound like a guidebook. But it seems strange to think that San Francisco hardly existed at a time when America was declaring independence from Britain. I really need to learn more about this place and how it was that Americans took it over from the Spanish. I want the boys to know all about it.

CHAPTER 7

As spring came to San Francisco in 1938, my mother took us to all of the San Francisco sights. We went to Fisherman's Wharf and the

Marina Green, which had a huge lawn, located right on the water, with a fishing pier that extended out onto the bay. We went to Chinatown, Playland at the Beach, and the Fleishacker Zoo, getting there by either bus or streetcar. We went most frequently to Golden Gate Park. And we had a lot to do and explore at the Presidio, where Mom often took us exploring in the woods that overlooked the craggy cliffs above the bay. Watching the ships heading toward the Golden Gate Bridge was exciting to our young eyes. One weekend in early summer, Dad borrowed a car and drove us down the Pacific Coast Highway to Half Moon Bay, where we had a picnic and went wading. What I remember about that was that the sun did not come out from behind the clouds until it was beginning to set and we were leaving.

Although life was good that year for the Booker boys, it was not so good for Dad, whose arthritis remained debilitating. My mother wrote that she thought it was the dampness of the San Francisco climate, but my father told her that the doctors at Lettermen believed his immune system was causing the inflammation to thrive throughout his body. The doctors asked if he had had any serious traumatic experiences in his life, and he responded that the worst was when he learned at just fourteen that his parents had been killed. According to Mom's diary, he told the doctors that after his parents' death, he had felt traumatized for a year and still thought about the loss of his parents to that day. Moreover, Mother learned that Dad had felt a lot of stress at West Point and had been sick a lot in his plebe year. And he felt great stress over the circumstances of his marriage, more than he ever showed. One of the doctors, apparently a psychiatrist, said that Dad needed to be more open about his feelings and that he left too much boiling inside of him.

Mom said she told the doctor that Dad was a very loving husband and father, and from what she could see, nothing ever bothered him. That was the problem, the doctor said: my father could express his love, but he could not ever admit to having any problems. He had to be the master of every situation. All I can remember about that time was that he was not so much fun to be around and that I worried about his health. Even though he was supposed to be working, he stayed home many days, because he was too fatigued. One day, my mother wrote, it took Dad ten minutes to go from standing to a sitting position in the bathtub.

In January of 1939, my father chose to take a medical discharge from the army. Instead of improving, his arthritis had, if anything, worsened over the past year, and the doctors agreed that they had no cure. Mom wrote that Dad felt relieved to have finally made the decision, because he had felt guilty about not being able to fulfill his military duties. We moved to a rented house on 8th Avenue near Mt. Sutro in the Inner Sunset District while Dad looked for a job. Surprisingly, Dad's arthritis began to improve, and he was able to go for long walks on the steep hills around our house. He usually took Jimmy and me on his morning walk, and Joe Jr., who had already started kindergarten, joined us in the afternoons. Mom also came along when she wasn't busy with housework or shopping. Dad's mood became more cheerful, he began to have fun, and he stopped limping. Thinking back, I realize that my father was out of work for nearly six months. I remember him getting dressed in a suit and going out for "meetings" on numerous occasions. When he wasn't looking for a job, he was exercising and reading and calling as many people as he knew to help him in his quest for work. The depression was still on, and finding work was tough, even for a West Point graduate. Finally, through the help of a distant cousin from Tupelo, Mississippi, who was working in Oakland, Dad got the name of a contact at the Standard Oil Company of California.

"Joe was so delighted when he came home tonight and announced that he was given a job paying $450 a month with Standard Oil and will start the first of next month," my mother wrote on June 15, 1939. "He brought home a cake for Danny's fourth birthday and we all celebrated. Joe has not seemed so happy since we left Ft. Riley."

I don't know exactly what my dad did with Standard Oil, but it had something to do with oversight of their scores of gas stations around the San Francisco Bay Area. His degree from West Point seemed to carry a lot of weight with the Standard Oil people—not that my father was not an imposing figure on his own, with his square-faced good looks and standing just over six feet and probably then weighing 185 pounds. One of the great benefits of the job was that Dad got a company car, a tan 1939 Plymouth sedan, which Dad said was the best-selling car in America.

Not much later, Dad bought a new house, and in October of 1939, we moved to the 1800 block of 28th Avenue in the Outer Sunset, which was twenty short blocks from Ocean Beach. The house, near the corner of Ortega Street, was only about one hundred yards from a grassy landscaped hillside, inside of which was a city water reservoir. The house was built by Henry Doelger, who at the time was mass-producing houses in San Francisco like Model T Fords. Doelger Homes were built on lots 25 feet wide and 125 feet deep. They were attached to other houses on both sides, though the walls were separate and not shared, as was the case with some other builders' homes. Our house had three bedrooms and a bath, a dining room, a kitchen, and a living room. The bedrooms were located in the back of the house, and one was built on columns that extended beyond the enclosed basement that made up the ground floor, where our car was parked and the laundry and the utilities were located. The Sunset at that time had more sand dunes than houses, so it wasn't anything back then like it is today, with every square inch of land taken. We kids had lots of adventures in those sand dunes.

"Thank goodness Joe invested his money from Tupelo so that we could afford to buy our house," my mother wrote on October 21, 1939. Actually, it did not take a lot to buy a Doelger home. They may be selling for more than $650,000 as I write this, but when my parents bought our house, it cost only $5,000. Of course, they were row houses, but they had a front lawn, an entrance patio, and a pretty good-sized backyard that was completely fenced. In early 1940, Dad built a playroom with a half bath in the back of the basement and put up walls of knotty pine with beige carpet, over which we had a variety of brightly colored throw rugs. We had a ping-pong table and a dartboard in the playroom, and we kept our toys there, including our lead soldiers and Lincoln Logs. For Christmas in 1939, Dad bought us a tricycle and a Flexi racer. Our block was level, but the 1900 block up the street from us was built on a steep hill that took a lot of nerve to go down on our Flexi, which was then a very popular item among kids in the Sunset. To drive it, you had to lie down on your stomach. You steered by maneuvering two bike-handle-like arms that when pushed downward also served as the brakes. If you got going too fast and twisted hard on the brakes, the Flexis had a habit of fishtailing and rolling over. That is how Joe Jr. got his three front teeth knocked out and cut his mouth open enough that he had to get stitches in his mouth at the emergency hospital in Golden Gate Park: it was Joe Jr.'s bad luck to roll into a rock garden that was part of the reservoir's beautification. Fortunately, it was a weekend, and Dad was home, so he drove Joe Jr. for his treatment. Joe Jr. was also lucky that all he lost were his baby teeth.

I don't know how young people starting out can afford to buy a home today, but Henry Doelger was a master of affordable housing. In the period from 1934 to 1941, Doelger built 25,000 houses in San Francisco that had an average selling price of $5,000—this at a time when interest rates on mortgages were only about 3 or 4 percent. Never before or since has San Francisco real estate been so affordable. That the houses were well constructed is probably best evidenced by the fact that sixty to seventy years later, almost all of them are still standing, in spite of the several serious earthquakes that ensued in those many decades.

Earthquakes were quite a common occurrence in San Francisco in the time in which we were growing up. But nothing serious happened that I recall in the 1940s, though I can remember numerous times when the foundation at home or at school would begin to shake and shift. Jim and I slept in bunk beds in the back room, and Joe had a room to himself. (To get to our room, Jim and I had to walk through Joe's room, and actually, the door was always open, so it was pretty much like we were all in the same room.) Earthquakes experienced from the top bunk (where I slept) were a bit more exciting than they are when felt from the floor. Just once, during one particularly sharp quake, I remember feeling like my bunk was going to tip over, but it didn't.

One of the things we kids heard about was the great San Francisco earthquake of 1906 that destroyed most of the city. My mother, the history scholar, wrote about it in her diary, having done her research at the Sunset Branch of the San Francisco Public Library. "It must have been a terrible experience, especially since it came at about 5:00 AM when most people were still sleeping," she wrote in her diary. "I talked with Joe about it and he said the army played an important role in maintaining order. He said the troops had shoot to kill orders to stop looters but they never had to shoot at anyone. At Joe's suggestion, I am going to look for a magazine article written a few years after the quake by Brig. Gen. Frederick Funston, who had been in charge of the army forces in the San Francisco area."

"I found Gen. Funston's article and it was clearly written and filled with facts," my mother wrote later, on December 8, 1939.

> Gen. Funston set the death toll from the quake and subsequent fire at 3,000, but more than 225,000 were injured and 300,000 were made homeless. Most of the destruction was caused by the fire, which was fueled by broken gas lines. Firemen could not put the fire out, because the quake had shattered the water mains. Communications were made extremely difficult by the fact the telephone system had been destroyed. The soldiers tried to stop the fire by dynamiting buildings but mostly to no avail. The fire burned for several days. There were a total of 1,700 soldiers involved in helping the police and firemen in maintaining order, and Gen. Funston, in his article, praised the fine work they did in making the best of a disastrous situation. He also congratulated the citizens of San Francisco for their tremendous spirit. Looking at the city today, it is hard to believe it was almost totally destroyed just 33 years ago. Joe says it is not

so hard to believe, because people always have a way of coming back much faster than you imagine. "Look at me," he said. "I am beating my arthritis."

Although the 1906 earthquake was a story of great interest to us kids in 1939, it was not nearly as compelling as the fact that war had started in Europe. My dad subscribed to *Life* magazine, and Joe and I would spend hours and hours poring over the pictures of death and destruction. The war machine of Nazi Germany was sweeping over Europe. I must say I remember being impressed by the look of the swastikas and the German uniforms. Of course, we all knew who Hitler was. My father said he was a madman. I remember listening to radio broadcasts in which the announcer described bombs falling in London. We boys were definitely against Hitler, even though America was not in the war.

Nonetheless, the war seemed quite a distant event, and my dad said he did not think America would get involved. When Dad came home at night, usually about 5:30 PM, he would immediately turn to the news on radio. He also subscribed to *Time* magazine, which he read avidly but which we kids never looked at it because of its lack of photos. Instead, we'd be listening to the long lineup of kids radio programs, including *Jack Armstrong, the All-American Boy, Captain Midnight*, and *Little Orphan Annie*, among others. I remember a lot of street games ending because kids wanted to listen to these programs. We usually ate at about 6:30 PM, and Mom, as I think back upon it now, made some pretty elaborate meals. We had meat almost every night—lamb chops, hamburger steaks, pork chops, spare ribs. We always had a salad, vegetables, potatoes, and bread, all topped off with a dessert, such as Jell-O with whipped cream on top or sometimes, a Three Musketeers candy bar, split three ways among us boys.

The Sunset District in those years was a great place to grow up. Just about every house on our block housed children, from babies to teenagers, with the majority between two and ten years of age. That meant we had all kinds of kids to play with in games like hide and seek, kick the can, baseball, or whatever else we could come up with. One of the great sports was climbing around the many houses under construction in the neighborhood. The most memorable experience for me was sliding down a supporting beam and hitting the tip of a nail that sliced into and down my chest for about ten inches in length, leaving a scar still in evidence more than sixty-five years later. There were many vacant lots, and in some areas, you could find wild strawberries.

About six blocks away from our house, there lived a junk man who had a wagon and horse that he would drive through the paved streets, calling out "rags, bottles, sacks!" People would give him all kinds of junk, but he was never very friendly with the kids, and we heard many stories about him doing mean things to kids. My father said to just leave him alone, and he wouldn't bother us. Of course, curiosity got the better of us as the months passed, and one day, we went to the shack where the junk man lived to spy on him. The shack was surrounded by a clump of bushes. In one of the bushes, there was a huge beehive, as large as a soccer ball. We went by the junk man's shack several times and he was never there. The last time we went, Joe got a bunch of rocks and began throwing them at the hive. He missed with his first efforts and edged closer. Finally, he hit the hive with a perfect throw. The nest broke apart, and suddenly, we could see what looked like hundreds of bees inside. Joe ran, but he could not outrun all those bees, and a dozen or so stung him on the arms and legs. As we were fleeing, the junk man was coming back, and he saw us, with Jimmy and me in the lead and Joe crying and screaming behind us. He didn't say anything, but he must have figured out what happened, because three days later, he came up our block when we were outside playing, and he stopped and told Joe, "If I ever see you kids around my place again, you'll live to regret it." From that time on, we kept our distance and never went back to the junk man's shack. Ultimately, Henry Doelger's building boom caused the junk man to leave for parts unknown.

In our first days on 28th Avenue, a milkman delivered bottles to our house from a horse-drawn vehicle. He would bring the bottles in through our patio and climb the steps to the front door, where he would place them next to the empties that Mom would leave, sometimes with a note for the milkman if she wanted something extra. Thinking back, this was definitely the end of an era. By the time World War II came, horse-drawn vehicles had all but disappeared from the streets of San Francisco.

We kids were free to come and go from our house, which was never locked. We knew most of our neighbors and their names. Sunset Playground was only a block and a half from our house, and it covered a whole city block and had a baseball diamond, a basketball court, and two tennis courts, plus swings and slides and other playground equipment for younger kids. Growing up, I spent thousands of hours there, mostly playing football and baseball. Unlike most of the families on our block, we did not go to church except at Easter and Christmas. Most of the kids were Catholics, and Mom said we were Protestants, which she later defined as

Episcopalian. I don't know why Mother never felt a need to go to church, especially considering that her father was still a minister.

CHAPTER 8

It was in early 1940 that I saw my grandparents together for the first and only time. My grandparents, the Rev. Pardon Crandall Connors, age seventy-one, and his wife, Mary Teresa Cosgrove Connors, age fifty-seven, arrived in San Francisco by boat from Hawaii on June 3, 1940. They had retired and were heading back to Boston after nearly forty years spent building up their church and school in what I later learned was an unfashionable area just outside Honolulu. By all accounts, they had done a splendid job—church attendance and the school's enrollment had more than tripled in size during their tenure. Although I was only two weeks away from my fifth birthday, I can clearly remember when Dad brought them to our house on 28th Avenue. Joe, Jim, and I were outside playing and waiting for them when Dad drove into the driveway. We kids were really excited, and we yelled for Mom to come down. I could not believe how tall my grandfather was. Grandmother, all five feet of her, led the way, giving huge hugs to each of us boys, knowing our names and saying we were all even better-looking than in the photos Mom had sent. Grandfather had a warm, friendly face with big creases around the mouth and many squint lines radiating from the corners of his eyes. He looked a lot older than our grandmother.

"Look at these boys, Mrs. Connors. God has truly blessed us all," he said. "Come and give your grandfather a hug and a kiss," he said to us.

Just then, my mother came down the stairs howling with excitement.

"Oh Daddy, Mommy, it has been so long!" she said, embracing them both, one arm around each. We kids joined in the circle, and we heard Dad say that he wished his camera was not broken.

"Well, I have mine," said Grandfather. "Constance, you look hardly a few years older; how long has it been?"

"More than six and a half years," my mother answered.

"Well, you were never prettier," he said, adding, "Joe, you must be taking good care of your wife and these boys, too. You make a perfect-looking family. God has certainly blessed us all."

My grandmother stood beaming through it all. It was she who dug into my grandfather's bag and brought out what I suspect now was a Kodak Brownie box camera. Durden Harley, one of our neighbors, was outside at the time and came over to introduce himself to my grandparents.

"I think you need a photographer; this is a picture for the ages," he smiled. Mom had told him about her parents and that they were only staying for a week. We posed for the pictures with Grandfather standing in the center and with Dad on his left, Mom on his right, and Grandmother at the front along with us kids. Mr. Harley took several different poses, saying each was "a beauty."

It's funny how our memories work. I have an absolutely vivid recollection of meeting my grandparents in our driveway and of how excited we all were, and it is good that I do, because I have never even seen the photos taken that day. What happened to them I have no idea, and I even searched through Mom's trunks just after she died, specifically looking for them. It is a shame, because it was indeed a picture for the ages. Those were the only photos ever taken of the Connors and the Bookers in a group. Thinking about it now, some sixty-five years later, I can't tell you how much I wish I had one of those photos.

The Sunday after my grandparents arrived, we all went to the Episcopalian Church on Nob Hill, where none of us had ever been. It was called Grace Cathedral, and today it is a San Francisco landmark. In 1940, it was open for services but still unfinished. My grandparents stayed at the church during their visit; our house was too small, and Grandfather apparently had some business to take care of with the bishop. My mother wrote in her diary that her father and mother were upset to learn that we were not regular churchgoers, and she told them that she made sure the boys said their prayers every night and that she and Joe both said their prayers.

"I felt embarrassed to say we did not go to church regularly but I could not lie about it," Mother wrote. "We all believe in God and Joe and I both believe our marriage was God's will. And God has certainly blessed us."

The most memorable part of our time with our grandparents was going to the Golden Gate International Exposition on Treasure Island. Somehow Dad got us all tickets to the biggest show, Billy Rose's *Aquacade.* It was performed mostly in a large, enclosed swimming pool, around which there were thousands of seats. I recall that we were sitting quite a ways from the pool high, up in the stands. The music and scores of swimmers were very exciting, as were the clowns and diving acts. We kids had never seen anything like it, nor, I suspect, had very many of the other people in the audience. The star was Johnny Weismuller, who played Tarzan in the movies and who had been an Olympic swimming champion.

The beautiful lady he swam with was, I learned later, a nineteen-year-old Esther Williams, who would go on to star in a series of highly popular MGM water-based musicals. The orchestra was led by Fred Waring and accompanied by his choral group, known as the Pennsylvanians. (I remember that, because my mother used to listen to the Fred Waring show on the radio. In those days, the radio was on in our house much like television is today.) The *Aquacade's* grand finale was performed to the tune of "Yankee Doodle Dandy." Everyone left whistling or humming and in a good mood; it was a great show. My grandfather said he had never seen anything like it. Funny, but I can remember being at that show about as clearly as I can remember watching the hit musical *Mame* on Broadway some roughly forty years later.

The San Francisco Golden Gate International Exposition was sponsored by the state of California and had been conceived as a way to celebrate the completion of the Golden Gate and Bay bridges. Some 17 million people attended the fair, which was a huge artistic success, if not financially profitable. Treasure Island was built adjacent to Yerba Buena Island (the land where the San Francisco and Oakland sides of the Bay Bridge connected) on a landfill that covered four hundred acres. The original plan was to have the fair open only in 1939 (from February 18 to October 29), but despite a loss of $4.1 million that first year, it was decided to open for a second season in 1940 (May 25 to September 29). Tourists and San Franciscans could not get enough of the fair, with its scores of exhibits, restaurants, children's rides, and events. On the fair's closing day, some 211,020 came via the Bay Bridge or ferries, setting the one-day attendance record. Another part of the original plan called for Treasure Island to be converted into an international airport after the fair's closing. But amid concerns that it would be too small, the federal government agreed to provide bayside land in northern San Mateo County (just outside the San Francisco County borderline) for the San Francisco International Airport in a trade that made Treasure Island into a U.S. Naval Base. In retrospect, that exchange made a lot of sense. It is not a pleasant thought to imagine today's modern jets dodging the bridges for landings and takeoffs.

Two days after the whole family had visited Treasure Island, my father took my grandfather back again to see the many adult-oriented exhibits put on by companies such as General Motors and General Electric. Grandmother came to our house and spent the whole day with us, but mostly spent it talking with mother. My mother wrote in her diary that she had a wonderful time. "We talked about everything. Mom said I was lucky to have three children, though she wished one of them had been a girl. She regretted she could only have one child but said that what she lacked in quantity she made up for in quality. Mom said she was looking forward to going back to Boston where she has dozens of relatives she has not seen since her one trip back from Hawaii in 1913, the year before I was born. Mom is such a sweet person, very considerate and she has been a great help to Dad."

"Dad and Joe got into a discussion tonight after dinner about the possibilities of America entering the war in Europe," Mother wrote on June 8, 1940.

> Joe said it seemed possible though he could not imagine under what circumstances. He said the American people, while supporting Britain in the fight against Nazi Germany, still

> seemed to have no appetite for sending troops overseas. Dad asked what Joe would do if America did enter the war and Joe said he would have no choice but to have his commission reinstated. He said the reasons for his medical discharge from the army had been cured, and he no longer had even a trace of the arthritis that had nearly crippled him for almost two years. Joe said he had talked with the commanding general at the Presidio and was told to stand by—he might be needed. I sure hope we don't go to war. I can't imagine what it would be like to have him off fighting a war in Europe. Lord only knows how long he would be gone. I refuse to allow myself to even think about what it would be like if something happened to him.

We kids were hazily aware of what was happening in Europe. It seemed the Nazis were unstoppable as they conquered one country after another, but the war seemed exciting rather than threatening. We played guns in the vacant lots behind our house and called each other "dirty Nazis." *Life* magazine continued to provide the most vivid pictures of the war, though the brief newsreel clips at the movies were even more exciting. We never thought about the reasons behind the war. We read comic books about Japanese atrocities in China, and *Life* carried a picture alleged to be of a Japanese soldier bayoneting a Chinese baby. The makers of bubble gum put war cards in the gum packages, and all of us kids collected them.

In September of 1940, I began attending kindergarten at the Lawton Grammar School. At five years and three months, I was one of the oldest in my class, but not one of the biggest. Joe was in first grade, and Jim would start kindergarten the next year. Mother brought me that first day and took me to my class, where I met Miss Beggs, a very sweet woman who seemed very kindly and made my mother's parting easier for me. The thing I remember most about that first day was that at some point, an awful smell suddenly filled the classroom. Miss Beggs asked everyone to line up, and she moved down the line, bending over and smelling everyone's backside. Donald McDonald was the culprit. He was wearing long white trousers, and I could see brown stains running down both pant legs. Miss Beggs quickly escorted him out of the classroom. I can't remember how the rest of the kids reacted, but it seemed to me to be the most embarrassing moment imaginable. I told my mother about it when I got home, and she said that poor Donald was probably sick to his stomach, and there was nothing he could do. It was two weeks before Donald returned to class. I spent three or four years at Lawton with Donald McDonald, and such is the perversity of the mind that every time I saw him, I inevitably thought about the one day he had crapped in his pants. Donald's father was a doctor, and the family left the Sunset District sometime during the war. I wonder if Donald remembers that day.

One of the things our family did almost every Sunday during 1940 and 1941 was go for a ride. We would drive to the beaches or across the bridges or south to the Peninsula or just to the various districts of San Francisco—the Marina district, Pacific Heights, the Mission, the Fillmore—or down to the Ferry Building and the nearby piers. We went to Playland at the Beach and to Sutro Baths overlooking Seal Rocks. Most of the time, the drives included a stop at a restaurant for either lunch or dinner. I especially liked Fisherman's Wharf because of the bins of live crabs and all of the fishing boats. My second favorite place was Fleishacker's, which had not only the world's largest outdoor swimming pool, but also a zoo with a merry-go-round. One thing about San Francisco—there were endless things to do.

CHAPTER 9

The year 1941 was our family's last full year together, and it is a year that I can remember well. Dad got a promotion at Standard Oil, and he resumed playing golf at Harding Park, teeing off each Saturday morning before 8:00 AM so that he could be back home in time for lunch. If the weather was nice, he and Mom would take us to Sunset Playground, which was a five-minute walk from our house. It was there that Dad taught us how to play baseball. He got us all mitts, and he had a bat and several balls. We played catch and tried to hit the ball. Dad or Mom would pitch to us underhanded, and Joe could hit, but I almost always missed. So did Jim. Dad's presence attracted a lot of other kids, and late in 1941, he started organizing games along with the director of the playground. Everyone looked forward to Mr. Booker's Saturday appearances, and he was quite a charismatic figure. We three Booker boys were very proud of our dad. We were also different from each other. Joe threw right-handed and batted right. I threw right-handed but batted left. And Jimmy was left-handed all of the way. Joe was tall and rangy even at age seven. I was much shorter and stockier. Jimmy was slim and graceful and had Mom's good looks. I took after Mom in only one way: like me, she threw right and batted left!

Sometimes on Saturday or Sunday afternoon (if we weren't playing baseball or going for a Sunday drive), Mom and Dad would take us to the Irving Theater. The Saturday matinee was best. You got to see two movies, a cartoon, a serial, the newsreel, and sometimes a short subject. It lasted more than four hours. Starting with my very first movie, *Snow White and the Seven Dwarfs*, which Joe Jr. and I saw with our mom, I was hooked. I loved Westerns, and I always identified with the hero. I remember well the first time we kids went alone to the Irving. Dad and Mom had something to do, so they dropped us off at the theater, giving Joe twenty-five cents. It cost ten cents for a child's ticket, but it was free if you were under five. So Jimmy got in free. We used the extra nickel to buy a box of Jujubes, which Joe divided among the three of us. Saturday matinees at the Irving could be pretty noisy with loud cheering and booing and sometimes waves of laughter, but it never got rowdy, and unlike the Lawton schoolyard, I never saw a fight, not once in the eight or nine years we attended matinees at the Irving.

It must have been July of 1941 that we went on a two-week vacation to Capitola, which is located just south of Santa Cruz at the north end of Monterey Bay. We stayed in a rented house underneath a train trestle next to the Soquel River, which emptied into the ocean only about two hundred yards away. The Larsens, friends of Dad and Mom, rented an adjacent house. Chick Larsen worked with Dad at Standard Oil as a sales executive. His wife, Holly, was a close friend of Mom's and was equally good-looking. The Larsens had a daughter and son, Jo, age eight, and Chick Jr., age seven. Dad and Mr. Larsen played a lot of golf together. We kids went to the beach every day with our moms. We also went canoeing in the placid, tree-lined Soquel River. Capitola was a perfect place, safe and with very little undertow in the ocean. There was also a pond at the beach formed at the end of the river. Jimmy spent a lot of time lolling about in the pond with several kids his age. I pretty much stuck by Joe Jr., and so did Jo and Chick Jr. We didn't normally go to the beach until eleven or twelve, because that was when the fog usually burned off. A pier ran out from the beach, so we would often go there just after breakfast to see what the fishermen were catching. One day, we were amazed to see a dead thirty-foot whale floating alongside the pier. We never did get the details, but it was huge. The next day it was gone. As for the fishing off the pier, I don't remember much action and had trouble understanding why people would stand there all day hanging a pole over the water. Much more interesting to me was the porpoise that appeared every day around the raft about a hundred yards out in the water. The older kids would swim out to the raft and had no fear of the porpoise, which sometimes would leap out of the water right next to a swimmer, causing excited howls. I guess the porpoise was playing with them.

One of the most exciting things we did was explore along the train tracks. But we never saw a train, so one day in the second week, we kids decided to walk across the trestle, which was about thirty feet above the Soquel River (which actually was more of a creek). In the middle, we encountered three teenage boys who were standing on the outside of the trestle and talking about jumping into the water. I remember edging up to the railing and looking down. I was in disbelief. The water looked shallow except for a small dark green area near the right bank. Thirty feet looked like a hundred feet when looking down. We must have stood watching for twenty minutes while the boys got up their nerve. Finally, one leaped off, screaming at the top of his lungs. He landed right in the middle of his target area, and a huge splash followed. He surfaced still screaming with excitement, obviously unhurt.

Moments later, the second boy jumped, despite a terrified look on his face. But he came up howling with laughter, shouting, "I did it! I did it!"

The third boy, looking even more terrified than the second, climbed back over the railing and said, "I'm going to do it tomorrow." I said to Joe that I was never going to jump off that trestle. Joe said he would do it when he got older. When we told my father about what happened, he said we should never go on the trestle again. I learned something about myself that day: I was not someone who gets a thrill out of doing something dangerous. But there are a lot of people who do.

One day during our Capitola vacation, Dad drove us over to Carmel, where we spent the day at the beach while Dad and Chick played the Pebble Beach golf course, then, as now, one of the world's greatest courses. The beach at Carmel was very steep, but it had the whitest sand I have ever seen, quite unlike the gray sand that we were used to seeing at Ocean Beach in San Francisco or at Capitola or Santa Cruz. Interestingly, when we went back to Carmel after the war, the white sand had disappeared. Mom said it was probably because of all of the oily shipping going past Carmel during the war. What I remember most about Carmel is all of the beautiful houses that were nestled in the woods rising up from the water. When we were taking the 17-Mile Drive in Carmel, Joe Jr. said he someday wanted to live in a place like Carmel. My dad said there were a lot of retired military officers living in Carmel.

Capitola was not so glamorous. It was a middle-class vacation area, quaint and simple. At about 1:00 PM each day that we were at the beach, Mom would take us to the Round House located next to the sand, where we ordered the most delicious hamburgers I have ever eaten. They were fried on an outdoor grill and covered with onions. We kids would stand by, eagerly watching our burgers cook. At the last minute, the cook would put the buns on the grill. Thinking back, they were pretty greasy, which made them taste even better. They also came with pickles, lettuce, and tomato slices. I can still taste them. Alas, the Round House is long gone. There is just no going back.

Capitola had an arcade with all kinds of games and amusements that cost a penny or a nickel. Some of them dated from before 1900. The town also had a bingo parlor and other attractions. Kids flocked to the arcade and boardwalk after dinner. We were allowed to go on our own, with our parents giving Jo and Joe Jr. the responsibility of seeing to it that we got back by nine o'clock. Dad and Mom stayed home mostly, talking with the Larsens and, I presume, having a drink or two. By the time we left Capitola, all of us kids were tanned a crisp brown. Everyone's hair got blonder, especially Mom's. I have some pictures from that vacation, and Mom, age twenty-seven at the time, never looked more beautiful.

Mom did not keep her diary during that vacation, so I can't say what was going on in her mind. In retrospect, I think she must have been concerned about the war raging in Europe and China. I remember that during the drive home, Joe Jr. asked if we could vacation in Capitola next year. Dad said something to the effect of "That's the plan, God willing."

CHAPTER 10

Anyone alive and out of diapers remembers where they first heard that Japan had attacked Pearl Harbor on December 7, 1941. It was a bright sunny day in San Francisco, and I was just walking out of our house with Joe Jr. and Jim when Durden Harley, our neighbor, asked if we had heard about "the Japs attacking Pearl Harbor." He said it meant the United States would be going to war and that he was thinking of joining the navy. Joe Jr. said it meant that Dad would be going too. At the time, Dad was playing golf at Harding. Joe went back into the house, and Jim and I followed. He told Mom. She looked sort of dazed, and I could see her mind racing through all of the possibilities. Young as I was, mine was racing too.

Dad got home about an hour later, and all of us listened to the radio for more news of the attack. Dad said that it was a dirty sneak attack and that the Japs would pay. Later that night, after we kids had been put to bed, we could hear our parents having a long talk.

"Joe has decided he has to go back into the army," Mom wrote on December 8. "He does not want to leave us but America has been attacked and every patriotic American will have to do their duty. As a graduate of West Point, Joe said it was particularly important that he serve. His training experience would be badly needed. He said he had been told that his greatest value to the army would be as a teacher. I can't imagine what it will be like without him but he is doing the right thing."

The next day was a half day at school. Dad went to work to inform his bosses that he would almost certainly be returning to the military. He said he might be able to continue until the end of the year unless he got orders to report to duty earlier. Mom and we kids listened to the radio as President Roosevelt made his memorable speech declaring war on Japan. President Roosevelt had a wonderful speaking voice, powerful and theatrical. Nobody I knew spoke like him, not even in the movies. When he talked of a "dastardly attack that will go down in infamy," it was quite moving. Of course, I had no idea about all the implications of going to war, nor could I even imagine how it would change all of our lives and the lives of just about every American.

In retrospect, I find it interesting that the United States did not declare war on Germany when it declared war on Japan. In fact, it was Germany that declared war on us because of its military pact with Japan. Honoring that agreement with Japan turned out to be a grave mistake, though given Roosevelt's desire to help the embattled British, I suppose he would have figured out some way to enter the war against Hitler even if Germany hadn't declared war first.

Just for the record, the attack on Pearl Harbor was launched from Japanese aircraft carriers sitting 274 miles west of Oahu, the island where Pearl Harbor was located. The first wave of planes struck at 7:53 AM, followed by a second wave at 8:55 AM. It was all over by 9:55 in the morning. The official American death toll was 2,403. Of the dead, 1,300 were aboard the battleship *Arizona*. Some 188 American planes were destroyed. Eight American battleships were destroyed or damaged.

Sometime in December, my father worked out the details for his reentry into the army. He received orders to report to Fort Knox, Kentucky, where what was to become the Sixth Armored Division would be formed. We spent Christmas and New Year's together as a family. It was a sweet but sad time. By the end of December, we had heard so much war talk and patriotic furor that we were proud and happy that our dad was about to help defeat Hitler and Tojo. We were not really feeling sorry for ourselves. Almost all the fathers on our block were talking about joining the military. If there were draft dodgers or people who did not feel it was an honor to fight for their country, we did not hear about them. Dad left for Fort Knox on January 7, 1942. We drove across the Bay Bridge to Oakland to take Dad to his train. Dad seemed excited to be going and sad to be leaving. He looked handsome in his uniform. He said that he was proud of his three sons and that he expected us to be brave and to take care of Mom while he was gone. When Dad gave me a farewell hug, I broke down crying in huge sobs. Joe Jr. and Jim followed suit, and we saw that Dad had a tear in his eye. Only Mom was tough. "Don't worry, boys. Your dad will be back. He won't be gone for long," she said. She then gave Dad a long kiss and hug while we kids watched. Dad was waving out the window as the train pulled out. We stood there on the platform for a long time, watching the train go out of sight. "Okay, boys, stiff upper lips. It's time for us all to be brave," said Mom.

Of course, that was just an act. Mom was more truthful with her diary. She wrote that she cried all night. "I have three strong willed and very different sons who will be growing up without a father for who knows how many years. I pray that God will give us the strength and wisdom we are going to need."

CHAPTER 11

Dad's departure and preparations for the war dramatically changed our lifestyle over the next twelve months. The first impact was that Mom had to return our car to Standard Oil. That was not nearly as significant as it might seem today. San Francisco had an excellent public transportation system. Lots of people did not have cars. From our house, it took just three minutes to get to the corner of 29th Avenue and Noriega to catch a bus that would take you to 25th

Avenue and Judah. From there, you transferred to an "N" streetcar that would take you downtown to Market Street in about thirty minutes. Buses and streetcars went to virtually every corner of San Francisco.

But our primary form of transportation was our feet. We walked to school. We walked to Sunset Playground, to Golden Gate Park, to the nearby shopping areas on Noriega Street. In summer, we walked most of the way to what we kids thought was the most compelling part of San Francisco, the northwest corner of the city. Located there in close proximity were Playland at the Beach (a fabulous amusement park), Seal Rocks, Kelly's Cove, the Sutro Baths (and ice-skating rink), and the Cliff House. I don't remember how long it took to get to this mecca of fun, but it was at least an hour's walk from our house. Sometimes, if we had the money, we would take the Noriega bus to 48th Avenue and then walk from there along the Great Highway that fronted the Ocean Beach, past the foot of Golden Gate Park, and thence a block or so to the entrance of Playland. The Sutro Baths, the largest indoor swimming complex ever built, were located just past the Cliff House. Coming home, we usually had to walk the whole way, having spent all of our money.

Sometime in January or February of 1942, air-raid sirens sounded and Lawton school was evacuated and everyone was sent home. We kids thought we might be bombed just like Pearl Harbor, but it never happened. In the early days of the war, serious preparations were made to defend San Francisco from air attack. We had air-raid wardens appointed for our block, and people kept buckets of sand to extinguish incendiary bombs. There was also the fear of sabotage. Army guards were posted at the huge reservoir near our house. All the Japanese people were rounded up and taken to places like the Bay Meadows racetrack. And it wasn't long before rationing came in for supplies such as sugar, gasoline, shoes, and butter. People who had cars and weren't involved in the war effort were allowed only four gallons of gas a week. We kids were allowed only two pair of shoes a year. I remember my mother breaking down into tears of gratitude when the lady who ran a dress shop at 25th and Noriega gave us her stamp for a pair of shoes so that Mom could replace my only pair that I had badly outgrown.

In early 1942, more and more men were disappearing from our block, replaced by stars hanging in the windows, signifying that someone from that house was serving in the military. Our neighbor, Durden Harley, did not go into the navy after all. Instead, he went to work in a defense plant in south San Francisco. He had to get up at 4:00 AM every morning, and Mrs. Harley once gave us fifty cents, asking that in return, we be quieter at night so that Mr. Harley could sleep. With the windows open, noise from our house, and there was a lot of it, carried not only next door, but beyond. We took the money, but I don't recall any of us ever saying to the others, "Be quiet—Mr. Harley is trying to sleep." But Mom was more sensitive, and she switched our bedrooms, which was a two-week project at least. She wallpapered our new bedroom and painted our old one. I can see her now wrestling alone with the project, trying to hang the long strips of paper. She had never done it before. But there was a war on, and people had to learn to do things for themselves. Mom really got into the war effort. She saved tin cans, grease, paper, and glass, all of which were dutifully collected and, we assumed, put to use in the effort to defeat the Japs and the Nazis.

Mom wrote to Dad every day, and he wrote back almost that often. Dad wanted to know everything we kids were doing. Unfortunately, he could not tell us much about what he was doing. So he talked about movies he had seen, personal events, friends he had made, and former West Point graduates he was with. Mom didn't tell Dad everything. For example, she never said anything about Jim getting caught trying to steal a dollar from her purse—or Jim getting caught stealing candy at the five-and-ten-cent store on Noriega. Jim was only six and had a mind of his own. The owner called Mom and told her all about it. Mom punished Jim on both occasions by depriving him of desserts for a week and, for the second offense, by also taking away his allowance (we all got fifty cents a week) for two weeks. Mom always gave advice with her punishment. "If you steal from others, God will see to it that others steal from you." She also said that being honest and trustworthy were about the most important things any person could be. "If people can't trust you, you will be in for a very hard life." She also said that kids make mistakes, and they can learn from them, and she believed that Jim was both honest and good. Her closing line was that she was not going to tell Dad about what Jim had done. That had the most powerful effect on all three of us. None of us wanted Dad to hear anything bad.

In September of 1942, Jim started first grade at Lawton and thus began attending school on a full-time basis. That meant we kids were away from about 8:00 AM until 5:00 PM, because we usually went to Sunset Playground after school or played in the sand dunes or on our street. That was when Mom started to look for a part-time job, restricting her search to the nearby business establishments. After a month or so of searching, she found one at the beauty parlor at 25th and Noriega, only three and a half blocks from our house. Mom would go to work Monday through Friday at noon and be finished at 5:00. After that, she would shop for our dinner and have it on the table by 6:15. That worked perfectly for us kids. We were glued to the radio between 5:00 and 6:00, listening to our adventure programs. Joe decided which programs we would listen to, though sometimes Jim would go into Mom's room to listen to something else. I don't know how Mom learned to be a professional beautician. She once told me that she had learned how to do hair from Alice Combs when she was at Fort Riley. Probably what got Mom the job was that she was the most beautiful woman in the Sunset. Mom loved the work, because it put her in touch with other women, many with children at home and husbands in the service.

Mom knew just about everyone on our block and those who shopped at the Noriega shopping area. Everyone liked her, and we kids noticed that men of all ages had a keen interest in finding ways to talk with her if they happened to see her walking by. Usually, the line was something like, "What do you hear from Capt. Booker?" (Dad had been promoted to captain in mid-1942). Our neighbor Mr. Harley was always asking if there was anything that needed fixed in our house. He invariably had a stupid smile on his face when he saw Mom.

Of course, at that time, we did not know that Mr. Harley was a secret drinker, who hid liquor on the top of his furnace so that his wife would not see it. We learned about that in late 1943 when Dad was home on leave. One night, Mrs. Harley started banging on our door in an almost hysterical state. Her two daughters were in tears, clinging to her skirt.

"Durden is drunk, and he has a knife, and he is threatening to kill us all!" she exclaimed, tears in her eyes and terror on her face. Dad told Mrs. Harley and the girls to come inside while he went to talk with Mr. Harley. I remember feeling very frightened for Dad and worried that Mr. Harley would stab him. Dad went next door and called for Durden to come out so that they could talk. We were all watching from the window. Dad repeated his call several times before Durden came out. He did not have a knife. Dad and Durden talked for maybe ten minutes. In the end, Durden put his arms around Dad and buried his head on Dad's shoulder. To this day, I don't know what Dad said to Mr. Harley, but it worked. Dad came up and got Mrs. Harley and brought her down to talk with Mr. Harley. Mr. Harley put his arms around his wife and began crying. They went inside. After a while, Mrs. Harley came to get her daughters.

"He's fine, now," Mrs. Harley said, adding, "Joe, I can't thank you enough." All of us were very proud of Dad. Thinking back, I wonder why he simply did not call the police and let them take care of the drunken Mr. Harley. Instead, he went out to find Mr. Harley, not knowing whether he might be attacked with a knife. I guess that Dad was confident that he knew how to handle men. I don't think I ever would have had the courage to act the way Dad did. Of course, I never went to West Point.

One of the things Mom reported to Dad in her letters was that Joe was winning a lot of praise from his teachers. He never got less than the highest grades. I remember my second grade teacher, Mrs. McLoud, telling me what a treat it had been to have Joe in her class the prior year. She said she was really looking forward to having me, assuming I would be just like Joe. Unfortunately, I never lived up to

Joe's reputation. Not only was I a bit slow in picking things up, but I was also disruptive. I talked in class when I was supposed to be listening, did not always pay attention, disturbed other children, and sometimes acted like the class clown.

Meanwhile, I was inept at doing a lot of things. In Mrs. Lacy's third grade class, the big project was for each of us to make a puppet. It was a two- or three-week ordeal for me. Most of the kids came up with finished products, but I never did. I botched the job so badly that the kindly Mrs. Lacy said, "That's all right, Dan; I think you are good in sports." I was quite relieved when she took my half-made puppet away from me and put it into a paper bag, which I assumed was mercifully headed for the garbage.

Mom also reported to Dad that Jim was the most popular boy in his first grade class and that his teacher said he was one of the brightest youngsters she had ever had. In one of his letters, Dad asked how I was doing in school. Mom replied that I did not seem as interested in school as either Joe or Jim but that I had become interested in reading, which was true. Mom read to us every night before we went to sleep, and I loved to hear her read. One of the books she read was *The Wizard of Oz.* I loved that book and used to run my hands across it and look in awe at the pictures that were taken from the Judy Garland movie. Eventually, I read more than a score of Oz books before graduating to the Tarzan books by Edgar Rice Burroughs.

Thinking back, I realize that I readily accepted that I was different from Joe and Jim. I knew that I had limitations and that there were some things I simply could not do. Of course, I did not totally absorb the lesson of learning one's limitations overnight, but the important thing I eventually came to understand was that there were a lot of things I could do—better to stick to sports or something else in which I would not make a fool out of myself, I thought.

CHAPTER 12

In early 1943, when Joe was eight, he got a paper route. He had to cover sixteen blocks on 17th and 18th avenues to deliver sixty-one copies of the *San Francisco Chronicle*. All papers had to be delivered by 6:30 AM, so that meant Joe had to get up at 4:30 AM, seven days a week. Mom had written Dad about Joe taking the route, and Dad replied that he thought it was a good idea. At this time, Joe had the only two-wheeled bike in the family, and he would ride up to 17th and Moraga, where his papers would be left bundled on the corner, along with an envelope that contained information such as complaints, starts, and stops. I went with Joe to help on several occasions, riding to the pickup point on the handlebars of Joe's bike. The trouble was that Joe could not carry both the papers and me at the same time, so I ended up trotting along while he zigzagged from one side of the street to the other. It was only on Sundays that I was of much help. We had to go to a vacant store on Lincoln Way where all of the delivery boys put together the various Sunday sections of the *Chronicle*. The building had very little light, and the other boys seemed much older and scary. I'll never forget the first time I went there and saw a chalked message on the blackboard: "Don't be late or I'll get you." It was signed "Dr. Cutyourpeckeroff." But there was never any trouble among the boys, and Joe paid me fifty cents for my Sunday efforts.

Joe had that *Chronicle* route for three months. He was making about $14 a month, a lot of money for a kid in those days. A Coke cost a nickel, movies ten or fifteen cents, and hamburgers fifteen or twenty cents. But even at age nine, Joe was analytical. One day, he told me he was applying for an *Examiner* route: "They have a much bigger circulation so that you only have to cover half the distance to deliver the same number of papers," he said.

The district manager for the *Examiner* was Mr. Bell. Joe had met him several months earlier when Mr. Bell stopped Joe on the street one Saturday afternoon and asked him if he wanted to earn a dollar by helping him unload Sunday sections of the *Examiner* to various distribution points in the Sunset and Parkside districts. Joe agreed. He was big and strong for his age, and he subsequently asked Mr. Bell for a route. But nothing was immediately available. Joe continued to pester Mr. Bell. In September of 1943, route B-26 opened, and Mr. Bell offered it to Joe.

The route began around the corner from our house at 27th Avenue and Ortega and ran down five blocks to Judah and then back up from Judah on 26th to Ortega, a total of ten blocks. There were 124 *Examiner* customers on the route, each of whom paid $1.25 a month for daily and Sunday home delivery. Delivering the papers was the easiest part of the job. The big headache was collecting from the customers. Joe had to make out separate bills for all 124 subscribers. The bills were printed in books of thirty or so and had carbon copies for the carrier's records, with the originals going to the customers. Finding people at home was a serious problem. Sometimes, you had to go back four or five times. After the first month of handling B-26 all by himself, Joe said he would give me $13 a month if I would carry the sixty or so papers on 27th

Avenue. He would do all of the billing and collecting. I readily agreed. I will never forget that first monthly payment. Joe paid me all in one dollar bills. I ironed them and counted them over and over again. I was eight years old and in the chips—thanks to Joe.

When I think about it now, getting up seven days a week at 4:30 AM month in and month out seems like it would be a tremendous hardship. But it never seemed that way to me then. It was just something that I was committed to doing. Having a nice disposable income made a big difference in our lives. In 1944, Jim got a route delivering the afternoon *Call-Bulletin*, but his route had only forty or so papers, and there was no Sunday edition, so the money was much less. But Jim said he definitely was not interested in a morning route.

Dad came home on leave in November of 1943 and stayed about three weeks. You can hardly imagine how glad we were to see him. He had been promoted to major, and he was tanned, lean, and handsome at age thirty-four. Mom wrote in her diary,

> It's true: absence does make the heart grow fonder. Having Joe back is like a second honeymoon. The boys could not be happier. He's done everything with them—gone to school, gone on their paper routes, taken them to two football games at Kezar Stadium, taken them ice skating, gone to the playground—and he even took us all to church at Grace Cathedral and a brunch after services at the Fairmont Hotel. The boys looked so grown up in their sports jackets and ties. I must say that everyone at church and at the Fairmont seemed to be watching us and smiling. Oh, we have such a beautiful family. Thanks to God. I can't wait for this war to be over when Joe comes back and we will have a normal life again.

A few days later, Mom wrote,

> Joe says I can't tell anyone, not even the kids, but he thinks his unit is going to be sent to England early next year. He thinks the invasion of Europe will come before July of next year, and he expects he will be part of the invasion force. He said the Germans seem more vulnerable, based on their fighting in North Africa and Italy, and he does not think it will be long after the invasion that the war will end. Still, he said, it will be a tough fight. He said he is not worried about himself so much, but he does worry about his family—more, he said, than I could ever imagine. I said I could imagine, because that is the way I feel about him. He said it was wonderful that after ten years of marriage, we were still deeply in love. I told him, "Even more." He just laughed and held me for a long time.

I remember Thanksgiving of 1943. Dad took us boys downtown to see the 11:00 AM showing of the latest Abbott and Costello movie at the Orpheum Theater. Mom stayed home to cook the turkey. On the way back, our streetcar went right past Kezar Stadium, where the crowd was just coming out. Lincoln, the three-year-old high school just six or so blocks from our house, had defeated Balboa for the city championship. Dad said, "Maybe we should have gone to the game instead of the movie." We dismissed that thought. Anything we did with Dad was the perfect thing to do.

The previously mentioned incident with Durden Harley happened two days before Dad had to return to Camp Chafee, Arkansas, where the Sixth Armored Division was quartered. Dad's bravery that night caused us to get more curious about exactly what his job was in the army. Dad said that he was the commander of a tank battalion and that virtually all of his men were drafted or had enlisted after the war started. He said he was almost as proud of his men as he was of his wife and sons. While on leave, Dad took the time to speak with each of us boys privately. That's when he told me about living with Uncle Jeremiah and going to West Point and meeting Mom. He wanted to know about my work in school, and I told him I was pretty average. He said that everyone was different and not to worry about it. When I told him that I wished I could do things like Joe, he said that Joe was a good model but that everyone had to be himself and not worry about being something they were not. He said all of his soldiers were different, but working together, each man learned to capitalize on his own strengths, and together, they got the job done. That, he said, was what life was all about. He said it was very important that everyone in the family think that way. He said a family was like a team and had to stick together and help each other. I've never forgotten that conversation.

Dad left on December 14, 1943. I won't recount the details. It was a scene that can still bring tears to my old eyes when I think of it. Suffice it to say his departure left an ache of vacantness in our hearts, a feeling stronger than I had ever felt before. It was like that for all of us. I thought about how Dad must have felt when he lost both his mother and his father at the same time in that car wreck. Mom said we should not worry about Dad, because he was a great soldier. And he would be coming back a hero.

CHAPTER 13

It was sad to have our father leave again, especially just before Christmas. But we boys quickly got back to normal. Dad had been gone for most of the past two years, so we were used to not having him at home. It helped that most of the other kids we knew didn't have a father at home either. American patriotism during World War II was a constant. Everywhere you went, you were reminded of the war. Movies, popular music, sign boards, newspapers, radio, comic books, and schoolteachers all carried the message that we were a nation at war, fighting to rid the world of tyranny. My brothers and I believed, along with virtually all Americans, that God was on our side and it was only a matter of time before we won. "I'll Be Home For Christmas," with its lyric "if only in my dreams," is a song I have heard hundreds of times since it first came out during the war, and it never fails to remind me of my father. I can remember hearing it on our radio while Dad was on leave, just before he left to go overseas. He said to Mom, "That's a beautiful song. I am sorry I can only be here in my dreams this year."

Jim asked Dad if he would be home next year for Christmas. And Dad answered, "You are darned right I will, God willing."

To this day, I can remember many lines from those wartime songs: "Good-bye, Mama, I'm Off to Yokohama"; "Let's Remember Pearl Harbor"; and "Praise the Lord and Pass the Ammunition."

I can still envision my mother ironing our clothes at night in our kitchen with the radio playing beautiful and sentimental songs such as "I'll Get By," "As Time Goes By," "I'll Be Seeing You," "Don't Get Around Much Anymore," and "It's Been a Long, Long Time."

The theme of separation from loved ones was ever-present. All of us missed Dad, but it had to be tougher on Mom. Still, she bore up well despite her loneliness. She had a can-do spirit about her, and she was always optimistic. She loved her work at the hairdressers' shop and took an interest in everything we kids did. She wrote to

Dad every day and to her mother at least once a week. Her parents had settled into retirement in Boston, and her Mom was talking about coming out for a visit. Of course, there was no way we could go back there, and it was far too expensive even to telephone, so letters were the only realistic means of communication. Correspondence from Dad was spotty during 1944, with his being mostly on the move. When a letter did arrive, Mom would read it first and then again out loud to us kids. If anything was bothering him or going badly, we never knew. And censorship prevented him from saying anything about where he was or what was happening from a military standpoint. So Dad's message was usually in reaction to what Mom had told him we kids were doing. He always expressed his love and admiration for how brave we all were. One of his most common phrases was "Boys, be sure to take care of your mom."

The fact was, Mom really did not need much taking care of. In retrospect, I see that she was the master of the stiff upper lip. And we kids were pretty much the same. In April of 1944, Joe told me he was going to quit delivering the *Examiner* and said that I could have the route all to myself if I wanted. I eagerly accepted, and Mr. Bell came by and talked to me about the responsibilities of the job, especially about collecting from the customers and paying the bill to him by the tenth of each month. I was almost nine and quite confident I could handle the job.

Joe, meanwhile, had hit upon another way to make money. For the past few months, he had been delivering prescriptions for the Noriega Street drugstore, known as Becker's Pharmacy; Joe would check with Mr. Becker after school to see if there was anything to deliver. We kids used to sometimes hang out there at the soda counter, sipping a vanilla Coke while waiting for Mom to get off work at the hairdressers' across the street. When word got out that Becker's Pharmacy had an afternoon delivery service, the number of Joe's deliveries began to increase. Joe did not like getting up at 4:30 AM to deliver our route, and he decidedly did not like doing the billings and collections. So he came up with the idea of an expanded delivery service. He went to the florist, the bakery, and the dry cleaning and laundry shops offering his services. All he wanted was twenty-five cents per delivery, but all the businesses said that was too much, so Joe settled for twenty cents. His delivery area was confined to the twenty square blocks surrounding the Noriega commercial zone. Joe's ingenuity and creativeness always impressed me. He built a wagon that attached to his bike to carry deliveries when the number was too great to fit into the basket on the handlebars. He later added a hanging bar on top of the wagon to carry dry cleaning. It wasn't long before Joe was earning four or five dollars a day, including tips, which was much better than he what he had received for what he considered much harder work delivering papers.

Joe was always doing things that surprised me, and he always included Jim and me in his projects. We usually just watched, especially me, who could not make a puppet. One of the first things I remember Joe doing was building a pigeon coop in our backyard, which was large enough to hold twenty or thirty pigeons. It was a serious structure, built on stilts and about six feet high. He also built a wooden den for rabbits, and we all bought our own to cuddle and take care of. It wasn't long before our population of pigeons and rabbits got out of hand. The pigeons always came home, but they also began flying around the neighborhood, leaving an ever-increasing number of "calling cards," which the neighbors took a growing exception to. Joe fed the pigeons corn and other seeds, and we got wilted greens from the grocery store for the rabbits. Our population of pigeons must have reached fifty at its peak. Often, they would swarm in a flock, sometimes landing together on the roof of a single house, where they would leave an abundance of calling cards. Johnny Tivinan, who lived nearby, got to calling the flock of pigeons "Joe's Shit Squadron." Finally, some of the neighbors went to Mom to complain. Mom did not rush to judgment, but in the end, she agreed that the pigeons were defacing neighborhood property. I remember asking Joe how we were going to get rid of them. Joe said, "Easy—we tear down the coop and stop feeding them." Joe was right. In a few days, they were all gone. None of us felt like we had done anything cruel. Then as now, there are seemingly tens of thousands of pigeons in San Francisco, and they all seem to get by without a house or a daily source of free food.

Next to go were the rabbits. We had bought eight at the start, but their number had grown to thirty-five or so. Despite the fact that we brought an increasing amount of wilted greens to feed them every day, they had insatiable appetites, and they ate practically everything in Mom's garden. The one benefit was that we no longer had to cut the grass. One day, Jim, who had the job of cutting our small front lawn, acting on his own, brought four rabbits from the backyard to the front, hoping they would save him from mowing the lawn. But instead, the rabbits all ran off, and one bit a neighborhood child who was trying to pick it up. The hysterical mother, fearing rabies, came storming over to our house. Only Jim was home. Jim said she should not worry, because he had been bitten several times, and nothing had happened. From there, the mother raced to the hairdressers' where Mom was working and expressed her outrage. Mom calmed her down, and the child did not get rabies, but alas, when we later found that the rabbits had dug tunnels into two adjacent backyards, Mom called the Society for the Prevention of Cruelty to Animals, and all the rabbits were carted away. Mom said the rabbits would be given new homes, but I always suspected that they probably got an early pass to heaven.

Not long after the rabbits left, Joe asked Mom if it was okay to buy a pet snake. Mom said, "Absolutely not." But three days later, Mom came home with a three-month-old black-and-white spaniel that we named Skippy. Skippy turned out to be a wonderful companion. She unfailingly went on my paper route with me every morning, and she accompanied Joe on his afternoon deliveries. She was housebroken after only about a week, and all in all, she was the friendliest, most loveable dog I have ever known. Skippy was patient with young children, and she never bit anyone or acted as if she might. We never had to put her on a leash. She came when called. She never tried to run away, and she never got into fights with other dogs. Her only downside was that she refused to learn any tricks, no matter how hard we tried. Mom had her fixed so that she could not have puppies. A stranger coming to our house could cause her to bark or growl, so in that sense, she was a good watchdog. We couldn't take her to Sunset Playground, but she could go virtually everywhere else. When Joe went from store to store to pick up his afternoon deliveries, Skippy would curl up and wait outside. We all loved Skippy and considered ourselves blessed by her presence. Skippy lived until 1956, by which time all of us boys had left home. I remember tears coming to my eyes when Mom called to tell me that Skippy had died.

When I remember my time with Skippy, it makes me think that everyone should have a dog. It is like the wisdom that holds we should always be reading a good book. Unfortunately, life and its complexities sometimes get in the way.

Another one of Joe's brainstorms was to go horseback riding. There was a place just past Fleishacker Zoo called the Mar Vista Riding Academy. He got Mom to take us there the first time, but after that we went on our own. For $15 we could rent three horses for three hours and ride on the many trails around Lake Merced and the surrounding countryside. We paid for the horses with our own money, though I think Mom might have paid for Jim.

I can also remember us renting three bikes near Fleishacker and cycling all the way down Highway l to Sharp's Park, a journey that in parts wound along steep ocean cliffs and that took nearly five hours roundtrip. Joe had no appetite for sitting around the house. He was the one who came up with all of the ideas for stuff to do. Somehow, he had the skill to bring us around to his way of thinking, whatever it was. Of course, sometimes he did things on his own, such as when he built a Marconi radio receiver—I was never into anything technical. However, in those war years, we mostly did things together. Both Jim and I realized that we were lucky to have a big brother like Joe. I think about it now—great dad, great mom, great brothers, great dog, plenty of money to spend—and I realize that we were lucky, very lucky.

CHAPTER 14

One day in April of 1944, my mother announced that she and Annette Morgan, the lady who worked with Mom and who owned the hairdressers' shop, had decided to form a club. Mom was quite excited with her news and said the club would be made up of twelve women their age, all of whom lived in the Sunset. The criteria for admittance, Mom said, was to be a customer at the beauty shop, to be fun and attractive, and to be willing to host the group in their home once a year. Mom said she and Annette had been working on the list for two months, and about fifty people had been considered for membership. She said everyone who had been asked had agreed to join, and they were equally excited about it. Mom said they would have meetings on the first Thursday of every month, and the first would be held at Annette's house on 15th and Ortega, a large house high on Twin Peaks with a fabulous view. Annette, who went to the University of California at Berkeley and was a member of a sorority there, was the one who suggested the club. I think Mom was excited, because a lot of the people on our block were not very stimulating, and she missed the kind of friends she had had at Fort Riley and at the Presidio. Mom always liked to be around intelligent people who enjoyed a good laugh. The second meeting of "The Club" (as it came to be known) was at our house, quite a comedown from Annette's. The ladies arrived at about 7:00 PM while we boys were still outside. They were all dressed up and looking glamorous. Mom knocked herself out on the food and drinks, and she had the living room and dining room filled with flowers, some from our yard and some from the florist.

The party lasted four hours at least. I usually went to bed at eight o'clock, because I had to get up at 4:30 AM for my paper route. But at ten o'clock, I was still awake. I have to say it was the noisiest group of women I have ever encountered. The laughter and the hilarity were nonstop, and it seemed to me that everyone was talking at once. For a while, we tried to listen to the conversations, but such was the din that distinguishing a single voice among the many proved impossible.

When I got back from my paper route the next morning, I was amazed to see that the house was cleaned with virtually no evidence that there had been a party—unless you went down to the garbage area of the basement, where I saw a lot of empty bottles next to brimming garbage cans.

Mom was sitting at the kitchen table, drinking a cup of coffee and reading the *Chronicle*. I delivered the *Examiner*, but Mom much preferred the *Chronicle*, even though Herb Caen was away in the service.

"Those ladies sure were noisy last night," I said.

"Were they?" she asked. "I don't think I even noticed, we were having such a lot of fun. I never heard so many jokes."

"How could you hear what anyone was saying?" I asked. "Everyone was talking at the same time."

"Danny, that is not true. I don't think I missed a word that anyone said."

"Mom, how can you say that? It sounded like a roar in our bedroom."

"I'm sorry if all the noise kept you up," she said. "You look a little tired. If you want to stay home and catch up on your sleep, I will write an excuse for you."

"No, that's okay," I said. "I'm not really that tired."

"Danny," Mom said, "I hope you understand that I am just like you boys. I like to have friends and have a good time. Most of the girls in the club have husbands who are away in the service. Two of them are in the South Pacific, where there is some terrible fighting going on against the Japanese. Their wives are very nervous right now. Last night helped put all our worries aside for a while. I think that is why everyone had such a good time. I hope you understand and are not upset with me."

"Mom, that's a laugh. I could never be upset with you."

Mom smiled and gave me a hug. "You know, deep down, you are a very sweet boy."

I should note that Mom remained associated with The Club for more than fifty years. She often said she should write a book about what happened to all of those ladies.

While Mom was adding to her stable of friends, I myself had someone new in my life. Her name was Mary Anne Nielsen, and she was two years ahead of me at Lawton, though, as I recall, she was only eighteen months older. I saw her every day at recess, and she was quite noticeable on two counts. One, she had almost white blonde hair. Two, she was the fastest runner I had ever seen.

Although I had looked upon her with admiration, I did not think much about her until I saw her at the 48th Avenue ice-skating rink. She looked very pretty. Mary Anne was an excellent figure skater and could perform jumps and formal spins with great agility. I was there on my first-ever attempt to ice-skate. It was crowded, so thankfully, she did not notice me. At that point, I had never actually spoken to her except to nod or say hello in the schoolyard. I can't remember everything that was going on in my mind about Mary Anne, but I do know that for the next six months, I went ice-skating three times a week. I got very good at hockey skating, because early on, I realized I could never succeed at figure skating. But using hockey skates, I could go backward almost as fast as I went forward. I was able to dart in and out among the skaters and throw up a huge spray of ice for sudden stops. If I sound like a showoff, you have it right. Ice-skating was the first thing in my life I was good at. Alas, Mary Anne never showed up at the rink in all that time.

Then, at about the time Mom had her first club meeting, when I was about to turn ten, Mary Anne, age eleven, showed up at the rink. The session had already started when Mary Anne and her older sister arrived. I was on the ice whizzing about. When Mary Anne came on the ice, she was quite shaky, not nearly the skater she had been six months earlier. That gave me the nerve to skate up to her and say hello.

"You have really learned how to skate," she smiled. "I saw you here the last time I came, and you could not even straighten your ankles."

"I didn't think you saw me," I answered.

"I can't believe you picked it up so quickly," she said. "Do you come here often?"

"Friday night, Saturday afternoon, and Sunday afternoon," I answered. "We play hockey on Sundays after the session closes, and Mrs. Campbell has me help clean the ice during intermissions, which means I don't have to pay admission."

She smiled again. While we were talking, I was skating backward while facing her, casually looking over my shoulder to make sure I did not hit any other skaters.

"How come you haven't been here?"

"My sister hurt her knee, so I had no one to come with," she answered. "My parents won't let me come alone. I'm afraid I am very rusty."

"It won't be long before you get it back," I suggested.

When the "couples only" sign went on, I asked Mary Anne to skate with me. She seemed very nervous. I would have been too, but somehow, being on the ice gave me tremendous confidence.

I told Mary Anne there was going to be a hockey game after the session ended, and I would be playing. Maybe she and her sister might want to watch, I suggested.

"I'll ask my sister," she said.

Most of the guys who played hockey were in their teens or early twenties. They called me "Little Danny." But I was a good enough skater to hold my own. There were two chairs at each end of the ice, and they constituted the goals. At one point early in the game, there was a major collision mid-ice, and the puck was pushed right into my stick. Five or six players were in the pileup. I raced toward the goal with only the goaltender there to stop me from scoring my first goal ever. I aimed to hit the puck into the left corner of the goal, but I broke my wrists too early, and the puck went right instead—and past the goalie for a score!

"Danny boy," said Art Fine, our team captain, "that's the best damn head fake I have ever seen!"

All of the other members of the team came by to congratulate me. Someone called from outside the rink, "He's only ten years old."

I looked up at the end of the rink, and there standing near the exit were Mary Anne and her sister. Mary Anne waved good-bye and smiled. I have had some good times in my life but I don't know if I ever felt any better than I did at that exact minute.

I saw Mary Anne the next day during recess at school. Summer vacation was not far off. She was a fifth grader about to go into the sixth grade, and I was only going into the fourth grade. To say that this constituted a major gulf would be a gross understatement. If Mary Anne had been ugly or unpopular, it might not have been so significant. But Mary Anne was pretty and popular in school. She was always surrounded by a group of girlfriends, and everyone knew that George Cable, who was a year ahead of her, was a serious admirer. He lived only a block away from the Nielsens, and he walked home with her and her friends every day. Alas, we lived in the other direction.

Anyway, Mary Anne said she probably would not be doing much ice-skating in the summer, but she did plan to play tennis every day at Sunset Playground. I said I played tennis, and maybe we could have a game. "I'd like to," she said.

So that is how I came to spend my summer playing tennis at Sunset. Mary Anne would show up at about 11:00 AM and stay until 3:00 or 4:00 PM. We played tennis about the same, and both of us were very competitive. She could sometimes beat me, but I think we probably broke even. One of the fortuitous offshoots of my friendship with Mary Anne was that coincidentally, Joe Sprinz and his wife frequently came to the courts at about noon and stayed for an hour and a half. Joe was the catcher for the San Francisco Seals, then a team in the Pacific Coast League; the Seals played all of their weekday games at night when they were not on the road. Mary Anne and I started playing doubles matches against Joe and his wife. Joe, at forty, was in the twilight of a baseball career. But he was a professional athlete and in good condition. Our matches against Sprinz and his wife were close and spirited. Several times, Joe Jr. and Jim came over from the basketball court to watch, as did a number of other people. Of course, Joe Sprinz was the celebrity draw. At first, we lost most of our doubles matches, but the tide turned in midsummer, and Mary Anne and I got so that we won quite easily. We played very well as a team. Joe Sprinz was complimentary to us both and said he was looking forward to the off-season so that he could bring his crippled son to the playground and start teaching him baseball.

I must have spent hundreds of hours that summer playing tennis with Mary Anne. At Sunset, like at the ice rink, our age difference did not seem to matter. She told me many times that I acted older than my age. On the other hand, Mary Anne seemed younger than her age. Unlike some of the girls in her class, she was flat-chested and had the figure of a slim boy.

In all of that time, I only kissed her once—at a birthday party for one of her friends, a party to which she got me invited. We were playing "spin the bottle." When it was Mary Anne's turn, she spun, and the bottle stopped at me. "Fate ordained," I remember saying, moving toward her to collect my kiss. I should have put my arms around her as they did in the movies. Instead it was a one-second kiss smack on the lips with arms down. Everyone squealed, because they knew we were good friends. Mary Anne and I both laughed.

When school resumed, I was out of my element. A fourth grader could not have a sixth grader as a girlfriend. Joe Jr. said Jim had girlfriends that were more than two years older than he was. Well, maybe Jim could pull that off, but I couldn't. Mary Anne and I saw each other at the ice rink a couple of times that year, and we played some tennis together. But the boys in her class were entering puberty and growing rapidly. It wasn't long before Mary Anne started developing breasts and wearing lipstick, and soon, she had a pretty sexy look about her. Meanwhile, I wasn't changing at all.

Instead of looking older to her, I suspect I was looking younger. Today, I imagine her saying to herself, "My God, what was I thinking?" Even so, I'll never forget the summer of 1944.

CHAPTER 15

While I was working on my tennis and baseball, Joe Jr. and Jim were developing their basketball talents, and World War II was reaching the decisive stage. On June 6, 1944, the Allied armies invaded France. Bitter fighting ensued, but an Allied victory seemed certain to us kids, though Hitler clearly did not think so. Dad, whose Sixth Armored Division landed at Utah Beach on July 18, 1944, was part of General George S. Patton's famed Third Army. The Sixth Armored immediately became involved in the struggle for Brittany that lasted until September 18. Casualties were heavy on both sides, but the Germans lost proportionately far more men than we did; in fact, the ratio was about three to one. In the years since, I have read detailed accounts of the fighting in Europe and of the part played by the Sixth Armored. There are thousands upon thousands of books written about the reconquest of Europe, so I won't attempt to recreate here what went on there, except to say that the Sixth Armored Division lost nearly a thousand lives.

At home, news of Allied successes dominated the front pages, and Mom and we kids paid close attention. We did not know where Dad was, but we knew he was somewhere in the middle of the action. We constantly read about Patton's tanks racing through France, liberating towns and cities at a breakneck speed. The newspapers made it seem easier than it actually was.

Mom made sure we prayed for Dad every night. We all believed Dad would survive. Only in the darkest corners of our minds lurked the thought that he might not. It was a thought that hung there, at least in my mind, never entirely going away, but never being acknowledged.

Meanwhile, San Francisco was booming. The Bay Area was the main staging point for servicemen going to and coming from the Pacific. Market Street was thronged with servicemen, and a lot of them met girls out for a good time. No matter where you went, you saw soldiers, sailors, and marines. The sailors seemed to be the most outgoing and the most successful in picking up girls. Treating servicemen well was part of the war effort.

A woman who lived on our block, Marilyn Smith's mother, used to bring home a different sailor every weekend. We used to play with Marilyn, who was two years older than Joe, and she once put on a show for us that she called the dance of the seven veils: that was the first time I ever saw a girl naked. Some of the older boys on our block heard about it and began visiting Marilyn quite frequently. At least one claimed to have "done it" with Marilyn, but the consensus was that she was a "prick tease." I never had any firsthand information, because Joe told Mom about Marilyn's striptease, and Mom forbade us to ever again go to her house. If we did, Mom said she was going to go directly to Mrs. Smith. But I remember being amazed one day before the war was over to see Marilyn and her mother coming up the block, each on the arm of a sailor. Marilyn's makeup was so heavy that it looked like war paint, and she was only thirteen or fourteen at the time. Well, some girls were never too young to serve their country. But actually, for all I know, all they did was play spin the bottle.

As promised, Joe Sprinz, the catcher for the San Francisco Seals, began coming to Sunset Playground every other day in the fall of 1944, bringing his son, LeRoy, who had a crippled right arm from polio. Joe wanted LeRoy to have as normal a life as possible. Even though the dozens of kids who came to Sunset in the fall liked to play choose-up tackle football, whenever Joe Sprinz came (usually Tuesdays, Thursdays, and Saturdays), we all played choose-up baseball, and Joe was the pitcher for both sides. Most of the kids were eleven or twelve, and some of them were pretty good. Joe told me I should try to be a catcher given that I was a left-handed batter. "Catchers who bat left-handed are in great demand," Joe told me. And that is how I became a catcher. Joe would bring bats and balls and catching equipment that was way oversized for me. Nevertheless, Joe insisted that the catchers for both sides wear his mask, chest protector, and shin guards, and it actually turned out to be a good thing, because several times every game, a foul ball would hit one of those protected areas. Joe taught me how to catch the ball and how to throw quickly from the right ear without a big windup.

Joe Jr. and Jim played in some of the baseball games, but inevitably, they preferred playing basketball. By the same token, I played some basketball, but I somehow lacked the coordination to shoot and dribble the ball. I am sure that if I had practiced twice as much as Joe and Jim, I still would have been half as good. In baseball, I seemed to have some natural talents, and I also had Joe Sprinz to encourage me. So that is where I spent my time. Without the inspiration of Mary Anne Nielsen, I pretty much stopped playing tennis.

Because of her work, Mom did not have a chance to come to Sunset except on weekends. One Saturday, I introduced her to Joe

Sprinz. Mom said she felt like she already knew him because, she said, "Danny talks so much about you." About three weeks later, Mom invited the Sprinzes to come to our house for dinner. They accepted, and Mrs. Sprinz brought a huge chocolate cake. Joe Sprinz told Mom that she had three very talented sons. He said that he had watched Joe Jr. and Jim play basketball and that they were the best by far for their ages out of any of the kids who came to the playground. Joe Sprinz was about five years older than Dad, and like Dad, he was the kind of man who commanded respect. He was a man's man, a natural leader. I have no idea why he was not in the service. Afterward, Mom said it was good to have someone like Joe Sprinz around as a role model.

"He seems to have taken quite an interest in you, Dan," Mom said. I replied that I thought that he appreciated that I was always kind to LeRoy, who was very quiet but highly intelligent and who got all As in school.

In addition to playing sports, we three boys went to as many sporting events as we could. We saw the Seals and Joe Sprinz play at Seals Stadium. We especially liked Sunday doubleheaders. Games cost only fifteen cents for kids age twelve and under. At the ticket window, you did not turn thirteen until you were at least fifteen! During the fall, we attended most of the games played at Kezar Stadium in Golden Gate Park. In the years 1943 to 1945, the football scene was dominated by service teams such as Del Monte Pre-Flight, St. Mary's Pre-Flight, Fleet City, March Field, and the El Toro Marines. Crowds of up to 50,000 turned out for the games.

College All-Americans were quite numerous on those service teams. One of my favorite players was Buddy Young, who was only five feet five and who weighed 155 pounds. I first saw him play in a newsreel that showed him make five long touchdown runs as a freshman for the University of Illinois in a 1943 game. Those heroics left an indelible mark on me that have never been erased. To see him play in person for Fleet City was a thrill indeed. The play I remember best of all was a touchdown he did not make. It was in a game Fleet City played against St. Mary's Pre-Flight. Young had broken into the clear with only one man between him and the goal. That man was Frankie Albert, the great Stanford All-American quarterback and future star and later coach of the San Francisco 49ers. Albert was famous for his running, passing, and punting, not for his defense. The speedy Young faked left and then right, but Albert brought him down with as clean and sure an open-field tackle as I have ever seen. After the game, Joe Jr. and I hung out by the locker rooms waiting for the players to come out. Albert, handsome and well dressed, joined some glamorous-looking people and got into a private automobile. He moved so fast through the crowd that we could not get his autograph. We went from there to the Fleet City bus, where the players were boarding. I got inside, and there was Buddy Young standing up in the middle of the bus, still sweating from his shower. He wasn't much taller than I was. Young was one of the few blacks to play on a major service team. There was still a lot prejudice in those days. But Young was so good he could not be ignored. Much later in his life, Young became an executive for the National Football League. I wish I still had the program he signed for me that day.

Naturally, as an avid sports fan, I read the sports pages of all four San Francisco newspapers, starting in about 1943. Of course, the *Examiner* and the *Chronicle* were the morning papers and the two best, but both the afternoon *News* and *Call-Bulletin* had solid writing talent. I may have drowsed through school, but I was an insatiable reader when it came to sports. At the time, I thought I wanted to be a sports writer. Alas, it never happened.

CHAPTER 16

My big Christmas present in 1944 was a chest protector, shin guards, and catcher's mask. Mom must have consulted with Joe Sprinz on where to buy them. They were professional grade and big enough that I could grow into them. I don't remember what Joe Jr. and Jim got for their big presents. By this time, being without Dad on Christmas was the norm for us. The last Christmas he had been at home was 1941. But we were thinking about him even more, because the war in Europe had taken a sudden turn for the worse. Hitler had gone on the attack, and the papers were full of the sudden change in the fighting. The papers reported freezing cold, heavy fog, and huge numbers of German soldiers in the kind of blitzkrieg offensive that had given Germany its victories early in the war.

Of course, we know now, decades later, what was going on, and we kids had a right to be concerned. Hitler had ordered three German armies, the equivalent of twenty-nine divisions, with a total of 500,000 men, to attack a weakly defended Allied line fifty miles wide in the Ardennes Forest on the German–Belgium border. The Allies were caught by surprise, because they did not think Hitler would attempt to attack on the difficult semi-mountainous and heavily forested terrain. It was known as the Battle of the Bulge. Hitler's strategy, according to historians, was to drive a wedge between British and American forces, reach the sea, retake Paris, trap four Allied Armies, and bring about a negotiated peace on the Western Front.

The German attack began on December 16, 1944, and initially enjoyed great success as thousands of American troops were trapped and forced to surrender. The Allied forces in the Ardennes eventually totaled more than 600,000 fighting men, including General Patton's Third Army, which had rushed into the fray to help reinforce the Allied line of defense. The Germans created a significant bulge in the Allied line, but they failed to encircle it because of heroic Allied fighting. The battle raged until January 25, when the Nazis were forced to retreat, having suffered 100,000 killed, wounded, or captured. Losses on the American side were almost as staggering, with 19,000 killed, 23,554 captured, and nearly 40,000 wounded.

During that time, we had no idea what was happening to our dad. They were anxious times, indeed. Mom said, "No news is good news," explaining that if anything had happened to Dad, we would have heard about it.

After more than a month of anxious waiting, we finally got a letter from Dad on February 16, 1945. It was dated January 30. All he said was that the fighting had been pretty fierce for a while but that he believed the Germans were on the run and ready to surrender. He said he was confident he would be home by that next Christmas. "You have no idea how anxious I am to see you and the kids," Dad wrote. "The experiences we have had here for the past six months make me realize what is most important to me, and that is to be with my family."

Getting that letter, together with the ensuing news about Allied successes, made us all greatly relieved. It seemed only a matter of time before the war in Europe would be over.

CHAPTER 17

The following story appeared on the obituary page of the *San Francisco Chronicle* on April 18, 1945:

> By Morton Griggs
>
> Lt. Col. Joseph Holt Booker, 35, whose family resides on 28th Avenue in the Sunset District, was killed in action on April 4 when a German fighter plane fired on a fuel truck, causing it to explode, according to a U.S. Army information officer.
>
> At the time of the attack near Muhlhausen, Germany, Lt. Col. Booker, a battalion tank commander with the Sixth Armored Division, part of Gen. George S. Patton's Third Army, was parked in a jeep next to the fuel truck. The ensuing explosion destroyed the jeep and the truck, killing instantly Lt. Col. Booker and the truck driver, Cpl. Richard Parsons, of Dublin, Ga.
>
> An army source interviewed by the *Chronicle* said the remains of the two were unrecoverable. Some 11 other soldiers were injured by the blast. The source said the air attack came as a surprise since Luftwaffe planes had not previously been operating in the area. The attack turned out to be part of a mini counter-offensive by the Germans that was quickly repulsed, the source said.
>
> Information about Lt. Col. Booker's death was delayed, because the army needed to confirm all details and notify the next of kin.

The army spokesman said Lt. Col. Booker had recently been awarded the Silver Star for risking his life to help pull two soldiers out of a burning armored personnel carrier during the Battle of the Bulge.

Maj. Gen. Robert W. Grow, commander of the Sixth Armored Division, said in an official statement, "Lt. Col. Booker was an outstanding leader whose professionalism, devotion to duty and bravery set a standard for all to follow. His loss is great indeed for his family, the army and his country."

The army said that Lt. Col. Booker was a 1932 graduate of the Military Academy at West Point. He grew up in Tupelo, Mississippi. His parents were both killed in an automobile accident when he was 14.

After graduation, Lt. Col. Booker served in various posts in Honolulu, Hawaii, Ft. Riley, Kansas, and the Presidio in San Francisco. Chronic illness forced him to take a medical discharge from the army in 1939, and he subsequently went to work for the Standard Oil Co. But he reentered the service in January of 1942 and became part of the founding of the Sixth Armored Division in Fort Knox, Ky., in February of that year. He was shipped to England along with the Sixth Armored in February of 1944 and landed in France at Utah Beach on July 18, 1944. The Sixth participated in the Brittany campaign and the battles for the Seille River, the Saar and the Ardennes and was often involved in heavy fighting. The Sixth crossed the Rhine River in March of 1945. On March 25, the Sixth helped capture Frankfurt and went on to cross the Main River. The small German counter-attack began April 4, the day Lt. Col. Booker was killed, the army source said.

Lt. Col. Booker is survived by his wife, Constance, and three sons, Joe Jr., 11, Daniel, 10, and James, 9. They all attend Lawton Grammar School. Mrs. Booker is the daughter of a

> retired Episcopalian minister and was born in Honolulu, which is where she met and subsequently married her husband.
>
> Mrs. Booker said in a telephone interview that Lt. Col. Booker was a wonderful husband and father who died for what he believed was a noble cause and further that his memory will live forever in the hearts of his family.
>
> Durden Harley, a neighbor of the Bookers, said in a telephone interview that "Joe Booker was a great man, a great friend, a man's man if there ever was one."

I think today that Morton Griggs must have put a lot of extra effort into writing Dad's obituary. Not all of our World War II dead got that kind of treatment. We heard the crushing news about Dad's death five days before the *Chronicle* published its story. Mom learned about it in person when an officer from the Presidio drove out to our house to give her the news. What happened over the next weeks is a blur to me now. Dad received a full military funeral service at the Presidio, which we all attended. Of course, there was no casket. Not even his dog tags. My grandmother, Mary Teresa, came out by train to stay with us for two weeks. She slept on the couch. I don't know who Dad's death affected more. We boys all cried when we got the news. But after that, I just felt a dull ache. Mom cried off and on for weeks. We tried to comfort her, but that only made her cry more. "It must be God's will," she said. "Thank God I have you boys."

The phone rang incessantly, and Mom received dozens of letters of condolences, mostly from military friends and people she knew in Hawaii. Neighbors came by with dinners and food and offered to do whatever they could. We were the first gold star on our block. A gold star in the window meant you had lost a loved one.

I started wetting the bed and continued to do so for the next two years. I can't tell you how embarrassing that was. I just could not wake up at night. Joe, who normally was a peacemaker and leader among his friends, got into two fights on the basketball court. I don't recall anything changing about Jim except that maybe he did not make so much fun of everything, and he worked at his basketball even harder.

Two months after Dad died, one of his fellow officers from the Sixth Armored came to visit us. His name was Richard Hamblen. He'd been wounded in the Battle of the Bulge, sent home, and discharged. He said that he was just starting a law practice in San Francisco where he had grown up and that while he and Dad were both fighting in Europe, Dad had asked Mr. Hamblen to please see if he could help Mom and us kids if anything ever happened to him. Mr. Hamblen, who was married, was a handsome man, about thirty-five with gray curly hair and a lot of wrinkles on his face. We all liked him immediately, and he proved a very valuable advisor to Mom and all of us.

CHAPTER 18

There is another perspective on my father's death. He was just one of 61 million fatalities in World War II, the majority of which were the responsibility of just one man, Adolf Hitler. Civilian and military casualties in the Soviet Union alone were 25.8 million. Germany itself lost 7 million, and Poland lost 6.8 million. The United States lost my dad among 295,000 military deaths. When I think of our family's grief multiplied by 295,000, or by 61 million, it seems an incomprehensible amount of suffering—and mostly the fault of a vile little man whose twisted, maniacal mind was allowed not only to come to power in Germany, but even to flourish. Make no mistake about it: at his peak, he was venerated by the German people. How egregious that one man could inflict death on so many. The Holocaust alone accounted for between 5 and 6 million deaths, mostly in Poland and the Soviet Union. How could one man promulgate such horrors with the complicity of so many? How could God have allowed it?

My faith in God was shaken after my father's death, but I continued to say my prayers. Mostly, my prayer was "Dear God, please don't let me wet my bed." I guess God wasn't listening.

The fighting in Germany ended May 6, 1945, just a month and two days after my father was killed. Japan surrendered on August 14, after we dropped atom bombs on Hiroshima and Nagasaki. Upon Japan's surrender, there was a huge celebration in San Francisco. Joe Jr., Jim, and I took the streetcar down to Market Street to be part of the celebration. The crowds in the street were so great that it took our streetcar an extra forty-five minutes to get to the Ferry Building, from which point we walked back up Market Street all the way to the Fox Theater. Servicemen were getting a lot of kisses from the girls who had come out to celebrate. It was pretty wild and a lot of drinking was going on. We were mostly just watching the excitement, enjoying being a physical part of it. By this time, we were reconciled to our father's death, but we hadn't totally recovered from it.

When we got home at about eight o'clock, Mom was not there. She had left a note on the kitchen table saying she was at Angelo's, a bar at 21st and Noriega, where The Club was celebrating. We made our own dinner. It turned out to be lucky that we did not stay downtown. That evening, the celebration turned ugly, with cars overturned, streetcars assaulted, and store windows smashed. The so-called peace riots in San Francisco did not end until four days later. The newspapers reported that eleven people were killed, and 1,000 were injured. Then as now, it made no sense unless one can just say that four years of war had created a lot of pent-up steam that had to be released. But that seems to be a stupid rationalization. I witnessed a similar occasion in 1984 in Detroit, when I attended the final game of the World Series that was won by the Detroit Tigers. As we left Tiger Stadium, I was amazed to see as many people celebrating on the surrounding streets as there were people inside. The crowd, virtually all white, was in a celebratory but unruly mood. We got away before a couple of cars were overturned and set on fire, one of them being a police car. There is a moral here: stay away from crowded victory celebrations where alcohol is flowing!

The postwar period slowly brought on a return to normalcy in San Francisco. The United States had put together a huge fighting machine, and it took time to unwind it. At the peak in July of 1945, the United States had 12.3 million people in uniform, with 7.4 million being overseas. Just a year later, total U.S. military strength had dropped to only 3 million, of which about 1.3 million were overseas.

Although the war was over, the 1945 football season was still dominated by the service teams, and there was a game every Sunday at Kezar Stadium. We boys attended all of them.

One of the great changes in 1946 was the return of all of the baseball players who had been in the service. Although professional baseball leagues had continued to operate throughout the war, the reservoir of players had been thin and the caliber of play substantially below prewar standards. Now there was great excitement across the country to see the great players like Joe DiMaggio, Ted Williams, Hank Greenberg, and scores of others.

Of course, our team, the San Francisco Seals, was in the Pacific Coast League, the highest-rated minor league in the country. There were a lot of players in the PCL in 1946 who would later become major-league stars. I probably attended twenty-five or thirty games that first postwar year. The Seals won the pennant under manager Lefty O'Doul. The stars were first baseman Ferris Fain, who hit .301, and pitcher Larry Jansen, who won thirty games and lost only six. Both Jansen and Fain went on to be major-league stars. Joe Sprinz was also on the team, but at age forty-four, it was his final season. Even so, he batted .280.

It was in 1946 that I heard something crazy about Joe Sprinz and asked him about it: I had heard that Sprinz had gotten all of his teeth knocked out trying to catch a ball dropped from a blimp in 1939 at the Golden Gate International Exposition on Treasure Island. Sprinz said that it was partly true, but that he had only lost five teeth. It seems that previously, Sprinz had successfully caught a baseball dropped four hundred feet from the tower at Treasure Island by Lefty O'Doul, as part of a publicity stunt, and he later got talked into making a try from 1,000 feet. Joe said several balls that were dropped from the blimp slammed heavily into the grass before he actually tried to catch one. "I had the line on it, and it was coming fast," he said. "I had my glove in front of my face, but the ball glanced off my glove and smashed into my mouth. The next thing I knew, I was in the hospital." In addition to losing five teeth, Joe had twelve broken bones in his face, and his recovery took three months. Some people said it was a brainless stunt, but Joe was not a stupid man. After his playing career ended, he became a Seals' coach and then a probation officer and lived to be ninety-two, no doubt helping a lot of people along the way.

As 1946 progressed, I continued to carry my paper route every day, sometimes getting up at 4:00 AM so that I could have time to work on my growing stamp collection before taking off for school. Stamp collecting had become a serious hobby of mine, my interest originally coming from a stamp book I got for Christmas in 1943. In those days, most kids collected stamps. I was quite serious, and I used most of my money from my paper route to buy them either through the mail or at the six or seven little stores on Market Street that specialized in stamps and coins. I was making about $60 a month from my route as of early 1946, and I was also making another $7 every week selling Sunday papers on the corner of Ninth and Irving. So all in all, I was making nearly $90 a month, a lot of money for an eleven-year-old in those days. Joe kept his delivery business and made pretty good money, but not as much as I did. Of course, he did not have to get up at 4:30 AM every day, either. But I don't think I ever missed a day in all those years.

Jim helped Joe with his deliveries but did not seem to have a need for much money. He cared about three things: basketball, girls, and school. Jim also did a lot of reading, mostly sports books, but also sea adventures and mysteries. The differences among us three brothers were growing more pronounced. I loved baseball the way they loved basketball. They both did very well in school, and I was only average. In fact, I seemed to always feel sleepy in class. Moreover, I did not remember a lot of the things I was supposed to and therefore did not do well on tests. I was pretty good at writing, but my spelling was awful. I did not like anything scientific, mechanical, or mathematical (except sports statistics). By contrast, Joe liked everything scientific, mechanical, and mathematical. I was good at world geography (because of stamp collecting) and did okay at reading, but thinking back, I was pretty much a dullard in school. I needed motivation to pique my curiosity. Why Joe and Jim were so different, I don't know.

It was in early 1947 that Mother told us we were moving to a bigger house. She said that we boys needed our own rooms and a better place to invite friends. I did not know much about our finances except that we got a check from the government every month and that Mom was doing well at the hairdressers'. She also had money from Dad's insurance and his stocks. We were comfortable. Because I had all the money I ever needed, I did not think much about the family finances. However, I subsequently learned that Dad's cousins in Tupelo, Mississippi, wanted to buy out Mom's inherited share of the furniture business. They originally offered something like $30,000, but they raised that offer after Mr. Hamblen flew back to Tupelo as Mom's lawyer and investigated the business. I think, in the end, Mom got $60,000, though part of that had to go to the government in taxes.

Anyhow, we had enough to pay $19,500 for a three-story, twenty-one-year-old house located on 29th Avenue a half block from Golden Gate Park. The houses built on that block were all prewar and beautifully maintained and landscaped. It was easily one of the prettiest blocks in the Sunset. Our house seemed like a mansion. In all, there were five bedrooms and three baths, and all of the rooms were bigger than our house on 28th, which we sold for $6,800. Mr. Hamblen insisted that Mom pay cash for the new house, which he considered a better investment than the stock market, because he feared the country was due for a steep recession, if not another depression. Joe, Jim, and I all had our bedrooms on the third floor. Mine looked out over the backyard, where there were a lot of mature trees, including a eucalyptus that was taller than our house. I could see all the way to the ocean from my room. Mom loved the house, and the girls from The Club were enormously enthusiastic and said Mom deserved something really good. There was no question that the new house perked up Mom's spirits. She knew she needed to get on with her life.

CHAPTER 19

It was not long after we moved into our new house in June of 1947 that my mother convinced me I should quit my paper route, ending nearly four years of getting up seven days a week at between four and five in the morning. She said I earned enough money selling Sunday papers, and she was going to give us all allowances so that we would not have to work on a daily basis. That meant that Joe would give up his delivery business, which was now quite a distance from our home. I gladly took my mother's advice. She had said that if I did not have to get up early every morning, I would probably do better in school. And I suspect she hoped it would help me stop wetting my bed. I don't know if the change in schedule was responsible, but shortly after I ended my tenure as a carrier for the *San Francisco Examiner*, I did stop wetting my bed. You cannot imagine how happy that made me. God did answer prayers.

It was a couple months later, in August of 1947, when I got a surprise. Ralph Grunnert, who sold Sunday papers in front of St. Anne's Church on 14th and Judah Street, quit that lucrative post, because his parents were moving to San Mateo. Many families were moving to the suburbs in that period. Anyhow, I was next in line for the St. Anne's post and gladly accepted. On my first Sunday, I sold all of my 450 *Examiners* and 125 *Chronicles* between 6:30 AM and 1:00 PM and made a profit of about $15. Really, all I had to do was insert the papers and count the money. The crush of buyers when mass let out was so great that everyone served themselves, putting down their coins, making change, and taking their papers. I never worried about people taking advantage of the situation. After all, they had just come out of church.

Three weeks after my first Sunday at St. Anne's, I went out to Seals Stadium and was talking with Joe Sprinz before the game started; Joe was now the bullpen coach for the Seals. While we were talking, a tomboyish girl in a baseball hat and jeans came up to Joe and started talking with him. Joe introduced me. Her name was Alice Tognotti, and she was the coach of a team called "The Baby Seals." The team featured sons of past and present Seals and included Tony Lazzeri Jr., Del Young Jr., and Gus Suhr Jr. Joe told Alice that I was a good player, and she ought to put me on her team. Alice, who had a lot of respect for Joe, said that they always needed good new players and that she would come by and pick me up in her truck at 10:00 AM the following Sunday. She would bring a uniform for me, too.

To say that I was ecstatic would be a great understatement. The thought of playing for the Baby Seals was a dream so remote and so fantastic that it had never crossed my mind. But now it was going to happen. Of course, I would have to give up my St. Anne's corner and $15 a week, but I never gave it a second thought. Joe and Jim were amazed that I would give up the job. Joe said, "Aren't you a little young for that team?" In truth, I was. They were mostly thirteen to fifteen, and I had just turned twelve.

I was outside on the fated Sunday a half hour early. Joe and Jim had rigged a basketball hoop onto a telephone pole outside our house and were playing a game against each other. I had my spikes, my glove, and my catching equipment all bundled up inside a canvas bag. Ten o'clock came and went. Joe said, "It looks like they forgot about you." At noon, I went back into the house, utterly crushed. I was fighting back the tears. Mom said that maybe the truck had broken down or maybe something had come up. She told me that I should not be concerned, because Alice Tognotti had said she wanted me on her team just based on Joe Sprinz's recommendation. But all I could think of was that I had given up my Sunday corner for nothing.

I never did play for the Baby Seals. Joe Jr. was right: I was too young for the team. But at least I eventually got a tryout. Alice said that she liked a lot of things about my game and that I should stick to it. I would get better when I got older and stronger.

The next spring, when I was in the seventh grade, I was named the starting catcher for the Lawton Grammar School team. All of the other kids were in the eighth grade. We won the City Championship by a landslide, frequently scoring more than twenty runs in a game. I was only five feet tall and weighed about a hundred pounds. Even so, those who watched those games said I was pretty cocky for such a little guy, stealing bases, taunting the opposition, and making a big show of catching the ball behind the plate. I was more show than talent. But I did have a tremendous desire to win and a very strong competitive nature, at least as far as sports were concerned.

One day, we asked our mother if she was ever going to get married again. She said that no man would be interested in a woman with three children. She said she was happy to have us boys, and she did not need another husband right now.

But Mom's diary told another story. I think she was infatuated with Angelo Santino, who owned his own bar on Noriega Street. Mom used to go there from time to time with friends. Angelo's was a friendly neighborhood bar, and everyone knew one another. Angelo Santino, in his thirties, was quite handsome, and he had a wonderful singing voice. On March 21, 1947, Mom's thirty-third birthday, she wrote that some of her girlfriends had invited her for a quick birthday drink after work. "Angelo seemed to be singing only to me even though there were four of us girls sitting in the booth," she wrote. "And we did not tell him it was my birthday. He sounds just like Russ Colombo and I must say he is very cute. Too bad he is engaged." Dad had been dead for almost two years. I remember going places with Mom at that time, and she always attracted a lot of attention, from both men and women. She was always friendly and always had something amusing to say, or at least she made people smile.

When we moved into our new house on 29th Avenue, Mom invited our two sets of next-door neighbors for afternoon refreshments. They were older than the people on 28th Avenue, which was not surprising given that the houses on 29th were a lot more expensive. One of our new neighbors was a doctor named Erickson, and the other, Robert Talbot, ran the Irving Street branch of Bank of America. Both men and their wives were in their early forties. Mary Talbot was quite good-looking for her age and had a substantial bosom. Dr. Erickson's wife, Carolyn, was cheerful and plump. Both couples had children in their late teens whom we never really got to know except to nod hello whenever we saw them, which was not often.

On that first visit, Mr. Talbot got Mom talking about us and about how Dad had been killed in the war just a month before it ended. They were all very sympathetic. Mom showed pictures of Dad, and they all commented how handsome he was. It turned out the Talbots were planning to go to Hawaii for the following Christmas, and Mom gave them a good description of the weather and things to see around Honolulu. When they were leaving, Dr. Erickson said that if we had any medical problems, we should not hesitate to give him a call; his office was at 19th and Irving.

After the guests left, Mom said she was very happy that we had such successful neighbors who were nice as well. Joe agreed, saying they were a couple of notches above the people on 28th. Mom said Joe sounded like a snob, but added, "But in this case, I think you are right." Clearly, Mom was pleased with her new circumstances.

Other early visitors were Richard Hamblen and his wife, Claudia, who was quite a glamorous and well-dressed woman. Mom served a delicious roast pork dinner, and Claudia pitched in to help with both the serving and the clearing of the dishes. Mr. Hamblen took the opportunity to ask us boys a lot of questions, such as where we wanted to go to college. Joe said he hoped to get into Stanford and wanted to play basketball there. Jim said he liked either California or Santa Clara. I said I did not know. Joe said he would be starting Lowell High in the fall of 1948. Mr. Hamblen said that was a good choice, because Lowell had the highest academic rating of all the San Francisco public high schools, and a lot of Lowell graduates went to Stanford. I said I would be going to Lincoln, because they had a good baseball coach, Milt Axt. Mr. Hamblen said Lincoln was a good school, too, and had a high percentage of its graduates go to college. Jim said he did not know if he would go to Lowell or Lincoln. He had heard Lincoln had the prettiest girls. Mr. Hamblen laughed and said that was an important consideration.

Not long afterward, the Hamblens had all of us over to their house, which was located in a secluded section of Pacific Heights on Vallejo Street, only a half block from the fence outside the Presidio between Baker and Lyon streets. Their home was a three-story brick building with a great view of San Francisco Bay and Marin County. There was no traffic at that section of Vallejo, because it was a dead-end. Then as now, Pacific Heights was the place to live in San Francisco. Of course, there were lots of other fancy areas such as St. Francis Woods, Sea Cliff, the Presidio Heights, and Nob Hill, and there were a lot of big houses along the avenues just off Lincoln Way where we lived, but nothing touched Pacific Heights in prestige or price. I have no idea how the Hamblens could have afforded the house. I don't know what they paid for it, but it would likely be worth more than $8 million today.

I liked both Mr. and Mrs. Hamblen, and so did Joe and Jim. They took a serious interest in all of us. As I mentioned, Richard Hamblen was a lawyer who was about as distinguished-looking as a person can be. Claudia Hamblen was tall like Mom, except Mrs. Hamblen had dark hair. The Hamblens did not have any children. Claudia and Mom got along very well. Thinking back, although Mr. Hamblen was a good friend of Dad's, he did not spend a lot of time talking about their time together. Of course, back then, I did not know that Mr. Hamblen had promised Dad to look after us if anything ever happened to Dad. Mr. Hamblen was certainly a man of his word, and he would have a great influence on all of our lives, not just in helping with the family finances, but in a lot of other ways as well.

CHAPTER 20

One of the outcomes of my quitting my paper route and Joe ending his delivery service was that our dog, Skippy, was not getting enough exercise. So usually, one of us boys was designated to take Skippy out for at least thirty minutes at some time during the day or evening. That usually meant going into Golden Gate Park only half a block from our house. The nearby area of the park was mostly woods. The closest attraction was the soccer and polo field complex about a third of a mile away. And there was a dog run down near the Sunset Boulevard park entrance. Skippy quickly learned to love the park, particularly all of the dog sniffing and playing that took place at the dog run. Personally, I preferred the soccer fields where there were frequently games being played. Hardly any of the players spoke English!

We never worried about getting into trouble in the park, although at times, it was a pretty lonely place, particularly when blankets of fog covered the Sunset, as they often did. Actually, the most common fog was a high fog that made everything bleak and overcast. Less common was the low ground fog, which sometimes could be so thick you could barely see fifty feet. The park could be pretty eerie in those circumstances. Mom said the neighbors had warned her that the park was not safe for young children, because there were perverts who would sometimes go there. But we boys never gave it a second thought.

One evening in early September, Mom took Skippy for a walk just after dinner. The fog horns were blaring as Mom crossed Lincoln Way into the heavily wooded area across from 29th Avenue. Both Skippy and Mom knew their way around the park, and they set off, heading due north and crossing two deserted roads before reaching the area just north of the soccer fields. Skippy raced ahead. Suddenly, Mom heard a faint woman's cry for help coming from a small hill off to her right. She stopped and listened. The cry was repeated but sounded muffled, as if someone had a hand over a woman's mouth. Mom called for Skippy, who immediately came racing back. She looked at Skippy and put her finger over her mouth, and they headed in the direction of the cries. Together they crept closer to the sounds. There in the bushes were two men, one on top of a woman whose dress was up above her waist. The other man was holding the woman's arms above her head. The man on top was fumbling to enter the wriggling woman. When he removed his hand from her mouth, the woman let out a tremendous "Help, help! Help me! Someone!"

That was all it took to ignite Mom and Skippy. They charged up toward the scene, with Mom yelling, "Stop it, stop it!" and Skippy barking at his loudest. The two men were taken completely by surprise. Mom was carrying one of Dad's old steel swagger sticks, which was about two feet long. She always carried it when she went for a walk in the park, mostly to fend off other dogs should they try to attack Skippy.

The man who was holding the girl down jumped to his feet. "Hey, lady, this is none of your business. You could get hurt." Just then Skippy lunged at the man, biting him ferociously on the hand and drawing blood. The man screamed and tried to kick Skippy but missed. He looked at his bleeding hand and exclaimed, "I'm seriously hurt!" Mom struck the second man, who was just rising, with her steel swagger stick, hitting him squarely on the shoulder at the base of the neck. It must have been a powerful blow, because the man went down, screaming in pain. Skippy turned on the second man and bit him hard on the leg. The first man shouted, "I'm getting out of here!" and ran. The second man looked at Mom as if he were going to attack her, but Mom screamed, "Come near me and I will bash your brains in!" Skippy lunged again, and the man fled.

Meanwhile, the girl on the ground, who appeared to be in her late teens, was in hysterics. Mom picked her up and held her in her arms, assuring her that everything was all right. But there was blood all over her dress. Mom held the sobbing girl in her arms for five minutes. "Thank you, thank you," the girl said to Mom, still sobbing. Mom said she needed to see a doctor.

All of us boys were out when Mom got back. She immediately called the police, after putting the stricken girl in the guest bedroom. She then called next door to Dr. Erickson, who came right over. Shortly afterward, the police arrived. When I got home just after dark, there was a police car in our driveway with its lights flashing. I got a sudden fright and rushed into the house, where I saw Mom talking with two officers in the kitchen. When I asked what was going on, Mom just said that a girl had been attacked in the park, and she would tell us all about it later. Meanwhile, Dr. Erickson drove the girl to the University of California Hospital. After the police left, Mom gave us a slightly laundered account of what had happened.

Joe's first reaction was "Mom, you could have been killed."

Mom replied, "I wasn't thinking about that. That poor girl needed help. And I had Skippy and Dad's swagger stick for protection." Instinctively, all three of us gave Mom and Skippy big hugs.

The next morning, the phone was ringing off the hook. Reporters from the city's four newspapers had read the police report on the rape and wanted to interview Mom. At first, Mom was not going to talk to them, but she called Richard Hamblen, and he said they would be bothering her for weeks if she didn't. He said he would take care of it so that she would only have to tell her story once to the press. That afternoon, Mom met for more than an hour with reporters from the *Chronicle*, the *Examiner*, the *News*, and the *Call-Bulletin*. And all four papers' editors shortly afterward sent photographers, no doubt having gotten word that Mom was "a looker."

The next day, all four newspapers carried photos of Mom and Skippy together with colorful stories about how they attacked and drove off the rapists. The story was front page on both morning papers and inside in the afternoon dailies. But the biggest pictures were in the afternoon editions. The *Call* had a shot that appeared over four columns and covered nearly a quarter of a page. Mom was shown holding the swagger stick over her shoulder with Skippy standing next to her on our kitchen table. The *News* had a lot of information about Dad and how he died in the war. "War Widow Thwarts Rapists," headlined the *News*. "The Charge of the Amazing Mrs. Booker," said the *News* subheadline. "Fearless mother of three attacks two rapists," headlined the *Examiner*.

The hype over the event went on for days. Mom did not seem to mind the attention and handled it well, though she thought the newspaper reaction was overblown. She really did think that anyone would have done what she did under similar circumstances. Fortunately, for Mom, she did not have to testify at a trial. It turned out that the two men, both in their early twenties, had met the girl in an Irving Street bar, and they had had a couple of drinks together. The girl told police she agreed to go to the park for a walk, thinking that they might do a little fooling around, but nothing more. She said she had no idea that the two men would try to rape her. Both men pleaded guilty to the rape charges and were sentenced to terms in San Quentin. The girl, Linda Wright, gave mother a specially made silver necklace that read "Thank You." Mother wore it on and off for years, and she and Linda remained in touch for at least ten years before Linda moved to Southern California.

Late that fall, Mother received a phone call from one of our neighbors, Cynthia Culver. Mrs. Culver was extremely upset and said she needed to see Mom right way. Mother wrote about the matter in her diary.

> Mrs. Culver startled me by saying she had caught her daughter, Cathy, in bed with Jimmy. They were only wearing their underpants and apparently they were fondling each other. She said nothing had happened but that it appeared that something might have had she not come home unexpectedly. She said she blamed her daughter as much as Jimmy and said she was aware that Cathy had had a serious crush on Jimmy since the first time she had seen him. Mrs. Culver said she had forbidden Cathy to ever talk to Jimmy again and she hoped I would do the same with Jimmy. I said I felt very badly about what she said, and I thanked God that nothing serious had happened. Both are only twelve. I spoke with Jimmy as soon as Mrs. Culver left and had a

long heart-to-heart talk with him. He said the whole idea of taking their clothes off was Cathy's, something I don't doubt. I said to him that was no excuse and that God had made him a very attractive person and that he should never take advantage of the situation. Jimmy said the problem was he was always thinking about girls, when he wasn't playing basketball. And he said a lot of girls liked him and a lot wanted to "do stuff." I told him his penis was a very dangerous weapon and could cause some poor girl to get pregnant. If that happened, I said, it would ruin his whole life and would bring disgrace to all of the family and the memory of his Dad. Jimmy was quite embarrassed by the whole matter, and he promised he would never get a girl into trouble and he would never talk with Cathy again.

CHAPTER 21

Joe's first year at Lowell High School was an unqualified success. When he began his freshman year in the fall of 1948, he was six feet tall and weighed 170 pounds. He was a serious student who worked hard at everything he did. Despite being in a school that attracted the best and the brightest college-bound students in San Francisco, Joe earned straight As and rated academically near the top of his class. But he made his biggest impact on the basketball court. Joe played only a few minutes in each of the first three games, but in the fourth league game, Joe started and scored 13 points. He was a regular starter after that, the only freshman starter in all San Francisco. I watched all of those games, which were played in the Kezar Pavilion. Joe was incredible. He scored most of his points on long set shots from the right hand corner of the court, one of the toughest shots in basketball. He was also good on defense and got his share of rebounds, not only because of his height, but also because of his relentlessness near the backboards. Joe scored in double numbers in every game he started, and at the end of the year, he was named to the third string of the *Examiner*'s All-City team.

One of the fixtures in the stands for Joe's games was Constance Booker, who attended with her now best friend, Claudia Hamblen. I will never forget the first time they came into Kezar Pavilion. Mom had never been there before, and she and Claudia decided to take seats at the far end of the court, just under the basket. To get there, they had to walk past the Lowell rooting section. As they passed, several boys began whistling at the tall blonde and the equally tall brunette. Soon, the entire section was whistling quite loudly. Mom turned to face the students with a big smile and a wave. The students erupted with a huge cheer. Of course, no one at Lowell knew it was Joe Booker's mother. Joe was on the court warming up when the incident happened. I could see he was quite embarrassed. But he could not help smiling when Mom waved and got the big cheer. That night, we all told Mom that parents and faculty always sat above the rooting section, and they never walked on the floor near the court.

We were all proud of Joe, and without a doubt, he was the pride of the family and had inherited all of the best characteristics of Mom and Dad. But I can remember Joe saying at that time that Jimmy was potentially an even better basketball player than he was. As for me, I never went near a basketball court for fear of being ridiculed. One of the more stinging insults I received at that time was from a kid who said, "There's no way you are Joe Booker's brother."

In February of 1949, Mom received a letter from her mother saying that her father, the Rev. Pardon Crandall Connors, was critically ill with a failing heart. He was eighty-two. Mom wanted to go back to see him before he died, but there was no way that she could leave us boys. It was Claudia Hamblen who came up with a solution. She knew a woman, Adele Hullen, who could stay with us, cook our meals, and make sure we stayed out of trouble. Adele had several times taken care of children whose parents were friends of the Hamblens. So Mom flew back to Boston. It was her first ride in a plane and the first time she had been away from her family.

Adele Hullen was well cast for her role. She was tough as a drill sergeant but had a good sense of humor and a hearty laugh. She was also an excellent cook. She had four grown sons of her own, and she had no trouble handling us boys. Actually, the only one at that time who took any handling was Jimmy, who liked to stay out at night with friends who lived on 33rd Avenue near Irving. Joe was a rock of discipline and did all of his homework every night and then some. I never had any homework, so I spent the evenings listening to the radio in my room, reading sports books and magazines, and thinking about playing baseball.

Starting in the fall of 1948, when I was thirteen, I was invited to join a team that was put together by Grove Mohr, the acting director of the "Big Rec" baseball fields located in Golden Gate Park between 9th and 7th avenues. Big Rec was known as "the cradle of the stars," and indeed, in those postwar years, it was bristling with activity. Our team was known as the Big Rec Juniors. We won the city championship in the C Novice division, and I was the starting catcher. Grove Mohr, who was to become one of the most influential people in my life, soon found a sponsor, a man named Harry Bristow, who owned a candy store in the Richmond District, and our team became known as Bristow's Candies. One Sunday,

Grove told me we were getting a new pitcher, a boy named Ed Cereghino. Like me, Ed was only thirteen, but he was six feet tall and muscular. When I first warmed him up and he unleashed his fast ball, he almost knocked me over. Ed struck out nineteen batters that first game. With Ed on the mound, we began playing against men's teams and beating them. I was one of the youngest players on the team and, I will be the first to admit, not one of the stars.

It was just before I turned fourteen in 1949 that I sustained an injury that almost ended my baseball career. I was trying to block the plate to prevent a runner from scoring on a throw from right field. My left leg was extended in front of home plate while I was facing to the right as the throw bounced in. I did not really see the runner, who must have weighed at least 200 pounds to my 120. He came in, flying high, and his spikes tore into my left calf, ripping it open. It hurt but it was not as painful as you might have expected. The umpire and Grove helped peel back my sock, and the sight of torn flesh and blood made me feel sick to my stomach. I was rushed to the Park Emergency, where the doctor used fourteen stitches to tie my calf back together.

The worst thing about the injury was that I would not be able to play for at least four weeks, possibly longer. That meant that Grove had to find another catcher, who turned out to be Bruno Mitchell, who was bigger and stronger and better in every way, defensively and at bat. Bruno was almost sixteen, weighed about 175 pounds, and appeared to be a professional baseball prospect. The bottom line: I had lost my job. I rode the bench so much I got the nickname "Splinters." But I kept practicing. Grove said to keep it up and someday it would pay off.

Pete Wilson, one of the pitchers on our team, once asked Grove why he kept me on the team. "He can't hit, he can't run, and he can't throw," Pete said. I overheard Pete say that, and I picked up a rake and charged after Pete, who was half a foot taller than I was. Pete retreated in fear before Grove restrained me. Unfortunately, Pete was more right than wrong. I was slow in developing. When I started Lincoln High School in the fall of 1949, I was five feet five inches tall and weighed 125 pounds, hardly the fine specimen of manhood that Joe was. And Jimmy, who was fifteen months younger, was already as tall as I was, though he clearly was not going to be as tall as Joe.

Thinking back on those days, I guess I had some ingrained sibling envy. But to be honest, I never really thought about it. In fact, I wasn't very thoughtful about a lot of things. In my first semester at Lincoln, I got an F in algebra from Mrs. Berkowitz, whom I hated, and a D in Spanish from Mrs. McIntyre, whom I loved. I was lousy at abstract thinking, and I had a poor memory for things that bored me—unlike Jimmy, who could remember almost everything he read or heard in school, I was average at best. Oddly enough, I still planned to go to college. Somehow, I had found out that I could get into San Jose State College without taking the normal college-prep courses (i.e., three years of math, science, and foreign languages). I did manage to pass first-year algebra and first-year Spanish, but those were the last college-prep courses I ever attempted. That left me plenty of time to practice my baseball and read the sports pages.

Pardon your narrator's digression. It is funny how one thought triggers another, bringing back clear memories of what one was thinking about more than five decades ago! To get back on track, Mom was away in Boston for three weeks. She said that her dad died at peace with himself and that he looked almost "beautiful" on his deathbed. The most interesting part of the trip, she said, was meeting the scores of her relatives from the Connors and Cosgrove families.

"They certainly come in all shapes and sizes, and the Cosgroves really like to have a good time," Mom told us. She said that most of her cousins in the Connors family were twenty years older than she was and that a lot of the Cosgrove men loved to drink and were in fact rather rowdy, quite the opposite of the Connors family. Mom said the visit gave a perspective she did not have before, and she said she could see the Connors and Cosgrove genes in all of us. But she gave no thought of ever living in Boston.

"Our home is San Francisco, and we are in the midst of building a great family," Mom said. "You boys are all going to get married and have children and make Rev. Connors and your dad smile down from Heaven." I know Joe Jr. believed that.

Mom was never quite the same after that trip to Boston. She did not change in any negative way, but I think she began to think more about her own life. For the first time, she realized she did not have to devote every moment to her children. She could go away for three weeks, and everything would be fine, as long as she had Mrs. Hullen. That's not to say that Mom wanted to go anywhere for three weeks, but she was feeling a sense of freedom that she hadn't experienced in years, since she was a teenager in Hawaii.

Mom was not writing in her diary so much in those years, and I regret that she never wrote about her trip to Boston. However, she did make an important entry in November of 1949. She wrote that she had decided to quit her hairdressing job. Most of the members of The Club were no longer living in the Sunset, having chosen to move to either Marin or San Mateo counties, where the weather was decidedly better than in the city, particularly in the fog-bound Sunset. And Annette Morgan, who owned the hairdressing shop, was thinking of selling the business and in fact offered it to Mom, who declined, saying there were too many hours of work involved, and she was still raising her three boys.

When Mom told Claudia Hamblen she might be looking for another job, Claudia said she had heard about something that might be perfect. Mom wanted to work five hours a day and only during the week, which is what she did for Annette. The job Claudia had heard about—it had been offered to one of her Pacific Heights friends who had just gone through a divorce—was as hostess at the Zebra Room in the Huntington Hotel on Nob Hill. The Zebra Room was building a reputation as a dining room that appealed to local celebrities and well-heeled tourists. They wanted the hostess to come in at 10:00 AM and make telephone contact with all those people who had made reservations. Then, when the customers arrived, she would personally greet them and then show them to their tables if she had the time or direct someone else to do it if she didn't. During lunch, she would drop by each table to see if everything was going well. The general manager of the Huntington said he wanted to create a sense of warm hospitality that was at once sophisticated and glamorous. Crucial to the job was the ability to remember names and to be able to make cheerful repartee. Of course, Mom was perfect for the job, and she got it some twenty minutes into her first interview. Claudia was Mom's coach, both for the way she dressed and as a source of background information on

San Francisco society. In time, Mom was working the Zebra Room as if she owned the place. Not only did she learn the names of all of the regulars, but everyone knew her name, too. Mom loved the job, and getting off at 3:00 PM made it easy for her to go to high school basketball games and baseball games.

Early in 1950, Herb Caen wrote in his widely read column,

> A new injection of glamour has been added to the Huntington's already glamorous Zebra Room, lovely and lithesome Constance Booker, who radiates her beautiful smile at those lucky enough to have luncheon reservations. Constance, astute readers may recall, is the widow of a World War II hero, Lt. Col. Joseph Booker. Last year, Mrs. Booker made headlines when she and her dog rescued a woman being attacked in Golden Gate Park. But our sports desk says her greatest claim to fame is that she is the mother of Joseph Booker, Jr., a sophomore at Lowell, who is touted as the best basketball prospect the city has seen in years. Prediction: Constance will marry a Pacific Heights millionaire and live happily ever after. Darn it. We ink-stained news wretches don't have a chance.

Mom's reaction to the Caen column was that it was silly. But it did raise the question as to whether Mom would ever marry again. Of course, she would first have to start meeting some eligible men.

CHAPTER 22

Claudia Hamblen introduced my mother to the segment of Pacific Heights society of which she and her husband, Richard, were a part, namely lawyers, business executives, and other professionals, many of whom were graduates of either Stanford or the University of

California at Berkeley. The really old San Francisco money operated on a different level, though Mom got more than a glimpse of them through her work at the Zebra Room. The Hamblens, who had become by far our family's closest friends—really, they were more like relatives—frequently invited Mom to dinner at their Pacific Heights home. Invariably, there was a single and eligible man among the guests. Many of these men subsequently invited Mom out on dates. Mom usually accepted but always came home saying that she had had a good time but that she had not fallen in love yet.

Strangely enough, Mom's first real romance was with a baseball scout. His name was Robert "Bobby" Crable. He worked for the Brooklyn Dodgers and was responsible for finding prospects in northern California, an area that in the past had produced scores of major-league players. Crable, in his late thirties, had been a pitcher with the Dodgers organization, but his career ended before he made the big leagues, because he tore some ligaments in his shoulder that cost him his fastball. Crable was about six feet four inches tall, and despite big ears, he was good-looking, always tanned, and slim. His best feature was his smile that caused wrinkles to radiate almost 180 degrees around his eyes. Crable was at once likeable and friendly, and he was well-known to everyone connected with amateur baseball in San Francisco. He and Mom met in February of 1951 at Big Rec, the baseball fields in Golden Gate Park. Mom was there to watch one of my games. I was fifteen years and eight months old and was now not only a regular again, but also one of the better players on Grove Mohr's team. My work for the past two years had paid off, and I had grown to be five feet ten, and I weighed 160 pounds without any fat. I had grown much stronger and was able to hit the baseball harder and farther. I moved from eighth in the batting order to fifth, and my batting average was well above .300.

Crable's opening line with Mom was something about wanting to tell her that Danny Booker was one of the most improved players he had seen all year. Because Mom had been through my "Splinter" days and was now enjoying my success, the comment earned a big smile from her. Easy conversation followed. Mom knew a lot about sports, and she knew about most of the high school baseball players and basketball players in San Francisco. So did Crable, whom Mom always called "Robert." We had a number of players on our team who were seventeen and eighteen and would be eligible to sign professional contracts once they graduated from high school that coming June. So there were usually several scouts in the stands when we played. Our star pitcher, Ed Cereghino, would not graduate until the next year, but a lot of scouts wanted to keep close tabs on his development. But nobody scouted our team like Crable, who showed up almost every Sunday, invariably sitting next to Mom.

Pete Wilson, our second pitcher, told me he thought Crable was spending more time scouting Mom than the players. "Look at him," said Pete, "he's always looking at your Mom. I don't think he sees half the game."

Pete was right. Crable was clearly infatuated with Mom, who told me that she found Robert to be cute and funny and that he made watching the games very enjoyable. Mom and Robert made a handsome couple. It turned out that Robert had been married just before the war but was now divorced. He had joined the navy in 1942 and was then shipped to the Pacific aboard a destroyer in 1943. He did not return to the mainland until the end of the war. While he was away, his wife, who was apparently five or six years younger, met and fell in love with another man and asked for a divorce. The couple had no children.

"I guess I did not want to be married to someone who did not want to be married to me," he told Mom. Mom told us that he was probably pretty broken up over the divorce, because he told her that he hadn't dated much since and that he had had no serious relationships. He and Mom had that in common. Mom had had no serious relationship in her life except Dad. When you looked at them, you could see the chemistry, the body language. They both appeared to be several years younger than their actual ages.

Mom invited Robert Crable to our house for dinner one Sunday in May. Joe and Jim had met him while watching my games, and they both liked him. We all had a good time. I think Mom and Crable began a relationship not long after that. Mom was exceptionally discreet and never wrote about it in her diary, but she made some marks that I think were her code for meetings with Crable. I suspect, thinking about it today, that it was a lusty relationship that unleashed long-pent-up emotions and feelings. At the time, we boys had no inkling about what was going on. Crable spent a lot of time at our house, and all five of us went out together to stores, restaurants, and shows (including the Ice Follies) or sometimes even to the movies, though we boys never sat with Mom and Robert. Everywhere we went, people would say hello to Robert, or "Bobby," which is what everyone except Mom called him. The relationship lasted almost eighteen months and ended when the Dodgers asked Crable to move east to become a minor-league manager for the 1953 season. Obviously, the Dodgers had a high regard for him.

Mom wrote in her diary in January of 1953 that Robert had asked her to marry him. He said he would forego the promotion and resign from the Dodgers if she would say yes.

"I love Robert and feel very affectionate toward him but I don't think we are meant for a long term relationship," she wrote. "Our mutual interests are based on my interest in what my boys are doing and those things are going to change. Claudia agrees that knowing Robert has been a wonderful and valuable experience for me but that marriage might not be a good decision. Claudia pointed out that Robert has no money, which is true, but that is not what is driving my decision. Really, I don't know for certain what is, except that in my heart I know it is the right one, even though I am very sad that Robert is passing out of my life."

Mom had a going-away party for Robert, and she invited Grove Mohr and a number of the players from our team and their parents for the barbecue in our backyard. Robert made a little speech, saying that becoming a team manager for the Dodgers organization was the dream of his life. He also said that knowing the Booker family had been the best experience of his life, and he said it with a big smile on his face. But I know he was feeling quite sad inside.

But I am getting chronologically ahead of my story. Jim enrolled in St. Ignatius High School in 1950. St. Ignatius was an all-male school run by the Jesuits. It was Richard Hamblen's suggestion that Jim go there, because first, it was an outstanding school, and second, there would be no female distractions. Jim agreed, though he did say he would miss the chance to play on the same team with Joe. I was then a sophomore at Lincoln, and Joe was a junior at Lowell, where he was the star of the basketball team and already ticketed to be heading for Stanford on a basketball scholarship. It must have seemed strange to some people, our having three brothers living in the same house but all attending different high schools. But it made a lot of sense. I never would have survived the academic requirements at Lowell or the discipline demanded at St. Ignatius, or S.I., as we called it. Jim could have handled Lowell easily, but both Mom and Mr. Hamblen agreed that the girls would distract Jim.

By the time the 1950–51 basketball season came around, Jim was five feet eight and weighed a wiry 130 pounds. He had sandy hair, bright blue eyes, a turned-up nose, and a square chin with a small cleft. But what was amazing about him was his coordination on the basketball court. He was virtually ambidextrous. He could shoot and dribble the ball with either hand. He could accurately pass the ball behind his back, and he was a confident playmaker who seemed to see everything that was happening on the court at once. From his guard position, he dominated the game, setting up plays and making incredible passes that caused other players to shake their heads in appreciation. Jim was a starter for S.I.'s 130 lbs.-league team in his freshman year and was named not only All-City, but also the outstanding player in the league. Most observers said Jim should have been playing on the S.I. varsity team. Jim did not shoot a lot, but he made a high percentage of those shots he did try, and he averaged 11 points a game, a lot in those days, when final scores were sometimes 26 to 23 or even 19 to 18.

In the San Francisco high school leagues at that time, defense was a huge focus, and Jimmy was also good at that. I think he had six or seven steals for goals during his first season. But Jimmy did most of his scoring using a jump shot. He would typically charge for the basket and then stop and fall back while using a one-hand push shot to loft the ball over the reach of the defender. The defenders knew it was coming, but they couldn't stop it unless they put two men guarding Jim. If they did, Jim would quickly pass to the open man, who would often score. Like a lot of people, I was in awe of Jimmy's talents. How could one guy have so much talent and good looks besides?

Mom attended all of Jim's games, and so did I. The 130 lbs. division always played their games as a preliminary to the varsity contest. Normally the crowds were pretty sparse, but as the word got out about the talents of Jimmy Booker, more and more people started arriving early. Among them were the prep sports writers for San Francisco's four newspapers, all of whom wrote about Jimmy in separate sidebar stories. All the stories included the fact that Jimmy and Joe were brothers and that their Mom was a well-known and beautiful fixture at every game. One of the writers said that Jimmy was a natural at basketball and that he already had the coordination and skills of a college player. Indeed, Jim had great natural talent. But the sports writer would have better informed his readers had he related that Jimmy had been honing his basketball skills almost every day for the past eight years under the tutelage of a very demanding and intelligent brother.

CHAPTER 23

The Korean War had begun in the summer of 1950, and I can remember Joe saying that if it was a prolonged battle, we boys might end up involved in it. Joe turned 16 on June 17, 1950, and in two years, he would have to register for the draft. Needless to say, we boys paid close attention to what was happening in Korea, especially after Red China sent its "volunteers" streaming across the Yalu River and temporarily forced the American soldiers into a major retreat. The question facing most teenage boys at that time was *when* would they be drafted, not *if*.

Two of the issues that we discussed around our dinner table were whether we should use the atomic bomb and whether we should attack the Chinese mainland. Joe argued that if we dropped a nuclear bomb on China and threatened more, they would be forced to withdraw from Korea and sign some kind of truce or cease-fire. Mom said Joe was probably right, but wondered how many innocent children and women might be killed in the process. Joe said it was the same principal as President Truman approving the drop of atomic bombs on Hiroshima and Nagasaki that forced Japan to surrender in World War II. Joe said that although many innocents were killed, tens of thousands of American lives were saved, because most believed that the Japanese would defend against an American invasion with the same suicidal ferocity they had shown in defending the Pacific Islands. Joe contended that if we fought the Chinese and the North Koreans "with one arm tied behind our backs," America would lose many thousands of fighting men. Joe was very persuasive. The trouble was that many thought that using the A-bomb could trigger a third world war. And others argued that if we used nuclear weapons, we would create a permanent enemy in China. Joe argued this was rubbish, because we had dropped the bombs on Japan, and they were now our allies and had welcomed American democracy to their shores under the emperor-like leadership of General Douglas MacArthur.

But President Harry S. Truman had other ideas. By mid-1951, the United States had more than 500,000 fighting men in Korea. The United States had thrown back the Communist invasion, and Truman, fearing an expansion of the conflict into Europe, sought to negotiate a peace. In the process, he fired MacArthur, who wanted to take all of North Korea. The leaders began talks, which took two years to be resolved. Truman did not seek reelection as president in 1952 and was succeeded by General Dwight D. Eisenhower, who hinted that he might use nuclear weapons unless the Communists agreed to a cease-fire. Just a month after Joe's nineteenth birthday, on July 27, 1953, the cease-fire was signed, but not before 36,574 Americans had been killed in the Korean theater. It has been estimated that as many as 2 million Koreans and Chinese were killed in the war, including civilians.

Although the end of the Korean conflict meant we boys would not have to go to war, we still faced service in the military. By war's end, Joe was at Stanford and was temporarily exempt from the draft until graduation. And I was about to enter San Jose State, where I too would get a temporary exemption. Such was the intensity of the Cold War with the Communists at that time that the draft was continued even after the war in Korea was over: the army could not maintain its desired troop strength relying solely on volunteers, as is done today. The marines, navy, and air force did not need draftees, because there were enough volunteers. A lot of my friends in that era joined one of those services so that they would not have to be in the army. That was especially true while the fighting was still going on in Korea. After the cease-fire, some friends requested to be drafted so that they could serve their two years on their own time frame and get the inevitable service over with.

My brothers and I were part of the lucky generation. We were too young for World War II and Korea and too old to serve in Vietnam. Also, because the birth rates in the first half of the depression-plagued 1930s were so low, we did not have a lot of competition when looking for jobs or trying to get into college. The baby boomers, who were born after World War II, would have to contend with Vietnam, though, like us, they were blessed by good economic times. One of the characteristics of our generation, the so-called "silent generation," was that we had respect for authority and the institutions of government, including parents.

President Eisenhower, whether you liked his politics or not—and most did—was a man of the highest character. The Eisenhower Years (1953–60), it can be seen now, constituted the end of an era as well as a high point for domestic tranquility. Church attendance in the United States reached an all-time high (69 percent) in 1960, Eisenhower's last year in office. By comparison, it was only 49 percent in 1940, and it fell back to 62 percent by 1970. During the 1950s, evangelists such as Billy Graham were touring the country and attracting huge crowds, many of whom stepped forward at the end of the sermon to commit their lives to Christ. Fulton Sheen, the Catholic monsignor, had an audience of 30 million for his weekly television show. Norman Vincent Peale, a Protestant clergyman, wrote best-selling inspirational books, his most notable being *The Power of Positive Thinking*, which sold millions of copies. I recall reading it, and I also attended a Billy Graham "Youth for Christ" meeting at San Francisco's Civic Auditorium. I did not go to church, but I believed in God.

Of course, there was evidence of what was to come. Hugh Hefner started his *Playboy* magazine in 1953, and the Kinsey Reports revealed that Americans were far more active sexually than most imagined. One Kinsey statistic showed that 50 percent of all men and 26 percent of all women had committed adultery by age forty. In my youth, girls were classified in two categories: those who did and those who didn't. The latter category was thought to include the vast majority of girls. But Kinsey reported that 50 percent of all females said they had had premarital sex.

The biggest change of the 1950s was the advent of television. In 1950, fewer than a million American households had television sets. By 1960, 90 percent had at least one television set, and many had two or more. Television ended dinnertime conversations in many households, though our mother refused to allow the television set to be on while we ate. She also discovered Jimmy's first copy of *Playboy* magazine, which she declared to be "filth" aimed at destroying morality in America.

Growing up in the 1940s and 1950s was vastly different from the way kids grow up in today's era of soccer moms and sassy, spoiled offspring who think of oral sex the way we used to about kissing.

My bottom line is that although a lot of us may have missed the sexual revolution (and the drug revolution), the period from 1934 to 1939 was a great time to be born in the United States. It is worth repeating that by and large, we respected authority, we respected our parents, we loved our country, and we believed that with hard work, we could not help but succeed, especially if we believed in God. Importantly, we did not have to fight in World War II or Korea or Vietnam. Indeed, we were the lucky generation. It is a small wonder that we kept our mouths shut! Of course, that may be why no one from the so-called silent generation was ever elected President of the United States. The presidency jumped from George Herbert

Walker Bush, a veteran of World War II, to William Jefferson Clinton, a baby boomer.

CHAPTER 24

Not only did my brother Joe lead Lowell to the city basketball championship in his junior and senior years, but he also excelled academically and finished second in his class. He found a girlfriend in his junior year, Claire Winstead, a lovely five-foot-nine-inch brunette who played and loved basketball and who was also an outstanding student. At the time, Claire's father, Charles, was a professor of journalism at San Francisco State, having previously worked at all four San Francisco newspapers over a period of twenty years. Joe frequently brought Claire to our house for dinner, and Joe often ate at the Winsteads, who lived two blocks away, just up from Lincoln Way, about a five-minute walk from our house. They had met taking the bus to school, and they had so much in common that Jim and I figured they might end up getting married; Jim said he wished he had one girl he liked well enough to go steady with.

While Joe was a star and leading his marvelously exemplary life, I got kicked off the Lincoln High baseball team in my sophomore year. The reason the coach gave was that I smoked (as did most of the baseball players I knew). But there was a lot more to it. I had originally decided on Lincoln because of its baseball coach, Milt Axt, a San Francisco legend who was also the football coach. Under Axt, I played on the Lincoln varsity in my freshman year and got into several games. Axt told a lot of people I was a future star, which made me feel pretty good. Unfortunately, Axt was transferred to

Poly High after my freshman year and was replaced by a man I will not even name. I will call him Blank.

Anyhow, Blank had never played any baseball in his life and knew nothing about the game. Blank's specialty was football. Under Axt, our practice sessions would begin at two-thirty in the afternoon and end around five o'clock. Under Blank, we were lucky to start batting practice by three, and Blank liked to wrap things up a few minutes after four. Obviously, Blank was just going through the motions. I was in my third year playing sandlot baseball for Grove Mohr, so I knew what a good manager did and what kind of commitment to practice was required if a team was to win. Under Grove, our sandlot team beat everyone. Under Blank, Lincoln was a disaster, despite having some pretty good talent.

I made the mistake of openly complaining about our short practice sessions. The word got back to Blank, and soon afterward, he called me into his office and told me I was off the team, because he had seen me sneaking a cigarette across the street from school during a break between classes. In fairness to Blank, it was the second time he had caught me. The first time, he had given me a warning: "If you can't discipline yourself, you have no place on our team," said Blank, who must have known that six of our nine starting players also smoked. And who was he to talk about discipline? I would have practiced six hours a day if we could have; in fact, that is how much we practiced during the summers at Big Rec. Looking back now, I should not have been smoking. Indeed, I have not had a cigarette for around fifty years. But Blank's agenda was to get me off the team. Blank was one of the few people in my life whom I really disliked. Why? Because he did not care about coaching baseball, and he did not like me for implying that he was a lousy, lazy coach. I was intense about it then, and I still am. I am surprised my attitude hasn't softened in all of these years.

Despite what had happened with high school baseball, the summer of 1951 was a great one for me. Our sandlot team, now known as Pomona Tile, played games all over northern California. We took on town teams, made up almost entirely of grown men, from Santa Rosa to Eureka. We played in St. Helena, Clear Lake, Reno, and Fort Bragg, to name a few of the venues. Although we were kids ranging in age from sixteen to eighteen, I don't think we lost a game. More importantly, we had a great time on those trips and a lot of laughs. Most of the guys on our team were Italian, with names like Santino, Scramaglia, Benedetti, Spatafore, Strazzula, and Cereghino. We also had a Russian named Suzdeloff and a Portuguese named LaCosta. Cereghino was our ace pitcher, and Pete Wilson was our second starter. I was playing the outfield that season, and my hitting was continuing to improve.

The high point of the summer for me was being named the starting right fielder for the *San Francisco Examiner* Baseball School All-Star game, a contest that pitted the best players from San Francisco against the best players from the surrounding suburbs. The game was played in Seals Stadium, and about 13,000 fans showed up for the action. Ed Cereghino, who was from Daly City, was the starting pitcher for the out-of-towners, and he struck out the first three batters he faced. I was hitting sixth and ripped a single into center field, the first hit off Cereghino, which got a huge cheer from the crowd, especially my mom, who had watched me play scores of games with Cereghino but never against him. To his credit, Ed struck me out my next time at bat.

The *Examiner* Baseball School was headed by Oscar Vitt, a former big leaguer who earlier managed the Cleveland Indians. The school was held for the first time in 1946, and the Hearst organization, which owned the *Examiner*, pulled out all of the stops. The "faculty" that first year included Ty Cobb, Babe Ruth, Rogers Hornsby, and Tris Speaker, the greatest players who had ever lived. I can remember standing as a gawking kid in their presence. Thinking back, that moment seems even more incredible now than it did then. Such were the benefits of living in a city like San Francisco.

Meanwhile, Mom's romance with Bobby Crable was just warming up that summer of 1951. Mom loved her job at the Zebra Room. She still managed to cook meals for her boys, do their laundry, and run a pin-neat house without any hired help. She even attended all of our games. Of course, we pitched in, and I learned to make great salads that usually included lettuce, tomatoes, avocados, cucumbers, onions, olives, and Roquefort cheese. Jim would make things like pudding and Jell-O, and Joe's specialty was making hamburgers or hot dogs, which he liked to cook on our grill in the backyard. Bobby Crable was often there when he was not on the road scouting talent. And when Joe's girlfriend, Claire, came, she pitched in setting the table and cleaning up afterward. She and Mom had an easy relationship, and Mom seemed to think Claire was more than worthy of Joe. That was about as high a compliment to Claire as Mom could give!

Conversations ran from the war in Korea to the growing number of black men in baseball. Bobby believed that Negroes, as they were then called, were naturally superior athletes, and he cited Willie Mays, the young centerfielder for the New York Giants, who Bobby said he had seen play and regarded as the best young player in baseball and a certain Hall of Famer. I asked Bobby if he thought Mays was better than Mickey Mantle, the rookie centerfielder for the New York Yankees. Grove Mohr had taken our team to see the Yankees play in an exhibition game against the Seals earlier that year, and we had watched Mantle in batting practice before the game. We had never heard of Mantle, but his power at the plate was the most awesome any of us had ever seen. Bobby said Mantle was a great prospect, but Mays was a better all-around player. Bobby heaped his greatest praise on Jackie Robinson, who was the first Negro to play in the big leagues.

"I know Jackie, and I pitched against him in spring training, and you can't imagine the amount of pressure that man was under," Bobby told us. "Many of the players came from places where Negroes couldn't eat in the same restaurants or drink from the same drinking fountains or ride anywhere but the back of the bus. In the South, Negroes had to sit in the back balcony seats at the movies. They called it 'nigger heaven.' You can't believe the names they called Robinson: snow ball, nigger, coon, you name it. But Jackie took it all. He had gone to UCLA where most whites accepted him as an equal. And Jackie was smart, damned smart. But playing for the Dodgers was a different story. A lot of the guys on the Dodgers were from the South, and they resented having a Negro on the team. At first some gave him the silent treatment to let him know how they felt."

Bobby could tell baseball stories twenty-four hours a day and never run out of material. One of the stories I liked best was his telling how Leo Durocher, who was managing the New York Giants the year that Robinson broke in, called a team meeting before a series against the Dodgers.

According to Bobby, "Leo said, 'Boys, we gotta have a new strategy with this Robinson fellow. He's killing us. We ride the hell out of him, call him every name in the book, and what does he do? He goes three for four, steals second, steals third, and steals home. So I'm proposing that we change the strategy. Let's start being nice to him. Tell him he's a credit to his race. Tell him he had a great series in St. Louis. Make him feel good.'"

I asked Bobby what the point was of being nice.

"That's what the Giants asked," Bobby said. "Leo Durocher said, 'Boys, have you ever heard the expression "let sleeping dogs lie"? Well, we want to put this guy to sleep. We know what happens when he wakes up. He kills us.'

"So that's what the Giants did," Bobby continued. "They were as nice as they could be, even the tobacco-chewing Southerners. What happened? Well it worked. Jackie got just one hit in that three-game series, and he made two errors. The Giants won all three games, and Durocher was beside himself, chortling to his players, 'Boys, never forget it. Let the sleeping dogs lie.'

"Of course, Jackie was too smart not to figure out what the Giants had done. In any case, Durocher had a big mouth, and he told lots of people how to deal with Robinson, and the story kept coming back to Jackie, which made him madder and madder. Durocher's strategy only worked once," Bobby finished, a big smile on his face.

CHAPTER 25

I was absolutely floored by the news, and so was everyone who knew Jim: Jim had been suspended. Jim was temporarily suspended from St. Ignatius for ten days in October of his sophomore year and was not allowed to play basketball in the 1951–52 season. The reason given was that he had violated the St. Ignatius code of ethics. Mom was called to the school and given the background, which she shared with Joe, but not me. Joe was furious with Jim, and I overheard Joe almost screaming at Jim, "What the hell were you thinking about? This is the dumbest thing, the stupidest thing, that I can imagine. How could you have let that happen? You've got the judgment of a four-year-old!"

I asked Joe what it was all about, but he refused to say. And Jim would not tell me, either. In fact, I did not find out until many years later. The local newspapers assumed that Jim had been caught cheating in school. The *Examiner* high school sports writer wrote, "It must have been a pretty significant violation to keep the best basketball prospect in the city off the team." St. Ignatius officials would only say that Jim had made a mistake for which he was being punished. But they added that he was an outstanding student and had promised never to violate the ethics code again. There were dozens of rumors about the suspension, but no one got it right. And it is a credit to those few who did know that the true facts never became public.

One of the most disappointing aspects of Jim's one-year suspension from basketball was that it meant Joe and Jim would not play against each other, something I had really been looking forward to. Lowell was the defending champion, but it was thought that with Jim, St. Ignatius could give them a run for the title. Without

Jim, the game was no contest, and Joe scored a game-high 19 points while Jim was relegated to watching the game from behind the S.I. bench.

Jim continued to play basketball at various playgrounds around the city where good players congregated. His arrival always sparked a stir, and pretty soon, there was a growing group of onlookers watching Jim make his flawless moves on the court. Jim also played in the YMCA men's night league and dominated every game in which he played, despite the fact that there were many former college players participating.

In the spring of 1952, Jim started going steady with a girl from Lincoln, Diane Haley, the prettiest girl in the sophomore class. She was also the sexiest-looking girl in school and attracted attention from the first day of her freshman year. I was a year ahead of Diane, and like everyone else, I was sort of drooling over her. But I never made any move to get to know her, because it was one of those "the line starts on the right" deals, and I figured it would be a waste of time.

But it was a different story with Jim. Girls talked about him the way we boys talked about Diane. Jim met Diane one Friday night at the Parkside Theater, a hangout for high school kids, mostly kids from Lincoln. She was sitting in the creamery next door to the theater with some girlfriends when Jim walked in with two friends from S.I. One of the girls invited Jim and his friends to join them, and Jim sat down next to Diane. There was an instant chemical reaction, and Jim later asked Diane if he could walk her home, no minor commitment given the fact Diane lived at 33rd and Pacheco. Normally, Jim would have taken the 19th Avenue bus to Lincoln Way and then another bus to 30th Avenue, two minutes from our house. But as Jim said later, the walk with Diane turned out to be a magic moment, mostly because Jim could not take his eyes off Diane, who was wearing a very tight skirt and a cashmere sweater under which popped an almost pointed bodice, a style of that time.

"We made out on her stairway for nearly half an hour," Jim told me the next day. "She said she had heard I was a star basketball player, and I had to tell her about my suspension. She didn't react much and seemed to think it was a routine incident. She was much more interested in knowing if I would be coming to the Parkside next Friday. I said I was and maybe we could meet there at 7:00 PM and sit together, and she said she would like that."

Jim told me he thought about Diane every day for the next week. The week after that, Diane and Jim began phoning each other, talking for hours at a time. Mom had gotten us two phone lines, but even so, Joe had to kick Jim off the phone when either Mom or I was using the other line. Jim was fifteen and apparently in love.

So both my brothers had girlfriends in 1952, and I didn't. Was I jealous? Yes, I was. Of course, I got in some making-out time with a variety of different girls, but never with the ones I considered my first choices. For example, there were the Lee twins, Ellen and Jean. They were in my class at Lincoln and were the two most popular girls in the school, as much for their personalities as for their looks. In our junior year, both started going steady with members of the Lincoln baseball team. Ellen went with our first basemen, Charlie James, and Jean went with our pitcher, Stan Cheyne. Both guys were good friends of mine. The twins came to all of our games. (Coach Blank had lifted my suspension for my junior year, only because I was easily the best hitter on the team. Even so, he did not like me. One day, he said, "What happened to your brother? Did he get caught smoking?" I wanted to punch him in the nose. But I just walked away.)

Anyhow, after our games, I usually went with Ellen and Jean and Stan and Charlie for a Coke. To say that I was attracted to the Lee twins would be an understatement. But they were unattainable. All of the girls I liked were seemingly unattainable. That summer, I went with a friend, Jack Kent, who had a car, for three days up to Russian River, and we ran into the Lee twins the first night at the Rio Nido dance hall. I danced with both Ellen and Jean.

"Hey, Book," said Ellen, "I didn't know you could dance. You're pretty good for a guy who has never shown his face at one school dance."

"I didn't know you were paying attention," I said.

"You need a girlfriend, Book," she said.

"The trouble is, you and Jean are taken," I said, conjuring up a big smile.

"There are plenty of girls around who would love to go out with you, Book. You just have to ask them." Ellen went on to say that she and Jean were going to make sure I had a girlfriend for our senior year.

The three days with the Lee twins were among the most enjoyable I have ever had. I really liked being in their company. Somehow, they had the ability to make you feel good about yourself. Their parents owned a cabin on the river, and we spent days at the beach and nights dancing and drinking beer. The conversations could get quite earthy. For example, Ellen revealed she was jealous of Jean, because Jean could pee standing up without wetting herself.

Neither John nor I ever tried to make out with the twins. They were committed to their boyfriends, who happened to be close friends of ours. We just laughed and made fun of everything. Until then, that was the longest time I had ever spent with girls ... three days and three nights.

About a month after our return from Russian River, Ellen asked me if I would take her to a movie. Charlie was tied up in some family event, and Jean had a date with Stan. Ellen wanted to see a particular movie that was on at the Irving Theater. I borrowed Mom's car for the occasion. After the show, we were sitting in the car in front of Ellen's house, sipping a can of beer.

"Book, you know, you are the first boy I have gone out with that I haven't kissed," she said. "Are you a good kisser?" With that she slid over in the seat with her back to the steering wheel and put her face only inches from mine. We kissed for a long time, and I felt myself getting dizzy, dizzy with delight.

"That was pretty good, Book. But you need to put a little more into it."

She renewed the connection. I can hardly describe how I felt with my mouth locked to the beautiful Ellen Lee, our tongues searching and teasing. I wanted to draw her totally into my being. Ellen, the unattainable Ellen, sure knew how to make a guy feel good, especially someone like me who could be shy and uncertain around girls.

"Book, that's a lot better. You really are a good kisser." Ellen then stunned me. She gently pushed her fist into my crotch where she gave a glancing blow with her knuckles to what she expected to find—a body part that was hard as a rock.

"That's what happens when you give a really good kiss, Book," she laughed, quickly adding, "I have to go in now."

"Don't I get a good-night kiss?" I said.

She leaned over and gave me a peck on the lips. "You've had enough kissing. A lot of girls are going to want to kiss you. Thanks for the movie, Book."

She was out the door and trotting into the house before I could react. I hadn't even walked her to the door. Needless to say, I was afterward even more smitten with Charlie's girl Ellen. And I knew she liked me, just not as well as she liked Charlie, who was taller, smarter, better-looking, and much more popular in school. Ellen had a power over boys, and I was just one of a dozen of so who had been exposed to her charms and who would have given anything to have her as a regular girlfriend.

Alas, I never again went on a date with Ellen, never again kissed her. But she was on my mind a lot in my senior year at high school. Fortunately, as Ellen said, there were plenty of other girls to date and make out with. I unintentionally specialized in dating the girls who didn't go "all the way," which thinking back, was a pretty good way to go. As far as I know, the Lee twins never surrendered themselves during high school. In fact, there were damned few girls at Lincoln who did. Girls from Lincoln had a reputation for being virtuous, not like the girls from Mission, Balboa, or Poly, about whom I had heard some highly detailed accounts from my baseball friends.

Jim's junior year at St. Ignatius exceeded even the highest expectations. Not only did he finish academically at the top of his class, but he also was named "player of the year" by the *Chronicle* and made their All–Northern California basketball team. St. Ignatius went undefeated, and Jim averaged seventeen points a game, an extraordinary number for a guard in that era of low-scoring games. Jim had reached his full height at six feet one inch, and he weighed a lean 173.

At the same time, Joe had begun his first year at Stanford and was a starter and a star on the basketball team. We greatly missed having Joe at home. But several times, Jim and I drove down on Sundays to visit the Stanford campus, a huge, sprawling place that looked like a mecca for the privileged, which it was, more so back then than it is today. Everywhere we went, whether into Palo Alto or to have a beer at a tavern in back of the campus, people knew who Joe was, and they gave him a greeting. A number knew who Jim was, too, and he got a lot of attention. Joe told us that the basketball coach at Stanford said he hoped "that little brother of yours is thinking about Stanford for his future."

Both of my brothers were celebrities. I think it is a pity that Jim never went to Stanford. Instead, he went to the University of California at Berkeley. I was never completely satisfied with Jim's explanation: "I want to make it on my own."

CHAPTER 26

We celebrated Mom's fortieth birthday two weeks early on a Sunday afternoon in March of 1954 because the hosts, Richard and Claudia Hamblen, had to be away on the actual date. About eighty people attended, including most of the ladies from Mom's club and their husbands and neighbors from both 29th Avenue and our former home on 28th Avenue. Joe's girlfriend, Claire Winstead, was there, as were her parents, Charlie and Barbara. Also there were Grove Mohr, my longtime baseball coach, and some of the parents and players for Pomona Tile. Other guests included people from the Huntington Hotel and the Zebra Room and Jim's girlfriend, Diane Haley, who got the most stares with her Marilyn Monroe–like persona. All in all, it was a motley group, but Claudia and Mom made sure everyone was comfortable, and outside caterers took care of the food and drink. Richard Hamblen made a toast, saying, "Constance is one of the most delightful people Claudia and I have ever met. Not only that, she is a devoted and extraordinary mother who has all by herself raised three of the finest boys you will ever want to meet." Everyone applauded and cheered and demanded that Mom say something.

"I feel blessed by having friends like the Hamblens, three boys like Joe, Dan, and Jim, and friends like all of you," she started. "I sort of feel like this is a moment of change in my life. Jimmy will be attending the University of California starting in September, so it will be the first time none of the boys will be living at home. I feel very sad about that. It has been a wonderful twenty years. But I could not be more proud of my boys, each quite different from the others, but wonderful, wonderful sons. I don't want to get too maudlin, because I am excited about their futures and being part of it. What is the old saying? 'Life Begins at 40.'"

Everyone cheered and Richard led a rousing chorus of "Happy Birthday."

The party lasted about four hours, and Mom had a great time—we all did. I was amazed to watch Mom work the crowd. She hugged and kissed everyone there at least once. She never looked more beautiful. I noticed that Richard Hamblen could not take his eyes off of her. I always suspected that maybe he was in love with Mom. But that would not have been surprising, she was easy to love.

The day after the party, I got $5,000 to sign a professional baseball contract with the Pittsburgh Pirates. I was just completing the second quarter of my freshman year at San Jose State (which operated on a quarterly system rather a semester system) and decided to sign, because I would get a chance to play more than one hundred games as a minor leaguer versus twenty-five or so in college. I would return to college in the fall. Richard Hamblen said signing was a good idea if for no other reason than I would learn a lot about myself. I left for Anaheim in late March for spring training at the Pirates' West Coast minor-league camp. After two weeks there, about fifty of us were flown back to Deland, Florida, where the Pirates had their main minor-league training ground. It was a hugely exciting time for an eighteen-year-old to be out on his own, playing a sport that he loved. In fact, I could write a whole separate book about those experiences, but others have already done that, many times over.

When camp broke up, about half the players were assigned to minor-league teams. The other half were thanked for trying and were sent home. Fortunately, I did not have to slink home in dishonor as did a couple of my friends. I was assigned to play for the Bristol, Virginia, team in the "Class D" Appalachian League, which was then the lowest category in minor-league baseball. It turned out to be a great four months. I fell briefly in love with an impish blonde who was from Dublin, Georgia, and was attending a nearby finishing school; when she went home for the summer, I became entranced with the popcorn girl who worked near the entrance to Twins Stadium.

We drew between 800 and 1,200 fans for each game. The other teams in the league were located at Johnson City and Kingsport, Tennessee, both towns being less than hour away by bus. We had to stay overnight in the other three cities, Pulaski, Virginia; Bluefield, West Virginia; and Welch, West Virginia. The latter two towns were in the heart of the depressed coal-mining region of Appalachia, and hanging out there during the day was educational for someone who had grown up in San Francisco and had never seen rural poverty. I shared the catching duties with a fellow from Sacramento, Harry Durston, and batted a respectable .274, not bad for a rookie. Although I had a lot of fun, by the end of August, I was yearning to get back home.

What I learned that first season was that I did not want to make a career out of playing baseball. I simply did not have the natural skills to make it to the big leagues as a starting catcher. The general manager for the Twins, who was responsible for the business side of the operations, encouraged me to come back for another season. He reasoned that if I did not make it as a player, he thought I had good potential to be in management. That was the furthest thing from my mind, though it did occur to me that I would like to be a broadcaster. Herb Epstein, from New York, was the "voice of the Bristol Twins," and he broadcast play-by-play descriptions of all of our games. Herb interviewed most of our team on the air at least once during the first month of the season. After that, he asked me if I would like to be interviewed before each game. Coming from New York, Herb probably reasoned that my California accent was better than the Southern drawls of most of our team. In any case, in answer to his questions, I would reel off answers about the strengths and weaknesses of the other team and what was going on with the Twins from a player's point of view. In all, the interview would last about five or six minutes, and I was pretty relaxed about it all. I never felt nervous in front of a microphone. Herb told me that I had a great radio voice and that I should consider going into broadcasting.

I will relate one anecdote about my Bristol experience. Our team got off to a terrific start, winning twenty of our first twenty-two games. However, in late May, two of our star pitchers were promoted to higher leagues. One of the replacements was a chubby, dumbo-eared pitcher from Pennsylvania, Bill Robards. He had been signed in June for a $15,000 bonus by Branch Rickey Jr., the son of the famed managerial genius who had built great teams in St. Louis and Brooklyn and who was building another winner at Pittsburgh. Junior, who had never played baseball, was known as "The Twig," which was not intended to be a complimentary nickname. The Twig personally drove Bill Robards to Bristol to watch his prospective phenom pitch. I have to tell you, a $15,000 bonus from the tight Pittsburgh organization was a hell of a lot of money. Rickey Sr., who had signed Jackie Robinson, thereby breaking the color barrier in major-league baseball, was renowned as a skinflint, perhaps the cheapest man in all baseball. But he was a great operator and a great judge of talent. Whether Branch Rickey Sr. ever saw Billy Robards pitch before The Twig gave him $15,000, I have no way of knowing, but I always suspected he did not.

Anyhow, Robards and The Twig showed up at the ballpark, and I was asked to warm him up. The first ball he threw at me was a knuckleball. I asked, "What the hell are you doing starting out with a knuckleball?"

He replied, "That's all I throw." I had never heard of anything like that before. Billy said he had a knuckle fastball, a knuckle curve, and a knuckle changeup.

While we were warming up, our manager, Jack LaTour, came over and asked me how he looked. "Not worth $15,000," I replied.

Jack watched Billy lob his knuckleballs for a while and then looked at me and rolled his eyes skyward. "He's the starting pitcher tomorrow night," LaTour said. "The Twig is insisting on it."

Billy Robards did get past the first inning against the Welch Miners. They scored nine runs on eleven hits before he was replaced. The leadoff batter for the Miners had missed Billy's first two pitches, both of which had danced unpredictably just as they reached the plate. The Welch batter then moved up in the batter's box, in front of the plate. He lashed the next pitch into right center field for a double. From that point on, all the Welch players moved up in the box, and it looked like batting practice.

Jack LaTour called timeout, we both went to the mound, and he looked at Billy, who appeared slightly shell-shocked. "What's the problem?" Jack asked me. I said the problem was that Billy's pitches were not moving until after they reached the plate. By moving up in the box, the hitters were making Billy's pitches easier to hit than watermelons!

Jack said to Billy, "Hey, hoss, make that damned thing break sooner." With that, he returned to the dugout.

To his credit, Billy hung in there, but not as well as the Welch hitters, who managed four doubles, one home run, a triple, and five singles off the softest-touch pitcher they had ever seen. The only outs were line drives that went directly at the fielders.

"You're finished—go take a shower," LaTour told Billy as he came in from the mound at the end of the first inning.

After the game, The Twig came down to talk to me, and I told him what I had told LaTour. He responded, "He must have been doing something wrong—he was un-hittable in high school." I suspected that he was imagining what his father was going to say when the report on the game reached Pittsburgh. Rickey Jr. left town the next day, and Billy stayed, though LaTour never once let him pitch in a game; it was not really an arbitrary decision. LaTour had Billy pitch batting practice.

"The first time I see you make somebody miss two of your pitches, I'll let you pitch in a game," LaTour told Billy. But we all knew what the deal was, so whenever Billy was throwing batting practice, we all moved up on the plate and belted his pitches before they knuckled. Having to carry Billy on our roster was not his only negative contribution to the team. Billy somehow met a man who sold pornographic pictures and comic books, and I first saw them on a bus trip to Pulaski, when Billy was passing them around to other players in the back of the bus. Most of our players, including me, had never seen such an abundance of porn before. In fact, all I had ever seen was a "Jiggs and Maggie" comic book at Sunset Playground years before. But Billy got a fresh delivery of stuff each week for five weeks. I always wondered how much of his $15,000 bonus Billy spent on that porn. Around the same time, our team went into a tailspin, and we fell out of first place, losing twenty-two out of twenty-eight games. I don't know if it was the porn or what, but our team seemed to have lost its focus. Jack LaTour, who always sat in the front of the bus with the announcer, Herb Epstein, did not get wind of what had been going on behind his back until about four weeks later. He erupted when he did.

"If I see anymore of this shit on this bus or anywhere around this team, I'm going to boot you back to Pennsylvania!" Jack told Billy in front of the whole team. "As for the rest of you guys, get your mind off your dicks and start playing some baseball." Jack LaTour had a wonderful way of making his points in language everyone could understand. One day, he said to me, "You know, Branch Rickey is one of the greatest general managers the game has ever known. He knows everything, except what an imbecile he has for a son. No, that's not it. I shouldn't say that. He's just human. You gotta love your own son, no matter what."

With our new focus, the Bristol Twins played respectably for the remainder of the year, and we finished the season in second place behind the Johnson City Cardinals. It had been a great experience, but I was eager to get back to California. I had seen all I ever wanted to see of Appalachia.

CHAPTER 27

I returned to San Francisco just after Labor Day in 1954. The cease-fire in Korea was still holding, and President Eisenhower had lived up to his promise to end the fighting there. Joe and Jim had been at home most of the summer, and Mom was in good spirits and delighted to have all three of us under her roof, albeit temporarily. None of us had to be at college for another two and a half weeks—Joe at Stanford, where he would be starting his third year; me at San Jose, starting my third quarter; and Jimmy at

Berkeley, the most highly touted freshman basketball player to come along in years.

Mom said she could not be happier about the way each of us had developed. Now, she said, we all had to prepare for change. "Sports have been the main force in all of our lives for the past ten years," she said. "But the time is not far off when there will be more important things, like setting goals, choosing careers, and having a family. Your dad was a great one for planning and goal setting; that was part of his training at West Point, but he also learned about it from his Uncle Jeremiah."

One night over dinner, Mom suggested we discuss what we might want to be doing in five years.

"I'm getting more certain that I want to go into journalism," said Joe, explaining that Claire Winstead's father, Charles, had been enthralling him with fascinating stories about his two decades working for San Francisco newspapers during the 1930s and 1940s. Winstead contended that reporting put you right into the middle of life in a way hardly anything else did except maybe big-time sports, and sports were really not that important in the long run.

Mom asked Joe if there was much money to be made in journalism, and he replied that was the only problem. Joe conceded he could make more money doing other things, including the possibility of playing professional basketball. But the money was not so important, because Claire wanted to work in public relations, and although they had no plans to get married until a year or two after they both graduated, Claire did not want to start a family until she had established herself in her work. Hence, Joe and Claire would have two salaries for the foreseeable future.

"Claire says that she does not want to be tied down with children too early," said Joe.

"I think she is right," Mom said quickly. "I was tied down from the time I was nineteen. Fortunately, I had you boys, and I really have never regretted it. The only regret I have in life so far is your father's tragic death. I can never reconcile myself to it deep inside, and it is a pity that none of you can really understand what was taken out of your life. The happy side is that we have become a very close and loving family. And the other good thing about marrying young and having three children in three years is that you are still young when you send your boys off to college."

That was typical of mother. She always had to turn the subject, any subject, to its brightest side. She really did believe life begins at forty, or, at least that it did not end there.

"With all of us gone, what are you going to do, Mom?" Jimmy asked. "You've spent most of your time outside of work feeding us, keeping house for us, doing our laundry, coming to our games, and being with us, and now that all is changed."

"Well, I will miss you boys, but I can live without the cleaning and the cooking. Anyway, I hope you boys come home on weekends and holidays at least some of the time," Mom said. "And I'll be at your games in Berkeley, Jim, just as I have seen a lot of Joe's games in Palo Alto. Thank goodness Claudia and Richard like to watch you both play as much as I do, so I never have to go alone. I can't wait until Cal plays Stanford."

"That's true, Mom, but your life is really going to change, just like you said at your fortieth birthday party," said Joe. "You know what I think? I think you should find a husband. There are lots of men out there who would be dying to marry you, and you don't have the excuse anymore that no man would want to marry a woman with three children at home."

Mom blushed slightly and smiled. "What makes you think I want to get married?"

"I agree with Joe," I said. "You could make some man very happy, and that would make you happy," I said.

"They are both right," said Jimmy. "Right now, it is as if you are married to the Hamblens. You go every place with them. I think they're great, but it would be better if you had a husband. You wouldn't feel so much like a third wheel."

"I don't think I am a third wheel, Jim," Mom said, almost sharply. "Claudia and Richard are like family, and they are the best friends anyone, including all of you, could ever have. Richard was in the army with your father in Germany, and he promised your father he would help take care of us if anything happened to him. Well, he's done that."

"Don't get mad, Mom," said Joe. "All we want is for you to be happy. Maybe we feel guilty, because we won't live at home anymore and probably never will. You have been the best mother anyone could have. We've talked about it, and we all agree. We've never met anyone who comes close to you as a mother."

"That's the truth, Mom," I said.

"If any of us finds a woman to marry as good as you, we'll be damned lucky," Jim said.

"I appreciate what all of you are saying," Mom said. "If the right man comes along, I might get married. But I am not going to marry just to be married. Furthermore, I fully expect to be seeing a lot of the three of you for as long as I live. Just because you don't live at home doesn't mean we can't be together. By the way, your grandmother, Mary Teresa, is coming out to visit next month. I hope I can talk her into staying. You boys will all be invited to a Sunday welcoming dinner when she arrives. She is your only living grandparent, and she would be so happy to see you. I know you will all be busy, but I hope I can count on you."

"It sounds like a command performance," Joe smiled, adding, "Don't worry, Mom. You are always going to be able to count on us. We appreciate what you have done for us, and we never want to disappoint you."

"Joe, that is very sweet," Mom said, her eyes misting.

Jim got up and put his arms around Mom and gave her a long hug.

"We could not love you any more than we do," he said. Jim could let that "love" word roll off his tongue in a way few young men could. Joe and I took turns giving Mom a hug. Mom started crying.

"Thank you, Joe and Dan and Jim. I love you all more than you can imagine," she said, pausing. "But let's not get too soppy," she laughed. "Well, we know what Joe thinks he wants to do after college—what about you Dan?"

"I haven't got a clue," I said. "But I am thinking of requesting to be drafted into the army in December when I finish the fall quarter."

"Are you kidding?" asked Joe.

"Look, I know I am going to have to put in my time, so I am thinking I might as well get it over with," I replied. "You and Jim are on full scholarships, but I have to pay my own way. I can do it, because San Jose costs nothing, and I have my bonus money. However, if I go in the army in December, I will be eligible for the

G.I. Bill when I come out. It pays $110 a month if you are going to college. The other thing is that the baseball manager at Fort Ord said he could get me on the base team if I could complete basic training by mid-March. The third thing is that I might get a better idea of what I want to do with my life after spending two years in the army. Maybe I will decide I want to stick with baseball."

"It sounds like you've given this a lot of thought," said Mom. Joe said he could not fault my logic since it was true that we would all have to serve in the military at some point.

"Playing baseball sounds like a good way to serve," Jim said, adding, "Mom, don't ask me what I want to be, because all I can think about is trying to live up to the expectations everyone has for me at Berkeley."

"Mom," said Joe, "what do you want to be doing five years from now?"

"Well, I guess I had better find myself a husband just to make you boys happy," she smiled.

CHAPTER 28

The luncheon crowd at the Zebra Room was one of San Francisco's most glittering. Located just off the Huntington Hotel lobby, the Zebra Room had caught on among the old-money crowd of the city and enjoyed a certain word-of-mouth cache among the more knowledgeable visitors. Of course, the food was good, but it was more the glamour of the place. Jackets and ties were required for the men, and most women dressed as if they were getting ready for a DeMille close-up. Beautiful, well-groomed women were in the majority, and they felt comfortable in the atmosphere that

Constance Booker helped create. I had lunch there with Joe and Jim and Richard Hamblen that fall of 1954 just before we all headed off to college. Mom moved about the room like the hostess at a party, not in a flashy way, but in a warm, smooth manner. Not only did she have great looks, but furthermore, she exuded class. Mom seemed to know everyone's name, and many of the customers knew Mom's name as well and greeted her as warmly as she greeted them. The day we were there, several of the customers noticed the attention she was giving our table.

"Those are my three sons," she told one group of four ladies who I assumed were regulars.

"My goodness, Constance, they look like your younger brothers," said one of the ladies. "They certainly are handsome, especially the one with your eyes," said another, in reference to Jim.

"Three sons will keep you young," said Constance.

"Or make you age pretty fast," quipped one of the ladies.

Richard Hamblen had invited us to lunch to talk about our plans for the future. He said he chose the Zebra Room, because he wanted us to get an appreciation of our mother at work. His comment made me even more certain he was in love with Mom. I could not blame him. But his affection was not going anyplace. Mom had too much integrity to mess around with a married man, least of all a man married to her best friend.

At this point, let me pause from the general narrative to make an admission. When I began writing this book at age seventy from my winter home in Los Cabos, Mexico, I have to confess that I saw it mainly as an exercise in reliving pleasant memories growing up in the Sunset with my mother and brothers. Now that I have covered some of my recollections from those early years, I realize that the story needs to be continued from an occasionally different point of reference if I am to convey the true nature of our family and its evolution. I will thus be writing about some events that I did not personally witness or read about in my mother's diary. Indeed, I will have to rely on my memory of countless conversations and events over a fifty-year period. When in doubt, I will be consulting with family and friends, making sure I have my facts straight. I also plan to use a limited amount of literary license in creating scenes and dialogue that give spark to events where I was obviously not present. Readers will have to trust me that I am being as scrupulous and faithful to the facts as I know them. And I hope that removing the clutter of sourcing and references will make for more enjoyable reading.

It was not long after our luncheon with Richard Hamblen that a whirlwind by the name of Desmond Archer Jr. came into Mom's life. Desmond, an Australian whose family owned several newspapers and magazines and, more significantly from a value standpoint, substantial mining interests, came to San Francisco to take delivery on a 116-foot yacht he had commissioned two years earlier. Archer, who was forty-five and divorced, had the reputation of being a ladies man and a playboy who lived ostentatiously. He used his magazines and newspapers to meet beautiful women and important and interesting people. He was used to being catered to, and in fact, when he made his reservation at the Zebra Room, he talked to Mom on the telephone and asked her if she knew who he was. She asked if he was the Desmond Archer from Australia, and he said he was indeed and hoped that he could get the best table in the Zebra Room, whatever that was.

Desmond Archer showed up with the Australian Consul General in San Francisco, Mathew Reynolds, and his wife, Anne, an attractive couple in their early forties whom Mom knew. When Reynolds made the introduction, Archer said, "Mrs. Booker, you are even more beautiful in person than you were on the telephone."

"You have to watch out for Mr. Archer," said Mrs. Reynolds. "He is a notorious flirt. But I am sure you have plenty of experience in dealing with his type."

Mom laughed a big hearty laugh.

Mom led Archer and Mr. and Mrs. Reynolds to their table. They were all still smiling over Mom's amusement at being able to handle flirts.

About twenty-five minutes later, Mom heard a commotion coming from Archer's table. She rushed over. Archer was red-faced and looked angry. He stood up, revealing a huge stain of red wine all over the front of his pearl gray trousers.

"Oh my God, this is a disaster," fumed Archer. "That bloody clumsy waiter snuck up on me with the wine glass."

Mother quickly sized up the situation and apologized, but did not try to clean off the stain, which even the waiter was not about to do, given its location.

"Where are you staying Mr. Archer?" Mom asked

"Across the street at the Fairmont," he replied.

"What if I sent a waiter over to get another pair of trousers from your room?"

"It's not a room; it's a suite. And I don't want someone I don't even know to go in there."

"What if I went?" Mom asked.

So that was how the matter was resolved. Mom retrieved the trousers and a pair of shorts, and Archer happily changed in the men's room while Mom had his wine-stained slacks and shorts sent to a four-hour cleaning service in the Fairmont.

"You know," Archer told Mom when he was leaving, "most people wouldn't have thought to also bring the shorts."

"You look the sort of gentleman who would wear shorts," Mom smiled.

That evening, two dozen roses were delivered to Constance's house. The note said, "Thank for being so cool and efficient in my moment of duress. I am going to be in town for the next five days. Perhaps you can join me for cocktails on my new yacht. I will give you a call. And thanks so much. I'm glad the wine was spilt. Desmond Archer."

The next morning, Archer called and asked Constance to come for a sunset cruise on the Bay. Constance said she appreciated the invitation, but she had a rule about going alone aboard men's yachts.

"Look, I just want to see you again," said Archer. "I'm not going to try to seduce you. In fact, bring some friends. I'll invite the Reynolds. It's a brand new yacht, and I'd love to have you aboard."

Constance said she would call him back, and she hung up and called Claudia Hamblen. Claudia said she and Richard would be delighted to go. Claudia wanted to know more about Desmond Archer. Was he a prospect? Constance wrote in her diary that Archer was not particularly handsome though he had a rugged outdoor look with bright red cheeks. And he had a nice smile and hearty laugh that offset his lack of height and slight paunch.

"He'll never win a beauty contest," she told Claudia."But he has a lot of confidence. I suppose that comes from having all that money."

Claudia countered, saying she knew a lot of wealthy people who were very shy and had little confidence. When they arrived at the water, Archer's new yacht, with a uniformed crew of eight, seemed huge anchored at the San Francisco Yacht Harbor. Wearing an ascot under a blue blazer with white trousers, Archer greeted Constance, gave her a well-muscled hug, and said how happy he was that she had come. He also gave a warm greeting to the Hamblens, embracing each. Archer said he had learned that Richard was one of the most respected lawyers in San Francisco.

"Before you leave tonight, Richard, there are a couple of things I'd like to talk with you about," Archer said.

Constance and the Hamblens greeted Mathew and Anne Reynolds, who had arrived earlier, dressed nattily as if they were going to a cocktail party at the Top of the Mark.

"Well, you're all looking quite lovely," said Archer. "Let me give you a tour while we keep the other eye on the sunset."

Claudia asked what Archer had named the yacht.

"It's right there on the stern: *Aussie Legend*," said Archer. Constance laughed, and Archer seemed to be happy that she got the joke.

"Why do you call it that?" Claudia asked.

"Well, my mates always say I am a legend in my own mind, and that's partly true, so what the hell," Archer smiled.

"I can't decide when he is serious," Claudia whispered to Constance.

"I think he is pretty unabashed," said Constance. "He's one of those people who really seems full of himself, but in a disarming way."

"You've already decided he is not Mr. Right," said Claudia. Constance laughed.

The cocktail cruise turned out to include dinner and lasted more than six hours. The party was held in the main cabin. Archer had a state-of-the-art sound system, and the background music was constant, starting with light classical and Broadway show tunes and then moving to some of the newly popular West Coast jazz, mostly Chet Baker and Jerry Mulligan. Last came the Frank Sinatra ballads. It was too cold to be on deck by then, even though it had been a wonderful and sunny Indian summer day.

Archer, it soon became evident, loved champagne and French wine, and it flowed freely, with the waiters immediately refilling any glass that got down to the one-quarter mark. Archer also liked caviar, and he conducted a tasting poll as to what was better, Russian or Iranian caviar. Interestingly, everyone chose the Iranian caviar, which was a medium gray in color. Archer said the caviar went best with a little Russian vodka, and everyone tried a small glass of vodka that came directly from the freezer.

Dinner, which took two hours to arrive, consisted of abalone steaks, artichokes, steak fries, salad, and San Francisco sourdough French bread. Mom wrote that she had never eaten so much, drunk so much, or laughed so much. Archer was never at a loss for words, though he could also listen.

"The secret to preparing abalone is pounding it with a wooden mallet before you put it on the grill," said Archer. "Most people don't pound it enough. You see, you can cut this abalone with a spoon. Of course, it helps if the abalone comes from Monterey Bay and was picked off the bottom by divers this morning at twenty feet below the surface."

"Where did you buy it?" asked Reynolds. "I'd like to serve it to some of our visitors. I have never tasted anything like this."

"My captain picked it up over at Fisherman's Wharf from a fellow who supplies the restaurants there," Archer answered. "By the way, the abalone is good, but it isn't any better than this sourdough," Archer continued, biting into a heavily buttered slice. "There is no place in the world with bread like this."

Mom wrote that Archer's enthusiasms seemed endless. He raved over the artichokes from Castroville. And he raved about the white French Burgundy wine, though he saved his best wine for the cheese course.

"You are all very special people and my first dinner guests aboard the *Aussie Legend*, so I want to make sure you remember our time together," said Archer.

"Desmond," said Anne Reynolds, lifting her nearly empty glass, "nothing could make us forget this dinner."

"A toast to our distinguished host," said Mathew Reynolds, "a credit to the spirit of Australia."

"Here, here," said Richard, "a toast to the perfect host."

"As I started to say before that splendid and altogether appropriate outpouring of appreciation, I've saved the best for last," said Archer, rising from his seat. "You will note these two lovely and already opened bottles on the bar that I am now bringing to our little feast. These, my friends, are Chateau Margaux vintage 1932, and Richard, may I request you to test to see if it is potable?"

"It would be the highest honor," said Richard, who first put his nose into the partially filled glass. "My, that is fantastic—what a distinct aroma. I don't think I have ever experienced anything quite like it."

"Taste it," said Claudia, a bit impatiently.

"Be patient, Claudia; your husband knows exactly what he is doing," said Archer. "Clearly, he is no stranger to fine wines."

Richard slowly rolled the wine around in his mouth. His expression was of absolute delight.

"I am without words to describe it," Richard said, at last. "I hereby pronounce this wine eminently potable." Archer and the others laughed.

Mom wrote that she had never tasted any wine so good. It took more than an hour to drink the two bottles, and Archer got Mother talking about her past, and she basically gave him her whole life story. There were three separate conversations going on most of the time, and the words flowed as easily as the wine. Claudia and Mathew Reynolds hit it off nicely, and so did Richard and Anne Reynolds. The conversation partners periodically changed, and everyone was having a delightful time. Mom wrote that you had to be there to fully appreciate how much fun everyone was having. Mom had not had many evenings like it.

While Archer and Richard were talking, Archer said he was interested in buying some newspapers in California and asked if Richard might be able to help him. They agreed to meet for lunch the day after next.

The party broke up about midnight amid effusive praise for the host, the guests, the food, and the wine and the general agreement that nobody could recall having a better evening.

"May I call you tomorrow?" Archer asked my mother. "I have an idea that might be fun." With that he gave Mom a short kiss on the lips and turned to say his good-nights to the others, which, Mom noted, also included kisses on the lips for both Anne and Claudia. Mom wrote that Desmond Archer was more charming than she had expected, almost too charming.

CHAPTER 29

Archer's three dozen roses arrived just before his 9:30 AM phone call.

"Good morning fair Constance, I'd have called earlier, but I didn't want to wake you," said Archer.

"Good morning to you, Desmond. I've been up since seven and am almost out the door. Work, you know," said Constance, adding, "Thank you for the lovely evening last night and the beautiful roses; they were just delivered."

Constance agreed to meet Archer at the Palace Hotel for tea after she was finished at the Zebra Room. It was a negotiated date. Archer had wanted to take her to dinner, but she begged off, saying she needed to rest from last night's marathon in which she had easily consumed more alcohol than she ever had anytime before in her life.

"This is a marvelous old place," Archer said later as he met Constance at the entrance to the Palace Hotel's vast lobby.

"This used to be the preferred hotel for famous visitors," said Constance. "I think it was Caruso, the great opera singer, who was staying here the night of the 1906 earthquake. Caruso, Lillian Russell—the famous visitors often stayed here."

At Archer's urging, Constance enthusiastically unloaded her trove of San Francisco history, from the Gold Rush to the building of the bridges. Archer hung on every word. When Constance suggested he might like to see the sunset from the Cliff House, Archer said, "There is nothing I would rather do."

They made it in Archer's rental car just in time, the sun being about fifteen minutes away from setting into the Pacific Ocean. Constance led Archer down an outdoor stairway next to the Cliff House, to a walkway overlooking Seal Rocks.

"Usually, the fog has rolled in by now, so you don't always get to see a sunset, but in the fall, it can sometimes be like this," said Constance.

"You've brought me to a rare place of beauty that I shan't forget," said Archer, moving closer to his lovely tour guide, whose face reflected the golden glow of the sunset. But she quickly moved away.

"Come down this way," said Constance. "You can see Ocean Beach for miles. Just look at those beautiful waves. I used to bring my boys here."

"It reminds me a bit of Australia," said Archer. "There is a delightful sense of raw beauty."

"There's more to see," said Constance. She led Archer up the hill beyond the Cliff House and Sutro's Baths to a circular parking area known as Inspiration Point, a renowned "make-out" place.

"This is where the teenagers come to park," said Constance. "You can see the entrance to the bay and the Golden Gate Bridge."

"I should have brought the car; we could pretend we are teenagers," said Archer, keeping a straight face.

"We'd better head back now; it is getting dark," said Constance, ignoring his comment. "I am glad you liked the tour. I love to show people around San Francisco, no matter how many times I do it."

Archer held Constance's arm as they walked back to his car, which was parked just below the Cliff House.

"Say, why don't we just pop in here and have a quick dinner," said Archer. "You don't have anything on tonight, no?" Constance hesitated. "Last time I ate at the Cliff House, the food was awful, but we're probably safe ordering a crab salad," she said. "Sure, let's do it. I can still get back in time to read my Edith Wharton."

The dining room was two-thirds full. Constance said she would have only one glass of white wine with her crab salad. Archer ordered a double martini and sand dabs with spinach, French fries, and salad.

Archer asked what Constance was reading, and she replied, "*The House of Mirth.*" She described it as a woman's book. The author, Edith Wharton, she told Archer, was born into an extremely wealthy New York family in the 1860s, and she wrote about how the rich lived.

"I've only been once to the East Coast to Boston for my father's funeral, and I have never seen the kind of wealth those people had, so it is great fun to read about it. Edith Wharton writes with so much detail you feel like you are there."

"People have money like that in Australia, but they don't make a big show of it," said Archer.

"Does that mean you have to hide your giant yacht?'" Constance smiled.

"Well, you got me there, but right on, we don't flaunt it. I guarantee you'll never see my yacht pictured in any of our newspapers or magazines. Actually, it is owned by our company, and it will primarily be used to entertain customers."

Archer ordered another double martini. He said that Hemingway was his favorite American author and that he liked F. Scott Fitzgerald and two new writers, James Jones and Norman Mailer, who had published books about their military experiences.

"Do you like Henry James?" Constance asked. Archer said he found him dull and unreadable.

"Well, you probably wouldn't like Edith Wharton."

Desmond Archer and Constance Booker talked more about books before switching to Senator Joe McCarthy, politics, the Cold War, and the White Australia Policy, the latter two subjects being dominated by Archer, who managed his third double martini before ordering coffee and apple pie. Constance relented on a second glass of wine, but passed on the pie and coffee.

"I ate so much last night, I won't be able to eat a full meal for a week," said Constance. "That really was a lot of fun last night."

"I am enjoying tonight just as much, maybe more, because I have you all to myself," said Archer. "Say, I like your friends, the Hamblens. They both seem to like you very much. Richard hardly takes his eyes off of you."

"Don't misjudge the situation," said Constance, who explained that Richard and her husband had been together in the war and that he fulfilled a promise to look after the boys and her if anything happened.

"That had to be the best assignment he ever had," said Archer. "Look, don't get me wrong. I'm not suggesting anything. I'm just saying that he looks at you like he ... well, like he cares a lot."

"Claudia and Richard are the most happily married couple I know, and Richard is a loyal and loving husband," said Constance. "By the way, do you always say exactly what you think?"

"Whoops, please forgive me," said Archer, adding, "Yes, I do say what I think too much, and it does get me into trouble. That is why I am not, repeat not, going to say how beautiful you are looking at just this minute."

Constance laughed but did not say what she was thinking, which was that Desmond Archer, charming though he was, drank too much.

Archer drove Constance home and made no effort to invite himself in for a nightcap. Constance had already commented on the lateness of the hour—it was almost 11:30—and Archer had gotten the hint, for which she was grateful.

"I'm having lunch with Richard Hamblen tomorrow," Archer said. "Is there any chance I can get the next leg of the Constance Booker Tour of San Francisco? I only have three more days here."

"If you'd like, I would be glad to," said Constance.

"I insist on seeing you to the door," said Archer, bowing gracefully as he opened the car door. Constance beat Archer to the punch by lightly embracing his shoulders and pressing her cheek to his, thereby avoiding the kiss on the lips that she guessed was coming. She was out of his arms before he could finish saying what a great evening he had had.

"Me too," she said, slipping inside the door.

Five minutes after Constance arrived home, the phone rang. It was Claudia Hamblen.

"Where have you been? I've been calling since eight o'clock, and I was beginning to get worried," said Claudia, adding, "Tell me all about it."

Constance gave Claudia a full description of what she said was a lovely evening. She said Desmond Archer could be quite charming, and she suspected he very badly wanted to get her into bed.

"He's rich and very eligible," said Claudia.

"Don't get your hopes up," said Constance. "I think he drinks way too much, and besides, he lives in Australia. And he's not going to get me into bed. I want to get married to someone I love, and I'm just prudish enough to think that you don't jump into bed with someone just because they are rich and charming!"

"I never suggested you should go to bed with him," said Claudia. "In fact, if you were looking to marry him, that's the last thing you should do."

"Well, I'm not looking to marry him, and I am not going to bed with him."

"Are you going to see him again?" asked Claudia. Constance replied that she had promised to take Archer on a tour tomorrow after work.

"He only has three more days in town, and he's fun, and he loves my San Francisco tours," said Constance.

"Good. Why don't you stop by our house for a quick drink when you finish," said Claudia. "We don't have anything on tomorrow night."

"Agreed. We'll be there about six," said Constance. "And thanks for the call and your concern, Claudia."

CHAPTER 30

Constance wrote in her diary about her tour with Desmond Archer and dinner afterward at the Cliff House.

> During dinner, Desmond said something that bothered me—in effect, that he thought Richard had romantic feelings for me. Of course, I denied it and said Richard was a wonderful friend who has helped us a lot, but who is a very happily married man to a woman who has become my best friend. I told Desmond that Richard had served with Joe in Europe and the two had become very close friends. I admit I love Richard as a person, but I have never ever had a romantic thought about him, never dreamed of kissing him or making love to him. In my mind, he is taken. How he feels about me, I really can't say. What I suspect is that he feels about me what I feel about him. The thought of adultery I doubt has ever entered his mind. Richard is like Joe, a man of character and high moral values who believes in his marriage vows. But what if Richard was not married? I think the situation would be very different. But it is silly to think that way, because Richard and Claudia are a perfect couple and my two best friends. We have known each other for nine years, and some of my happiest moments have come from being with them. And Richard has been indispensable in helping with the boys and our finances. I would not want to change our present situation, and I don't think Richard would either. I am so grateful just to have them in my life.

CHAPTER 31

Desmond Archer showed up at the Huntington Hotel shortly after 3:00 PM, riding in the backseat of a dark blue Cadillac convertible with the top down. Archer waved at Constance, who was smiling, but slightly surprised to see the convertible and driver.

"My, what is all this about?" she said, smiling in a way that indicated she was happy to see him.

"Hello, Constance darling, this is such a beautiful day that I thought we really ought to enjoy it," said Archer while reaching to give her a hug. "I thought we would enjoy the tour more with Leonard doing the driving."

The temperature was in the low seventies, not totally unusual for San Francisco in November, because the city has its best weather in Indian summer.

"This feels like spring," enthused Archer, reaching to hold Constance's hand. "Where are we going?"

The tour lasted until six o'clock and covered virtually the entire city. At Constance's suggestion, Leonard drove from Nob Hill on California Street down to the Ferry Building, thence along the mostly abandoned piers and back up to Coit Tower on top of Telegraph Hill. Archer said he loved the city's ethnic neighborhoods, particularly Chinatown and North Beach. Constance said she loved eating at unpretentious Chinese and Italian restaurants, which she said were often both cheap and full of atmosphere. Constance directed Leonard to drive through the Marina district and then into the Presidio, where she showed Archer where she had first lived when her young family moved to San Francisco in 1938.

"I can see the army treated its officers pretty well," said Archer, commenting on the size of the wooden structure that looked almost exactly the same to Constance as it had sixteen years earlier.

"We were very happy here," Constance said. This was the first time in years that Constance had looked at that house, and she later wrote in her diary that she had been suddenly overcome with grief at the sight.

Archer put his arm around her shoulder and said it must have been very hard to confront an old memory that is part of a tragedy.

"I'm sorry, Desmond. I'm fully reconciled to what has happened, or at least I thought I was," Constance said. Moving past the moment, she said, "Leonard, let's go over to Golden Gate Park and drive through it down to the beach. Then we can come back along the ocean to Lake Merced and then over Twin Peaks to City Hall."

Constance rattled off information throughout the drive.

"Constance, you are the best tour guide I've ever had," said Archer.

"Can you guess what famous event happened here at City Hall last January?" asked Constance.

"Give me a hint," he said.

"Well, it was an event 90 percent of all American men would have liked to attend," Constance teased, adding, "and most of them wouldn't have minded trading places with the man involved."

"Sounds like a wedding," said Archer. "You are not going to suggest we get married, are you?"

"Definitely not, but you would have loved to marry the woman involved."

"Okay, I give up."

"Right over there, City Hall, is where Marilyn Monroe and Joe DiMaggio got married, January 14, 1954."

"You sound starstruck, Constance," said Archer. "She is beautiful, but I would rather be with you."

"Actually, I had dinner with Joe and Marilyn at his restaurant about six months before they got married," Constance said, adding, "I'm not really starstruck, but I can tell you that Marilyn is even more beautiful in person than she is on the screen. She has the whitest, softest skin I have ever seen."

"Like a baby's bottom, I have heard," said Archer. "How did you happen to have dinner with them?"

Constance explained that Richard Hamblen had been doing some legal work for the DiMaggio family, and Joe had invited Richard to come to dinner at the DiMaggio family restaurant that night so that they could do some talking. When Richard told him he already had a dinner commitment with his wife and her friend, DiMaggio surprisingly said to bring them along.

"Joe is a pretty reclusive person and doesn't even know how to drive a car," said Constance. "But he likes and trusts Richard a lot. We had no idea that Marilyn Monroe was going to be there. She said they had been dating on and off for eighteen months. She turned out to be very sweet, and you could tell she respected Richard, who is not one to be intimidated by baseball stars or Hollywood stars. He's pretty suave that way."

"Richard again," said Archer. "It is a pity he already has a wife."

"You are going to make me mad again—we've been all through this," said Constance.

"I just like to see some color come to your cheeks; you are quite lovely when you are mad. Anyhow, I am just kidding. But I am really jealous of Richard. He's tall and good-looking and as cool an operator as I have ever seen." Constance did not respond.

"I was sort of surprised that Joe would want to marry someone like Marilyn, who loves the public spotlight," Constance said. "Joe, according to Richard, is just the opposite. He likes to stay home."

"What about you, Mrs. Booker?"

"I like to go out, but I don't have to go out all the time. When I was growing up, I went out every chance I had, but later on, with my boys growing up, I was home almost every night. They were always good company, and I learned to enjoy reading during those years—and frankly, some of my happiest times are just reading,"

"You are too beautiful to stay at home," said Archer. "You need to be out so that people can appreciate what a rare creature you are."

"Didn't anyone ever tell you that looks are transitory and that what is inside is what counts?" said Constance.

"What a joke," laughed Archer. "Are you telling me you look at a beautiful orchid and instead of appreciating its delicate colors and shape, you say, 'too bad—it is going to wilt'? You just got through telling me how beautiful you thought Marilyn Monroe was."

"No, I am just saying looks are not everything."

"That's easy for you to say. What if you were plain and not beautiful?"

"I don't think of myself as beautiful."

"Well, you are. You are absolutely at the peak of your bloom."

"I'm just preparing myself for the day when I start wilting," said Constance, letting out a big laugh, her signal that the conversation was not really serious.

"Mrs. Booker, your modesty and charm are overpowering."

"Okay, Desmond, I want to show the mansions in Pacific Heights before we stop for drinks at the Hamblens'," said Constance. "We have saved the best for last."

Leonard drove them to their last tour area. “Obviously, people in this town make a lot of money,” Archer said after a block-by-block tour of the Pacific Heights mansions.

“Would you like to live here, Constance?”

“Not really. My house is already too big, and I have nice neighbors, and I like to be able to walk in Golden Gate Park,” Constance answered.

“The trouble with you is you are too easily satisfied,” said Archer.

“I am more picky than you might think,” Constance smiled.

Constance and Desmond arrived at the Hamblens’ house a little after six. It was already almost dark, and the temperature had dropped into the low sixties.

The Hamblens’ house was a three-story Tudor, with the living room on the back of the second floor affording sweeping views of both bridges and Marin County.

“From the street, I had no idea you would have such a magnificent view,” said Archer. “I love all of the lights. It must be fabulous in the daytime.”

“The only negative is the view of Alcatraz,” said Richard. “It is a bit depressing to think of the men imprisoned there.”

“I hope none of them were your clients,” said Archer, laughing. “I might have to rethink our little arrangement.”

Claudia served shrimp and crab legs, and Richard handled the drinks. Archer asked for a martini on the rocks with three olives. The others drank white wine.

“Constance has taken me on the most magnificent tour,” said Archer. “If it wasn’t for the fact we have all of our businesses in Australia, I could be tempted to move to a city like this.”

"Well, if we can find a newspaper for you, that would give you a chance to become a regular visitor," said Richard.

Just then the doorbell rang. It was Mathew and Anne Reynolds.

"I thought it would be nice to reassemble the cast from our lovely dinner aboard the *Aussie Legend*," said Claudia.

Archer greeted Mathew and Anne with enthusiasm.

"Let me say this before anyone accuses me of having too much to drink," said Archer. "You three ladies ought to be in the movies. I can see you playing together in one of those sophisticated drawing room comedies Hollywood used to make before the war. Let me propose a toast to our hostess and her two lovely costars."

The cocktail hour extended past eight o'clock, and all six were in a merry mood, Archer being the merriest, having consumed four martinis before switching to white wine. Richard talked privately with Archer about buying a newspaper, and the three ladies and Mathew talked about San Francisco. Mathew and Anne Reynolds had only been in San Francisco for seven months of what would likely be a three-year posting.

"I can't imagine we will ever have a more beautiful place to live," said Anne, who added that with the Australian diplomatic service, they could not ever predict where they might be assigned. She said Mathew's next job would likely be as an ambassador, and she guessed the Philippines was a strong possibility.

"I have friends who used to live in the Philippines," said Constance. "Of course, that was before the war, but they said Filipino society was quite sophisticated, and servants cost next to nothing."

"I wish that was true here," said Claudia. "We have a cleaning lady twice a week, but that is all."

"You are looking at the cleaning lady," said Constance.

"Here's a toast to the servants," said Mathew. "Constance, tell us about where you took Desmond on this tour he has been raving about."

"Better yet, I will just take you and Anne," said Constance. "I don't know why, but I really love to take people to places they have never been, like walking around the damp fortress at Fort Point, where many times you won't see a single other soul. It is right under the Golden Gate bridge and is totally deserted—no guards, no fences—you can just walk right in."

Constance went on to talk about the other harbor fortifications that went back one hundred years and from which nary a shot had ever been fired, unless you counted the prison riot at Alcatraz.

"I have lived here all my life, and I don't know nearly as much about San Francisco as Constance," said Claudia.

"Claudia knows the best places to shop for anything or everything, whether it is downtown, Chinatown, the Mission, or North Beach," said Constance. "She also knows everything that is going on at the theaters, the opera house, the night clubs, you name it."

Claudia brought out six whole crabs, all at least seven inches across, a huge tossed salad, and two loaves of French bread.

"This is very informal," she said, inviting everyone to use a lap tray for their food. "This is not up to Desmond's abalone, but I hope it will do."

Richard kept the wine glasses full, and the only trouble with the conversation was that there was too much to catch it all. Constance wanted to hear everything, but it was impossible with as many as four people talking at once!

As the meal concluded, Archer rose to his feet, complimenting Claudia on her wonderful dinner and her beautiful house, saying he felt like he was with new friends who were old friends.

"I truly feel like I have known you all much longer than just a few days," he said. "Therefore, I hope you will forgive me if I make a last-minute proposal that will extend our friendship—and that is for you all to come with me on my yacht on a two-day voyage to Monterey and Carmel. We can leave tomorrow night, which is Friday, and return on Sunday. I realize this is short notice, but as you know, I am leaving Monday morning to fly back to Sydney."

"We have a dinner at the Grahams on Saturday," said Claudia, looking at Richard.

"We can always have dinner with the Grahams," said Richard. "Why don't we just say something has come up, and we have to go out of town. Constance, do you have anything you have to do?"

"No, it sounds good to me. What about you Anne?" said Constance.

Anne looked at Mathew, and they both smiled.

"Three Americans and three Aussies—should be great fun!" said Mathew.

"Wonderful," said Archer. "I will spend tomorrow doing the planning."

As Leonard drove toward Constance's house, Desmond Archer and Constance rode in the backseat with the top up. Constance managed to deftly handle his groping and gave him a peck on the lips when they arrived at her house.

"Thank you for the tour today and yesterday; it has been a spectacular four days of knowing you," said Archer, giving her a powerful hug at the door.

"Thank you, Desmond. I am really looking forward to the trip."

CHAPTER 32

The party was in a jovial mood as the *Aussie Legend* motored from the San Francisco Yacht Harbor toward the Golden Gate Bridge. The remains of the sunset cast a deepening red glow on the skyline. Once out on the ocean, the 116-foot fan-tailed motor yacht began to rise and fall, gently at first but more heavily as time went on.

"I hope you all have your sea legs," said Desmond Archer to his five guests, gesturing with his martini toward the rising ocean. "The swells could get to eight or ten feet, according to the coastal weather forecast."

"I've steamed through typhoons in the South Pacific," said Mathew Reynolds, who had served as an officer in the Australian navy during World War II. "I got sick the first time I went out, but I learned just to relax after that, and everything was fine."

"If anyone wants some pills for seasickness, I have them," said Archer. No one responded.

"I've never had any problems," said Richard, "and neither has Claudia."

The cocktail hour lasted only until 8:00 PM, and it seemed everyone was reducing their intake of alcohol, perhaps, Constance thought, because of the heavy drinking that had gone on both Tuesday and Thursday nights. Every night can't be New Year's Eve.

Archer introduced the chef before they sat down to eat, a lovely Chinese woman named Betsy Ling, a third-generation San Franciscan. Betsy was pretty and appeared to be about thirty. Archer said she was an award-winning chef who had agreed to sign on for the trip to Monterey.

"We are dining very simply tonight," said Betsy in a broad California accent. "We have for the main course poached Pacific salmon, steamed asparagus, and boiled potatoes with a lovely hollandaise sauce on the side for those who like it. But first we have a thick crab soup followed by slices of tomatoes and avocados. And Mr. Archer has selected a very crisp California white wine, which will go beautifully with everything."

Richard Hamblen applauded and said he was glad Betsy was keeping everything "simple."

Constance said nothing. The thought of food was beginning to sound quite unappetizing.

"Are you all right, Constance?" Archer asked.

"I think so, but I do feel a bit queasy," she said.

Archer got up from the table while the others, none of whom felt sick, offered their sympathies to Constance.

"Take three of these pills with a glass of water, and then drink this shot of brandy," instructed Archer. "You will feel better in no time."

Archer also called the captain and told him to reduce speed so that they would arrive at the north end of Monterey Bay no earlier than 7:00 AM

"We can have an early night of it and then get up at dawn so that we can see the whales," said Archer, who explained that the gray whales were now heading south from Alaska to their winter spawning grounds along the southern coast of Baja.

"We might also see some blue whales, humpback whales, and, if we are lucky, some killer whales," said Archer, now returned to his seat. "If this were spring, we might see one of the great dramas of the sea. I've read that the killer whales lay in wait near Monterey for the gray whales as they come back from Baja with their new offspring. The killer whales like nothing better than eating baby grays."

"Will you excuse me," said Constance. "I think I have to lie down for a while." She had eaten only a bit of her soup.

Archer jumped up again and said he would escort Constance to her room.

"I think she will be all right after a nap," said Archer, upon his return. "Let's all eat and be merry."

Constance had to get up three times during the night to throw up. She felt as miserable as she could ever remember. The motion of the boat was all the more bothersome as the southerly course put the vessel astride the heavy swells, causing it to rock sideways as well as fore and aft. Unbeknownst to Constance, Claudia had excused herself from the dinner table before she was halfway though her salmon, and ten minutes later, Anne had excused herself as well, looking only slightly green.

"Well, this proves that men are the superior gender," chortled Archer, evoking smiles from both Richard and Mathew. The men stayed up until eleven, talking about the sea and marine life. Mathew told some interesting stories about his life in the Australian navy serving aboard a destroyer in the waters around New Guinea and the Dutch East Indies. He said that while on shore leave in New Guinea, he and his crew met some authentic headhunters who were quite friendly and with whom they got drunk on some local concoction that gave them thirty-six-hour headaches.

"You are lucky those boys didn't eat you," said Archer.

"The way my head felt, I would not have minded," said Reynolds. "I did not have another drink for two years."

Later, on his way to bed, Archer knocked gently on Constance's door. There was no answer.

Hours later, Constance looked at her watch. It was 6:00 AM. She had been in bed more than nine hours. She felt better, but there was an ache and emptiness in her stomach. She got up and dressed and went to the top deck, where the first mate was in the pilot house overseeing the vessel's sophisticated radar and automatic piloting system.

"Can I get you some coffee, ma'am?" asked the first mate.

"That would be wonderful, if you have some heavy cream to go with it," said Constance. "I was a bit seasick last night."

"Coming up, ma'am. I guess you weren't alone," said the mate. "I understand all the ladies had to retire early."

"Constance, there you are, I have been looking all over for you," said Archer, suddenly appearing behind her. "Are you all right?"

"I'm feeling better, I think. I'll tell you more after I finish this coffee," she said, taking the cup from the first mate. "I'm sorry I had to leave during dinner last night."

"Don't apologize. You weren't the only one, and as a matter of fact, I was not feeling so well myself when I went to bed," Archer said. "Come, put on this foul-weather gear, and we can go stand at the bow. It's the best way I know to clear your head."

"This is refreshing," said Constance moments later, the cold wind and spray from the water lashing her face. For a change, Archer did not say much. The two of them leaned forward on the railing, watching the bow cut gushing white waves left and right while rising and falling in a way that no longer bothered Constance. Then came the sun rising over the mountains, out of a cloudy sky to their left. It was an intoxicating moment, and neither Constance nor Desmond said anything.

It was Constance who finally broke the silence: "I think I have my sea legs."

"You must be hungry," said Archer.

"I'm starved. Can we get breakfast?"

What a difference ten hours had made. Constance started with oatmeal and orange juice followed by two fried eggs, hash brown potatoes, bacon, and toast and jam.

"That is an impressive recovery," said Archer, who ate only oatmeal. "I'm not much of a breakfast person."

"I feel completely recovered," said Constance.

"You are an amazing woman," said Archer. "Let's go back on deck. We should be just outside Santa Cruz now, and we might see some whales."

By eight, everyone was up and standing at the bow as the *Aussie Legend* plowed slowly through the rich waters of Monterey Bay. The first sightings were three porpoises that were swimming northward and that came out of the water in regular intervals.

"If I had to come back as a mammal," said Claudia, "it would be as a porpoise."

Anne asked Claudia if she believed in reincarnation.

"Well, I wouldn't say I believe in it, but I can't rule it out, either," said Claudia. "I mean, we know so little, so how can we say something is impossible?"

"I used to think that when we died, we went to another life," said Constance. "Actually, now, while I believe there is a God, I am not sure about the heaven and hell my father used to describe. That's one of the most interesting things about dying. We'll know the answer to whether there is a life after death."

"Constance," said Mathew Reynolds, "you must have studied the philosophy of David Hume, the eighteenth-century Scottish philosopher, who said he was eagerly awaiting death, because it would bring the answer to the greatest question concerning mankind, that is, whether there is indeed life after death. And if there wasn't, he said, what would be better than a deep sleep from which you remember nothing?"

"That almost sounds comforting," said Richard Hamblen. "Except it does not address the question of heaven and hell if there is a life after death. Personally, I don't believe God would make people suffer in the way hell is sometimes described."

"Well, there are a lot of awful things God lets happen right here on this earth," said Archer. "But you know what, I'm not even thinking about it. I take my life one day at a time, and as the cowboys say in the movies, I let the chips fall where they may."

"One can only infer, Desmond, that deep down, you don't believe in hell," said Reynolds.

"No, I didn't say that," Archer responded. "What I am saying is I don't think there is any way I can know about heaven and hell and God, so I don't waste my time worrying about something I can't find the answer for."

"Until you die," Constance interjected. "I believe we should conduct our lives as if there was a God and a heaven and hell. That way you have nothing to lose."

"Except maybe a lot of fun," laughed Archer.

"Now, you are getting to the question of whether there is more pleasure to be found in virtue or sin," said Hamblen.

"The answer to that is very simple," said Reynolds. "Sin is more fun in the short term, but not over the long run. That becomes clearer the older we get. Of course, that introduces the question of whether or not there is a devil who is luring us all into temptation."

"Here I am, the devil incarnate," laughed Archer. "This conversation is getting a little bit heavy for me. Who would like a Bloody Mary?"

Both Reynolds and Hamblen thought that was a good idea.

"I think I have some of my father's religious genes," said Constance. "Deep down, I know there is a God."

"You are among the blessed, my dear," said Archer. "I wish I could feel that way."

The conversation on religion continued until Archer shouted, "Look over here! Three gray whales heading to Baja." Archer directed the captain to move closer and to keep pace with them. The rather ugly backs of the whales were visible just above the water's surface. Then one disappeared, only to leap out of the water in an almost complete breach.

The group let out a collective gasp at the size of the whale.

"He must be thirty feet," said Archer. The whales continued their easy pace, seemingly unconcerned and uninterested in the *Aussie Legend*, which had gotten to within thirty yards of the huge mammals. The small convoy moved along together for perhaps five miles until Archer said it was time to head into Monterey, where a car was waiting.

"Being so near those whales was very exciting," said Constance. "Thank you very much, Desmond." Richard and Mathew hoisted their almost empty drinks in a salute to the smiling Archer, who was pleased that the weekend outing had gotten back on the track he had imagined.

CHAPTER 33

A black Cadillac limousine was waiting in the parking lot near the dock. Archer suggested the party could spend two hours or so walking around the Monterey waterfront before taking the limo to Carmel.

"This is John Steinbeck country," Richard Hamblen said to Constance as Archer led the group to the pier. "Have you ever read him?"

"Only *Cannery Row*," said Constance, "but I want to read more—he's a wonderful writer."

"I've read everything he has ever written," said Richard. "He writes about very ordinary people with such a wonderful passion that you are caught up quickly in their lives."

"My father used to say that the more you learn about something, the more interesting it becomes," said Constance.

"Your father must have been a great influence on your life," said Richard.

"Much more than he ever thought," said Constance. "And I guess his influence is probably even greater now. I mean I can see the wisdom of so much of what he said."

"I think you and I both agree about God, that he exists," said Hamblen. "But then we agree on a lot of things."

"I hadn't thought about that, but I suppose you are right."

Richard and Constance walked together for most of the hour the group spent on the pier, which was dotted with fishermen, none of whom seemed to be catching anything. The group drifted apart in pairs, Archer with Claudia and the Reynolds with each other.

The temperature was in the fifties, but a light wind made it seem colder. Constance began to shiver.

"Do you want my jacket?" said Richard. He put his arm around her shoulder and gave her a squeeze. "I think you are still a little weak from last night."

"Thank you, Richard, but I don't need your jacket. You'll freeze to death," said Constance, leaning into Richard's arm. Richard continued his hold.

"Say, what is going on here, Hamblen? Are you trying to steal my girl?" said Archer, looming from behind.

"She's shivering from the cold," replied Richard, removing his arm.

Claudia stepped forward and put her arm around Constance.

"She certainly is shivering," said Claudia. "Richard, you were doing the right thing."

Archer put his arm around Constance and said he would take responsibility for keeping Constance warm. Constance laughed heartily.

"I certainly appreciate all of this attention," she said.

"Come now, let's get back to the warmth of the car," said Archer, pulling Constance in tightly next to him, "We need to warm this girl up." Constance laughed again.

Constance recommended that they take the famous 17-Mile Drive just off Highway One that winds from the hills above the ocean down to the rocky shoreline where some of the world's most spectacular golf courses are located, including the famed Pebble Beach golf links.

Neither the Mathews nor Archer had ever before been to Pebble Beach.

"Small wonder this place is so famous," said Archer as the group sat down for lunch at the Inn at Pebble Beach overlooking the eighteenth hole. "By comparison, the golf links in Scotland and Ireland are quite bleak. Here the ocean is spectacularly alive with waves crashing on rocks, deer grazing on the fairways, marvelous houses, wonderful woods, and a cozy town. This really is a storybook setting."

"When we first came here before the war, Joe said that one day, he would like to retire here," said Constance. "He loved golf, and he played this course."

"I've played here and at Cypress Point, which we passed just before we got to Pebble," said Richard. "Some people believe Cypress is even better than Pebble, but Cypress is a private club, so very few people are lucky enough to play there."

"I wouldn't mind joining," said Archer. "Is it hard to get in?"

"For most people, very hard to get in," said Richard, "but for someone like you, I think it is possible."

"Well, having a house here and belonging to a good golf club would be a nice way to live part of the year and entertain my mates from Australia and elsewhere," said Archer. "Are houses available?"

"I could look into that for you," Richard said, "and the club as well. How large a house would you be looking for?"

"Nothing grand, maybe six or seven bedrooms, with a nice view of the water, preferably on the golf course if something is available," said Archer.

"Do you have a price range?" asked Hamblen.

"No limit—because from my very limited knowledge, anything you buy here is just going to go up in value," said Archer. "This is one of the prettiest places in the world."

"Do you always make up your mind so quickly?" asked Claudia.

"I'm forty-six years old and have been almost every place in the world worth seeing, so when I see something like this, it doesn't take long to appreciate the value, never mind the prospective lifestyle. And at the end of the day, California is on the way to becoming the largest state in population, soon to surpass New York—and in wealth as well. The American economy may not be quite so hot right now, but it is going to get better. When it does, places like Pebble Beach will soar in value."

Mathew Reynolds said he concurred completely and wished he had the money to make his own investment.

"Desmond is one of the fortunate few who has the capability of putting his money where his mouth is," said Richard, adding that he would wire information to Archer within the next thirty days.

"Well, that's done," said Archer. "Where do you suggest we go next, Constance?

"I suggest we drive south down to Big Sur and have tea there and then come back," said Constance. "I think we can make it back before dark."

"Won't that make you miss shopping in Carmel?" said Archer. "I believe you said they have some wonderful shops there."

"We can come here anytime," said Richard. "It is really only three hours by car from San Francisco, and I suspect you will enjoy seeing Big Sur."

"I've got an idea," said Archer. "Instead of going back to San Francisco tomorrow morning, why don't we spend the day in

Carmel and leave at just before dark so that we can get to the city early Monday morning in time for all of you to get to your jobs or whatever?"

"That would be fine with us," said Richard. "But I can't speak for the Reynolds or Constance."

"I really don't need to shop but it is always fun; Anne, what do you think?" asked Constance.

"Let's do it," said Mathew.

"All agreed," said Richard. "Perhaps we can get a chance to look at some houses tomorrow."

"Oh, I'd love that," said Constance. "There are few things I like better than poking around houses, especially nice ones."

"Then it's off to Big Sur," said Archer.

As it turned out, the trip to Big Sur was an even bigger success than Constance had imagined. The temperature had risen to the high sixties, and the group went on a hiking trail overlooking the spectacular seascape below. Archer was enchanted by the ancient redwood trees and huge ocean swells crashing on giant rocks. The path went on for several miles.

"I've been on hikes in Ireland overlooking the sea, but there is nothing this spectacular," said Archer.

"I think we had better head back," said Richard. "The light is fading, and the fog seems to be dropping and getting thicker."

"Don't worry, I have a flashlight," said Archer.

"Desmond, in some ways, you remind me of my husband," said Constance. "He always thought of everything."

"I'll take that as the highest compliment; Richard has told me what a fine person he was," said Archer.

The group did not arrive back at the dock until after 8:00 PM. Archer suggested that they forego their dinner reservations in Carmel and eat on the boat.

"Have a shower and a bit of a rest, and we'll meet for drinks in the lounge at nine o'clock," said Archer. "I think we can scrape up some abalone."

Constance decided to take a short nap, and knocking on her door soon awoke her. It was Desmond telling her it was past nine and wondering if there was anything wrong. She said she must have been more tired than she thought and apologized for not being on time; she would be in the lounge in fifteen minutes.

Everyone was on their second round of drinks when Constance arrived. Archer insisted that she needed to overcome her fatigue with one of his patented, very dry martinis. She agreed that she needed something and drank it down in three gulps.

"Would you like another?" asked Archer.

"I do feel a lot better. Maybe one more," said Constance.

"Be careful, Constance," said Claudia. "You've heard that old ditty: 'Oh, I never have a martini, well maybe two at the most. Three I am under the table, and four I am under the host.'" Everyone laughed.

"Where did you learn that?" asked Richard.

"Didn't know your wife knew such stuff, huh," said Archer. "It is my experience that women among themselves can be as raunchy as any man, except for Constance here, to whom I will not serve a third martini—unless of course, she wants a fourth."

Constance and the others laughed. "I guarantee you this is my last martini. I don't know how anyone can drink more than two.

But I have to admit they taste pretty good, especially when you are tired."

"Martinis cure just about everything," said Archer, "everything from fatigue to depression to boredom to fear. A friend once told me after his fifth martini that 'martinis ought to be against the law.' With that, he passed out right there at the table with a smile on his face."

"What were we talking about this morning—that sin in the short run is a lot more fun?" said Reynolds.

"I'll drink to that," said Archer, looking straight at Constance. "I'm on my fourth martini right now. Claudia, do you have a rhyme about a host having four martinis?"

"I'll try to think of something," said Claudia.

"Don't include me in it," Constance laughed.

"I've come up with something," said Claudia, who was on her third glass of wine. "There was a man who loved martinis, to compensate for his tiny weenie."

Constance erupted in laughter.

"Of course, I am not referring to any present company," said Claudia. "I say that, because I have noticed evidence to the contrary beneath those crisp white trousers.

"Claudia, I think you are getting drunk," said Richard.

"See, I told you women are the raunchy sex, going around checking out crotches," laughed Archer.

"I think people are naturally checking out everything," said Anne.

"That's why men wore cod pieces in their trousers centuries ago," said Mathew. "They knew that women were checking out their crotches."

"Maybe they wore them to attract other men," said Richard. "I can't imagine a real man wearing a cod piece. After all, what would happen if he seduced his subject and then had to introduce a reality that was less than advertised?"

"He wouldn't care at all," said Archer. "At that point, he would have achieved his end."

"So long as you get the woman into bed, anything is justified, is that it?" asked Claudia.

"Lord, no," said Archer. "But almost anything," he laughed.

"I think this conversation has deteriorated to a level that is beneath us all," smiled Richard. "I move we change the subject to President Eisenhower."

"You mean, you want to talk about the romance he had with his female British driver during the war in London?" said Archer. Everyone laughed.

"I agree with Richard. There are more interesting things to talk about, like what we are having for dinner," said Constance. "I am famished."

CHAPTER 34

Betsy Ling was in the dining room awaiting the diners. It was nearly 10:30 PM.

"You have had a very long day," Betsy said to Archer. "I hope you have brought your appetites. We have some very tender abalone poached in butter, and we are starting with artichokes."

"Is there any more of that crab soup from last night?" asked Archer. "I'd like to start with that. Eating an artichoke is too much work for me. Constance, would you like another martini?"

"Heavens no," she laughed.

"I'd like to try one," said Claudia. "What do you think, honey?" she said, turning to Richard.

"I think what I say is not going to matter, because I know you well enough after all these years that when you say you are going to do something, you do it," said Richard. "Personally, I prefer not to mix the grain with the grape. It can have some repercussions the next day."

"That's my Richard," said Claudia. "He is always right. I am going to try one of Desmond's famous martinis."

"Coming up, my dear," said Archer. "Anyone else?"

Mathew and Anne said they were sticking to the white wine, as did Richard. Constance said she was going to follow Richard's advice and not mix the grain and the grape.

"You mean you are not going to have anything more?" asked Archer. Constance said some water would do, because the two martinis made her feel like she had already had a bottle of wine.

"Such discipline," said Archer. "I wish I had it."

"I have it too," said Claudia, "except not tonight."

Betsy had the steward bring out a cup of crab soup for everyone, and she accepted Archer's offer to have a glass of wine.

"Tell us about yourself," said Archer. "How did a beautiful woman like you ever decide to become a chef?"

"It is a family thing," said Betsy. "My grandfather worked as a cook in a small Chinese restaurant on Grant Avenue, and my father followed in his footsteps and finally owned his own restaurant, which was quite successful. Unfortunately, my father died a few years ago at only sixty. Now the restaurant is run by my two brothers. I went to a culinary arts training school in Connecticut and have been working in Western kitchens in San Francisco for the past six years, including Scoma's at Fisherman's Wharf and the Fairmont Hotel, which is where I work now during the week."

"Are you married?" asked Archer. Betsy blushed slightly and said she was not.

"Well, you are going to make someone a wonderful wife," said Archer. "This crab soup is even better than it was last night."

Claudia switched back to wine during dinner while Archer ordered another martini. Richard and the Reynolds drank sparingly, and Constance stuck with her water, but devoured her food and asked for a second helping of abalone.

After dinner, Archer suggested that everyone work out the kinks by dancing.

"Claudia has promised to teach me how to do the Charleston," said Archer. "She and Richard are going to demonstrate how it is done. Constance, do you know how to Charleston?"

"A little bit, but that was a long time ago, at Fort Riley before the war," said Constance.

Archer found several Charleston records, and the Hamblens put on a spirited display of prowess that brought applause when they finished.

"Okay, let's all try it," said Archer. "Claudia, you teach me, and Richard can refresh Constance, and Mathew and Anne, please join in."

The three couples danced the Charleston for half an hour.

"Hey, we are getting pretty good at this," said Archer, perspiration dripping from his forehead. "But I'm getting tired. I'm going to put on some slower music."

"Put on a tango," said Claudia. "I'll teach you how."

"I need to get some fresh air," said Constance. "I'll be back in a minute. I'm just going to go on deck."

Claudia ordered another wine and Archer another martini.

"We have to fuel the engine for all of this work," said Archer.

"I'll drink to that," said Claudia. "Now, the tango is not going to be easy to teach you, but we are going to try."

Mathew and Anne said they would like to learn as well.

Richard quietly slipped outside to the deck, where Constance was leaning over the railing. The lights of Monterey gave a sparkle to the night and reflected off the water. No one seemed to be on any of the nearby boats sitting in the harbor. The air was windless, and the fog had given way to a starry sky.

"Are you having a good time?" Richard asked.

"Oh, you surprised me, Richard," said Constance. "Yes, I am having a perfectly wonderful time, though I wish Desmond did not drink quite so much."

"He has a problem, all right," said Richard, "but he can be a lot of fun. I don't think he is the man for you. You know, in the ten years we have known you, I don't think we have ever spent as much time together as we have this past week. I wish we did it more often. We have Archer to thank for that. You know how much both Claudia and I enjoy being with you. Claudia was saying tonight as we were dressing that she had never seen you look more beautiful, and I have to agree. Right now, you look as lovely as I have ever seen you."

"Thank you, Richard. It must be the fresh air and the two martinis," Constance laughed. "Or maybe it is all that wine you have been drinking. I'm just kidding. You know how I feel about you and Claudia and how much I appreciate all you have done for me and the boys."

"Constance, there is something I want to tell you," said Richard.

"Sounds like you are going to make a confession," said Constance.

"I am. I just want to say what I feel in my heart about you. If I wasn't married, and happily so, I would be deeply in love with you. I would like nothing better than to take you in my arms and kiss you forever, but I know that is never going to happen. Actually, I *am* in love with you, a platonic pure love dictated by the circumstances of our lives and our beliefs. I am happy just to be with you and near you."

"Oh, Richard, if you were not married … but you are. You know I love both you and Claudia. You are a very attractive man. Who wouldn't fall in love with you? You and Claudia are also my best friends in this world. I appreciate what you have said, but I don't want to change anything; I don't want to risk losing what we have to a passion that can only burn out."

"I agree," said Richard. "The love I feel for you will never burn out."

Richard leaned forward and kissed Constance softly on the lips.

"I think we had better go back in now," said Constance.

Claudia and Archer were dancing slowly to a Frank Sinatra record. Mathew and Anne had apparently gone to bed. It was almost 1:00 AM.

"Hey, where have you guys been?" asked Archer.

"We've been on deck; the air is beautiful," said Constance. "You have to come out."

"I hope you two haven't been smooching out there," said Archer. "Claudia, you have to watch out for that husband of yours. I think he has a thing for Constance."

"Claudia doesn't need to watch out for anything," said Constance.

"I am sure you are right," said Archer. "I believe you can handle any situation. C'mon, Constance, how about a dance?"

"I would be delighted, but just one. I've been up since six o'clock."

Richard took Claudia in his arms and said he wanted to dance with his beautiful wife.

"I thought you had forgotten all about me," said Claudia. "I might as well dance with the most beautiful man here."

Archer danced well, but he crushed Constance against his body.

"Constance, the divine," said Archer. "Tall, beautiful, slim, sweet, funny, Constance the irresistible. I can't think of anything better than holding you in my arms."

"Your compliments leave me speechless," said Constance, as she pushed back from Archer's pelvic press that she could feel was having an effect on him. Archer pushed forward.

"Let's just sit down and talk," said Constance.

"We're going to leave you two lovebirds alone," said Claudia. "We're going to bed, and don't wake us up too early." Richard looked intently at Constance and waved good night.

"I finally have you alone," said Archer, who walked to the bar and mixed himself a martini. "Can I get you a third and fourth?" smiled Archer.

"I'll just have a water," said Constance. "How many of those martinis have you had?"

"I've already worked off half of them dancing with Claudia," said Archer. "I shouldn't tell you this, but I think she is a little jealous of you. She knows how Richard feels about you."

"That's ridiculous," said Constance.

"No, it isn't, Constance. You are truly the kind of woman everyone falls in love with, including me. I'd marry you in a minute if I thought you would have me, but I have already figured out you are not going to leave your sons and live in Australia. My only hope is that we could be lovers."

Archer moved to put his arms around Constance, but she pushed him off and laughed.

"I think I hear those martinis talking, Desmond. You know I am not going to become your lover, even though I find you fun and amusing, and I can see where many women would find you very attractive. You are quite handsome in a rugged kind of way. I just don't think we have that much in common."

"You prefer the more sophisticated types like Richard," said Archer.

"I don't know what I prefer, but I like you a lot, Desmond, and we have had a lot of fun together this past week. You have been a very generous and thoughtful host, and we have all had a great time. Hopefully, we will all see each other when you come back."

"And four I'm under the host," laughed Archer. "Pity you only had two martinis. I think it is time for bed, but first, I am going to fight off this feeling of rejection with my very last martini."

"Do you really need another?" said Constance, thinking he had probably already had at least eight. "I don't know how you can hold them and not be falling down drunk."

"It takes a lot of training," said Archer.

"Well, I'm going to leave you, Desmond. I'm exhausted. Thank you for a lovely day." Constance walked over and gave Desmond a kiss on the cheek. He tried to grab her, but she deftly backed away, smiling and blowing him a kiss.

"You are as slippery as an eel!" muttered Archer as he put the tiniest amount of vermouth on the top of his glass of gin.

Constance took only a few moments to fall into a deep sleep, but not before she had pondered what Richard had said to her. Yes, she had to admit that she loved him but that it was a love never to be consummated. And she had to smile at the fact that in a single evening two men had said they loved her. It reminded her of her high school days in Hawaii when lots of boys said they were in love with her.

Constance hadn't been asleep for more than an hour or so when she was awakened by a woman's screams. She bolted up in bed. They were screams of anger. It sounded like Betsy Ling, but Constance could not be sure. She got up and put on her bathrobe and rushed out into the hallway.

Archer was stumbling out of one of the guest suites on the starboard side of the yacht.

"She stabbed me," said Archer, holding his hand to his blood-drenched shoulder.

Richard suddenly appeared, asking what had happened.

"She stabbed me! Betsy stabbed me," Archer repeated.

"You are darned right I did," said Betsy, appearing in the hallway, still holding a butcher knife in her hand. "He came into my room and tried to rape me, the bastard. If I didn't have a knife under my pillow, he would have."

The blood continued to rush from Archer's upper right arm.

"Take your shirt off, we need to stop the bleeding with a tourniquet," said Richard. "Where's the first aid kit?"

"There's one in the pilot house," said Archer.

"I'll get it," said Constance.

When Archer was bandaged, Richard suggested they go to the salon and talk, inviting the still-agitated Betsy to join them. Constance had her arm around Betsy, trying to calm her down.

"We are going to have to take Desmond to have that wound stitched up, but I don't think we can get a doctor at this time, and I would rather not take him to the emergency room just yet," said Richard.

"Oh, God, I am sorry," said Archer. "I had too much to drink. Oh, Betsy, I am sorry. I was out of my mind."

"It seemed to me you knew exactly what you were doing," said Betsy. "I had that knife under my pillow because I was worried about a couple of the crew who had been leering at me. I never thought I would have to defend myself against the owner, a drunken pig. I want to call the police and press charges. You came into my cabin and tried to rape me. You deserve to go to jail."

"You are right, Betsy—I do," said Archer. "All I ask is that you forgive a stupid drunk."

"I'm not falling for that stupid drunk line," said Betsy.

Richard said he wanted to speak privately with Betsy. They went into the adjoining dining room, leaving Constance and Archer alone.

"Why did I have that last martini?" said Archer. "I am such a weak-willed idiot."

"Does your arm hurt?" asked Constance. "I'm sure it must."

"Do you think Richard can talk her out of pressing charges?" Archer asked.

"Is that what he's doing?" asked Constance.

"That's what good lawyers do," said Archer. "I am ashamed to say this is not the first time I have been in a fix."

"You mean you've tried to rape someone before?"

"No, not that. Never mind. I am just sorry, especially sorry that it happened with you around, someone I really care for," his voice trailing off pathetically.

"My father always said everything happens for a reason. You have to figure out what that reason is," said Constance.

"I know what it is," he said. "I'm never going to take a drink again, and I am going to try to do something more useful with my life. I just hope I don't have to go to jail, though if I do, I'll have to live with it."

"Not drinking would be quite a change for you," said Constance. "I'll pray that you can stop. With your energy, I am sure you can accomplish a lot of good."

After about thirty minutes, Richard came back into the room alone. He asked Constance if she would go talk with Betsy.

"She's agreed to not file any charges if you meet certain conditions," Richard told Archer. "How would you like to finance a restaurant? You put up all of the money as a loan, and you get 25 percent of the profits while Betsy has complete control and 75 percent of the profits. Betsy doesn't want anything to do with you, and she asked that if there is an agreement, I act as the go-between."

"Whose idea was that?" asked Archer.

"Well, it was mine, actually, for a lot of different reasons, including tax considerations, plus what I can only assume are considerations for your own companies," said Richard. "We agreed that you will not have to invest more than $150,000. Personally, Desmond, I recommend that you accept. Otherwise, she's going to press charges and wants to call the police right now."

"Okay, it's a deal—what choice do I have? God, I feel awful. But you have done your job well, Richard. I am very grateful to you. Be sure and send me your bill, but let's put our other plans on hold for a while. I need to get back to Australia and get my life straightened out."

"But first, you have to get that arm treated and stitched," said Richard. "We'll get a taxi and go to the emergency. We'll have to think of some excuse as to how it happened."

Archer and Richard rejoined Constance and Betsy. Constance still had her arm around Betsy, and they were talking quietly. Constance had told Betsy she was a brave woman and had done the right thing.

"Constance, you and Betsy ought to get some sleep while Desmond and I go to the emergency," said Richard. "I suppose it is fortunate that Claudia, Mathew, and Anne slept through it all."

Shortly after dawn, Richard made arrangements for Betsy to be driven back to San Francisco. He told her to start looking for a restaurant and suggested that perhaps they could meet in a week or so.

"How do I know he is going to come up with the money?" asked Betsy.

"Because he has agreed to give me a certified check for $150,000 on Monday," said Richard.

"Betsy," said Archer when she was leaving, "I know I don't deserve to be forgiven, but I thank you for your understanding and I wish you great success."

"Perhaps in time this will heal," said Betsy.

Archer, with bloodshot eyes and a beaten down, remorseful countenance, said that he was going to fly back to the city and that he needed to be alone. Richard said he thought that was a good idea.

"You take everyone back in the boat," Archer said to Richard.

"Desmond, I'll see you tomorrow. I suggest you delay your flight to Sydney until Tuesday," said Richard. "There are some things we need to finalize."

"Agreed. I need to spend some time with the captain as well; they are supposed to have some shakedown problems taken care of before they leave for Sydney later in the week."

Betsy and Archer were both gone. Claudia was still asleep, and so were Reynolds and his wife. It was still only 8:45 AM. Richard went to his cabin.

"Where have you been, honey?" said Claudia. "Oh, I have a terrible hangover. Honey, could you get me a coffee?"

Richard told Claudia the whole story.

"You mean all that happened while I was sleeping? I can hardly believe it," said Claudia.

"I don't think Archer ever had another drink," my mother wrote in her diary years later, when she was recounting her most memorable experiences.

Claudia and my mother often talked about that trip, and both agreed that it had changed the lives of both Archer and Betsy. Once I heard my mother say it had changed her life, because it indirectly led to her meeting Ken Thatcher, who was to become a very important person in her future.

CHAPTER 35

Joe, Jim, and I came home for a week for the Christmas holiday in 1954, and we were all happy to have the whole family together again. Joe was still going with Claire Winstead, and she was around a lot. Jim brought his new girlfriend, Cynthia Flowers, on several occasions. Cynthia was beautiful, and she oozed sex appeal. She could not keep her hands off of Jim and was always reaching out to hold his hand or lean into him or whatever. I got the feeling their relationship had passed the platonic stage. The most notable thing about Cynthia was her lush figure, which, oddly enough, she did not flaunt, but could not hide, even under loose-fitting clothes.

Mom and Claire got on well and worked together with great efficiency on the meals. Cynthia, like Jim, was a freshman at Berkeley. She said she was an only child whose parents lived in Napa, where her father was in the wine business. That did not seem so glamorous then. I mean, you could buy California wine for less than a dollar a bottle!

Jim was a celebrity at Berkeley from the start because of his widely publicized basketball talents. He was getting a lot of playing time in the early season games and was averaging 13 points a game. No one was surprised. In Jim's final year at St. Ignatius, he had been named both All City and All State by the San Francisco newspapers.

Joe, meanwhile, had been a standout for the Stanford team for his first two seasons, though the star was Ron Tomsic, eventually a Stanford Hall of Fame player. The Indians, as they were known then, had a strong team, and Joe was regarded as an excellent team player, feeding his teammates rather than trying to take more than his share of shots. Even so, he averaged 14.6 points per game in his sophomore year, and he was off to a good start in his third season. Physically, there was quite a difference between Joe and Jim. Joe had put muscle on his six-foot-five-inch frame, and his weight was up to 215 pounds, all the better for the tough physical beating he had to take fighting for rebounds.

Jim, if anything, had lost some weight. Four inches shorter than Joe, he weighed at least thirty-five pounds less. But Jim had an agility, honed by constant practice, that was responsible for his reputation as a highly gifted player. Jim was gifted, but I knew firsthand from growing up with him how hard he worked at his game.

Mom, who had attended Jim's first two home games and one of Joe's, said she was tremendously excited about seeing her two boys play against each other in January. But that was a game I would not see, because I had to report to the army induction center in San Francisco as part of my request to be drafted. Assuming I passed the physical, I would be in Fort Ord starting basic training when Stanford played Cal and Joe faced Jim for the very first time. There had been several newspaper articles hyping the Booker-versus-Booker aspect. The game, to be played in Palo Alto, was already a sellout.

"Who is going to score the most points?" Cynthia asked during dinner two days before Christmas.

"I think Jim will outscore me just because he has to," laughed Joe. "But he is going to take a lot more shots than me, and we are going to win the game. That's what counts, winning the game."

"I'll make you a bet right now, Joe," said Jim. "I don't know about scoring more points, but I will bet you anything I have more assists than you."

"You're a guard, and I'm a forward: you're supposed to have more assists," said Joe.

"I thought you were suggesting I was a shot hog and not a team player," said Jim.

"I was just kidding, Jim. You are a great team player, and I tell everyone you are better than me," said Joe. In fact, that was true. I frequently heard Joe say Jim was the more gifted player.

"You are both great players," said Mom. "You just have different styles that suit your size."

Cynthia asked me if I played basketball. Joe and Jim laughed.

"Dan is the professional athlete in the family," said Jim. "He signed a bonus contract with the Pittsburgh Pirates, and he played last season for the Bristol Twins in the Appalachian League, where he fell in love with the girl who sold popcorn. But he doesn't have a picture of her."

"The Booker brothers are very different," said Claire Winstead. "It is amazing that they came from the same mother and father."

"I think God sees to that," said Mom. "But there are some similarities you might not notice. For example, they genuinely like and respect each other, and they seem to know what each other is thinking most of the time."

"Constance," said Claire, who had long ago started calling Mom by her first name, "what the Booker boys have in common is you, and they are very lucky to have you as their mother, and they all know it."

I asked Mom about an item that had recently appeared in Herb Caen's column that mentioned her and the Hamblens and a rich Australian.

"Oh, that. It was just a silly piece based on nothing," said Mom.

"I saw that item," said Joe. "He wrote that 'the ever lovely Constance Booker of the Zebra Room was being wooed by Australian media tycoon Desmond Archer' and that you and the Hamblens and some other couple had gone on Archer's huge yacht down to Monterey and had been seen eating lunch at the Inn at Pebble Beach."

"The part about the yacht trip is true, and we had a lovely time, but let me assure you that there is nothing going on between me and Desmond Archer," said Mom, adding that Archer had gone back to Australia in mid-November and probably wasn't coming back anytime soon.

"Caen also said that you and Archer had been seen dining alone at the Cliff House," said Joe.

"That's also true, but I was just showing him around the city; you know how I love to do that," said Mom.

"Caen seems to want to get you married off to a millionaire," said Jim. "That's not a bad idea."

"I bet it is just a matter of time before some handsome and charming guy sweeps you off your feet," said Claire.

"I suppose it could happen, but I am not counting on it," said Mom. "Actually, I am really enjoying my life right now. I have more freedom than I have ever had. The only thing I don't like is the thought of Dan going away for two years in the army.

"Mom," I said, "my deal is that I am going to stay at Fort Ord the whole two years playing baseball. I hope to be home a lot."

Who could have known as we enjoyed our Christmas together how swiftly things would change? I never played baseball at Fort Ord, and Joe and Jim never faced off on the basketball court.

I was just starting my second week of basic training in January when an orderly came into my barracks just after 11:00 PM on a Sunday night. I was asleep. He said I had an emergency, and I had to call my mother on an extension at a number I was not familiar with. I was immediately overcome with a sense of foreboding. Trainees were not allowed incoming phone calls except in case of the most serious emergencies.

"Stanford Hospital," the operator answered. My stomach sank. Mom answered on the extension.

"Danny, Joe has been very seriously injured in an auto accident," said Mom, barely able to control her voice. "The doctors say he has a good chance to survive, but it is not a certainty."

It turned out that Joe was riding in a car with three other friends on the Bayshore Highway when another car crossed over the double line. Both cars were going at the speed limit when they collided head-on. Two people from each car had been killed in the accident, all of them riding in the front seat. Joe was napping in the backseat after having spent the day on a biology field trip to Monterey. He suffered severe concussions to his head, which was swollen to twice its normal size. His right knee was shattered, and his right leg was broken, as were his left collarbone and his left arm. Almost no part of his body escaped injury. The *Chronicle* ran photos of the two cars, which were smashed beyond belief, under the headline "Bloody Bayshore: Four Dead, Stanford Cage Ace Miracle Survivor." The paper also ran a file photo of Joe.

Mom said that the Hamblens and Claire were with her and that Jim was on the way. She said Richard was going to try to engineer a compassionate leave for me.

"If ever you pray, this is the time," said Mom. As we talked, Joe was being operated on, and Mom said it would probably take all night. She said the critical part was relieving the swelling on the brain. Joe had been out from the time of the accident, which had occurred at about 6:00 PM.

It took two days for me to get a leave. Mom was with Joe when I arrived at Stanford Hospital. He was mumbling, but very hard to understand. Mom said he was heavily sedated to ease the pain. What shocked me was the terrible swelling of Joe's head. I wondered if his brain could survive such a beating.

"The bones are all going to heal, but Joe's knee is so badly shattered he may never play basketball again," said Mom. That is what the newspapers were saying. Looking at Joe, my big brother, my idol, the best person I'd ever known, made my heart ache, literally. Tears welled up uncontrollably in my eyes. I had never felt that way in my life before. I must have let out a sob.

"Don't worry, bro," Joe slurred. "I'm okay." Obviously, he was alert enough to have perceived my pain. Mom and I held each other, and I grabbed Joe's fingers and squeezed them.

"I can feel that," said Joe.

I spent three days with Joe and Mom at the hospital. We had to limit the number of visitors. Joe was taken out of the critical care ward on the day I returned to Fort Ord. The doctors said he was out of the woods. I saw Jim on just one of the days I was at Stanford. Of course, he had been there the first two nights when I wasn't. Jim took Joe's injury as badly as I had. We both realized how much we loved our big brother, who we thought was indestructible.

"If you could have seen him down in the emergency ward, you would have been certain he could not survive," said Jim. "It was the worst thing I have ever seen."

It is funny how we get blindsided by events in life. You go along taking a lot of stuff for granted, seldom ever thinking disaster could be lurking just around the corner.

Joe spent four weeks at Stanford Hospital before Mom brought him home. He stayed with Mom for the next few months while undergoing a massive rehabilitation program at the University of California Hospital on Parnassus Street, about ten minutes by car from our house on 29th Avenue. For the first month, Mom drove Joe to his rehab workout, dropping him off on her way to work. Then Claudia Hamblen would pick him up so that Mom could continue with her work; she needed the income. Stanford picked up all of the medical bills not covered by insurance and also subsequently agreed to pay the transportation costs to rehab, which made it a lot easier on Mom and Claudia. Stanford also said that Joe's full scholarship would remain in force even though it was clear he would never play basketball again. Stanford had always been a classy school. Joe finally returned to classes for the summer session of 1955. His reconstructed knee caused him to limp badly, but the doctors said all Joe's hard work in the rehab program had paid off, and Joe's body had recovered better than anyone had expected. Importantly, there was no evidence of brain damage.

Meanwhile, I returned to Fort Ord with a different attitude.

Going through basic training seemed much less forbidding in the wake of what had happened to Joe.

CHAPTER 36

Joe's injuries had badly shaken Constance Booker, and it showed in her face. I first noticed the beginnings of dark circles under her eyes when I came home on leave from Fort Ord in April of 1955. She also had put on some weight, not much, but maybe five or six pounds. She said she hadn't been going out much, what with taking care of Joe. Jim got over from Berkeley once every week or so.

Mom was worried that Joe was depressed, though Joe himself seemed okay to me. He said he was reading almost a book a day and had read all of the great Russian novels, including *War and Peace* and *Crime and Punishment*, which helped take his mind off his own troubles. He was also reading books by journalists about their careers (the public library was full of them), and he was more and more convinced that he would go into journalism. Claire Winstead had been steadfast through it all, and she came home from Stanford every weekend. A couple of times a month, Joe and Mom would have dinner with Claire and her parents. Charlie Winstead was a rumpled, slightly overweight man with a sharp wit and gift for telling stories. Like many newspapermen, he had an endless array of anecdotes to fit any situation. We all came to love and appreciate Charlie's spirit-lifting persona, and he was good for both Mom and Joe. I heard that Charlie Winstead was extremely popular among his journalism students at San Francisco State.

One night over dinner, Joe asked Charlie what he thought was the best way to get started in journalism. Joe said he had learned that the San Francisco newspapers liked to hire graduates from Cal and Stanford and employ them as copy boys for starters while gradually giving them reporting and writing jobs that would determine if they would be put on permanent staff.

"That's one way to go, Joe," said Charlie. "A lot of people have started their careers that way. But I think you are better off going to work for a small paper where you get to write about everything almost from the start. I started with the *Santa Cruz Sentinel* in the 1920s, and in the first year, I was reporting on the courts, city hall, the police beat, the sheriff's office, everything. I bet I wrote three or four thousand words a day. I also covered high school football. The *Sentinel* was not a very good paper, but the key thing was that I got to do virtually everything, and as they say, experience is the best teacher. You don't get that on a big metropolitan paper."

Joe asked how long it would take to make it to San Francisco.

"That depends on a lot of things, but mostly on how good you are," said Charlie. "It also helps if you know the right people. Another thing about San Francisco, the newspapers here put a great store on cleverness. They want to entertain their readers, make them eager to pick up the paper from the front steps or buy it on the newsstand. They are all in a competitive fight for survival now, and circulation is critical. So you have to show that you can cover the news and do it in an entertaining way. I have to tell you that is not true if you work for the *New York Times* or the *Washington Post* or even the wire services. Those people want the facts, and they don't want reporters who are constantly trying to prove how clever they are. They are paid to inform, not entertain."

"I think I would ultimately like to be a foreign correspondent or a roving national reporter, a least for awhile," said Joe.

"There aren't many of those jobs available," said Charlie. "It takes a lot of luck and talent, but Joe, you are smart and disciplined, and you have a chance, all the more so if you have your goal set. And one thing you might consider is television. They are getting more and more serious about news. But in any case, the small newspaper experience is best for whatever you want to do in journalism."

"That's really helpful," said Joe.

"What about me?" asked Claire, with a grin on her face. "Are you going to dump me and go to Indochina?"

"I know you say that with a smile, but I know you well enough to take you seriously," said Joe. "I thought we agreed that we both wanted to get started in our careers. We will be graduating within six months of each other, and also, you are twenty and I am twenty-one, way too young to get married. If you are in San Francisco, and I am someplace like Santa Cruz or Salinas or Santa Rosa, we'll be close enough to see each other every weekend." Claire agreed that it made sense.

I had to admire Joe's positive outlook. Here he was still using a cane, but eagerly thinking about his future in journalism and with the willowy and lovely Claire Winstead. Meanwhile, I was eight weeks from being sent overseas for eighteen months and had three years to go on top of that before I would get my degree. And then there was the question about possibly trying to make baseball a career. I really had no specific view about what I wanted to do with my life after college. By comparison, Joe was putting together a clear strategy. I was more like Mom—I really had no plan except to deal with things as they arose. Jim was a lot like that too. Joe, on the other hand, was like our father—smart, analytical, and disciplined. Jim was smart and had an almost photographic memory, but he was not as analytical as Joe. As long as he could play basketball and had a sweet girl, he was happy. I never heard Jim say what he wanted to do after college.

In the summer of 1955, Constance wrote the following in her diary:

> With Danny in Germany and Joe back at Stanford and Jim working at Lake Tahoe for the summer, I feel more lonely than at any time since those early days at Fort Riley when Joe and I were first married. Claudia has become very active in the San Francisco Public Library Foundation and is also spending a lot of time in Republican Party activities. She is a big supporter of Vice President Nixon and knows him from his days as a Senator. Richard sometimes gets his name in the newspapers for his legal work, and he is becoming one of the best-known lawyers in town. He certainly deserves to be. It seems he is involved in many of the big civil cases. I feel grateful that if I need help, he will drop whatever he is doing to be there, as he was when Joe had his accident. Unfortunately, since our trip to Monterey, I have not been seeing so much of Claudia and Richard. Given what Richard said to me and that Claudia may suspect that Richard was or is in love with me, I don't feel right in initiating get-togethers with them so much as I used to. Claudia and I talk on the phone almost every week, but there is no doubt our relationship has changed. I really miss Danny. He writes me every week from Germany, and I am happy he is enjoying his time there. But he is such a long way away. And Jimmy more and more has created his own life. Unlike Joe and Danny, I don't really know what Jim is thinking about, but at least he is happy. Well, I guess all this is part of life. Dad always said that the purpose of life was to overcome obstacles. I'm not sure why, but I feel I am at a critical stage of my life right now. I have to start thinking about filling the voids that have developed. For one thing, I want to lose 10 pounds and do more exercise. I looked at myself in the mirror the other day, and I could see the first signs of age—wrinkles around the mouth and

> eyes and slightly dark circles under my eyes. I still think I look okay for 41, particularly in comparison to some of the girls in The Club who are my age, but age takes its toll on all of us. Thank God for my job at the Zebra Room. It gets me out every day, and I love the people there and being around people who are leading exciting lives. I am afraid my life is rather dull right now. I am going on a diet starting tomorrow, and I am going to do some jogging in the park. Maybe that will get my spirits up.

A month later, my mother wrote,

> I can't believe how much better I feel since I began jogging. I am up to two miles without stopping, and I do it in sixteen minutes. When I started, I had to stop four or five times, and it took about twenty-five minutes. It is amazing how fast one can turn things around with a little dedication. I have also lost five pounds, and all I have done is give up desserts and soft drinks. Several people have commented that I am looking very well, and I can see a difference in the mirror. I have been invited to a formal dinner party in Tiburon next Saturday night being given by Tim and Mary Ryan. He is the president of American Steamship Lines, and I know them from the Zebra Room. They are celebrating their twentieth wedding anniversary and are having about 100 people, according to Mary. She said they had tried to strike a balance between the unattached men and women, though it will be mostly married couples. The Hamblens are not invited, so I will have to drive over to Tiburon by myself. I always feel a little uneasy when I have to go somewhere alone, but I need to get out more, and who knows, maybe I will meet someone.

CHAPTER 37

The June sun was still shining brightly as Constance drove her 1953 Ford sedan over the Golden Gate Bridge to Tiburon. The invitation from the Ryans said cocktails would begin at 6:30 PM, with the "rededication" ceremony at 7:30, followed by dinner at 8:00. It seemed the Ryans were going to celebrate their twentieth anniversary by renewing their marital vows. Constance planned to arrive at 7:00 PM. The temperature was in the high seventies, and Mary told Constance that weather permitting, they would serve dinner around the pool. Unfortunately, Constance got mixed up with the directions and did not reach the Ryans' sprawling ranch-style hilltop home until 7:40 PM, just in time to hear all of the applause as Tim Ryan gave Mary an enthusiastic kiss, as a Catholic priest looked on.

When the moment had ended and people had begun talking among themselves, Mary moved toward Constance. "Oh, there you are, Constance! We were getting worried about you," said Mary. Constance explained that she had gotten lost and had visited three hilltop enclaves before finally finding the Ryans' home.

"Never mind—you made it, and that is all that counts," said Mary. "We have eight tables of twelve, and I have you with some interesting people. Come, let me introduce you to one of your dinner partners."

"Kevin Keagan, I want to introduce you to Constance Booker; she is one of the dearest ladies you will ever meet," Mary effused. The glass of champagne in her hand was not her first. "Kevin, will you please take care of Constance? I have some things to do before we all sit down."

Kevin was just under six feet, slim with dark hair and a florid complexion that told Constance he was Irish and probably liked to drink. He appeared to be in his mid-thirties.

"I've seen you many times, Mrs. Booker, and always wanted to meet you," said Kevin. Constance looked puzzled. "No, you wouldn't have noticed me. I used to be the high school sports writer for the *San Francisco News*, and I saw you at your sons' basketball games."

"Of course, Kevin Keagan, forgive me. I loved your writing," said Constance. "My son Joe used to think you were the best. What happened? Why did you stop?"

"I needed more money to make my alimony payments, so I went into public relations with P. K. Thatcher, at least on a part-time basis, and I write magazine articles and do some stuff for Herb Caen."

"My, that sounds very interesting," said Constance. "What do you do for Herb Caen?"

"I feed him items from time to time. I also do some stuff for Stanton Delaplane, the *Chronicle* travel writer."

"You sound like a busy man with an exciting life, Kevin," said Constance.

"Constance, can I call you Constance? How about a glass of champagne? Tim Ryan is serving the best tonight."

The sun had just gone down, and the view from the Ryans was a mind-boggling panorama that included the lights of Belvedere, San Francisco, and the Golden Gate Bridge. All the men were wearing tuxedos and the women long, light summer dresses with wraps at the ready.

"This is exquisite," Constance said to Kevin, who bowed while presenting her drink. "I've never been to anyone's house in Tiburon, and I never thought about the kind of views people here have."

"The only trouble is you have to cross the bridge to get here. I'm a city person myself; there is no action over here."

"Except for tonight," smiled Constance. "But I agree about living in the city."

"How is Joe doing?" asked Kevin. Constance gave him a full update.

"I think he was one of the best and brightest players I ever covered," said Kevin. "I interviewed him three or four times over the years, and I was always taken by his maturity and intelligence."

"He takes a lot after his father," said Constance.

"I remember the story about you saving the girl from being raped in Golden Gate Park, and there was a line about your husband being killed right at the end of the war."

"You have an excellent memory, Kevin," said Constance.

"Some stuff does stick," he smiled. "You've had a pretty rough go, though you don't show it."

"My father was an Episcopal minister; he said you had to cope."

"Mine was a bartender, almost the same business."

Constance smiled as another couple moved up to join the conversation

"Ken and Stacy, may I introduce you to Constance Booker, who we are fortunate to have sitting at our table tonight," said Kevin. "Constance this is P. K. Thatcher, my boss, otherwise known as Ken, and our mutual good friend, Stacy Hollings, who is God's gift to readers of the *San Francisco Examiner*.

"I've read many of your stories," Constance said to Stacy. "You write very well, though I am hardly a judge."

Ken Thatcher extended his hand and smiled intently, looking Constance deep in the eyes. Constance felt just the slightest twitch as she returned Ken's gaze. He was about six feet two or three and slim with a full head of prematurely gray hair that was in striking contrast to his thick black eyebrows. His large brown eyes were widely spaced. He had a strong jaw and nose and wonderful clear skin. *Very handsome*, Constance thought.

"You are a good judge of writing talent, Mrs. Booker," Ken said. "Stacy is the best writer in town. And the best thing about her is that she says almost nothing."

"I've found that I don't learn much when I'm talking," smiled Stacy, who was about five feet five and very thin with an almost boyish look, despite delicate features. The right side of her mouth curled up when she talked. "And let me tell you, Constance, I do plenty of talking when I am not around these two. I bet you and I could have a very nice conversation."

"I'd like that. One of my sons wants to have a job like yours, and I'd like to find out how you did it," said Constance.

"You could be treading on some dicey ground there," said Kevin. "However, I can tell you that there are no rumors that Stacy used feminine guile on her road to success, unlike a number of her contemporaries."

"The truth is," said Ken, "the last two city editors at the *Examiner* fell in love with Stacy, and it is to her credit that she barely acknowledged their existence."

"They were lovely creeps," laughed Stacy. "Temptation they were not."

Kevin asked Stacy if she was going to attend a press conference that the Thatcher firm was holding for a client the following Tuesday. She said it was akin to a command performance, and she would be there. Ken turned to Constance and said he wanted to say how sorry he was about Joe's injury. Ken was a University of Southern California graduate, and he had seen Joe play twice against the Trojans in Palo Alto.

"It is a tragedy that he will never play again," said Ken. Constance thought she saw his eyes mist up ever so slightly. "If he is the son who wants to go into journalism, I will be glad to do what I can do. And so will Stacy."

"Thank you for your thoughtfulness. I'll tell Joe what you said."

Constance spent most of the dinner talking with Ken, who was seated on her left. Kevin was on her right, but talked mostly with Stacy, who also had to field questions from others around the table. Someone asked Stacy what she thought of Nixon.

"He's a loser who always seems to win," said Stacy. "Never underestimate a guy who does his homework."

Ken smiled and said to Constance that he and Stacy and Kevin went a lot of places together. "Strictly platonic," said Ken. "She's in love with a Pan American pilot. Actually, I introduced them. He is currently flying out of Los Angeles. He hopes to get reassigned here, but until then, we help keep her out of trouble. He comes up most weekends if he is not flying."

"Stacy is lucky to have such protectors," said Constance.

"I am sure you have the same," said Ken.

"I have my sons and maybe one or two others," Constance smiled.

"Do you mind if I say something rather personal?" Ken asked. "You don't look old enough to have three grown sons. You look about the same age as Stacy, and she is thirty-four."

"That's a very nice compliment, Ken. Do you have any children?"

"A daughter and two sons, ages fifteen to twenty-two," Ken answered. "The only one left at home is living with her mother in San Rafael. My wife and I separated four years ago. We're both Catholic, so divorce is not an option, but we have decided to go our separate ways."

"I'm sorry to hear that," said Constance.

"Don't be," said Ken. "My wife is happy, and I am happy that I am no longer making her unhappy by never being home and living a kind of life she hates. My wife loves staying at home, and I'm just not like that—never have been. And even if I wanted to stay home, my work would never allow it. When the kids were young, she didn't seem to mind me having to be out. For my part, she was a perfect mother, and we were in love for many years until her unhappiness killed it all."

"I'm still sorry," said Constance.

After dinner, there was dancing. Kevin asked Constance to dance.

"Ken doesn't dance," said Stacy. "Thank goodness for Kevin."

"I don't do much dancing, so watch your feet," said Constance.

"What do you think of Ken?" asked Kevin.

"He seems like a very interesting man," said Constance. "I don't think I've met anyone quite like him, though that is just a first impression. When you talk with him, he makes you feel there is no one else around."

"That's Ken; you've got him," said Kevin. "I love the guy, and he's about the only one I would fall on my sword for."

"Have you ever had to fall on your sword for him?" laughed Constance.

"Sometimes, but not that often," Kevin smiled.

The party broke up starting at just before eleven. Ken asked Constance if she would like to accompany them to see Shelly Berman performing at the Hungry I in San Francisco. Ken said he had reserved a table. But Constance said she had her own car and had gotten lost once tonight and better not risk getting lost a second time.

"Why don't I ride with you?" said Ken. "We came in Kevin's car. You'll love Shelly if you haven't already seen him."

Constance agreed. *Why not?* she thought. *This is the most attractive man you have been around in a long time.* As Ken walked her out, heads turned. They made a striking pair. Mary and Tim Ryan were delighted that Constance was being escorted by Ken to the Hungry I.

Shelly Berman turned out to be hilarious. He was a bit raw, but the jam-packed crowd loved him. The group's table was in the front row, and Berman briefly stopped by to say hello.

"How the hell do you do it, Ken?" said Shelly. "An old white-haired codger like you always surrounded by beautiful women."

"He's harmless, that's why," said Stacy.

"They don't say that about you, Stacy," said Berman, then turning to Constance: "The power of the press. But you look too respectable. How did you get mixed up with this group?"

Constance let out a huge laugh. Shelly waved and left. He was not one to miss a classic exit cue.

Ken ordered a last round of drinks at 1:55 AM, five minutes before the serving curfew. Constance loved being part of the group. They were certainly different than any people she had encountered before and a lot more world-wise than Constance, but she felt she could hold her own. She hoped P. K. "Ken" Thatcher would make good on his promise to call.

CHAPTER 38

P. K. Thatcher's office was located mid-distance between San Francisco's downtown financial district and Telegraph Hill. He liked the location, and the rent was modest for a space of 2,400 square feet, about a third of which he used for his private office.

"What did you think of her?" Keagan asked the Monday following the party at the Ryans, as he brought two cups of coffee and put them on Ken's desk.

"Almost too good to be true," said Thatcher.

"I think she had a good time," said Keagan. "Have you sent your report to Archer?"

"Not yet. Later today probably if we get the detective's report," said Thatcher.

"I saw that look in your eye, Ken. I think you are going to give her a charge," Keagan smiled.

"I've thought about it, but I don't know. The paint has hardly dried on Rose. Do I need another involvement? We've got a lot on our plate right now."

"You must figure women like Constance grow on trees," said Kevin.

"Well, let's see what Shine has to say," said Thatcher. "For all we know, Archer is right and that angel face is banging her best friend's husband."

"I can see why Archer liked her and also why he figures he has no chance with her," said Kevin. "Is it true that he has quit drinking?"

"That's what he claims," said Thatcher.

"That's a helluva a hit on the gin makers," said Kevin. "I don't think I ever saw him when he wasn't at least halfway in the bag. Remember that cocktail party in Sydney when he tried to get that Qantas stewardess to give him a blow job in the men's room? A real class act."

"But a rich one," said Thatcher. "And he seems to care about Constance Booker, along with that little Chinese gal whose restaurant he is financing."

"Betsy Ling, a very shrewd lady," said Kevin.

"I'm still trying to figure that one out," said Thatcher.

At noon, Thatcher and Keagan walked fifteen minutes to the Iron Horse Restaurant on Maiden Lane, where the owner greeted them like his best customers, which they were. As soon as they sat down, a telephone was plugged into a wall socket near Ken, and two drinks arrived, a Dewar's and water for Thatcher and a Bombay Gin martini for Keagan. There was very little water in Thatcher's drink.

"Anyone joining you today?" asked Sam, the owner.

"Yeah," said Ken, "a couple of guys from KRON-TV. We want them to do an advance piece on the summer Olympics in Sydney next year."

"That's a long way to go," said Sam, who fancied he knew a lot about the public relations business and the cheapness of most media.

"Qantas has agreed to comp them all the way," said Thatcher.

"Kenny boy, you cover all the bases," said Sam.

Thatcher returned to his office at just before 3:00 PM. Detective Albert Shine was waiting.

"We staked Hamblen out for a month," said Shine. "All we found out is that he works his ass off, puts in twelve to fourteen hours a day, and then gets dragged out by his wife three or four times a week. He is probably too tired to get his dick up at home, let alone anywhere else."

"I don't necessarily buy that," said Ken. "I know a lot of guys who don't get it up at home who have no trouble on the road."

"You wouldn't be talking about good Catholics like us, would you?" smiled Shine. "Anyhow, Mrs. Booker has some gal friends she goes to movies with, and she also sees Mrs. Hamblen from time to time. She's pretty friendly with a couple of her neighbors, one a doctor and his wife. And she sees some professor and his wife from San Francisco State. Her longest trip was to Palo Alto, where she visited with her son and his girlfriend. Of course, she works five days a week at the Huntington Hotel, roughly from ten to three, and lots of times she goes downtown shopping from there, usually alone, but a couple of times with Mrs. Hamblen. She jogs every day in the park. The bottom line, boss, is that she isn't doing any slinking around to mysterious places. And if she is having an affair with Richard Hamblen, they took the last thirty days off."

"Did you do any listening on their phones?" Thatcher asked.

"I don't know what you are talking about, Mr. Thatcher," said Shine, then adding, "There is nothing there, either."

Archer was right, thought Thatcher: a woman like Constance Booker ought to be out and around more often, so she could be appreciated. There was a whole great big world out there beyond the Zebra Room.

Constance had been thinking about Ken Thatcher. It wasn't a conscious effort. His face just kept popping up in her mind. Well, for one thing, he might be quite the man about town, but he was no Desmond Archer, who had flooded her with roses after their first two meetings. Of course, that was good and bad, but mostly good. No, Mr. Thatcher was a pretty cool customer. And for that matter, so were Kevin Keagan and Stacy Hollings. They were all three single people who seemed to know how to enjoy themselves and get the most out of every day. Constance pictured herself being part of the Thatcher entourage, going to all the right places and meeting a lot of exciting people, not the stodgy married couples Constance had met so often at the Hamblens'. Constance was surprised at her own thoughts. It was P. K. Thatcher who was driving them. She could not get him out of her mind. It took several days for the thought of Thatcher to finally subside. By the next week, she scarcely thought of him at all. Obviously, he was not going to call. Maybe she would call Stacy Hollings to talk about Joe's journalism career. No, that would seem too obvious.

Constance's mother was scheduled to arrive September 27, 1955, for a twelve-day visit. Grandmother Mary Teresa, who was a vigorous and healthy seventy-seven, said she wanted to visit both Joe and Jim at their respective campuses rather than drag them home for a Sunday dinner. That would mean visiting each campus on separate weekends. No problem, thought Constance.

Prior to her mother's arrival, Constance had a very pleasant four days at home with Joe and Jim just before they went back to classes. Jim had spent the summer working as a lifeguard in Lake Tahoe, which he said was pretty easy work, because the water was too cold for most people to go swimming. Jim said his knee—which had bothered him most of his freshman year, causing him to miss several games and spend a lot of bench time in games he did play—was much better, and he thought he would be as good as new for the 1955–56 season. Joe sensed that Jim had been disappointed over his failure to do as well as he thought.

"Injuries happen, and the key is not to force yourself back before you are ready," Joe told Jim. "I've seen a lot of players end their careers doing foolish stuff. What happened to me, no one can predict or control. But what you have is reversible if you keep doing the therapy."

"My knee is almost totally back to normal," said Jim.

"You know that, but does your knee know it?" Joe asked.

Ken Thatcher called the evening that Constance had gone to the airport to pick up her mother, whose flight from Boston had been delayed by bad weather. Ken stopped calling at eleven o'clock, just minutes before Constance and her mother walked in the door.

Ken tried again over the weekend but again got no answer. Constance and her mother were overnighting in Palo Alto for their visit with Joe, who had gotten them tickets for a football game at

Stanford Stadium and had worked out a full schedule for Mary Teresa, who found it all terribly exciting.

Constance was out jogging when Ken called again on Monday morning. Mary Teresa did not pick up the phone.

Later that morning, Ken called Kevin into his office and told him to call Sam and let him know they would not be lunching at the Iron Horse that day. "And call the Zebra Room and get us a table for lunch today," said Ken.

Kevin came back a few minutes later and said he had talked to Constance Booker at the Zebra Room. There were no tables available for either Monday or Tuesday because of a medical convention that had taken over the Fairmont, The Huntington, and the Mark Hopkins Hotels.

"We're booked for the rest of the week, boss, so I told Constance we'd get back to her. By the way, she said to give you her best regards."

"You know, I've been trying to reach her for five days," Ken said. "For a woman who has no life, she sure as hell seems busy."

That afternoon, at just before three, Ken had his secretary get Constance Booker on the telephone.

"I am happy to finally get to talk with you, Constance," said Ken. "I've called your home several times, but I never seem to get an answer."

"My mother is here, and we've been pretty busy," said Constance. "I am sorry to have missed you. What were you calling about?"

"I just thought it would be nice if we could get together again," said Ken. "I have some tickets for the new play at the Geary for Saturday night. Can you join me?"

"Darn, I'd like to," said Constance. "Unfortunately, we are going to spend the weekend at Berkeley with my son Jim. I hope you will give me a rain check."

"Well, that's too bad," said Ken. "I'll give you a call next week."

"I'll look forward to it," said Constance, who was quite pleased to learn that Ken had been unsuccessful in trying to reach her. *Serves him right for not calling for two weeks*, she thought.

CHAPTER 39

It had been almost a month since she had first met and last seen Ken Thatcher. Constance left her car at the Huntington and walked down from Nob Hill via California Street, cutting over from there to Union Square to kill an hour at I. Magnin's, the fashionable women's clothier. Ken had invited her to meet him at his office at about five. He said that he wanted to show her where he worked and that he had a couple of people dropping by whom she would enjoy meeting. Later, he said, they could have a quiet dinner at a new restaurant that had opened only a couple of months before.

Kevin Keagan greeted Constance when she arrived and introduced her to Ken's longtime secretary, Jane Bowers, and three other staff people.

"Ken is in with Colonel Andres Soriano right now, and they should be breaking up any second," said Kevin, who asked Jane to let Ken know Mrs. Booker was here. Moments later, Ken opened his office door.

"Hello, Constance," said Ken. "So nice of you to come. Colonel Soriano, may I introduce you to Constance Booker, the mother of two of the finest basketball players ever to come out of San Francisco."

"Oh, I've met Mrs. Booker at the Zebra Room," said Colonel Soriano, who was the owner of, among other things, the San Miguel Brewing Co. of the Philippines. He reached for Constance's hand, bowed, and gently passed his lips over the back of her hand without actually touching. "It is a pleasure to see you again."

"We've missed you at the Huntington, Colonel Soriano. It has been at least a year, if I am not mistaken," said Constance.

"You have an excellent memory; it has been thirteen months," said Colonel Soriano, who was in his late sixties, had white curly hair, and had the look of a Spanish aristocrat, which he was.

Ken moved toward Constance and gave her a hug.

"You look even better in the daytime," he smiled. "Why don't we all have a drink?"

"You know, it isn't because I don't love San Francisco that I have not been here so often as usual," said Colonel Soriano, looking at Constance. "We have a very active president in my country, and he is changing many things that have created some turmoil."

"I have read about President Magsaysay defeating the Communists," said Constance.

"That is almost true; there are a few Huks left, but they have retreated and are not a factor just now," said Colonel Soriano. "No, he is a great president, a man of the people with great energy and integrity. The trouble is that he is trying to break up all of the traditional family estates, and that is creating the turmoil. I personally support him, but the very rich, all of my friends, are against giving up their lands without what they deem adequate compensation."

"Is it not true, Colonel, that the greater the prosperity among the masses, the more beer they will be able to drink?" said Kevin, smiling.

"That is true, but that is not why we support the uplifting of our poor," said Colonel Soriano. "The world has changed. We are not living in the nineteenth century anymore, though some of my compatriots don't seem to agree.

"That is why I am trying to talk my friend Ken here into moving to the Philippines to help me with the education of our people and our politicians," he continued.

"Ken, we will continue our talk, and I want you to think about what we have discussed. You would have two newspapers, eleven television stations, and twenty-eight radio stations under your direct control. Meanwhile, I must go. Mrs. Booker, you have been the highlight of my day."

"My," said Constance, after Colonel Soriano left. "What a charming man."

"He's a lot more than charming," said Ken. "He comes from a very old and rich family, but he is a brilliant businessman with a strong social conscience. There are not many Filipinos like him."

"He looks Spanish," said Constance.

"Probably as pure as any Spaniard in Madrid, but he regards himself as a Filipino, and his family goes back three hundred years there," said Ken. "Sometime, I will get him to tell you how he left the Philippines in 1942 for Australia with General MacArthur just before the Japanese forced the surrender of our military. He's a great man in so many ways."

"It is interesting to think I have just been talking to a man who was a friend of General MacArthur, one of my late husband's idols," said Constance.

Just then, Stacy Hollings came into Ken's office. She seemed surprised but happy to see Constance and said it was nice to see her again.

"I bumped into your meal ticket getting into his limousine outside," said Stacy. "Ken, when are you going to learn that you don't make your clients come to your office? You go to theirs. San Miguel has a much nicer office than this, though the last time I was there all they served was beer."

Stacy accepted Kevin's offer of a scotch.

"There are exceptions to every rule," said Ken. "When people come to your office, they usually have something they want from you. And there happens to be something Colonel Soriano wants from me that I am not free to discuss."

"Let me guess," said Stacy. "He wants you to take over his so-called media empire in the Philippines. That's no secret, Ken; you told me that six months ago."

"Well, it is now a concrete offer, and I am giving it some thought," said Ken. "Being at the mercy and whim of twelve clients is not always fun."

"Come on, Ken, you love every minute of it," said Stacy. "What do you think, Kevin—do you think Ken is going to take over Soriano's rag of a newspaper and the lowest-rated television station in Manila that has a signal so weak half the people can't get it?"

Constance erupted in a hearty laugh, and Ken joined in.

"You don't make it sound very glamorous," said Ken.

"Only because I have been there on that Philippines Air Line junket you engineered," said Stacy.

"You said you loved it," said Kevin. "I remember you saying you got more propositions during that five-day trip than you had in the previous five years."

Constance laughed again.

"Filipino men are quite the ladies' men," said Stacy, "or at least they think they are. Constance, have you ever been around them? They all think they are Errol Flynn."

"Sounds like I am missing something," smiled Constance.

"Well, I really wouldn't know, never having accepted any of their propositions," said Stacy.

"You didn't have to say that, Stacy. We all know that if you were not a newspaper reporter, you would be in a nunnery," said Kevin.

"Yes, Kevin, and if they served martinis at communion, you'd be a priest," said Stacy.

"Let me change the subject," said Ken. "But first, I am not moving to the Philippines, now or ever. I just can't tell that to Colonel Soriano right now. The subject I want to pursue is the Down Under restaurant for which we have been hired as of this week to help publicize. The restaurant has only been open for a couple of months, and business has been slower than expected. They need some hype."

"How about serving kangaroo meat?" said Stacy.

"Not the worst idea I've heard," said Ken. "They are trying to sell Australian beef, but the problem is it is a little tough by American standards."

"What if they pounded it the way they do abalone steaks?" asked Constance, remembering what Archer had told her.

"Hey, that could work," said Kevin.

"Well, Constance and I are going there tonight, and you two are welcome to join us," said Ken.

"I can't make it, thanks," said Stacy.

"I can only go for a little while," said Kevin, "but I want to see the place and meet the owner if we are supposed to be of help."

"Okay, Kevin. But Jack Walling was supposed to be here by now, so would you wait for him here, and we will meet you at the Down Under?" said Ken.

"Whatever you say, boss," said Kevin. "Stacy will keep me company."

Ken Thatcher explained to Constance as they walked to the Down Under that Walling was the public relations director for Qantas Airlines, one of his larger clients. The issue was finalizing arrangements for a film crew from KRON-TV to fly to Sydney to do an in-depth program on preparations for the 1956 Summer Olympics.

The Down Under restaurant was located on Geary Street, a block and a half up from Union Square. It was a twelve-minute walk from Ken's office.

"I hope you don't mind walking," said Ken. "It is just about my only exercise."

"I love to walk, particularly on a nice evening like this," said Constance.

When they arrived at the restaurant, Ken started to introduce the owner.

"Oh my God," said Constance. "It's you, Betsy! Betsy Ling!" The two women hugged like sorority sisters.

"Constance, it is wonderful to see you again," said Betsy. "How did you meet Ken?"

"At a dinner party in Tiburon about a month ago," said Constance.

"How did you two meet?" asked Ken.

Constance let out one of her big laughs and said it was a long story, clearly signaling she was not going to tell it now.

"Constance, every one I try to introduce you to already knows you," Ken smiled. "You are amazing."

"The truth is I know very few people, but you can keep on being amazed if you like," Constance smiled back. "Betsy, your restaurant looks terrific; can you show us around?"

The décor was simple, and murals of the dry Australian countryside filled the walls, including life-size depictions of all the wonderful and strange animals that are exclusive to that continent.

"We can seat ninety-six people at one time, counting the private room, which seats twelve," said Betsy. "The bar can hold thirty to forty people, and the kitchen is oversized, because eventually we expect to get into the catering business. But first we need to build up our clientele and our reputation, and that is why I have asked Ken to do for us what he has done for the Iron Horse."

Ken looked around the restaurant, which was about half full and said, "It takes time, sometimes years."

"I'm famished," said Constance. "I understand the specialty is Australian beef."

"It is one of the specialties, though it is a kind of acquired taste," said Betsy. "Australian beef cattle are grass-fed, not grain-fed like most cattle in the United States. The result is that Australian beef cattle grow more slowly and are therefore older when they are slaughtered, which usually means the meat is less tender."

"Constance was wondering if you can tenderize it by pounding it the way you do abalone," said Ken.

"We do that sometimes," said Betsy. "And we marinate it, but the most important thing is to buy your meat from the right ranch, because it turns out that certain bulls have a tendency to sire offspring whose meat is more tender than others."

The subject of tenderizing meat was one on which Betsy could talk for hours.

"We have some wonderful tenderloin cuts I'd like to serve you tonight along with some creamed spinach and steak fries," said Betsy. When Ken excused himself to go to the restroom, Constance said she was surprised that Betsy had opted for an Australian format, given what had happened.

"I got over it, and he was very drunk," said Betsy. "I'm glad I didn't kill him. Actually, he's been pretty helpful in lining up sources for meat."

Kevin arrived just as the orders were going to the kitchen.

"We're all set with Qantas," Kevin said to Ken while looking around. "This place could use some warmth. Reminds me of the Museum of Natural History in New York."

"More people—that is what this place needs, and that is our job," said Ken.

Constance sat fascinated as Ken and Kevin kicked ideas back and forth. Betsy came and went, keeping a close eye on her customers and the service they were getting and on how they were eating their food. Constance said her steak was delicious, and she loved the creamed spinach.

At the end of the evening, Ken told Betsy there were two things they thought could help jump-start things. One was to launch a radio campaign on three radio stations that specialized in playing old standards, offering half-price meals at the Down Under for anyone who served in Australia during the war. And any Australian citizen could also qualify. The second idea was to bring in six San Francisco 49er football players to see who could eat the most Australian beef. The sole purpose would be to create an item for Herb Caen's column, which would not lose sight of the fact that the Down Under was run by a third-generation San Francisco Chinese woman.

"I like it," said Betsy. "Let's see what happens."

After they had said good night to Betsy and Kevin had left, Ken asked, "You have seen my office; would you like to see where I live, Mrs. Booker?"

"Oh, I'd like to do that, but not tonight," she smiled. "I don't like to try to absorb too much in just one night. Maybe we could start at your place next time."

"Excellent. How about tomorrow night at six? We can watch the sunset at my place and then go to the Iron Horse for dinner."

Constance agreed and laughed that it was quite a coincidence that she had already met Colonel Soriano and Betsy Ling. Ken hailed a cab and dropped her at the Huntington to pick up her car before being taken to his Telegraph Hill apartment. He was looking forward to tomorrow night.

Chapter 40

Thatcher's apartment was located on the southeast side of Telegraph Hill in a building with three other units.

"This is spectacular," said Constance, standing on the deck, looking at downtown San Francisco and the Bay Bridge.

"I fell in love with it the first time I saw it," said Ken. "There are actually two floors. On this level we have the living room and dining room, the kitchen, a half bath, and a small office. Downstairs, there is another deck, the master bedroom, a sauna, a large bathroom, and a workout room, plus a small wine closet."

"I like the decorations—very manly," said Constance.

"If you like a lot of leather," said Ken. "It was done by a decorator. The previous tenant was a health nut, and he put in the sauna and what amounts to a gym. It was filled with weights and workout equipment when I first saw the place. Come on downstairs."

The workout room, about twelve by fifteen, fronted on the deck, as did the master bedroom, which was much larger.

"What a wonderful sauna! It's huge," said Constance.

"It seats six," smiled Ken. "The shower has three spigots, and it could probably hold six people too. I try not to imagine the previous uses of this place."

Constance let out one of her big laughs.

"Did the bed come from the previous tenant?" asked Constance, eyeing the first perfectly round bed she had ever seen."

"That's a long story," Ken laughed. "Let's go upstairs and watch the sunset."

"This is quite a large place for just one person," said Constance.

"Not counting the two decks, it's 3,000 square feet, 1,500 on each floor," said Ken. "By San Francisco standards, it's huge. A garage also comes with it, which is nice, because I seldom use my car. My office is just a fifteen-minute walk from here."

"You have your life very nicely organized," said Constance.

"It is a nice change from being married with three children and an unhappy wife," said Ken. "The only problem is I'm supporting two households, and that has forced me to take on more clients than I should. Saturday is my only day of rest. Sunday I usually spend with my children in San Rafael."

Ken and Constance sat on the deck for nearly two hours. They told each other more details about themselves. Ken was born in Los Angeles in 1910, which made him forty-five, four years older than Constance. He was married during his senior year at the University of Southern California and upon graduation went to work for the *Los Angeles Examiner* as a newsroom trainee. He worked for the *Examiner* for five years and eventually got to cover some major stories. He said he got the most attention for a humorous piece he had written about life in a nudist colony.

"Actually, my mom and dad belonged to the camp, which was located in the hills out in San Bernardino," Ken said. "My mother was pure Swedish and quite comfortable walking around naked. My father was part English, and it took a long time for him to get comfortable with it.

"Anyway, my parents were excited when I said I was going to do a story on their camp, though not if they were there. It turned out to be a lot easier than I thought, and frankly, one of the conclusions I reached was that most of the people would have looked better with their clothes on."

Constance laughed and said maybe that was what it was all about, being comfortable with your own body regardless.

"Were you nervous?" asked Constance.

"No, I was only twenty-six or twenty-seven and in pretty good shape," said Ken. "I think I take after my mother."

Ken said he left the *Examiner* and went to work for a small public relations firm and later joined Trans World Airlines, eventually becoming director of public relations. He said when the war started, he tried to enlist, but was turned down because of a bad back. In 1948, Ken moved his family to San Francisco to take a job running Bank of America's public relations department. Two years later, he formed his own company, putting together a group of clients he had met while doing work for Bank of America, including the San Miguel Brewing Company.

"Norma refused to live in the city," said Ken. "So we bought a nice house in the hills of San Rafael, and she was quite happy with everything except me. I was working hard trying to get my business started, and I neglected my family. Getting involved with Filipino companies meant entertaining a constant stream of visitors who loved to stay out all night. I spent many a night at the Fairmont back in those days.

"Finally, it got so bad that Norma and I decided to go our separate ways," said Ken. "She was convinced I was fooling around, and our love had turned to bitterness and distrust on her part. I was so miserable I moved out and found this place.

"You know, my life has changed and it is still changing, especially since I have met you," said Ken.

"Being around someone like you is quite a change for me," said Constance. "I have been more of a homebody."

"That is a natural consequence of being a mother to three sons," said Ken. "But you're free now to do exactly what you want. I think you should find that exciting."

"I guess I do," said Constance.

Soon, they left for dinner, and Ken was treated like a king the moment he entered the Iron Horse.

"Is this the beautiful lady from the competition?" asked Sam as he greeted Ken. "No wonder I hear the Zebra Room is always packed for lunch."

"Thank you," said Constance. "Do you ever have any empty tables at lunch? Perhaps we could direct some customers your way?"

"She has a sense of humor," laughed Sam.

"Seriously, Sam, visitors are always asking me to give them the name of a good restaurant around Union Square; can I have them call you?"

"Sure, we usually have space after 1:30 PM," said Sam. "Constance, I'm liking you already."

"Your restaurant is warm and cozy," said Constance. "Women love subdued lighting like this."

Sam escorted them to the corner table and plugged in the phone while a waiter put a Dewar's and water in front of Ken.

"What will you have, Constance?" asked Sam. "I am sorry that our staff feels the need to get Ken his drink within thirty seconds of his sitting down."

"Why don't you have a glass of champagne?" suggested Ken. "It will go well with that Chablis you had at my place." Constance smiled agreement. The booth they were sitting in could hold six people but it was always reserved for Ken, even if he was eating alone and the restaurant was packed. Usually, Ken was accompanied by a wide assortment of interesting people, the kind of folks who made Herb Caen's column. Often as not, Sam would join the party, ordering extra drinks or a bottle of wine, compliments of the house.

Ken and Constance talked for three hours as the Iron Horse gradually emptied of patrons. Sam left them alone. Constance talked about her marriage and her sons and her work. Ken talked about each of his clients and said that doing the PR for the Olympics would be time-consuming, and he was about to hire a former associate, Pete Rozelle, from the Los Angeles Rams to help with the extra workload.

Constance loved to listen to Ken talk. He had a low, very pleasant voice and an interesting face. Somehow, he made whatever he was saying sound interesting. He was also good at listening and never seemed to be distracted when she was talking.

Ken asked Constance if she was free on Saturday, because if she was, he would introduce her to his physiotherapy routine, which included a massage, yoga, and a sauna.

"If you can get to my place at 10:00 AM, you can join me for yoga training," said Ken, adding that his masseuse was a 300-pound Australian woman named Annabelle who would be arriving about 11:30.

Constance said she had never had a professional massage before, and she knew very little about yoga.

"But it all sounds very interesting; I hope I won't be intruding on your normal routine," she said.

"You'll feel fantastic afterward," said Ken. "Bring some workout shorts and a light sweatshirt for the yoga. You won't need anything for the massage."

"I hope your 300-pound masseuse doesn't leave black and blue marks," Constance said. Ken assured her that she was remarkably gentle. Outside the restaurant, a taxi was waiting, and Ken dropped Constance at the Huntington, where she had left her car again before walking from work to Ken's home. He gave her a short soft peck on the lips and said he would see her in three days.

Constance thought about Ken a lot those next few days. The downside was that Ken was married, and because he was Catholic, he was not about to get a divorce. Did she want to become Ken's girlfriend? Or was she really looking for a permanent relationship that would lead to marriage? The trouble was she was terribly attracted to Ken—exactly why, she was not sure, but a lot of it was physical, and a lot of it was her perception that being around Ken was fun. And maybe it was because she was starved for love. Oh, she loved Richard Hamblen, but that had to be different. And she loved her sons, and they loved her. She did not feel unloved; in fact, she felt quite loved. Maybe it would be less complicated to just be a friend of Ken's like Stacy Hollings. What would her father say? She knew. He would be totally against her becoming anyone's de facto mistress and would be shocked that she would even consider it. What would God think? One could rationalize that question. Ken was estranged from his wife. She had been a widow for ten years. Could love be wrong?

CHAPTER 41

When Saturday arrived, Constance had decided she was not going to get involved with a married man, which is exactly what she wrote in her diary. It had been a mistake to even consider it, because it ran against everything she believed in. What, for example, would she tell her sons? Having a relationship with a divorced man like Robert Crable was not the same. Constance vowed to let her head rule the situation.

Ken greeted Constance wearing gym shorts and a t-shirt. He gave her a hug and thanked her for being on time, because the yoga trainer had a tight schedule. Constance was surprised that instead of an Indian or some intriguing foreign person, the instructor was Stan Fetterman, a reed-thin San Francisco accountant who said he had studied yoga in Bombay while on a two-year business assignment there.

"Mrs. Booker, I understand from Ken that you have never done any yoga before," said Fetterman, who overcame his unattractive oversized features with a healthy glow to his skin and an animated though calm demeanor. "What we will do in the next ninety minutes is assume a variety of poses that will both stretch and relax your entire body. These are poses that have come down through the ages and that over time will make you more supple, more relaxed, and more comfortable physically and mentally. If you are serious about what we do, you will derive great benefits. Let us begin with some very simple arm stretches and neck exercises before we do the poses. Ken, if you don't mind, I am going to focus my attention on Mrs. Booker."

Constance found assuming the poses easier than she had expected.

"You are one of the few I have seen be able to do a perfect lotus pose on your first try," said Fetterman. "Your legs are quite flexible."

Toward the end, when they got to the shoulder stand, Constance was easily able to rotate her legs over her head, touching her toes to the floor with her legs straight.

"That is a lovely position," said Fetterman. "Now come back up with your feet pointing again to the ceiling and hold it while breathing deeply. Ken, look at that wonderful posture. I think Mrs. Booker is a natural. It took Ken six or seven sessions before he could rotate his feet to the floor from a shoulder stand."

"That's because women are naturally more flexible," said Ken. "They don't have any muscles to tighten."

The final five minutes of the yoga session were spent in meditation lying on the floor.

"Picture yourself floating through space with every muscle in your body totally relaxed," said Fetterman. "Feel the joy, the euphoric weightlessness that permeates your being. Picture yourself moving through space. You are arriving at someplace you would like to be. Perhaps it is a tropical island, and soft breezes are caressing your body. You feel warm and very, very relaxed. You could not feel any better or more at peace with yourself."

Fetterman was silent for the final two minutes, letting his previous words reverberate in the minds of his students.

"Okay, that does it," said Fetterman. "How do you feel, Mrs. Booker?"

"I feel like—where has this been all my life?" she answered. "I don't think I have ever felt so relaxed."

Constance gave Stanley a hug as he prepared to leave.

"Please call me Constance, Stanley. You are a terrific teacher," said Constance. "I very much want to do this again."

"You can do the poses we learned today in your home," said Stanley, "and I strongly recommend it, but it is also true that most people do better working with a teacher."

Ken pressed some money into Fetterman's hand and said that he would see him next Saturday and that he was inviting Constance to be there as well.

"It is my pleasure to work with you both," said Fetterman.

"Annabelle should be here any minute," said Ken. "I am glad you liked Stanley and doing yoga. I've been doing it for a year now, and it helps override some of my sins, like not exercising the way I used to and perhaps drinking a bit more than I should."

Thirty minutes later, Annabelle arrived.

"Sorry I'm late, mates," said Annabelle, giving Ken a hug with her huge body and then turning to Constance, saying, "I've heard about you; you're even prettier than he said." Annabelle put her arms around Constance, pressing her to her enormous bosom. "I'm so happy to meet you."

Constance thought Annabelle had gone well beyond three hundred pounds. Even so, her jolly persona and warmth seemed to indicate a person filled with the capacity to give love.

"I love coming here," said Annabelle. "Ken was kind enough to buy a massage table, which saves me the trouble of bringing mine. It's bloody hell finding a parking space around here."

"Okay, Annabelle, I think Constance should go first, and I'll go upstairs and do some dictation," said Ken.

"You don't need any clothes for this," said Annabelle. "I'm going to go into the bathroom and wash up and you can just get on the table under the sheets lying on your stomach."

The massage lasted ninety minutes and was more painful than Constance had expected. Annabelle explained that to be effective, the massage had to reach the deepest parts of the muscles and tissues, and that necessarily led to some discomfort. When Annabelle leaned her 300-plus pounds into a joint or a muscle, it was indeed a powerful force.

"Your body is in excellent shape," said Annabelle, adding she wished she had Constance's body. "I think we are about the same age, but I just can't stop eating. When I was twenty-one, I used to have a figure like you, but now, fourteen years later, I am two hundred pounds overweight. I blame it on my first husband. He kept telling me I was getting fat and that I had to go on a diet. Meanwhile, that lout was chasing every skirt he saw, and I reacted by eating more and more. Once I started eating too much, I couldn't stop. I've tried every diet there is, but no luck."

"You have a very pretty and young face," said Constance. "I don't think you have any wrinkles at all, and you have lovely skin."

"Ah, Ken said you were very sweet and that I would like you," said Annabelle. "As usual, he is right."

Annabelle said she had been giving Ken a massage every Saturday for the past year. A pilot at Qantas had recommended Annabelle to Ken.

"I do all of the Qantas pilots, and do they need it," said Annabelle. "Flying the Pacific cooped up in those tiny cockpits is murder on the body."

Annabelle said Ken was tight as a drum when he started doing massage but had shown great improvement.

"He's got a lot on his plate with work—never mind having to deal with that wife of his," said Annabelle. Constance did not comment.

"Ken's one of the most elegant people I've ever met, a gentleman and thoughtful and a nice sense of humor," said Annabelle. "I wish I would have met him when I had a figure like you. By the way, do you mind if I ask how old you are?"

"I'm forty-one," said Constance.

"That's right; Ken told me you had three sons in college. You sure don't look your age. I thought you were my age, thirty-five."

"Thank you, Annabelle. I wish it were true. Alas, I have permanent wrinkles around my eyes, and I've had dark circles under my eyes, too."

"I don't see any circles, just a very faint shadow that frankly looks pretty good. And the wrinkles at the corners of your eyes, those are also attractive, especially when you smile."

Annabelle asked if Constance did any exercise. Constance said she jogged two miles in Golden Gate Park at least four times a week.

"That explains how those long, lovely legs of yours are in such good shape," said Annabelle.

Ken knocked on the upstairs door, asking if he could come down.

"The coast is clear," said Annabelle, adjusting the sheet covering Constance.

"I'm afraid I have to call time," said Ken. "Annabelle will massage you for three hours if you let her. But I know she has a two o'clock appointment with a needy, fagged out Qantas pilot."

"I was just finishing," said Annabelle.

Constance rested on the deck upstairs while Ken had his massage. It was a nice, though cool, sunny day, and Constance wrapped herself in a blanket and let the sun play off her face. She felt better than she had in many years. Yoga and massage, back to back—what a combination.

Ken was in his robe when he and Annabelle came upstairs. He said Annabelle had to leave immediately, because she was late for her next appointment.

"Lovely meeting you, Constance; you are my new inspiration," said Annabelle, giving Constance an almost suffocating embrace.

After she left, Ken turned to Constance, putting his hands on her shoulders and looking her warmly in the eye.

"You certainly made a hit with Annabelle and Stanley," said Ken. "I've never heard Annabelle rave about anyone as much she did about you."

Ken leaned forward, kissing her fully on the lips. She found herself responding in a way that made her feel dizzy, a very pleasant dizziness. She felt her body suddenly shake.

"Are you all right?" Ken asked.

"You took my breath away," she answered. "I felt a little dizzy."

"I have just the cure for that," said Ken. "Actually, it is a treatment for a hangover."

Ken explained that his "treatment" involved sitting in the sauna for eight minutes and then taking a cold shower, a process that had to be repeated three times. After that, he said, she would be ready for anything.

Ken wore only a towel around his waist and he suggested that Constance maintain decorum with two towels, one around her neck and the other around her waist.

"You can take them off whenever you want—it gets pretty steamy in here, and you can't see anything."

Constance knew what was happening. That is what she wrote in her diary. She was in the hands of an expert. Once in the steam-filled sauna, she dropped the towel from her shoulders and leaned back on the wooden bench, stretching her arms in the air.

"Oh, the heat feels wonderful," she said, looking at Ken, who she realized could see the foggy outline of her body.

Ken moved closer to her and gave her a kiss that made her almost faint. She could not remember ever quite feeling this way.

"I think the eight minutes are up," she said. "Time for the cold shower."

They both walked naked out of the sauna and into the shower.

"Oh, my God, this is freezing," said Constance, throwing her arms around him. He kissed her again, and this time she felt neither faint nor dizzy, just aroused.

"Back to the sauna," said Ken. "Do you mind if I say you have an incredible figure and an even more incredible mouth." Once again he embraced her, this time pressing his loins against hers. The two bodies in the steamy sauna were oozing perspiration as their hands explored one another while they kissed.

"Let's go to the bedroom," he whispered.

"We shouldn't really," she responded.

"I know, but I don't think we will ever regret it," he said, putting his arm around her shoulder and leading her to the bedroom with the perfectly round bed.

Ken took his time. He was an expert all right, Constance said in her diary. They cuddled, napped, and made love twice over a space of four hours. Afterward, she felt relaxed and happy. Abstinence has its benefits, she wrote. So much for her resolution not to be involved with a married man. She marveled at how naturally it had all seemed to happen. No doubt about it, she was hooked and happily so. Yoga, massage, sauna, cold shower, sauna, four hours of intimacy. A very nice way to spend a Saturday. She felt no regrets.

CHAPTER 42

No matter how you look at it, 1956 was an important year. When I was a kid, the worst fear I had was getting polio. I used to walk past the Shriners Hospital on 19th Avenue, and you could see the bedridden kids crippled from polio looking out the window. If President Roosevelt could catch it, anyone could. One of the kids on our block on 28th Avenue had polio. He had to wear heavy leg braces, and he could not play any sports, about the worst thing imaginable to me. The number of polio cases in the United States was near epidemic proportions in the post–World War II period, reaching 20,000 in 1952. But all that ended in 1956, when most American kids were inoculated with the anti-polio vaccine developed by Dr. Jonas Salk.

Another critical event in 1956, as seen today from the eyes of this seventy-year-old, was a speech given by Soviet Communist Party Chief Nikita Khrushchev to the Communist Party Congress in which he denounced the tyrannical rule of Josef Stalin. The contents of Khrushchev's remarks were not intended for the Soviet citizenry but rather were a warning to the Soviet leadership that the nasty blood purges that had characterized Stalin's Soviet Union would no longer be acceptable. This was a first step in the journey over four decades that finally brought the end of the Cold War.

And 1956 was the midpoint in those wonderful Eisenhower years. President Eisenhower had enjoyed huge personal popularity during his first term in office, with approval ratings as high as 79 percent. Ike had signed the Korean War Armistice in 1953, and the economy was in good shape. Ike made everyone feel good, and it was not just his smile. For a while, it was feared Ike would not seek a second term because of a 1955 heart attack. But once Ike decided to run again, his opponent, Adlai Stevenson, had no chance. Stevenson's most potent argument was that reelecting Ike put Vice President Richard Nixon a heartbeat away from the presidency. Indeed, Ike himself tried to get Nixon off the ticket by saying he would make him Secretary of Defense, which he argued would increase his chances for a 1960 presidential bid. Nixon declined to rise to the bait, and Eisenhower left him on the ticket.

The 1956 Republican National Convention was held in San Francisco's Cow Palace. One of the criticisms of Eisenhower's presidency was that he did not address the civil rights issue in any serious way, which was true. However, I remember being surprised to read at the time that one of the Republican speakers was Nat King Cole, the legendary black singer.

Ike polled 57.6 percent of the vote in scoring his landslide victory, although the Democrats won control of both the House of Representatives and the Senate. Ike was a lot more popular than the Republican Party itself.

There were about 150 million people living in the United States in 1956. And the average annual wage was only about $3,000. Life expectancy was 65.6 years for the average man and 71.1 for the average woman.

In 1956, Ike signed the Federal Highways Act, which led to today's marvelous network of interstate highways that span this nation.

Down in San Jose, IBM workers completed design of the IBM 350, billed as "the world's first computer storage device with random access to large volumes of data." No one called it Silicon Valley in those days.

Elvis Presley, age twenty-one, cut his first big hit record, "Love Me Tender." Ken Venturi, a fellow I knew from high school, college, and the army in Europe, was the third-round leader as an amateur of the prestigious Masters Golf Tournament in Augusta, Georgia. Alas, he shot an 80 in the final round and finished in second place. No amateur has ever won The Masters.

The New York Yankees, with Mickey Mantle, Whitey Ford, and Yogi Berra, won the 1956 World Series over the Brooklyn Dodgers, four games to three. The series was highlighted by perhaps the greatest game ever pitched, Don Larsen's no-run, no-hit masterpiece in which not a Dodger reached first. That feat was all the more amazing given that the Dodger lineup included such greats as Jackie Robinson, Duke Snider, Roy Campanella, and Carl Furillo, among others.

Speaking of sports, my great love, the San Francisco 49ers, had a backfield that included four future National Football League Hall of Fame selections: Joe Perry, Hugh McElhenny, John Henry Johnson, and Y. A. Tittle. Even so, they finished 5–6–1 under first-year coach Frankie Albert.

Also in 1956, Ken Thatcher involved Constance on the roller-coaster ride leading up to the Olympic Summer Games being staged in Melbourne, the first time ever in the southern hemisphere. Constance and Ken attended the games, which opened November 22 and closed December 8. It was Constance's first trip overseas, not counting Hawaii.

Watching Ken in action, dealing with all kinds of people, including the much-reformed Desmond Archer, caused her admiration of her boyfriend to soar. Constance described him to members of her club as "the silver fox, tall, gray and handsome."

The problem leading up to the Olympics was whether enough countries would show up to hold them. When France and Great Britain invaded the Suez Canal after Egypt had proclaimed ownership, Iraq, Lebanon, and Egypt pulled out of the Olympic Games in protest. When Russia brutally crushed the Hungarian rebellion, Spain, Switzerland, and the Netherlands pulled out. West and East Germany, which were then run as separate nations, were forced by the Olympic Committee to compete as one country, and for a while, no one was certain whether they would participate. Three weeks before the games were to begin, China pulled out in protest over the committee's decision to allow Taiwan to compete as a separate nation. The Chinese, then as now, contend Taiwan is a part of China. In the end, sixty-seven nations participated.

Constance said the most exciting moment in the Olympics was watching Hungary defeat the Soviet Union in water polo, 4–0, a game in which some brawling broke out, and Russian noses were bloodied.

The U.S. basketball team was led by two University of San Francisco stars, Bill Russell and K. C. Jones. The Americans finished 8–0 and won most of their games by 40 points or more.

But in this year of the Cold War, the Soviet Union could take great pride in winning the race for the medals with a total of ninety-seven, including thirty-seven golds. The United States finished second with a total of seventy-four medals and thirty-two golds. Australia stood a surprising third with thirty-five medals and thirteen golds.

Constance said she was exhausted for a week after the grueling pace required to keep up with Ken. She said being there with 102,000 other people for the opening and closing of the Olympic Games and all the activities in between constituted one of the greatest, most exhilarating things she had ever done. That was life with P. K. Thatcher.

In thinking about the mid-1950s now, I can see that it was clearly a very different time from today. For those of you who were not alive back then, think about a world with no cell phones, no telephone answering machines, no personal computers, no Internet, no birth control pills, and no cable television. Commercial jet aircraft travel was still three years away, and fast food restaurants were just beginning in Southern California. There were no Walmarts, no Costcos. The pace of change has been so incredible it makes me wonder what the world is going to be like fifty years from now. I suspect people will be living to 120 or more by then.

Meanwhile, Constance was living one day at a time. She was the happiest she had been in years. She saw Ken an average of three times a week, but sex was usually limited to long and languid Saturdays, because Ken worked most nights. Anyway, Ken was more into quality than quantity, which was fine with Constance. They spoke on the telephone every day, and Ken kept her informed regarding most of what he did. One of the things Constance liked about Ken was that he was never too tired to tell her in detail what was going on, and usually, in dramatic fashion. In fact, Ken was a born dramatist and storyteller, which was one of his most compelling aspects. It especially worked in business and with the media.

CHAPTER 43

I need to digress a bit to tell you about an incredible event involving Ken Thatcher. Two months before the start of the Melbourne Summer Olympics, Ken was flooded with work. The trouble was of his own making. His clients had come to expect that he would personally and immediately handle any problems that arose. On October 9, 1956, Ken got an urgent request to help with a labor problem that had flared in Hawaii. So the next day, Ken flew to Hawaii aboard a PanAm Boeing Strato-Cruiser, a nearly eight-hour flight in those days before the introduction of jets. He did not want to make the trip, but he had no choice. Fortunately, the labor problem was resolved, and Ken booked his return aboard PanAm Flight 943, which departed Honolulu at 10:00 PM on October 15 and was scheduled to arrive in San Francisco at 7:00 AM, October 16 (Pacific Coast time).

As Ken recounted later, he could not have felt better. First Class in the Strato-Cruiser, a converted B-29 Flying Fortress, had sleeping births, and Ken tucked himself in an hour after takeoff, intending to get at least six hours of sleep. However, shortly after 2:00 AM, a stewardess awoke Ken and other sleeping passengers and advised them all to dress, because there was a problem with one of the engines.

Ken looked at his watch. The plane had been aloft for four hours and was roughly halfway through the flight, probably 1,000 miles from San Francisco, not a good place to lose an engine. A few minutes later, the captain announced that the no. 1 engine had been shut down and that the no. 4 engine was also shut down. He said he was in consultation with the mainland as to whether to try to make it to San Francisco on the two remaining engines. Fortunately, the captain said, a U.S. Coast Guard weather ship, the Pontchatrain, was located immediately below and was aware of the situation. He added that there was a possibility that the plane would have to be ditched. Ken said afterward that he suspected there was no alternative to ditching. But he thought the chances that it could be done successfully were slim. The pilot brought the plane down from its 21,000 feet cruising altitude to 1,500 feet and began circling the Pontchatrain. It was dark, and the pilot, Richard W. Ogg, mulled over whether to try an ocean landing immediately or wait until daylight. The captain of the Pontchatrain reported that the seas were calm, but there was no guarantee they would remain so. Captain Ogg decided he would wait until daylight. That meant at least four more hours of circling.

"They say that for people jumping off buildings, their whole lives flash before them as they plunge to their deaths," Ken told Constance afterward. "Imagine what it is like if you have four hours to think."

There were thirty-one people aboard the double-decked Strato-Cruiser, twenty-four passengers, including three children, and seven crew members. Capt. Ogg came back to talk with them twice during the long night, appearing calm and encouraging, explaining that he considered themselves lucky to have the Coast Guard ship on the scene and ready to rescue them as soon as they hit the water. He also said that it was fortunate that the seas were calm and that assuming they remained so, he felt he could hit the water smoothly enough to keep the aircraft upright.

Ken said there was no panic among the passengers, in no small part because of the demeanor of Capt. Ogg and the rest of the crew. Ken also began to think perhaps he was not about to die, even though he had never heard of a large aircraft that had ever successfully been ditched on the open ocean.

Ken said he talked with virtually all of the other passengers and was surprised at his own calmness, although he felt the possibility of imminent doom gnawing inside him.

When daylight finally came, the Pontchatrain laid down a 2,500 strip of foam that served as both a fire retardant and a landing target for the Strato-Cruiser. It was exactly 8:14 AM when the plane lumbered at 90 knots into its ocean landing. All the passengers had been moved to the second deck and were hunched over in their seats wearing life vests when the plane slammed into the water, bouncing so hard that the tail section broke off from the main fuselage. However, the lower deck cushioned the crash, and no one received more than a bruise. The crew sprang into action and had all passengers into lifeboats within five minutes of impact. The plane sank after eight minutes, and all thirty-one of those aboard the Strato-Cruiser were aboard the Coast Guard vessel within fifteen minutes.

I recently went to the downtown branch of the San Francisco Public Library to see what the *Chronicle* had reported on the crash. Incredibly, three days after the event, the newspaper had published an amazing photo taken by a Coast Guard photographer showing the Strato-Cruiser just before it hit the water. They also had photos of the plane floating in two parts with the rescuers from the Pontchatrain picking up the passengers and crew.

"It was the best-managed near-disaster I have ever encountered or even heard about," Ken said afterward.

Three days after the miracle landing, the passengers and crew, who had been traveling with the Coast Guard, arrived at Pier 9 at the foot of Broadway.

Ken was wearing a perfectly fitting blue blazer and gray slacks with a Brooks Brothers shirt and tie when he saw Constance among a host of friends who had come to greet him. Ken appeared slightly drawn from the experience, but he was in a good mood as he greeted everyone, giving Constance a kiss and a hug.

"How do you like these clothes?" said Ken. "We gave our sizes to Pan Am the day we were rescued, and they were delivered by Coast Guard cutter this morning twelve miles from the Golden Gate."

The welcome reception lasted about thirty minutes. Ken gave Capt. Ogg a full hug and said if he ever had to make a crash landing at sea, he wanted Capt. Ogg in the pilot's seat. Capt. Ogg thanked Ken for helping to keep everyone calm.

Kevin Keagan, who had driven Constance to Pier 9, said that he would take Ken wherever he wanted.

Ken looked at Constance and asked her if she wanted to take a walk. She nodded, "Sure."

"I just want to feel some terra firma," Ken explained. They walked over to Filbert Street and climbed the steep, multitiered stairway that would take them to Ken's place on Telegraph Hill.

Ken and Constance talked the whole way, and she said she was grateful that she was sleeping when the story broke and that the first news she heard was that everyone had survived, basically unhurt.

"Thank God I did not have to go through any suspense," she told Ken, putting her arms around him as they stopped on a landing halfway up the hill.

"It wasn't all bad," said Ken. "It made me realize how much I love you. I thought of you more than anyone or anything."

When they got to Ken's place, Constance fixed him a scotch on the rocks that Ken drank in the sauna. Ken fully intended to make love to Constance, but somehow, he fell asleep. Constance wrote in her diary, "Ken looked so handsome sleeping and so at peace that I just watched him for more than an hour before I fell asleep. I never felt so grateful to God."

CHAPTER 44

Constance loved working at the Huntington, but alas, hotel management decided that the Zebra Room needed a major remodeling, after which it would be known as Romanoff's. The prospect of being out of work for six months or more was not something Constance could afford. So in January of 1956, Constance went to work for Betsy Ling at her now prospering Down Under restaurant. Constance worked the luncheon shift five days a week. In addition, on Tuesdays and Fridays, she hosted the room for dinners. This greatly relieved Betsy, who, in addition to managing every detail at the restaurant, had also been acting as hostess, which meant she was putting in fourteen- to sixteen-hour days six days a week. Moreover, Betsy's catering business was growing, so she viewed having Constance come to work with her as a godsend.

In April of that year, Ken Thatcher suggested Constance might want to form her own business together with Betsy. He said San Francisco needed a high-quality catering company. Ken personally could generate a lot of business through his clients and friends and said that Constance herself, well-known from her years at the Zebra Room, could do the same if she put her mind to it. Thus, International Catering Inc. was born. Ken said he would provide a loan of $75,000 to get the company started, which included the purchase of two vans, dining ware, portable tables and chairs, and three tents. The loan was to be repaid over a period of ten years and carried an interest rate of 6 percent. Most of the cooking was to be done at the Down Under's oversized kitchen. Betsy sold the food to International Catering at wholesale rates. Although the fledgling company got off to a slow start, it was not long before the company's reputation for excellent service began to spread. During the Republican National Convention, International Catering handled eighteen different events. Betsy was responsible for the food and beverages while Constance handled everything else. One of the things Constance learned about herself was that she had the capacity to remain calm and keep several balls in the air at the same time. It turned out that she was as good at managing people as she was at greeting them and making them feel comfortable. It was not long before Constance had lined up a staff of highly professional people who were willing to work part-time as needed. At Ken's suggestion, Constance owned 51 percent of International Catering, and Betsy had 49 percent. That was fine with Betsy. She had complete control of Down Under. What neither Constance nor Betsy knew was that the $75,000 working capital loan hadn't come from Ken Thatcher, but from Desmond Archer. Ken had talked him into it, saying that

6 percent interest was a good rate and that Constance and Betsy were in fact a highly talented team who would not fail. Ken, himself, would see to that. Archer did not take much convincing. He had been on the wagon for nearly eighteen months, and his feelings toward Constance had not cooled.

Betsy and Constance agreed that each would be paid by International Catering based on the actual hours worked. Any profits would go to pay back the loan, the sooner the better, a manifestation of the streak of independence that ran through both women.

When the project was first being considered, the Hamblens had invited Constance to a Sunday lunch, and she had told Richard and Claudia all about it then. Richard had volunteered to act as her attorney, saying that there were certain things she needed to have in her agreement with Betsy, including a buy-out clause, and further, that he wanted to look at the details of the loan. Constance had agreed and set up a meeting between Ken and Richard.

The two men had a lot in common. Both were in their mid-forties and were tall, handsome, and at the peaks of their careers. And both men had done work for Desmond Archer, though Richard, at first, had no idea that it was Archer who was putting up the $75,000 startup loan for International Catering. Ken knew a lot more about Richard than vice versa, and he could see how Constance could be attracted to a man like Richard. He admired Richard for apparently not taking advantage of Constance. As it happened, Richard and Ken took a liking to each other, though Richard had mixed feelings about Ken's romance with Constance. He knew from Constance that Ken was married to a Catholic who would not consider a divorce. But he was pleased to see that Constance was very happy.

By the fall of 1956, International Catering's business had increased so much that Ken suggested Constance hire a full-time manager to help her in coordinating the business. The extra person was definitely needed. Many weeks, Constance had been putting in sixty to seventy hours, and she had been looking tired. Constance welcomed the idea, which, among other things, meant that she could attend the Olympics in Melbourne. Ken helped Constance in her search for a business manager, and together and separately they interviewed more that fifteen candidates before selecting a handsome young Italian named Anthony Santino, who had run his father's North Beach restaurant for five years but was now looking for a change. Tony regarded Ken and Constance as quality people who could take him to a higher level.

With Tony aboard, Ken began to pull back from his involvement with International Catering. Ken and Constance saw each other less, because both were up to their ears in their own jobs. But Saturdays at Ken's remained the high point of the week for them both.

CHAPTER 45

I would be remiss if I did not write a bit about my experience in the U.S. Army from 1955 to 1956. Enduring basic training at Fort Ord, California, located on the sand dunes overlooking Monterey Bay, was jarring and traumatic, to say the least. I never realized how free and unthreatening my life had been growing up. Nobody had told me what to do. Although playing baseball had introduced me to a wide variety of people, I had spent little time around either black people or people who had had limited education. Lincoln High in San Francisco was all white when I went there, no black students and no Chinese or Hispanic students either. San Jose State had all races represented in its student body, but the atmosphere was subdued, well mannered, and civilized. The army, in retrospect, made me feel I had lived a somewhat sheltered life.

The makeup of my basic training company at Fort Ord was about 10 percent black, with a sprinkling of Hispanics and Asians. Among the whites, there was a segment that came from rural backgrounds, and some hadn't finished high school. At the low end were the high school dropouts who had enlisted in the regular army for a four-year stint. They were mostly eighteen-year-olds. At the other end were the college graduates who had been drafted for two-year hitches. I fit more toward the upper end with my one year of college and one season as a professional baseball player. Moreover, I expected to be a member of the Fort Ord baseball team once I completed my eight weeks of basic training. That put me in a special category, or so I thought.

Of course, it was the job of the drill instructors to remove any such distinctions.

"Cruits," intoned my platoon sergeant on that first day of training, "and that is what every one of you pathetic swinging dicks are, cruits—that stands for recruits—we gonna make soldiers out of your pathetic asses. I am Sgt. Masters, and for the next eight weeks, all your sorry asses belong to me, and cruits, you gonna learn to jump when I speak—when I yell shit, you come sliding in! Do you hear me? Come on, sound off like you got a pair!"

Fort Ord was an infantry training center. We were awakened at 4:30 AM six days a week, and lights did not go out until 10:00 PM.

The food was lousy, and there was never enough of it. By 6:30 AM we were usually on the march, heading for the site of that day's training. The drill sergeants never missed a chance to jump on someone who had screwed up.

"What are you, some kind of eight ball?" I recall one sergeant asking a young trainee during a break in an outdoor lecture on the M-1 rifle. The trainee looked puzzled.

"You don't know what I mean, cruit," the sergeant persisted. "Well, maybe you don't, but let's see if anyone here can tell me what's wrong with eight ball here. You there, cruit, what's wrong with this eight ball?" The sergeant was speaking to me.

"Get over here closer and look at this eight ball, Private Booker—what is wrong with him?"

"Sir, I can't see anything wrong, sir," I replied.

"Well, we have another eight ball! Private Booker can't see anything wrong. Give me thirty push-ups, Booker, cuz you're stupid," said the sergeant.

"Where is one of you college graduate cruits?" asked the sergeant. "I need somebody with some brains who has the power of observation."

No one said anything.

"Hillman, I understand you went to the University of California and you got your degree," said the sergeant. "Get your ass over here and tell what is wrong with this eight ball."

"Sir," said Hillman, "I think Private Ekedal forgot to shave."

"That's right, Private Hillman, you are right. But you don't look very strong. Give me thirty good push-ups, and maybe your body will catch up with your brain. And you, Private Booker, give me another thirty push-ups to put some more muscle on you cuz God knows you don't have any brains."

Poor Ekedal—the sergeant made him dry-shave himself in front of our platoon when we got back to the barracks that evening.

"If I see any of you swinging dicks laughing or snickering, your ass will be the star of the show tomorrow night," said the sergeant.

It was during basic training that I learned the broader meaning of the term "motherfucker."

"That motherfucker stole a motherfucking candy bar out of my motherfucking locker," charged one black recruit. Another classic line I overheard was "that motherfucker would fuck his own motherfucking mother." That translated to meaning the chap in question could not be trusted.

It didn't take long before our company segregated itself, with most making friends with people who came from similar backgrounds. Red Howell was early on a dominant persona, a redneck bully from California's farm country by way of Oklahoma. Red was big and strong and usually angry. The first weekend we were at Fort Ord, Red got drunk and came back to the barracks around midnight on Saturday night. He was making a lot of noise, and someone shouted for him to shut up so they could sleep.

The main lights were out, but Red demanded to know who had said that. He pulled three young men out of their beds, demanding to know if they had told him to shut up. Each said they hadn't and he flung them to the floor. Red finally decided he knew who it was.

"Boscacci," he said, "Where the fuck are you? I know it was you."

"I'm over here, Red, trying to sleep. I haven't said shit."

Boscacci stood up next to his bunk. Red stumbled over toward him in the dark. He was six inches taller than Boscacci and fifty pounds heavier.

"I'm going to kick the shit out of your dago ass," said Red.

"He didn't say anything," I said to Red. "Go to bed, and you can sort it out tomorrow."

"What the fuck, Booker—who asked you anything?"

Red lunged at me and drove his big head into my stomach, knocking me against the metal pole of my bunk bed. My head felt like it was exploding, and my brain went swirling in circles; within seconds, I was knocked out. I was told later that Boscacci and three others jumped on Red, but two of Red's friends got into the fight, which lasted for several minutes. I was oblivious to what was going on. Red focused on Boscacci and smashed him repeatedly in the face, breaking his nose and causing blood to spurt all over both of them.

The hero of the night was Mitchell Francis, a six-foot-five-inch black recruit who came into the barracks during the brutal fracas and turned the lights on. Mitchell and Boscacci had both gone to Commerce High School in San Francisco.

"What the fuck are you doing, Red?" Mitchell asked. "Is that my man Boscacci you beating on, you chicken shit?" Red got up, ready to face his new adversary.

Mitchell pulled out a knife.

"You come near me, you motherfucker, and I'll cut your throat," said Mitchell.

Red backed up.

"Get the fuck out of this barracks, Red," Mitchell said.

"Okay, man," said Red, "we will settle this later."

"I see you beating on anyone in this platoon, Red, and your redneck ass is history."

I came to just as Red was leaving. Boscacci was still on the floor, bleeding profusely. Mitchell said somebody should get a towel and clean up all the blood.

"Booker, you and Boscacci better go see the medics, but don't go telling anyone what happened," said Mitchell. "We gonna settle this on our own."

I suffered a mild concussion and was kept in the hospital for overnight observation. But poor Boscacci was in excruciating pain and had to be hospitalized for three days and have his nose reset.

"Thanks for sticking up for me, Booker," Boscacci said when I left the hospital that Sunday afternoon. That night, Mitchell and some of the others decided to have a "blanket party" in honor of Red. At just before 2:00 AM, while Red was sleeping in his lower bunk, the group surrounded the bed and threw a blanket over Red, which four of them held down while the others kicked and smashed fists and elbows into the hulk. Red was screaming in pain but could not free himself. The pummeling went on until there were no sounds from under the blanket. Red didn't make the company formation the next morning. His squad leader said he was sick. Sgt. Masters went in to check with Red and found him barely conscious, huddling in pain under the covers.

Red was taken to the hospital and placed in a ward with Boscacci, who had been told what had happened.

"Hey, Red," said Boscacci, "I hear you been given a lesson in barracks democracy." Boscacci told me afterward that Red did not respond. We never saw Red again. I think Sgt. Masters eventually learned exactly what had happened, but he did not try to get anyone punished. He knew Red was a bully.

In my fourth week of basic training, I caught an upper chest infection that was known as the "Fort Ord Crud." It didn't help that I had not been issued a field jacket and thus was subjected to near-freezing temperatures in the early morning while wearing only my fatigues. We often marched for up to an hour in the morning to get to classes, working up a sweat in the process, especially when we marched double time. Then we would sit down in the outdoor arena, still sweating and motionless while the cold of the morning combined with the sweat to send me shivering. I had a fever of 103 degrees when I was admitted to the hospital and had to stay for four nights of heavy sweating before the fever subsided.

One of my still-vivid memories of being in the hospital was looking out the window, where I could see the lush greenness of Monterey some six or eight miles away. It just as well might have been six light-years away. I was in what to my mind was prison. The upshot of my illness was that I missed two weeks of training and had to be transferred to another company. The company to which I transferred was designated as a "carrier company" and was bound for Germany, but not before an additional eight weeks of advanced infantry training. I tried mightily to get sprung from my company after the first eight weeks were completed, but I was told there were no exceptions; the whole company was Europe-bound. So I never played baseball at Fort Ord. In the end, I would not have had it any other way.

The best part of my sixteen weeks of infantry training was a two-week bivouac at a remote military reservation one hundred miles south of Fort Ord. We slept in tents and engaged in numerous simulated combat exercises designed to make us use all the skills that we had learned. The most comforting aspect was "knowing" that we would never have to use these skills in actual combat, so certain were we that the United States was not going to get into another war after the disaster that was Korea. Not under Ike, we thought. The training ended with a twelve-hour, all-night march over a mountain, with full field packs and our ever-present M-1 rifles, which, if I recall correctly, weighed nine pounds.

I finished basic training in the best shape of my life. After a two-week home leave, our company was flown from Monterey to New York, and we spent two glorious weeks waiting at Camp Kilmer, New Jersey, for a troop ship that would carry our company to Bremerhaven, West Germany. With nothing to do but wait, most of us spent our time visiting New York, where we went to the top of the Empire State Building and climbed the arm of the Statue of Liberty and went to Lindy's, the Copacabana, and the jazz joints on 52nd Street. We saw the Dodgers play in Brooklyn's Ebbets Field, the Giants at the Polo Grounds, and, of course, the Yankees at Yankee Stadium. They were the best teams in all baseball that warm June of 1955, and it was a thrill to see the likes of Mickey Mantle, Willie Mays, and Jackie Robinson.

Daytimes, I mostly read, having only recently discovered F. Scott Fitzgerald, all of whose books I devoured. During basic training, I had read *From Here to Eternity*, the great book on the prewar army by James Jones. As a matter of fact, I did more reading for pleasure in the army than at any time in my life. Seeing how the other half lives spurred me to want to better myself, and I vowed that when I got out of the army, I would take my college studies a lot more seriously.

When we arrived in Germany, our company was temporarily assigned to the First Infantry Division Headquarters in Wuerzburg and scheduled to be sent down to the regimental level at Stuttgart, where we would constitute the first line of defense in the unlikely event that we went to war with Russia. I was not looking forward to spending two weeks a month in the field preparing for the possible attack. Luckily, I was one of several who were told we were being removed from our company and assigned to division headquarters to form a so-called defense platoon composed of forty men.

I soon learned that we defense platoon members ranked at the bottom rung among enlisted men in the elite headquarters unit, whose offices were filled with draftees with four-year college degrees and IQs in the ninety-fifth percentile. A number had come from Ivy League schools. They played bridge and chess, read a lot, learned to speak some German, and systematically saw all of the myriad and important tourist and cultural attractions. Just as the lower end of the people spectrum was unfamiliar to me, so was the intellectual and well-educated upper end. I liked being around people who were smarter than I was, and I had no trouble finding them at the First Division Headquarters. I soon learned to play chess and bridge, but it was hard finding anyone I could beat.

That September, I was sent to the Seventh Army NCO Academy in Munich for a six-week course attended by two hundred or so men, most of whom were regular army with little education. I ended up as an honor graduate and was promoted to corporal upon completion of the course, which meant my pay jumped to $125 a month (from $86), a fortune in Germany in those days when the mark was exchanged four to the dollar.

We GIs lived like kings in postwar Germany. Upon returning from Munich, I was lifted out of the defense platoon and made an instructor for the weekly infantry training of the desk jockeys who populated our elite headquarters. When April arrived, I joined the First Division Headquarters Company baseball team, became the starting catcher, and ended with the second highest average in our league, .373. For four months, all I did was play baseball and read! We traveled throughout the American zone for games and even to Salzburg, Austria. When the season was over, I took a two-week leave to visit France and England.

I could write at great length about my experience in the army. Looking back, it was one of the most eye-opening, educational, and motivating experiences of my life. It is too bad in these days of the all-volunteer army that not everyone gets a chance to serve.

I put in for an early discharge for September of 1956 so that I could return to San Jose State. There was no war on, and my request, along with the requests of thousands of others, was granted. So it was that I returned to college a much more mature and motivated individual.

CHAPTER 46

In 1959, which does not seem like nearly fifty years ago to this aging author, the lives of all four of the San Francisco Booker family were on the threshold of change. For my brothers and I, there was excitement about new jobs. Meanwhile, our mother, although she was excited for us, was facing a tough but inevitable decision with respect to Ken Thatcher.

Let me start with Joe. He was winding up two-plus years of reporting experience at the *Santa Cruz Sentinel* and was, at Thanksgiving 1959, about to go to work in the San Francisco bureau of United Press International, then a great news agency that competed around the world with the Associated Press. Joe signed on with the promise that if he did well, he would be considered for an overseas assignment. Joe took a salary cut to go with UPI, whose bureau chief, John Madigan, told him that sometimes you have to take a step backward to take two steps forward. I always thought that was a brilliant response. UPI had a reputation for being so tight that employees were asked to sign out for pencils in some bureaus. Claire Winstead, who was now working in the public relations department of the Union Oil Company, eagerly welcomed Joe's return to San Francisco.

Jim, whose knee had never fully recovered and who thus never became the basketball star we had expected, had graduated from the University of California the previous June. He had been working as an insurance claims adjuster for five months, but was entertaining an offer to become a sales representative for a San Mateo radio station. Meanwhile, I was about to graduate from San Jose State in January, six months behind schedule, because I had played another full season of baseball in 1957. I was twenty-four years old, but that was not too old to be graduating from college given that I had served twenty months in the army and had played two full seasons of professional baseball.

I still did not know what I wanted to do. But I had majored in business administration with a minor in journalism, and Ken Thatcher had promised he would make some inquiries with friends at some of the smaller San Francisco radio stations where he thought I might be able to catch on preparing newscasts from wire copy.

"What you need to do is get your foot in the door," said Ken. "I can help you get a job, but after that, it is up to you," he said.

Mom put together a huge feast for Thanksgiving and invited Ken Thatcher, Claudia and Richard Hamblen, Betsy Ling, and Claire Winstead and her parents, making it a party of eleven. Neither Jim nor I had a girlfriend we wanted to invite. The guests came around 2:00 PM and stayed until 10:00 PM.

No one had a better time than Mom. She was surrounded by people who loved and respected her. Betsy and Claire helped in the kitchen while Ken did the bar chores. That was the first time I realized that Ken was not a moderate drinker, or at least on that occasion he wasn't. He must have had five or six scotches on the rocks before switching to wine at dinner. Richard Hamblen was much more moderate. Both Ken and Richard were very handsome men, almost strikingly so, and both were damned smart. I would have traded places with either one of them. Actually, Jim was still the best-looking man in the room.

Joe got into very serious conversations with Richard about California politics. I was impressed at how knowledgeable he had become. When Joe spoke, there was an air of gravitas about him that belied his twenty-five years. And he looked well. He still limped from his accident, but it was not so noticeable.

Jim spent a lot of time talking with Claudia about San Francisco nightlife, fashions, movies, and restaurants. Jim had a prodigious memory and could remember menus, lines from movies, and the names of headwaiters and bartenders and supporting actors in a way that made most everyone react in awe.

Betsy told me that she loved working with Mom, who had a great head for business. Weddings had become the staple of International Catering's business, and well-heeled couples could turn over the entire event to I.C. and everything would be taken care of, including, if requested, music and photography.

"I never believed it would work out so well," Betsy said. "We have paid off almost all of our debt and we are making a good profit, much more than my restaurant."

Mom overheard Betsy's comments and came over to put her arm around Betsy.

"This woman is a dynamo," said Mom. "And do you know we have never had a single disagreement or harsh word during our four years together?"

"Sounds like the first four years of my marriage," said Ken, clinking the ice in his otherwise empty glass.

"And what is that supposed to mean?" asked Mom in a tone that sounded slightly annoyed.

"I don't know," said Ken. "I guess I was trying to be funny."

Clearly, the fact that Ken was a married man was still a sensitive subject for Mom.

Richard asked Ken how his business was doing, and Ken said it was about the same, too much work and too little time to do it.

"I know what you mean," said Richard. "I wonder sometimes why we work so hard, why we don't spend more time enjoying ourselves. I love my work, but does working sixty hours a week make sense?"

"Enjoy it while you can," said Charlie Winstead. "It doesn't last forever. I love retirement, but I sure miss working. I think the secret is to not burn yourself out. I almost did that working twenty years in the newspaper business, drinking every lunch and dinner, never getting any exercise. Fortunately, I began teaching, and it changed my whole outlook, gave a balance to my life, gave me time to think about prioritizing what was important."

"Well, here's a man who has it figured out," said Ken. "Pay attention, gentlemen; Charlie knows what he is talking about. I've been down that near-flameout road, and it isn't pleasant."

"That's hard to believe," said Joe. "You make everything look so easy."

"It's a deception," said Ken. "The truth is everything is harder than it looks."

"Ken, it sounds like you deserve a vacation, a good long one," smiled Richard.

"Well, I am flying to the Philippines in December and will likely be there for three weeks or so," Ken said. "It is a command performance requested by Colonel Soriano, my biggest client. I am trying to get Constance to come with me, but so far no luck. Thank goodness I will be able to fly on a Boeing 707 jet, which PanAm is now using for the Manila run. That makes a huge difference in flying time—twelve hours versus almost an entire day."

"I wish I could come," said Constance, "but we have so much work over the holidays there's is no way I can get away. I hope you will be here for Christmas, Ken, along with the boys."

"That's a date," said Ken.

Richard asked Constance if she was thinking of selling her house. He said it was awfully large for just one person.

"I don't think so right now," said Constance. "My mother is coming out for Christmas, and the boys still have their rooms, and I expect they will be using them."

Joe said his salary at UPI was so low that he would probably stay at home until he passed the third-year experience tier of the Wire Service Guild, which would raise his salary to $110 a week from the second-year level of only $89.49. I said I didn't even have a job lined up and might have no choice but to live at home.

"You are all welcome to stay as long as you like, though I won't be doing your laundry," Mother smiled.

Ken asked Jim about his job selling radio advertising. Jim said he hadn't made the final decision yet, but if he took the job, it would be with a San Mateo station that played Western music.

"That sounds like a great learning experience," said Ken. "You will learn to deal with rejection, and that is a must in sales."

"I hadn't thought about it that way," said Jim. "But the station has a dedicated group of listeners who represent a demographic segment that is impossible to reach in any other really targeted way, or at least that is what the station manager told me."

"You already sound like a pro," said Claire Winstead, who listened to a lot of advertising pitches in her job at Union Oil.

Ken said to me that if I could come to the city in January, he would set up a couple of interviews for me. I said I hoped I would see him at Christmas, and we could talk about it then. One thing I knew, I did not want to be out on the road selling or working in Santa Cruz. I loved San Francisco, and that was where I wanted to stay.

CHAPTER 47

Christmas of 1959 marked the beginning of the end of the Eisenhower era in America. Under Ike, it had been a great seven years. None of us had any reason to expect the tumultuous times that would lie ahead. Mom had decorated our house with great care, including outside lights framing the eight windows that faced the street. Many of our neighbors had even more elaborate decorations, and our block became a sort of attraction for motorists cruising around, soaking up the Christmas spirit. Mom bought, and we all helped decorate, the eleven-foot Christmas tree that filled the bay window in our living room.

Mom gave a cocktail party on December 23rd, and about fifty people attended. Included were neighbors, friends, and business associates. The only person missing was Ken Thatcher. He had cabled that the press of business would keep him in Manila until after the first of the year. Mom was greatly disappointed, but she chose to focus on the fact that all three sons were with her, not to mention the Hamblens, Betsy Ling, and the members of her beloved women's club. There were parties almost every night until after New Year's, and that was no problem for Mom and Joe and Claire Winstead—they were what Ken's associate Kevin Keagan described as "serious under drinkers." I, however, was unable to curb my appetite for alcohol and ended up hungover on several occasions. At our party and a couple of others, I spent a lot of time talking with Kevin Keagan and Stacy Hollings, the *Examiner* reporter who for years had had a pilot boyfriend who was never there. Stacy was a tough-talking and, to me, very attractive lady, who was full of playful wisecracks.

She broke the ice with me by saying that she had concluded that I was the luckiest of the three Booker brothers.

"Joe is too tall and too smart," said Stacy. "Jim is much too good-looking."

"So how does that make me the luckiest?" I asked.

"Well, it's obvious, isn't it?" she replied. "No one is really expecting much out of you. I think you are going to exceed expectations, and I don't see how Joe and Jim can exceed anyone's expectations, because everyone thinks they have it all and can't possibly fail."

"Maybe that is because they've succeeded in everything they have done so far," I replied.

"And you haven't?"

"Well, if you go by grades in school, both Joe and Jim got straight As, while I was lucky to pull a B now and then. And they were much better as basketball players than I ever was at baseball. Jim could have been one of the best ever if he hadn't wrecked his knee, and Joe was fabulous at Stanford until his accident."

"I know. I saw them both play," said Stacy. "But let me tell you something. High grades don't correlate with success in work or life. And being a great athlete helps you make contacts, but it doesn't make you a success. I say you are the luckiest, because you feel like the underdog, and you have to work harder. Most great people at one time or other in their lives felt inferior. It is known as the importance of feeling inferior."

Stacy went on to say that she, herself, always felt too skinny, too gawky, and too flat-chested.

"I was twenty years old before I even had a boyfriend," she said. "I had to work at developing a personality. I knew I wasn't going to make it on looks."

"But you look fabulous—you have great skin, good features," I said.

"The braces worked, and the freckles mostly faded when I reached my twenties," she said, adding "I think you are going to get better-looking as you get older, too."

"Can you wait?" I asked, raising my glass. Then I did something that even surprised me. I leaned forward and gave her a peck on the lips.

"It doesn't take long to coax you out of your shell," Stacy said.

"I just need to be encouraged," I said. "Actually, I am just expressing my gratitude for your encouragement."

"I understand Ken wants your mother to move to Manila."

"I hadn't heard that," I said.

"Probably because your mother is not going to go," Stacy said. "She's not going to move away from her three sons and her friends and give up her business. What, to live in a place where the temperature is ninety degrees every day and the humidity is so thick you can cut it with a spoon—for a man who is married to a woman who won't give him a divorce?"

"Why would Ken leave San Francisco?" I asked.

"Maybe you have not heard, but effective January 1, he is giving up his Australian business, Qantas, the Tourist Board, and Desmond Archer's media company," said Stacy. "Ken has gotten very tired of having to take care of a dozen different clients. He's been drinking more, he looks tired, and in fact, he is starting to look his age. He's getting close to fifty, and Colonel Soriano, whose brewery is booming, wants Ken with him full-time to run his newspaper, television, and radio stations. The Philippines is a very political place, and Colonel Soriano has the highest regard for Ken's public relations skills. I've been to the Philippines, and I've watched Ken operate there. The Filipinos love him."

It turned out that Stacy had it right. Ken came back in the middle of January and did his best to talk Constance into moving with him to Manila. It was a futile effort. I think there was no question that she still loved Ken, but there was no way she was moving to Manila. I learned many years later that Mom and Ken agreed that Ken's departure would end their physical relationship. They could be friends, but Constance was not going to be available for trysts when Ken made periodic visits back to San Francisco. Both would no doubt be dating others in the future, and it was important to Constance that the break with Ken be clean and final.

In the long run, the split with Ken was a good thing. Mom was never comfortable having a relationship with a married man, even though it had been many years since Ken had actually lived with his wife. Truth be known, Joe, Jim, and I were also happy the relationship had ended. We all wanted Mom to get married. And so did she.

After I graduated from San Jose State, I moved back home and began looking for a job. Ken had given me the names of several radio station managers and had sent them letters on my behalf while he was back in San Francisco closing out his affairs and turning his public relations business over to Kevin Keagan. In April of 1960, I landed a job with a small Oakland radio station, KOAK, which played only jazz music and had a pretty sophisticated audience. The pay was $90 a week, and my job was to prepare five-minute newscasts that were read by the disk jockey at the top of each hour. Basically, what I did was select news from the UPI radio wire, which carried both local and national stories, and I supplemented these news pieces with the odd public relations releases and stories from San Francisco's four newspapers, which were brought to the station as soon as they were available. KOAK's offices were in downtown Oakland, and the daily commute took me forty minutes by car; I had recently bought a 1951 Kaiser for $300.

Joe was also living at home, though he spent a lot of time at Claire Winstead's. She was at our place a lot too. Mom and I got pretty close during 1960. We went together to the Irving Theater to see Alfred Hitchcock's *Psycho*, the top box office hit of that year. The murder of Janet Leigh in the famous shower scene was the most surprising thing I have ever seen in a movie. (Thinking back, that sudden murder was a harbinger of the changing times. We didn't know it then.) That same year, Mom read James Michener's *Hawaii*, which she said brought back memories of her childhood. She insisted that I read it too. I did and found it to be a wonderful book—for me, the best thing that Michener ever wrote. It made me feel much closer to my mother's roots.

Mom and I both hoped that Nixon would be elected president, so we were disappointed when Senator John Kennedy won with a popular vote margin of just over 100,000 out of some 68 million cast. There was a lot of speculation that the Kennedys had stolen votes in Illinois, Missouri, and New Jersey, but Nixon refused to pursue the claims, saying it would create a constitutional crisis. Nixon had a lot of faults, and he lacked charisma, but he was vastly more knowledgeable and more honest than John Kennedy, who was, we learned many years later, a bogus creation of his father, himself an undisputed criminal. But John Kennedy had irresistible charm, a good sense of humor, and movie star good looks. He became a very popular president. Years later, when all the books came out exploding the myth of the Kennedys' "Camelot," my mother would phone me, demanding to know if I had read this book or that book that told the real story of the corruption of the Kennedys.

"We were right about him, weren't we, Danny?" Mom said, adding, "It is all so sickening. When I compare John Kennedy with a man like your father, it is very, very sad."

Gasoline was only thirty-one cents a gallon in 1960, and a first-class stamp cost four cents. Inflation that year was just 1.4 percent, though the average cost of a house had climbed to $16,000, higher in San Francisco. I figured our house on 29th Avenue was worth at least $40,000, and Mom owned it free and clear.

My favorite book that year was William Shirer's *Rise and Fall of the Third Reich*. Shirer had been a reporter in Germany during the 1930s and personally witnessed the rise of Hitler and the start of the war. Shirer had an amazing command of detail, and he almost made you feel you were part of the Hitler era. That I had lived in Germany for fifteen months made the book all the more compelling. Even though Hitler had caused the death of my father, I had a fascination with that evil man, much as I might be mesmerized by a conversation with the devil.

I got Mom to read Shirer's book, which was a huge best seller. She read about half of it, the first five hundred pages, but quit with the descriptions of the war. That was too close to home.

If Mom missed Ken, she did not show it. In fact, she seemed quite happy having Joe and me living at home and doing things together. Jim had his own place, a small apartment in Burlingame, just south of San Francisco. We saw him a couple times a month when he would come home for a Sunday dinner, usually bringing a very attractive date with him. Coming home to introduce a new girlfriend to Mother was no big deal for Jim. He had a different girl almost every time.

My own love life was pretty sparse, though I did date several girls I had known from San Jose State who were now working in the city. Nothing serious, though. I was hoping to meet a girl like Stacy Hollings.

Mom had a couple of casual dates during 1960, but she did not meet anyone she really found interesting. She was looking for someone like Richard Hamblen—I know because she wrote that in her diary.

CHAPTER 48

Joe got the news that he would be assigned to Asia by United Press International in December of 1960. He was to leave shortly after New Year's Day and would first go to Tokyo for a breaking-in period at UPI's Asian Headquarters and then move either to Singapore or Djakarta. He was tremendously excited about the transfer that would launch the kind of career he had read and dreamed about.

Even though Claire Winstead had known all along what Joe wanted to do, the reality of Joe's leaving was more depressing than she could have imagined. Joe and Claire had been going together since high school. Neither had ever doubted that they would get married. Joe told Claire that his plan was to succeed to the point where he had enough money so that they could get married in two years. He would be getting only $125 a week from UPI, but he hoped his performance would lead to more money.

He hadn't yet learned that the Asian Division of UPI was one of the cheapest in the company, though he did know that UPI was generally regarded as the most penny-pinching organization in all journalism. But of course, these are the reasons they selected Joe for Asia: he was cheap and single. UPI operated on the theory that you could get talented people who were just starting out at very low salaries. Once they had proved themselves, they would be hiring targets for other more prestigious companies. When they left, new blood—and there was always plenty of it available—was hired to take their place. It was a never-ending cycle. UPI executives liked to point out that Walter Cronkite had worked for UPI for twelve years before he joined CBS. Many other highly successful journalists had gotten their start with UPI. Of course, a few talented reporters and editors spent their whole careers with UPI, and some were well paid, but they constituted a tiny minority. It did not take Joe long to figure out that he had to use UPI as a springboard to something better, like a job with *Time* magazine.

The boss of UPI in Asia was Earnest Hoberecht, a colorful promoter who cared primarily about profits, from which his own bonus was determined. Ernie had made a small fortune by writing two books about romances between American soldiers and Japanese women. Ernie dictated the books in choppy, potboiler English and had them translated by a talented Japanese poet. Ernie's first book came out in the late 1940s during the American occupation, a time when the Japanese faced severe restrictions in what they could publish. Thus, there was no competition on the bookshelves, and Ernie's first book became a runaway best seller. He quickly followed it with a second. The lucrative books made Hoberecht a celebrity in Tokyo, and he rode around town in a chauffeured black Oldsmobile sedan and was given to wearing tailor-made suits and homburg hats and carrying a silver walking stick.

When author James Michener came to Japan in 1951, already famous for his *Tales of the South Pacific*, he gave a lecture to a group of Japanese university students on great American writers, naming Hemingway, Fitzgerald, Steinbeck, and Faulkner. The Japanese asked, "What about Hoberecht?" Of course, Michener had never heard of him. But shortly afterward, Michener did meet Ernie at the Foreign Correspondents Club of Japan. Michener was taken by Hoberecht's flamboyant personality and subsequently wrote a magazine article on him called "America's Greatest Writer." It was written tongue in cheek and recounted that when Ernie's first book was published in the original English, *Newsweek*'s reviewer said it was the worst book he had ever read. Ernie protested in a letter to *Newsweek*, saying, "What are you talking about? I have written much worse."

When Joe first met Ernie, an Oklahoman in his early forties by then, Ernie asked him what he wanted to do with his life. Joe said he wanted to be a foreign correspondent.

"Writers are a dime a dozen," Ernie told Joe. "What I need are people who can sell the news. Out here in Asia, UPI is the number one news service. We sell our news service to more newspapers than the Associated Press or Reuters. That's because we have the best-written, liveliest service, and we know how to sell and take care of our customers. If you are going to work for me, you have to understand that. If I send you down to Singapore, which I am planning to do, in addition to being a damned good correspondent, you are going to have to look after the *Straits Times* and the other newspapers down there. If you want to make more money, you can start by taking away some of the Chinese newspapers that are using the A.P. and by getting us some rate increases that we badly need. The managers we have had there in the past haven't had the guts to raise rates. I can't do it all from here, so it is going to be up to you. We need more money out of your area, and it is going to be up to you; it is your first priority."

Joe was numbed by Hoberecht's crass explanation of what he wanted.

"I have never done any selling, but I will see what I can do," said Joe, believing he had no other alternative.

"Of course, I know you will get some great stories," said Ernie. "You have a wonderful territory. You will love Malaya and North Borneo. That Sultan in Brunei has more money than God. See if you can get an interview with him. And Malaya is fighting off the last vestiges of a Communist uprising that is worth reprising. And make sure you get to know the Singapore prime minister, Lee Kuan Yew. He is one of the smartest s.o.b.'s I have ever met. The Brits are still running Singapore's foreign affairs, but it won't be long before Singapore is completely independent. By the way, you'll love the Brits. The bastards all look and talk like they stepped out of a British movie."

Joe arrived in Singapore in late February of 1961. His official title was UPI Manager for Singapore, Malaya, British North Borneo, Brunei, and Sarawak. He was still only twenty-six years old. His office was in the Cable & Wireless Building, and the staff consisted of twelve locals, including six editors, a secretary, an accountant, and four messengers who delivered news and photos around town. The editors were responsible for cleaning up incoming news sent by radio-teletype from UPI's Asian transmitter in Manila and another radio-teletype service from Europe. The copy was then relayed by landline to clients in Singapore and Malaya. The bureau was open twenty-four hours a day, seven days a week. Joe was the only one who could write in English for the UPI world service, so in effect, Joe was on call every minute of every day. Fortunately, there was not that much breaking news of import to the outside world.

Joe had written home that he loved Tokyo and said it was the most exciting place he had ever been. He said that Singapore was equally fascinating and that it still looked and felt like the British Crown Colony that it had been for hundreds of years. He loved being in charge of the UPI bureau, and in his first six months, he was introduced to scores of people, all the movers and shakers in the news business, government, and foreign diplomacy. Standing six feet five inches and with a serious though pleasant demeanor, it was not long before everyone knew who Joseph Booker was. He stood out in a crowd, especially when the crowd was Chinese. Though he was as thrilled as a kid by the venue and the people he met, Joe wrote that he tried to project a cool, professional image.

Prime Minister Lee invited him to a private dinner in May of 1961. After that, he got a dozen or so invitations from assorted others, including the American Consul General, the British High Commissioner for Southeast Asia, the Managing Director of the *Straits Times*, plus his new friends in the foreign correspondent corps. They all wanted to know what Prime Minister Lee had told Joe, primarily because at the time, Lee was playing the West off against the Communists. Joe's take was that Lee did not sound like a Communist, but he would be willing to use them to gain an advantage, an assessment that turned out to be accurate.

Joe wrote to Mom once a week describing his experiences, usually sending clippings of stories he had recently written. I was frankly pretty jealous about the exciting life into which he had so suddenly been thrust.

It was in another meeting with Prime Minister Lee, this one in July and attended by five other foreign correspondents, that Joe got information that ultimately led to his becoming a hero in the eyes of Ernie Hoberecht. The meeting took place over lunch, and Joe asked Mr. Lee what he would do if the *Straits Times* became critical of his regime. Lee said nothing but gestured with his hand, chopping toward his neck, clearly implying he would figuratively chop the head off of the *Straits Times*. The next day, Joe was with the editor of the *Straits Times*, Leslie Hoffman, and he mentioned the incident. Two hours later, the *Straits Times* convened an emergency meeting of its executive staff, and Joe was requested to attend and give them a report on the Prime Minister's threatening gesture. The interrogation lasted twenty minutes, and Joe was repeatedly asked to describe the exact angle of Lee's chop to the neck. Afterward, Hoffman thanked Joe and said he had been very helpful. It was not long afterward that the *Straits Times* moved many of its executives to Kuala Lumpur, the capital of Malaya (which the next year became "Malaysia," a joining together of Malaya, Singapore, British North Borneo, Sarawak, and Brunei).

What made Joe a hero in Ernie's eyes was that the *Straits Times* had the UPI service under cancellation, and everyone at UPI feared that the cancellation would stick. Hoffman had told Joe that spring that the cancellation was a done deal. But six months later, just when the UPI contract was about to expire, Joe proposed to Hoffman a new five-year contract for the UPI service, which included a 20 percent rate increase. Following a week of tense waiting on Joe's part, Hoffman called Joe and said his proposal had been accepted.

"Joe, this is because we respect you and also because you have been wise enough not to bring your overbearing Mr. Hoberecht down here," Hoffman said in a friendly voice.

Joe immediately cabled the news to Hoberecht, leaving out Hoffman's insult.

"Super Congrats Brilliant Heroic Straits Times News," Hoberecht cabled back.

Joe was amazed that the business side was so easy and took so little time. Basically what he did thereafter was keep in close touch with the major clients, seldom ever trying to sell, but rather working to create a relationship of trust and respect. The editors all liked Joe, because he was obviously intelligent and had become very knowledgeable about Southeast Asia. Importantly, he was not the stereotype of the overbearing American that the Brits and their colonial clones had come to loathe.

At the end of the year, Hoberecht wrote Joe that the business outlook for the new year was not good and that UPI had imposed a salary freeze for all management. Nevertheless, Ernie said he was getting Joe a $10 a week raise to $135 a week. Joe was greatly disappointed. He wrote back that he would be making more money back in San Francisco just based on the Guild salary table for reporters with four years of experience. Ernie replied that it was a foolish argument, because Joe was not a union member; he was part of management with all of the perks that entailed.

"You are living a life you could never live in the States," Ernie wrote. "You have a maid and a nice apartment; you are invited to parties every night; you rub elbows with prime ministers, diplomats, politicians, generals, foreign correspondents, editors, and publishers. You have a first-class expense account. You have a life others only dream about."

Of course, Ernie was right, especially about the expense account. When Joe entertained customers or news sources, it was inevitably at the Raffles Hotel or the Goodwood Park. When he traveled, he stayed in the best hotels and ate in the best restaurants. He bought impeccable tailor-made suits for $55. UPI managers in Asia lived very well.

Joe's only problem was trying to figure how he could get Claire Winstead back into his life. He missed her a lot, but he wasn't about to marry her on a salary of $135 a week. He could not even afford to fly back to the United States, and UPI had no home-leave policy.

CHAPTER 49

Joe's glamorous life in Singapore was in sharp contrast to my nightly work at KOAK putting together 500-word newscasts every hour, about half of the copy being from the UPI wire that did not require retyping. Meanwhile, Jim was learning to deal with rejection at KVSM in San Mateo, the only country music station in the Bay Area. The good news was that he was doing better than his predecessor in selling advertising, and his boss told him he was off to a good start. Jim said making all of the personal visits to ad agencies and other prospective advertisers was a great opportunity to meet girls. Jim fixed me up a couple of times, and we went out together, but it usually ended up with the girl designated for me becoming enthralled with Jim. And Jim would encourage them with smiles and touches and intent listening. He loved to win hearts, and he did it so easily. My defense was to be decidedly uncharming—and don't ask me to explain that.

Anyhow, there was a blonde secretary at KOAK who had my interest, and we started dating on weekends. Her name was Helen Sinclair. She was twenty-two and decent-looking with an excellent figure. She came from Chico in northern California and had a degree from a secretarial school. Helen was hired a month after I was. Her hours were 9:00 AM to 5:30 PM, and I came in at 1:00 PM and worked until 9:00 PM. I was expected to brown-bag it for lunch at my desk; we were a nonunion station. Helen's desk was about ten feet from mine in the cramped KOAK offices. She was outside the door of the station manager, and I was next to the glass-enclosed broadcast studio. We both did a lot of coming and going to and from our respective desks and at first gave each other foolish smiles every time our eyes met.

Helen spent half her day facing the news writer who came to work at 5:00 AM. His name was Skip Amos, and although he was only twenty-five, he must have weighed 260 pounds. Even worse, the intellectual strain of putting together the newscast caused him to perspire profusely under the arms. By the end of his shift, the arcs of sweat had circled all the way down to his belt. It was particularly noticeable when he wore a blue shirt. There was always a faint aroma of salty dampness in the air when I arrived to replace Skip. In Helen's second week, she told me, "You can't believe how much I look forward to your arrival." She then looked into the direction of the departing Skip Amos. I gave Helen a big smile. It is great to be on the favorable end of an invidious comparison. Now I knew how Jim must have felt all of the time.

When I first considered asking Helen for a date, I thought perhaps I would also invite Skip to tag along, though I had no idea if he perspired when he wasn't writing news, at which, by the way, he was very good. In fact, I used to study his copy, doing so at the suggestion of the station manager. And actually Skip was a very sweet guy. After I got to know him, I suggested he try Arrid Extra Dry, but unfortunately, the only result was a sickly sweet smell that permeated the office. Skip's arcs of perspiration still got down to his belt-line. Skip wore the Arid only once.

I told Mom about Helen and Skip, and she got a kick out of my description of poor Skip, but she said Skip needed to go on a diet and lose some weight.

Meanwhile, Skip made me feel almost dashing and handsome vis-à-vis Helen, who seemed genuinely excited when I asked if she wanted to see *Some Like It Hot*. It was the funniest film I had ever seen, and Helen and I spent most of the time in hysterics. It was an auspicious start.

Helen lived in an apartment in Berkeley with another girl, and I was still living at home, so getting together on weekends involved some logistics. Fortunately, Helen liked San Francisco, and she would often meet me someplace there. After we had been going out for three months, I invited her to spend the weekend at our house. I assured her that my mother would be there and that she would be staying in the guest bedroom located on the same floor as my mother's bedroom. Helen had told me she was still a virgin and planned to stay that way until she got married, a concept imbued in her by her mother, who was a devout Baptist. But she trusted me and agreed to spend the weekend in San Francisco. Mom liked Helen a lot and thought she had a lot of character.

Meanwhile, I was trying to figure out some way to get my career going. Writing anonymous newscasts was good experience but did not exactly put me on a fast track to success. Sometime in late 1961, I got the idea to write a series of twelve-minute feature programs—about a thousand words—on famous figures and events in San Francisco history. It wasn't exactly an original idea, but at the time, there was nothing like it on the air. I talked it over with the station manager, Glen Albaugh, and he said I should put together a pilot on my own time, and he would decide if it was worthy of a sponsor. If we went ahead, Glen said I would get a share of the advertising revenue.

I got Helen involved in the project, and she agreed with my choice of a subject for the pilot program: Adolph Sutro, who had made millions in silver mining in Nevada, which he had then invested in San Francisco real estate. At one point, he owned 8 percent of the entire city. But what made Sutro a great subject was that he was not just another multimillionaire who believed in grand living. Sutro was an enormously generous humanitarian, and he believed that the human condition could be elevated through education. He also owned what was generally believed to be the best library in the United States and had a brilliant and creative mind.

Sutro's first big impact came in the Ocean Beach area, where in 1881 he bought the Cliff House overlooking Seal Rocks. Under the old ownership, the Cliff House had been a tawdry place with gambling and prostitution. Sutro, who was born to a wealthy family in Prussia and was a religious man, promptly cleaned it up so that it became an attraction for respectable families. When the Cliff House burned down in 1894, he replaced it with a grand structure. More importantly, he developed the hilltop above the Cliff House into what became known as Sutro Heights, where he built a conservatory and a sprawling garden and installed statuary, all open for the public, who came in droves to see the smashing views and formal garden. Sutro so loved the magnificent view combined with the sound of the waves crashing on the rocks below and the barking sea lions that he built there a private mansion for himself and his family.

As a further attraction to the area, he conceived the idea for Sutro Baths, a magnificent complex of six saltwater swimming pools and one freshwater, designed to accommodate 10,000 swimmers and viewers at the same time. A two-acre glass dome covered the pools, and the elaborate entranceway was filled with tropical plants and glass encased treasures and curiosities, including mummies. *Scientific American* magazine called the network of pools and their replenishment by seawater an engineering marvel. To make sure the public could get to the Sutro complex, Sutro built a streetcar line from downtown.

Because of Sutro's vision, Seal Rocks, the Cliff House, Sutro Heights, and Sutro Baths became San Francisco's top tourist attraction at the turn of the century. The best hotels arranged carriage rides to and from the area, which became known nationally and were the subject of numerous magazine and newspaper articles. Rich and poor alike enjoyed the Sutro complex.

When I went over the highpoints of Sutro's life with Glen Albaugh, he said he thought it was a great subject that would take more than one program to properly cover. Tentatively, he said he thought there could be four programs: one on the life of Sutro himself, one on the Cliff House, one on the gardens, and the fourth on the baths. I agreed that would make it easier. It took two months to get the first segment together. At Helen's suggestion, I gave my final script to Skip Amos for his review. Skip took it home and two days later brought back a significantly revised script that I recognized immediately was far better than mine.

Skip said he thought I had the voice to do the narration, and we got one of the disk jockeys to help us with a proper mix of music. I must have done twenty versions of the narration before finally agreeing to let Glen Albaugh hear it. Albaugh's reaction was that it was a great first effort, worth shopping around to some institutional advertisers, with Bank of America being his primary target. Two months later, just before Christmas of 1961, the Wells Fargo Bank agreed to the sponsorship for a total of twenty-six programs to be produced in 1962 and to be called *San Francisco Memories*. Each program would be run three times every other Sunday—the first at 8:00 AM, another at 4:00 PM, and the final at midnight—the assumption being that there would be a different audience for each broadcast time.

The first show on the life of Sutro, who I should note was elected mayor of San Francisco for a two-year term in 1894 and who sadly died at age sixty-eight in 1898 in a state of severe dementia, was a huge hit. One of the entertainment writers at the *Chronicle* who loved jazz and was a regular listener to KOAK, happened to hear the midnight broadcast and gave it a nice plug in his column, mentioning me by name as not only the narrator, but also the program's creator. I got several phone calls from friends who had heard the show and liked it very much, two commenting that I had a great voice for radio. Albaugh got six letters praising the show and one that erroneously disputed the date of the second fire at the Cliff

House. He said that was the most mail he had ever received on any show at KOAK.

Helen and Skip and I all went out to celebrate the next Saturday night. Albaugh had said that I would be allowed to work two days a week on the show, and Skip would be given one working day to do the final version of the script. Wells Fargo agreed to a 40 percent increase in its ad rate when the ratings book came out in April.

By the end of 1962, Albaugh asked me if I thought I could do a show once a week. I said there was no shortage of subjects if we could focus on dramatic events large and small. I added that the longer we did the show, the more time it would take to find appropriate subjects. Albaugh agreed that the never-ending challenge was to be interesting and dramatic. And, of course, we had to deal in facts, without literary license. Even so, we came up with a set of programs on haunted houses of San Francisco and another on the adventures of early fishermen who went out each day past the Golden Gate. We did one particularly well-received show on the Robin Hood of California, Joaquin Murietta, and another on the founder of the Bank of America. Wells Fargo did not complain about the BofA show, apparently recognizing that for an old San Francisco bank, being tied to our program was an association made in heaven.

I don't want to mislead readers into thinking that I had become a celebrity as a result of *San Francisco Memories*. But after the first year, I hardly ever met anyone who was not aware of the program or who did not tell me they loved to listen to it and that I had a good voice for radio. No one ever suggested that I do the show for television.

At the start of 1963, I was making more than $300 a week, a huge sum of money for a twenty-seven-year-old. Helen and Skip and I were the best of friends, and we sometimes went out as a threesome. Skip lost some thirty pounds in 1962, and not only did he look good, but his armpits had largely ceased to flow also. Helen remained a virgin, though our moments of passion together led me to believe she had some strong and healthy desires that were only trumped by her mother's inculcated religiosity.

CHAPTER 50

Joe wrote in the early summer of 1963 that he was being temporarily assigned to Saigon to help out in the coverage of the so-called Buddhist crisis. Two monks had gotten worldwide attention by immolating themselves on separate occasions while thousands looked on, including Western correspondents and photographers. Photos of the burning monks were published throughout the world. The grisly suicides were said to be in protest over the discriminatory treatment of Buddhists by South Vietnamese President Ngo Dinh Diem, who, like 15 percent of the population in the former French colony, was a Catholic. At the time, the Communist insurgency, being orchestrated from North Vietnam, was thought to be under control and winnable. The United States had 15,000 "advisors" in South Vietnam that summer, but they were not supposed to be involved in any fighting.

The Buddhist crisis exacerbated matters by causing Diem's autocratic leadership style to come increasingly under fire. David Halberstam, the Saigon correspondent for the *New York Times* in 1963, repeatedly referred to "The Catholic Government of Ngo

Dinh Diem" in what he invariably described as an "85 percent Buddhist nation." Joe said that he had gotten to know Halberstam pretty well, because David often worked out of the UPI Saigon office, which was run by Neil Sheehan, a Harvard classmate of Halberstam. Joe wrote that Halberstam and Sheehan were both very smart and hardworking, but that they seemed to have lost their objectivity. Halberstam was particularly critical of the U.S. Ambassador Frederick Nolting, and the U.S. Army Commanding General Paul Harkins. Several times in private conversations, Halberstam referred to Nolting and Harkins as "assholes." Joe was taken aback by the disrespect and privately wondered how Halberstam and Sheehan had become so cynical about the American leadership, men thirty years their senior. In fact, both Halberstam and Sheehan believed that the U.S. government was lying to them about the war, trying to put a good face on a bad situation. And they felt Diem was a despot.

Joe arranged to interview Ambassador Nolting, bringing along a Movietone News cameraman. Movietone, which sold news film worldwide, was partly owned by UPI. Most of Joe's Nolting interview was about the Buddhist crisis, and when the cameraman said he had enough film, Joe said he wanted another three minutes on the war.

"That's right," thundered Nolting. "Let's talk about the war. I have been in this country for two years, and I have never seen a single incidence of religious persecution. Yes, let's talk about the war. We are winning the war."

Nolting went on to say he believed the Buddhist protests were strictly political to undermine the Diem leadership.

Joe went back to the UPI office and typed up an account of his exclusive interview. As a courtesy, even though Joe had worked for UPI two years longer than Sheehan, Joe gave Sheehan a copy of his story before he filed it by cable to Tokyo. Sheehan showed the copy to Halberstam, who happened to be in the UPI office at the time.

"What bullshit," said Halberstam. "He doesn't know what he's talking about."

"I guess that makes it a pretty good story," said Joe.

"I wouldn't run it," said Halberstam. A long discussion ensued on how the story could be balanced. Halberstam suggested detailed qualifications to refute what Nolting had said. Halberstam believed the Buddhist complaints were valid.

"I'm sorry, fellows, but I am going to file the story as it is," Joe said. "This is an interview with the ambassador of the United States. I have no way of knowing whether he is right or wrong, but I know what he said. If he is wrong, history is going to prove him wrong, not me."

Joe's story got good play in the United States. When Joe set up a similar interview with General Harkins, Sheehan called him the morning of his scheduled meeting with Harkins and told Joe he had to immediately get to Hue, because he had heard rumors of unrest there. That meant postponing the Harkins interview. Joe went to Hue, but there was nothing going on. Joe later said he thought Sheehan and Halberstam did not want him to do the Harkins interview, which likely would have produced comments that ran contrary to what the pair had been reporting on the Buddhist crisis and the state of the war.

Later that summer, Joe returned to Hue and ended up with what he thought was a six-hour beat when a monk immolated himself in a local pagoda. Joe got the beat, because he was sleeping on the floor of the U.S. Consulate in Hue when the overnight officer in charge woke him to tell him about the immolation. Joe called Sheehan at 3:00 AM with a bulletin on the monk's death, citing the source as the U.S. Consulate. Instead of filing Joe's exclusive, Sheehan went back to bed.

Joe, just after daybreak, went to the pagoda, where he was the first to obtain a photo of the burning monk. The monks were eager to publicize the suicide. Joe rushed to the airport and gave a packet containing the photo together with $40 to a U.S. Army pilot flying to Saigon and asked him to call the UPI bureau as soon as he arrived to make arrangements to hand over the photo. Sheehan got the pilot's call, but waited twenty-four hours to get the photo, unbeknownst to Joe. Joe flew back to Saigon the next day feeling exuberant over his two beats. Upon arriving, he was shocked to see a "rocket" from New York saying the A.P. had an exclusive photo on the Hue immolation.

Joe asked Sheehan what the hell had happened, exclaiming that he had practically risked his life going to the pagoda, which had been surrounded by government troops, to get the photo. Sheehan, who had a reputation for not caring about the photo side of the business, told Joe he didn't have time to pick it up.

"Jeez, Neil, I told you it was an exclusive," said Joe, adding, "New York said *Paris Match* ran it as a double truck, and you don't even bother to pick up the photo that I got hours ahead of the A.P."

Joe said he practically went through the roof when he read the news file and found that Sheehan had not filed the story on the immolation until seven hours after Joe had first called.

"I wanted to get proper confirmation," Sheehan claimed.

"What the hell is the U.S. Consulate?" Joe demanded. "I got that beat, because I was sleeping on the floor of the consulate, and Peter Arnett was sleeping in a very comfortable sampan on the Perfume River. I come back here thinking I have two great beats, only to find that because of you, I don't. I can't believe it."

Years later, Joe conceded that Sheehan had been working seven days a week for nearly a year and was physically and mentally exhausted.

One of the things that his Saigon experience caused Joe to realize was that he was a rare Republican in the ranks of the news media. This came into focus for Joe when the *New York Herald Tribune* sent its Pulitzer Prize–winning correspondent Marguerrite Higgins to unearth what was really going on in Saigon. Halberstam hated Higgins, not just because she was from a rival newspaper, but because he alleged she was a lackey for the U.S. government, a charge that was accepted by much of the press corps. Joe spent a lot of time with Maggie, and her contacts with the military and CIA were extensive. Maggie had been married to an army general, and Joe was the son of a West Point graduate. They had a lot in common.

One night, Maggie set up a dinner with John Richardson, who was the head of the Central Intelligence Agency in Saigon. Joe told Richardson that Halberstam had once complained to him that Ambassador Nolting had never bothered to invite him to lunch. Halberstam clearly believed that as the representative of the *New York Times*, he was worthy of special treatment.

"I admit the ambassador could do a bit more outreach," said Richardson, conceding that Nolting was not good with the press corps.

"The Buddhists are much better at public relations," said Joe, adding, "When I go to press meetings with the Buddhist spokesman, the sessions invariably began with a round of hugs and giddy laughing." Joe said Halberstam was among the most effusive. It was a sharp contrast to the edgy meetings between U.S. officials and the press corps. Joe told Richardson that Halberstam seemed to believe that the war could only be won if a more democratic leader replaced President Diem. Richardson said the problem with that was there was no one who could fill that role.

"If we get rid of Diem, there will be chaos," Richardson said.

In the end, Halberstam's view prevailed over the view that Richardson expressed that night over dinner. President Kennedy, who read the *New York Times* every morning in bed (according to Pierre Salinger, his press secretary), agreed to the overthrow of Diem, who was killed in the process. Kennedy was assassinated less than a month later and did not live to see the chaos that led to the decade-long quagmire that was the war in Vietnam. The lack of leadership in South Vietnam forced the United States to send more and more troops to maintain order. Before the war was over, the United States would suffer 58,000 deaths and 350,000 casualties. More than 2.7 million Americans would serve in the war, and somewhere between 1 and 2 million Vietnamese would die.

Joe, many years later, said he had been in Saigon at the last point when deep U.S. involvement in the war might have been averted.

"If we had followed Richardson's advice, things might have turned out differently," Joe said. "We could have just walked away as the French did. The problem with that is that a lot of people agreed with the so-called domino theory, that if South Vietnam went Communist, all of Southeast Asia would follow. So maybe we were stuck in a fight no matter what."

Halberstam won a Pulitzer Prize for his reporting in Saigon and went on to become a successful and prolific author, though his subjects over the years trailed off from *The Best and the Brightest* to more prosaic sports figures. Sheehan joined the *New York Times* in Saigon in 1964 and later was the reporter who was given the Pentagon Papers. He finally got the Pulitzer Prize (which many people thought he deserved for his Saigon coverage) for a book on Vietnam called *A Bright Shining Lie*, a biography on Colonel John Paul Vann that took Sheehan fifteen years to write.

As far as Joe's personal life was concerned, Claire Winstead wrote him a letter in late October of 1963 to say that she was breaking off their engagement. They had been apart for nearly three years, and Joe had broken his promise to come back home after two years overseas. Upon receiving the letter, Joe immediately phoned Hoberecht and said he needed a transfer back to the United States. Hoberecht said that he personally did not have the authority to give Joe the transfer, but that he would talk with New York. The response from headquarters was that there was an opening on the New York foreign desk and a good possibility that a post would be available in Europe within a year.

So Joe resigned from UPI in November of 1963 and flew home to San Francisco. I don't think Tony Bennett had recorded the relevant song yet, but clearly Joe had left his heart in San Francisco. Joe was able to save his relationship with Claire, and shortly afterward, Joe and Claire were married in Reno. Instead of immediately looking for a job, Joe decided to write a novel about a young reporter in Southeast Asia. It was total fiction but was set against an authentic Asian background. Joe had a natural instinct for writing fiction, and although his book was more exciting than profound, he found a publisher who gave him a $5,000 advance. The book was entitled *Joseph Brady in Asia*. The fictional Joe was nothing like the straightlaced real Joe. "Joseph Brady" was a womanizer, a hard drinker, and an adventurer who got involved in dark plots to get exclusive stories. When Claire asked Joe how he could write about someone so different from himself, he said Joseph Brady was a composite of several journalists he had met in Asia.

"And I have to admit I just made a lot of it up," Joe had said. Claire said she hoped that was true of a highly detailed sex scene that ran for five pages. Joe laughed and said he only wished it were based on real-life research.

The *Chronicle* gave *Joseph Brady in Asia* a favorable review, and Joe was interviewed on the San Francisco Public Broadcasting television station. Sales of the book reached 22,000 by the end of 1964, and a paperback edition promised more revenues. Joe's agent was dickering with Universal Studios over the movie rights, and his publisher asked Joe if he could produce another Joseph Brady adventure. Mother was a bit shocked by the details in Joe's book, but she thought it was a lot of fun to read.

"I don't think it is great literature," she told Joe. "But I could not put it down. In fact, after the first fifty pages, I had completely forgotten that you wrote it, and I was eager to find out what was going to happen next."

I told Joe that his book would make a great movie and that he ought to keep writing Joseph Brady adventures.

"That's the plan," said Joe.

CHAPTER 51

Constance Booker was delighted with the progress of her three sons, but disappointed with her post—Ken Thatcher love life. Her catering business had grown to a point where, despite the competent presence of Tony Santino to help her manage things, she was back to putting in many twelve-hour days and working too many six-day weeks. She greatly missed Joe during his nearly three-year stint in Asia. Adding to her loneliness, Jim had gotten a job in Los Angeles working for a firm that represented independent television stations seeking national advertising. I was still around, but had moved to my own apartment in mid-1962 following the success of the *San Francisco Memories* series.

In the fall of 1962, Richard Hamblen suggested to Constance that she consider selling her house on 29th Avenue. She had complained to Richard and Claudia that although she loved it very much, the house was too big for one person. Richard said that she could get at least twice what she had paid for it and that she might be happier investing part of the money in a Pacific Heights flat, which would be far more convenient. I agreed that Mom should make the move, because I did not think any of us would ever move back home again.

Constance, with a lot of help from Claudia and other friends, searched for eight months before she found something that she liked and that also fit her pocketbook. It was a second-floor flat located on Pacific Avenue with about 1,900 square feet and offering a spectacular view of San Francisco Bay from the combined living room and dining room. It had a fireplace, twelve-foot ceilings, three bedrooms, and two baths. There was also an airy step-down deck off the living room designed to not interfere with the views from inside.

The flat had its own private entrance, reached via a brick stairway in front of the house. Also included were two parking spaces in the basement, plus a screened storage area. The flat was only a fifteen-minute walk from the Hamblens.

The owner of the real estate agency who sold Constance the house was a charming gentleman named Conrad Sutro, a distant relative of Adolf Sutro. She had been introduced to Sutro by Claudia Hamblen who said he used his many friends to find houses that hadn't yet been put on the market. Conrad, a widower whose wife had died of cancer only two years earlier, took a liking to Constance and got deeply involved in her transaction, much to the surprise of his employees, because he was normally not a hands-on manager.

After several business meetings with Constance, Sutro asked her if she would like to go sailing the coming weekend together with another couple. Constance accepted, though she was not particularly fond of sailing. She found Conrad Sutro to be an attractive man. He was fifty-two years old, had graduated from Stanford with a degree in liberal arts, and had gone into the real estate business with his father's firm. He hadn't married until he was thirty-one, and he had the reputation of being something of a playboy who made up for his rather average looks with a wonderful smile, impeccable manners, and a keen interest in other people. He also exuded a great deal of confidence and knew all the members of San Francisco's old-money set, though he had many friendships outside that group. Conrad had tried to enlist in the army during World War II but was rejected, because he had only partial vision out of his left eye, the result of a childhood accident.

Conrad lived in a large three-story house on Broadway in Pacific Heights, which he had inherited from his parents. His father had died a decade earlier, and his mother had passed four years after that. Conrad and his wife had had only one son, Adam, who was now sixteen and still living at home, along with a full-time housekeeper, Rosario, who had been employed when Mrs. Sutro became ill. Rosario cooked, mostly for Adam, but sometimes also for Conrad, who was out more evenings than he was home.

Conrad owned a share of a winery in Napa County that included a rambling ranch-style house located on the estate. His office was located on Fillmore Street near California, and he naturally specialized in Pacific Heights. When Conrad got a listing, he often sold it to friends who had asked him to be on the lookout for certain kinds of property. Pacific Heights homes frequently sold without the general public ever knowing they were available. Such was the case with the flat bought by Constance. Conrad Sutro had received the listing from friends, gotten two professional appraisals, and set the price. No dickering was involved. Match the sellers' price, and it was yours, which is what Conrad told Constance. Although it had taken nearly eight months to find the flat, agreeing on the terms was only a matter of twenty minutes. The owners, who were pleased to sell to a person like Constance, said they did not want to close for another three months, which was fine with Constance, because she had not yet put her own house up for sale. She had already arranged for the preliminary work to be done by a respected Sunset realtor, Stephen Lane, who assured her he would have a buyer at her price within a month. In the end, it took six weeks. Richard Hamblen represented Constance for both closings.

Hamblen and Conrad Sutro were reasonably good friends, and they invited Constance to have lunch with them on the day of the closing. During the lunch, Conrad talked about his investment philosophy.

"I believe in the future of California, and I believe in the future of computers," Conrad said. "I own only two stocks, Bank of America and International Business Machines."

Afterward, Richard said he was impressed by Conrad's logic and suggested Constance invest the excess money she had made on the sale of her house in those two stocks. They would make a fine pension for her old age, he said. Actually, Constance was saving more than she was spending, up until now having put her extra money into mutual funds, a strategy recommended by Richard. Constance was grateful that never in her life had she ever had to really worry about money, because she had always managed to keep her expenses in line with her income. With Richard's help, she managed her assets very conservatively and was never given to any kind of extravagance.

From Constance's view, Conrad Sutro was very different. Not only did he have plenty of money, but he had no hang-ups about spending it, either. He belonged to both the San Francisco Golf Club and the Olympic Club. He was also a member of the Union League Club, and he was considering buying a house in Carmel and joining the Cypress Point Golf Club. During their years together, Conrad and his wife had made five trips to Europe, and he spoke passable French. Clearly, Conrad had been a very happily married man until tragedy struck in the form of lung cancer, taking his wife in less than a year. Conrad said his wife had been a smoker since high school, and so had he. He quit when he learned his wife had lung cancer, which was three years before he met Constance.

Conrad liked to do crossword puzzles, and he was very good at it. He also liked to play bridge and was a reasonably good chess player. He enjoyed reading, usually nonfiction, but he was not above reading racy novels and best-selling fiction, too. Like most San Franciscans, he was an avid fan of the 49ers football team and was learning to like the San Francisco Giants, who had moved from New York in 1958. However, he would attend only day games at Candlestick Park, saying he had gone once to a night game and had almost gotten frostbite. As a Stanford graduate, Conrad usually attended the annual "Big Game" between Cal and Stanford, and he always had season tickets to the San Francisco Opera.

Conrad liked golf, but he played only fifteen to twenty times a year. He also enjoyed tennis but played that even less. His forty-two-foot sloop sat idle in the harbor 355 days a year. He got most of his exercise walking around Pacific Heights, which was also good for his business—many a listing had come from a chance encounter on the streets. Cocktail parties were one of his best sources of leads, and he seldom failed to show up when invited, which was often.

Conrad began dating a year after his wife died and was surprised that much younger women seemed to be attracted to him, and he found little difficulty reverting to the lifestyle he enjoyed in his bachelor days. Gradually, he came to realize he was more comfortable with women in their forties, who had much more in common with him than their younger counterparts did. Of all of the women he had met, he found Constance Booker to be the most attractive. At first, he thought she was in her early or mid-forties, but when she told him about her sons, he realized she had to be older. In fact, that summer of 1963, she was forty-nine years old.

Constance invited Conrad Sutro to dinner along with the Hamblens at her soon-to-be-vacated 29th Avenue home. I was invited also and brought along Helen Sinclair. Conrad Sutro was definitely old money, but he was very polite and affable and, I judged, much smarter than he let on. He said he had heard my radio shows on his great uncle, Adolph Sutro, and had found them to be well done and accurate. He asked if the series was my idea, and I said it was.

"Excellent, congratulations," he said.

He wanted to know why I had selected Adolf Sutro to kick off the series, and I replied that I thought Adolf Sutro was San Francisco's first Renaissance man, a man of rare intellect with the ability to get things done.

"He saw his ideas through to fruition," I said, adding that as a kid, Mom had taken us many times to Sutro Baths, the Cliff House, Seal Rocks, and Sutro Heights. Those places, along with Playland, were my favorite part of the city when I was a child.

"My father always said he was an incredible man," said Conrad Sutro. "Unfortunately, his combination of genes are seldom passed on, I regret to say."

"He's perfect," Helen told me after the dinner. "I can see he really likes your mother, and he's got everything she could want."

"Does he have everything you want?" I asked playfully.

"He is out of my league; I'm just a secretary from Chico," said Helen. "Besides he is a little too old for me."

I had to agree with Helen's assessment of Conrad and my mother, but I wondered if Mother in fact would ever get married.

She could have married Bobby Crable but passed. And I am sure something could have happened with Ken Thatcher if she had really wanted to marry him.

"I don't think my mom is going to jump into anything," I said. "But I really like Sutro. He knows how to enjoy life. I think he has a lot of those Sutro brains he says he missed. Actually, I wish Mom would get married to someone like Conrad. She needs to give up that job of hers and enjoy life. She has spent her last twenty-nine years either raising children or working—or both."

"You care a lot about your mother, don't you, Dan?" said Helen.

"We are pretty lucky to have gotten her as a Mom," I said.

"I think your future wife has a pretty tough standard to reach," said Helen.

"Do you think so?" I said. "I never thought of that."

CHAPTER 52

In the spring of 1964, I was quite surprised to get a letter from Carole Andersen, a former girlfriend from San Jose State. I hadn't seen her since the summer of 1960. Of all of the girls I knew at SJS, Carole was the one I had cared about most. She was three years younger, but we were in the same year of school, and we met early in our senior year. She had a rare combination of dark hair and bright blue eyes that highlighted a pertly pretty face. She was small-breasted, and she thought her legs were too heavy for the rest of her body, but I found her quite attractive. When we first met, she was impressed that I was older, had been a professional baseball player, and had served in the army in Germany. For a college student, I was, relatively speaking, a man of the world. Carole loved to drink, and she was not a serious student. She fit in nicely at San Jose State.

We must have gone on thirty to forty dates, and we had a lot of fun together, especially wrestling around in the front seat of my car. (But Carole was just one of a lot of girls I never went all the way with). As often as we went out together, she sometimes dated other guys. At the end of my final term, I told Carole how much she had meant to me and said I was feeling anticipatory emptiness at the thought of her not being around. She said she was going to miss me too but that she was keen on moving home to Beverly Hills, where her parents ran a florist shop on Rodeo Drive. Carole loved flowers and liked working in the shop, especially dealing with the shop's highly interesting clientele, including a lot of people in the movie business.

We corresponded during that first summer, and in September, I drove down to visit Carole, staying with her at her parents' house. Mr. Andersen was quite interested in what I was doing in San Francisco, and I suppose he was disappointed when I described my new job writing news stories for an obscure radio station that was actually located in Oakland. He seemed more impressed when I told him that my eldest brother was about to be a foreign correspondent in Southeast Asia and my younger brother was a television sales executive working in Los Angeles. Carole insisted that we invite Jim over for dinner. Jim was delighted to accept and showed up at the Andersens' Brentwood home bearing a two-pound box of chocolates and dressed smartly in a summer suit that set off his deep tan.

"Why, you look like a movie star," Mrs. Andersen said when she greeted Jim at the door.

"Are you Carole?" Jim asked with a warm smile.

"I'm her mother," said Mrs. Andersen.

"I can't believe you have a grown daughter," said Jim, a master at flattery. Actually, Mrs. Andersen did look far younger than her forty-five years.

Carole had met Jim only once before, but she greeted him as if they were best buddies, with a long hug and kisses on each cheek. Mr. Andersen told Jim he had the posture and bearing of a West Point graduate.

"My father would be proud to hear you say that, sir," Jim responded. "Our dad was a graduate of West Point and became a colonel in the army during World War II."

"Dad," said Carole, "Colonel Booker was killed in Germany just before the war ended."

"I'm sorry to hear that, boys, but I am sure he is proud up there in Heaven to have three fine sons," Mr. Andersen said.

Jim was the center of attention throughout the dinner, and he told some interesting stories about the television business in Los Angeles, with Carole asking a lot of questions about the various personalities. Seeing Jim in top form made me realize just how gifted he was and what a spell he could cast on people. I knew Carole well enough to know that she was mesmerized by Jim's looks, by what he had to say, and by how he said it. The Andersens were equally taken. When Jim left, he promised to come by the Andersens' florist shop the following week.

"You have a wonderful brother," said Mr. Andersen. "I can tell you I've seen a lot of young men who became very successful, and your brother can succeed in anything he puts his mind to. Dan, I think you're going to be a big success too, but you are going to have to work at it a lot harder."

"Thanks, Mr. Andersen. I appreciate that advice and I know it is true," I said.

Later that night, Carole asked me if I was jealous of Jim.

"What, just because he's better-looking, more charming, and more intelligent?" I said. "Who the hell wouldn't be? But, you know, I understand that I am who I am, and I'm playing the cards I was dealt. Nothing is going to change that, so I'm not going to worry about it; I won't even think about it."

"That is one of the things I like about you, Dan," said Carole, giving me a kiss on the lips.

"You mean that I've learned to fake confidence and manliness?" I smiled.

"No," she chortled, "that you can always make me laugh."

I drove back to San Francisco thinking warm thoughts about Carole and thinking that we would probably continue to write, but in the end, that did not happen. In fact, by the time I heard from Carole again, it had been two years since she had written, and she had slipped further and further from my mind as my relationship with Helen Sinclair deepened. I did hear from Jim that he had visited the Andersens' florist shop and that he had taken Carole out three times but stopped, because he had met another girl. Jim was always meeting another girl, and I could not even venture an opinion as to how many hearts he had likely broken. That was one cross I did not have to bear.

When Carole wrote that spring of 1964, she said that she had heard that I was a huge success in radio and had developed a program on San Francisco history that everyone listened to. She said she had thought of me often in the past nearly four years and that she would like to come up for a visit. I immediately telephoned her and invited her for the following weekend.

My apartment was located on Vallejo Street, just off Columbus Avenue near Grant and at the foot of Telegraph Hill. It was near the area of North Beach that the beatniks had taken over in the 1950s but had since largely abandoned. The Haight-Ashbury district was where the action was in 1964, a just-emerging mecca of free love and drugs. My apartment was on the top floor of a three-story complex whose main feature was a swimming pool. From my living room, I could see Nob Hill and Russian Hill and rooftops located to the west. There was a nice airiness about it, and the rent was only $240 a month. The apartment had two bedrooms and one and a half baths.

Helen Sinclair and I had continued to date, and I thought many times that she was the person I would eventually marry. Helen and I had many of the same thoughts, not surprising given that we had been going together for more two and a half years. When I told her that an old school friend was coming to stay with me for the weekend, I said it was a platonic relationship and she did not have to worry about me being unfaithful.

Helen was upset, but she put a good face on it, saying, "Don't worry, Dan. You are the most trustworthy person I have ever met. Look at me—you have kept me a technical virgin! Anyway, Skip will entertain me this weekend." Good old Skip Amos, the ever-faithful friend.

I picked Carole up at the airport. She looked even prettier than I remembered.

"What a fabulous place to live," she said as we climbed the stairs to my apartment. "Nice," she said, surveying my furnishings. "I like the conversation pit," she smiled. "Where did you get that rug?"

"Mexico," I replied. "I mean, I bought it here, but it was handwoven in Mexico."

"It looks wonderful under the glass coffee table," said Carole. "Let me see the seduction palace," Carole laughed.

My bedroom was pretty straight, just a queen-size bed, a bedside table, a lamp, a chest of drawers, a chair, and a couple of throw rugs. There were two movie posters on the walls, one for *Some Like It Hot* and the other for *Casablanca*.

"What, no mirror on the ceiling?" she smiled. "I'm disappointed, but I like your posters."

I showed her the guest room, and she said it no doubt helped in getting girls to stay overnight.

"Actually, I don't have many guests," I said.

Carole threw her arms around me and said the trouble with me was that I was too shy, not at all like my brother Jim.

"Have you been drinking?" I asked.

"Funny you should ask, because that's just what I'd like right now, a very dry martini," she said. "And in answer to your question, I came up here first class and did have two or three gin and tonics on the airplane. I'm ready to party in San Francisco with the famous Danny Booker, the toast of San Francisco radio."

"I love your sources," I said. "Shall we go?"

The compelling thing about where I lived in North Beach was that it was near the center of most of San Francisco nightlife. The nightclubs and strip joints on Broadway were a huge attraction, and there were more than a score of good restaurants within five walking minutes of my apartment. There were quiet coffee shops on the north end of Grant Avenue, and south on Grant, across Columbus Avenue, Chinatown began. I took Carole to the park across from the shimmering white steeples of St. Peter and Paul's church, a San Francisco landmark. We sat in an outdoor restaurant, enjoying the view while sipping our martinis. Carole was impressed when the waiter called me Mr. Booker.

"Danny, this is really wonderful seeing you after all of this time," said Carole. "I don't know how it happened, but we sort of disappeared out of each other's lives."

One of the problems, Carole said, was that her father had suffered a stroke and was partially paralyzed on his left side, so she had taken over the running of the florist shop. She said her Dad now came in every day for at least a few hours, but he mostly just sat there.

"Mom is so busy taking care of Dad that she doesn't have time to do much else," said Carole. "Fortunately, business is better than ever, and I have been able to hire some good people so that I don't have to work such long hours. We started advertising on radio, and our delivery business has quadrupled in the last year."

"That is too bad about your dad. I really liked him," I said. "I wish you would have let me know."

"I should have; I'm sorry," said Carole. "Dad liked you a lot. He said you would make a much better husband than Jim."

"He probably got that right," I smiled. "Jim has too many worlds to conquer."

"You mean too many girls to conquer," said Carole.

"Did that include you?" I asked.

"What, you think I believe in incest?" she laughed. "Where are we going to eat?"

"Do you want to eat inside or outside?"

"Let's eat outside. I like watching the people," said Carole.

"I've got the perfect place, right at the corner of Broadway and Columbus," I said.

"You seem to know everyone around here," said Carole, impressed that a lot of people were greeting me by name as they passed.

"This is my neighborhood," I smiled. "Everybody knows everybody."

And everybody knew that my girlfriend was Helen Sinclair, but no one said a word about the beautiful, blue-eyed temptress who was on my arm this night. But the questions would come later from just about everyone I saw that weekend.

I ordered a bottle of California cabernet from Buena Vista Wineries labeled "Owner's Reserve."

Carole was eating the sourdough bread and munching on green olives when the wine arrived. I tasted it and directed the waiter to pour her a glass.

"Oooh, that is fabulous" she said, smiling at me first and then at the waiter. "Danny, you have come a long way from those seventy-five-cent bottles of Petri you used to buy in San Jose. And by the way, I am paying for this dinner," she said. I just smiled at her and said she was in San Francisco, where no one would allow her to pick up any check.

Dinner lasted three hours. I ordered simply, as I did in those days. We had a thick minestrone soup, tomato and avocado salad, spaghetti in a zesty red sauce, and thinly sliced veal in a delightful lemon sauce. Don Benedetti, the owner and a friend of mine from my baseball days, came over and sat with us for the cheese course. We had finished our second bottle of wine, so Don ordered another bottle, a Mondavi merlot that was even better than the Buena Vista.

"This goes well with the cheese," said Don, whose father had just retired, turning the business over to Don and his brother, Mario. Don soon learned that Carole was from Southern California and had just taken over the family florist shop. The two fell into animated conversation about what it was like taking over a family business. Don, short, dark and handsome, had his charm roaring on the front burner, and Carole was delighted at the attention.

Don, perhaps realizing he was being a bit too charming with the date of his good friend and customer, suddenly stood up, saying how delighted he was to meet Carole but that duty called in the kitchen. He kissed Carole on her hand and winked at me.

"You two make a beautiful couple," he smiled.

"Wow, he's a dynamo," said Carole.

"Would you like to listen to some music?" I asked.

"Sure, it's only eleven thirty," said Carole. "May the adventure continue."

One of my neighbors owned the Jazz Workshop located only a half block from the restaurant. I forget if it was the Modern Jazz Quartet that was performing that night, but it was West Coast jazz a la Jerry Mulligan, Chet Baker, and Stan Getz, the kind of music Carole and I had liked in college. It was a Friday night, and the Jazz Workshop was packed, but we were squeezed into a mid-room table, which I preferred to being up close, because the acoustics seemed better to me.

I put my arm around Carole as we sat down and gave her a kiss on the ear, saying how much I had missed her. I guess we were both pretty looped.

"You are not a hard guy to love," she said, kissing me first on the cheek and then on the lips.

"What if I said that being with you tonight makes me realize that I love you like I have never loved anyone else?"

"Do you mean that, Dan?"

"Yes, but I didn't know it before tonight," I said. I was looped.

We sat listening to the music until the 2:00 AM mandatory closure came. We talked between sets, and I told her about my work and about Helen Sinclair. It turned out Carole was also dating someone, an aircraft engineer who worked for Lockheed and came from a wealthy family. They had been going together for nearly two years, but Carole said she did not know if she loved him enough to get married. I said I was sort of in the same boat with Helen.

"Oh, it is so good to see you, Dan. I think you have really matured," said Carole. "You seem a lot more confident."

"Thanks, Carole. It helps to have a little success."

When we got to the apartment, Carole said, "Are you going to try to seduce me?"

"I've been thinking about it all night," I said. And I fully intended to and definitely would have if Carole hadn't fallen asleep while I was ardently kissing her on the neck.

CHAPTER 53

I woke up the next morning fully dressed on my leather sofa. Carole was not there. It took a moment for me to recall what had happened, or, more correctly, what hadn't happened. It seemed to me that Carole had been eager to be seduced. But alas, a day and night of drinking had worn her down by 2:30 AM. I must have crashed only moments afterward. Not surprising for me. Drinking almost always puts me to sleep if I have the chance. My energy level is strong when I am out doing something, but the minute I get home after a session of drinking, I am invariably overcome by a heavy drowsiness. I think Carole and I had that in common.

I could see the sun reflecting on the buildings atop Nob Hill. It was 8:00 AM, and it looked like a perfect June day. I had made no plans. In San Francisco, whatever you decide to do is fun if you are with someone you like. And I was feeling some delicious thoughts about Carole, who, I realized, was showering. I got up and put on the coffeepot. Carole emerged from the bathroom wearing only a large white towel that she had artfully wrapped around herself.

"That was a wonderful evening last night, Dan. San Francisco can be so much more charming than L.A.," she said, moving forward and wrapping her arms around my neck.

I leaned forward, and we kissed with increasing intensity for what must have been more than a minute. Her cheeks were flushed and hot. I put my hand on her back inside the towel and pushed out, causing it to fall away. I stepped slightly backward to let the towel give way at the front. Carole made no effort to stop it.

"Aren't you warm in all of those clothes?" Carole smiled, moving away so that I could see her in all her nakedness. I quickly took off my shirt and trousers and boxer shorts.

"Wow, look at you," she smiled.

"It is only nature," I said, pulling her toward me as we kissed again.

The weekend with Carole was like a honeymoon. We spent Saturday and Sunday sightseeing in San Francisco, eating wonderful San Francisco food, and having totally unabashed sex. I drove Carole to the airport early Monday morning.

"Thanks for everything, Dan. I think that's the most wonderful weekend I have ever had," she said when we parted. "I want you to come to L.A. Do you think you could make Fourth of July weekend?"

"Sounds perfect," I said, adding how fantastic she was. "I think we wasted a lot of time in our last year in school."

"No," she said. "I wasn't ready for it, and neither were you. It was perfect this way."

I had to agree that it could not have been any better.

I went back home afterward to clean up the apartment and get dressed for work. I was just about to leave for work when the telephone rang. It was Skip Amos.

"Just want to give you a little heads up," said Skip. "I took Helen to the Jazz Workshop on Friday night, and we saw you and your friend arrive. We were sitting about five tables behind you guys, and Helen saw all the smooching going on, and she was furious. I have to admit, Dan—it looked like you two were dying to get into the sack together. Helen said a lot of nasty things about you, Dan, and she called in sick this morning."

Skip's news was disturbing, mostly because I did not want to hurt Helen, who had been about as true and loyal a friend as I had ever had.

I told Skip that Carole was the amorous type who was all show in public and pretty restrained in private. Nothing had actually happened, I said.

"Helen's not going to buy that any more than I do," said Skip.

"I guess it looked pretty bad," I said. "Look, I'll call Helen, Skip. Thanks for the heads up."

I got to thinking about Helen. Being with Carole had made me realize that although I loved Helen, I didn't feel deeply in love, and I certainly did not feel the passion for her that I did for Carole. Maybe, I thought, the easiest path was to apologize to Helen, but not to go begging for forgiveness. What a joke that turned out to be. Helen, in fact, was unconsciously looking for a way to end our relationship, because she had fallen in love with Skip Amos, who had lost more than one hundred pounds in the past two years while engaging in a vigorous physical fitness program. It was only later that I learned he was doing it for Helen, with whom he had fallen in love just shortly after they had met.

Helen had always been aware of Skip's feelings, but she had never taken him seriously, though she liked him very much. It was only after seeing me with Carole in the Jazz Workshop that Helen took a good look at Skip, who had become almost handsome in his slimmed-down image. Sweet and thoughtful, he always was, but now he looked sexually attractive to Helen too. Skip and Helen were married that September and I was the best man.

I never did visit Carole in L.A. She called to say her rich engineer boyfriend had asked her to marry him, and she had accepted. We talked for quite a while on the phone as she explained her reasoning: she knew that passion like we had known so briefly would soon burn out, and there were other things that mattered more. Then Carole blew my mind and took the sting out of her news when she told me at the end of our conversation, "You are a much better lover than your brother."

About a month after Carole's call, I saw Jim in San Francisco, and I asked him if he'd ever had sex with Carole. Jim sort of smiled and said he could not remember.

"Come on, Jim, you've got the best memory of anyone I've ever met," I said.

"Are you thinking of getting back with her?" Jim asked.

"No, she's getting married pretty soon," I answered.

"All right, I screwed her on the second of our three dates," said Jim. "She was pretty wild."

"How come you stopped taking her out?" I asked.

"I think I met someone else," he said. I did not tell Jim that Carole thought I was a better lover.

CHAPTER 54

If you thought I would be depressed at seeing both Carole Andersen and Helen Sinclair get married, you would be mistaken. In fact, I was happy for both of them, and I was happy for me in that I was not married to either. Carole had sown some wild oats with me and had almost certainly known she was going to marry her wealthy boyfriend before she made her little trip to San Francisco. And Helen was never going to be the exciting and stimulating girl that Carole made me realize I was seeking. Helen clearly got that message when she saw me in the Jazz Workshop with Carole. Skip, who was conservative and square, was far better suited for Helen. Moreover, Skip's new image was a startling change and showed in his posture, general confidence, and more relaxed demeanor. Skip and Helen and I continued to work together on the *San Francisco Memories* show for WOAK, and by the start of 1965, we were entering the show's fourth year. Wells Fargo continued to sponsor our weekly effort, and we had not yet begun to run out of material, though it was getting tougher and tougher. Unfortunately, our ratings began to slip a bit, but Glen Albaugh, the station manager, said that was to be expected.

Lyndon Johnson defeated Barry Goldwater by a landslide in the 1964 presidential election, an event that made none of the Booker family very happy. Alas, none of us particularly liked Barry Goldwater either. Nixon would have been our selection, but we thought he had ended his political career by running and losing the race for governor in California in 1962, acidly telling the press they would not have Nixon to kick around anymore.

The mid-1960s were a terrible time in American history, despite whopping spending on social welfare for LBJ's "Great Society." The main factor was the growing unpopularity of the war in Vietnam, not to mention an increasingly heated civil rights movement.

Joe was the most vocal of our family in his criticism of Johnson's wartime leadership.

"The only way we can win is to invade North Vietnam and fight the war on our terms," said Joe over dinner one night in 1964 at Mom's Pacific Heights apartment, where eight of us were celebrating her fiftieth birthday. Conrad Sutro said he thought an invasion of North Vietnam carried the risk of China entering the battle and could even lead to nuclear warfare involving the Russians.

Richard Hamblen said the United States was caught in a dilemma the likes of which he had never seen before.

"That is right," said Constance, "no one has a solution, and I suggest we change the subject." Mom never liked to pursue subjects that left little room for optimism.

Conrad Sutro stood up after dinner and said he wanted to make a toast to Constance, describing her as "the most wonderful person who has ever come into my life."

Jim got up to say that she was "the most wonderful person in all of our lives."

Joe and I chimed in with "Here, here."

Then Mom rose, looking very pretty and smiling her brightest. "Thank you, Conrad, and thank you, Jim and Joe and Dan," she said. "And thank you, Claudia and Richard, my dearest friends for almost twenty years. You all know I did not want to have a big birthday celebration. I am not sure turning fifty is something I want to brag about. But there is really no escaping it, and I have to say that I am utterly happy to be with the people I love most in this world.

"And I am especially happy that Claire and Joe are going to become parents before the end of the year. Dan and Jim," she said, turning to us, "that's going to make you two boys uncles, Uncle Dan and Uncle Jim. And I will be a grandmother, and Claire, I am looking forward to being the most helpful grandmother I can be.

"My life has been blessed. I could not ask for anything more. I may not be happy to be fifty, but I'm happy at fifty. I'm happy that Joe's book is selling well. I'm happy that Dan's *San Francisco Memories* continues to be a big hit, and I'm happy that Jim is such a wonderfully successful businessman. And I am happy to have a daughter-in-law like Claire who I could not love more if she were my own daughter.

"And I am blessed to have Claudia as a friend and sounding board to whom I can confide my most private thoughts. Thanks to Claudia, I have never needed a psychiatrist! And I'm blessed for all the help and wisdom Richard has provided the whole Booker family over these many years.

"And finally, I am exceedingly happy that Conrad has come into my life. Conrad, you are a constant delight, and I treasure your companionship, your sense of humor, and your sense of fun. You make me very happy."

I could not help but marvel at my mother's ability to say unabashedly what she felt. She did so in the most natural, straightforward way. Why were most people I knew unable to be so open? It was my mother's gift from birth, I long ago concluded. I knew I could never be that way.

Three weeks after Mom's fiftieth birthday, Conrad Sutro proposed, and they were married in Grace Cathedral on June 14, 1964, before a glitzy crowd of nearly six hundred. Stories and pictures of the wedding were carried in all the San Francisco newspapers. Mom had sold her share of International Catering to Betsy Ling, and she and Conrad went on a ninety-seven-day honeymoon that took them around the world by plane, train, and boat. Afterward, Mom said it was an exhausting trip, but the most fun she had ever had. Mom was radiant when she came back, though I noticed she had added a bit of flesh around her waistline. Signs of the good life. She deserved it.

Mom, of course, moved into Conrad's mansion, and she told Joe and Claire she wanted them to live in her apartment, rent-free. As a consolation to me, she "loaned" me $30,000 to buy an apartment. She told Jim she would also "loan" him $30,000, but even though she made it clear to Jim that he would not have to pay it back, he declined, saying he did not need it. But he said he might want to borrow some money at some future date.

I bought an apartment on Telegraph Hill just a block below Coit Tower for $53,000. It was actually a third-floor walk-up flat, 2,934 square feet in size, and it had great views of downtown, the Bay Bridge, and the East Bay. The flat had a large window-lined combination living room and dining room, three bedrooms, two and a half baths, and a study with bookshelves lined the walls. I also had sole access to the roof for sunbathing, growing flowers, or whatever. A single-car garage was included, as was a screened basement storage area for which I had no use. It was much more than I needed, far too spacious for my furniture and especially excessive for a thirty-year-old bachelor. But Richard Hamblen advised me that it would be the best investment I would ever make. Conrad Sutro agreed. Of course, they were right.

CHAPTER 55

The success of *San Francisco Memories* combined with my new apartment enhanced my image with a number of old friends from San Jose State. I asked a couple of former fraternity brothers to spend the weekend with me in the summer of 1966. One was Dick Applesworth, who was working as a sports columnist for the *Palo Alto Times*, and the other was Jim Wiles, who had become a sales manager for a San Jose Ford dealership. The three of us had played a lot of golf together in college and shared an affinity for the beach at Santa Cruz.

We all belonged to Kappa Alpha, a good fraternity, but not as highly regarded as Sigma Alpha Epsilon or Delta Upsilon. And finally, we all worked as "hashers" at the Delta Gamma sorority house. We cleaned up in the kitchen in exchange for our meals. But the real deal had been getting to meet the ninety or so Delta Gamma members. The D.G.s had the reputation of taking pledges on the basis of looks and resultantly had more good-looking girls than any other house on campus. And I should note that although San Jose State did not enjoy high academic standing, it was famous for the loveliness of its female students. In fact, there were more females than males at San Jose State, which was founded in the nineteenth century as a teacher's college. When Dick Applesworth, Jim Wiles, and I were at SJS, most of the girls were studying to be schoolteachers, elementary and high school. And a lot of the guys we knew majored in physical education and wanted to be coaches. Dick majored in journalism with a business minor, and Jim was business all the way. I was sort of in between with my business major and journalism minor.

Of the three of us, only Wiles had any great success with women, and he had no qualms about telling us who he had made it with. Six years after college, Applesworth and I had added some luster to our images by virtue of what we did for a living. Wiles, as a car salesman, had fallen a notch or two, but he was making $1,000 a week, or so he claimed. Applesworth was, best case, making $150 or $175 a week, which was far less than my $475. All of us were working more than fifty to sixty hours a week, so my proposal for a weekend together was greeted with enthusiasm. We started Friday afternoon by playing golf at Stanford, where Applesworth was able to get us on free. We made it to my apartment by 8:00 PM, in time to start receiving guests that I had invited, guests whom we had all known in college. In all, there were twenty of us, nine guys and eleven women. We cooked out on the roof and had a keg of beer, and a case of white wine. By 3:00 AM, we had drunk it all! I can't recall everything that went on that night, but some who attended said it was the best party they had been to since leaving college. In reality, that is what it was, a college frat party for people between twenty-eight and thirty. I think for all of us it was a rare chance to turn the clock back. Dick reported later that he had tried to go to bed around 2:00 AM, but the door to his guest bedroom was locked.

"Some people were using my bed as well," said Jim. "I think people were screwing all over the place."

"I think it was just a couple," I said. "I know nothing happened on my bed, though Bev Belturn asked me if I wanted her to stay over."

"God, I hardly recognized Bev," said Jim. "We were freshman together, and I can't believe how awful she looks."

"I think she parties a lot," I said.

I had scheduled an afternoon starting time at Harding Park, so we cleaned up my "cool pad" and headed back out to the links. None of us played very well, and we decided to have a quiet dinner with some intelligent conversation.

One of the subjects we covered was San Jose State. It was the only halfway decent college any of us had been able to get into, and it was gloriously cheap. Tuition when I started was less than $15 a quarter. It had gone up slightly by the time I returned from the army, but my $110 a month in G.I. Bill of Rights funding covered most of my expenses, and I was driving a car. Among Bay Area schools, the generally agreed-upon pecking order was Stanford, California, Santa

Clara, the University of San Francisco, St. Mary's, San Jose State, and San Francisco State.

"The beauty about San Jose was that you didn't have to have top grades in high school to be accepted," said Applesworth. "I was a C student in high school—all I cared about was sports, and I never studied."

"I found out you could get into San Jose State without taking precollege courses like geometry, physics, and advanced languages," I said. "I had a lousy memory, and most of all, I was lazy and bored with school. So I took a lot of electives at Lincoln that didn't require any effort, knowing I could still get into San Jose."

"Look at you, Dan—you are a success in radio, but you were too dumb to get into Cal or Stanford," laughed Wiles. "School brains are not as important in real life as a lot of people think. I spend a lot of time with car salesmen who never got past high school yet have street smarts far superior to most of our customers. We love to sell cars to college professors. They mostly haven't got a clue!"

I asked Wiles what he wanted to do in the next five years.

"I hope to have my own dealership within the year," he replied. "I've been talking with some Japanese automakers, and they are willing to help me finance the start-up."

"Japanese cars?" said Applesworth. "They are pretty cheap and tinny. Do you think they will sell in the United States?"

"The quality is getting better, and they cost a lot less than American cars," said Wiles. "Anyhow, there is no way I could qualify for an American car dealership. But I will be hedging my bets in a way, because I plan to sell used European sports cars at an adjacent lot. Bank of America said they will help to finance the lots and the cars if the Japanese finance the dealership sales and maintenance facilities. Of course, I will be putting up all of my own savings, $42,000, so that seems to carry a lot of weight with everyone."

"Wow, Wiles, it sounds like you are going for a home run," said Applesworth. "What is the name of the Japanese company?"

"Toyota," said Wiles. "They are the biggest."

"Jim always could sell anything," I said.

"It is all about figuring out what people want and then giving it to them, but you have to listen hard, because sometimes people don't really know what they want, and you have to help them along."

Applesworth let out a big laugh. "What about you, Dan—what do you want to be doing in the next five years?"

"I sort of live day to day," I replied. "I like what I am doing now, though I am not sure how much longer I can come up with ideas for *San Francisco Memories.*"

"Get yourself a plan, Dan," said Jim. "What about you, Dick?" asked Jim.

"I'm like Dan, one day at a time," Dick answered. "But the truth is I wouldn't mind becoming a columnist for either the *Chronicle* or the *Examiner*. By the way, you guys would be interested to know that I have been invited to give talks to Stanford journalism classes three times in the past year."

"Holy cow, do they know you're from San Jose State?" asked Jim.

"Sure, but they think I write well and want to know how I do it."

"What do you tell them," I asked.

"I say they should never write from the top of their heads. I tell them that good writing usually means presenting a lot of facts, facts that you mostly don't get sitting in the office. I say they have to get out and talk to people, see what makes them tick, what motivates them, discover the drama in their lives, in their games."

"No wonder I always find your writing meaty," I said.

"Thanks, Dan. The harder I work at reporting, the better my writing gets," said Dick.

"It's the same in the car business—the harder you work, the more cars you sell," said Jim.

"Radio writing is the same," I said. "I sometimes go through six drafts of a show, and each script is better than the last."

"Funny," said Dick, "we were all goof-offs and lazy students in high school and college but have changed our approach to real life."

"I worked a lot harder in college than I did in high school," I said.

"Did you work as hard in college as you do now?" Dick asked.

"No, not by a long shot."

It was great seeing Dick Applesworth and Jim Wiles, and I was happy that we had the time together. When we parted, we promised to make it a yearly event, though maybe next time we would forego the beer bust.

CHAPTER 56

It was late in 1966 that I got the bad news from Glen Albaugh, the general manager at WOAK. The owners of the station had sold to a group of stations headquartered in Chicago who planned to switch the format to twenty-four hours of rock music. There would be no more prepared newscasts. Under the new format, the disk jockey would rip and read the news from the UPI teleprinter. No preparation was needed, and the format had no room for *San Francisco Memories*. Glen said he thought that if I could hold onto

Wells Fargo as the sponsor, I could probably move the show to another station. I talked it over with Skip and Helen, and they both said it was worth a try.

Unfortunately, Wells Fargo had a new advertising and marketing director who had decided that more than four years of *San Francisco Memories* was enough. Actually, I was relieved. To be honest, I had gotten tired and a little bit bored with doing the show, and I was running out of good ideas. The problem was that I was getting $475 a week, a lot of money in 1966, and I didn't know a way I could match that.

I needed some advice and decided to call Ken Thatcher, who had just moved back to San Francisco. Ken was very cheerful and wanted to know about Mom. He asked me to meet him the next day for lunch at the Iron Horse restaurant. We both arrived exactly at noon. Ken was in a magnanimous mood. He told me about developments in the Philippines. He had left, because Ferdinand Marcos had been elected president of the Philippines, and he had backed the incumbent, Diosdado Macapagal. Ken said he had violated his own number one rule in life: never burn a bridge. During the presidential campaign, he had burned a bridge with Marcos, a onetime close friend, by approving a newspaper editorial saying he was unfit to be president. The people at San Miguel wanted Ken to continue working for them, but now he would do that from San Francisco.

On his third scotch on the rocks, Ken said, "Maybe I wanted out of there. Maybe I was sick of the Philippines. Subconsciously, maybe I knew exactly what I was doing."

We were still talking at 4:00 PM. Ken wanted to know more about Mom, and I told him how happy she was with Conrad Sutro. Ken said he had met Sutro and knew that he had a good reputation.

"I'm glad," said Ken. "Your mother is the best."

Ken asked a lot of questions about my work at WOAK and about the *San Francisco Memories* series. He had heard several installments when visiting San Francisco, and he thought they were very professional.

"You've got talent, Dan, and you are imaginative and creative," said Ken. "How much are they paying you in severance?"

"They are talking about three months," I replied.

"That works out," said Ken. "Why don't you come to work for me for a few months. I can only pay you $125 a week while you are collecting your separation pay, but I have something in the works that is coming up in February of next year that could pay you a lot of money, more than you were making at WOAK."

"What is it—can you say?" I asked.

"You are going to have to trust me on this," said Ken.

I told Ken I would accept.

"Let's finish this off with a little B&B," said Ken, as he motioned to the waiter to take their drink order. "I am looking forward to working with a second generation of the Booker family."

CHAPTER 57

I told Mom about my meeting with Ken Thatcher, and she was curious as to how he was. She had heard that he was back and that things in the Philippines had gotten pretty messy for him, what with picking the wrong side in the presidential election.

"He looks great," I told Mom. "He is still the silver fox. He wants me to work for him and says something very big is about to happen, but he can't say just what."

Mom said that Ken had a tendency to drink too much but that he seemed to be one of those rare people in whom it did not show.

"Of course, eventually, it will catch up with him," she said.

"He speaks very highly of you and wanted to know all about your marriage," I said. "I told him you were very happy and that Conrad was a fantastic guy."

"Well, that is the truth," Mom said.

"He said he was very happy for you and that you were the best," I said.

"I think you will get some good experience with Ken, and he can teach you a lot, but make sure you don't get dragged down into his lifestyle," Mom warned.

Of course, that is exactly what happened. In February of 1967, Ken told me he had been offered the job as commissioner of the newly formed National Professional Soccer League, with headquarters in New York. He said he wanted me to be his deputy at a salary of $25,000 a year. I said I did not know anything about soccer, and Ken said he didn't either. Ken explained that he had interviewed for the job because of his former associate and longtime friend Pete Rozelle, now the highly regarded commissioner of the National Football League. Ken said that two of the owners of the fledgling NPSL had asked Rozelle if he knew anyone he thought would be a good commissioner—who could help sell the game to the American public and who had a lot of skills with the media. Pete, who had worked for Ken on the Melbourne Olympics, said he had just the man they were looking for, Ken Thatcher. The NPSL owners flew Ken to New York and after a day of meetings gave him a three-year contract at $80,000 a year. Ken said he thought I would be a good assistant, because I was single, knew sports, and was creative and hardworking.

Ken himself worked sixty- to seventy-hour weeks (if you counted drinking with business associates), and the silver fox was not a lone wolf, as I was to learn. He wanted me at his side most of the time to keep track of promises made. Occasionally, that included social drinking with his pal Pete Rozelle, who, I have to say, was the most charismatic person I had ever met. Together, Pete and Ken were a formidable pair who loved to get together after work and have drinks. Both were great storytellers, and it was fascinating to hear them talk. I seldom opened my mouth except to laugh or ask a question. Pete, who liked his drinks as much as Ken, had rules about drinking. Number one was never to drink in the same establishment more than once a week. That way, if he had a few too many, the owner (inevitably the owner took care of Pete) could say it never happened more than once a week.

Another close friend of Pete's was Bill MacPhail, vice president of CBS Sports; Pete and Bill had negotiated the NFL's first big television contract together. CBS had signed the NPSL to a one-year contract for $1 million, and I was ultimately made the league contact with CBS. By coincidence, I rented an apartment at 201 East 66th Street only to find that MacPhail also lived there, on the very same floor. I spent a lot of time at CBS and with Bill and the people who worked for him, mostly the producers and directors of the NPSL game of the week. I also got to know CBS sportscasters such as Pat Summerall, Jack Whitaker, and Frank Gifford, all of whom matched Bill drink for drink when invited. One night at the

21 Club, Bill fell asleep, facedown in his soup. It was amazing how fast the 21 staff got Bill up from the table and into a limo. I asked Summerall if someone should go with Bill, and he said not to worry; the 21 staff knew where he lived, and they would get him safely inside his apartment. Apparently, this was not the first time Bill had been overserved.

MacPhail was the son of Larry MacPhail, a well-known baseball executive, and the brother of Lee MacPhail, who subsequently became president of the American League. Bill, a bachelor, was known and liked by virtually everyone in the world of professional sports. Through Ken, Pete, and Bill, I must have met hundreds of sports celebrities, the kind who flocked to Toots Shor's, always stopping by to say hello to Rozelle or MacPhail.

Pete Rozelle was married at the time, but his wife, I was told, was in a sanitarium, so Pete was free a lot at night. That meant that when he met people for drinks, it would often turn into dinner. I will never forget one night when I was having a drink after work with Ken's secretary, Barbara Driscoll, in the bar of the Warwick Hotel, where we had set up our temporary offices. Rozelle and MacPhail came in for a drink and asked if they could join us. I think they both took a fancy to Barbara, who was young and lovely and could hold her own in any circumstance. The party lasted until 11:00 AM the next day, having moved from the Warwick to the 21 Club for dinner, to Shor's for drinks, to MacPhail's apartment, to a jazz joint, to Rozelle's apartment, and finally to my apartment. I don't remember everything that happened, but I do recall somehow being encouraged to put on my German accent while spoofing mutual friends of Pete and Bill whom I did not know. The calls we made were mostly to West Coast friends, because it was two or three in the morning in New York.

"Vee understand zat you have engaged in zertain zexual improprieties about vich vee must inform your vife," I recall saying to Ken Flowers, a West Coast broadcaster for CBS who had been an All-American basketball player at USC and was a close friend of Bill's.

I carried on the charade with Ken until he finally said, "Who the hell is this?"

Then Bill came on the line laughing the laugh of an all-night drinker. There must have been six or eight similar calls that night. A lot of the people were in bed asleep when the call came. It all seemed very funny at the time, especially with a dozen or so drinks apiece under our belts.

I think Barbara was the nucleus holding our little group together that night. All of us later tried to get her into bed. I failed, despite a valiant effort. Barbara said it was a mistake to have a sexual relationship with someone from the same office. I don't know about Pete or Bill, but Pete may have been successful. Barbara liked Pete a lot.

Alas, the party broke up on a sour note. Pete refused to go to a restaurant for breakfast, as Bill was suggesting. Bill got so upset he began to cry. But Pete had the good sense not to be seen in public after an all-nighter.

Years later, I saw Pete in San Francisco and reminded him of that night. He smiled and said he remembered it well.

"We don't have as much fun as we used to," he said, smiling.

By then Pete had remarried and cleaned up his act. His new wife made sure Pete's drinking pals were seldom around for her high-toned social gatherings. Meanwhile, MacPhail quit drinking sometime in the 1980s and spent the rest of his career working for Ted Turner's CNN as president of sports. Alas, both Pete and Bill are dead now, but I knew them when they seemed invincible.

Although working for the soccer league was fun, it was an ill-starred venture from the start. The players who signed to play in the league were mostly washed-up former stars from Europe. Unscrupulous European agents convinced the naïve American owners to pay these aging stars large salaries, much more than they would have commanded at home. The result was that the caliber of play was mediocre at best, despite the owners' belief that they were bringing in first-rate talent.

Making matters worse, CBS hired a former English soccer great, Danny Blanchflower, to announce the games. Danny, whom I got to know pretty well, was used to watching first-class soccer, and he repeatedly characterized NPSL play as the equivalent of fourth-division English soccer, or football, as Danny and everyone else in the world calls what we Americans call soccer. The owners were furious that Blanchflower would disparage what they were trying to sell as major-league soccer.

Actually, the television ratings that first year were decidedly better than the average attendance. Research showed that the listeners loved Blanchflower for his irreverent commentary and candor, commodities uncommon among American sportscasters.

In 1967, you could not get people to come to the games even if you gave away the tickets. I even hired a guy to see if he could pad the house at Yankee Stadium for a New York Generals game, and he spent two weeks giving away thousands of tickets, but less than 4,000 showed up at the game. You understand the meaning of the word "pathetic" when you stand on the field at Yankee Stadium at game time and see only 4,000 people in the stands, which then had room for 73,000. The only consolation was that I got to stand at home plate where Babe Ruth and all of the other Yankee immortals had stood, imagining what it would be like to sock one into the seats down the right field line.

As that first season reached its conclusion in September of 1967, it was clear that soccer was not going to be the success the owners had hoped. Losses that year were probably upward of $30 million. Meanwhile, I had gained twelve pounds from all of the eating and drinking. I loved the partying, especially being with fascinating people, but I did not like what I felt like when I got up the next morning. I would come to the office looking like hell and feeling worse, whereas Ken, who had probably drunk a lot more the previous night, was always clear-eyed and fresh, another reminder that life was not fair.

Ken performed heroically in the lost cause, snagging numerous interviews with top newspaper columnists, making radio and television appearances, and keeping the increasingly agitated owners under a semblance of control. He also ran the board meetings with skill and oversaw player discipline with a sometimes-severe hand, dealing suspensions and stiff fines for dirty play.

His greatest success was engineering a merger with the rival United Soccer League, which had planned to open its first season in 1968. He also carried out the owners' instructions to have CBS get rid of Blanchflower in favor of someone who would be more supportive and positive. When the rival owners of the two leagues could not decide who should be commissioner of the combined league, known as the North American Soccer League, Ken suggested that he be made chairman and that Dick Walsh, his counterpart at the United Soccer League, be named president. Ken further suggested that Walsh stay in New York, and Ken would move our office to San Francisco. How the owners bought that I could never understand. Of course, they kept the two former commissioners, because each had an unbreakable three-year contract and in any case would have to be paid.

Bill MacPhail told the owners that one reason CBS was opting for another season, despite heavy losses, was because I had done a fantastic job coordinating matters between the league and the network. I think Bill thought my job might have been at stake.

So Ken and I moved back to San Francisco in January of 1968. The only problem was I had rented out my apartment for a year and could not get back in until April 1. Mom suggested that I stay at the Sutro mansion, saying that Conrad was insisting on it. So there I was, thirty-two years old, single, and living back with Mom. More worrisome was that I knew my job with Ken was not going to last beyond the end of the 1968 season.

CHAPTER 58

I am going to skip ahead to 1970. That was when my mother was diagnosed with breast cancer. She was only fifty-six years old. The year before, her own mother, Mary Teresa Cosgrove Connors, had died of heart failure in Boston at age eighty-six. Mother had been with my grandmother for her last month and was at her bedside when she finally died, a simple, undemanding woman who believed she was about to join her husband in heaven.

"She was at peace and was looking forward to ending what she considered a blessed and full life," said Constance to those who asked. "Her body was worn out, but her mind and spirit were bright right until the end. It was as peaceful a death as you could ever imagine."

My mother's first reaction to the news that she had cancer was mostly surprise. Then she thought there was now no guarantee she would reach eighty-six. Before this, she had always enjoyed good health; she exercised a lot and kept her weight under control, she did not eat sweets or sugar, she avoided fats, and she ate a lot of fruits and vegetables. She drank wine, but never smoked. Plus, many members of both her father's and her mother's families had lived into their eighties.

"I suppose we can never know why these things happen," Constance wrote in her diary.

> God may have decided I needed a bump in the road. God knows that I have been very lucky in my life—three wonderful sons, two wonderful husbands, three perfect grandchildren, hundreds of good friends, good health, decent looks, and good fortune. I have been far more fortunate than so many people I know and I have always felt grateful to God that He has given me so much. I don't know what I have done to deserve such luck. Nothing, really—it is just the luck of the draw, I suppose.
>
> Dr. Boothby is recommending that my right breast be completely removed and I am having a hard time with giving up a part of me. He said he might get by removing only the tumor but he said he did not recommend it and that it was a lot less risky for the long run to remove the entire breast. He said that for the long run the removal of both breasts was the safest and smartest approach. I am not going to decide anything until I

> talk with more people. Conrad agrees and he is urging me to go to Stanford Hospital for another opinion. Dr. Boothby says I need to make a decision quickly, because even though only a small amount of cancer was revealed in the biopsy, there is a real danger that it can grow rapidly and spread to the lymph nodes. Thank goodness Dr. Boothby promised me he would not automatically do a radical mastectomy if they found cancer in the biopsy operation. One of the girls in my club went in for a biopsy last year and came out with her left breast completely removed. She said it was the normal practice if they discovered cancer. After that, even though her cancer had not spread, she had to undergo radiation therapy just in case there was still some cancer left. She was exhausted for months from the radiation. Dr. Boothby said that it was the current best medical thinking to be very aggressive in dealing with breast cancer. He said my cancer was an early stage type, but still it needed to be dealt with as swiftly as possible.

In the end, Constance opted for a lumpectomy rather than having her entire breast removed. The surgery was done by Dr. Frank Sullivan at Stanford, who believed that the medical profession was too prone to do radical mastectomies when a removal of only the cancerous tissue was often all that was needed, if indeed the cancer had not already spread. He had reached that conclusion when his own wife was diagnosed with breast cancer and had a radical mastectomy. She was only thirty-three and was so traumatized by her loss that she ended up deeply depressed and had to undergo a year of psychotherapy. Dr. Sullivan was thus intimately aware of the psychological damage that losing a breast could cause, especially to young women such as his wife (most readers may know that the practice of removing breasts during biopsy procedures has been ended and that radical mastectomies are today far less common than they were thirty-five years ago).

Mom's experience with breast cancer caused a major change in her life. Not long after her operation, she wrote in her diary that she felt something was missing. It was not love. She knew Conrad adored her, and she loved him very much, as she did the rest of her family, including her three young grandchildren produced by Claire and Joe. Of course, her big disappointment was that neither Jim nor I was married. Beyond that, she felt she needed to be making more of a contribution. She took good care of Conrad, and she knew that what she did, sometimes just being there, was important to him. She also helped with the grandchildren, but Claire had quit working, and Joe was writing at home, so there were no urgent needs there.

Her years as a working mother and, later, her years with her catering business had been demanding and had left her with little idle time. But since her marriage to Conrad, she had stopped working and spent most of her time having fun, going to sports events, sailing, traveling, playing tennis and golf, and attending a never-ending round of parties with Conrad's Pacific Heights friends and old pals from Stanford. Oh, there were breaks. Conrad bought a house at Pebble Beach and joined the Cypress Point Golf Club, and they went there for a weekend at least once a month, often alone, but sometimes with one or two other couples. Constance loved it when they went alone, sitting by a fire at night, walking on the beach, or playing golf as a twosome. They also spent a few days at the winery in Napa once a month. Conrad liked to have dinner parties at home five or six times a year, usually inviting sixteen to twenty people. Once a year, Conrad gave a huge cocktail party at home for three hundred people.

Constance liked it all and worked hard to make each event a success, but there lurked a sense of guilt about living so well. She did not think her father would have approved of her affluent lifestyle. Her dad, the Rev. Connors, had told her that life was the process of overcoming challenges and doing the Lord's work, and although Constance had never bought into organized religion, deep down what her father had said still resonated. As a young wife and working mother, she had felt fulfilled. Now, after nearly six years of marriage and a series of seemingly endless social events, she yearned to do something really useful. She had no idea how much longer she was going to live. Suddenly, her cancer had made that an issue. She had not followed the prevailing opinion in treating her cancer. It could strike again at anytime. Maybe the cancer was God's way of telling that she should take a fresh look at herself. Maybe God did not believe in all of the high living she had engaged in since marrying Conrad Sutro.

Of course, Conrad, "to a manor born," felt no guilt. He was happy with his life, and he counted himself very lucky for finding someone like Constance, whom he loved more now than when they first married. He took his money and his lifestyle for granted. Conrad also loved helping people buy and sell their dreams. He vicariously enjoyed seeing people find a home in the best section of the world's best city. Conrad had enough money that he did not have to work, but he loved what he did. All of the social events and networking were part of his job. He enjoyed every minute of it. That was not true of Constance. Though she found many of Conrad's set both attractive and interesting, her dearest friends remained Claudia and Richard Hamblen, whom she saw often.

"I feel like I have to find what is missing," she wrote in her diary. "I love being married to Conrad, and I love being a grandmother, but I need something else. I just wish I knew what it was."

CHAPTER 59

The late 1960s and early 1970s brought shocking change to America. The Communist TET offensive in South Vietnam in January of 1968 ignited widespread antiwar sentiments and a growing loss of confidence in American leadership, even though Communist losses were vastly exceeding those of the Allies. Lyndon Johnson decided not to seek another term so that he could concentrate on winning the war.

The assassination of the popular civil rights leader Martin Luther King Jr., in April of 1968, was followed two months later by the murder of Robert Kennedy, the likely Democratic candidate for president. The two deaths stunned the nation. America had lost two great leaders.

And then there was the fluke of the 1968 presidential election. Alabama governor George Wallace had abandoned the Democratic Party to run for president on a third-party ticket. Republican Richard Nixon, running on a law and order platform, won the election with a popular vote of 31.7 million, in comparison with 30.9 million votes for Democrat Hubert Humphrey, who had been vice president to President Johnson. Wallace polled 9.9 million votes, a majority of which likely would have gone to Humphrey had Wallace stayed in the Democratic ranks.

So Nixon entered the White House in January of 1969 having received only 43 percent of the popular vote. Many people respected

Nixon for his intelligence and general competence, but he was not a beloved figure. In fact, he was much easier to hate. Our family, and we had all watched Nixon closely since his days as a congressman, saw him as a positive and patriotic leader whose strong points outweighed his lack of charisma. Indeed, he created an alliance with China and eventually got us out of the war in Vietnam, but there was a lot of turmoil on his watch, principally the ongoing struggle in Vietnam. A sidelight to that time was the horrible 1969 disclosure of the murder of actress Sharon Tate and others at the hands of the satanic family of Charles Manson. The grisly details dominated the headlines for months. In all, Manson and his young followers claimed to have murdered thirty-five people. For some, the Manson episode symbolized America out of control.

Even more wrenching in 1970 was the news that National Guardsmen had opened fire on 1,000 war protestors at Kent State University in Ohio, killing four students and wounding eight. The previous week, Nixon had expanded the war by ordering U.S. troops into Cambodia to go after North Vietnamese soldiers. Meanwhile, peace talks were underway in Paris. Even so, war protests continued across the country. Young American men did not want to be drafted to fight a war that a majority of Americans did not support.

Clearly, the world was on the threshold of great change. In 1970, the population of the world was 3.7 billion, and there were 203 million living in America. Thirty years later, the world's population rose to 6.45 billion, and the United States grew to 296.4 million.

Despite the turmoil and change in the world, life went on pretty much as usual for the Bookers. Constance had just survived her cancer operation and was actively looking for a new challenge in her life. The National Professional Soccer League folded at the end of the 1968 season, and I, at the recommendation of Richard Hamblen and with the enthusiastic approval of my stepfather, Conrad Sutro, decided to become a stockbroker. I joined a trainee program at Sutro & Co., an old-line San Francisco firm with which Conrad had no connection. I could have stayed with Ken Thatcher, but I was tired of public relations. Fortunately, I had saved a good bit of money that enabled me to get through my first two years as a broker.

Jim continued to work in Los Angeles as sales manager for the television firm and was making a lot of money. Joe's fourth book had just been published and was expected to sell 70,000 copies in hardback and about 250,000 in paperback. Joe worked at home and could look out on San Francisco Bay as he concocted plots for his exciting tales of life as a foreign correspondent, not as he lived it, but how he fancied others had. Joseph Booker III had been born on December 30, 1964, and Robyn Booker had followed on March 15, 1966, with Karen arriving June 20, 1968. Joe wrote about four hours a day and spent a lot of time taking care of the children. When Joe had to leave to do research, my mother would volunteer to babysit. The kids loved her.

Claire had taken a part-time job three afternoons a week as a volunteer in the headquarters of the Salvation Army. "I do it, because it preserves my sanity," Claire told me one night at dinner. I spent a lot of time with the Joe Booker family in those years. I loved being around them all, and I ate there at least once a week. Joe was the most intelligent and well-informed person I knew, and he invariably had a fresh or novel take on the events of the day.

Little Joe, as we called Joe III, had an incredible vocabulary, and by the time he was five, he spoke in complex and compound sentences. At age six, he was reading books on animals and the nature of life and the universe. He said he wanted to be a doctor when he grew up. Robyn was less precocious than Little Joe, but she was pretty and blonde and seemed to take after her grandmother, Constance. Karen, as a two-year-old, had a very chubby body and an even larger personality that commanded attention for her every whim. Claire was a conscientious but demanding mother who was a much stronger disciplinarian than Joe. Television was limited to one hour a day.

My mother and Conrad Sutro were frequent visitors there, and they often entertained all of us at "the mansion," which is how we referred to the Sutro home. Conrad was delighted with the wonderful sense of family created by Joe and Claire and the children. Of course, we talked about all of the issues of the day. Joe remained hawkish on Vietnam and staunchly pro-Nixon. Conrad increasingly thought America should abandon the war, quoting one of his friends as saying "Let's quit and say we won." We all agreed that Nixon's overtures to China were a stroke of genius that had huge implications for the balance of power with the Soviet-led Communist bloc.

Conrad was very helpful to me as I sought to establish myself as a stockbroker, recommending me to friends as well as tipping me off to information he had picked up on Bay Area companies whose shares were sold publicly. Richard Hamblen was equally helpful, and I never saw him when I did not ask him if he had any stock tips. Richard was the first to recommend Hewlett Packard to me, on which I made lots of money for my clients, including a bit for myself. Richard said the most important thing I could do was establish relationships with a number of leading Bay Area companies that had growth potential. He said that it was tough to miss in California, what with the incredible growth in population. San Francisco's population was holding steady at about 760,000, but the metropolitan area around it was growing rapidly. Richard thought that Bank of America and Pacific Gas and Electric were sure bets on the burgeoning California economy. He also liked IBM and McDonald's.

Conrad Sutro gave me $200,000 to manage for him in late 1969, saying I was free to make whatever trades I wanted. He said he would judge after the end of the first year whether he had made the right decision. By the end of 1971, I had built Conrad's account up to $261,000. Conrad was delighted and recommended me to still more of his friends. I regularly consulted with Richard Hamblen, who, because of the recommendations he had given me, in fact was responsible for at least half of Conrad's gains. I hasten to add that no insider information was involved.

By the end of 1972, I had 232 clients and was earning upward of $60,000 a year, not counting what I gained in my own stock account. Jim and Joe both opened accounts with me, and so did Glen Albaugh, my former boss at WOAK. Ken Thatcher came aboard, and so did several of Ken's friends. I spent time in San Jose, visiting with several old friends who were in the auto business running their own agencies. My good friend Jim Wiles, who now owned four auto agencies, gave me $50,000 to manage, saying he would give more, but he needed his capital for future dealership acquisitions. Two other former Spartans who had become car dealers, Don Marcus and Bob Walsh, had been investing their profits in Santa Clara county real estate, which was rapidly rising in value. Fifteen years out of college, both were already multimillionaires. I talked each into diversifying with a small amount of their assets to be invested in Santa Clara County companies. Bob and Don knew a lot of successful San Jose people, and through them I added still more clients and sources for stock tips.

Nixon was reelected in a landslide in 1972, gaining 46.7 million votes to only 28.9 million votes for the hapless George McGovern. He won the electoral vote by a crushing 520 to 17. The Dow Jones 30 Industrials topped 1,000, and my clients were all making handsome profits. My work kept me so busy that I hardly had time for dates. But I very badly wanted to find the right girl and settle down and raise a family. There were plenty of girls who seemed attracted to me, but the ones I was attracted to were not that interested in me. I did not have the movie star good looks I was looking for in a partner. Was I really looking for a perfect someone like my mother?

CHAPTER 60

I met Veronica Rodgers in April of 1973 at the Sutro mansion. Veronica was a distant relative of Conrad Sutro, though he had never met or heard of her until she called his office one day, saying that she was David Rodgers's daughter. David Rodgers was a third cousin to Conrad whom he had met only once on a trip with his family back to Cleveland before World War II. Veronica told Conrad she was on vacation, traveling alone, and was going to be in San Francisco for a week. She said she worked for a travel agency in

Cleveland and wanted to get to know everything she could about San Francisco given that it was a popular tourist attraction, and she thought seeing it firsthand would her help in her business. Veronica said her father had suggested she give Conrad a call before she embarked on her trip to ask for some suggestions. Conrad insisted that no relative of his was going to stay in a hotel and that she had to stay at his house.

"You will love my wife, Constance," Conrad told Veronica. "She knows more about San Francisco than anyone I know."

Veronica arrived at midday, and Constance picked her up at the airport. Mom called me afterward and asked me to come that night to their house for dinner.

"What is Veronica like?" I asked.

"She is very quiet but is a very intent listener," Mom answered.

"Is she good-looking?" I asked.

"Not in any classical way, but there is an intangible something about her that makes her attractive," Mom said.

"How old is she?"

"Mid-twenties, I would guess."

When I first saw Veronica, I was a bit disappointed. Her skin was pale and had some acne scars. She wore her almost scruffy brown hair short and had slim hips and long legs that did not quite match her oversized bosom. Her mouth was small, and so was her chin. She was tall, maybe five-seven, and she had small hands and feet. She was definitely not a classical beauty.

Veronica said very little at dinner, at least at the outset. Conrad asked about her parents. She said that they divorced when she was five and that they had no other children. Her father, she said, worked as a salesman for a tool manufacturer, and her mother had died twelve years earlier of an accidental overdose of sleeping pills.

"I'm sorry to hear that; it must have been very difficult for you," said Constance.

"Actually, it did not change much; I already lived with my father," Veronica said. "My mother was an alcoholic. She was better off dead."

Constance reached over and put her arm around Veronica.

"You poor dear, what a thing to have to experience," said Constance.

"It made me stronger, I guess," said Veronica. "My father was away a lot during the week on sales trips, and my aunt used to come over and stay with me. She taught me yoga and meditation. I still do them every day."

Veronica took off her glasses and looked in turn at Conrad, Constance, and then me. Her large eyes were a dark brown, and her pupils seemed oversized. She looked almost beautiful, the very dark eyes contrasting against the ashen skin that suddenly seemed to have taken on a healthy glow in the candlelight. She reminded me of one of those paintings by the San Francisco artist Walter Keane, the paintings featuring little girls with huge, soulful eyes.

"Now you know," she said, falling into silence and looking down at her napkin.

Veronica was certainly a study in contrasts—strong yet fragile. Overriding it all was an air of seeming detachment, an existence devoid of emotion. But was that right?

Conrad and my mother did most of the talking that night, telling Veronica about all of the places in the city that she should see.

Veronica nodded with excitement as they planned out the next three days.

"I have to work," I said. "But I'm free at night and would be happy to show you around to some of the places that Mom and Conrad won't take you."

"You don't have to do that," said Veronica.

"No, I want to," I said. "I insist on it."

Veronica smiled. It was the first time all evening that I had seen her break into a full grin. She had nice teeth.

"We're going down to Pebble Beach for the weekend," said Constance. "You'll love it down there. You have to come with us, Veronica. Maybe we can talk Danny into coming too."

"I may have a problem with that," I said, not certain I wanted to go.

At ten o'clock, Veronica said she was tired, because she was still on Eastern time, and had to do her yoga exercises before she went to sleep.

"This is exactly what I'm going to do," said Constance.

"Danny's going to join me for a brandy so that we can talk about the stock market," said Conrad. "I'm afraid this stupid Watergate business is going to destroy the market."

I came by to pick up Veronica at seven the next night. It was remarkably warm for an April evening, with the temperature still in the sixties and no sign of the usual fog.

"I have a lot of things we can do, but let me first ask you what you want to do," I said.

"I want to walk around the Haight-Ashbury district, go to a strip club, visit a porn shop, and go to a gay bar," said Veronica. "Those are all things I've heard San Francisco is famous for, and I would like to have the experience," she said.

"Ha, very funny," I said. "I have not done any of those things either, except I've been in a porn shop—I will admit that."

"You don't have to take me to those kinds of places," said Veronica.

"No, it sounds like fun, but I think we should have dinner first," I said.

As it turned out, our dinner at the folksy New Pisa restaurant in North Beach stretched out over more than three hours, and we never went anywhere afterward, except a block away to a small bar, not gay, to have a nightcap. Veronica was a lot more talkative than she had been the night before. It turned out she was twenty-eight and had reached the stage in life where she realized that time was passing her by, and she was experiencing a growing feeling that she had to be more adventurous and live life to the fullest.

"I've always been very conservative, afraid to do things, afraid to say what I think," she told me. "Actually, I am not very good at conversation, because words just don't flow from me like they do with others—like you, for example."

"I'm not an extrovert, and I don't think you are deep down an introvert," I said.

"What if I told you that I am still a virgin?" she asked.

"At twenty-eight in this day and age of free love?" I smiled.

"I've been with boys and men, but I have never gone all the way," she said. "Each time I think I might, something always happens, or I suddenly get a change of heart. I don't have a healthy outlook on sex. I think it's because of my parents. When I was very young, I saw my parents doing it, but my mother got mad at my father when he stopped, and she swore at him and said he was not much of a man. I guess he was impotent, at least that night.

"My mother started drinking a lot, and she brought men home during the day, and several times, I saw her doing it. One time, she caught me watching, and she jumped up naked and called me a nosey little brat. I could see the man's thing, and it seemed huge, all red and slimy. I got sick to my stomach. It wasn't long after that that my parents divorced, and my father and I moved into an apartment in a nice section of Cleveland."

"What were you, about five?" I asked.

"Yes—I don't know why I'm telling all of this to you. It must be the wine," she said. "How old are you?"

"I am almost thirty-eight," I said.

"Have you ever been married?" she asked.

"No, no one ever wanted me badly enough," I said.

"That's a joke," she said. "Have you ever lived with a woman?"

"I've restricted myself to sleepovers," I replied.

"You never wanted to get married?"

"I didn't say that, but it takes two to make a marriage, and I guess I just have not found the right person. My friends say I am too picky. One girl told me I would never get married, because I judged all women by my mother, who everyone, including me, thinks is perfect."

"I can't believe she's almost sixty," Veronica said. "She is still very beautiful and wonderfully sweet. I can see where someone might say you would never find anyone like her."

Veronica gave me her whole life story, and I gave her mine. Veronica said she did not have many friends, but the few she had were good ones, all living back in Cleveland and married with children. She went to Ohio University and afterward went to work for Booth's Travel Agency in Cleveland, where she was still employed. She and her aunt, Henrietta Fenner, shared an apartment in Cleveland.

"I don't like to be alone, even though it seems I often am," she said. "That's why I like working for Booth's—people are always calling for help."

"Do you date much?" I asked.

"Most of the people I meet are married, and I don't hang out in bars or belong to a church, so I don't meet many men. I do belong to an exercise class, and I jog, which is how I've met most of the guys I've dated.

"I was engaged once to a policeman who had been married before and had two kids, but I broke it up because I don't think I really loved him. He was a very sweet and gentle person, surprising for a cop, a great big Irish guy who was like a teddy bear. He knew I was a virgin and said I should stay that way. He was a practicing Catholic."

Veronica said that she and her aunt went to the movies at least twice a week and that she read a lot, mostly magazines, but often the best sellers that her aunt got through her book club as well.

"Compared with yours, my life is pretty pathetic, but I really don't mind it," said Veronica. "It is just recently that I have had this itch to break out and do a lot of new things."

It was eleven o'clock when Veronica asked if I would take her home. She said she had enjoyed talking with me, and she thanked me for listening to her problems, but she was still jet-lagged.

I walked Veronica to the door and blurted out, "The more I look at you, the more beautiful you get."

She flashed a rare smile and said I was very sweet. I kissed her on the lips. She held her lips together, and the kiss did not last long.

"Would you like me to take you on a tour tomorrow night?" I asked.

"Okay, but you don't have to."

"No, I really want to," I said. She smiled again and disappeared inside the door.

As I drove home, I tried to figure out what it was about Veronica Rodgers that I found so attractive. After all, she was certainly no Constance Booker Sutro.

CHAPTER 61

By 1973, the Haight-Ashbury district was mostly over as a hip place. You could tell by the tour buses plying the sixteen square blocks that made up the once trendy area where the Grateful Dead performed free concerts and artists and writers sought to expand their thought processes with LSD. You could tell by the down-and-out look of the young people likely influenced by Dr. Timothy Leary, the Harvard professor who exhorted anyone who would listen to "turn on, tune in, and drop out." The first wave of hippies had long since departed to be replaced by a new wave, who came to party but brought little else.

"These people look so unhealthy and dirty," said Veronica as we walked down Haight Street near Buena Vista Park, heading toward Hippie Hill at the edge of Golden Gate Park. "This is the first disappointing thing I have seen in San Francisco," she said as we completed our hour-long trek.

"Well, if you want free love and drugs, you'll have no trouble finding them here," I said.

"I can just imagine what the rooms look like where these people are living," said Veronica.

"You have to be stoned, and then you won't notice the sordid details," I smiled. "You know, the same thing happened in North Beach along Grant Avenue, which became famous for the beatniks. It only lasted a few years. When a place goes from being cool to popular, the exodus of the truly hip begins."

"Shall we go to a gay bar?" Veronica asked.

"This is your night," I smiled. We drove over to Polk Street, a few blocks up from California, where I had been told we would have a choice of several gay bars.

Veronica was holding tightly to my arm when we entered. It was a medium-sized bar with perhaps twenty-five stools and eight or so tables in the back. It was a Friday night, and the place was packed, with two or three people standing around each bar stool. The noise level was that of a two-hour-old cocktail party.

"There is not another woman here except for the waitress," said Veronica, as we threaded our way through the crowd at the bar, heading for the lone empty table. Veronica got a few quizzical glances and a couple of winks, but no one said anything. I pretty much got the same thing. I ordered us each a martini on the rocks.

Our table faced the bar, so we could watch the action, and there was plenty of it going on.

"Most of these guys are very good-looking," said Veronica. "It is hard to believe they are all gay."

Just then, I felt a tapping on my shoulder. I turned around to see an older guy, maybe forty-five, smiling down at Veronica and me.

"What's your gig?" the man asked. "Whatever it is, it looks pretty interesting; do you mind if I join you?" He sat down before we could answer, saying his name was Brian Fitzsimmons.

"Danny Booker," I began, "and this is Veronica. Glad to have you join us," I finished, extending my hand. I expected a soft, clammy hand, but instead got a weight lifter's grip.

"We don't get many couples here, though we do get a few," said Brian. "A few years ago, I got friendly with one couple, and we had some pretty good times together. I think they got a bit of an education," he added, letting out a laugh.

"Veronica is just visiting San Francisco, and there are several things she wanted to see, one of which was a gay bar," I said.

"So you wanted to see what us queers look like," said Brian.

"I'm impressed by how many handsome and fit men there are in here," said Veronica.

"You have to stay trim to make it in the bar scene or the bathhouses," said Brian. "I spend five hours a week lifting weights, and I am very careful about my diet so I don't look like a flabby middle-aged old fool."

"It seems to be working for you," said Veronica. "You know, you don't look gay."

"Actually, dear, I was married for five years before I realized my heart was not really in it. I met a man, and he taught me things I enjoyed much more than what I did with my wife. I never looked back."

"So you don't consider yourself bisexual?" I asked.

"Once you try it, you never want anything else," said Brian.

"What happens in the bathhouses?" Veronica asked.

"You really don't know?" asked Brian. "To be honest, I don't go to them. It is pretty sordid—lots of men naked performing sexual acts on each other."

"Isn't that against the law?" Veronica asked.

"Yes, but it happens anyway," said Brian. "Can I buy you two a drink?"

"Thanks," I said, "but we have some other places we have to see."

"Let me invite you up to my apartment—it is only two blocks from here and has a nice view," said Brian. "I have some pictures from bathhouses, Veronica. You might like to see them. Have you ever been to a bathhouse, Danny?"

"Two or three times, but I didn't like it," I lied, getting a surprised look from Veronica. Brian said he did not believe me.

A couple dancing came near our table and began kissing, slowly at first and then with rising passion.

"Ah, young love. Two perfect specimens," said Brian, wistfully.

I stood up, smiling, and extended my hand to Brian while calling the waitress over for our check. I gave her $20 and said, "Buy my good friend Brian here a drink."

Brian smiled and said, "Well, it wasn't a complete waste of time." Turning to Veronica, he said, "I think you are a kindred spirit. I live a life where rejection is a constant."

Outside, the fog had rolled in, and it was almost ten o'clock. The streets were wet and quite lonely looking.

We drove over to North Beach, where I promised I could show her both a porn shop and a strip club.

"But first I have to eat," I said.

"I'm famished too," said Veronica. "What do you think that man meant when he said I was a kindred spirit?"

"Maybe he thought you were a closet lesbian," I laughed.

"I don't even know what lesbians do," she said.

"I'll show you once we get to the porn shop; they have sections for everything—gays, lesbians, couples, groups, you name it."

We ate at the counter of New Joe's restaurant, where we had sand dabs, a salad, and a plate of pasta and shared a bottle of Chianti.

"I guess I have lived a pretty sheltered life," said Veronica. "I still can't get over all of those men. Have you really been to a bathhouse?

I told Veronica that no, I had been joking, and that the thought of kissing a man made me want to throw up.

"One day, maybe twelve years ago, I was in a downtown building and had to use the rest room and happened to notice two sets of legs inside one of the toilet cubicles. One man was obviously sitting on the lap of the other. It literally made me sick. Another time, I was in a bathroom at a theater, and the line was moving very slowly, and one guy wasn't moving at all. When I finally got up to the urinal next to him, he was just standing there with a huge erection, just holding it. I couldn't believe it. I looked over at him and said, 'Move it before I call the cops.' I walked away, but he was still standing there. Lots of men seemed to be fascinated, but I wasn't. In other words, I have never been in a bathhouse."

"Sounds like an exhibitionist," said Veronica. "One time, I answered the door at our apartment for what I thought was a telephone repair man. The man was just standing there looking down at his penis. I slammed the door in his face. My aunt told me he was an exhibitionist and said that we should call the police, even though she said exhibitionists were usually harmless. I don't think the police ever caught the guy, because they never called back."

The porn shop was located only half a block away and was brightly lit with maybe fifteen or so people browsing around, mostly men, but a few women as well. The proprietor sat at an elevated checkout counter from which he could keep track of what was going on.

"Where would you like to start?" I asked, suddenly wondering to myself what my mother would think if she knew I had brought Veronica here, or even had visited by myself, for that matter. I let out a small laugh.

"Why are you laughing?" asked Veronica.

"I'll tell you later," I said. "Okay, let's start with the straight couples."

We spent more than an hour there. Veronica was fascinated. She went through all of the sections, including some movies that you could watch in a booth in the back that cost twenty-five cents for about five minutes of grainy action.

We both had had enough to drink that we had shed any inhibitions we might have had while sober. Inside the booth, I pressed against Veronica from the rear, placing my hands around her waist and my chin on her shoulder so that I could watch the movie too. She backed up slightly, right into my alert groin. She let out a soft "oh" and stepped forward, breaking contact.

"I can see you are aroused by pornography," Veronica smiled, turning her head to look back at me.

"Most men are," I said. "What about you?"

"Not really," she said. "I'm more interested in the physical aspects of the people and the stuff they are doing. I feel pretty detached from it. I really did not like the group things. It was like a bunch of animals. Those women can't have any self-respect. I think I learned a lot, some of which I didn't really need to know."

"On to the strip show," I said.

Actually, I took Veronica to a place that I had been told was more than a strip show. We got a table just in front of a dimly lit stage. We had to order champagne at $50 a bottle on top of a $10 cover charge for each of us. After about fifteen minutes, a couple came onto the stage and began to undress. The lights had been dimmed to a point where it was impossible to see very well. The show lasted about half an hour and was a great testimony to the man's staying power.

"I think they are really doing it," said Veronica. I knew they were. I watched Veronica as much as the couple on the stage. She was staring intently at the moving figures as they rotated around in pleasure. It was as hot an act as I have ever seen. (And a week later, the police raided the club and shut it down.) The crowd of about seventy-five people gave a loud round of applause when the act was over. The lights came up, and the pair took a nude curtain call amid shouts of bravo. The man looked like he was ready for another act!

"Thank you, Danny," said Veronica as we walked back to my car. "It was all a bit overwhelming, but educational and interesting and, I admit, quite entertaining." She put her arm around my shoulder and gave it a squeeze.

"Now that I have plied you with liquor and introduced you to the seamy side of San Francisco, perhaps you would like to see my apartment?" I asked.

"Sure," she said. "But I am not having sex with you."

And she didn't, much to the disappointment of my aching testicles.

CHAPTER 62

Veronica agreed to stay overnight with me after seeing that I had a comfortable guest bedroom. I think she trusted me enough when I said I had never raped a girl in her sleep at this apartment. I was too tired to drive Veronica home in any case. Constance and Conrad had driven to Pebble Beach that afternoon with the understanding that we might or might not join them there on Saturday. So there was no one waiting up for Veronica at the Sutro household. Before we went to bed, Veronica said that she had had one of the most interesting evenings of her life and that I was a very dear person to take her exactly where she wanted to go.

"I've done it, and I don't have to do it again," she said. "I think I have a lot better understanding of some things, and I have you to thank for that."

"Wisdom at 3:00 AM!" I said. "Time to go to bed." I was too tired to even brush my teeth, and I was asleep the instant my head hit the pillow.

The sun was hitting me in the face when I awoke. It was 10:30. Veronica was already up, and I quickly deduced she had cleaned my apartment, washed the dishes in the kitchen, and gone to the store for orange juice, eggs, bacon, and whole wheat bread. The bacon was cooking very slowly on the stove, the smell from which mixed nicely with the fresh air pouring through the open windows. Outside, it looked like a perfect late April day, blue skies and no fog.

"It is nice on a hill like this, being able to see so much of the city and the bay," said Veronica, sounding quite chipper, as I walked into the kitchen. "Did you sleep well?"

"I must have—I don't remember a thing. How about you?"

"I had some weird dreams, but I was wide awake at eight, so I got up," she said.

"Thanks for the cleaning up and the shopping," I said.

"I hope you don't mind that I threw some things out of the refrigerator," she said.

"I usually clean everything up on Saturday," I said. "I used to have a maid once a week, but she quit and I have been too lazy to replace her."

"You need someone to look after you," said Veronica, coming over to give me a hug, pressing her large breasts firmly against my chest. "Good morning."

"Good morning to you," I said. "You look pretty good in the morning." I gave her an extra squeeze, which was all it took to get my manhood preparing for action. For a virgin, Veronica seemed remarkably attuned to the male condition.

"I'm not changing what I said last night," she said.

I gave her a kiss on the lips and was surprised that she parted her lips and put some gusto into it.

"What makes you think I am interested in having sex with you just because you have great breasts and lovely long legs and dark eyes that look magical?" I said.

"I am not going to give in to the cheap desires created by sex acts and porn," she said.

"Wait a minute," I said. "Last night was all your idea, not mine."

"I said I wanted to see a strip show, not two people doing it ten feet away from me," she replied.

"I am sorry about that; I didn't realize it was a sex show," I said.

"Don't apologize—I liked it. It gave me a more intimate view of sex. In the dark, it did not seem as seedy at all. But it was still a cheap thrill."

"So it did get you aroused," I said.

"Were you aroused by it?" she asked.

"That's not hard to do," I said. "No pun intended."

"I guess I was aroused, if my dreams mean anything," she said.

"What did you dream?"

"I dreamt you and the man from the gay bar were both in bed and doing things to me that felt wonderful, and I was not protesting or fighting. Then you and the man started doing stuff to each other, and you stopped paying any attention to me, even when I tried to get in on the act. I felt like I was in a porn movie, and I felt rejected."

"I wish I was good at dream interpretations, but let me assure you that I am not getting into bed with Brian Fitz or whatever his name was or any other man, so you miscast me in your dreams," I said.

"There was also a woman in my dream who I'd never seen before, and she was sitting on the edge of the bed, shaking her head in disapproval and at the same time beckoning me to come to her. That's when I woke up."

"From virginity to group sex in one night," I said, smiling. "I guess your subconscious added the girl to provide some balance." Actually Veronica's dream seemed quite puzzling, perhaps significant. I put my arms around her and gave her a kiss that she returned for a full twenty seconds but then broke off.

"You're still under the influence of last night," she smiled. "Do you like your eggs straight up or over easy?"

Veronica said she would prefer to stay in the Bay Area rather than drive all the way to Pebble Beach that day, so we drove across the Golden Gate Bridge to Point Reyes, where the weather was quite blustery and cold. From there, we drove to Muir Woods, where it was warm and pleasant. Veronica was impressed by the majesty of the ancient redwood trees.

"The San Francisco Bay Area is so different from Cleveland," Veronica said. "There is so much to it. I could move here in a minute."

"You've seen a lot, but not everything by any means," I said. "Wait until you see the Sierras, Lake Tahoe, the wine country, Pebble Beach. There are so many great places—the Feather River, Mendocino, Russian River, Clear Lake, Mount Shasta, San Simeon, Palo Alto, Tiburon. The beauty of San Francisco is that there is so much to see, all within three or four hours, and some places, only thirty minutes to an hour."

Veronica looked at me with those soulful eyes as we stood in the deep shade of the huge trees.

"You really love it here, don't you?" she said, putting her face directly in front of mine.

There was no one around, so I put my arms around her and gave her a kiss.

"I bet you would like to do it right here behind those bushes," she laughed.

"Is that your idea?"

"No, but I am good at mind reading."

A family of six or seven came noisily up the path.

"Let's go up to the wine country," I said. "We can be there in an hour. There are a lot of good restaurants there, and it is a pretty drive."

"Ocean to forest to wine country all in two hours. Pretty neat," Veronica said.

"It is nice being with you," I said, giving her a hug, which like the earlier kiss was purely spontaneous. I don't know exactly why, but I found myself being increasingly attracted to her. Maybe it was because deep down I wanted to find someone to be my wife and have children. The trouble was I did not really know much about Veronica, except that she was a distant relative of Conrad Sutro and claimed to be a virgin at twenty-eight, a virgin who wanted to be introduced to graphic sex but did not seem anxious to get any firsthand experience.

I vowed to myself that over dinner and drinks I would find out more about her.

We had dinner at the St. Helena Inn, a romantic old place in the Napa Valley wine country. The temperature was in the seventies, and the sky was clear and full of stars.

"Another lovely place," said Veronica, taking my hand as we were escorted to our table overlooking a waterwheel and a pond.

I ordered a bottle of Sauvignon Blanc and some goat cheese and French bread to get us started.

"What is it like to live in Cleveland?" I asked Veronica.

"I think it can be nice," she said. "It depends what you like. The suburbs are very preppy, conservative, and Republican—everybody knows everybody if you are part of a certain crowd. I've known people who were fourth-generation Clevelanders who would never think of leaving. Most of them live in Shaker Heights, belong to country clubs, went to Ohio State or an Ivy League college, and have trust funds and usually like to drink a lot.

"We lived on the edge of Shaker Heights when I was growing up. But we were pretty isolated. My parents were never very social, according to my aunt. And my parents got a divorce when I was only five, and after that, I lived with my dad. He was pretty much an introvert, even though he is a salesman. My dad is very bright, and he knows a lot about complex machinery and engineering, which is why I think he has been successful in his work."

"My grandfather, Timothy Rodgers, married a second cousin of Adolph Sutro, or something like that," Veronica said. "I don't really know all of the details, and I have to get Conrad to fill me in. It was sort of out of the blue when my dad suggested I call Conrad for advice for my trip to San Francisco. Actually, it is about the best suggestion he has ever given me."

Veronica said she and her dad had never been close. He was gone a lot and did not say much when he was around. But she was close to her aunt, Henrietta, who was her mother's never-married sister.

"Henrietta has been great," said Veronica. "She is a little weird and likes to talk to the spirit world through a pendulum. She has worked thirty years as a secretary in a law firm, and she has had a boyfriend at the firm for twenty years. The trouble is he is married. They have been meeting once a week all this time. He says he is going to get a divorce, and Hen believes him. I don't."

I was beginning to get a clearer picture of Veronica. She obviously had had acne in high school, based on the scars on her face that somehow no longer seemed as noticeable to me as they had when we first met. She said she had never been invited to a high school dance. In college, she lived at home and worked part-time in a department store. She dated a bit but never had a steady boyfriend, not until she had graduated and gone to work. She did say she had a lot very nice girlfriends with whom she kept in touch, though the time they spent together was dwindling, because most of her friends were now married.

"We are talking too much about me," said Veronica. "You are the one who has had the interesting life."

"You've had a much tougher life than mine," I said. "But you have come through it pretty well. You have a good job that you like, and you are interested in seeing new places and learning new things. You have a lot of energy and enthusiasm. I have no doubt you are a very diligent travel agent."

"Tell me about being a stockbroker," she said. "You own a sensational apartment, and you drive a Jaguar convertible. You are a very interesting man and obviously very successful. I have to admit that when we first met, I wasn't so impressed. I mean that as a compliment. Actually, I have had people say that about me. Do you like me better now than when we first met?"

"I like you better now that I am getting to know you better," I said. She reached across the table and held my hand.

"Isn't that waterwheel beautiful?" she asked.

CHAPTER 63

We slept in the same bed and smooched a bit, but Veronica was so emphatic about no sex that I did not really pursue the matter. She was up by 6:00 AM and said she would love to see Pebble Beach.

"It's about a five-hour drive from here," I said.

"If we leave at seven o'clock, we could be there in time for lunch," she responded.

"Okay, we'll take the coast route, starting just south of San Francisco."

It was a beautiful sunny morning in St. Helena, and we drove with the top down. Veronica's short hair was whipped into a puffy frenzy, and she was clearly happy to be off on another adventure. Unfortunately, by the time we got to San Rafael, the fog was creeping over the mountains, and when we reached the Golden Gate Bridge, the fog was so thick you could not see the top half of the towers. We stopped in Golden Gate Park to put the top up and drove to Ocean Beach and then picked up Highway One. South of San Francisco, Highway One curves along steep cliffs some four to five hundred feet above the crashing sea. Veronica insisted we stop at Devil's Slide so that she could see the surf pounding into the rocks below.

The wind was blowing, and it was cold and damp. Veronica put her arm around me for warmth and squeezed hard. I suggested we get back in the car, and she insisted we stay a few minutes longer.

"This is nature in the raw," she said. "It's beautiful. I love the fog and the ocean."

"It can be a bit depressing in large doses," I said.

We did not get to Carmel until two in the afternoon, having made several stops along the way, one of which was my doing. I could see that the surf was up as we drove past Davenport above Santa Cruz, so I made a little detour to show Veronica "Steamer Lane," a popular surfing spot at the north end of Santa Cruz. Veronica said she had never seen people surfing on big waves, and standing on a low cliff as surfers whizzed by parallel to the shore scarcely thirty yards away thrilled her. The surf was breaking at about ten feet, and there were a number of wipeouts that caused Veronica to let out a loud "ooohhhh."

"Do they ever drown?" she asked.

"They get hurt, but a drowning is very rare, especially among the kind of surfers you see here," I replied. "They never surf alone, and they are always watching out for each other. Of course, every once in a while, you read about a surfer being attacked by a great white shark. Sometimes they escape with just a lost limb, but sometimes they don't."

"Are there any Great Whites around here?" Veronica asked.

"Once in a while, someone sees one," I said. "Some people say the sharks confuse the surfers with sea lions because of their black suits. But who knows the mind of a shark?"

"Who knows the mind of anybody?" Veronica said. "I don't even know my own mind."

We drove through Santa Cruz and then south via Watsonville and on to Fort Ord, where I had undergone basic training with the U.S. Army eighteen years earlier. It was an exhilarating experience every time I drove past Fort Ord, so much had I hated my time as a recruit in the army.

"I never realized how spoiled I was until I got into the army," I said. "I don't think I inherited any of my father's genes. He went to West Point, and I am sure that he went through all of the crap they handed out at Fort Ord."

"Did you know your father pretty well?" Veronica asked. I told her everything I remembered about him.

"No wonder your mother loved him so much," said Veronica. "She told me about your father the day after I arrived, when we were touring the Presidio. She showed me where you lived, and she also showed me the house in the Sunset where you moved in 1939."

"You know all about my past," I said.

"Yes, your mother could not stop talking about you growing up, your baseball, your time in Europe, your radio show, your time in New York, and your success as a stockbroker," said Veronica. "She said she was blessed that all of her sons had turned out well and that she was herself very fortunate to be surrounded by people who she loved and who loved her."

"My mother is a remarkable woman," I said.

"I wish I was one-tenth of what she is," said Veronica.

"Now you are fishing for a compliment," I smiled.

"You caught me," she laughed. "But not really."

When we arrived in Carmel, Mother and Conrad were having tea on the terrace of their cottage, which was located on a wooded half acre along the famous 17-Mile Drive that winds from the highway down to the ocean.

"You have such beautiful homes," said Veronica.

"Conrad likes to keep this his refuge, informal and relaxing," said Constance. "It suits his nature."

"How about a real drink, Danny boy?" Conrad asked. "I want to hear what you two have been up to."

I said a beer would be fine, and Veronica asked for tea. I told them what we had seen and done, and Veronica jumped in to rave about the surfers and the stark beauty along the cliffs of Highway One. She repeated that she would love to live in the Bay Area.

"Veronica, dear, you are looking quite lovely," said Constance. "I think the fresh air agrees with you." I wondered if my mother was imagining that Veronica was glowing from several nights of sex with her wonderful son. What a laugh!

We had dinner at a small restaurant in Carmel. Conrad and I drank a lot of wine and talked about the slowing down of the stock market as a result of the confusion created by the Watergate scandal.

"I think the market is going to be headed south," he said. "I think you might consider putting more money into cash until everything is settled."

"That's funny that you say that, because Richard Hamblen and I were talking about the same thing last Friday," I said.

"Hamblen in a very wise man," said Conrad.

"I intend to have my customers 80 percent in cash by next week, including you," I said, adding, "We will be taking some nice long-term profits."

I overheard my mother ask Veronica if she ever wore her hair longer.

Veronica said she had always worn it short, because she liked never having to do anything with it. "I don't wear much makeup, just mascara and some lipstick, and I guess I don't spend much time on grooming."

"Good for you," said Constance. "You have to be your own person."

"To be honest, I never felt there was much I could do about my appearance," said Veronica. "I had a pretty bad case of acne in high school, and it didn't really clear up until college, and then it left some scarring."

"Have you ever tried to do anything about it?" Constance asked.

"I've tried some creams, but they did not do much good, and I refuse to cover my face with pancake makeup like some girls I have known. It makes them look like prostitutes!"

"Veronica, I think you are a very attractive person," said Constance. "I want to do some checking with a friend a mine about those scars, which, frankly, I hardly notice. Your eyes attract all of the attention. They are so dark and beautiful and large."

"Thank you," said Veronica, looking down. "You are very kind to say that."

I told my mother that night at the cottage that Veronica and I would be sleeping in separate bedrooms, and when she raised an eyebrow, I told her we were not sleeping together.

"She says she is still a virgin," I said.

"My, that is unusual from what I read about young people today," she said. "But it is also nice. I was a virgin before I met your father. On the other hand, I wasn't twenty-eight. Even in my day, I don't think many girls held out that long."

We all drove back to San Francisco on Monday morning. My mother took Veronica on a tour of the Mission District on Monday afternoon, and they visited Mission Delores. The Mission District in those days was growing ever more ethnic, but in the 1970s it was a lot seedier and less trendy than it has become today. Apparently, Veronica and Mother did a lot of talking. I found out later that Veronica told my mother all of the details of our sex tour of San Francisco, and Constance said she had never been to any places like that.

I took Veronica to dinner on Monday night in Tiburon, and we ate outside, overlooking the water. Veronica said she could not believe her week was soon coming to an end. Her flight to

Cleveland was scheduled for 8:00 AM on Wednesday morning. My mother had invited us to have dinner at home with them the night before Veronica's departure, and she said Richard and Claudia Hamblen would also be there.

"So this is your last night to lose your virginity," I said.

"Your mother said I would never regret saving myself for marriage," said Veronica.

"You told her you were still a virgin?" I asked.

"No, you did," she replied.

I had to be in the office at 6:00 AM the next day, so I took Veronica home early.

"Danny, you are a very sweet and understanding person," Veronica told me when I walked her up to the door of the Sutro house. She then put her arms around me and gave me a long and wonderful kiss. She backed away with a big smile and said, "Good night, Danny."

Dinner with Mom, Conrad, and the Hamblens the next night was a delight. The Sutros and the Hamblens had become ever-closer friends, and they laughed a lot and had intelligent conversations. Veronica, who looked quite beautiful in the soft light, was fascinated with Richard. She said he was the most handsome and distinguished man she had ever met, though she quickly added that it was just as much fun being around Conrad, who she said really had a great sense of humor. Later, Veronica said Constance was right about how lucky Constance was to have so much love in her life. Veronica also told me that she could tell there was great chemistry between Richard and my mother.

"Your mom is so fortunate," Veronica said.

"She deserves it," I said. "She raised three boys alone while working, and I never heard her complain. On the contrary, she always said how lucky she was to have three sons."

"Some of us are destined for different things," said Veronica.

"What do you mean by that?" I asked.

"I don't know; it just sort of came out," she said.

Veronica was very affectionate and effusive at the airport. She said that her visit to San Francisco was the most exciting thing she had ever done and that being with me was her nicest experience with a man. We both promised to write. I told her I liked her very much and enjoyed being with her even though she did not believe in sex. We kissed. Veronica had a tear in her eye.

"Maybe we can do a vacation together, maybe go to Europe in the fall," she said, as she walked away. "I could do all the planning."

"Sounds good," I said as I waved my farewell. I knew I was going to miss her. But I had a lot of stocks to sell.

CHAPTER 64

About a week after Veronica returned to Cleveland, I got a call from my brother Jim, who told me he had finally met the girl of his dreams. He was planning to bring her to the city to meet the family on May 12 and 13, and he hoped I would be around.

"She must be one helluva babe to catch you, Jimmy," I replied.

"Wait until you meet her; she is definitely different," said Jim.

I have been remiss in not reporting on Jim's life. He had been running the largest independent television station in Los Angeles for the past two years and was in negotiations to buy a company that represented more than three hundred independent broadcast stations across the country. The company, called Burson's, was the largest broadcast rep firm in the business, though it was losing nearly a million dollars a year. Jim and I talked frequently on the telephone, so I knew a lot of the background. Two brothers had inherited Burson's from their father, a legendary broadcast salesman, but none of the father's talent had passed to either son. In the midst of their struggles, the Burson brothers approached Jim, offering him a 50 percent interest in the company if he would come in and run it. When Jim first told me about the offer, I was excited for him.

"I'm not going to take it," said Jim. "Those two clowns want to stay on the payroll as chairman and managing director, draw big salaries, and do nothing except demoralize the staff. I told them I would give them $1 million cash over three years and assume their $650,000 loan. I said that left to their own devices, they would be bankrupt within a year. It was a take-it-or-leave-it offer."

Six months into the negotiations, Burson's was on the brink of bankruptcy, and the Burson brothers agreed to Jim's terms. The first thing Jim did was sell the declining radio rep business, for which he got $375,000. He next cut back the number of television stations Burson's represented to the largest thirty-two and laid off half of the 160-person staff.

Burson's main office was in New York, where most of the major ad agencies were located. The second-largest office was Los Angeles, and Jim was convinced he could run the company from there, or at least he said he was going to try it. The main reason he did not want to move to New York was Jill Landis, whom he had been dating for three months (a record for Jim) and whom Jim planned to bring to San Francisco.

"She has skin as soft as the underside of Marilyn Monroe's breasts," Jim told me on the phone. "And she is the most gorgeous creature I've ever seen."

"Does she have a personality?" I asked.

"She is not a big talker, and that's what I like about her," said Jim. "She is more the earthy, sensual type, and does she ever love sex! By the way, she studied at UCLA for two years."

"You said she was a movie starlet?" I asked.

"She got into films by accident," Jim replied. "A couple of guys who majored in moviemaking at UCLA asked her if she would play a small part in a film they were making for one of their classes. Somehow, some guy over at Warner's saw the film and immediately became interested in Jill. It turned out that all the guy wanted was to get into Jill's jeans. She slapped him in the face when he tried to grope her in his office, and she stormed out."

Jim said that as Jill retreated through the reception area, Albert Rankin, a prominent director at Warner's, stopped her. He inquired what was wrong, and she burst out crying. He invited her into his office and told her that she was an extraordinarily beautiful woman and that he would like to arrange for a screen test. She agreed, and Rankin subsequently offered her a small role as an ingenue in a comedy.

"That led to several other small roles, but so far, she hasn't been able to get beyond that," Jim said. "She takes acting lessons four times a week, and she is really working at it. One problem is her voice; it is low and kind of scratchy. But for me, that just adds to her sex appeal."

I asked Jim where he had met Jill, and he said at a party in Malibu. She was there with Rankin, who was in his forties, at least twenty years older than Jill. During the party, Jill noticed Jim about the same time he noticed her, and the two began to talk to see if there was anything else beyond the obvious physical attraction.

"Jill immediately wanted to know what I did, and I told her that I ran Channel 5 but was in the midst of buying a company," Jim said, adding that she seemed happy to learn he was not in the movies.

Jim asked Jill if he could take her home, and she said she had come with Rankin and could not dump him. But she agreed to have dinner the following week. Two weeks later, they were sleeping together, and a month later, Jill moved into Jim's house in Hollywood Hills, a spectacular Spanish-style hacienda with good views of the surrounding hills when the smog lifted. Meanwhile, Jim had completed the purchase of Burson's and had turned over the general manager's chair at Channel 5, all in all a very heady time for Jim.

"Running your own company is the only way to go," Jim told me a month after taking over Burson's. "I work as hard as I have ever worked, but at the end of the day, I am not the least bit tired, and I'm ready to take Jill out for dinner and dancing, which is what she loves to do. By the way, Jill is a huge asset with our clients. I took her to New York for meetings with our big customers, and she had them drooling," Jim laughed.

"I am dying to meet her," I said.

I picked Jim and Jill up at the airport on the Friday night they arrived, and it was fascinating to see the effect they had on the crowds in the terminal. Jill was even better-looking than I had imagined and Jim more handsome than I remembered. I had not seen him for six months. As usual, he was tanned and healthy-looking, though he had more wrinkles than before, and his curly hair was graying at the temples. Jill, by contrast, was pale with luscious, unlined, and glowing skin. I kept thinking of the underside of Marilyn Monroe's breasts. Passersby unabashedly stared at this lovely couple, neither of whom seemed to notice. Obviously, they were used to it.

Jill was quite bubbly in the car, saying that San Francisco was her favorite city and that Jim had told her all about me making a fortune in the stock market.

"Not this week," I said. "Maybe you haven't heard about it yet, but Nixon fired John Erlichman, Bob Halderman, and John Dean, and it looks like Watergate is worse than anyone thought," I said, adding that the stock market was taking a beating.

"I hope my stocks aren't going south," said Jim, who had given me $35,000 to manage two years earlier. I told him that I had put all of my clients into cash two weeks ago and that he had $60,000 in cash and about $20,000 invested in Knight Newspapers.

"See what I mean, Jill? Danny is as sharp as they come," said Jim.

"Don't believe him," I said to Jill. "All I do is get advice from people who are six times smarter than I am."

"That not only takes brains; it takes humility too," laughed Jim. "Who are your advisors?"

"Well, for this latest go-around, they were Conrad Sutro and Richard Hamblen," I said.

"That's good, bro. How is Richard these days? Is he still in love with Mom?"

"Nothing has changed, except the Sutros and the Hamblens are as close as you can get," I replied. "Richard and Conrad have become real buddies, and Mom and Claudia are still each other's best friend. It is a great relationship they have, but if something ever happened to Claudia and Conrad, I bet Richard and Mom would marry. But I can tell you Mom is in love with Conrad. He's a fabulous guy."

Jim asked Jill if she thought a woman could be in love with two men at once.

"I was once in love with three boys when I was in high school," Jill laughed. "Sure, I think it's possible."

"What if you were married?" I asked.

"That's different," said Jill. "Maybe you would have the feelings for the other person, but you would keep them to yourself."

"I think that is the way it is with Mom and Richard," I said. "I'd bet a million dollars he has never made a pass at her."

"And I would bet a million that if he did, Mom would stop him in his tracks," Jim said.

"Your mom sounds like a saint," said Jill.

"I never thought of it that way," said Jim. "But maybe she is."

"Other than getting knocked up at age nineteen," I joked.

"You mean your mom had to get married?" asked Jill.

"Mom always said it was God's doing and that she and Dad probably never would have married otherwise, because he was being shipped from Hawaii back to the mainland," I said.

"Oh, Jim has told me about your dad, how he was killed just as the war was ending," said Jill. "It must have been awful for you two and your Mom. I could think about that if ever I have to cry for a scene in a movie. I mean that seriously; I mean, I could cry about it even now."

"We had better change the subject," I said. "Jim tells me you have acted in six films—are you serious about being an actress?"

"Breaking into the movies is about the hardest thing there is," said Jill. "The competition is incredible. There is so much talent around and so few roles. You have to be willing to sacrifice everything, and I am not sure I am, though sometimes I think I am."

"Is it true that a lot of the women in movies get parts because they are willing to sleep around?" I asked.

"If you don't get propositioned at least once a day, it is a rarity," said Jill. "And you can't believe how old some of the guys are—married with grown kids, but dying to get into bed with someone thirty years younger. Of course, that's how a lot of girls got their start."

"Sounds as tough as I've heard," I said.

"Before I met Jim, all I could think about was getting a good role, a featured-player role that could lead to my becoming a star," said Jill. "Now I am not so optimistic. I don't have Mr. Rankin helping me anymore. But Jim is helping me find a good agent. Jim thinks I could be the next Marilyn Monroe."

CHAPTER 65

Dinner at the Sutro house was a family affair and included Mom and Conrad, the Hamblens, Jim and Jill, me (unescorted), and Joe Jr., Claire, and their three children—Joseph Booker III, now age eight; Robyn, seven; and Karen, four. Conrad turned the bartending over to me while he prepared the terrace grill for steaks, hamburgers, and hot dogs.

Jill's presence and her remarkable good looks added a sense of electricity to the gathering. It seemed that hardly anyone could keep their eyes off of her, at least for the first hour. It was a coolish evening, and Jill was wearing a pink jacket, a white blouse, and a beige skirt that ended at the top of her knees and inched much higher when she sat down. She had slim ankles and well-formed calves, and her thighs were sturdy. She looked younger than her twenty-six years, mostly because of the glowing skin and animated, wide-eyed look she had. Her eyes were blue, and her hair was blonde, not a platinum blonde like Marilyn Monroe but a streaked blonde like Carole Lombard. Her chin receded ever so slightly, and she had a small mouth, but a wide face with high cheekbones. Next to her, Claire looked middle-aged (she was thirty-eight at the time), and Mother looked, well, grandmotherly (at fifty-nine). Robyn kept staring at Jill, and little Karen was equally fascinated.

"My father says that you have been in the movies," Robyn said to Jill. "You look like a movie star."

"Uncle Jim says you are the most beautiful woman ever," said Karen.

Jim picked up Karen and lifted her to the ceiling.

"Do you always go around telling everything you hear?" Jim smiled at Karen, herself a very pretty towhead. "You could embarrass people by saying things like that."

Jill got up from the couch and took Karen in her arms and said, "Don't you listen to him. Tell me everything."

"You are the first girl Uncle Jim has taken out for more than two months," said Robyn. "All the girls fall in love with him."

"That will be enough talk like that," said Joe Jr., rising to his full height of six feet five inches with a stern look on his face. "When I was your age, my father used to say 'loose lips sink ships.'" The two girls blinked in confusion.

"Come on, kids, come out on the terrace and help me with the barbecue," said Conrad. The children looked at their father, who nodded, and they scampered out.

"You have very lovely children," Jill said, smiling at both Joe and Claire. "Of course, I am not surprised, looking at you both. It is a pity, Mrs. Sutro, that you did not have any daughters."

"I really don't think I can complain," said Constance. "With two granddaughters, I can have all of the fun without the responsibility."

Claire said she thought Robyn looked a lot like Constance. Richard agreed, and so did Joe.

Claudia thought Karen also looked a bit like Constance, adding, "I think they are both going to be beautiful, inside and out."

Richard asked Jill which parent she took after, and Jill said she really did not look much like either of her parents.

"My mother always told me I looked like her grandmother, but I never saw my great-grandmother in person; she died when I was little," said Jill.

"Are both your parents still alive?" Richard asked.

"Yes, my dad just retired from Lockheed, where he worked in the aircraft design section," she answered. "My mother has been working as an elementary school teacher, but she is quitting next month, and my parents are thinking of moving to Hawaii. But they are just thinking about it. I am an only child, and they don't want to be too far away, so maybe they won't move. My dad has been playing golf every day, and my mom says she would like to do that when she retires."

"Hawaii is lovely. I grew up there," said Constance.

"Jim told me you lived there and that your father was an Episcopalian minister," said Jill.

Jill said both her parents had graduated from UCLA, and that both had been born in the Midwest but had come to California with their families in the 1940s.

"A lot of people decided about that time that California was the place to live," said Richard. "The state has been booming ever since."

The talk went on until midnight; the grandchildren had been temporarily put to bed in one of the spare bedrooms. Conrad told Jill that Joe had sold the movie rights for two of his Joseph Brady books, and she asked Joe if he might be coming to Hollywood. Joe responded by saying he had read so much about authors coming to grief working on movies of their books that he would never agree to go to Hollywood.

"I've sold the movie rights, but nothing is currently planned for production. When they buy the rights to make a movie of one of my books, that's all they get," said Joe. "I can make a very good living staying right here with my family, never having to do anything I don't want to."

"It is a rare man who can say that," said Richard.

"I love taking out the garbage," Joe smiled, winking at his wife.

Conrad said he had read the first four Joseph Brady books and asked what the next one was about.

"It is set in the Caribbean and Miami and covers the politics and intrigue of the 1969–72 period," said Joe. "In the draft of the book, Brady interviews Papa Doc, the Haitian dictator, and sneaks into Cuba with a false Canadian passport, where he is discovered and imprisoned. He escapes but is caught in a hurricane. Naturally, along the way, he meets several exotic women whom he seduces.

"I have not worked out all of the details yet, especially the tie-in between Castro and Papa Doc," said Joe. "The book will also cover the state of Communism as it exists in the various islands and the attitudes of the Cubans in Miami. I am taking the whole family on a four-week tour of the Caribbean next month after school gets out so that I have the places properly described."

"I think your writing is very realistic and factual, even though you do make your hero into something of a journalistic James Bond," laughed Conrad.

"That's what makes it fun. You have to have a little fantasy," said Joe.

"That is what keeps you home and faithful—all those vicarious thrills," said Claire.

"Do you model your protagonist after yourself?" asked Jill.

"He is a composite of several people I have known," said Joe. "He's also a product of my imagination blended with actual events."

"You should read his book on Vietnam," Constance said to Jill. "Joe spent a lot of time there in 1963."

"I want to," said Jill. "Constance, you have such successful sons—a writer, a stockbroker, and Jim, running his own company. You must be very proud."

"Don't jinx it, honey," said Jim. "We are still losing money."

"That's right; you can't declare victory until the game is over," said Richard. "I regret to say that I have known many people who were successful early in their lives and then subsequently fell flat on their faces. A wise man once said that life would be a lot easier if everyone understood how hard it was."

"So you are saying, Richard, that even if you become a millionaire, you shouldn't stop saying your prayers," I said. Richard nodded.

"Arrogance comes before the fall," said Joe. "I think it is going to happen to our beloved President Nixon."

That set off an hour-long discussion on Watergate. Only Conrad and Claire contended that Nixon should be booted from office.

One of the interesting things about Booker family conversations was that often, only one person spoke at a time—not always, but usually. So on this memorable May night in 1973, when one person was talking, everyone else listened. Of course, that was not true over dinner, but it was afterward. In Mom's house, the men did not separate from the women after dinner. If there were more than ten people there, one conversation was impossible, which was why Mom preferred three or four couples. Anyhow, I note the conversational discipline at Mom's simply because I have never encountered it anywhere else, except in a well-ordered classroom.

With the evening's lively group discussion, I did not get a chance to zero in for a private conversation with Jill. I was totally enthralled with her looks and obvious intelligence and wanted to get to know her better. So did everyone else. Jill was amazingly relaxed, despite being around seven adults she had never met before who were obviously sizing her up.

The next day, all of us, including the grandchildren, went to Fisherman's Wharf for lunch. It was a beautiful breezy day, and we took a long walk afterward. Jill wore a wide-brimmed hat, sunglasses, and lots of suntan lotion. She absolutely looked like a movie star, and almost everyone who saw her gave her a second or third look. I walked beside her for a bit and asked if it was possible to combine a career in the movies with marriage.

"I don't know. I've never had either," she laughed.

Richard hosted a dinner in a private room at the Union League Club on Saturday night and gave a welcoming toast: "I want to congratulate James on two counts, firstly for acquiring his own company, at which I predict he will be a great success, and secondly, and more importantly, for bringing the lovely Jill into our lives."

Everyone applauded, and Constance gave a rousing "Here, here."

James got up and returned the toast. "Thank you, Richard, for inviting us here tonight. It isn't often all of our family gets together these days, so it is with all the more conviction that I also say thank you to our mother for making it all possible."

"Here, here," said Jill, smiling. Everyone applauded and stood up, raising their glasses to Mom.

"I'm not going to make a speech," Mom said, rising. "I just want to say you all make me very happy. My only remaining goal in life is to have a few more grandchildren, and I am counting on Danny and Jim to fulfill that dream."

"Darn," said Conrad. "I was hoping you'd want to have some more children yourself. You certainly are fit enough."

"Let me also say it is very nice to have a husband who is a shameless flatterer," Constance smiled.

I was seated next to Jill at dinner. She told me that she wished she had brothers and sisters and that she was almost bowled over this weekend, saying that never before had she been in the company of such exceptional men and women.

"Even the grandchildren seem to have an aura about them," she said.

"I'm the only ordinary person here," I said.

"Is that really how you feel?" Jill asked.

"Well, let's put it this way—you wouldn't want to have to compete with my brothers," I replied.

"Looks can sometimes be a detriment. People get mesmerized by your looks to the exclusion of you as a person," said Jill. "I remember a line Marilyn Monroe had in *Gentlemen Prefer Blondes.* She said, 'A man being rich is like a girl being pretty. You might not marry her just because she's pretty but, my goodness, doesn't it help?'"

"Hey, that's pretty good. I guess I'd better make a lot of money," I said. "Have you memorized many of Marilyn Monroe's movie lines?"

"Just a few short ones, like the line in *Bus Stop*, when she was playing a pretty pathetic floozy. She said, 'I just got to feel that whoever I marry has some real regard for me, aside from all that lovin' stuff.'"

"I remember that," I said. "I liked her better in happier films like *The Seven Year Itch* and *Some Like It Hot.*"

Jill put an impish look on her face and said, "'You know what I do when it is hot like this, I put my undies in the ice box.' That's from *Itch.*

"Now you've got me started," she continued. "How about, 'I want you to to find happiness and stop having fun.' Or, 'I can be smart when it's important, but most men don't like it.' Those are both from *Gentlemen Prefer Blondes.*"

"Can you lip-synch her movies?" I asked.

"You are kidding me," she smiled. "Actually, I have a much greater appreciation of Bette Davis, who was really an actress. In her early career, she could play sweet young things, even though she had average looks at best, and in the end of her career, she could play wicked, hateful, and ugly with almost unimaginable conviction. The trouble with me is that I could never be Marilyn Monroe or Bette Davis. And there are a thousand actresses, like me, who fall somewhere in between."

"You are a stunningly beautiful woman, Jill," I said. "Don't underestimate yourself."

"Okay," she said, "as long as you don't underestimate yourself."

As you might guess, I was very much taken with Jill Landis. But I somehow had trouble picturing her settled down and married to a man like Jim, or any man for that matter.

CHAPTER 66

James Crandall Booker, age thirty-seven, married Jillian Landis, twenty-six, on February 14, 1974, in Las Vegas, Nevada. The couple had flown to the gambling mecca aboard a chartered airplane with their forty-two best friends, a noncelebrity group from the film and television industries. The decision to marry had come only two days earlier and therefore had precluded, Jim said later, inviting any members of either family, because doing so would inevitably have delayed the Valentine's Day merger of two of Southern California's most beautiful people. The Los Angeles press carried nothing on the marriage, which was not surprising given that bit film players and ad sales types were hardly news. However, a photo of the couple on their wedding day would sell for $5,000 two years later.

Constance Sutro got over her great disappointment about not attending the impromptu wedding and insisted that she and Conrad be allowed to hold a reception for the couple in San Francisco. Jill, still in a high state of excitement, readily agreed to a February 28 date for an event attended by some three hundred people and reported in all of the San Francisco newspapers.

"Former Cage Ace Weds Hollywood Beauty," headlined a story in the *Chronicle*. A three-column photo of the couple together with Conrad and Constance Sutro accompanied the story. I must have received a hundred comments from friends and acquaintances about the beauty of my new sister-in-law, and Jim looked like the happiest man alive during the couple's three-day stay in San Francisco.

"I proposed, and she accepted and agreed we should do it right away," Jim told me. "I did not want to give her time to change her mind. Actually, Jill said she wanted to elope and not have a big wedding, because she did not want her parents to pay for it. She said that she had seen the Booker side of the family and that there was no way her family could afford the kind of wedding she assumed they would expect. And she didn't want Conrad to pay for anything. So I chartered the plane and got a gang together on thirty-six-hours' notice so it would be a memorable occasion for Jill. And believe me, it was. We stayed up and partied all night long."

"Well, Jim, you have married a fabulously beautiful woman," I said. Jill was standing nearby and overheard my remark.

"I have married a fabulously beautiful man," she said, coming over to us and putting her arm around him. "And I am now part of a wonderful new family with especially nice brothers-in-law."

I leaned forward and gave Jill a kiss on the cheek, which was even softer and smoother than advertised.

Meanwhile, I had been corresponding with Veronica, and I confess that the visage of Jill had sort of blocked her from my mind.

Veronica wrote in March of 1974 that she had been in contact with a travel agency in San Francisco and was discussing a job with them. She asked if I thought that was a good idea. It had been nine months or so since we had seen each other, and I replied rather reservedly that it was up to her. Frankly, I did not want to be committed to anything or to take responsibility for her coming out west. I had been dating a wire service reporter to whom Joe had introduced me and was having a lot of fun with her, though she was clearly a very free spirit and not the marrying kind.

Veronica telephoned a week later and said that despite my lack of enthusiasm, she was coming anyway and that I did not have to take any responsibility for her.

"I fell in love with the San Francisco Bay Area, and for the past nine months, I have been debating whether I should make the move," she said. "Part of my affection for the city was how gracious you and your family were to me, but I'm not expecting any repeat of that."

"Hold on, Veronica," I said. "I was very happy that you were thinking of coming out. I just did not want there to be any assumptions on your side that might be misleading. When are you coming, anyway? I want to meet you at the airport."

"You don't have to," she said.

I almost did not recognize Veronica when she arrived at the airport at midafternoon on Friday. She was immaculately dressed in a form-fitting tan suit and looked glamorous. She had let her hair grow out, and it was pulled back into a ponytail, which gave her a bouncy, lively look. The biggest change was her skin. It was glowing and much smoother than before. Only the large soulful eyes were the same.

I put my arms around her and said how beautiful she looked.

"Thank you, Dan. You are looking just the same, healthy and prosperous."

"I don't know about prosperous—Watergate is killing the market," I said. "Anyway, I'm really glad to see you, and I have cleaned up my spare bedroom, so you can stay with me."

"That's very thoughtful of you, Dan, but I've arranged for a small furnished apartment on Larkin Street, and if you could take me there, I would really appreciate it," she said.

"My, you are organized. Have you landed that job yet?"

"I start on Monday," she smiled. "I'm really excited. I am still mostly on a commission, but I am making more base pay than I did in Cleveland."

Veronica's flat was a four-story walk-up, and carrying her two heavy bags was a reminder that I was letting myself get out of shape. The landlord, Dolly Fong, was a Chinese lady who lived on the ground floor. She gave Veronica one key to the front door and one to her apartment.

"No need two sets of keys, no?" Dolly said.

"No, I am living alone," Veronica smiled.

"Good," said Dolly. "Nice view, but very small apartment."

"Oh, I love the view of the Bay and Alcatraz," Veronica said as we looked over what must have been about eight hundred square feet of living space. "Of course, the view is nothing like your place or the Sutro house, but it is a view. For what I am paying, I am lucky to have it."

I suggested that Veronica unpack while I went downstairs to move my car, which I had left in the driveway of Dolly's apartment house.

"Oh, you don't have to stay," she said.

"I'll be right back," I said, ignoring her exit line.

I had to go two blocks away to find a parking space, and then it took me a half hour to buy a mixed bouquet of flowers and two bottles of wine, some cheese, and crackers.

By the time I returned, Veronica had changed into light slacks and a loose-fitting dark blue sweater. She had taken her hair out of the ponytail, and it now fell to her shoulders.

"I was beginning to think you were not coming back," she said. "Oh, you brought flowers and goodies. That's very sweet of you."

I could not get over how different Veronica looked. Letting her hair grow out had made a huge difference. She had lost some weight, though none of it in the place where it was appealing. She was not wearing a bra under her sweater.

"I don't think I ever really gave you a welcome kiss," I said, putting my arms out and drawing her toward me, pressing my chest against those free-flowing and very ample breasts. She gave me a peck on the lips and smiled.

"It is so wonderful to be here," she said, backing off, still smiling warmly.

"How about some wine and cheese?" I asked.

"It is seven o'clock in Cleveland; that sounds terrific."

We drank both bottles of wine over the next two hours. I had a lot more than my share, but I weighed 195 to Veronica's 120, and that was about the ratio of our consumption.

"This is more wine than I've had since I left here," Veronica said. She told me she had joined a gym and was working out four days a week. She said she was also on a diet that limited her intake of meat, and she did not eat any sugar. She was also drinking eight glasses of water a day, the only drawback being the frequency of her trips to the bathroom.

"I eat a lot of fish and chicken and occasionally pasta," she said. "The key thing is to also eat a lot of fruits and vegetables."

"Well, whatever you are doing, don't stop," I said.

"You should try it and start working out," she said. "I noticed you were breathing pretty hard coming up the steps, both times."

"I can't argue. My mom has been doing what you are for at least fifteen years, and she has been pushing me to do something for at least two years."

"She's the reason I got started," said Veronica. "And she is the one who gave me the name of the doctor in Cleveland who helped me clear up my skin."

"She's going to be impressed when she sees you," I said.

I suggested we go to North Beach for dinner. Veronica said she would prefer to go somewhere nearby.

"I want to get to know this area and try all of the restaurants," she said. "And by the way, I am buying this one," she said.

"Oh good, I was hoping you would. I'm a little short." That made her laugh.

"I'm glad you still have your sense of humor," she smiled. "Let's go."

We ended up at a small French restaurant on Polk Street. Veronica wanted to know all the news of our family, and she was fascinated by the story of Jim and Jill. I ended up doing almost all of the talking, because there was so much to tell.

I had told my mother about Veronica's return, and she had said I must bring her over for dinner on Sunday night. When I told Veronica this over Friday's dinner, she said she would be delighted to go, but she turned down my offer for help shopping on Saturday and said she just wanted to stay home by herself that night. The trouble was that I wanted to be with the new glamorous and seemingly independent Veronica. But I did not argue, and instead, I said I could understand her wanting some time to relax, especially with the start of her new job on Monday.

"Danny, I just don't want you to feel responsible or obligated to help me," she said, as we were saying good night.

"I promise I won't do a thing that I don't want to do," I replied. "You know I like being around glamorous women."

"Do you think I am looking glamorous?" she smiled.

"Definitely, I do," I said, putting my arms around her and giving her a hard, take-charge kiss on the lips. Veronica did not resist. It was a wild, passionate embrace that ended with Veronica saying almost breathlessly, "Wow, I am bringing out the animal in you." When I sought to once again engulf her in my arms, she smiled warmly and said, "I think that is enough for now. I will see you Sunday."

CHAPTER 67

"Oh, my goodness, look at you!" said Constance as she greeted Veronica and me at the front door on Sunday. She gave Veronica a long hug. "Danny said you were looking pretty glamorous, but that is an understatement."

Conrad let out a wolf whistle and kissed Veronica on both cheeks.

"I am delighted you are going to live here," Conrad said. "There are about fifty members of the Sutro family I will have to introduce you to. You are going to make a fine addition to the clan, but you have to know that not everyone speaks to each other."

"I am happy that you consider distant cousins part of the family," said Veronica, smiling.

Standing behind Constance at the doorway was Adam Sutro, Conrad's only offspring from his first marriage. Adam had just returned from El Salvador, where he had spent the last two years working for the Peace Corps. Constance said Adam was joining us for dinner and would be living at home from now on.

I had seen Adam on only three previous occasions. He was always away. Now at twenty-six or so, he had matured nicely and was a slimmed-down version of his father with a ready smile but not quite so garrulous. Conrad had told me that Adam took after his mother: "That's where he got his brains and ambition."

Adam was a graduate of Harvard, from which school he also earned a graduate degree in business administration before joining the Peace Corps. He said he was planning to go into the real estate development business.

"Adam has declined my offer to go into business with me," Conrad said. "He says he wants to make it on his own first."

"I can understand that," said Veronica, smiling at Adam, who was two years younger than she. "It is much more satisfying when you are able to accomplish something on your own."

"Well, Veronica," said Constance, "you have certainly done that. We would have been very happy to help you find a place to live here in San Francisco and find a job. But it is to your credit that you did everything on your own. And we're just happy to have you here."

"Veronica has some good Sutro blood coursing through her veins," said Conrad.

"Does that mean I can't ask Veronica out on a date?" Adam smiled.

"Adam, my boy, Veronica is dating Danny."

"Oh, we're really just friends. Danny has been wonderful to me, like a brother," said Veronica.

My mother glanced over at me, and I smiled weakly back at her. Veronica's comment hurt more than I wanted to admit.

"Just call me brother, the helper of all," I said, at once regretting that I had said something so insipid.

Veronica came over and put her arm around me and said, "Danny, you are more than a brother."

"I guess that settles that," smiled Adam.

"I need a drink, let's go to the balcony," said Conrad.

Veronica talked a lot with Mother during dinner while Conrad, Adam, and I discussed San Francisco real estate and the stock market and agreed they were both underpriced. We also agreed that President Nixon was underappreciated and that gasoline was still overpriced.

"I'm going to be very surprised if Nixon is still in office at the end of this year," said Adam. "The Democrats control both the House and the Senate, and I think they are out to impeach him."

"They will never get the needed two-thirds vote in the Senate," I said.

"I'm willing to bet you $100 even money Nixon is gone by December," said Adam.

"You're on," I said, extending my hand.

Alas, Adam proved right. Nixon resigned on August 9, 1974, the culmination of an eighteen-month witch hunt that had started with a silly, small-time burglary of the Democratic offices in the

Watergate complex, a crime that Nixon knew nothing about. In the end, Nixon's rationale was that even though he could survive a Senate vote on impeachment, the process would take many months and would leave the nation without a credible leader until resolved. In my view, and that of historians such as Paul Johnson, this was a mistake, but an honorable one.

So Gerald Ford replaced Nixon as president, and I paid Adam $100. Adam said he would buy me a fancy lunch, and I accepted. He proved to be well informed about real estate, and I guessed right then that he would be a success. I liked him a lot. He had an air of leadership about him, and I concluded he was a hell of a lot smarter than I was. He was also a lot richer. He had a $2 million trust fund that he had been given at age twenty-five, and he stood to inherit still more. Over lunch, I asked that he consider giving me $50,000 to manage for him in the stock market.

"Dad says you are great; I'd like to start with $100,000," Adam said.

I put all the money into newspaper stocks, and Adam had tripled his investment by the start of 1977. By that time, I was managing money for an annual fee of 1.5 percent and 10 percent of all gains, computed annually, in excess of the rate of inflation. The money was rolling in!

I was not so lucky with Veronica in the months following her move to San Francisco. She turned down about half my requests to see her, and she quite openly said she planned to date other guys. I said I was going to do the same, even though my relationship with the wire service reporter ended when she decided to marry the head of the Time-Life bureau in San Francisco.

As I look back on my thinking at that time, there is no doubt that Veronica's elusiveness and her seeming indifference fueled the flames of my feelings toward her. She had obviously been stung by my initial, lukewarm reaction to her moving to San Francisco. But that was before I had seen her new look and increased confidence. I found myself thinking about her a lot, more than I wanted. At odd times of the day, her face would pop into my mind. I could not stop it. I was beginning to think that I was in love. The harder she was to get, the more I wanted her. I seemed caught in an age-old game.

One weekend just after Labor Day, Conrad invited us for a Saturday afternoon sail on his boat, after which we would dock and dine at a waterfront restaurant in Sausalito. Adam was invited and brought a lovely-looking lass who had been a year behind him at Harvard and who was now working as a financial analyst with Bank of America. Her name was Lillian Graff, and she came from an old-line California family. Conrad knew both her parents and her grandparents.

Lillian turned out to be an expert deckhand and bounced confidently around the boat along with Adam.

"I can see they are both sailors," I said to Veronica, as we stood together with Cokes in hand. Richard Hamblen and Conrad were talking to each other over the helm while my mother and Claudia were seated aft. It was a sparkling, Indian summer day on the bay, and I think all of us were in a good mood. I was certainly happy to have Veronica at my side—except that as the afternoon wore on and as dinner progressed at the restaurant, Veronica grew more and more quiet, and I could tell by the look on her face that she was not happy. Her attention seemed to be on Lillian, who had a great laugh and was obviously bright and gifted. Richard asked Lillian a lot of questions about what she was doing for the BofA and she replied that she was helping to select stocks for several large pension funds and that it involved visiting companies in both California and New York and occasionally spots in between.

"You and Danny have a lot in common," said Richard. "Danny is one of the best portfolio managers I know."

Lillian smiled at me and said, "I'll buy you lunch next week." I nodded and said I would phone her.

Lillian said she had heard from Adam that Constance was an expert on General George Custer and that she wanted to hear all about him. Constance, ever-ready to be the tour guide, responded with a ten-minute description that we had all heard before but that left Lillian enraptured. I overheard Conrad say to Richard, "Lillian is going to make someone a very good wife."

"She's got the breeding," said Richard. "She's just right for Adam."

"We should be so lucky," said Conrad.

All of those comments were perfectly fine except that Veronica happened to overhear the exchange.

"Would you order me a scotch on the rocks," she whispered to me. "I don't feel like any more wine."

I beckoned the waiter and ordered two double scotches on the rocks. Constance looked a bit quizzically at me.

"We didn't drink on the boat," I smiled. "Anyhow, I thought I would introduce Veronica to one of Conrad's favorite drinks, which, when the market is off fifty points, is also one of my favorite drinks."

Constance looked at Veronica and asked if she was feeling a bit queasy from the boat ride.

"Maybe that's it," said Veronica. "I'm not feeling so hot."

After dinner, back at my car, I asked Veronica if she would like to come to my place for a nightcap and listen to some old records. The drinks had improved her mood, and she said she would if I would give her another scotch and ice.

I put on a stack of records—Brook Benton, Dinah Washington, Johnny Mathis, and Frank Sinatra.

"I love Johnny Mathis," Veronica said, finishing her drink. "This could be the night I lose my virginity. Don't you think it is about bloody time?" she asked.

"Not tonight," I said. "First-time sex doesn't go with double scotches."

"Who's talking about first-time sex?" she said. "I said I was a virgin, but I never said I hadn't had sex."

"Well, it is the same thing," I said.

"That's what you think," she said, getting up and heading for the bathroom.

I must say I was of two minds. I did not want to take advantage of Veronica. She was somehow jealous of Lillian, and I had already guessed that that was the reason for her earlier unhappiness. I probably should not have ordered doubles. Just then, Veronica appeared at the door of the bathroom wearing only her panties.

"I just want to give you a private showing of what working out in the gym has done for me," she said, striding toward the couch.

"Wow, you look great," I said, my resolve suddenly melting. She sat on my lap and pushed her breasts into me.

"I seem to remember you are a pretty good kisser when you want to be," she said, pressing her lips hard against my mouth. Dinah was singing "What a Difference a Day Makes."

We lay on the couch kissing and touching through all of Dinah's numbers. We were both naked when Frank Sinatra began singing "Always."

"I'm ready if you are," she whispered.

Does a dog have fleas?

CHAPTER 68

Veronica and I were married in Grace Cathedral on December 14, 1974. Veronica wanted to elope, but I could not break a promise I had made to my mother, who herself had had only about thirty people at her wedding. More significantly, both my brothers had eloped and left Mom out of it. Conrad and Mom paid for everything, and Mom insisted that the guests be seated randomly on both sides of the aisles given that 95 percent of the three hundred guests would have normally sat on the groom's side. Veronica's father was there, as were six of her girlfriends, who all served as bridesmaids. Veronica's aunt was in attendance too, along with several distant relatives, at least two of whom had a tiny amount of Sutro blood. Veronica's side held up nicely, and there were no embarrassments, though a couple of my friends from baseball got totally smashed at the reception, albeit in a happy sort of a way.

The *Chronicle* ran our picture over two columns and gave about two hundred words to the event, far less coverage than Jim and Jill had received. Veronica looked beautiful in her white gown, and her face was radiant, set off by her wonderfully large and dark eyes. In the months leading up to the marriage, I had had occasional second thoughts, and so had Veronica, but Mom and others said that was par for the course.

During this time, Veronica had changed yet again. When I told her in early October that I wanted to marry her, she agreed much faster than I expected. Our sex life had taken interesting turns as well. Veronica did not have an orgasm our first four times together, despite what I considered some heroic efforts on my part. Finally, a week after our first time together, she climaxed in a way that made me glad my apartment had thick walls. After that, she wanted to have sex all of the time. It was as if she was trying to make up for all of that time being a virgin. Not only that, she wanted to try every variation imaginable, including some things I was not familiar with. The longtime virgin had turned into a sexual wildcat, often initiating the action in some pretty weird places, like Golden Gate Park, for example. I could write an erotic novel just based on the things that Veronica wanted to do. A week before the wedding, I suggested to Veronica that we not have any sex until our honeymoon so that we would still have some bedroom excitement left. Frankly, I wanted to restore myself; I was finding it more difficult to get and maintain the third erection of the night after our first month of sex. Veronica got a bit upset one night when I said I was not up to a third effort.

"You did it five times in one night last month," she said. "I hope you are not losing interest in me."

I told her that most married men in their thirties hardly ever did it more than once a night, with an average of maybe of three or four times a week. And they still loved their wives.

"I hope you don't get that way," she said, unzipping my trousers.

At that stage of our marriage, Veronica never seemed to get enough sex. She insisted that we go to one of the porn shops and buy an assortment of marital aids and sex toys, plus a lot of porn magazines of all types. It is a pity Viagra wasn't around in those days. I would have been taking fourteen pills a week.

Veronica continued to work at the travel agency and said she was developing a pretty good clientele. Of course, she got some help from the Sutros and the Hamblens, and she was not shy about asking for business. As for my work, because it was related to the New York stock exchanges, I got up at 5:00 AM every morning and was in the office at 6:00 AM. I was usually able to break away by four, and at least a couple of days a week, I would pick up Veronica at her office, and we would go jogging together, often at Ocean Beach or Golden Gate Park. Afterward, we would have dinner out, often talking over the meal about children, which we both wanted.

Conrad had introduced Veronica to all of the Sutro relatives and frequently included us in social events at their house. We had free use of the house at Pebble Beach if it was not otherwise taken, and we went there whenever we could. We often dined with Joe Jr. and Claire and their children, occasionally at our apartment, but mostly at their home because of the logistics with the kids. We always brought the wine and beer and sometimes precooked food such as a ham or a turkey. Veronica loved playing with the kids, and she looked dreamy-eyed when she did; when she looked like that, I knew she was thinking about having her own. Veronica was pleasant with everyone but not very talkative. She and Mom talked, but not nearly with the degree of intimacy Mom did with Claire. She wrote regularly to her aunt in Cleveland and talked to her dad by phone about once every three months. She said she wished her father would find someone and get married, but she doubted it would ever happen.

"He's married to his work," she said on several occasions.

With Ford in the presidency, the stock market began to rise. The Dow Jones average had hit a low of 600 during the Watergate fiasco, but it had climbed back over 1,000 by the end of 1974 and continuing into 1975. Not only did that help my business, but it also helped Veronica's. More people had the money to travel.

Mom and Conrad went to Australia and New Zealand in April of 1975 and actually came back via Singapore and New Delhi and London, so in fact, they circumnavigated the globe. They were gone forty-five days, and both looked in great health when they returned. Conrad invited all of the family over for a slide show from their trip in early June. Unfortunately, Jim and Jill could not make it. Jim said he was still swamped with his new company, trying to make it profitable, and was spending a lot of time in New York. Meanwhile, Jill had resumed her acting classes and had reconnected with Warner Brothers director Albert Rankin, and he was close to landing her a good role in a forthcoming film starring Gerhard Reich, a German-born screen heartthrob.

Jill and Jim did come to San Francisco over the Fourth of July holiday in 1975. Jill looked more beautiful than ever, but Jim looked a bit stressed out, though even the look of an overworked executive made him appear more interesting, or at least that was what Veronica told me.

Jill said her chances of getting a significant part in the Gerhard Reich film appeared good, and she would know the next week. She said the part she was vying for had a love scene with Reich early in the picture, though her character would die shortly after that.

"The role is central to the film, and the girl I would play is the love of his life for the Reich character," Jill said. "The story is about how the Reich character recovers from the loss of his first love and finds meaning to life. There are a lot of flashbacks. I am supposed to meet Mr. Reich next week, because he has the approval rights on all of the main characters. That's how big a star and how powerful he is."

"I've seen Gerhard Reich in two or three films," said Constance. "He's awfully handsome, and he has a wonderful accent."

"You had better watch out, Jim. You may find yourself with serious competition," Conrad said, kiddingly.

"Jim doesn't have to worry about Mr. Reich," said Jill. "First off, he is married, but more importantly, I am totally devoted to my marriage, and Jim and I would never do anything to wreck what we have. Another thing, Mr. Reich is too old, and he's not nearly as handsome as Jim."

That struck me as an awfully long answer. She would have been better off just laughing.

Veronica later told me she feared the worst for Jim's marriage. I asked her why, and she said she thought Jill was so irresistible that men would do anything to have her. She had talked with Jill about what goes on in Hollywood, and Jill had said that adultery is commonplace, especially when stars are shooting on location.

Big news, I thought.

"Of course, Jill said that a lot of stars don't get involved that way, and she was definitely going to be in that category, but saying and doing are two different things," Veronica said.

I asked Veronica what she would do if she were in Jill's place.

"I can't answer a hypothetical question," smiled Veronica. "But if you want my honest answer, I wouldn't do anything. If I wasn't married, that would be a different story."

Veronica asked me what I would do.

"Honey, I can't handle any more than you," I smiled.

"Don't ever change," said Veronica, putting her hand on my fly.

CHAPTER 69

Jill Landis got the part in the Gerhard Reich movie, *No Greater Love*, a film destined to make history of a sort. Actually, it was more what happened on the set that brought the notoriety. The first information I got about what was happening came from Veronica, who had struck up a close friendship with Jill. The two talked on the telephone and wrote each other quite a bit during the second half of 1975, when the film was being made. Hearing the details of Jill's life in Hollywood seemed to give Veronica a vicarious thrill. (Of course, I did not learn the whole story until years later when Kitty Kale wrote the scorching biography on Gerhard Reich.)

Veronica told me that Jillian had a two-hour interview with Gerhard before she was actually offered the role. The famous actor was interested in finding out if Jill could be comfortable doing the critical love scene that would likely cover six to ten minutes of screen time and would probably take six to eight hours to film. He explained that she would have to be partially naked for some of the shots and that it was essential that the filming be as realistic as possible. Jill said she believed she could do it if she focused on the fact she was just acting. Gerhard said the kissing aspect was crucial, and she would really have to throw herself into it as if she were with the greatest love of her life.

Gerhard then asked Jill if she would be willing to do a test, right there in the office. Jill told Veronica she did not know what to say at first and hesitated. Gerhard said, "I can understand how you feel, not knowing me at all and being a very beautiful woman who has had to fend off many would-be lovers."

Jill said that in person Gerhard looked even better than he did on the screen, much younger than his forty-something years. In just a few minutes, he won her confidence. Gerhard began kissing her slowly at first and then at a gradually increasing rate of passion. Jill told Veronica that she had no idea how long the kiss had lasted but that she had never been kissed like that before. She felt breathless. Jill said that she had put everything into it. When he finished, he said something to the effect that he thought she could do it but would require more passion for the actual shooting.

Jill said that for the first three weeks of shooting, Gerhard scarcely spoke with her. In fact, she concluded he was deliberately ignoring her, a matter that she tried to rectify by seeking his advice on some small scenes she had to do with her screen family, building up to her meeting with Gerhard. He responded by saying he would only work with her on the scenes they had together. She concluded that Gerhard did not really like her.

Jim was relieved that Gerhard seemed to be comporting himself as a gentleman, and therefore, he was not at all concerned about having to spend an increasing amount of time in New York. Moreover, Jill was very aware of the fragile nature of beauty, and she felt and looked her best if she got a full eight hours of sleep. She also had her family and friends right there in case she needed anything.

In the fourth week of shooting, Gerhard and Jill began doing their talking scenes together. Jill was understandably nervous, a state exacerbated by Gerhard's impatience at having to reshoot several scenes because of mistakes Jill made.

Two days before they were supposed to begin shooting the love scene, Gerhard came to Jill's dressing room with a dozen roses and a simple gold necklace. Jill said he was so sweet and respectful that he seemed like another person. Gerhard talked to Jill for more than an hour about the importance of the scene and about how for it to work they both had to give it everything they had. She said he was mesmerizing when he talked, using a soft voice and staring intently into her eyes. Gerhard told her he had not had sex with his wife for more than two weeks so that he would have the stamina and vigor to get through the more than six hours of shooting time that their scene would probably take. Gerhard said you really couldn't fake it in front of cameras that put your image on a giant screen. Jill didn't say anything, but because of Jim's travels and draining work at the office, it had been at least ten days since she and Jim had any sex too.

At Gerhard's insistence, the set was cleared for the love scene. Only the director, the lighting technician, and three cameramen were present. For the first hour and a half, the shooting involved kissing on the mouth, the ears, the neck, and the breasts, with each wearing towels around their waists. Jill told Veronica it was a dizzying experience, and she felt as if she was floating in a sea of rising passion. Both Gerhard and Jill were perspiring when the director suggested a break.

After forty-five minutes away from each other, the pair returned to the set in a greatly reduced state of ardor. Jill said she felt back in control of herself until the director explained that the next shots were going to require full nudity. Gerhard exhibited no qualms about being in the buff, and Jill was somewhat stunned by the size of his penis, which she told Veronica was the largest she had ever seen, though she had only seen it fleetingly because each of them had small hand towels to cover their private areas while setting up for the various shots. But she felt him in every scene, and she had no trouble believing he had abstained from sex for two weeks. The shooting went faster than expected. Jill said that she completely forgot about the cameras and that other people were in the room.

The final scene was to be shot from a ceiling camera located directly overhead. Gerhard was to be lying on top of her while her legs were widely spread. The camera was to zoom in and out, alternating between full-length body shots and the passion on her face. Gerhard had positioned himself so that the full weight of his body was pressing on her, his pelvic bone pressed directly on hers. He told her to wrap her legs around his waist. She could feel his penis bending downward over her clitoris, with the end touching the opening of her vagina. He kissed her fiercely on the neck as he rocked slowly and heavily against her mound. They stayed that way for several minutes, and Jill found herself rocking ever so slightly. She felt a rising tide in her groins, and she let out several moans. The pulsating in her clitoris was intense. She thought Gerhard's technique was much better than the normal in-and-out sex she had had with Jim and others. Gerhard barely moved his lower body but continued to kiss her. Suddenly, she felt him partially enter her, and she let out an involuntary "oohhh." Her body was drifting; the sensations were incredibly intense. She had forgotten everything; only the moment was a reality.

The next thing she knew, she was being wrapped in giant towel by one of the ladies from wardrobe. The director told her she had been magnificent.

Gerhard, wrapped in a white bathrobe, came over and gave her a hug. He asked her to drop by his dressing room for a glass of champagne, saying she had earned it.

Though weak-kneed and confused, Jill was at his door only minutes later. She was still tingling. She entered, and he wrapped his arms around her and kissed her hard.

"My darling, I think we have some unfinished business," he said. She was his to do as he wished.

Shortly after the love scene between Gerhard Reich and Jill Landis was completed, rumors began abounding in Hollywood that the couple had taken their love scene on the screen very seriously and had gotten so caught up in the moment that they had actually had sex before the cameras. This was hardly the first time a story of this nature had gotten out. But in this case it was not some publicist's dream. The word was that all you had to do was watch Jill's face in the rushes to know she wasn't faking it.

Gerhard and Jill became the hottest item in Hollywood, and there were rumors that they spent their lunchtime together each day in his dressing room. Jill told Veronica that Gerhard had more charm than she thought was imaginable. Although she fought hard against it, at last she admitted that she was madly in love with the German, and there was no turning back.

When Jim heard the rumors about his wife, he flew back from New York and confronted her. She was crying, Jim told me later. She told him she was in love with Gerhard, and there was nothing she could do about it. She said she felt terrible about hurting Jim, but she would not lie: she still loved him, but Gerhard had become the love of her life. She guessed the only solution was a divorce. Jim was stunned and felt a sinking in his heart and light-headedness. He told me that he had almost gone into shock looking at his beautiful, angel-like wife telling him it was over. No woman had ever said that to him. He had dumped dozens of brokenhearted charmers, but none of them had been his wife. He said he and Jill talked for an hour. He had three drinks, all scotches on the rocks.

"I realized it was over, and there was nothing I could do to change it," Jim said. The night they talked, Jill said she would be moving out the next day. She didn't say where.

So that was it. The date was September 22, 1975. The marriage was over after nineteen months.

Constance was more stunned than anyone, and she said she cried for two days when she learned of the breakup. She blamed it all on the lack of morality in Hollywood, but most of all, she grieved for her son. She caught a cold in early October, and it took her three weeks to get over it, spending much of the time in bed. Veronica said Jill had been caught in a web of circumstances few women could resist. I told her to keep that opinion to herself around the Booker family.

Jill's romance with Gerhard Reich made all the tabloids. Reich filed for a divorce from his wife, who had returned to Germany, and said he planned to marry Jill as early as possible. *No Greater Love* was a box office hit, and Warner signed the lovers for a second film to be shot on location in Munich. Meanwhile, Jim found no shortage of women eager to console him, and he buried himself in his work, at last turning Burson's into a profitable company by the end of 1976. Jill did not ask for any alimony. In the end, it was an amicable breakup, though my mother was unforgiving.

"How could that filthy German treat his wife and two children that way? How could he break up two marriages and still go around like God's gift to the world?" Mom asked me one day.

"He's not the first German to bring us grief," I said.

"Yes," she said. "It is hard to believe your father has been dead for more than thirty years."

CHAPTER 70

One night in late April of 1976, Constance and Conrad decided to give their driver, Umberto, the night off after he dropped them at the Geary Theater. It was Umberto's wife's birthday, and Constance felt that was the least they could do for a safe and responsible driver. Upon leaving the theater, Constance asked Conrad when he had last walked up to Nob Hill from Geary Street. Conrad said it had been many years, but if Constance wanted to make the climb, he was up for it. After all, he said, it was a good evening for walking, with a high overcast fog and the temperature in the low sixties. They held hands with their heads bent forward as they made their way up the steep hill on Taylor Street. It was only five blocks from Geary to California, but it was a demanding walk, and there were not other pedestrians making the trek upward. The Sutros had just crossed Bush Street and were about a third of the way into the next block when they heard a voice:

"Rich motherfuckers, too fucking cheap to take a taxi, you motherfuckers?"

Conrad turned around and saw walking behind them a tall Negro dressed in ragged clothes and carrying a bottle wrapped in a brown paper bag. He was staggering and apparently had been standing in a darkened doorway. He had a scraggly beard and a decidedly ugly, antagonistic look on his face.

"What's an old motherfucking fart like you doing climbing this hill?" the man said to Conrad. "Don't you know you could get a motherfucking heart attack? Hey, old man, you might even get robbed or beaten up, maybe both. Who's that woman you got with you, your daughter?"

"What do you want?" asked Conrad, stepping in front of Constance.

"Maybe I want that white bitch you got there," the man answered, taking a step toward Constance. "Here, let me take a look at you."

"Don't you dare touch her," Conrad said.

"Give him your money," Constance said. "That's what he wants."

"The lady got that right," the man said, approaching Constance again. "Let me see that purse."

"I told you not to touch her," Conrad said, pushing the man. The man stopped Conrad cold with one long arm. Conrad swung wildly and missed and then in frustration kicked the shins of the robber, who brought his bottle down on Conrad's head. Conrad fell to the ground just behind his assailant. The man looked down at Conrad and began searching for his wallet.

Suddenly, the attacker straightened, looking down the street as a car passed through the intersection of Bush and Taylor. Just then, Constance pushed the man from the side, sending him toppling over Conrad's body. The man was caught completely by surprise. He was unable to break his fall, because he was still holding the neck of the bottle in his right hand. His head hit the pavement, and he was momentarily knocked unconscious.

Constance rushed into the street and hailed the passing motorist, who could see the well-dressed lady was in trouble. There were two men in the car, both in their thirties. Meanwhile, Conrad and his assailant had staggered to their feet. They were about fifteen yards apart. The robber saw the two men getting out of the car and Constance pointing at him, screaming that he had tried to rob them. The robber turned and fled down the hill.

Constance looked at Conrad. His head was covered with blood. The two men drove them to St. Mary's Hospital, where he got eight stitches to sew up his scalp. Constance tried to get the names of the two men who had helped them so that she could send them a present, but they declined and said they were happy to have come along when they did. Conrad asked Constance what had happened, and she told him.

"Damn, honey, that was mighty brave of you," he said.

"When he hit you over the head with the bottle, I was in a rage, and I didn't really think about what I was doing," said Constance.

"Say, I still have my wallet," said Conrad.

The next day, Constance and Conrad filed a report with the police, giving a detailed description of their attacker. Two weeks later, they were asked to come to the station to possibly identify a suspect who closely fit their description. There were five men in the lineup, three with beards and two clean-shaven. Conrad at first said that none of them looked like the attacker.

"That's him," said Constance. "I would recognize those high cheekbones and those eyes anywhere. The only difference is he shaved off his beard."

"By God, you're right," said Conrad.

The police detective asked if the Sutros wanted to press charges.

"I think we have to," said Conrad, looking at Constance. "If we don't get this guy off the street, he's only going to do it again to someone else."

"I agree," said Constance.

But the trial of Alonso Washington never took place. The district attorney decided to accept a plea bargain to the reduced charge of aggravated assault, which resulted in a six-month jail sentence. Washington's court-appointed attorney had told him it was, under the circumstances, a very good deal. It turned out that Washington had been arrested before on numerous occasions for petty crimes and public drunkenness, but he had no felony convictions. Constance could not believe that Washington was only thirty-five. She told me afterward that she was touched at the preliminary hearing when Washington saw her and mouthed "I'm sorry" to her.

"You know," she told me, "he looked like he really meant it. I must say he looked like such a forlorn figure that I felt very sorry for him, even though he could have killed us both for all I know."

"I'm afraid there are thousands of people like him on the streets of San Francisco, dirty, smelly—and some, like your guy, aggressive—indigents," I said.

"Well, we don't know how they got that way," my mother said. "They have no work and apparently no families who care about them, a lot look like mental cases. They have no place to live except the street or the shelters, and their spirit is gone, drowned in drugs and alcohol. Maybe it is not fair to judge until you know the whole story."

"Why don't you find out about Alonso Washington?" I said, adding that Conrad knew people who could help her get access to public records.

"What if I visited him in jail?" Mother asked.

"That sounds like a really bad idea," I said.

"I'm going to talk to Claudia," said Mom. "Claudia has been involved with some of the homeless charities. Maybe there is something that I can do."

Three weeks later, my mother told me she had indeed visited Alonso Washington in the San Francisco County Jail, not once, but three times. Mom had picked up his whole life story, and it had taken two visits before she got all of the details. Briefly, the highlights were that Alonso was born into a fatherless family in Atlanta, Georgia. He played football in early high school, but he flunked out of school in his sophomore year because, he said, he had hooked up with the wrong crowd and started drinking and using drugs. Alonso's older brother helped him get a job as a "gofer" with a construction crew. Alonso learned how to drive, and by the time he was twenty-two, he had landed a job driving a dump truck. He kept out of serious trouble, met a girl, and got married.

When he was twenty-seven, he was offered a job doing long hauls between Atlanta and Midwest cities including Chicago, Kansas City, St. Louis, and Detroit. The job paid well and gave him more money than he had ever dreamed of having. But he was away from home four or five nights a week, and his wife filled the vacuum by sleeping around. She was also apparently unable to have children.

When Alonso was thirty-two, his wife left him, and he began to drink heavily. He was convicted twice of drunk driving, and he lost his job. Atlanta police arrested him twice for drunk and disorderly conduct. On the second offense, he was sentenced to ninety days in jail. One of the men he met in jail told Alonso he was going to San Francisco the moment he got out. Alonso said the man told him San Francisco treated homeless people better than any city in America with generally clean and safe shelters, free food, medical clinics, and psychiatric help. They even let people sleep on the street.

Alonso told my mother that he had come to San Francisco two years before their violent encounter and that it was a lot better than Atlanta. Even so, he said, he was still embittered that his wife had left him and that he had become an alcoholic. All he cared about, he said, was how and when he was going to get another drink. He begged for money on the streets, and people were so intimidated by his size that they usually gave him at least a dollar, sometimes more. He told Mom that he really had no intention of robbing her and Conrad. He said it was only when Mom said to Conrad that he wanted their money that the thought occurred to him to commit a robbery. He said he was too drunk to think straight, the proof of which was that he had never before robbed anyone. So Mom concluded that the whole mess was partly her fault.

When Alonso was about to be released, Mom and Claudia arranged for him to get part-time work doing cleanup jobs under close supervision at various homes in Pacific Heights. Mom said she had gotten to know Alonso pretty well, and she trusted him almost completely. She told Alonso that if he could stay sober, he could get his driver's license and go back to truck driving. Alonso liked the plan, but probably just as important was that someone believed in him. Conrad arranged for Alonso to join an Alcoholics Anonymous chapter in the Fillmore district that was attended by both black and white people. Alonso made some good friends in that group, one of whom offered him a room, which was far better than sleeping in the nearby shelter run by the Catholic Church.

Alonso became religious, began writing his mother in Atlanta, and managed to stay sober, thanks to the daily encouragement of his friends in AA. Subsequently, he got a job driving a delivery truck for a large retail chain. He met a girl in church, and in 1979 he married her, and they eventually had four children. Alonso and Mom stayed in touch, and she and Conrad attended his wedding.

"Richard Hamblen told me that Alonso was a very unusual case and that street people are hardly ever rehabilitated," Mom told me years later. "That is true from what I know now, but if Alonso hadn't been successful, I doubt that Claudia and I would have gotten so involved in helping these people."

Mom and Claudia eventually contributed substantial sums of money to the Catholic shelter for the sole purpose of giving these hard-core derelicts some tools to reach for a better life. The shelter used the money to clothe, educate, and motivate homeless people and to probe into each individual for redeeming qualities. Only a small percentage actually changed, but for those who did, the help was like a gift from heaven. Alonso, of course, was the star, and he became an excellent speaker and motivator. He always ended his inspirational story by saying that he owed it all to a lady he had once tried to rob.

CHAPTER 71

To backtrack a bit, just after the foiled attempted robbery by the then-unknown robber, Herb Caen had run a longish item about it in his column. Caen noted that Constance Sutro had pushed the robber to the pavement after he had knocked her husband out by bashing a bottle on his head. Clearly, said Caen, the robber did not know with whom he was dealing, recalling that back in the 1960s, Constance and her dog had driven off two men in the midst of an attempted rape in Golden Gate Park.

"Constance Booker Sutro is one of the grand ladies of our lovely city, and despite her more than five decades, she's still a looker," Caen wrote. "And a warning to any would-be assailant: Mrs. Sutro is now armed with mace."

Veronica asked me how Caen had gotten all that information. I said I did not know, but probably from the police. I found out later that it was Conrad who had called Caen, and I told Veronica.

"He sure is proud of your mom," said Veronica. "I wish you felt that way about me."

"Come on, honey, I love you—what more can I say?" I said. "I couldn't live without you. We're best friends. You're better-looking now than ever, and you love San Francisco and the life we have here together."

"You say all the right things, but words are cheap," she said.

"What are you talking about?" I said.

"You haven't touched me in a week, and we are only in our second year of marriage," Veronica said. "How are we ever going to have a baby?"

"Honey, it is not for lack of trying. I've produced enough sperm with you to populate China," I said.

But despite all of our trying, Veronica did not get pregnant. She suggested we seek medical advice. Eight weeks later, the doctor recommended that we consider adopting, because it did not appear that Veronica could produce a child; she was not producing any eggs. We sought second and third opinions, but the answer was the same.

Veronica sank into a deep depression and began to drink more. Moreover, she spent more and more time at work, often not getting home until after eight. She said she was quite busy. A couple of times in the evening, I called her direct line, but she did not answer. When I asked her where she had been, she said she had been in the office but perhaps had missed my call, because she had been working a lot in Donal McMurtry's office, putting together package golf vacations to the United Kingdom. I knew McMurtry, and I did not like him—mainly because he was a big, good-looking single guy with a great sense of humor. He was drunk on three of the four social occasions where we were together. Even worse, he was very solicitous of Veronica and seemed to like her a lot. Veronica said that Donal was creative and that his ideas on developing golf vacations were looking very doable and profitable.

The tip-off that something was drastically wrong with our marriage came when Veronica lost her seemingly endless appetite for sex. In fact, she began turning down my overtures. I questioned her, and she said it was just a cycle she was going through. I asked her if there was another man in the picture, and she said I was getting paranoid.

In June of 1976, Veronica informed me that she was making a three-week business trip to England, Ireland, and Scotland to finalize arrangements with a number of golf clubs and hotels.

"We feel that we have to see all facilities firsthand before we recommend them to clients," Veronica said.

"Who is 'we'?" I asked.

"The agency," she said. "Actually, Jack Peters, the owner."

"Are you going alone?" I asked.

"Someone else will probably go along, but that has not been decided," she said.

"What if I went along?" I asked.

"Dan, it is a business trip, not a vacation," she said.

"So your husband is not welcome," I said.

"Don't make a big thing about this, Dan. It doesn't become you."

Another thing that bothered me was that Veronica no longer wanted to spend much time around my family.

One day, when I was visiting my mother and Conrad to talk about investment matters, somehow the subject switched to Veronica.

"She seems very distant these days, Dan. Is there something wrong?" my mother asked.

"She's been pretty upset about not being able to have a baby," I said.

"Why don't you adopt a baby?" Conrad suggested.

"She's got a serious hang-up about that," I said.

"She'd change her mind if she could see the baby in advance," Mom said.

"It takes months to find a child; there are long waiting lists," I responded.

"There are ways I might be able to help," said Conrad, who promised to quickly get back to me.

I later told Veronica what Conrad had said, and she showed no interest.

"I told you I don't want somebody else's baby," she said.

Two weeks later, Veronica said she would be flying to Dublin on August 1 and would not return until August 24.

"We are visiting twenty-one golf courses and thirty hotels, and we'll be driving all over Ireland, Scotland, and England," said Veronica.

"You seem pretty excited," I said. "Have they decided who is going with you?"

"Mr. Peters said it had to be Donal McMurtry, because he is the only one who plays a lot of golf," said Veronica.

I got a sinking feeling in my stomach. I did not know what to say. The thought of Veronica spending all that time with Donal McMurtry made me sick. He'd have her in the sack by the third night. Maybe they had already started an affair.

I poured myself a drink, a double scotch. I just sat in my chair, looking out at San Francisco Bay. The sun was almost down, and it was a warm and clear July night. I poured another scotch, not bothering to add any water.

Veronica was busy in the bedroom, doing what, I did not know. She finally came out and asked, "Are you getting drunk?"

"I'm just having a few farewell drinks to our marriage," I said.

"What are you talking about?"

"Just that if you take off for three weeks with Donal McMurtry, it is going to end our marriage," I said.

"I have to go—it is my job," she said.

"You don't have to work," I said, knowing the statement was a mistake the minute it left my mouth.

"What do you want me to do, sit home all day and do nothing?" she said. "Work is what keeps me going, and if you have so little respect for me, so little trust in me, maybe we shouldn't be married."

That was it. She had said it: "maybe we shouldn't be married." It reverberated in my numbed brain. I said nothing.

Veronica went to the kitchen, saying she was going to make some dinner given that we were obviously not going out. I poured another drink and said nothing. What was there to say? Nothing. It was over. Endsville. Donal McMurtry, big stud. Fuck him. Fuck her.

Veronica came into the room with a TV tray.

"I made some scrambled eggs and salad," she said. "You'd better eat. You've had too much to drink. You started three hours ago."

"I haven't had enough," I said.

"You are drunk," she said.

"Screw you—and Donal McMurtry too," I said.

"I can't stand to be around you when you are like this," she said.

"You are getting me mixed up with Donal McMurtry," I said. "He's the one with the drinking problem, not me. I only get drunk if my wife tells me to go fuck off."

"Why don't you sleep on the couch," Veronica said.

"You don't want me in the igloo?" I said.

Veronica turned and went to the bedroom.

Screw her, I thought.

I woke up at five in the morning. I remembered everything—and I cringed at the recollection. What the hell was I doing getting drunk? What a jerk I was. I showered and by 6:00 AM was at my desk. Veronica was still sleeping when I left home. The great thing about my work was that I found trading stocks and watching markets to be so absorbing that I thought of nothing else. It was only when I went home to my empty apartment that the reality of what had happened caused me to once again cringe at the situation. Veronica had left a note saying she would not be home for dinner, no reason given.

I called my brother Jim at his home in Los Angeles. His maid said he was in New York, staying at his apartment in the Hampshire House. I caught him moments after he had walked in the door. I told Jim I had to get his opinion about my marriage and proceeded to give him a detailed thirty-minute backgrounder.

Jim asked lots of questions about our sex life, and I told him it had ceased to exist starting about six weeks earlier. He also asked how long Veronica had been working nights at the office. He wanted to know every detail I could give him about Donal McMurtry.

"You think she is having an affair with McMurtry, don't you?" I said.

"Just because it looks that way doesn't make it so," he said. "I take it that Veronica has made up her mind about making the trip, no?"

"Yes, she is leaving in ten days," I said.

"Do you want my advice?" Jim asked.

I grunted.

"Let her go. Don't mention anything about the trip again, or McMurtry. See how she handles it. If she brings up anything, just tell her you have been thinking things over and that you are going to do what she said: trust her."

I followed Jim's advice. It was hard, but I did it. And I didn't have more than one drink at home while Veronica was still there. The night before Veronica was to leave for her trip, we went out to dinner in North Beach, where we both knew a lot of people. There was not a lot of time for private talk, but we actually had a pretty good time. When we got home, she apologized for still being in her cycle of not wanting sex.

"I don't know what has happened to me," she said, giving me a kiss before we went to sleep. As I was leaving for work the next morning at 5:30 AM, she sat up halfway in bed and waved a kiss at me. She was gone when I got back from work, gone for more than three weeks with Donal McMurtry.

I had been talking with Jim, and he seemed to think my situation was more hopeful. He asked if I could give him over the phone the first four hotels Veronica would be staying at. He said he might be able to find out whether Veronica was sleeping with Donal McMurtry.

Jim called three days later and said Veronica and Donal had booked separate rooms at each hotel, and none of the sets of rooms were adjoining.

"That doesn't really prove anything except that they probably aren't stupid," said Jim, asking me to give him the entire rest of their itinerary in the United Kingdom. "We need a bit more detective work."

Jim called a week later.

"I've got some bad news and some good news, bro," said Jim. "The bad news is that Veronica and McMurtry have been sleeping together. The good news is that some photos are one the way. They were taken in Manchester by a very aggressive private detective who managed to get inside the room where they were staying. They were both nude and on top of the covers when he threw open the door and took three photos. Apparently, McMurtry charged after the detective, but gave up the chase down the hallway when he realized he was naked."

"Well, it proves my fears were right," I said. Somehow, I felt a little relieved. Somebody once told me that bad news was better than doubt. I had been living for nearly two months suspecting the worst of my wife, but I hadn't been sure. Now, somehow, I felt relieved to know the truth, as horrible as it was.

"By the way, bro," said Jim. "There is another little wrinkle. Veronica and McMurtry weren't alone. There was another naked woman on the bed with them."

I wasn't as surprised as I should have been.

The next day, I called Richard Hamblen and asked to see him in his office. He postponed two appointments to see me when I told him briefly what it was about.

Richard worked out the arrangements for a divorce with Veronica. She went to Reno for six weeks, where she got an uncontested divorce on the grounds of mental cruelty. I gave Veronica a check for $50,000 in lieu of any alimony.

My mother wrote in her diary that she had never felt "so heavy of heart."

"I could never have imagined how awful I could feel over the ending of both Jim's and Dan's marriages. They are both so wonderful. They just married the wrong kind of women. Joe used to say that character was everything. And not everyone has it—certainly not Jillian or Veronica. They are part of a new generation that doesn't seem to have the same values as my generation. I am so glad my father is not witness to what has happened. Fortunately, Jim seems to have gotten over his breakup with Jill. He now jokes that he is famous for once having been Jill's husband, especially since she is now one of the top stars in Hollywood. He says women are chasing after him more than ever. The one I worry about is Danny. He's very different than Jim."

CHAPTER 72

The Booker-Sutro family got together for Thanksgiving in 1976 at the Sutro mansion. I was fresh from my divorce, and the party helped to lift my spirits. Jimmy Carter had just defeated Gerald Ford for the presidency with 297 electoral votes to 241. Carter, who had campaigned on the slogan "I'll never lie to you," turned out to be an ineffectual idealist whose greatest contribution might have been that he set the stage for the election of Ronald Reagan in 1980. Actually, Richard Hamblen, who was a staunch supporter of Reagan during his two terms as governor of California, had been part of a campaign to have Reagan nominated for the presidency in 1976. But the effort failed narrowly. At the time, we thought that was the end of Reagan because of his age, but we all underestimated the Gipper.

Mom, now sixty-two, was her same old self, though her hair was now more gray than blonde, and her figure was shifting to the middle, despite her regular tennis, brisk walks, and light weight lifting. There was no question her face showed some of the sorrow of her sons' two divorces. But on this day, it was bright with the excitement of the family gathering. She was particularly delighted with Jim, who had come from Los Angeles with his new, steady girlfriend, Pamela Langer, a lovely Eurasian woman from Singapore who was half Chinese and half German. Pamela, an airline flight attendant and only twenty-five, was tall, with long black hair, an ivory complexion, and beautiful delicate features. But the best part was her lovely British accent and her ready laugh. She doted on Jim in a way that Jill never had. Mom took an immediate liking to Pamela and went out of her way to make her feel at home. In fact, everyone did, including the budding socialite Lillian Graff, the fiancée of Conrad's son, Adam Sutro, who was making remarkable progress as a real estate developer.

Pamela told Lillian that she had met Jim on a United Airlines flight from Los Angeles to New York. She had recognized him from a photograph of him and Jill Landis that had been published in *People* magazine.

"I remembered that photo, because I could not understand why Jill Landis would leave that beautiful man for an aging German," said Pamela, laughing. "I can tell you Germans are not prizes as husbands. I love my father, but he is so old-school, so set in his ways. Of course, my mother doesn't see that. My father found a perfect wife. They have been married for thirty-one years."

I must say that I was happy for Jim and also jealous. My split with Veronica, despite the circumstances, had left me more than a little depressed. I was forty-one years old with no wife and no children and no prospect of having either. Worse, I did not feel particularly good about myself. When I compared myself with my brother Joe, it was strictly no contest. Joe had a great wife who adored him and three lovely children. His books were selling well, and he lived, it seemed to me, a charmed life. The worst thing that ever happened to Joe was pretty awful: the grisly auto accident on the Bayshore that ended his basketball career and nearly killed him. But now, one of his books was even about to be made into a movie, a circumstance helped by a process started by Jill Landis when she was still married to Jim.

I know that Jim had been devastated by his breakup with Jill, but he had a great ability to accept the blow and move on. Perhaps it was because, in his case, there was an endless stream of beautiful women who considered him the Prince Charming they had always dreamed about. Jim, at forty, was more handsome than ever, and his business was prospering, so much so that he was talking about setting a goal to retire at age forty-five. The truth was that although Jim was a great people person when he wanted to turn on the charm, he really did not like the top-level salesmanship that went with romancing the television station owners and managers that his firm represented. Joe used to kid Jim about having to "suck up" all of the time, something Joe, as a newspaperman and a writer of fiction, never had to do. Jim said he envied Joe's independence.

I too had to do some selling in my job as a portfolio manager and securities broker, but I likened myself to a person who was basically showing people how to make an above-average return on their investments. The truth of the matter was that I was quite lucky to have Conrad Sutro and Richard Hamblen as my advisors; they were blessed with remarkable judgment and excellent contacts in the world of business.

Of course, Richard had been handling my mother's investments for years before I became a broker, and he had done exceptionally well by her. In retrospect, no one in my family ever had to worry about money. However, I don't think anyone took money for granted, either, Mom especially, who had to manage a modest income during the depression and then the war. But even then, we were lucky. Dad was an army officer, and his pay and benefits were better than most.

After my divorce, I began drinking more than before, often coming straight back to my apartment after work, skipping exercise, but never skipping a third martini. When you start drinking martinis alone, you are in real trouble. But I could not get motivated. I had lost some zest for living. Was it wounded pride? I found myself feeling lousy in the morning and increasingly aloof from other people, some of whom I began to duck.

However, there was one woman I was interested in. She worked as a buyer for I. Magnin's, and I had recently met her at a party. Nancy Shofner was thirty-one years old and divorced, and I found her exceptionally attractive. I took her out twice, and I thought we got along pretty well. But when I asked her out a third time, she said she did not see the relationship going anywhere, because she was looking to get married again and have children, and she felt I was too old for her. I said the difference was only ten years, but she said she wanted someone more her age. I later found out that shortly after my and Nancy's first date, she had met another man with whom she had almost immediately fallen in love. Why not—he was younger, richer, and better-looking! But I did not know that at the time she broke up with me. Then, I thought she was rejecting me in favor of nothing. Well, nothing was what I felt like. I could not seem to shake it.

Mom and Conrad hosted the annual family Christmas party that year. It was fun, and I kept a good face on my inner sadness, or at least so I thought. I did not think that anyone had noticed my three martinis or how my wine glass at dinner had required constant filling, but then Conrad called a taxi to take me home, saying it would not be prudent for me to drive my own car. I did not argue. I was never an obstreperous drunk.

During the week between Christmas and New Year's, I had separate invitations for private lunches with Richard Hamblen, Conrad Sutro, and my brother Joe. Mom invited me for dinner on a night Conrad was going to be out, and Jim called from Los Angeles wanting to know if he could help me get out of my funk.

"I've never known you to be so down, bro," said Jim. "Veronica is certainly not worth any prolonged sorrow any more than Jill Landis. We Bookers are tough; we just get on with it. Look at Mom. I can't recall her ever sitting around feeling sorry for herself."

The others all gave a similar message. I decided they were right. I was going to get on with it. The trouble was I felt a void inside myself, a loss of interest in life. I had a great family. They all loved me. But somehow I did not love myself.

In March of 1977, Conrad invited me to spend a week with him in Arizona to watch the San Francisco Giants in spring training, just the two of us. Conrad knew practically everyone in the Giants organization, and we had dinner with a number of the players, the most notable and most fun being Willie McCovey, the future Hall of Fame first baseman then in the twilight of his career. I told Willie I had seen him in his major-league debut with the Giants in 1958 in a mid-season game played at Seals Stadium. McCovey, then twenty-one, had just been called up from the Phoenix Giants.

"If you were there, man—what'd I do?" McCovey asked.

"You hit four doubles, two down the right field line and two down the left field line," I said.

"Hey, man, you *were* there—gimme five," said McCovey, adding, "Hey, Conrad, this dude's all right. That was eighteen years ago."

Spending a week in the warm Arizona sun and hanging out with people who had succeeded in a game I knew well was a lot of fun. I loved the endless stories, and I even managed to get myself some new clients. When we returned to San Francisco, I felt better than I had in months. Mom commented that the trip to Arizona had been just the tonic I'd needed. She was right.

Conrad invited me to eight Giant day games once the season began, and Mom and Joe and some of his kids would often come along. Conrad's seats were in a box right behind the Giants dugout. Unfortunately, the Giants had a pretty awful team in 1977, and they finished fifth in the National League West, well below .500, but we still had a great time.

Conrad was a great believer that life was meant to be fun. Being around him meant being amused almost all of the time. He was especially fun at golf and had a respectable 13 handicap. We must have played fifteen rounds together that year at the Olympic Club in San Francisco and at Cypress Point and Pebble Beach in Monterey.

"You are a good influence on Conrad," Mom said to me. "He's played more golf this year than I can remember."

In the fall, Conrad insisted that I join him and his usual crowd of people for Stanford football games on Saturdays and 49er games on Sundays. Everywhere Conrad went, he knew lots of people, and his ready smile and joy for life were contagious. As I look back, I see that 1977 was my year with Conrad, and it was the year I broke out of my funk and learned to have fun once again.

CHAPTER 73

The late 1970s were a pivotal time in American history. Richard Hamblen, San Francisco's most distinguished lawyer, was incensed when President Carter agreed to turn over the Panama Canal to Panama. It was Hamblen's view, expressed at a dinner at the Hamblen household, that too many lives had been lost and too many dollars spent to simply give it to the Panamanians, even if the handover was to be twenty-two years in the future. Moreover, he questioned whether the Panamanians had the skills to operate the canal in an efficient manner. He also was worried the Panamanians would try to raise prices beyond reason.

Conrad Sutro said he thought it was a good political move with respect to America's relations with Latin America. Second, he said, there were a lot of well-educated Panamanians who were smart enough to run the canal, and it was in their self-interest to run it efficiently. Twenty-two years was plenty of time to get a management team in place. The fact was, he said, there were alternatives to using the canal, most notably coast-to-coast American rail service, in addition to sailing around the tip of South America, which took longer, but involved no tolls.

"If the Panamanians don't do the job, they will lose a lot of business," said Conrad. Richard said he hoped Conrad was right, while noting neither of them would likely be around to see the actual results.

"I hope to be around, and I think it is a lousy idea," said brother Joe, as ever the ardent rightist. "Carter is the kind of guy who doesn't want to keep score in kids' sports games so there won't be any losers. How did we ever elect that nerd to be president? He's a born loser."

"He didn't lose to Ford," I said.

"Don't tell me, Danny, that you are becoming a Carter fan," said Joe. "You've been spending too much time with Conrad."

"I voted for Ford," I said.

"I think we all did, including Dad," said Adam Sutro. "Dad is a liberal Republican, and I think the rest of us are just a lot more conservative, though Dad may be responsible for moving Danny more to the center."

"I confess I have fallen under Conrad's spell," I said. "He gives me two-foot putts on the golf course, and the rest of you are so mean-spirited you make me putt them out."

"Adam is right; I did vote for Ford," said Conrad. "The reason was I could not bring myself to vote for anyone who does not play golf."

That brought laughter and cheers from the gathering.

"I am glad our family doesn't have fierce arguments like some," said Mom. "Yet there is conversation about serious matters and even differences of opinion. I happen to agree with Conrad that if we are going to have the respect of people outside of this country, we have to respect them. By agreeing to give the canal to Panama, we are sending a very positive message about the truly altruistic intentions of the United States."

"Constance," said Richard, "I have always said you would have made a great lawyer or diplomat."

"Are you now supporting the turnover, Richard?" Conrad asked.

"Of course not," said Richard. "I just like the way your wife expresses herself, and Conrad, I have to say that I consider you one of the most reasonable and affable men I have ever met."

"None of this sugarcoated, soft-boiled dialogue would ever make it into one of my books," said Joe, laughing.

There was no doubt that our family got along well and, unlike many families, genuinely liked to be together. That was especially true of the women. Claudia Hamblen and my mom had been best friends for more than thirty years. And Mom, and the rest of us, dearly loved Joe's wife, Claire, who we had known for more than twenty years. Jim's girlfriend, Pamela Langer, fit right in and had remarkable political intelligence and was totally at ease. It was a slightly different story with Adam's future wife, Lillian Graff, who could sometimes be a big standoffish and remote. But Mom was working on her and making progress, an effort that did not go unrecognized by Adam, who treated Mom with enormous respect.

One of the subjects that invariably came up at family gatherings was whether I had met any nice girls. If Conrad was within earshot, he would interrupt, saying, "I don't want to hear any war stories that are going to make me jealous," which he followed with lascivious laughter. But the fact was, as Conrad knew full well, that I did not have any serious love life, though I confess I did not live an abstemious life, either.

I decided to quit drinking on September 1, 1978, not for good, but for the time being. I was forty-three years old and looked older. I had gotten out of shape and weighed 204 pounds, which was too much on my five-foot-ten-inch frame. My hair was thinning and turning gray. My face had a slightly bloated look from too much drinking and not enough rigorous exercise. Moreover, my diet consisted of too many steaks, hamburgers, and french fries and too much coffee. I even decided to cut out the odd Cuban cigars that I loved to smoke with a brandy after the three martinis, big steak, and french fries.

But I had gone through periods of abstention before, and I knew if I was going to succeed, I would have to replace all of these very enjoyable pursuits. So instead of heading to a bar or home for drinks after work every night, I walked from my Montgomery Street office to the YMCA near San Francisco City Hall, which took twenty-two minutes. On Mondays, Wednesdays, and Fridays, I jogged around the track for one mile in nine minutes, over time increasing to three miles in twenty-four minutes, and I followed that with a one-hour yoga session. On Tuesdays and Thursdays, I swam laps for fifteen minutes before going into a one-hour meditation course. Then I would have dinner with friends or clients (those whose lives did not revolve around drinking) or go home and cook for myself. Instead or ordering steaks, I began eating a lot of fish, salads, and vegetables. I cut down to just two cups of coffee a day and ate absolutely no sugar. I never cast a shadow on McDonald's or any other fast-food place. Between meals, I snacked on fruit.

I told Joe about my new program, and he laughed and said it sounded like one of his New Year's resolutions.

"I resolve to drink less and exercise more every year, but it lasts about a week," he said. "I wish you luck."

My mother said she liked my new program, but thought I should also address the mental side, not just the physical.

"You can overdo the self-absorption," she said. "You need to get involved with a good cause—do some good for other people to give your life a proper balance."

Of course, my mother practiced what she preached and had become extremely involved with the plight of homeless people in

San Francisco. Interestingly, in 1977 my mother had had a brief association with Rev. Jim Jones, who ran the People's Temple on Fillmore Street on a property formerly occupied by a synagogue.

Jones was a charismatic preacher who had begun his ministry in Indiana and then moved to Ukiah in northern California in 1965 before moving to San Francisco. Jones was a socialist who believed that a commune was the ultimate lifestyle. He had a tremendous knack for self-promotion, and his dark hair and black eyes gave him a surreal look. Jones became politically active in San Francisco, and his congregation of devoted worshippers grew to nearly 2,000. He gave significant financial support to George Moscone in the mayoral election, and when Moscone won, he appointed Jones as director of the city's Housing Authority. About half of Jones's congregation was black, and many of them believed that Jones was capable of performing miracles, including the cure of cancer.

When Jones went back to Indiana for a vacation, he bumped into an old friend who was working as a newspaperman. The former friend noticed the enormous change in Jones, who was wearing a fancy suit and was accompanied by two burly bodyguards.

"When you've reached the top, you have to play the part," Jones was supposed to have said. Meanwhile, Jones's initial reputation in the city was that of a progressive minister who sought to create racial harmony. Not surprisingly, Jones became a friend of Willie Brown, the all-powerful speaker of the California State Assembly, a very savvy black politician who later became mayor of San Francisco. California governor Jerry Brown also sought out Jones.

My mother attended services at the People's Temple a few times at the request of some of her homeless friends, and she came away with a mixed reaction. She found Jones to be a masterful speaker, but she thought some of the "cures" invoked by Jones were questionable. Even so, my mother made a significant contribution to the People's Temple that got her into a one-on-one meeting with Jones. Jones said he had heard of my mother's work with the homeless, and he praised her for her generosity and understanding. He said that he hoped that she would be a regular member of the People's Temple and that she would not be asked to be any more generous than she had already been. My mother left the meeting wanting to do even more.

Richard Hamblen had opposed my mother's $10,000 donation to the People's Temple, because he had heard some nasty rumors about Jones. It was one of the few times my mother did not follow Richard's advice.

A few months later, a local magazine wrote a scathing exposé on Jones, spelling out his sexual activities plus his increasing financial demands on members of his church. Jones responded that these were all lies perpetrated by his enemies. But the media would not relent, and more and more incriminating stories were brought to light, including information that Jones asked his followers to sell all of their belongings and make a total commitment to the People's Temple. Many did.

My mother said it was hard to believe all of the terrible things that were written about Jones.

In the end, Jones led nearly 1,200 church members to Guyana on the heavily jungled north coast of South America, where four years earlier, he had purchased three hundred acres of land on which he hoped to create a perfect commune in a socialist country far, far away from his enemies.

Jones's exodus was huge news in San Francisco, and I remember my mother saying the press had hounded a good man out of town. One who did not agree was Congressman Leo Ryan, a friend of Richard's from San Mateo. Ryan had heard complaints from several of his constituents that Jones was keeping some of his congregation against their will. Ryan agreed to make a firsthand investigation, and in November of 1978, he flew to Guyana with several newspeople and others. There were some 1,100 members of the People's Temple in Guyana at that time, but only fifteen said they wanted to return with Ryan to the States. When Ryan and the fifteen defectors arrived back at the airport, an armed group of Jones's followers appeared and opened fire, killing Ryan and three others. The next day, more than nine hundred of the members of the People's Temple died of poisoning in what was purported to be a mass suicide ordered by the preacher. Jones himself died of a gunshot wound that may or may not have been self-inflicted.

All of us were appalled at the grisly tale, and my mother said she had never in her life been so wrong about another person.

The next week, San Francisco mayor George Moscone was murdered in his office, along with Harvey Milk, a city supervisor. They were killed by a former supervisor, Dan White, thirty-two, a self-styled conservative who did not like the liberal ways of Moscone. It was not a proud time for San Franciscans.

Also in 1978, the religious right took satisfaction in the shooting of *Hustler* magazine publisher Larry Flynt, who was paralyzed for life.

There was good news in the late 1970s too. Margaret Thatcher was elected prime minister of the United Kingdom in 1979. Bill Walsh was named coach of the San Francisco 49ers, the beginning of the great 49er dynasty. Formal diplomatic relations between China and the United States were established. The Soviet Union invaded Afghanistan, an action that most believe was the beginning of the end of the Soviet Union as a global superpower. Egypt, Israel, and the United States signed the Camp David Accord.

But also in 1979, Iranian students stormed the United States Embassy in Tehran, where they held fifty-two American hostages for 444 days, an act that brought focus on Jimmy Carter's soft underbelly and as much as anything paved the way for the election of Ronald Reagan in 1980.

I held onto my pledge not to drink during that entire period starting on September 1, 1978, until the Reagan's inauguration in January of 1981, by which time I was a happily married man.

CHAPTER 74

There was a shortage of American heroes as the 1970s mercifully came to a close. President Carter's approval rating was a dismal 30 percent. Legendary Ohio State football coach Woody Hayes was fired after he punched an opposing player who had intercepted an Ohio State pass in the Gator Bowl. Famed Indiana basketball coach Bobby Knight, in Puerto Rico as coach of the U.S. basketball team, was sentenced to six months in jail for assaulting a policeman. Nelson Rockefeller, former vice president and four-time governor of New York, died of a heart attack while allegedly having sex with a young woman; it was subsequently reported that another young woman was also present. Billy Carter, the president's beer-loving brother, received criticism from the Jewish community for being friendly to Libya; he replied, "They can kiss my ass." John Wayne died at age seventy-two. Chrysler was near bankruptcy, inflation was in double digits, and the prime lending rate reached an all-time high of 15.5 percent; a decade of economic malaise was ending on a decidedly sour note. Iran seized the U.S. Embassy in Tehran. U.S. Steel announced it was closing eight U.S. plants and laying off 13,000 workers. OPEC announced it was raising oil prices to $30 a barrel. Economists said the action would bring on even greater inflation and a likely recession in 1980.

It was no small wonder that my income was off sharply in 1979. But I was confident a turnaround was in the offing. Ronald Reagan seemed a cinch to get the Republican nomination and would surely beat Jimmy Carter in 1980. Carter's chances for reelection appeared so dim that scandal-scarred Senator Edward Kennedy announced he would seek the Democratic nomination. Of course, he never had a chance. Reagan said America had a "rendezvous with destiny," a sharp contrast to Carter, who seemed intent on downsizing America's role in the world. Reagan said he stood for traditional American values, lower taxes, free enterprise, and a strong military that would stand up to the Soviet threat.

On September 4, 1979, I weighed in at 180 pounds. In one year and four days, I had lost twenty-four pounds. My waist had shrunk from thirty-nine inches to thirty-five. People said I looked ten years younger. I had not had a drink in more than a year. Amazingly, I did not miss it. A year earlier, before my rigorous exercise program, I felt I was spiraling downward through middle age at a rapid clip, with much more behind me than ahead. But now I felt just the opposite. I was convinced the best was still to come, even though I conceded that my life had been up to that point good in every department except matrimony.

The first time I met Karen Brewster was at the office of Ken Thatcher. She was there working on an ad campaign for one of Ken's clients. She was wearing heavy-rimmed glasses, an oversized orange sweater and white blouse, and a khaki skirt. Her long, sandy-colored hair was in desperate need of combing. She looked like a librarian who preferred reading books to arranging them.

Ken, now in his late sixties, wore his thick white hair over his collar and was as handsome as ever. He had cut back on his drinking. Ken and I had maintained our relationship since our soccer days together, and he had a modest equity account with me from which he made enough money to help keep up his traditional lifestyle in those months when his expenses exceeded income. He had lost the San Miguel Brewery account when the Soriano family lost control of the company to some Marcos cronies, but he had enough clients to keep him involved and happy.

"Danny, this is Karen Brewster, who is working on the Sea World campaign," said Ken. Karen put out her hand without really looking at me.

"Danny will make you some money in the stock market if you ever get out of debt," Ken added.

"Fat chance of that happening with my mortgage payments," said Karen.

"Where do you live?" I asked.

Karen looked up at me and appeared to be deciding whether or not to answer the question. It was as if I had brazenly asked for her telephone number, a thought that did not cross my mind.

"On Baker, near the Panhandle," she said. "Where do you live?"

"I have an apartment on Telegraph Hill," I replied, adding, "Baker Street is a great location, dead in the center of the city."

"It's my piece of the pie," she said, turning to Ken, asking if there was any chance Sea World could increase its budget for print advertising.

"I think we can get good response from family discount coupons," she said.

"I agree," said Ken. "Say Karen, why don't you join Dan and me for lunch?"

"Sure," she said. "I like being seen with handsome older men and buffed stockbrokers."

It was hard to tell what kind of body Karen had under her loose-fitting attire, but I liked her description of me as buffed! In fact, I was buffed for the first time in my life. I had been seeing several different women since deciding to clean up my act. Most of these girls were still in their late twenties. I judged that Karen had passed that milestone and was somewhere in her mid-thirties.

Over lunch, Karen wanted to know if Ken had ever met Mother Teresa, who had just won the Nobel Peace prize for her work with the poor in India.

"Funny you should ask," said Ken. "Actually, I went to Calcutta five years ago to give her mission $50,000 that was raised by some of my Catholic friends. They chose me to go, because I had spent a lot of time in Asia. Unfortunately, and this did not surprise me, I never got to meet her, but I was able to pass the money to her through a priest and later got a nice thank-you note from her."

"Why wouldn't she see you?" Karen asked.

"She prefers to spend her time helping the sick," said Ken.

"I guess she's a living saint if there ever was one," I said, adding that while in the army, I had actually met a woman who would probably be made a saint one day.

"Really?" said Karen, suddenly showing her first sign of interest in what I had to say. "Who was that?"

"Therese Neumann of Konnersreuth, which is a tiny town in Bavaria near the Czech border," I said. "She was a stigmatist, born in 1898 on Good Friday, and after she became an adult and went through a long health crisis, she developed all of the wounds of Christ and had these incredible visions."

"How'd you happen to see her?"

"I read about her in one of the army newspapers. I was stationed in Wuerzburg at the time, and I guess I had been searching for a long time for proof that God existed. The story about Therese Neumann made it sound like she was living proof. Anyway, I got to talking about what I had read to our lieutenant, a devout Catholic, and he said we should go see her."

"What kind of living proof are you talking about?" Karen asked.

"Oh, there was a lot of stuff," I said. "A lot of it very impressive. For example, she did not eat any food, saying the only nourishment she needed was Holy Communion."

"And you believed that?" said Karen.

"Actually, the church was skeptical, and back in 1927, they decided to do a foolproof check by watching her nonstop for fourteen days. Two doctors set up the tests, and four nuns rotated watching her. She was never left alone for a minute. They took her temperature, weighed her, took her pulse—even sent body secretions and blood to a laboratory. At no point was she given any food except for her daily wafer at Holy Communion. At the end of the two weeks, she weighed exactly what she had at the start of the test. The doctors were incredulous, and news of the peasant woman from Konnersreuth swept Germany."

I went on in great detail about what I had read about Therese Neumann's childhood as the eldest of eleven children growing up on a small farm in Konnersreuth, where she had only seven years of schooling. When she was twenty, she was injured in a fall that began a six-year period in which she ultimately had a complete breakdown in her health, becoming both deaf and blind and completely unable to take care of herself. Doctors believed death was near. In 1923, Therese dumfounded her doctor and her family by miraculously regaining her sight. From that day forward, she ceased to eat or drink any earthly food. Subsequently, all of her illnesses went away. In 1926, she had a vivid vision of Jesus, and at the same time, she felt a sharp pain in her left side, and blood began to trickle down. That was just the beginning."

"Ken, do you believe this?" asked Karen.

"Thanks to Danny, I have read two books about Therese Neumann, and I don't think she had the education or the motivation to try to fool people," said Ken. "She ultimately had thousands of visions in which the wounds of Christ opened and bled. Tens of thousands of people in total saw her endure these day-long visions, including scholars who said that she repeated words in the language of the time of Jesus that she could have had no way of knowing."

"So you actually met her?" Karen asked me.

"Yes, Lieutenant Cheney and I and his interpreter drove over to Konnersreuth on a Monday morning. We were riding three in a little two-seat M.G. convertible, and it took us four hours to get there. When we arrived, our interpreter began asking where we could find Therese Neumann. It took more than an hour to learn that she might be working at a house outside of town. We went there, and there she was, alone, holding a shovel in her hands and wearing a white scarf and a full-length black peasant's dress. We walked up to her, and I confess I could feel a chill go through me. I could clearly see the blackened stigmata on the back of her hands. Lieutenant Cheney bowed before her and crossed himself. I sort of hung back. The interpreter said we had come from Wuerzburg. She replied that it was a long distance away and that perhaps we had better start back. We said it was a thrill to meet her, and she smiled and returned to her work. That was it."

Ken said that Therese Neumann was probably the most visited stigmatist who had ever lived. Between 1926 and her death in 1962, hundreds of thousands of people flocked to Konnersreuth to see her, many actually being present for the ecstatic visions when her wounds opened and bled. A lot of American soldiers were included in that number. Ken said Therese had these visions thirty to thirty-five Fridays a year.

"So, Dan, you saw her, but Ken has become the expert," said Karen.

"You know," said Ken, "they say that if she was faking it, she would have had to be the greatest actress in all history."

"I think one of the great things about her was that she recognized that God had chosen her for a purpose and she made herself available to see people," I said. "I have seen pictures of her during her visions in which she is sitting up in her bed with blood all over the place, and people are there, just watching."

Karen asked a lot more questions, and we spent virtually the entire lunch talking about Therese Neumann.

"Have they made her a saint?" Karen asked.

"The Catholic Church moves very slowly in such matters, though I understand there are many petitions to do so," said Ken.

"Well, this has been a very different kind of lunch, being with two evangelists who don't drink!" Karen smiled. "We'll have to do it again sometime."

CHAPTER 75

About a week after my lunch with Ken and his colleague, I was a bit surprised to receive a telephone call from Karen Brewster. I had not given her a thought since that first meeting. Karen said that she had been fascinated with what we had told her about Therese Neumann and had gone to the library to read more about her.

"I'd like to talk with you about her," said Karen. "Frankly, you have introduced me to a subject that could change my whole notion of God."

We agreed to meet for coffee the next afternoon. Karen showed up looking as she had at Ken's office: baggy clothes, messy hair, and the same unflattering horn-rimmed glasses.

She smiled warmly when we met and said she appreciated my valuable time.

"No problem," I said. "The New York markets are closed."

"You said when you met Therese Neumann, you were looking for evidence of the existence of God," she said. "I could identify with that, because frankly I've been pretty skeptical about organized religion since my days at the University of California in Santa Cruz.

I don't think any of my friends there believed in God, and if they did, none of them ever showed it. In the years after I graduated, starting with my divorce, I began to think about God. My family was never religious, and my mother has gone through four husbands. Actually, my father does go to church once in awhile, but we have never had a really serious conversation about God. He and my mother only lived together for three years, after which he moved to Los Angeles, so I did not see him more than once or twice a year growing up."

"What does your dad do?" I asked.

"He's a movie cameraman for Paramount," said Karen. "He married a set decorator twenty years ago, and they have a great marriage and live in the San Fernando Valley. I have two half brothers and a half sister. I visit them whenever I can. Actually, my job gets me to L.A. five or six times a year."

"What about your mom?" I asked. "She must be a pretty attractive woman to have had four husbands."

"She looks pretty good, takes care of herself, and has a weakness for younger men who don't believe in monogamy," said Karen. "She's a waitress at the Palace Hotel—been there twelve years."

"That's a coincidence," I said. "My mother used to be a hostess at the Huntington Hotel."

"Ken told me your mother married a millionaire," Karen said.

"Actually, my mother dated Ken Thatcher for a couple of years before she met Conrad Sutro," I said.

"She must have good taste," said Karen. "What happened?"

"Ken's work took him to the Philippines, and my mother refused to go, because my brothers and I were still in school, living at home. And Ken was still married, though he had been estranged from his wife for years. The trouble was that both Ken and his wife were Catholics and did not want to be excommunicated over a divorce."

"That's why I don't believe in organized religion," said Karen.

"I don't go to church, either," I said. "But I believe in God, most definitely. My mother's father was an Episcopalian minister, and I think I have some of his genes."

"Ken said you were married but got divorced," said Karen.

"Why did he tell you that?"

"I was just asking about you—don't take it personally," said Karen. "I like to know about people, interesting people. Ken said you were a minor-league baseball player and that you created a great radio show on San Francisco history, worked with him when he was commissioner of the soccer league, and now are one of the top stockbrokers in town."

"Did Ken tell you he used to work for Howard Hughes?" I asked.

"No, did he? Tell me about it," said Karen.

I spent the next thirty minutes telling Karen about Ken's days in Southern California when he worked for Trans World Airlines, then owned by Hughes. Karen hung on every word. She really was interested in people.

"Did you say you were married?" I asked.

"Who told you that?"

"You did, before we started talking about Howard Hughes."

"Oh. Yes, I made a foolish mistake in my senior year of college and married a gorgeous surfer I met at the beach, just the sort of man my mother would have fallen for. We were both twenty-one. He delivered pizzas when he wasn't surfing or painting or running around with his pals. Actually, he was a wonderful artist, and I hear his paintings have found a market in Santa Cruz and Monterey. But he was no more prepared to be married than I was. We split after less than a year when I came to San Francisco to work."

"As they say, youth is wasted on the young," I said, smiling.

Karen laughed and said it was certainly true in her case.

"I'll be thirty in a couple of months," she said. "And the worst part is I look even older."

"You look like the talent side of the ad agency business," I said.

"Whatever that means," she replied. "How old are you, Dan?"

"Ken didn't tell you?"

"I forgot to ask."

"Guess," I said.

"I think you are thirty-nine or forty."

"You've made my day. I'm forty-four."

"Too bad—you're too old for my mother," Karen smiled.

"I thought you wanted to talk about Therese Neumann?" I said.

"I did, but I have to go now. I have some work left to do on a presentation I have to make."

"It's after six o'clock," I said.

"No one keeps regular hours at my office," she replied. "We live off deadlines."

"I tell you my age, and you suddenly have to leave," I smiled.

"I like older men," she said. "They make me feel young."

"You are young, Karen."

"I bet my ex-husband doesn't think so," said Karen. "I am sure he is still chasing teenagers. But that is no concern of mine. I would like to talk about Therese Neumann. Can you meet me here next Monday for coffee?"

I unconsciously thought about Karen over the next couple of days. She was younger than I had thought, younger than she looked, and too young for me. A fifteen-year age difference was an insurmountable gap as far as I was concerned. Conrad Sutro was only two or three years older than my mom, and they were a prefect fit age-wise. No way I could consider someone fifteen years younger.

So why was I thinking about Karen so much and looking forward to our forthcoming coffee date? Well, for one thing, I didn't feel forty-four. I had never felt better in my entire life. More importantly, Karen seemed to be interested in me. She had called to ask me out for coffee, and she had obviously grilled Ken Thatcher about my past. Then she had asked for another coffee date. Also, she had told me things about herself that one doesn't usually tell on a second meeting, about her mother's love life, about her own aborted marriage.

Karen was a bit like Veronica was when I had first met her, a tacky, unstylish dresser in need of a serious makeover. But I didn't sense the same level of insecurity in Karen that had lurked in Veronica. Karen seemed more stable, less complicated, more direct, more honest. And if you studied her closely, you could see she had nice skin and good features and pretty, pale blue eyes with long, dark lashes, which probably were magnified by her glasses, which I had never seen her without. Still, I had to ask myself, what was I thinking? A relationship with a woman fifteen years younger? No way! But what if she did see the age difference as an obstacle? Hell, I had thought she was thirty-four or so, and she had assumed I was thirty-nine or forty. That's only a five-year age gap! I decided to let the cards play out.

Karen appeared for our coffee date with her hair pulled back in a ponytail and wearing a beige business suit and high heels with a light blue scarf that seemed to set off her eyes. The glasses were gone.

"Pardon my appearance," she said. "I had to make a client presentation this morning."

"I hardly recognized you," I said. "You look like you just stepped off the cover of *Glamour* magazine."

"Thanks," she said. "But this is not the real me. I much prefer the comfort of dressing down and forgetting the makeup. And I like to be able to see!"

"Well, put your glasses back on," I laughed. "I don't want everyone to think you are my daughter."

"Don't worry, Dad; they would never think that."

"Dad? Is that a Freudian slip?" I asked. "You are making my point."

Karen laughed. "A weak joke."

Karen finally got around to the dilemma posed to her by Therese Neumann.

"I have come to believe that there is a God, a creator, someone who planned everything, including the stars billions of light-years away from Earth," she said. "It is impossible for me to believe that the perfect order of our universe was created by chance. I mean, look at the complexity of the human brain, or the eye or the ears, or the reproduction of zillions of living things—for me, there is no way there is not a God. But I find it hard to believe the Bible stories, that man is made in God's image and that the earth and the heavens were all created in seven days. I don't know what God looks like, but I don't think he looks like us. The earth has been around for billions of years. I believe God has been around all of that time, but not in the human form. All organized religion has been created by man, not God. I think it is well intended, but I don't think it is real. Now, I do believe that God somehow has a role in our lives. Maybe we are part of God or God is part of us. I think God answers prayers. But I don't believe some priest can absolve you of all of your sins just because you have laid them all out in a confessional."

"A lot of people feel like you," I said. "In fact, I agree with most of what you say."

"Yes, but don't you see—that is why Therese Neumann creates a dilemma," said Karen. "If she is what she appears to be, and what you and others believe her to be, the stories about Christ in the Bible are likely true. So what does that imply about the veracity of the rest of the Bible?"

"Maybe the part about Christ is true, but some other things are merely made up by the Bible's authors," I said.

"I think we need to do more research into the life of Therese Neumann to see if there are many people out there who think she was a fake."

Karen had raised a question I had not really thought about. It had been twenty-four years since I had seen Therese Neumann, and I—foolishly, I now thought—had failed to think all of the implications through.

"Do you want to spend the weekend in the library?" Karen asked.

"Sure, let's do it," I said.

CHAPTER 76

I left work early the Friday before I was to meet Karen Brewster at the library and, being in a meditative and reflective mood, decided to take a long walk, despite the fact that rain was falling lightly and was expected to get heavier by early evening. On this day, I decided to forego my visit to the Y. I needed time to think about my life and where it was headed. I was forty-four, divorced, financially successful, and physically fit, but I still felt something was missing. The simple truth was I still wanted to get married, to have children, but I had no prospects. Karen, bless her, was too young. Maybe I was too picky. My mother was the standard. Why could I not find someone like Constance Sutro? My brother Joe had found Claire Winstead in high school. My brother Jim had more beautiful girlfriends than anyone had the right to and was now linked with the lovely Pamela Langer. Women were attracted to Jim because of his charm and good looks, categories in which I felt relatively insufficient.

Market Street was crowded as I walked toward the Ferry Building. The rain was soft, but the air was cold. I wore a tan trench coat and had my umbrella open. It was an effort to dodge oncoming walkers who had their umbrellas lowered into the wind. Who were all these people? I wondered if they were happily married with children.

At the Ferry Building, I turned left and walked along the mostly empty piers in the direction of Fisherman's Wharf. I could hear the roar of the hated Embarcadero Freeway above me to the left and occasionally the sloshing of boats on the bay to my right. There were only a handful of pedestrians along the Embarcadero. I walked to the end of one of the piers and could see the heavy traffic on the Bay Bridge and two large cargo ships heading to the Port of Oakland. A ferry was leaving a dock near the Ferry Building, crowded with East Bay commuters. I felt alone in a vast complex of humanity.

What had I accomplished in my life? When I died, would there be anything anyone would remember? Would anyone remember the pinch-hit home run I hit in 1957 when I was playing for the Waco Pirates in the Big State League? It was my second and last season as a professional baseball player. Why didn't I give baseball a better chance? Why did I not go to spring training with New Orleans that next year? Pittsburgh had given me a contract. They must have thought I had a chance to make it to the big leagues. Instead I decided to stay in school, get my degree, and get started in the real world.

One thing a lot of people would remember was my *San Francisco Memories* radio show. That was good. Maybe that was the high point of my life. People knew who I was then. Why did I not try to continue the show on a San Francisco station when KOAK changed its format? But television had become the medium of choice, supplanting radio. I had a great voice for radio, but I never saw myself as visually suitable for television. Of course, leaving radio got me to New York with Ken Thatcher and the National Professional Soccer League, where I had a glimpse of the lifestyles of the sports celebrities. That was fun. I could have gotten other jobs in New York—I know I could have—but I was pulled back to San Francisco. Stockbrokers can make a lot of money. But they can also lose a lot of money when times get bad, and you make the wrong decisions.

Why did I not marry Helen Sinclair? She was sweet and plain and simple, and I think she loved me. If only I had not met up with Carole Anderson again and started smooching with her while Helen, unbeknownst to me, was watching the whole stupid business. Helen and Skip Amos have three beautiful children. That could have been me. No, not really. I didn't really love Helen. But maybe I did love Helen and was too stupid to know it. She now seemed very loveable in my mind.

Finally, the Embarcadero Freeway ended at Broadway, and I could hear the squish of the local traffic on the wet streets, the sound of the rain falling slightly more heavily into the growing puddles. It was four o'clock, but the sky was dark, and it seemed later. Lights were on in the houses on Telegraph Hill, and traffic was beginning to thicken as commuters worked to beat the worsening storm for their drives home. In the old days, I would have interrupted my walk for a stop in a neighborhood bar for a drink. But not now. I loved the rain, and I loved not being dependent on alcohol to feel good.

There was no question that marrying Veronica had been a huge mistake. She was psychologically disturbed. She was a professional virgin who had become a sex maniac. Maybe it was my fault. I loved her, but the signs were all there from the start. What a marriage! It was great for a while, but it lasted less than two years. I wonder how Donal McMurtry feels about himself these days. Stealing another man's wife! The drunken lothario probably hasn't even given it a thought over the years.

The restaurants at Fisherman's Wharf were nearly empty. I decided to go over to Scoma's for dinner for one. The bar was half full, and I thought to myself how great a martini would taste right now. No, make that two martinis and the accompanying feeling of release and joy. Maybe even a third. Instead, I asked for a table by the window. I had abalone and a small salad and was out in less than an hour. As I was leaving, I noticed the bar had filled up, mostly with groups of people and couples. I was glad I did not see anyone I knew.

The forty-minute walk to my home near the top of Telegraph Hill seemed easy, and my legs felt strong. The rain was coming down harder, but I did not mind. I wonder how I would have felt if I had had those three martinis that seemed so deliciously inviting just an hour earlier. Gosh, I was glad I had stopped drinking. I was excited about seeing Karen the next day. If I had not met Therese Neumann twenty-four years earlier, I doubt Karen and I would have ever reconnected after our lunch with Ken Thatcher. Were there powerful forces about to play a role in my life?

CHAPTER 77

Karen Brewster and I spent the next day at the San Francisco Public Library in the Civic Center. It was early November of 1979, and the rain that had begun falling the day before was expected to continue throughout the day. It was a perfect backdrop to our quest for the real Therese Neumann. Although we found references to fraudulent stigmatists, there was nothing incriminating on the peasant from Konnersreuth. It was Karen who came up with the most compelling information in an unexpected place, a book on the life of an Indian Yogi. The book, *Autobiography of a Yogi*, was written by Paramhansa Yogananda and was first published in 1945. The thirty-ninth chapter of the book was devoted to his meeting in 1935 with Therese Neumann. The Indian Yogi had just finished fifteen years in the United States and was heading home via Europe. He had heard of Therese Neumann and wanted to see her, so he and two students made the lengthy side-trip to Konnersreuth.

"Yogananda was totally convinced that Therese was authentic, a very saintly person who could not have been lying," Karen whispered to me in the main reading room. "He asked her point-blank if she ever took food or water, and she said only a daily, paper-thin wafer. When he said she certainly could not live on only that for twelve years, she replied she lived by God's light. Listen to what the Yogi wrote: 'I realized at once that her strange life is intended by God to reassure all Christians of the historical authenticity of Jesus' life and crucifixion as recorded in the New Testament and to dramatically display the ever-living bond between the Galilean Master and his devotees.'"

Karen continued, "Yogananda was allowed to watch Therese during one of her trances, and he said it was such a bloody scene that one of his students fainted. He also talked with a lot of people about Therese, including her family and the family doctor. One of the brothers said Therese slept only one or two hours a night. The doctor said when he and others traveled with Therese, they had to eat at least three meals a day to keep up their energy. He told Yogananda that Therese never ate and never got tired and in fact always looked fresh and rested."

Karen's enthusiasm was enormous. She said it was even more amazing that I had actually met Therese. I told Karen that the youthful, unlined face Yogananda had described was not what I had seen; in fact, she had looked her age in 1955—fifty-seven—and was seemingly heavy, although her bulky peasant clothes could have made her seem heavier than she actually was.

"You know," said Karen, "if Therese Neumann was a fake, she would have had to carry out her sham for thirty-six years. And do it in a small town where she lived under what must have been the closest of scrutiny from her family, her doctors, her priests, and what must have been hundreds of thousands of visitors. That seems so improbable. How could she have learned ancient Hebrew and other languages she repeats in her visions? Yogananda mentioned that a Dr. Fritz Gerlick, editor of a Protestant German newspaper, went to Konnersreuth to expose her but ended up writing a flattering biography."

I asked Karen how she felt now about organized religion and the New Testament.

"I don't know," she said. "Therese Neumann was a devout Catholic, and from what I read, her religious experience was largely related to the sufferings and teachings of Christ. If Therese is real, and it certainly seems that no one has been able to prove otherwise after all of these years, then you have to believe that Christ was real and what he said was real. And that may include most of what is in the New Testament."

But Karen added she was not sure this virtue applied to the Catholic Church. I agreed, saying that the church had been corrupted at many stages in its long history.

"So what does it all mean to you and the way you live your life?" I asked.

"Christ said we are all sinners, and I believe that," she smiled. "I think I will try to live more by the Golden Rule, doing unto others as I would have them do unto me. But there is a lot I still have to consider. What about you?"

"I have to think about it some more," I replied. "If you cannot refute the legitimacy of Therese Neumann, it is pretty hard to dismiss the teachings of Christ. On the other hand, there are myriad aspects that need to be studied and analyzed. My problem is I am lazy, and I've never been the scholarly type. It is true that merely following the Golden Rule and the Ten Commandments simplifies things. But easier said than done."

"I know," said Karen. "Maybe what comes out of all this is knowing that we should all try harder."

By the time we left, we had been in the library for more than six hours. Outside, it was already dark, and the rain was still falling. I offered to give Karen a ride home, and she accepted and invited me inside to see her recently purchased second-floor flat. I asked her for a rain check, saying I had other plans I could not get out of. Actually I had a date at 7:00 PM with a stewardess who was flying in from Los Angeles. She was a friend of Jim's girlfriend, Pamela.

"I'll give you a rain check for when it is not raining," Karen smiled. "Thanks for a very interesting day. You don't know how important it has been to me. I want to read more about Therese Neumann and whether or not her visions and bleeding might be internally produced, a kind of psychosomatic phenomenon."

"Let me know when you figure out the eating bit! Anyway, it was fun being with you." I gave her a brotherly hug.

Driving through the rain, I wished I didn't have a date. In fact, I did enjoy being with Karen. I liked her energy and her enthusiasm and the way she thought. In many ways, she seemed very mature for a woman just under thirty.

On Wednesday of the next week, I had to fly to New York and Boston for a series of meetings given by newspaper-industry companies in which I had taken significant positions for my clients. I also took the opportunity to see some of my old friends at CBS, so I did not return until late Saturday night. In my mail when I arrived home was a very sweet letter from Karen, thanking me for introducing her to Therese Neumann. She said she hoped I would call her so that we could do something together. She said she liked being with someone who did not have to always have a drink.

I laughed out loud when I finished reading, mostly, I think, because what she said made me happy and partly out of irony as I reflected on how many times I had unsuccessfully sought to establish a relationship. And here was Karen, who had asked me on two coffee dates, had asked me to the library, and now just wanted to do something together. She was making all of the moves.

I called Karen at her office late Monday afternoon. Her secretary said she was out of the office for a week. The next night, I got a call at home from Karen, who was in Los Angeles on business, but staying with her father and his family.

"I was glad you called yesterday," she said. "I thought maybe you did not want to deal with a religious zealot."

I laughed and said she was right, but I had changed my mind. She asked if I was busy on Friday night and wondered if I wanted to go see Woody Allen's movie *Annie Hall*, which she had missed when it first came out two years earlier. She said if I had a date Friday night, maybe we could go to a matinee on Saturday or Sunday. In fact, I did have a date for Friday—my regular monthly poker game—but I said I would be delighted to go with her, and we arranged to meet for coffee beforehand. I suggested we have dinner afterward.

"That would be nice, but you don't have to do that," she said.

"I've only seen you drink coffee," I said. "I want to make sure you are not a starving stigmatist."

"You shouldn't make fun of Therese Neumann; you'll be punished," she jested.

I love Woody Allen. He has to be one of the most physically unattractive men ever to win the girl in the movies. Karen had told me she liked to be around older men, because it made her feel young. I liked being with a date at a Woody Allen movie, because it made me feel like a relative stud. Of course, Woody was brilliantly funny, and he obviously had something, or he would never have attracted a gorgeous woman like Diane Keaton in real life. He proved that a clever sense of humor can trump good looks.

Karen thought *Annie Hall* was one of the best films she had ever seen. She said she thought Woody's self-deprecating persona and hilarious and insightful views on life and romantic relationships made him the freshest voice on the screen. She raved on, recalling scenes and quotes in a way that had us both laughing.

"Did you used to drink a lot?" Karen asked me, changing the subject.

"Why do you ask that?" I said.

"My mother said most men who don't drink are probably reformed alcoholics," she said.

"I don't think I am an alcoholic. I can overdo it, but I can also quit. I haven't had a drink for almost fifteen months."

"Why did you quit?"

"I was drinking too much and did not feel good about myself, and I thought I had better get myself into shape so I wouldn't look like most of the faces looking back at me in our wonderful San Francisco bars."

"You look good; you really only look a few years older than me," she said.

"I think Woody Allen and I are about the same age," I said.

"You look a lot better than he does, but I still think he is attractive; I mean his wit is marvelous if you think a pessimistic outlook on life is okay.

"He lost Diane Keaton in the movie," I said. "His pessimism was correct."

"She was pretty bad—ungrateful after all he taught her and did for her," Karen said.

"I think in real life it was Diane Keaton who broke off the relationship," I said. "I have read that *Annie Hall* was based on the relationship between Diane and Woody."

"Right, I think that is totally believable," said Karen. "They are both sort of kooky. But he's the smart one. Opposites attract."

Karen was dressed with two sweaters and a very long skirt, and she had brought with her an ankle-length raincoat even though there was no forecast for rain. She drank four glasses of water with dinner and, to put it frankly, ate like a horse. She had soup, salad, lamb chops, spinach, steak fries, and a chocolate sundae. She was wearing her unattractive horn-rimmed glasses, but now and then, she would take them off, revealing very pretty eyes and wide cheekbones. She wore only a trace of lipstick and no perfume that I could detect. Her hair often fell messily onto her face. Was she truly this comfortable with herself? I envied her.

"I'm going to take a walk with a girlfriend tomorrow," she said. "She lives next door to me, and we are going to walk from the Panhandle to the Ocean Beach. Would you like to come with us?"

I was supposed to go to the Stanford game the next day with Conrad Sutro and some of his friends. "I'd love to," I said.

CHAPTER 78

I invited Karen to come to the annual Thanksgiving party at my mother's house, but she turned me down, saying that she was going to spend the day with her mother, who would otherwise be alone. She said she was disappointed not to be able to come, because she knew I had a wonderful family, and she was looking forward to meeting them. But the day before Thanksgiving, Karen called and said she now could come if the invitation was still good. Apparently, her mother had received a last-minute invitation to Lake Tahoe for the Thanksgiving weekend and had managed to get all four days off from her job at the Palace Hotel. Karen did not offer any details of her mother's sudden change of plans. I was beginning to think I knew all I needed to about her mother.

The gathering at Mom's included all of the usual suspects, with the special addition of Jim and his girlfriend, Pamela, who had flown up together Wednesday night from Los Angeles. They brought with them good news: they were planning to get married in Singapore, where Pamela's mother was insisting they have a big wedding to which we would all be invited. In other good news, Adam Sutro, now thirty-two, who had married Lillian Graff in a huge wedding in 1977, announced that Lillian had finally become pregnant. Last, Brother Joe showed up with his family, and they made an overpowering entrance. Joe, at six feet five, had seen his weight rise to 240 pounds from too much good living and not enough exercise. And although Joe's presence filled the room, "Little Joe," now fifteen, was already two inches taller than his father and was slated to be the starting center for the Lowell high school basketball team, just as his dad had been thirty years earlier. Also like his dad, Joe III was a straight-A student. Joe's thirteen-year-old daughter, Robyn, was far less serious at five feet eight inches, and she had the lanky look and impish face of someone who enjoyed herself at every opportunity. Little Karen, the youngest at eleven, was just five feet tall and had a freckled face and braces and a sweet, deferential personality. She clearly idolized her brother and sister. While Joe Jr. had gotten, well, huge, his wife, Claire, had remained lean and vibrant, and she was still my mother's closest friend, not counting Claudia Hamblen.

When I think back on all the wonderful Thanksgiving gatherings at my mother's house, the one in 1979 was probably the high-water mark. Even though my mother was sixty-five and Conrad was sixty-eight, they both seemed indestructible. And so did Richard Hamblen, who at nearly seventy had grown ever more distinguished-looking with his wavy, curly hair now all gray. Claudia was sixty-six and, like my mother, could easily pass for a woman in her late fifties. My mother said it was hard for her to believe that Joe was now forty-five, I was forty-four, and Jim was forty-three, nor could she quite come to terms with the notion that her grandchildren were fast approaching adulthood.

"The years are just speeding up," she said. "It seems like yesterday that your dad and I took you kids on the ferry across San Francisco Bay on our way to the Presidio. My gosh, that was forty-one years ago."

Jim said, "Mom, don't get upset; you are going to live another forty-one years."

"I'm not sure I want to live past ninety-five," Mother said. "But I might change my mind if I actually get there."

Karen Brewster, as the only newcomer to the gathering, came under close scrutiny. She was the first woman I had introduced to my family since my divorce. Karen, in honor of the occasion, showed up in her client-presentation persona, wearing makeup with her hair neatly combed into a ponytail. She wore a snug-fitting long, gray wool skirt and a dark blue cashmere sweater tucked in at the waist. Her attire revealed her ample curves and slim waist, attributes usually hidden, but which I had first noticed the week before on our walk to Ocean Beach.

Karen and I had been out together seven or eight times, but it was strictly a platonic relationship, and I still felt uneasy over our fifteen-year age difference, which, somehow, did not seem to bother Karen.

It was the slightly snobbish Lillian who first cornered Karen, wanting to know where she went to school, what her parents did, and where she worked. But the ever-vigilant Conrad broke into the conversation by asking Karen if she was responsible for "those wonderful Sea World ads" he had seen lately.

"Excuse me, Lillian," said Conrad, grabbing Karen by the arm, "I want Karen to tell Robyn how she got into advertising; she thinks that is what she wants to do."

Just then, I put my arms around Lillian and kissed her on both cheeks, saying how wonderful and radiant she looked as a newly expectant mother. She did not seem to notice that Karen had been removed from her probing clutches. Conrad loved his daughter-in-law, but he did not want her to upset Karen.

"Danny, darling," said my mother. "You did not tell me that Karen was beautiful." Turning to Claudia Hamblen, she remarked, "All he said was that she was fun to be with."

"Beautiful girls are always fun to be with," smiled Claudia. "I used to be a lot of fun when I was her age. How old is Karen?"

"She will be thirty pretty soon," I answered.

"Claudia," said my mother, "don't be jumping to any conclusions. They hardly know each other."

"We're really just friends," I said.

"Maybe that's what you think, but you can't see yourself looking at her. You can't fool your old Aunt Claudia."

"Claudia, dear, have you been drinking too much wine?" my mother said.

"Of course," she said. "It's Thanksgiving."

Conrad and Mom saw to it that Karen had a chance to talk with everyone there, and Karen seemed to be enjoying herself immensely. So was I.

Karen invited me up for a cup of coffee when I took her home, not for any romance, but for talk about my family.

"Danny, I really had a fantastic time," she said, after showing me her very cluttered flat that was filled with old books, pop art, and a wide variety of semi-antiques and well-worn furniture.

"I love the high ceilings and warmth you have created here," I said.

"Do you realize how lucky you are to have such a family?" she said.

"They are so beautiful in looks and in spirit, and they really made me feel so welcome. By the way, that Richard Hamblen is gorgeous. I've seen his picture in the papers many times, but the photos do not do him justice. He seems so wise and judicious and patient in the most kindly way. What is his relationship to you?"

"Actually, he is not a blood relative," I said, telling Karen how Richard had served with my father in Germany during World War II.

"He and your mom seem very close," said Karen.

"We have known Richard and Claudia for thirty-four years, and it seems they have always been a key part of our lives," I said. "And when Mom married Conrad, the Hamblens became his new best friends too. Actually, Richard and Conrad are very close, even though they are quite different."

"Conrad is a loveable darling, so sweet and so relaxed," said Karen. "He and your mom make a perfect couple."

"Mom told me they have never had a serious argument in the fifteen years they have been married," I said. "Conrad has been like a second father to me. He is always fun to be with, because he is happy and positive all of the time."

"Must be that old money," Karen laughed. "I wish I was like that."

"But you are," I said.

"Thanks, but not really—I can have my mood swings. I think you are a bit like Conrad."

"I'm trying, and I've learned a lot from him," I said. "We do a lot of stuff together—go to baseball and football games and play golf. I probably see him more than Adam does. Adam is a workaholic, and he's really keen on his development projects, such as shopping centers and office buildings. That does not leave him much free time for anyone but his wife."

"She struck me as high maintenance," said Karen.

I laughed. "You certainly have Lillian figured out."

"Your brother Jim is awfully good-looking," said Karen. "And I think Pamela is absolutely gorgeous and wonderful. Is he a lot older than she is?"

"I'm not sure—maybe sixteen years," I said.

"She adores him," said Karen. "Did you notice how she watched him all of the time—got his food and drinks, held his hand, gave him kisses? I've never seen anyone so attentive."

"Jim has always brought that out in women," I said. "I have been jealous of him all of my life."

"You can be Conrad Sutro to his Richard Hamblen," laughed Karen. "You don't have to be beautiful to be loveable."

"American women would never act like Pamela," I said. "Joe, who used to live in Asia, says Asian women are taught to please their men, knowing in the long run they will gain ascendancy in the marriage and ultimately control everything."

"Pamela does not look that diabolical to me," said Karen.

"She will be well taken care of in any case," I said. "Jim's company is worth millions, and I think he is going to sell it in a few years."

"Why? He's so young."

"He just wants to do something else," I said.

"That is typical," she said. "People achieve something, and they want something else."

"It is built-in—God's way of achieving progress for the human race," I said. "We can't have everyone as happy and satisfied as Conrad. We need more people like Adam who will change things!"

"I think your niece Robyn is really going to be a beautiful girl," said Karen.

"I think she is cut in the mold of my mother," I said. "On the other hand, I suspect Joe III is going to be like Adam, very serious and very ambitious."

"What are you, Dan?"

"I'm a Conrad wannabe, but it's not yet a comfortable fit. I'm trying to just be happy all of the time," I said.

"Do you know what makes you happy?" she asked.

"I like being with you," I said.

"I'm glad you said that, because I like being with you, too; I hope we can spend more time together," she said, moving closer to me. It was our first kiss, sweet and loving. Our age difference seemed to melt away.

"I'm glad my mother went to Lake Tahoe," said Karen.

CHAPTER 79

I hate to harp on Jimmy Carter's presidency, but there was a made-up story going around in 1980 that pretty well summed up the negative sentiment that some American people, including our family, felt toward Carter. I heard it first from Richard Hamblen, who was working hard to help get Ronald Reagan the Republican nomination.

As I remember the joke, Jimmy Carter was working late in the Oval Office when the ghost of Teddy Roosevelt suddenly appeared. Jimmy jumped up and offered TR his chair, but TR declined, saying "You are the president now; I'm just haunting the place." Then he asked Carter how things were going.

"Not so good," President Carter responded. "The Iranians have imprisoned fifty-two of our diplomatic personnel."

"So you sent in the marines, right?" said TR.

"Well, no, but I registered a strong protest at the United Nations."

TR seemed upset and asked "Anything else?"

"Well, the Russians just invaded Afghanistan."

"I hope you retaliated with every weapon in our arsenal," said TR.

"No, but I withdrew our athletes from the Olympic Games," said Carter.

TR exploded in anger: "The next thing you are going to tell me is that you have given back the Panama Canal!"

Inflation was still rampant, and oil prices were at historic highs. Adding to the gloom of the sports-loving members of my family was the fact that the once mighty San Francisco Giants had become sad also-rans with no stars of note. The San Francisco 49ers in 1980 were equally noncompetitive under second-year coach Bill Walsh, winning only six of sixteen games, one consolation being that they won four more games than they had in Walsh's first season. A second consolation was that second-year quarterback Joe Montana had wrested the starting job from Steve DeBerg. He definitely appeared to be a star of the future, though none of us guessed how extraordinary he would become.

Karen and I dated all through 1980, mostly on weekends. My work kept me extremely busy during the week. I had more than two hundred clients, many of whom were active in the markets, not just buying and selling equities, but also exercising puts and calls and doing what later became known as day trading. A few were even hardy enough to want to short the market, but I always tried to talk them out of it. There was a hard core of perhaps thirty clients with whom I spoke at least once a day and often a lot more than that. Some liked to have regular lunches and some even dinners.

Moreover, there was a lot of interest in the emerging technology sector, and many of the leading companies were located south of

San Francisco in what was becoming known as Silicon Valley, which started in Palo Alto and extended just south of San Jose. Companies such as Hewlett Packard, Sun Microsystems, 3-Com, and dozens of others had captured the fancy of investors as the world of computers continued to evolve along with office automation systems. It was my job to keep in close touch with analysts who followed those companies. I also maintained my own sources at the most important firms. And I continued to keep tabs on the newspaper industry, which had made me a lot of money, as well as blue chips like Bank of America.

I remained unrelenting in my program of exercise and abstinence from alcohol. I mostly ate healthy foods, the key word being "mostly."

Once in a while, Karen and I might go to a movie during the week, but otherwise we saw each other on weekends. Starting in the spring of 1980, when we finally went to bed together, Karen and I made numerous trips to the dozens of lovely venues in northern and central California, everywhere from Lake Tahoe to San Simeon and less well-known spots such as Ukiah, Placerville, Mendocino City, and Lakeport. We spent several weekends with Constance and Conrad at their Pebble Beach house, and we also went with them to Conrad's wine estate in Napa. The fact that the Giants and 49ers were doing poorly made it a lot easier to miss their games.

By this time, I was more in love with Karen than I had ever been with anyone in my life. I was beyond happy that she even considered me worthy of her. I always felt she could have done much better, and frankly, I was amazed that the relationship continued. Karen made me feel like the only man in the world she was interested in, though she did rave about all of the men in my family, particularly Richard Hamblen. I asked her once why, if she was so taken by Richard's looks, she went out with me. She replied she appreciated looking at handsome men, but would not want to marry one again. I understood that comment better when I learned more about Karen's first husband, a twenty-one-year-old hunk who was not a very considerate husband, or lover, for that matter.

Karen's interest in sex was healthy but not as wild and animalistic as Veronica's had been. In that regard, Karen and I had a nice balance of interest. I was in love with her as a woman and a person, and the sex act was almost incidental, though I confess we always enjoyed it. Karen said she liked older men, because they were better lovers. I asked her how many older men she had made love with.

"Just you," she said. She explained that before me, she had mostly gone out with men either her own age or just a few years older.

"They must have been a bunch of yuks," I said.

"You are not far off," said Karen. "They were mostly in it for themselves. Because I had been married, most guys thought they could have me no later than the second date. Some of them did. And sometimes when it was so easy, I'd never hear from them again. I was pretty attracted to one guy, but he dropped me after about six months. He said I was the marrying kind, but he did not want to get married for at least another five or six years. So that was when I stopped sleeping with men—more than eighteen months ago, it was. I didn't sleep with anyone again until you forced yourself upon me after five months of dating!"

I laughed. "If I was still drinking, I probably would have attacked you on the second date," I said, only partly in jest.

"I'm glad you don't drink. Do you miss drinking?"

"Actually, I do," I said in total candor. "Alcohol loosens me up, makes me less self-conscious, more happy. I've had hundreds of great nights when I drank more than I should. The trouble comes when you sober up, you feel lousy, your brain isn't working, you have no energy, and you look like hell. It gets worse as you get older. I think that's one of the things that got me, seeing what booze does to people over a period of time. The old saying that liquor spoils good looks and health faster than anything is beyond dispute. Did you know that Jackie Gleason was once widely considered handsome? Look at him now. But it is more what it does to your brain and your energy and your feelings of self-worth; those are the things that are important to me."

"Have you ever tried to drink in moderation?" Karen asked.

"I've never been the kind of guy like Richard Hamblen who can have two drinks and then stop, or go to a big dinner party the night before he has an important trial and not drink anything. Watch Conrad—he'll have three drinks at the most, and he mixes his scotch with a lot of water. Someday I will return to drinking when I think I can do it only in moderation."

"The Romans used to say that if you were not your own best doctor by the time you were forty, you hadn't been paying attention," Karen said.

"Where did you read that?" I asked.

"When I visited Rome, I bought a book called *Everyday Life in Ancient Rome*, and that is one of the things it said," Karen smiled.

"When I think of Therese Neumann not eating, my quitting drinking does not seem like a big deal," I said. "I still wonder why she got so hefty-looking. Maybe it was to blend in with all of the other Bavarian peasant women. You know, when I first met you, Karen, I thought you were sort of fat."

"That's a fast change of subject," said Karen.

"It was because all of your clothes were so baggy. And I couldn't see how pretty your eyes were behind those horn-rimmed glasses. And your hair covered your face. We had three dates together before I realized you had a terrific body."

"That was when we went walking to Ocean Beach, right?" said Karen.

"So you knew what you were doing? Surprising me, that is?"

"It crossed my mind," she laughed.

Karen reached over and pinched my waist, first with her left hand and then with her right.

"I bet you used to have pretty big love handles before you reformed yourself," said Karen.

"Why do you say that?" I asked, laughing.

"Because I saw a photo of you at your mother's that must have been taken three or four years ago, and you were chubby and looked middle-aged. I must say you look a lot better now."

"What did you look like three years ago? Were you dressing for failure?" I said.

"I gave up drugs two years ago," she said. "Like most people I knew, I used to smoke a lot of pot and do some coke once in awhile. I quit, because I didn't like myself. That's all I am saying. I have put that part of my life behind me, and maybe the way I dress reflects that."

"I think you are wonderfully understated, but I admit I like it when you are in your client-presentation mode or, better yet, when you are completely naked. I really like to be naked with you."

"Do you ever want to have children?" Karen asked.

"Veronica and I tried, but it turned out she could not be a mother," I said. "It wasn't me firing blanks. What about you?"

"Yes, I guess I want to be a mother more than anything," she said. "Maybe I will now that I have found the right man."

"Who might that be?" I said.

"You, stupid," she smiled.

"Let's make one right now," I chortled, throwing my arms around Karen, almost crushing her in a hug.

"Does that mean you'll marry me?" said Karen.

"I was hoping you'd ask," I smiled, locking her in a deep kiss.

Karen and I were married on January 20, 1981, in a small wedding in a chapel at Pebble Beach attended by eighty people. She was thirty, and I was forty-five. It was the same day that Ronald Reagan took the oath of office as president of the United States and that the Iranians released the American hostages. It was perhaps the happiest day of my life. I could not believe my good fortune in finding Karen. And the crazy thing about it was that she felt the same way about me.

CHAPTER 80

Naturally, one of the first things Karen wanted to do after we got married was change the furniture in my manly apartment. It was a measure of my love for her that I said "go ahead." And a further measure of her love for me that she kept my favorite leather chair and sofa. Down came my movie posters, and out went the huge, wooden coffee table and the leather-shaded lamps. Gone was the wonderful and rich wall-to-wall carpeting, so dark there had never been a visible stain or a sign of dirt, not that they weren't there aplenty. Karen loved the makeover, and I loved watching her make her very thoughtful transition. I liked the exposed hardwood floors, the Oriental rugs, the Asian art, the glass coffee and end tables, and the modern lamps. I liked flowers everywhere and big leafy plants consuming all of the carbon monoxide. I loved the new king-sized bed, so decadently soft that the sink factor was eight to ten inches. Only the spectacular city views remained the same.

I never asked Karen why her own apartment (which she sold for a handsome profit that I invested for her) had had such an informal and lived-in look with stuff everywhere—books, semi-antiques, Japanese and Chinese art, dying plants, and more. But she told me her marriage was a new start and she was changing everything. Indeed, she did. The baggy clothes and heavy glasses disappeared. She opted for the client-presentation look on a full-time basis. Before, when we walked down the street, people seldom gave Karen a second glance. Now, I noticed that not only did men give her a second glance, but a few even tried to catch her eye for a bit of passerby flirting. I am glad we did not go to bars in those days. Karen, with her new look, would have attracted a lot of men, all the more given that I was on the borderline of looking like her father. Why she changed her "look" was a puzzle to me, and one day not long after our wedding, I asked her.

"I feel better about myself, thanks to you, and I want to look nice for you," she said.

"How did I ever get such a wonderful wife?" I said, while still thinking deep down that her transformation had to be more complex than that.

I tried to figure out what she really saw in me. Probably the most important thing was that she knew I loved her, and deep down, she knew that I did not believe I was worthy of her. I mean she was young and very attractive, especially now that she lightened her hair and combed it on a regular basis. When well-groomed, Karen was a 9.5 to my 5.8.

Even so, we had a lot in common. We both liked healthy, simple food, good movies, sports, walking, Mozart, Broadway musical soundtracks, reading, and entertaining small groups of friends. I was pretty easy to please, and I had learned from Conrad Sutro how to relax and enjoy life. Nonetheless, I worked very hard and was making a lot of money.

And also, unlike Karen's first husband, I was not a womanizer, and in that sense, I probably provided her a nice mix of emotional and financial security, both important considerations for a woman whose main goal in life was to become a mother. She also loved my family and was becoming a part of it. I suspected that deep down, she hoped for some of those Booker genes in our children. Just as I sought to emulate Conrad, I think Karen wanted to make herself into a woman like my mother, who was so unlike Karen's own mother.

Another key element in our relationship was that although neither of us went to church, we both believed in God, the Ten Commandments, and the Golden Rule, and we shared the knowledge of Therese Neumann, whose life, or at least our mutual interest in it, had been the catalyst for our relationship.

Of course, we never know the whole story of why we feel the way we do, but it is fair to say that whatever the reasons, Karen and I were both very much in love and most happily married.

In May of 1981, Karen announced she was pregnant, which resulted in a family celebration over the Memorial Day weekend. Everyone was in a festive mood until late in the day, when my brother Joe said he had been suffering from a severe headache for the past two days and had to leave the gathering early.

My mother asked him if he had taken any aspirin, and he said he had been taking three every four hours. Richard Hamblen suggested that Joe go to the hospital for a checkup and told him that he knew a specialist Joe could call. Joe said it was nothing serious, but Richard decided to call his doctor friend anyway, and the doctor suggested that Joe come to see him first thing in the morning at the University of California Hospital on Parnassus Street, at the foot of Sutro Forest. Joe agreed to go, but he never made that appointment.

Claire later told us that during the night, she heard Joe get out of bed and then fall to the floor. She jumped up and was shocked to see a contorted look on his face. He tried to talk, but the words were senseless. She immediately called for an ambulance and then called Constance. It was 3:00 AM. Constance listened to Claire's description of Joe's condition in a growing state of horror. She consulted with Conrad, who suggested she call Richard for the name of the neurologist he had recommended.

Upon hearing the details, Richard said it sounded like a stroke and could just be a mild one. Richard called Claire and suggested she accompany Joe to the UC Hospital in the ambulance and said that Claudia would come to their house to take care of the kids. Richard then called Dr. Edwin Weinberger, who said he would be at the hospital in thirty minutes.

About an hour after Joe's fall, he was being treated at the UC Hospital, where Dr. Weinberger and his associates concluded that

Joe had suffered a hemorrhagic stroke. Blood was leaking into Joe's brain. Three hours after his fall, Joe was in surgery as doctors drained the leaking blood from his brain and dealt with the source of the leakage. The operation took four hours and twenty-three minutes.

Afterward, Dr. Weinberger told Richard that Joe had almost certainly suffered permanent brain damage and would likely be paralyzed on one side for several months and possibly permanently. He commented that if they had waited another hour or two to perform the surgery, Joe likely would not have survived.

Joe had turned forty-seven just a couple weeks earlier, on May 17. Before his stroke, he had been absolutely at the top of his game. He had written eight successful books, one of which had been made into a profitable film. He was the father of three wonderful children, and his marriage to Claire was a fit made in heaven. He had been a great basketball player at Stanford and might have become an All-American had it not been for the horrible auto accident that had ended his career. But that had not stopped Joe. He had become a noted foreign correspondent who covered the war in Vietnam. And then he had given that up to be a husband and father who did not travel, who, in fact, worked at home, writing books about the exploits of an imaginary hard-living foreign correspondent. His writing no doubt had furnished Joe with sufficient vicarious thrills and pleasures to compensate for his comparatively quiet life at home

To be truthful, I had been a bit concerned about Joe. He had added fifty pounds in the last five years, and I knew he had high blood pressure, though he would never supply any details, saying merely that his doctor had told him to be more careful about what he ate and to get more exercise. Joe kept saying he was going to do that, but he never went beyond the talking stage.

To say I was grief stricken over Joe's plight would be a gross understatement. When I first heard from Mom what had happened, my chest tightened, and I was nearly overcome with nausea. I thought I was going to vomit. Tears welled in my eyes. I could barely breathe. It was amazing how words spoken over the phone could so suddenly change my physical being. Joe had always been my hero—big, handsome, smart as hell, a great father and husband, and a talented writer who loved his life. He had hundreds of friends, but he kept his focus on his family. I had never tried to be like Joe, because he was so superior to me in every way. Yet Joe had always treated me with respect and affection. I could not have had a better brother, and suddenly, there he was, flat on his back in the hospital, unable to speak coherently, paralyzed on the left side, with none of us knowing whether he would ever have any semblance of his former life. The only thing we knew for sure was that he would never be the same.

The next three months were a terrible time for the Booker family. Joe came home from the hospital in late June in a wheelchair that he could not operate. His speech had partially returned, but he did not always make sense. He did not seem to comprehend totally what had happened to him. Dr. Weinberger had warned that stroke victims are often unable to see themselves or understand the effect they have on other people.

To his great credit, Joe worked hard on his physical therapy, and Dr. Weinberger said he believed Joe might walk again. Conrad volunteered to pay for a full-time therapist to work with Joe. Joe's office was converted into a therapy center, and Dr. Weinberger urged Claire to have him try to do as much for himself as possible. Visiting Joe continued to be a shock. His brain was recovering, but it had lost its edge, and he was not above complaining about the treatment he was getting from Claire. He said his children were acting differently too. My mother came to see Joe every day, and she frequently took Claire out to do something afterward.

Specialists were brought in to help with the therapy, and slowly, Joe began to improve. Dr. Weinberger had told us that improvements would take place for about six months. After that, there would be little hope for further improvement. In late August, Joe was walking with the use of a cane and the assistance of another person. But he had no feeling and no movement in his left arm.

Karen suffered along with me over Joe's plight, except that it was worse for her, because her pregnancy had led to severe morning sickness. At my encouragement, and with a lot of support from my mother, Karen quit her job at the advertising agency in the sixth month of her pregnancy.

I spent a lot of time with Joe's children, and Karen and I often took them on outings, though the truth of the matter was that they had developed lives of their own and did not need coddling. Still, we knew they appreciated the constant reminders of the love of their extended family. I attended all young Joe's basketball games, and he was every bit as good as his father had been in his junior year at Lowell, making All-City. My brother Joe came to young Joe's last game and watched from his wheelchair at courtside, near the Lowell bench. Before the game, the basketball coach of Lowell presented a special award to Joe for his heroics on the basketball court and in life. The crowd gave Joe a huge ovation, and the *Chronicle* carried a story and photo of him the next day, with young Joe standing next to his humbled father. All of us were teary-eyed during the brief but moving ceremony. Joe waved to the crowd with his right hand, sporting a crooked smile on his face, clearly a brave shadow of his former self.

CHAPTER 81

It was some time in July of 1981 that I received a phone call from a man who identified himself as Alfred Booker. He said that he was a freelance journalist who worked from his home in Tupelo, Mississippi, and that he was probably a third or fourth cousin of mine. I had never been to Mississippi and had never been in contact with any of my relatives there. Alfred asked me about Joe and said his tragic situation, which he said tied into the piece that he was just starting to write that might be either a long magazine article or even a book. His working title was *The Curse of the Bookers*. Alfred knew all about my father's death in the final stages of the war in Europe and how his parents before him had died in an automobile crash.

"Your father's death may have been the last strike by a German fighter in World War II," said Alfred. "It was a fluke, just like your grandparents' death. I mean, what are the odds that an oil truck would spill oil on a wet road just minutes before your grandparents came along?"

"It sounds like you have a lot of information I don't have," I said.

"Well, you should hear about all of the gory deaths suffered by Booker family members in the eighteenth and nineteenth centuries," Alfred continued. "Did you know that at least a dozen Bookers died in the Civil War, one in the Spanish-American War, and eight in World War I? Your dad was one of five Bookers who died in World War II. What is most striking is that all the deaths occurred under some weird circumstances. And there were dozens of other Bookers who did not die of natural causes. The more I research, the more I find that really makes me believe the Booker family is under some kind of curse." Alfred kept talking until I got tired of the conversation.

"Alfred," I said, "let me know when your work is published. I'm not sure I want to read it, but in any case, let me know."

"Thanks, Dan. It was good talking to you, and I appreciate your assistance. And good luck, Dan."

"Yeah, good luck to you, too, Alfred. I don't happen to believe in curses."

I never heard again from Alfred, and that made me happy. I hardly wanted to see a book that would make members of our family believe they were cursed! I wish I had never talked with Alfred.

The impact of Joe's stroke was constantly with us in 1981. Everyone got more health conscious and began to watch their diets. My younger brother Jim vowed anew that he was going to sell his business no later than 1983, and he admitted that he was wrestling with the same high blood pressure that affected Joe. Karen insisted that I go in for a thorough medical checkup, and I did. The doctor told me I was in great shape with blood pressure of 115 over 68, cholesterol of 158, and no signs of bodily deterioration.

"Keep doing whatever it is you are doing," said the doctor. "Everything looks good. You have the cholesterol of a Japanese fisherman." I did not tell the doctor that in my previous physical three years ago, my blood pressure was 145 over 90, and my cholesterol was well over 200. I probably should have. Clearly, my decision to exercise had paid off in more ways than one. I know that I never would have hooked Karen if I was still flabby and aging faster than the clock. I just wish Joe had started a similar program when I did. To this day, one of the great mysteries of my life is how and why an intelligent person such as Joe could have let himself go the way he did. Was there some internal conflict that caused him to be irresponsible about himself?

In the aftermath of Joe's stroke, it seemed ironic that I had greatly envied Joe upon first starting my program of clean living—as he sipped a brandy after dinner while smoking a Cuban cigar on his balcony, and I sat nearby drinking my insipid glass of water while listening to his stories and opinions. Suddenly, we had changed positions. It made me very sad.

One thing Joe and I had in common was that we had wonderful wives. Karen marveled at the strength Claire showed in dealing with Joe and the children. How she managed to remain so cheerful and positive was hard to believe. I am sure that deep down she was aching over her beloved husband being a shell of his former self. And he literally was that shell; he had lost fifty pounds since his stroke and had a gaunt, unnatural look. My mother told me that Claire had broken down a couple of times when they were alone but had quickly pulled herself together. My mother told everyone that Claire was a saint. Joe's stroke probably hit my mother as hard as it did Claire. But Mother said she thanked God that Joe was still alive and getting better. Indeed, by December of 1981, Joe's speech was dramatically improved, though it was still slightly distorted, and he could not marshal his thoughts as in the past. But he was more of a person again.

At the end of that year, on December 29, 1981, Jonathan Conrad Booker was born, weighing in at eight pounds, one ounce. He had all of his fingers and toes, attached to an angular body. Karen thought she saw evidence of the Booker genes. I had always thought newborn babies were ugly. But Jonathan was clearly different. When you wait as long as I did to have your first child, you may be excused for having a passionately biased view of what constitutes beauty. Karen was ecstatic and said she was going to nurse Jonathan for no less than six months, possibly longer.

"You don't mind slightly sagging breasts, do you, honey?" she smiled.

"I sure like them the way they are now," I said. "You look like Jayne Mansfield."

The first six months of 1982 were as happy a time as I have ever known, and Karen felt the same way. Baby Jonathan was a nice offset to the tragedy that had befallen Joe. We had family visitations to see Jonathan virtually every week, and Joe's eldest daughter, Robyn, liked to come over to visit with Karen and the baby whenever she could. Of course, my mother was there almost every day, and she and Karen formed a strong and warm bond.

Jim and Pamela came up from Los Angeles at least once a month to see Joe and the rest of the family. Pamela was trying to get pregnant, but so far, nothing had happened. Jim began looking at real estate in the Portola Valley, thirty-two miles south of San Francisco and situated near the Stanford campus. Jim said when he sold his company, he was going to move north, but he had been spoiled by the weather in Southern California and could not bring himself to live in what he called fog-bound San Francisco. He had a point. The weather on the San Francisco Peninsula south of the city was usually ten to twenty degrees warmer, and the Portola Valley, like neighboring Palo Alto, had relatively little fog.

So Jim looked at virtually every house that came on the market in the Portola Valley. Conrad told Jim it was a hot location that had excellent upside potential, though in 1982 the market, like the economy, had been soft for a couple of years. But it was beginning to come around under Reagan's economic policies. In July of that year, Jim successfully bid $750,000 for a house with five bedrooms and four and a half baths—a total of 5,830 square feet on three-quarters of an acre. That seemed like a lot of money to me at the time for a house that needed nine months of renovation, but Jim said it was an investment that would outperform the stock market. Conrad agreed. (Between 1980 and 1989, the Dow Jones Industrial Average rose 267 percent. And between 1990 and 1999, it grew another 362 percent. Those two decades constituted the greatest bull market in Wall Street history. Depending on where you lived, housing prices rose nicely, but not nearly as sharply as the stock market, which was led by the frenzied investor interest in technology stocks. Alas, the market fell steeply in the technology crash of 2000, but not before a lot of folks made some serious money—and that included a number of my clients. After 2000, housing dramatically outperformed the stock market.)

Looking back, I can never remind myself too often how lucky I was to be born in the 1930s. My father's generation had to weather the Great Depression. My generation had the greatest bull market ever.

One of the problems that Joe had to confront was what to do with his time. He watched a lot of television, especially sports. Cable news as we know it today did not exist then. Joe tried to do some writing, but he lost interest when he failed to live up to even his own reduced expectations. But my mother finally found something to capture Joe's interest. She brought him his old postage stamp album that he had been given for his sixth or seventh birthday. Joe and I both had been avid collectors during our youth, me more than Joe, who probably stopped collecting before he turned ten. But the sight of his nearly filled old album kindled in him an interest that surprised all of us.

"I found this in an old trunk, and I thought you might like to see it," my mother told Joe. He seemed delighted to hold a long-forgotten relic of his youth. He carefully turned the pages, admiring the stamps, and said he was amazed that he had been able to fill so many of the spaces.

In the ensuing months, Joe became a collector again, specializing in postage stamps from the United States, Germany, and Africa. He seemed to have a particular fascination for the German stamps printed during the twelve years of the Third Reich. Through a dealer, I was able to purchase more than a score of issues depicting Hitler, and I gave them to Joe, who was ecstatic. Actually, the Hitler stamps were cheaper to buy in 1982 than they had been during the war, a commentary on the demise of stamp collecting in the United States. Although baseball cards would have been a better investment, Joe loved his stamps and spent hours every day working on what was to become a most formidable collection.

Claire and my mother both assisted Joe and arranged for dealers to come to his house. Prices had plummeted, and it was easy to acquire very old stamps well below catalog prices. Joe also got in touch with other collectors by phone, by mail, or in person, and over time, his hobby became an avocation. He not only bought whole collections from estates, but also began selling to other collectors.

"Thank God for Joe's stamps," Conrad commented. "It has given him a new lease on life."

In other developments during that time frame, Joe and all the rest of us got a huge lift over the performance of the San Francisco 49ers, who won the Super Bowl in January of 1982 after compiling a regular season record of 13–3 under third-year coach Bill Walsh. On the field, 49er quarterback Joe Montana performed brilliantly in a 26–21 victory over the Cincinnati Bengals in the Silverdome in Pontiac, Michigan. Karen had insisted that I join my mother and Conrad and the Hamblens to see the game, even though Jonathan was only three weeks old. God, what a great wife!

The Detroit area was hit by a huge blizzard, and temperatures at game time were hovering around zero, which made getting to and from the covered stadium an ordeal. Ken Thatcher had gotten us the seats through his pal Pete Rozelle, the commissioner of all football. After the game, I learned that Ken had collapsed outside the 49er dressing room and had been rushed to a hospital, where doctors determined he had had a mild heart attack. When I saw Ken back in San Francisco a week later, he said it had just been a fluke reaction to all of the excitement. But he had a gray, exhausted look on his face. When we parted, I felt a hollowness in the pit of my stomach, a feeling that disappeared only when I got home to my beautiful wife and month-old son, who was becoming ever more alert and handsome.

CHAPTER 82

March of 1983 was probably one of the most significant months in American history. Of course, that is merely my own personal opinion, and I am hardly a historian—but hear me out. On March 8, President Reagan denounced Soviet Communism "as the focus of evil in the modern world." As such, the Soviets could not be trusted, never mind the various arms agreements that had been signed in the prior decade by the two superpowers. Then, on March 23, President Reagan announced his "Star Wars" missile defense system, which the White House said would likely involve lasers directed from satellites with the capability of shooting down enemy missiles before they reached the United States.

By 1983, the Soviet economy was a disaster. By contrast, the American economy was beginning to benefit from the Reagan tax cuts. More important, Soviet technology was already estimated to be three generations behind the United States. For the first time, Soviet leadership realized they could not compete with the United States, either militarily or economically. For those of us who had lived through the Cold War from 1945 until the 1980s, its ultimate end was huge, even if Ronald Reagan's Star Wars defense remains to be completed more than two decades later. Many liberals criticized Reagan's aggressive stance toward the Soviets. But history proved him right. And 1983 was the year it all began.

It is funny how events large and small present themselves, though at the time we have no understanding of their long-term significance. Such was the case one late summer day in 1983. Karen and I had brought Jonathan to lunch at the Sutro house. Afterward, my mother, Conrad, Karen, and I decided to go for a walk down to the Marina Green. We left the baby napping under the trusted eye of my mother's maid. The walk to the Marina Green, mostly down steep hills before the flatness of the Marina District, took an hour or so. It was a perfect day with clear, blue skies and the temperature in the high seventies. Karen, who had lost most of the weight she had added during her pregnancy, was in a happy mood and kidded Conrad about walking so slowly.

"It is just because I like the view from the rear," he said, playfully.

We spent an hour reveling in the beauty that is San Francisco, seeing both bridges bathed in bright sunlight and eyeing a mostly well-toned crowd of younger people, including some obviously gay men, a few wearing what some called "fruit bowl" bathing suits. I swear some of them had bananas stuffed in their crotches. My mother and Karen were giggling. Lots of people were just sunbathing, stretched out on blankets. Others were walking, like us, taking in the sights, which included sailboats bouncing along in the Bay where the winds were clearly stronger than on land. Conrad and I bought rocky road ice-cream cones that we shared with our ladies.

It was getting on toward five o'clock, and Conrad asked if anyone thought we should get a cab back to the house. We all said we wanted to walk. So we headed back to Pacific Heights via Webster Street. When we got to Union Street, just before the steep hills that would take us home, Conrad said he was not feeling very energetic and would like to find a cab, which we did, twenty minutes later.

That was the first time I had ever seen Conrad run out of gas, but I confess I did not think much about it. Conrad had always seemed indestructible, and I never thought of him as being seventy-one years old, two years older than my mother, who struck me as still being young middle-aged.

Karen asked after we got home if I'd noticed how pale Conrad looked when he suggested a cab. I said that I had but that he was just tired.

"One of my uncles, Mom's brother Calvin, got that way when he was visiting us, and about three weeks later, he had a heart attack," Karen said.

"I think I had better talk to my mother," I said. "I doubt it is anything serious, but it could be," I said.

"That's all your mother needs, another serious illness in the family," said Karen.

The next day, I spoke to my mother, and she surprised me by saying she had already arranged to have Conrad see a heart specialist; the appointment was for the coming Friday.

"Good news," my mother said after Conrad had had his physical. "The doctor said he was in good health and did well on his stress test."

"That's a relief," I said, suddenly feeling as if a heavy burden had been lifted from me.

"But the doctor said Conrad needs to lose about twenty pounds and get his cholesterol down," my mother said. "He also said he should cut back to just one drink a night and get more exercise and eat more fish and vegetables."

"If he is so healthy, why all the recommendations?" I asked.

"The doctor said it is just precautionary, because Conrad does have a profile that makes him a candidate for a heart attack, even though the tests indicated he was in good health."

"You are going to have a hard time getting Conrad to give up his meat and potatoes and that second drink," I said.

"Don't underestimate your mother," she replied. "I am insisting we cut back on our social life, and we are going to spend a lot more time at the cottage in Pebble Beach, where we can go for long walks and eat fresh fish in Monterey. We both love to read and play golf, and we like the weather there, so cozy in the fog with a fire going."

"I'm getting jealous," I laughed.

Later, when I told Karen about the conversation, she said, "Your mother is not one to sit back idly and let things happen."

"She can be an inspirational nurse," I said. "I can remember her telling me when I was a little kid that my father had rheumatoid arthritis and needed to get his rest and that we should not bother him. He had it so bad he had to be discharged from the army. My mom took good care of him, and he completely recovered, although Mom always said Dad did it by his own willpower. The doctors were amazed, my mother told me later."

"She is awfully good with Joe," said Karen.

"You can edit that sentence down," I said.

Karen paused and smiled: "Right, Constance is awfully good."

My mother and Conrad had been married for eighteen years, and I think they were still as fond of each other as they had been at the start. They never seemed to tire of one another's company, though Conrad was clearly the more extroverted of the two and had a need to surround himself with people. For years, Mom had been spending a lot of time working at the homeless shelters, but had cut back when Joe had his stroke. When Conrad's health became an issue, she ceased all regularly scheduled activities, but remained on two shelter boards to which she was a significant financial contributor. She knew her priorities and now she was needed on the home front. And at sixty-nine, she had a right to ratchet back a bit.

On December 29, 1983, we had a party to celebrate Jonathan's first birthday. It was a lovely affair at our flat, and Jonathan had learned to grunt and scream and laugh and cry to fit his many moods, which helped to make him the center of attention all the more. He cried out and hid behind his mother's skirt when his cousin, Big Joe, all six feet and seven inches of him (the reason he could no longer be called Little Joe), loomed through the front door. Big Joe reached down and lifted Jonathan up to the ceiling. Jonathan did not know how to react at first, but when he saw everyone else smiling up at him, he let out a scream of excitement that was followed by a wide smile. Behind Big Joe was his father, smiling crookedly, stooping over, and leaning heavily on his cane, with Claire at his left side, followed by Robyn and Karen, both tall and attractive teenagers. Big Joe, who would turn nineteen in just two days, was a freshman at Stanford. Robyn, seventeen, and Karen, fifteen, both attended Lowell, the top public high school in San Francisco, from which both their father and brother had graduated.

It was just a small gathering. Karen's mother had moved to Santa Monica, where she was working at a hotel and was involved in a new love affair; Adam and Lillian Sutro were committed to attend a party given by her parents; Jim and Pamela were in Singapore; and the Hamblens were in Hawaii. Jonathan was to learn that having your birthday over the Christmas and New Year holidays had its drawbacks.

My mother complained it was getting confusing with two Joes and two Karens.

"Call my handsome son Big Joe and my distinguished husband Joe Senior," said Claire. "And our Karen's friends call her 'Kare.'"

"'Big Joe' makes sense to me," said his father. "But just call me Joe, just plain Joe, an ordinary guy, just like in the song."

"No one ever said you were ordinary, son," said my mother.

Big Joe was turning into a chip off the old Booker block. I had a long talk with him that day, and he struck me as far more mature than his years.

"Dad's stroke has changed things a lot," said Big Joe. "I think I admire him even more for the way he is dealing with his limitations, but it is very sad. Mom and my sisters have been heroic, and I feel like maybe I am not contributing enough, being away at school. I offered to delay starting college for a year, but neither Mom nor Dad would hear of it. They both came down for the season opener, and Dad insisted that there be no introduction. He likes to fly under the radar. I scored 14 points, and I thought that was pretty good since I played only half the game. Oops, I forgot—you were there, Uncle Dan. But the point is Dad told me later that he had scored 18 points in his first college game. So he still likes to compete, and he loves to play me in chess. He always wins. That part of his brain is still as good as ever."

Joe was not above boasting and in fact did quite a bit of it in his new persona, but he was good-natured about it.

"Big Joe is pretty good, but he has a long way to go before he catches up to where I was at his age," said Joe.

Big Joe let out a laugh and said, "I probably would have scored 30 points against the midgets you were playing against, what was it, nearly thirty years ago?"

"I give you that," said Joe. "Where are all these seven-footers coming from?"

So it went. Joe told me his books were continuing to sell well, and he had a steady stream of revenue. Also, Hollywood was looking at the possibility of making two more into movies, and his agent was feeling pretty confident.

"It's like when Hemingway died, there was an increase in sales of his books," said Joe. "The readers think I am a corpse," he laughed.

Joe looked over at Jonathan, who was basking in loving attention from Robyn and young Kare. Joe turned to me and said it didn't look like Jonathan was going to be nearly as tall "as some of the Bookers."

"Maybe he has those Cosgrove or Brewster genes," Joe said, referring to our maternal grandmother and Karen's father, Ed Brewster. "Well, no big deal—look at you, Danny," Joe continued. "You have the Cosgrove genes, and you've done pretty well; in fact, you have surprised the hell out of me. I never thought you were going to make a lot of money or have a wife as lovely as Karen."

My mother winced slightly, and I said Joe was turning into the hard-boiled correspondent he wrote about in his books. Of course, what he had said was true, but slightly tactless.

Young Kare wanted to know what was wrong with Cosgrove genes. "Grandmother says I remind her of her mother, who she said was a very sweet lady all of her life," she said.

"The Cosgroves produced splendid ladies," said Joe. "It is the men who were suspect, short people who drank a lot. That's probably why Grandmother married Pardon Crandall Booker; he was a minister who was well over six feet tall and did not drink."

"I don't think genes are all that important," said Conrad. "The real test is how you play your hand. We all live our lives one day at a time, though I think a lot of people spend their lives always thinking about the future or some bygone days they have fantasized were better than they were. There is a lot of good advice out there to live one day at a time. All we have is the present. Play the cards you are given. I see some pretty good hands around this room."

Just then, Jonathan started turning blue in the face with strain. Karen jumped up and rushed him out of the room.

"I guess Jonathan doesn't think so well of your sermon, Conrad," laughed Joe. "He picked just the right time to have his bowel movement."

CHAPTER 83

Constance and Conrad were playing the sixth hole at Pebble Beach, a longish par 5 that climbs to a cliff overlooking the ocean. It was a cool, foggy day in middle March of 1984. My mother told me later that when they reached the top of the hill near the green, Conrad complained of a sharp pain in his chest. He said he felt dizzy. The color drained out of his face, and he sat down in the fairway. The caddy said it looked like something serious, maybe a heart attack. Fortunately, a foursome was behind them, riding in carts. The caddy, at my mother's urging, ran back and explained the situation. One of the foursome said he was a retired physician and drove with the caddy to where Conrad was now stretched out prone on the grass. His face was ashen.

It took fifty-five minutes to get Conrad to the emergency room in Monterey.

He was dead on arrival. My mother was so stunned she went into shock and had to be hospitalized. She was not able to call me with her terrible news until the next day when she reached me at my office. I simply could not believe it. Aside from my mother, wife, and son, I think I loved Conrad more than anyone I had ever known. I felt like something was ripping away at my innards and that my own heart was in danger of stopping.

I told Mother I was leaving immediately but would first call Adam to let him know about his father. It was the toughest call I have ever had to make. Adam was speechless at first and then began sobbing; in fact, both of us were sobbing into the phone. Adam said that he had a friend with a plane and that we could fly to Monterey together. I said I would prefer to drive and would meet him at the hospital; we could decide later how to bring mother back.

Karen was as stunned as I was when I told her what had happened. She said she would call the rest of the family. As it was, I reached the hospital before Adam. The drive down was like falling out of a building. My whole life flashed before me with a focus on a thousand different things I had done with Conrad—Giants baseball, 49er football, Stanford football, and golf a hundred times, all fun, all relaxed, seemingly never-ending good times, now gone, forever. But the fatherly advice, the support and affection—they would never die. Then my mind turned to my mother. Nineteen years with a man I know she deeply loved, maybe even more than she had loved my own father. My eyes welled with tears at the thought of her suffering.

My mother was dressed and sitting in her hospital room, waiting for me. I don't remember what I said. We embraced, and I held her for a long time. We were both crying. Then she stepped back and looked at me.

"I've been crying for the past twenty-four hours," she said. "But I have also been thinking how lucky we have been, having Conrad in our lives for twenty years. I am truly grateful to God for that, and I know that is the way Conrad would want us to be thinking right now."

It is too painful for me, even now, twenty-two years later, to recount the funeral except to report that it was attended by more than 1,000 people at Grace Cathedral. Both Adam and I spoke, as did Richard Hamblen. Conrad Sutro was a man loved by many, and there were no dry eyes at Grace Cathedral that day.

The next six months were difficult, but slowly the sense of loss numbed. Mom spent two nights a week with us, two with Joe and Claire, and one with Adam and Lillian. She said she could not live full-time in the Sutro home, which by the fall of 1984, she proposed to relinquish to Adam, even though Conrad's will had stipulated that the house would go to Adam only after Mom's death. Mom decided to buy a 2,600 square foot apartment on Pacific Avenue with a beautiful view of the bay, which Adam insisted on paying for.

"Constance, you are going to live to be one hundred and could have lived forever in Dad's house, so it is the least I can do," Adam argued when mother protested she could pay for it herself.

"I have plenty of money, thanks to Conrad, Richard, and Danny," Mother said.

"The money you save can go for larger trust funds for your grandchildren and great-grandchildren," said Adam.

"My goodness, I hadn't thought of great-grandchildren," Mother said. "Adam, you are very sweet, and I know your father would be proud of your generosity, which, on behalf of my future great-grandchildren, I accept."

Mom gave Adam a warm embrace. I think Adam felt as much love for Constance as I did for Conrad, even though I had spent much more time with Conrad than he ever had with Constance. Adam was an extremely smart and rational man. And he was also generous. He never begrudged my relationship with his father. Adam, because of grueling work schedule, did not have the time I had, especially during the hiatus between my two marriages. I think Adam regarded me as an older brother whom he could trust, and the Lord knows I have always had the greatest respect and admiration for him, even though he was completely different from his father.

By January of 1985, Mother had moved into her new apartment. Suddenly, it was almost impossible to reach her by telephone. She had reconnected with a lot of her lady friends from The Club, the once-young women from the Sunset District who had banded together during World War II. They had continued meeting after all of these years, though the gatherings had been reduced to twice a year, and only nine of the original twelve were still in the San Francisco Bay Area. But the original members all had close friends they now wanted to include, so in fact, the circle was greatly increased. Then there were all of Claudia Hamblen's friends, almost all of whom loved Mom. So Mom had plenty of opportunities to go to concerts, plays, restaurants, and countless other things. But her main focus remained on her family.

"I think I am as busy as I have ever been," my mother told me. "It is such a blessing to have a close family and wonderful friends."

My mother did keep the house at Pebble Beach. She knew I loved going there, and so did Jim after he sold his company and retired to Portola Valley, or I should say, began to prepare himself for his new career as a consultant. The cottage at Pebble, located midway up the 17-Mile Drive, had been expanded and now included five bedrooms and three and a half baths, plus a separate sleeping annex with a triple-sinked bathroom, in sum suitable for four or five kids.

Jim emerged from the sale of his company in late 1984 with $11 million, after taking care of a lot of his key employees with bonuses of appreciation that he did not have to give. We were all happy to have Jim back in northern California. He and Pamela invited the family for three days over Christmas that year, and it proved to be a lot of fun for everyone. The women all pitched in to keep the house looking perfect in spite of nine guests. Adam and Lillian were invited, but they were in Lake Tahoe with Lillian's parents. The Hamblens came by for Christmas dinner. Big Joe brought his girlfriend, whose parents lived in nearby Atherton. Her name was Ashley Robinson, and like Joe, she was a sophomore at Stanford. Ashley had medium-brown hair, blue eyes, and enviable thick dark eyelashes. She was also tall and athletic and was on the Stanford varsity women's volleyball team.

Ashley surprised me by saying she had not met Big Joe at school but rather the previous spring, when playing volleyball at Cowell's Beach in Santa Cruz.

"Basketball players at Stanford are sort of like isolated in their own little world, especially if they are like Joe and, like, serious students, which Joe is," said Ashley—three "likes" in one sentence from the cream of America's youth. Frankly, I did not think that crutch expression could last, but, like, I guess I am very wrong, like twenty-plus years later!

Robyn told me she had decided to go to Berkeley next year, and Kare said she was not looking forward to being the last one left at home—nor, I knew, was Claire excited about another one of her children leaving home.

The vacuum created by Conrad's sudden passing was filled by increased attention to Jonathan, who had become a demanding three-year-old with a strong-willed mind of his own. As I recall, when my brothers and I were growing up, we were compliant and respectful of our elders. Not Jonathan. He would throw food off of his plate if he did not like it. He sometimes seemed frustrated that he could not express all his thoughts. He hit my mother once when she tried to pick him up and then ran to his mother for comforting. Sometimes I was his favorite, because I was not at home all day, as was Karen, who had to discipline him if he refused to take a nap, eat his food, or sit on the toilet.

Karen never complained to me about Jonathan in front of him, but she kept me abreast in private of his youthful transgressions. I tried to show him as much unconditional love as possible, and so did Karen. At night, he would often balk at going to bed, putting up a terrible and unpleasant scene. During the day, he would sit for hours watching cartoons on television and would not answer when spoken to. I became so aggravated with him one night that I said I was going to get rid of our two television sets. He charged across the room and began to hit me. That night, Karen and I had our first argument over Jonathan. I don't remember the specifics, but it had to do with my wanting to give him a spanking, which Karen opposed.

Karen said we needed to focus on the positive things that Jonathan did to reinforce appropriate behavior. One thing Jonathan did like was being read to, especially at night. Most kids in my experience go to sleep about ten minutes into any reading. But not Jonathan. After an hour, he would still be wide-awake and asking for more before finally slipping off to sleep, exhausted. Karen and I often stayed in Jonathan's bedroom together during reading time, sharing the reading duties. Afterward, Karen herself was often so exhausted from her sixteen-hour day that she was not interested in sex, though she desperately wanted another child.

I talked to my mother about Jonathan's behavior, and she said not to worry—that it was just a stage he was going through. I said I did not remember my brothers and I being so disobedient.

"That's because there were three of you, and you kept control of each other, and Joe was a good example for you and Jim to follow," my mother said, adding, "I hope Karen gets pregnant again; she told me she wants to."

Though Jonathan had his disagreeable side, when he smiled, he lit up the room. When I came home at night, he would get up from whatever he was doing and run to me, screaming in excitement and holding his arms out to jump into my arms. Sometimes Karen would join in the welcome, putting her arms around me and giving me a warm kiss on the lips. It didn't get any better than that.

One night after Karen and I had had a most pleasant sexual encounter, I said to her, "You know what—I wouldn't mind dying like Conrad. He had one of the two great deaths you can have. I mean he was playing Pebble Beach with the woman he loved, and he had only a brief sharp pain before passing out and dying. He never really knew what happened. I'll take that any day."

"What's the other great death, dying for your country like your father?" asked Karen. "He never knew what hit him either."

"Dad had a good death, but that is not what I was thinking about. If you know men, you know they often kid about dying in the saddle—you know, having sex."

"They are obviously selfish slobs who think nothing of the woman," said Karen.

"Oops, you got me there, honey," I said, laughing and putting my arms around her, which is how we fell asleep.

CHAPTER 84

Growing older should not be a surprise, but there are long periods in most people's lives when they don't give it any thought and really take a lot for granted. That's probably healthy if you are living one day at a time. I recall my mother remarking on the subject:

"You are a young mother, and suddenly you wake up, and you have reached your biblical life span of three score and ten, except in my case I feel like I am fifty, which is the age you boys are getting closer to." The occasion was mother's seventy-first birthday on March 1, 1985.

"What are you trying to say, Mom?" asked Joe.

"I guess I just want all of you to know that time passes very quickly, and you should take advantage of every day you have," she replied.

"It helps if you believe in God," said Karen. "If you really trust in God then there is nothing to worry about."

"Except if God decides to test you as he has Joe," said Jim.

"If collecting stamps and following sports equates to being tested, I can tell you it is not so bad," said Joe, smiling his crooked smile.

"Joe, you have the most marvelous attitude," said Mother. "I know a lot of people who would be feeling sorry for themselves, because events had made them different than they once were."

"I think Joe is passing the test," said Jim.

Joe indeed was passing the test but I missed the old Joe, who was much more substantial, much more intellectual, much more a force in family affairs. The post-stroke Joe was often superficial, and his sense of humor could be cutting and cruel at times, though I think it was unintentional, more a reflection of lost brain cells. All of this took its toll on Claire, who had aged considerably. Her hair was graying, and her face had become heavier, though her figure remained trim thanks to regular workouts and walks, often with Constance.

But Claire did her best to remain cheerful, and her energy had not diminished. She attended all of Big Joe's Stanford basketball games that were played in the Bay Area, along with Joe and, frequently, Karen, Mom, and me. Of course, Jim and Pamela made all the Stanford home games, the arena being only a ten-minute drive from their Portola Valley home. Claire was also involved in her daughters' lives and outside activities, not to the extent of today's soccer moms, but more so than most mothers. Of course, just shopping and cooking took a lot of time, because she did it mostly by herself now; before Joe's stroke, he had liked to work in the kitchen, which served as a nice break from his writing.

Constance recognized the burden Claire had assumed and did a lot of things for her, like taking the girls shopping. Mom seemed to sense when Claire needed a break, and she was almost always there to provide it.

Our family circle was diminished with the change in Joe and the loss of Conrad. But offsetting this was the fact that Big Joe, Robyn, and Kare were becoming more distinct in personality and consequently more interesting and fun to be around. And my wife, Karen, and Jim's wife, Pamela, made us a more female-dominated family. Unfortunately, Adam Sutro was not around as much as we would have liked because of his wife's close-knit family.

Richard Hamblen and his wife, Claudia, continued to attend most of our family gatherings, and they frequently invited Constance out to social events, only some of which invitations she accepted. Fifteen months after Conrad's death, Mom began to get asked out on dates, but she respectfully declined them all.

Jim and Pamela invited all of the family down on Memorial Day of 1985 to celebrate the opening of their new fifty-foot heatable swimming pool. Karen and Jonathan and I drove down with Mom. Joe and Claire were there with their three offspring, plus Big Joe's girlfriend, Ashley Robinson. Also present were the Hamblens and Adam and Lillian Sutro.

At one point in the afternoon, Jim and I were chatting with Richard Hamblen. It was a beautiful day with the temperature in the low eighties. We were all in our bathing suits, and Jim said he was amazed at how lean and trim Richard was. "How do you manage it?" Jim asked.

"I think it is genetics more than anything," Richard said.

"I wonder," said Jim, who himself was twenty-five pounds heavier than he had been in his college days, with most of that gained weight having gathered about his middle. "Danny here was twenty pounds overweight all of his life, and now look at him—he's lean and mean."

"It's the only way I could get Karen to marry me," I said.

"I don't doubt that," said Jim. "Richard, what is your secret? I don't believe that your health and physical condition are only the result of your genes."

Richard replied that his father had lived to be ninety-one and had weighed the same all of his life. On the other hand, Richard said that his own brother had died at fifty-nine; he had been under stress most of his life and often drank too much.

"He was an air traffic controller, and early on, he got into the habit of having two or three stiff drinks to unwind after work," said Richard. "He hardly ever exercised; even when he played golf, he never walked—always took a cart. His wife was heavy, and not surprisingly—because she was a fabulous cook."

"I've never seen you take a cart," I said to Richard.

"Not if there is a caddy available or if pull carts are allowed," said Richard.

"Conrad used to like to take a cart," I said. "Except when he played with Mom; she always insisted they take a caddy."

"I think it is pretty clear that Conrad would have lived longer had he not been overweight and had he exercised more," said Richard. "He loved rich foods and desserts. Near the end, he tried to change his ways, but it was obviously too late. However, I would have to say that of all of the people I have known in my life, Conrad was one of the happiest and was a great pleasure to be around. I miss him very much. Would he have been the same if he'd always been worrying about what he ate or about getting enough exercise? There are trade-offs, obviously."

"Yes, but look at you—you seem to enjoy your life every bit as much as Conrad did his," said Jim. "And Danny here is happier than I have ever seen him, and he hasn't had anything but wine in several years."

Jim spent the next half hour asking Richard and me about our exercise and eating habits. Oddly enough, I had never before told

Jim about my physical fitness program and the kinds of foods I was either eating or avoiding. I told him maintaining discipline was the hard part.

"Most people know what they should be doing, but they don't have the discipline," I said.

"I'm not sure I agree with that, Dan," said Jim. "I've spent most of the last twenty-four years working with businessmen and women, many of whom are hard-driving sales people who believe that working hard and playing hard are perfectly acceptable ways of life. Most of them, in their thirties and forties, think they are indestructible. Look at the number of overweight people in the crowd at the 49ers games. Those guys don't look like they are worried about their weight, not if you look at the food consumed at those tailgate parties or at the lines for beer and hot dogs inside the stadium."

"I would say that is true," said Richard, "But it is even more so in New York than in San Francisco."

In late August of 1985, Jim phoned and said he wanted to bounce some ideas off of me. He came to the city, and we met for lunch at the Iron Horse on Maiden Lane.

"You know, I have spent the past couple of years trying to figure out what to do with the rest of my life," he said. "I'll be forty-nine next month, and I think that is way too young to retire. When I first sold my company, I thought I would become a business consultant and a career advisor to middle-aged executives. I've done a lot of study in those fields, and I've already started doing some consulting, and up to a point, I like it. But getting clients is hit-or-miss, and I really prefer to have a bit more critical mass to what I do. So what I am thinking about, and this is what I want to bounce off you, is starting a proactive health center. I have to tell you, I have been influenced by what happened to Joe and Conrad as well as by what you and Richard have told me. When I say proactive, I mean doing the things that will prolong the quality of life. You say that discipline is the hardest thing to maintain, and I could not agree with you more. I've been trying to lose weight for the past three months, and all I am down is two pounds."

"What will happen at your health center?" I asked.

"Everything," he said. "I am talking about an investment of up to $2 million. I've been talking with a lot of physical fitness people and doctors, and what I want to do is create a one-stop center for all of people's proactive health needs. I am going to need at least 40,000 feet of space, and I have found a former supermarket in Menlo Park that would be perfect."

"Wow, that's a lot of space," I said. "Do you need it all?"

"I just hope it's enough," he replied.

Jim outlined his plan. His proactive health center would even have space for doctors to conduct physicals, blood testing, and stress tests and take urine samples.

"The idea is that the optional first step would be a complete physical that would result in a fitness diagnosis. I've talked to several young doctors from Stanford who tell me they could devote at least ten hours a week for appointments with clients. They aren't willing to work in any way except by appointments, which makes a lot of sense.

"We also would have a dietician, probably full-time after a while, who would add an ongoing personal touch for at least monthly consultations. The facilities would include a large weight-training room with personal trainers and an assortment of strength-building machines, a massage area, whirlpools, a large general exercise room for aerobics classes, yoga, and stretching, and a smaller exercise room for smaller classes. There would be a separate room for exercise bikes and treadmills, with individual cassette tape players and headphones for each station so that everyone can move to their own music.

"We'll have saunas and steam rooms. And there will be a small candlelit room with pews for people to meditate. Of course, we will have first-class men's and women's locker rooms. There could be more stuff, including a vitamin and health food concession, but I think we'll hold off on that until we open."

I told Jim that it sounded like a great idea and that he was going to need all of his energy to pull it off.

"The key is hiring the right people and putting together a marketing plan," Jim said. "I have no doubt there is a need for something like this, but it has to be sold and resold—you have to keep the people sticking to their programs. You have to create a lot of word of mouth. I think it is a lot easier for people to discipline themselves in some kind of program with other people as opposed to doing it entirely on their own."

"I agree. Are you looking for investors?" I asked.

"Would you be interested?" he asked.

"Yes," I said. "If your center works, you could get them going all over the country, go public, make yourself a new fortune."

"First things first," he replied. "The truth is I just want to do something useful."

CHAPTER 85

Jim briefed me the next week in more detail on his plan to establish his health center on the El Camino Real in Menlo Park, about twenty-seven miles south of San Francisco, just a few miles up the road from Palo Alto and Stanford. At his request, I talked about it on a confidential basis with a dozen or so of my more erudite business friends. Almost to a person, they thought it was a good idea if it was well executed, though a few wondered about the return on invested capital. All of our family liked the idea, and both Richard Hamblen and Adam Sutro indicated they would be willing to invest in the project. The most enthusiastic supporter was Mom. She said she would be there three times a week and would be coming with friends. Claudia Hamblen said she wished it was going to be located in San Francisco, but Jim said he wanted to work near his home.

After Jim signed the lease for the onetime Safeway store in Menlo, he hired a well-known architect to create the layout. Jim had done his homework in every respect, and his charisma and enthusiasm helped him get free input from experts in the fields of preventive health and training. A perfectionist when his heart was in it, Jim sought out the best of everything, from treadmills to massage tables to weight machines to tape players and on and on. No details were glossed over. To validate his assumptions, he organized three focus groups, each composed of twelve participants, led by a professional, to describe the concept and solicit opinions. Several of the women recommended that hairdressers be available within the complex and suggested that lectures on health, skin care, menopause, and other subjects might be made part of a program for members. Another participant suggested facials, manicures, and pedicures. A couple of men said they thought the inclusion of a rehab capability would be a plus.

In the end, Jim decided to limit investors to family members, with units of $100,000 each. Each unit would be worth 3 percent of the business. Richard Hamblen, my mother, Joe, Adam Sutro, and I each bought a single unit so that collectively we owned 15 percent of the business to Jim and Pamela's 85 percent; they were putting up $2 million.

"If you were all just investors and not family, I would take at least 90 percent," said Jim. "But you are family, and I want you all to be part of it. You will all be on my board of directors."

For the next year, Jim and Pamela worked twelve hours a day, six days a week, putting together the myriad details that went into the project. My wife Karen got involved in the advertising for Pro-Active Health, the name of the center. My mother and Claudia Hamblen made a major contribution, coming up with more than 1,000 names and addresses of "movers and shakers" living between Burlingame and San Jose. The list was used for a direct mail campaign.

It was Richard's idea to have an open house for members of the medical community. Karen suggested that the press be included. The ensuing coverage was worth a million dollars in advertising.

"Onetime Cal basketball star Jim Booker, and his lovely Singapore-born wife, Pamela, have created what may be the world's most complete health spa," intoned WPIX-TV reporter Ginny Adams, "and also one of the most glamorous. This used to be a Safeway market, but the new façade makes it look like a Greek temple." The camera panned a dozen eighteen-foot-high pillars and then passed through huge double glass doors that opened into a marble lobby, where a giant fountain sent water halfway to the ceiling in a dramatic crescendo.

"Want to improve your mind and body?" asked Ginny. "Well, whatever you need, Jim and Pamela Booker are making it available under one tent covering 40,000 square feet and at a cost of millions."

The KPIX cameraman and Ginny toured the entire building, talking with various staff professionals about the multitude of services available.

"This place is to die for, and it officially opens its doors next week," said Ginny. "I don't know about you, but I'm coming back."

Similarly gushing coverage was on KGO-TV. All of the Peninsula newspapers ran photos and stories. The *Chronicle* dubbed Pro-Active Health a "Preservation Pleasure Palace."

One columnist wrote that if he were to take advantage of all of the available services, it could easily consume a whole day, not counting the optional physical exam, which he strongly recommended for people who hadn't had one in the past year.

Ken Thatcher telephoned me the week of the opening and said that in all of his life he had never seen so much free publicity for the grand opening of anything.

"You probably have to go back before my time to the opening of the Sutro Baths to match all the hoopla Jimmy and Pamela have generated," said Ken. "It proves the old adage that if you do something classy and original, you are going to get the attention of the media."

In the first month, 719 people plunked down $200 as an initiation fee to join Pro-Active Health. In addition, they agreed to pay dues of $25 a month, which gave them a locker and use of the weight room, aerobic machines, running track, meditation room, saunas, showers, and general training room. They could also attend the weekly health lectures that were held in the main classroom. Everything else required a special fee. Personal weight training, acupuncture, and massages were priced at $25 to $50 a session. Aerobics classes, with up to fifty people, were an additional $5, and yoga classes for twenty people were $7. Package discounts were also available. Consultations on health matters with the part-time staff doctors were variously priced, usually about the same as a visit to a doctor's office. The basic physical, including a stress test, cost $100, and urine and blood testing were charged separately at a discounted rate Jim had negotiated with a nearby medical laboratory.

"I can't believe how well it is going," Jim told me. "The women love Pamela's lighting, especially the candles in the massage and acupuncture rooms. And the subdued lighting and Indian background music for the yoga classes have gotten terrific response. We tried burning incense, but a couple of ladies said they were allergic to the smoke."

I went through a screening exam conducted by a thirty-something doctor from Stanford who was a strong advocate of preventive medicine and who also believed in taking vitamins, especially fish oil. He told me that his brother was a chemist for a drug manufacturer and had started insisting that the doctor take fish oil ten years earlier. He said his brother contended that fish oil, with a high omega-3 content, was the closest thing there was to an overall health cure-all. He insisted I give it a three-month trial.

"From what I have learned," the doctor told me at the end of our session, "staying healthy is easiest when you control stress and your weight, when you exercise regularly, when you are optimistic, and when you eat a balanced diet. It is not complex, but it requires discipline. Of course, smoking is out, and you need to get your rest."

"What about alcohol?" I asked.

"It's great, but I don't drink during the week," he said. "Some people say it is better to have one or two drinks every day, and they may be right. But my wife and I have a lot of friends our age, and there is a tendency to party a bit on the weekends, not to the point of getting drunk, but we will have more than two drinks. I never drink on Sunday night, unless we are entertaining. I work ten- to twelve-hour days, and I need to keep my head clear and energetic."

"Any other tips?" I asked.

"Try to avoid arguments—getting mad, raising your voice," he said. "Learn how to disagree tactfully; it will add years to your life."

When I talked to the dietician, she stressed that eating fish two or three times a week was a huge benefit to overall health, just as eating processed foods and too much red meat could be a serious negative. She also stressed the value of eating a lot of fruit and vegetables. She said she did not eat sugar, though she did allow herself some low-fat ice cream once in awhile.

"If you feel a strong urge to eat something sweet, try eating some grapes or fresh pineapple, and that will quell your sweet tooth," she said.

"You look like you have been taking good care of yourself," the dietician told me. "Your skin is clear and you have a healthy glow about you."

"It helps to have a happy marriage," I said.

"More than you know," the dietician said. "I have clients who do everything right, but because they are deep down unhappy, they don't look and act nearly as healthy as they should or could."

"I find if I am unhappy about something, I do strenuous exercise, and that helps to calm me down," I said.

"Whatever works," she said. "Personally, I prefer yoga and meditation to get me on the right track. Really, there is no one way to achieve your goals. Truth be known, you can eat almost any kind of diet in moderation and be healthy as long as you are happy about yourself and what you are doing."

"But you are that much better off if you don't eat sweets and fats, no?" I said.

"Of course," she said, "but you don't have to be too exacting on your diet; the human body can handle almost everything that is not done to excess."

Claudia Hamblen did not do well on her stress test, and the doctor recommended that she see a heart specialist for further testing. Richard Hamblen, on the other hand, like Mother, was proclaimed a marvel for his age with no apparent problems. Karen had some loose fat around her middle that she had not been able to shake since her pregnancy, and the weight trainer said it would be gone in six months. Pamela was in fabulous shape in every respect. Joe was told he could improve himself a lot by doing weight training, aerobics, yoga, and meditation and by cutting out sweets, which he admitted he ate far too often. Claire, who passed her tests with flying colors, promised that sweets would be banned from their household.

Adam Sutro, it turned out, had high blood pressure and high cholesterol and needed to exercise more. He was also fifteen pounds overweight, and the doctor said he needed to mitigate the stress in his business life by doing either yoga or meditation, while also engaging in some form of regular exercise to get his heart rate up. The doctor said it would be a good idea to stop drinking at lunch.

For the first six months that Pro-Active Health was open, all of our family was keen in pursuing the path to optimum health. The fact that we were working with others helped motivate everyone. But after six months, the intensity began to lag, not significantly, but noticeably. Jim said that attendance among the original members was showing a similar lag. Maintaining motivation became Jim's newest challenge. He said that although the original members' declining attendance was not hurting his business, he felt a need to address the issue. I said to him that the less frequently people came, the more new members he could sign up.

"Danny, I am not in this to make money so much as I am to give something back," Jim said. "We defeat that purpose if we don't jump all over the backsliding and figure out how to keep people motivated."

"Maybe you need to keep people motivated by keeping score," I said. "If scores weren't kept in golf or bowling, I can guarantee you that hardly anyone would play."

"Danny, my brother, I think you have something there," Jim said. "We just have to get people to keep score."

CHAPTER 86

In the mid-1980s, America found its bearings and got its confidence back. January 20, 1985, brought two events that gladdened the hearts of the Booker family. First, their beloved San Francisco 49ers won their second Super Bowl by defeating the Miami Dolphins 38–16. And second, Ronald Reagan was sworn in for his second term in office, after defeating Walter Mondale in forty-nine of the fifty states, garnering 59 percent of the vote.

Perhaps the most important event of that time was Mikhail Gorbachev's rise to the top leadership post in the Soviet Union, succeeding Constantin Chernenko, a hard-liner who had served only briefly. Gorbachev proved more interested in seeing growth in the Soviet economy than anything else. I always suspected that Gorbachev was influenced by his wife, whose un-Kremlin-like tastes included French fashions and perfumes. Reagan and Gorbachev met for six hours of private conversations in Geneva in November of 1985, and the genial Reagan said afterward, "We got very friendly." Gorbachev said the talks were "productive."

The big issue of disagreement was Gorbachev's insistence that the United States drop its plans to build space-based weapons systems, known as Reagan's "Star Wars" program. When Reagan refused, Gorbachev said the Soviets would build their own system.

"Mr. President," Gorbachev told Reagan, "you should keep in mind we are not simpletons." Gorbachev was playing poker, but he did not have the cards. In April of 1986, Soviet vulnerability was exposed to the world when the nuclear generating plant in Chernobyl exploded, forcing the evacuation of an estimated 135,000 people from the Ukrainian countryside surrounding the plant. The Soviets had to ask West Germany and Sweden to help them deal with the crisis, which subsequently was revealed to have caused thirty-one deaths and hundreds of injuries, not to mention the proliferation of cancer deaths that pocked the landscape in coming years.

That same month, Reagan flexed his muscles by ordering the bombing of Libya in retaliation for its role in the bombing of a Berlin nightclub, in which American soldiers were killed and injured.

In justifying the attack, part of which was launched from Great Britain (France refused to allow its airfields to be used), Reagan said, "I warned that there should be no place on earth where terrorists can rest and train and practice their deadly skills. I meant it when I said that we should act with others, if possible, alone, if necessary, to ensure that terrorists have no sanctuary anywhere."

Libya's leader, Muammar Khadafy, got the message. He ceased to sponsor terrorist attacks.

Although many liberals criticized Reagan over the Libya bombing, it did not hurt relations with Gorbachev, whose revolutionary policies of *perestroika* (restructuring) and *glasnost* (openness) had caught the fancy of Americans. When "Gorby" came to Washington in December of 1987, his motorcade was cheered as it passed. Gorbachev several times ordered his car to stop so that he could get out and work the crowd, not unlike an American politician. More importantly, the two leaders signed a historic agreement providing for the first bilateral reduction in nuclear weapons. The Soviets agreed to dismantle 1,750 weapons and the United States 860.

The late 1980s were a good time in America. A popular song was Bobby McFerrin's 1988 classic "Don't Worry, Be Happy."

With the end of the Cold War on the horizon, with the American economy having recovered from its doldrums, and with the inflation rate below 5 percent (down from double digits a few years earlier), the stock market roared ahead, and the public seemed to be happy indeed. Pro-Active Health was operating at near capacity by mid-1988. Jim always said part of the success was that we had figured out a way to reduce backsliding among many of the customers.

The program to increase and maintain motivation was put together by members of the Booker family in a joint meeting held at Jim's Portola Valley home in late 1987. Jim and Pamela had invited us all down for the weekend. The participants at that meeting were as follows:

James Booker, age fifty-one, Chief Executive Officer of Pro-Active Health
Pamela Booker, age thirty-six, President
Richard Hamblen, age seventy-seven, Chairman of the Board
Constance Sutro, age seventy-three, Vice Chairman
Joseph Booker Jr., age fifty-three, Treasurer
Daniel Booker, age fifty-two, Secretary
Claudia Hamblen, age seventy-three, board member
Karen Booker, age thirty-seven, board member
Claire Booker, age fifty-two, board member

Shareholders present included Joe's three children: Joe III, age twenty-two, a senior at Stanford; Robyn, age twenty-one, a junior at Stanford; and Karen, age nineteen, a freshman at San Jose State. Our son, Jonathan, soon to be six, was also there, as was Big Joe's girlfriend, Ashley Robinson, now twenty-one. The only ones not present were Adam Sutro, age forty, and his wife, Lillian, age thirty-seven. Adam said he was proud to be an investor but did not want to be on the board of Pro-Active Health, because he was too busy and needed any free time to devote to his own family, which included twin boys, Alan and Richard, age six.

After lunch on the first day, Jim gathered everyone in the huge living room with the exception of Jonathan, who went for a walk with the dogs and Ashley. He stated that the challenge was to come up with some kind of scoring or record system that would motivate users of the spa and gym to sustain their interest.

He cited statistics concerning resignations (about 23 percent) and persons whose use of the facilities was declining (66 percent).

"We are operating at 93 percent capacity right now, but I feel strongly that we ought to try to stop the backsliding," said Jim.

I noted the company would make more money if people who had paid their initiation fee of $200 dropped out and were replaced by new members, especially considering that there had been two freezes on membership when the facilities had become too crowded.

"Danny, we have already talked privately about that, and I told you it is a matter of principle with me," Jim said. "We started this business, because we wanted to help people. If all I was interested in was making more money, I would have kept my television rep company."

"I agree with Jim," said Constance. "I think what Danny is saying is important, because there is no doubt a high turnover rate would be more profitable, but that is not what we are worried about."

"Well, fortunately, the company is making a profit, albeit a small one," said Richard. "I think Jim's moral bearings are something I am comfortable with."

"If we were a public company, we would be obliged to try to make the most profit possible," I said. "But we are not, and I don't think we should ever become one."

"So we all agree to spend some time today and tomorrow to come up with a plan to reduce the backsliding, even though it may cost us some money?" asked Jim. Everyone agreed.

The discussion went on for the next two days. Jim was marvelous at running the brainstorming discussions. Obviously, he had done a lot of it in his work. One of the ground rules was that no one could belittle anyone else's ideas.

"There is no such thing as a bad suggestion, and no one should feel any trepidation about speaking out," Jim said. "Sometimes, what at first seems like a silly idea becomes a catalyst for a great idea. So if you don't like something, don't say it. We will put all of the suggestions on the blackboard, and then we will go back and pick the top four or five suggestions. It often happens that the best idea turns out to be a combination of two or three separate ideas."

Hours of talk revealed that there were no shrinking violets among the board members, and some of the discussions became intense, though good manners prevailed. Everyone had so many ideas that it eventually became clear that the plan, if it was to succeed, had to be as simple as possible.

We finally agreed upon and implemented a computer-based card system that included insertion devices in every department of the complex. When a client entered the premises, he or she was required to enter their card, which recorded the time and date. Similar card-entry points were located at each individual facility in the complex. For example, if the client was going to the weight room for a training session, the trainer would make sure the card was entered into the system for billing purposes as well as to record the activity. If the person was doing weight lifting on his or her own, the card would be entered into a different slot upon arrival and departure. Once a month, each client was signaled to report to the medical facility to have his or her weight and blood pressure recorded at no charge. Those who wanted a cholesterol test could get it done at a nominal fee.

Three computers were located in each locker room, where monthly activity compilations were available for each account. It had taken three months to develop the special software for the program, and it had cost nearly $200,000, including the computer network. But we knew the system would pay for itself, because clients were required to have their credit cards automatically debited for monthly dues and individual costs for classes, treatments, and training. This greatly reduced both the need to bill customers by hand and the cost of doing that.

My mother proudly showed me her first monthly printout. She had participated in twelve sessions with her personal trainer, four massages, four acupuncture treatments, four yoga classes, and twelve stretching classes. She had scheduled her weight-training sessions just before her stretching classes. And she had scheduled her acupuncture treatments on the same days as her yoga class and her massage. Mom was at Pro-Active Health four days a week. Her monthly bill, including facials, manicures, and health foods, ran more than $2,000, and she insisted on paying. To my surprise, there were a couple dozen women, and even a few men, who ran up even larger bills.

"I really think I am getting in the best health possible," said Mom. "Look, you can see this chart on my blood pressure—it is down to 108 over 58. When I started, it was 115 over 65. And my pulse is now averaging 66 compared with 72 before."

"What about your weight?" I asked.

"It is up from 118 six months ago to 122 now, but my trainer says the gain is mostly muscle," she replied. "This program takes time, but I can't remember feeling so energetic, and you know, I need less sleep. I've been reading at night past midnight, which is not like me. I just love having so much mental energy. At my age, I should be deteriorating, but I really think all this training is making me better. Of course, I realize how lucky I am to be able to have the time and the money for it. Most people aren't so lucky."

CHAPTER 87

My nephew, Big Joe, graduated magna cum laude from Stanford in the spring of 1988, having been a starter on the basketball team for four straight years. Although he could have sought a career in professional basketball, he reasoned that among the pros, he would be at best a mediocre player, not a star. At six feet seven inches, he was relatively small for a forward.

Job opportunities abounded for Joseph Booker III, though, and after two months of soul searching and much consulting with family members, he decided to accept an offer to become Adam Sutro's executive assistant. The Sutro & Partners Development Co. was headquartered in San Francisco and in 1988 owned four major shopping centers in northern California, thanks to strong financial backing from the Bank of America. Adam's company was also working on developing two more major shopping centers. Adam was attracted to Joe III's intelligence and integrity, and for his part,

Joe thought that Adam was brilliant in business and a man he could trust and look up to.

Everyone in the family thought Joe had made the right decision, especially Mom, who loved the serious-minded Adam as if he were her own son. She liked the idea of Adam and Joe working together and imagined it would similar to the close-knit Booker family involvement in Pro-Active Health.

The younger Joe was in my opinion the most gifted and fortunate of all the Bookers, smart, good-looking, even-tempered, a great athlete, and born into money with an excellent family. He had weathered the tragedy of his father's stroke and subsequent personality change with remarkable maturity. One of his strongest traits was to always seek out advice. Over the years, he had often asked me questions about what I would do if I were in his shoes. After his Dad's stroke, Joe and I had many conversations about his future. For awhile, and I took this as a compliment, he thought of becoming a stockbroker. I suggested he would be better off owning a piece of the action or, better yet, running his own company. I was also probably influential in Joe's decision not to pursue a career in pro basketball. It seemed to me that being a has-been at age thirty-five or even sooner was not a smart career choice if you had the talent to do almost anything, as Big Joe did. When Adam told Joe that if he did well, he one day would own a part of the company, I told Joe I thought it was a deal he could not refuse.

"Of course," I said, "success won't automatically happen, and Adam will be a stern taskmaster. Just look at the hours he puts in. He's going to expect the same from you."

"I understand, Uncle Dan, and that is one of the reasons I want to work with Adam. I did pretty well at Stanford, because I think I worked harder than most of the people. I don't think I am going to change, and I can't—because the only thing I really know is that I have a lot to learn about the real world of business."

"Joe, you are a recruiter's dream, talented and humble," I laughed.

"I'm not sure I am humble, just realistic," said Joe. "One of the things I learned at Stanford is that there are a lot of people out there who are a lot brighter than me."

"You'll find out in the real world that there are lots of brilliant people who don't ever succeed the way they should and some pretty average folks who are enormously successful," I told Joe.

"Why is that, do you suppose?" Joe asked.

"Well, a lot of the brightest people lack people skills," I replied. "And don't ever underestimate the value of luck, good and bad. The successful people I've met have had the ability to focus on what they were trying to achieve, often to the exclusion of almost everything else. Opportunity knocks at one time or another for most people, but not all are ready to answer. Successful people usually seize the opportunity when it comes, and they often have good practical judgment, which is not always true of the most brilliant minds. It is important to work hard but even more important to work smart, putting the emphasis on achieving your top priority."

"You should write a textbook on management," Joe smiled.

"I've read a few, but if you want to see good management in action, go spend some time with your Uncle Jim at Pro-Active Health," I said. "He is a perfect role model for you."

A few months later, in the fall of 1988, bad news came. Claudia Hamblen, age seventy-four, wife of Richard Hamblen for forty-nine years, died of complications following open-heart surgery. For forty-two years, Claudia had been Mom's friend—ultimately her closest and most intimate friend.

A 90 percent blockage in two arteries had made the operation necessary, and Claudia's sudden and unexpected death made the front pages of the *Chronicle* and the *Examiner*, both of which carried photo layouts describing her as the glamorous wife of San Francisco's most prominent attorney. One of the pictures showed Richard and Claudia with Constance and Conrad Sutro at the latter couple's wedding in 1963.

I have not written as much about Claudia in these pages as I might have. She was an intelligent, fun-loving woman who was the epitome of understated style, who devoted thousands of hours each year to worthy causes, and who was a constant and loving companion to her husband. For at least thirty-five, years she had been Mom's best friend, and being childless herself, she was deeply involved in the lives of the Booker boys and their wives and friends. She loved people and parties and was not above having a third or fourth drink on certain occasions. When young, she was, like my mother, a stunningly beautiful woman, and she aged gracefully, never losing her attractiveness. She was always good company and could be unpredictable with her views on any subject. She enjoyed shocking people with an outrageous remark—she had, for example, once announced that she doubted that Richard and Pat Nixon had had sex during the last twenty-five years.

When we boys were younger, it always seemed to us that Claudia knew the score of what was really going on, not like the usual out-of-touch adult. She managed to be contemporaneous all of her life and had friends in all economic levels. She and Mom worked together for many years with homeless people.

"The difference between these poor alcoholics and some of the highly successful people I have known is not always that great," she once told me. "Sometimes it is nothing more than a bad marriage or an unexpected illness or some kind of tragedy that sets off a chain of events that leads to a downfall. Did you ever see the movie *My Man Godfrey*? William Powell plays the role of a man living as a hobo, and he meets a very spoiled and rich young lady played by Carole Lombard, who hires Godfrey as her butler. It turns out that Godfrey, the hobo, is smarter and wiser than everyone else in the film. I forget how it ends, but the point is that when your mother and I worked together with the homeless, we were often surprised at how intelligent these tragic figures could be. What I am saying is that the difference between success and failure in life can be amazingly small and subtle."

Richard Hamblen was stricken with grief by his wife's sudden passage. The doctors had assured him the operation was serious but not life-threatening for a person in Claudia's good general health. Richard and my mother were both at the hospital while Claudia underwent her surgery. They were together when the doctor brought word of her death.

In the ensuing months, Richard decided to retire from his law practice, though he would remain a consultant to his firm. He was seventy-eight. He said he could not continue with his normal life. He put his large house up for sale and signed on with a group of friends to go on an around-the-world trip that would last for three months and was arranged by a local travel agency. He asked Constance if she wanted to join the group. At first, Mom hesitated.

She said she felt some uncertainty about the propriety of going off with the husband of her now-dead best friend. She told me she did not know the answer to her dilemma.

"You are going to be with a lot of other people," I said. "Richard has been the best friend we have ever had, and I think he needs you; it is the least you can do for him."

So Mom agreed to go. All of the family were delighted. Both Richard and Constance felt the persistent gnawing feeling that so often goes with the sudden passing of a loved one. Together they would do much better than alone.

Vice President George Bush was nominated in 1988 by the Republican Party to succeed Reagan, and he handily defeated Governor Michael Dukakis, though few people, including me, thought he was Reagan's equal. When the Gipper stepped down in January of 1989, I felt a further sense of personal loss, but nothing like what I had felt when Conrad Sutro died while playing golf, or when Claudia had expired during a routine operation, or when Joe was stricken with his terrible stroke. Now my mother and Richard Hamblen were somewhere in the South Pacific. My world and the people who were in it had shrunk. Thank God for Karen, who was an awesome, devoted, thoughtful, and diligent mother who still made me feel like the most important person in her life. I always suspected that somewhere along the line, she had vowed to be just the opposite of her mother, who flitted from one man to another, whose face-lifts and body tucks gave her advancing age a graceless quality. Jonathan, meanwhile, seemed to take more after his mother and was becoming quite a handsome youngster who had only a slight interest in sports but a keen interest in anything scientific.

In those early months of 1989, Joe and Jim and I and our families spent a lot of time together. We knew that our lives had changed and we were now on the brink of becoming the older generation. There was nothing really wrong with that. It just took a bit of getting used to. I felt good that my mother had Richard to stabilize her life, and vice versa.

CHAPTER 88

Our family received a deluge of postcards from Mom during her trip, starting at first from exotic islands in the South Pacific. The bottom line, reading between the lines of Mom's colorful descriptions, was that she was having the time of her life.

"Getting away like this has been the best possible antidote," she wrote. "The only thing that would make it better would be to have Claudia and Conrad with us."

In early April, when the three-month trip was supposed to end, Mom called from Rome and said six of the ten people on the tour had decided to take a villa outside of Rome for two weeks and then spend two weeks in Paris and two weeks in London before heading home.

"We've been eating huge meals and drinking more wine than I can ever remember, and I don't think any of us has gained an ounce," Mom told me on the telephone. "Richard says to give his love to Karen, Jonathan, and you. He is doing amazingly well."

Word that Mom and Richard were an item reached San Francisco in March as a result of an accidental meeting in Bombay with a San Francisco couple, regulars on the Pacific Heights social scene. I heard thirdhand what was being said from one of the vice presidents at Bank of America, a chap I sometimes went jogging with after work.

"Everyone is delighted from what I hear," my friend told me.

Indeed, my only worry had been that they would not become a couple, that Mom would invoke her old-fashioned morality and construe that somehow it would be wrong. Mom later told me that when she was reminded how compatible she and Richard were in the first weeks of their travels together, she ceased to think that anything was wrong. After all, she said, they had slept in separate rooms for the first three months of their trip. However, she said, upon arriving in Italy, they had begun sharing a room.

Mom and Richard returned home on May 19, 1989, and a few days later, Jim and Pamela hosted a welcome-home party. Mom, despite being seventy-five, was looking radiant, as if she had just spent six months in a health spa. Richard, according to my wife Karen, was "the best looking seventy-nine-year-old man in the world."

None of us had seen my mother for four and a half months, and I had almost forgotten the charm of her presence and how she could infuse love and affection into our family gatherings. She told us about all of their stops, which included Tahiti, Micronesia, New Zealand, Australia, Singapore, Malaysia, Thailand, Burma, India, South Africa, Zambia, Kenya, Egypt, Spain, Italy, France, and the United Kingdom.

"I could do it all over again in a minute except that I could never be away from my family for so long again," Mom said. Both Robyn and Kare hung on every detail of Mom's descriptions.

"In Kenya we were on a safari in the middle of lion country when we got a flat tire," Mom said. "The problem was we were surrounded by a pride of lions, who paid no attention to us and had no fear of our Land Rover. It was amazing that the lions would sit right down on the road next to us, showing absolutely no fear whatsoever. It was a hot late morning when we got the flat, and we were just heading back to the lodge for lunch. The lions were having their siestas, so our guides could not get out to change the tire."

"Why didn't they shoot a gun off and scare them away?" asked Joe.

"That's what I wondered," said Richard. "But our guide told us that if we fired a gun or tried to scare them, they wouldn't be so comfortable in the future, and other tourists might not have the thrill that we had, parked amid a pride of absolutely wild lions."

"What about the lion that got under the truck?!" said Constance. "Imagine, a big lion getting out of the hot sun right underneath us. We had to sit there for three hours before the last of them ambled off."

"Did you see any tigers?" Jonathan asked.

"Tigers don't live in Africa, Jonathan, but when we were in India, we went on a six-hour safari to try to see a tiger, but we only saw these huge paw tracks and droppings," Mom answered. "We did see snake charmers, Jonathan, with cobras in baskets weaving back and forth right in front of our hotel in Bombay."

Pamela wanted to know about Italy, and both Constance and Richard said the food and wine there were the best they had ever had.

"Jim has promised to take me there for a month next spring," Pamela said. "I want to see Rome, Florence, and Venice."

Richard said the cities were wonderful, but the countryside was even better, though he agreed you had to see the cities first.

"I have friends who go to Italy every year," said Karen, looking at me and adding, "Danny, we can go there with Jonathan; he would love it."

Mom's enthusiasm had the travel bug biting!

"I only saw Denmark, Germany, France, and Spain when I went to Europe last summer," said Robyn. "I want to go back this year, and Dad and Mom said it is okay if Kare comes with me, if she doesn't have to take any makeup classes."

"All I see is northern California," said Big Joe. "Adam never takes any time off; he's a proverbial slave driver."

"Don't worry, son," said Joe. "Your time will come."

"I know, Dad," said Big Joe. "I love what I do and working for Adam, and I was really just kidding."

Mom wanted full details on Pro-Active Health. Jim said it was making a surprisingly good profit, and applicants now had to wait up to three months to become members.

"We've been working nonstop for more than three years," Jim said. "And it has been worth every ounce of that effort. You wouldn't believe how many people have told me how their lives have been changed for the better."

"You and Pamela look so fit and healthy, Jim—you should pose for your ads," said Mom. Everyone laughed in agreement.

Karen told Mom that she was planning to go back to work part-time and hoped to hook up with an advertising agency. Mom thought that was a good idea. Robyn said she would finish her master's degree in biology in June and hoped to be teaching in a Bay Area high school by next fall. Kare said she did not know yet what she wanted to do except that she wanted a job in San Francisco.

"After the boys were all in school, I went to work in a beauty parlor," said Constance. "It was the first job I had ever had, and it was a lot of fun. I made a lot of friends. That was during the war, and almost all of the women had husbands in the service."

"Was that when my father's Dad was killed?" Jonathan asked.

"Yes, just three weeks before the fighting stopped," Constance said. "Your grandfather was a colonel and commander of a tank battalion, and he won a Silver Star for bravery."

"You can all be very proud of Colonel Booker," said Richard. "We served together in Europe for eighteen months, and all he could do was talk about getting home to see his wife and three boys. The happiest I have ever seen anyone was when he got mail from home."

"I wrote him every day, and the boys also wrote letters, especially Joe," said Constance.

"The trouble was we were constantly on the move after we left England, so sometimes it would be two or three weeks between mail deliveries," said Richard. "If he had a chance, Colonel Booker would take his bundle of letters and read them over and over again for as long as the time allowed. I will never forget the look of pure joy on his face whenever he finished, even though we had to resume fighting a very grim war, especially during the Battle of the Bulge when Hitler made his famous counterattack."

Joe, Jim, and I had all heard Richard's account of his time with our father, as had all three of Joe's children. But Jonathan was fascinated by what Richard had to say and wanted to hear more. Richard promised he would tell him all about it the next day.

"Do you boys remember when I first came to see you right after the war, and you were all living on 28th Avenue in the Sunset

District?" Richard asked. We all nodded that we did. "I don't mind telling you I was pretty unsettled about having to tell you kids what a hero your dad was and what a great and brave soldier he was and how much he loved you all. You were about the finest-looking family I had ever seen. You could have all been in a poster depicting the American homefront. I can't believe that was almost forty-five years ago."

"Richard," said Mom, "may I propose a toast to you? I know I speak for all of the boys in saying how grateful we are for all your help, advice, and friendship over these forty-five years."

Joe, Jim, and I all stood up and toasted Richard with smiles and cheers. He stepped forward and gave us all a full Mexican abrazo. He then put his arm around Mom and said, "You can't imagine how much the Booker family has meant to me and Claudia."

It was great having Mom and Richard back. None of us were surprised when Mom said she was inviting Richard to live with her.

"Neither of us wants to be alone," said Mom. "I hope none of you are scandalized."

We all laughed. After all, we were closing in on the last decade of the twentieth century, and times had changed mightily since 1914 when Mom was born.

CHAPTER 89

In June of 1989, I had what I thought was an innocent conversation with a friend of mine over lunch at the downtown Olympic Club, a conversation that actually ended up causing me trouble. The friend was Charles T. Wagner, the chief financial officer of Zephyr Semiconductors, a Mountain View–based technology company on which I had made a lot of money for my clients and myself. I had known Charlie for many years. His dad had been a baseball scout for several major-league teams and had in fact offered me $7,500 to sign with the Boston Red Sox farm system. (I declined and later got less money going with the Pittsburgh Pirates.) In any case, I kept tabs on my fairly substantial holdings of Zephyr stock by having lunch with Charlie two or three times a year. On this particular occasion, Charlie evinced none of the usual bravado and optimism I was used to hearing from him when we discussed his company. I asked him only one direct question with respect to Zephyr's outlook for the rest of the year. He replied that nothing had changed since the last conference call with financial analysts. We talked a bit about product development, but we spent most of our lunch talking about our respective golf games. Charlie said that his handicap was down to four and that he was playing the best golf of his life. His mood went from subdued to enthusiastic on the switch of subject to golf.

Two days later, I decided to sell all the Zephyr shares in my clients' accounts as well as 25,000 shares that were in my own account. The total was more than 300,000 shares. Why did I decide to bail? First, we would be taking a fat capital gain, with most shares going for two or three times their purchase price. But more importantly, I did not like the way Charlie had sounded. His subdued demeanor when talking about Zephyr was so unlike him that I inferred something must be wrong, despite the fact that he told me there was no change in the company outlook.

Five weeks after my and Charlie's lunch, Zephyr reported a second-quarter loss that stunned Wall Street and sent Zephyr shares down by 35 percent in one day. The problem was that outside auditors had demanded that Zephyr restate the company's profitability. The bottom line was that Zephyr had been posting phantom revenues during an eighteen-month sales slowdown, apparently figuring they could cover their actions when business improved. They must have figured that doing otherwise would mean seeing the share prices plummet, which is what happened when the truth got out.

When this news broke, virtually all of my clients called to thank me for getting them out of Zephyr, and a few asked how I had made the decision. I said it was luck based on the proven notion that taking big profits when you can is good business.

"You didn't sell Microsoft," one of my clients said. "We have a quad there."

"Zephyr is no Microsoft," I answered.

"Obviously," my client said. "Whatever, I thank you for getting me out."

In early September, I received a call from an investigator from the Securities and Exchange Commission. He said he was doing routine fact-finding with respect to some large trades in Zephyr shares that had taken place shortly before the price plunged. He asked for an appointment to discus the matter. I told him the next day would be fine with me.

If I had been smart, I would have had a lawyer with me. At the very least, I should have called Richard Hamblen, just to get his thoughts on the meeting.

The SEC investigator, Vincent Martell, arrived at 9:00 AM, and he did not leave until after 11:00. Martell asked about my dealings in Zephyr stock and wanted to know the number of shares held by my clients and by me. He wanted to know who I knew at the company, which in fact included all of the top officers. He wanted to know about my selling more than 300,000 shares of Zephyr stock over three trading days.

"I just decided to take a profit for my clients and myself," I said.

"Did you consult with your clients before you sold?" Martell asked.

"All of the accounts that owned Zephyr are discretionary, and I have full authority to buy and sell, so no, I did not."

"Do you ordinarily sell everyone out of a single stock as you did with Zephyr?"

"I've done it once or twice before," I said. "Sometimes you decide it is time to sell."

"Who was the last company official you talked with?" Vincent asked. I stalled and said I would have to check my calendar, which I did, and then told him about my lunch with Charlie Wagner, the CFO.

"Did he give you any information about Zephyr?" Vincent asked.

"We talked mostly about golf; we have known each other a long time. The only thing he said when I asked how the company was doing was that nothing had changed since the last analyst meeting."

"So you have lunch with an old buddy who tells you everything is fine, and two days later, you start to sell all your stock in his company," said Vincent. "Any prudent man would have to conclude that something went on at that lunch, that you learned something that caused you to sell. Mr. Booker, were you the recipient of anything we could call inside information?"

"No, he told me nothing. I know it sounds strange, but I am telling you the truth," I said.

Martell continued his probing. It was clear he did not believe me. When he left he said, "Mr. Booker, I will be making a report to my superiors, and they will have to decide whether this case warrants further action and whether it should perhaps be brought into a Federal District Court. There is clearly incriminating circumstantial evidence that requires further investigation, which is what my recommendation is going to be."

When Martell left, I sat stunned and almost mortified at my desk. If I was charged and convicted of insider trading, it could be the end of my career, never mind the public disgrace. I could even be sentenced to jail. But in my own mind, I had done nothing wrong. Charlie Wagner would confirm that he had given me no inside information.

I subsequently learned that violating insider trading laws could carry a maximum prison sentence of ten years, a fine of up to $1 million and triple damages for any implicit savings or gains as a result of the illegal transactions.

I telephoned Richard Hamblen. Unfortunately, he and Mom were still on a vacation trip to Mexico and were not due back for a week. So I called one of Richard's former partners and arranged a meeting for the next day. That night, I told Karen about the meeting with Martell but portrayed it in a positive way so that she would not worry.

"I hope you are not taking this too lightly," Karen said. "I think your selling of the Zephyr stock would look pretty suspicious to someone who did not know you."

My meeting with the lawyer from Richard's old firm did not help me to feel any better, but he counseled that because I had not been charged with anything, I should just sit tight. And under no circumstances should I call Charlie Wagner.

"I am certain they are going to want to confirm your story with Charlie Wagner, so you don't want to be having any conversation with him." the lawyer said. "I can see where Martell was coming from and why the S.E.C. is probably going to follow up. When they do, make sure you have a lawyer with you. Richard Hamblen would be perfect."

The next two weeks were agony. Never in my life had I had anything like this hanging over my head. On the second weekend of the ordeal, Karen had taken Jonathan to Southern California to make separate visits to see her mother and her father and his family. I was going to drive with them, but distraught over the Zephyr matter, I decided not to go. Karen said she understood, though she and Jonathan were very disappointed.

That Saturday night, with nothing to do, I gave Ken Thatcher a call, and we agreed to have dinner. Ken was in his late seventies, but he still had all of his gray hair. We met at the Iron Horse. I was driving up from an afternoon at Pro-Active Health in Menlo Park, so I parked in the Union Square Garage and walked from there to Maiden Lane, where the Horse was located. Ken was already there, sipping on a martini.

"Ken, I thought you quit drinking," I said, shaking his hand warmly.

"I did, many times," he smiled. "Actually, I got some news yesterday from my doctor, and this is absolutely my very last night drinking. I'm really glad you called, Danny."

In the past couple of years, I had resumed what I considered very moderate consumption of wine, one or two glasses with dinner, and once in a while maybe three, but that was on special occasions.

"Bring Mr. Booker here one of these," Ken told the waiter, pointing at his Bombay Gin martini on the rocks. I should have protested, but I didn't. I hadn't had a martini in many years, and I wondered what it would taste like. Ken held up his glass when my drink arrived.

"Here's to the son of probably the greatest woman I have ever known," he said. I was a bit surprised. Ken always expressed his fondness for my mother, but never called her the greatest woman he had ever known. Knowing Ken's attractiveness to women, and vice versa, that took in a lot of territory.

"To the incomparable Constance Booker," I said. The martini tasted just as I thought it would, wonderful and bracing. I knew I was going to have another.

"My doctor told me the other day that I have a partial blockage in my heart, and he wants to do open-heart surgery," Ken said, looking pale but emboldened by the gin. "I'm not going to do it. Look what happened to Claudia Hamblen. I am going to take some blood thinners and let nature take its course. I've got so darned much wrong with me after all these years of hard drinking and hard living, hell, I never thought I would live this long. I'm ready to go," he added, emptying his glass with gusto and calling for another round.

I don't know if it was the pressure that had been building over the Zephyr matter or the fact that I was away from my family, but I had consented to a third drink before we had even ordered dinner, by which time I could almost feel the room spinning. When the food came, Ken ordered a bottle of red wine. We sat and talked for four hours, the last of it over several cups of coffee. I told Ken the whole story about the Zephyr shares. Ken's reaction was to ask why

I hadn't bought any for his account. Ken wanted to know all about my mother, and I told him.

"God, I loved your mother," Ken said. "I was so stupid. I should have gotten my divorce and married her and stayed in San Francisco. To think I did not because of the Catholic Church seems so ridiculous to me now. Well, I made a lot of mistakes in my life, Danny. I guess we all do."

My head was almost clear by the time we left. Ken caught a cab, and I walked over to the garage to get my car. On the way home, I was rear-ended at the intersection of Grant and Vallejo. The back bumper of my car was crushed, despite it being a slow-speed collision. When the police arrived, they could clearly see that it was the other driver's fault.

"He slammed on his brakes and caught me by surprise," the other driver said in a slightly slurred voice. The officer asked me for my license and insurance card. He shone a flashlight into my face and asked if I had been drinking.

"I had a couple of drinks over dinner, but that was hours ago," I said.

He said that my eyes were totally bloodshot and that I looked like I had been on a bender. I explained that I had been having trouble sleeping and that that was the reason my eyes were tired. He then asked me to get out of the car, lift one leg, and put my finger on my nose. I apparently flunked. He then asked me to walk an imaginary line, and I strayed only slightly.

"Sir, you were not at fault in this accident, but I am asking you to come to the station to check your alcohol level," he said, politely.

"What are you talking about?" I demanded. "If you take anyone in, take that guy—he's the one who banged into me."

"He's going in too," the officer said.

"This is ridiculous," I said. "I'm not agreeing to take any test; I only had two drinks."

"In that case, sir, you will probably pass the test," the officer said.

I argued, but to no avail; I was officially placed under arrest, handcuffed, and taken to the station, and my car was towed away. I had once been told to never take a breath test, because they were not always accurate, so I was unrelenting. By the time I was booked for drunk driving and put into a cell, it was after 2:00 AM. Fortunately, I was able to reach a criminal lawyer friend of mine, and I was out on bail by 4:30 AM. I was ordered to be in municipal court on Monday morning at 8:00 AM.

My God, I thought, what was happening to my well-ordered life? I was suddenly in deep trouble and on the verge of being a disgrace to my family. That bothered me more than anything. Suddenly and quite inadvertently, I had become caught up in circumstances that were swirling beyond my control. Words can hardly describe my angst and fears. It seemed my whole life was about to implode. I could not sleep more than two hours at a stretch. Thinking back, I realize it was the low point of my life.

CHAPTER 90

I entered a plea of not guilty to the charge of driving under the influence of alcohol. My case was set for a court trial in four weeks. Ken Thatcher had called the day before to say how much he had enjoyed our get-together, and I told him the grim tidings of what had happened after he caught his cab.

"Hell, you weren't drunk," he said.

I went over all of the details of my arrest and told him the officer said I looked like I had been on a bender, because my eyes were bloodshot.

"I noticed that, too, before you even had a drink," said Ken. "We drank nothing but coffee for the last two hours together. No way you were drunk at 12:30 AM."

But Ken said he thought I was smart not to take the breath test.

"I've heard a lot of stories that those tests are inaccurate, and the police and courts know it," Ken said. "What is the name of the judge who is hearing your case?"

"Sean Kaler," I replied.

"I've met him," said Ken. "He's a good friend of Kevin Keagan. There is a chance we can do some good with him. Darn, Danny, you don't need a DUI case now, not with the Zephyr deal too. I feel badly about this. I never should have forced those martinis on you."

"Don't blame yourself, Ken. I was the one who drank them. The guy I blame is the drunken jerk who rear-ended me! I was four blocks from my garage when he hit me."

I told Ken that Richard Hamblen was returning at the end of the week and that I would be talking with him. Ken said he would call Keagan.

The next five days were continued agony for me. I kept thinking about the old bromide that bad news is better than doubt. At least with bad news, you know what you are dealing with. With doubt, the imagination can run rampant, conjure all kinds of negative outcomes like a year in prison and a million-dollar fine. The drunk-driving charge was just salt on the wound, but even by itself, it was very serious. Not only was it humiliating, but I could lose my driver's license too.

It got worse. The *Chronicle* carried a two-paragraph item saying that Daniel Booker, a prominent securities broker, had been arrested for drunk driving and had entered a plea of not guilty in municipal court. I got at least twenty calls in response to that article, not including embarrassing communications from my family. I said I was not guilty and blamed the charge on my bloodshot eyes. Of course, I made no mention of why my eyes were bloodshot—lack of sleep over the pending SEC matter.

Two days later, the *Chronicle* carried another story saying that the Securities and Exchange Commission was conducting an investigation involving insider trading of Zephyr Semiconductor shares just prior to the crash in the stock price. No names were mentioned. Two days after that, my friend Charlie Wagner and the Zephyr CEO were indicted by a grand jury, following an investigation by a federal prosecutor who had moved swiftly based on the findings of Zephyr's outside auditors. They were charged with falsifying the company's accounts in order to sustain the company's stock price. I felt awful for Charlie, though I confess to feeling even worse for myself. I knew Charlie to be an honest man. He had a lovely and devoted wife and four children. I guessed Charlie was pressured by his CEO into cooking the Zephyr books. Surely, he must have understood that the outside auditors would catch up with their skullduggery. Charlie could be facing more than a year behind bars.

I met privately with Richard Hamblen for two hours on the Monday after he and my mother returned from Mexico. I recounted my meeting with Charlie Wagner and my subsequent meeting with the SEC investigator. Richard listened avidly, made notes, and asked far more questions than the SEC's Vincent Martell.

"Had I been with you, I would have suggested you tell Martell more than you did," Richard said.

I was puzzled and asked Richard what he meant.

"I would have recommended that you tell Martell the real reason you sold the stock," said Richard. "What you said was fine as far as it went. You decided you just wanted to take a profit. And that was true. But something else was driving you too: you were bothered by the way Charlie was acting during your lunch. If you don't mind, I suggest that we have a meeting with Mr. Martell to clear the air. You were operating on gut instinct when you sold, and I don't think it will hurt to get it on the table."

Vincent Martell agreed to meet with us on the stipulation that he have present a lawyer from the federal prosecutor's office. The meeting lasted about ninety minutes. I don't have the transcript of what was said, and I hesitate to put quotes around what Richard said, because I could never recapture the elegance of his language. What he argued was that I obviously did not think I had anything to hide, because I had agreed to meet with Vincent Martell the very day after he requested a meeting. More importantly, I had not had an attorney with me for that first meeting, obviously feeling one was not necessary. I had not told a single falsehood with respect to my discussion with Charlie Wagner, who gave me no inside information whatsoever. However, said Richard, I had left something out that needed to be told. Richard then turned it over to me, and I told them the truth, which was that Charlie was much more enthusiastic about his golf than his company.

"So the question is, assuming you are telling the truth," said Vincent Martell, "can body language and comparative demeanor be construed as inside information?"

"What I think we have here is a gray area," said the lawyer from the federal prosecutor's office. "Mr. Hamblen, Mr. Martell and I thank you for being forthcoming and bringing your client in to complete the record. I cannot tell you what the next step will be. We have not completed our investigation. We will keep you posted."

The most encouraging thing that happened was on the way out. The federal attorney said to Richard, "It has been an honor to meet you."

I mentioned that comment to Richard afterward, but Richard said that kind of talk was common among lawyers, and it could be translated in any number of ways, one of which was "I'd love to tangle with a big shot like you in court."

"My gut feeling is that is not what he was intending," I said.

"Well, your gut feelings are pretty good; let's hope you are right again," said Richard.

"Actually," Richard continued, "I don't think they have a very strong case against you. The feds don't like to prosecute gray and nebulous areas, especially in a case that would likely generate a lot of publicity.

A month later, an agonizing month later, a month so awful I can't bring myself even now to write about how wretchedly I felt, Richard Hamblen received a phone call from the justice department lawyer.

"Daniel Booker is no longer the subject of an investigation," the lawyer said.

When I got the news, I felt as though I had escaped from a tomb, felt so light that I could fly. I was joyous, relieved, and thankful for dodging a 1000-pound cannonball! Now all I had to worry about was the drunk-driving charge, the trial for which had been postponed twice.

I had no idea what to expect when we went to the court of Judge Kaler two weeks after the Zephyr matter was resolved. Richard Hamblen's arguments were concise and to the point.

"It seems to me that the principal reason for arresting my client was that he had bloodshot eyes," said Richard. "My client has never before been arrested for drunk driving; he has not even had a moving violation in at least fifteen years. He was innocently stopped at an intersection when his car was struck from behind. My client was not driving recklessly or erratically; he was just sitting there, waiting his turn to go through the intersection. According to the arresting officer's testimony, my client did not miss by much passing the sobriety tests given him. I submit that those near misses were a result of two things: He was asked to perform the tests on an uneven surface, and he was tired from a week of very hard work that had caused him to miss his usual amount of sleep. He had not had a drink for nearly three hours before he was arrested, and he had had only two drinks and a glass of wine with dinner. He did not agree to take the breath test, because he had been told for years that they were not accurate. Had I been with him, I would have advised him to take the test, because based on what he had to drink and when he had it, he surely would have passed the test."

The judge seemed to hang on every word uttered by Richard. It was a rare moment for Judge Kaler's court to see a man of Richard's renown argue a case.

"There are a number of aspects to this case that are serendipitous," said Judge Kaler. "The defendant is found not guilty." The whole proceedings had taken less than fifteen minutes.

Winston Churchill was reputed to have once said that there was nothing so exhilarating as to be shot at and missed. I was doubly exhilarated, having dodged two cannonballs, thanks in large measure to Richard Hamblen. But those two episodes over three months had taken a toll. A look in the mirror revealed a graying and receding hairline as well as dark circles under my eyes. I think Karen and I had had sex only twice in those last two months. I had put on eight pounds and had not been doing nearly enough exercise. The stress of my ordeal had taken a very quantifiable toll. Now, I felt like a new man. But I was also a changed man. I would never again sit behind the wheel of a car having had a drink. And I would never allow a friend to drink and drive. More importantly, I was going to do my best to eliminate stress from my life. I was going to renew my efforts to be more like the late Conrad Sutro.

Karen had seen the changes in me during my ordeal—or our ordeal, I should say. She was with me every bit of the way. She knew the truth. She knew I was very lucky. She knew my story to the court that I had had only two martinis was a lie. I had told her the number was three and probably two glasses of wine, not one. I did not want to ever have to lie again. In a way, I had lied to Vince Martell too by saying that my decision to sell Zephyr stock was merely normal profit-taking. In fact, my decision was based on information unwittingly given me by Charlie Wagner. It was indeed a gray area, and a more reckless federal attorney might have prosecuted. I felt both contrite and lucky.

My friend Charlie Wagner ended up testifying against his boss, who had ordered him to falsify Zephyr revenues by booking them in advance based on existing contracts. He pleaded guilty to a lesser charge and was given a suspended sentence. His boss was sentenced to one year in prison and was fined $2 million. Interestingly, none of the Zephyr executives had sold any of their own stock. Charlie told me months later that he had been asked about our lunch together and that he had said he had not given me any inside information. Had Charlie sold some of his shares before the announcement of the accounting fraud, I might not have fared so well.

Another event that contributed to my suddenly high spirits was the San Francisco Giants making it to the 1989 World Series against, amazingly enough, the cross-bay rival, the Oakland A's. Oakland won the first of two games played in Oakland, and our family had fourteen box seats all together for game three, which was scheduled to start at 5:30 PM. Karen, Jonathan, and I got there at 4:00 PM so that we could watch batting practice. The A's were led by two formidable sluggers, Mark McGwire and Jose Conseco. Jonathan was thrilled to see them repeatedly bash the ball over the fences. Just after five o'clock, Richard and my mother were walking down the aisle when suddenly the whole stadium began to rock. Being a San Franciscan, I had experienced plenty of earthquakes, but never anything like this.

"Oh, my God," said Karen, reaching out to bring Jonathan from a standing position onto her lap. I could see the light towers swaying. The players still warming up on the field stopped in their tracks. The whole stadium was shaking. It seemed strong enough that I feared the partial roof of the stadium could come crashing down. My mother was leaning forward, holding onto the back of an empty seat next to the aisle. Richard was holding onto her.

When the quake stopped after perhaps twenty seconds, the crowd, which had been hushed, let out a cheer of relief. Half-filled

Candlestick Park, perhaps the most maligned stadium in all baseball, had survived without any visible damage.

Those inside the stadium had no idea of the enormous damage that the quake had caused outside. When the dust settled, the death count was sixty-two, with 3,757 people injured and total damage estimated at $10 billion. It was the worst quake since 1906. A section of the Bay Bridge collapsed, killing only two people, fortunately. The collapse of a section of the Nimitz Freeway in Oakland resulted in forty-two deaths.

Most of the houses in San Francisco survived without serious structural damage, but the Marina District suffered immensely, because most of the houses there were built on reclaimed land from the bay, and many foundations gave way in the soft fill.

Some ten minutes after the quake, the stadium was still filling up.

"Play ball!" someone shouted, starting a chorus. But when baseball officials learned of the destruction around the Bay Area, the game was postponed. It took three days to restore electricity to the entire city. The quake had caused twenty-four fires, but unlike in the 1906 quake, firemen had plenty of water to put them out.

The quake struck on October 15, 1989. The third game of the World Series was not played until twelve days later. By that time, no one much cared, and the A's, who swept the series four games to none, did not even have the customary victory champagne in their locker room. Who could celebrate when so many people had suffered?

My mother later observed that one good thing resulted from the quake: the badly damaged Embarcadero Freeway was to be torn down and replaced by a lovely ground-level boulevard running along the waterfront.

"My father used to say it is an ill wind that does not blow some good," she said. "He was certainly right. I hated that freeway from the moment they started building it back in the 1950s."

CHAPTER 91

It seems strange writing about what happened in 1990, just over fifteen years ago. I say strange, because I can visualize events from the 1930s, 1940s, and 1950s often more vividly than what happened last month. Somehow, looking back now, the 1990s seem somewhat dull, a view that is no doubt related to my advancing age. Those who were teenagers in the 1990s would no doubt view that decade much differently than I do. One personal disappointment was that my generation was passed by for the presidency of the United States. George Herbert Walker Bush, who succeeded Ronald Reagan in 1989, was a fighter pilot in World War II. He was born June 12, 1924, in Milton, Massachusetts. His successor, Bill Clinton, who managed to avoid service in the Vietnam War, was born July 6, 1946, in Hope, Arkansas. So no one with any of the experiences of those born in the late 1920s, 1930s, and early 1940s ever made it into the oval office. Although I loved Reagan, I never thought much of the first George Bush, who struck me and others as wimpy. I found Clinton to be a glib scoundrel, likeable but hard to respect.

Perhaps it was the lack of tension caused by the end of the Cold War that made the 1990s seem so humdrum. The Soviet Union was broken up, Germany was united, and the United States was the world's sole superpower. Henceforth, it seemed (wrongly as it turned out) that wars would be fought on economic fronts.

The only real excitement, outside of the exploding world of technology, was Iraqi dictator Saddam Hussein's invasion of Kuwait in 1990. To his credit, George Bush, with a lot of moral support from United Kingdom's prime minister, Margaret Thatcher, rallied United Nations approval for military intervention to end the Iraqi occupation of Kuwait. Operation Desert Storm was launched on January 16, 1991, and the conflict turned out to be much easier for our side than anyone expected, but that was not the case for the poor Iraqis. In the end, an estimated 200,000 Iraqis died in the war (mostly from air attacks), compared with only 148 Allies. But Bush, thinking that the humiliating loss by Hussein would embolden the Iraqi people to revolt, allowed the dictator to stay in power. Hussein dealt mercilessly with the incipient rebellion and for more than a decade thumbed his nose at the Western world. At that time, no one could foresee the pitfalls that would ensue from that war, not even when a group of terrorists tried to blow up the World Trade Center in 1993. Other big stories of the 1990s were the O. J. Simpson murder case and the White House sex scandals.

Also during this time, significant developments in California were a harbinger of the change this country and this world will be seeing for the rest of the twenty-first century. I refer to California's population growth. When my family moved to San Francisco in 1938, the state's population was about 6 million. By 1990, it had reached 29.7 million, and by 2000, it was 33.8 million. Between 1990 and 2000, while the overall population rose 13.8 percent, the percentage of white residents fell by 7.1 percent, dropping from 17 million to 15.8 million, thus making whites only 46.7 percent of the total population.

The fastest growing segment of the population was Hispanics, who grew from 7.7 million to 10.9 million, a rise of 42.6 percent. Most of the Hispanic growth came in Southern California. Next was the Asian population, which rose from 2.7 million to 3.6 million, a gain of 38.5 percent, much of that growth coming in northern California. The black population rose only 4.3 percent, from 2.1 million to 2.18 million. But most importantly, a whole new category was created for the 2000 census, which was designated as "multi-race," totaling 903,115 persons.

I remember a family discussion after the 1990 census figures had been released in which Richard Hamblen predicted—quite accurately, as it turned out—that whites would be in the minority in California by 2000. He said he thought the rise of the Hispanic and Asian populations was a good thing, an extension of the assimilation that had been going on for two centuries in the United States. He spoke most highly of the Asians, who he said were naturally intelligent, family-oriented, and willing to work endlessly to achieve long-term goals.

"That's not so true of the Mexicans," was my brother Joe's opinion. "They seem willing to take the most menial jobs and don't have the same ambition as the Chinese and Vietnamese."

"That's because they don't have the education," Richard said. "You will see Hispanics getting a bigger piece of the pie as they become better educated. And all of the races are going to benefit by an ever-increasing number of interracial marriages. Science shows that a diversified gene pool breeds more talented people."

"We need to have more breeding between whites and blacks if we are ever going to have diversified basketball teams," said Joe. "If it keeps going the way it is now, there won't be any white men left in the NBA."

"Joe," said Richard, "you need to look a bit more closely. There are a lot of light-skinned black men in the NBA."

"I don't think 'breeding' is the appropriate word for human beings," said Constance.

"What would you think if your granddaughter Robyn married a black man?" asked Richard.

"To be perfectly honest, I might have trouble with it," Constance replied. "But if Robyn wanted to do that, then I would support her, because I know her well enough to believe she wouldn't marry someone who was not nice and worthy of her."

"I probably wouldn't mind if she married a light-skinned Oreo," said Joe, who was not above making racist remarks since his stroke.

"What is an Oreo?" asked Constance.

"Someone like O. J. Simpson, a black on the outside, but white inside, like an Oreo cookie," Joe said.

"I've met O. J. at several parties," said Richard. "He's a very charming man, has a lovely wife, and doesn't seem to have any of the hang-ups that most people do."

It seems ironic to think back now on that conversation in 1991, when O. J. Simpson was an icon in San Francisco. Three years later, Simpson, the highly likeable movie star, corporate pitchman, hall-of-fame football player, and general all-around good role model for the black community, blew it all. He was charged with murdering his former wife and her boyfriend. A jury may have acquitted Simpson, but everyone knew he did it, and indeed, he was held responsible for the crime in a civil case.

At the start of the 1990s, one could already see the huge contribution that Asians were making in Silicon Valley, where many worked in the development of new technology, integrated into groups of people whose only criteria for entrance was high intelligence.

But even though the population of California had exploded, San Francisco's population had remained unchanged, at about 750,000, though the ethnic makeup of that population had changed dramatically, with many more Asians. Also by 1990, San Francisco had within its population an estimated 100,000 gay residents who raised cultural levels if not the number of kids in school.

Of course, a lot of parents had decided that the suburbs, with their better weather and arguably better schools, were a nicer place to raise a family. But for me, San Francisco was the best place to live. I tuned out the liberal politics. I never tired of the beauty of the city. It was there to see and enjoy every day. The gorgeous bay with its dramatic bridges, the moody weather, the opulence of Pacific Heights, the wide variety of restaurants, the cable cars, the spectacular views in almost every part of town, tourist-packed Union Square, Fisherman's Wharf, the Embarcadero, the Presidio, North Beach, Ocean Beach, Golden Gate Park, Chinatown, Japantown, Telegraph Hill, Nob Hill, Russian Hill, the fast-changing Mission District, the unchanging Seal Rocks, the Cliff House, the ruins of Sutro Baths, the Opera, the Symphony, the museums, the Olympic Club, the Union League Club, the Marina, and the full menu of major-league sports events, especially the Giants and the 49ers.

CHAPTER 92

I suppose I will reveal a certain amount of hypocrisy when I say that we did not send our son to a public school. Jonathan attended the Cathedral School for Boys on Sacramento Street in Pacific Heights. Neither Karen nor I attended church, but we felt a private religion-based school would give Jonathan a good foundation for later life, if not the real world.

Jonathan was nine years old and in the fourth grade at the Cathedral School when he asked, "How come we don't go to church?"

It was not the first time he had raised the question, but this time, he seemed more persistent.

"Don't you believe in God?" he continued in a tone that not only seemed critical, but that also demanded a forthright answer.

"Of course, I believe in God. He gave me you and your mother, the two greatest blessings of my life," I said.

"Jonathan, all you have to do is look around at how marvelously everything works, and you know there has to be a creator," Karen said. "I can't believe it when evolutionists say our world is all an accident, that life evolved over hundreds of millions of years starting from some oozy swamp."

"The Bible says God created the earth in seven days," said Jonathan.

"That has been a controversial part of it all," I said. "The problem is scientists estimate that the earth may be 4.5 billion years old, and man has been around for only a tiny fraction of that time, so scientists tend to disbelieve that the earth and heavens were created in seven days. That does not mean that they don't believe in God. Many scientists do, and some say that the seven days referred to in the Bible may relate not to time, as we know it, but to time the way only God may know it. It is a difficult concept for many people to deal with, especially if you believe—as many churches teach—that the Bible was written at the direction of God. I don't happen to believe it was. I think the Bible was written by men, well-meaning and religious men, but only men and not God."

"Jonathan," Karen interjected, "you have seen movies about dinosaurs and cavemen, right? Well, scientists have studied their bones, and they can prove they are hundreds of thousands of years old."

"Why didn't the Bible tell about that?" Jonathan asked.

"When the Bible was written, people did not know about carbon dating or have all the scientific tools that are available to scientists today," I said.

"But God knew," said Jonathan.

"Of course, He knew. But I am convinced that God put men and women on earth so they can learn to solve the mysteries of the world, which is exactly what is happening. I believe God has given mankind the freedom to discover these things and the right to choose our own destiny. But I don't mean to suggest that God does not play a role in our lives. I believe He hears our prayers. I believe He has hopes for each of us, and He has given us the talents to fulfill those hopes, whatever they may be. But it is up to us."

"So why don't we go to church?" Jonathan asked.

"I guess growing up, I never got in the habit of going to church. And your mother was the same way. But we both believe in God, a master creator, a divine intelligence."

I told Jonathan some of the details about my visit to Therese Neumann in Germany many years earlier. He seemed impressed and asked if she was proof that God supported churches, because I had said Therese Neumann went to church. I replied that one could take it that way.

"Why don't we all go to church this Sunday?" suggested Karen. I agreed and said we would invite my mother and Richard Hamblen to join us. It meant I'd have to give up my Sunday morning golf game at the Olympic Club.

I mention this little episode in our family life, because I think it reveals a level of hypocrisy on my part, but also my inherent skepticism about organized religion. As I told Jonathan, I was a firm believer in the existence of God, mainly because I felt there was no other explanation. How could the incredible complexity of life be anything but the work of a master creator? I also believed that Jesus had been sent by God to provide guidance to mankind, as were other great religious figures throughout history. But the vastness of space and the unfolding knowledge revealed by science have fueled my strongest convictions. Science tells us that our universe is one hundred billion light-years across. That is a vastness of inconceivable proportions considering that light travels at 186,000 miles per second. And some scientists suggest there may be an untold number of other universes out there.

Another thing I have long found interesting about God is that He constantly changes things. Of all of His earthly creations, more than 99 percent are now extinct. Man clearly was His most sophisticated species creation on earth, as far as science can tell. But I have a feeling that man will evolve into a far more sophisticated entity as science continues its relentless, ever-faster advance. In 1,000 years or less, I suspect we will be able to greatly augment our brains and download their contents into perfectly formed bodies that you will be able to buy just as you might a Rolls Royce. I will not try to imagine what life may be like 10,000 years from now.

Jonathan became keenly interested in the origins of man and our world, so I tried with my limited abilities to convey to Jonathan the vastness and smallness of things, both of which constituted frontiers of learning that might still be unresolved in half a million years.

"I believe there has to be a God," Jonathan said.

"Well, we agree on that," I said. "By the way, Albert Einstein, one of the most brilliant scientists who ever lived, believed in God."

I also told him about Max Planck, the Nobel Prize–winning originator of quantum theory, who said, "All matter originates and exists only by virtue of a force. We must assume behind the force is a conscious and intelligent mind. This mind is the matrix of all matter."

In the succeeding years, Jonathan's interest in science grew ever more fervent. By the time he reached high school, he had decided that he was going to become either a cosmologist or a small particle physicist. He was far ahead of Karen and me with respect to the science of the heavens and the impossibly small world of particle physics. Yet he still strongly believed in God.

I won't spend much more time writing about religion in this book. However, if I may borrow language from the old Barbra Streisand song, people who believe in God are the luckiest people in the world. I say that because I was facing criminal prosecution on two fronts at the time, my thoughts turned to God in a way they seldom do when everything is going well. Although I didn't attend church or consult with a pastor, I'd frequently listen to religious sermons on the radio while driving in my car. Religious programming can be found at all hours of the day and night seven days a week. I found the thought of God and the teachings of Jesus most comforting. However, I often found myself disagreeing with some of the fundamentalists who regarded every word in the Bible as sacred text written with the total approval of God. Science has disproved many assertions in the Bible, but not the existence of God as creator of all that surrounds us.

Although I have no idea whether there is a heaven or a hell, I think God wants us to do the best we can in our lifetime, which, if we live until eighty, as many do, adds up to a total of just over 700,000 hours. I am reminded of my college fraternity initiation rite that included the line, "Think thee of thy past and of thy future, how much of evil, how much of possible good?"

I hate to think how many of those 700,000 hours I have or will have squandered by the time I reach the end of the trail. I grow ever closer to the time that the question of the ages will be answered for me: is there life after death? If there is life after death, it makes a lot of sense to believe in God and religious ethics. Of course, even if there is no life after death, it still makes sense to follow the Golden Rule.

CHAPTER 93

In a surprise that caught everyone in the family off-guard, my brother Jim announced that he had received an offer from a group of investment bankers to buy Pro-Active Health for $8 million, prospective buyers who we later learned wanted to set up franchises in various affluent areas around the country. The Menlo Park facility was making about $400,000 a year, but its success related in large measure to the hard work put in by Jim and Pamela. Jim explained to the board that he had grown tired of the long hours. Indeed, he looked quite fatigued, had lost weight, and had dark circles under his eyes. Moreover, he seemed preoccupied, at times a bit morose. Pamela also seemed different and was not her usual lighthearted self. The board unanimously approved the sale.

Jim said he was thinking of investing his share of the capital gain in a Silicon Valley start-up, though he had not made his final decision. Pamela said she wanted to start an adoption agency, bringing orphans from Asia and finding them homes in California. Jim said he would construct the agency as a nonprofit charitable institution.

"Even though we have not been able to have any children of our own, we can at least make a lot of children happy," said Pamela.

"I'd like to contribute my profits from Pro-Active Health to your project," said my mother.

"Constance, that would be very nice," said Pamela. "I hope you are also willing to help in some other ways."

Jim said he expected that the adoption agency would not need any money once the start-up phase was completed. He said he calculated that the adopting parents would be paying $5,000 for each adoption. That would cover the agency's costs.

"We believe having affluent adoptive parents is key to giving the children security," said Pamela. "The home environment is also very important. We want to make sure the parents can provide the love that is needed. I can tell you from my personal experience that it is not always easy being an Asian in the United States, especially when you are half white."

"Come on, Pamela, everyone who has ever met you falls in love at first sight," laughed Joe.

"Listen to Pamela, Joe," said my mother. "If she says it can be tough, imagine what it can be like for girls not so beautiful and smart."

"Mrs. Sutro, all Asians are smart," said Joe.

Pamela laughed at Joe's stereotyping

"Anyway," said Jim, "we want to carefully inspect the homes we are putting these children into, and we also want to do serious due diligence at the adoptive end to make sure we are getting the best possible candidates."

"What Jim means is that we want to meet the actual parents if possible," said Pamela. "Or at least members of the immediate family. By the way, we know that 99 percent of the children available for adoption will be girls."

"Asian customs foolishly put a greater value on boys," Jim said. "That is the good news for us because down the road we may have more people like my beautiful wife."

"Here's to more Pamelas," said Joe.

The discussion about the adoption agency lasted for several hours. I could not help but notice that the enthusiasm that had been ignited over Pro-Active Health was quickly transferred to the new project. My mother, who was seventy-seven at the time, was talking excitedly about making trips with Pamela to China and Vietnam.

Later the same day, Karen and I got into a discussion about Jim. She said he looked terrible, which did not make sense, because he had been working out almost daily, ate right, did not smoke, and was a light drinker.

"Jim's only vice has been a weakness for girls," I said. "It's been true since he was eleven years old."

"You don't think that Jim is cheating on Pamela?" said Karen.

"Even if he was, that would not account for the change in the way he looks," I said.

"Do you think he has some illness, like AIDS?" said Karen.

"Well, I don't know how he would get it; he's not gay, and he doesn't use drugs," I said.

"I've read you can get AIDS from women," said Karen.

A week or so later, I called Jim and asked him to lunch. He seemed to be in good spirits over the sale of Pro-Active Health and expected it to be finalized in four weeks.

"Running the health center has been a great experience, and I think we have helped a lot of people," Jim said. "The only disappointment is that, in spite of all our efforts, only 62 percent of the members stick with the program for more than a year."

"It is hard to stay motivated; even the dullest minds can come up with creative reasons why they should not exercise on any given day or eat the right foods," I said.

"Temptation carries the day," said Jim.

Before we parted, I asked Jim about his health. He said that in the last six months, he had noticed a lack of energy and a loss of appetite and said he hadn't been sleeping well. He said he kept thinking that it would go away and that he'd been remiss to not consult the doctors who did physicals at Pro-Active Health.

"A year after we started the gym, the doctors all said I had gotten into great shape," he said. "Really, until the last six months, I had felt better than anytime since college. I guess I need to get a thorough checkup at Stanford. It could be I have picked up a bug of some kind at the gym. We sanitize the weight machines every day, but not after every user."

Joe and Claire invited Karen and me for dinner shortly after my lunch with Jim. We talked mostly about the adoption agency. We were all enthusiastic. I could tell Claire saw it as a chance to do some traveling and get out from under the day-to-day strains in her life. Joe's stroke had been life-changing for both of them, but I never heard Claire complain. She was from the old school and took her marriage vows seriously, for better or for worse.

While the women were cleaning up after dinner, Joe and I went to his study, where he showed me some new and rare stamps he had recently acquired.

"Stamps are losing value, because there are so few collectors compared with before," Joe said. "But these zeppelin stamps keep going up, because there are so few of them, and these happen to be in excellent condition."

Joe had a way of suddenly changing subject. "Do you think Jim has AIDS?" he asked. "I hear the women have been talking about it."

"I think he has something wrong with him, but I would doubt very much it is AIDS," I said.

"I never told you this," said Joe, "but the reason Jim got suspended from basketball in his sophomore year in high school was that he got caught getting a blow job from the towel boy."

"C'mon, Joe," I said, "Jim is not gay."

"Well, he's always loved sex; maybe he's tired of women," Joe replied.

"That's the dumbest thing I have ever heard you say," I replied, but then regretted having said it. My brother Joe was operating on half a brain.

CHAPTER 94

Few things can torment a person more than doubt and uncertainty. Such was the case with Jim and all the members of our family. We knew there was something wrong with Jim, that he might even have AIDS. Jim spent two days at the Stanford Hospital and was given the most thorough possible examination, according to what Pamela and Jim told us afterward. When nothing conclusive was found, Jim's primary doctor suggested a consultation with a specialist in rheumatoid arthritis. That meeting lasted more than two hours, and the doctor asked Jim to recall everything he could about the time when he had started to feel bad.

Jim related that his problems began with a case of the flu that he assumed he had caught at the gym. It had lasted about two weeks and was the worst case he had ever had, replete with fever, fatigue, and muscular soreness that seemed to migrate from one part of the body to another.

The doctor asked if Jim had any other symptoms, such as a rash, palpitations of the heart, or any trouble with his eyes. Jim could not recall any of those symptoms. Pressed further on his health since recovering from the flu, Jim said from time to time his knees would swell and become painful. He also said his stomach bothered him, which it had never done before. Occasionally, he would feel a strange light-headedness. Sometimes he experienced tingling in his legs. He also said he suffered from a stiff neck, and he felt his usually prodigious memory was sometimes slipping. He said he was constantly tired, sometimes depressed. However, on some days, he had no symptoms at all, which is why he had waited so long before seeking medical help.

The doctor asked Jim about his personal life, about how he spent his time, and about whether he ever went camping in the woods. Jim described his life and said that he had never been camping but that he did walk in the wooded hills around his Portola Valley home. The doctor wanted to know if there were deer in the area, and Jim said he saw some from time to time.

"I think I have a hunch of what this might be," the doctor said. "But there are a few more tests I would like to have done. The good news is I don't think what you have is in any way life-threatening."

Pamela phoned everyone with the news that Jim did not have a life-threatening disease.

It turned out that Jim had an advanced case of Lyme disease (which I had never heard of), which he had no doubt contracted during a walk in the woods, when, presumably, a tiny Western black-legged tick had attached itself to some part of Jim's body and stayed there for at least thirty-six hours. The tick transmitted to Jim's system a bacterium that multiplied and began to attack his system.

Jim told us that Lyme disease hadn't been discovered until the mid–1970s, in Lyme, Connecticut, though it no doubt had been around for years. Fewer than 1,000 people a year were diagnosed with Lyme disease in the United States during the early 1990s, and most of those were in the Northeast, though northern California had a number of cases as well.

Jim was treated with a four-week course of antibiotics, and by the middle of 1992, he had thrown off all symptoms and was practically as good as new. He looked years younger.

"It is funny how life works," Jim told me at the opening of the P&J Adoption Agency office in Palo Alto late in 1992. "This whole adoption thing wouldn't have happened if I hadn't contracted Lyme disease. The reason I wanted to sell Pro-Active Health was that I was so drained, I didn't have the energy to carry on."

"God maybe wanted you to make a change," I said.

Getting the adoption agency started turned out to be far more complex than anyone imagined. Bringing children in from overseas involves the U.S. Immigration and Naturalization Department, which has strict rules that are overseen by the intercountry adoption program. For its part, the state of California has the Department of Social Services, which implements the California adoption laws.

It took more than six months to complete the requirements necessary for state and federal approval. Without the skills, contacts, and prestige of Richard Hamblen, the agency most likely never would have been approved. The agency was named the P&J Adoption Agency in honor of Pamela and Jim, with a goal of finding homes for at least one hundred Asian infants during 1993. It was an ambitious target, and the work involved serious and time-consuming due diligence in investigating the homes and circumstances of those wishing to adopt. Fortunately, through a contact Richard got from one of his friends, an orphanage in Shanghai was identified as possibly being interested in working with an American adoption agency. Pamela and Jim flew to Shanghai with Bonita Everest, a professional social worker with a PhD in social welfare, who was hired full-time to actually run the program. Arrangements were completed to bring in infants ages three months to one year, at the rate of two a week. The start-up cost more than $560,000, the great bulk of which was put up by Jim and Pamela.

The media was the principal target for the cocktail party announcing the formation of P&J, and they gave it excellent coverage. About thirty members of the media were present, along with a sprinkling of officials and Booker family friends—in all, about 120 people. Most of the news stories focused on Jim, the former Berkeley basketball star who they said had made millions in television advertising and another small fortune in developing and selling Pro-Active Health.

"My wife and I are doing this, because we believe we will be able to change lives," Jim said. "Making money is a lot of fun, but it is even more fun to be able to give it away to a worthy cause like finding good homes for orphaned children."

Jim introduced Dr. Bonita Everest, who spoke briefly about the professionalism of the organization created by P&J. Jim said that Richard Hamblen was serving as chairman of the P&J board, which was made up of Booker family members and Dr. Everest.

The news coverage for this opening was not nearly as great as it had been for the opening of Pro-Active Health, but it was enough to cause Ken Thatcher to phone, saying it was a pleasure to see the Booker public relations machine getting the family back in the limelight. It turned out that Ken was calling from the UC Hospital and that he had suffered yet another heart attack.

"I'll be out early next week," Ken said. "I think it is your turn to buy me lunch. Give my best to your mother."

Two days later, I got a call from one of Ken's sons, who reported that Ken had died in his sleep the night before. He was in his early eighties, though he had always claimed to be younger than he actually was. He had lived an incredibly active life and had seldom had a boring day. As my mother said at Ken's funeral, "Ken was always where the action was. It was exciting just to be around him."

His passing was another powerful personal loss for me. If I have learned anything so far in writing this book, it is the inescapable nature of the ticking clock, which we mostly don't think about. We only realize how brief and temporary life is when someone near to us dies.

"You can't replace people like Ken," I said to my wife.

"That is why it is so important to keep making new friends and keep a close involvement with the younger generation," said Karen. "You become to the younger generation what the older generation meant to you."

That was nice of Karen to say, but I doubted I could ever be as influential to others as Conrad Sutro or Ken Thatcher had been to me. In my mind, they were great men who had lived great lives, taking advantage of seemingly every moment while spreading a lot of happiness along the way. Fortunately, I had Karen. She had done wonders for my confidence, and her love was my most precious asset, though my mother and brothers were not far behind. Of course, Jonathan, the budding cosmologist and small-particle physicist, was the apple of my eye. On December 29, 1992, we celebrated Jonathan's eleventh birthday, and the whole family turned out, including Adam Sutro, his wife, and their twin sons, Alan and Richard, who were now twelve.

Joe Jr., Claire, Joe III, Robyn, and Kare were there as well. None of Joe Jr.'s offspring had yet married. Big Joe had gone with Ashley Robinson for five years, but she had broken off the relationship, apparently contending that Big Joe was a workaholic, not surprising considering that he was now in his fifth year working for fellow workaholic Adam Sutro's highly prosperous real estate development company. As he promised he would, Adam had given Big Joe 20 percent of the company when Joe was twenty-eight, a prize clearly earned, no doubt at the cost of his engagement to Ashley Robinson.

The team of Sutro and Booker was already well known throughout the West Coast in the world of land developers, most notably for the company's nine shopping centers. However, with Joe on board, Adam sought to diversify, and he, with the help of Joe, began acquiring office buildings and refurbishing them principally in the San Francisco Bay Area and Sacramento. Their firm employed more than one hundred people and had close working relationships with the best builders and contractors in northern California.

Robyn was twenty-six now and had dated a fellow student at Stanford, but they had broken up a year after graduation, when he was offered a job as an engineer in Saudi Arabia. Robyn was devastated that he would take the job whether she would agree to go or not, but apparently she was not so much in love that she would live in Saudi Arabia for three years. My mom told Robyn it was the best thing, and it would give her a chance to live life before she became tied down raising children. After two years as a high school biology teacher in Oakland, Robyn had recently joined Citibank in its executive training program, a decision that resulted in her moving temporarily to New York in 1993.

Kare, age twenty-four, was the free spirit of the family and had been working as a stewardess for Southwest Airlines for the past eighteen months. Fresh-faced and impish to match her persona, Kare said she was not planning to get married until she was thirty.

"I'm having too much fun to get tied down to just one man," Kare told my mother.

"That's because you really have not fallen in love yet," said my mother.

"Oh, I've been in love four or five times, but never to anyone I wanted to marry," said Kare.

I suspected that Robyn and Kare had been negatively influenced about marriage by their father's stroke, which had made life very difficult for their mother. But that was only a guess. Perhaps their attitude toward marriage was typical of their generation. I know my mother's feeling was that times had changed greatly since she was young.

"Mother," I said, "weren't you a bit like Kare with lots of admirers in Hawaii before you met Dad?" I asked.

She replied, "I think it was different then, more innocent, sweeter. Today, from what I read, girls are out doing the things the boys in my era wanted to do, but really didn't get to very often, if ever."

"That's pretty convoluted, but I understand what you're saying," I said. "The pill and women's rights have changed things, and I'm not sure it is for the better. Fortunately, I'm married to a throwback to the old values."

"You wouldn't have said that if you'd known me in college," smiled Karen.

"Karen, we have agreed that you did not exist before we met and that I am not interested in war stories about wild oats," I replied, laughing, but with a certain sense of seriousness. Karen smiled and crossed her finger over her closed mouth.

I had not had a chance to talk with Richard Hamblen about politics since just before the presidential election in 1992, so we had that discussion at Jonathan's birthday gathering as well.

"You were right, Richard—Ross Perot took away enough votes from the Republicans to give the election to Bill Clinton," I said.

"The only word I have for Perot is 'despicable,'" said Richard. "That he got 18 million votes surprised me, but it still never would have happened if Bush hadn't broken his pledge not to raise taxes. Maybe a change will be good."

CHAPTER 95

One of the nice perks of my job as a more-or-less independent stockbroker with Sutro & Co. was an annual trip to New York, ostensibly to attend financial analyst meetings and confer with various money managers. Karen often came with me, and we would attend several plays during the week and dine with New York friends, many of whom dated from 1967, when I was working in New York with Ken Thatcher. Unfortunately, Karen decided not to make the trip in February of 1993, because her part-time work in advertising was being squeezed by her volunteer efforts at the P&J Adoption Agency.

Karen suggested that my niece, Robyn, who was on a three-month training assignment in New York with Citibank, would love to attend plays and go to dinner with me. So I called Robyn, and she said she would clear every evening but Thursday and sounded quite excited about running around the town with Uncle Dan. Robyn, at twenty-six, had developed into a poised and very striking woman. She was five feet eight inches tall and had a slim and elegant figure, excellent posture, beautiful skin, and an intelligent and lovely face. In fact, she reminded me a bit of Constance and had her grandmother's bright blue eyes and sandy blonde hair. Robyn was also a keen listener, and she asked a lot of questions, often ones that were hard to answer.

"Why doesn't San Francisco have more live theater?" she wanted to know. "New York has twenty times as much going on."

"I think it is because New York has more business visitors than San Francisco," I lamely offered. "And people who live in New York seem to attend plays and cultural events in a much greater proportion than do people in the Bay Area. I don't want to get ethnic, but New York has a huge Jewish population, and they love and support culture and live theater."

"And the Chinese don't?" Robyn said.

"Certainly not to the same extent," I said.

I took Robyn to the 21 Club, and we got a good table on the ground floor, mainly I think because Robyn looked so beautiful.

"How can they charge $28 for a hamburger?" she asked.

"That's to keep the riff-raff out," I smiled. "In New York, when you go to a famous restaurant or hotel, you expect to pay top dollar. Most of the people are either rich or on an expense account—and often both. My whole trip is covered by my expense account, except that I will not charge your half of our meal or the cost of theater tickets, because you are not a client or a source of business information."

"I bet a lot of people do charge everything," said Robyn.

"I don't doubt it, but I would not underestimate the number of honest people out there, either," I said.

"Uncle Dan, you are a very sweet man," said Robyn, leaning forward and giving me a peck on the cheek.

"Be careful, Robyn—people will think you are my date," I said.

Robyn let out a gleeful laugh that reminded me of Constance.

"I see several men here your age with women in their twenties," Robyn smiled. "I hope you are not embarrassed."

"On the contrary, I am proud to be here with you as my niece, but I am the jealous kind, and I don't want you going out with any other men my age."

"I promise," she smiled.

Robyn could operate on a lot of levels, I learned during our week together. She was fascinated by art, a subject about which I knew little. She had also acquired a taste for classical music and the opera. She loved going to good movies and could remember plots and even dialogue. She was like her uncle Jim in that regard. Her knowledge of economics and finance was mostly book-learned, but it was nonetheless impressive. Importantly, she said she was picking up on what she said she perceived as a significant difference between academia and the real world of business.

"I'm getting the notion that more goes on because of personal relationships than because of raw business dynamics," she said.

"You have that right," I said. "A lot of deals result from friendship, but make sure you keep greed and power in your equation."

Robyn also had a younger side. "Oh, guess who I saw on 5th Avenue today?" she said to me excitedly on the way to a play. "Al Pacino. Nobody was paying any attention to him. I walked right past him and smiled, and he gave me a big smile back. He's a lot shorter than I imagined. The top of his head was just above my shoulders. I had heels on. But he is still a very attractive man and a great actor, to my mind, one of the very best. He has such enormous versatility."

I found being around Robyn a lot of fun. She had a wide range of enthusiasms. Citibank did not consider her master's degree from Stanford in biology to be a drawback; the company was no doubt impressed by the total package. At one point during the week, I suggested that she might keep in mind the thought of joining a smaller company, where she could get stock options or a piece of the ownership action.

"My brother Joe is certainly doing well with Adam," she said. "I think that Adam was very smart in giving Joe 20 percent of the business, because I think Joe would've eventually gone out on his own if Adam hadn't. Joe is so smart and so hardworking, but I don't blame Ashley Robinson for breaking up with him after all of those years. He's been working seventy to eighty hours a week and has very few outside interests except sports. I think a woman wants more than that—I know I do."

"I don't blame you for not going to Saudi Arabia," I said. "Three years there would have to be pretty stultifying for someone with your interests and energy."

"It was a no-brainer," she laughed. "I feel that my real life is just starting. I'm not worried about getting married and having children. I think that's going to happen, just not right away. I'd like to first achieve some success in business, but I have no desire to be like Joe. I want to have time for a life outside of work and become well-rounded like Grandma."

"Well, I can tell you that your grandmother thinks you are a lot like her, even though she was married at nineteen, while you, at that age, were on your way to a brilliant education at Stanford."

"Grandmother seems very well-educated to me," said Robyn.

"That's true, but it was just never a formal education," I said. "She has, like you, a very curious nature and a lot of energy. And she's spent her life around some very smart and successful people—Richard Hamblen, for example."

"Oh, Richard Hamblen," sighed Robyn. "There aren't many men like him. He's the sexiest eighty-year-old man in the world. I bet it was hard for Claudia being married to him all those years, with every woman in town chasing after him."

"I have it on good authority that Richard never once was unfaithful in his marriage, even though I think he was in love with two women, his wife and your grandmother."

"Do you really think it is possible to love two people at once?" Robyn asked.

"I don't know—maybe if one of the relationships is strictly platonic, or at least that seems to have been the case with Constance and Richard," I said. "And keep in mind that your grandmother was very much in love with Conrad Sutro for the entire time of their marriage."

"I think it's different for my mom," said Robyn. "She still loves Dad, but his stroke has made him much different."

"Your dad's stroke was a great tragedy. You can't know how much your uncle Jim and I worshipped him growing up. He wasn't only our big brother, but also like a father to us. After he went to work, he was a great foreign correspondent and then a highly successful author. He was cut down at the very prime of his life. I give him a lot of credit for the way he has handled it. He lost a large part of his brain to that stroke, and yet he carries on, takes care of himself, and stays busy. He's just not the same person."

"He can be pretty exasperating some of the time, and I don't think he gives Mom the proper appreciation," said Robyn.

"That's part of the brain he has lost," I said.

"I guess we should all be happy he is still alive," said Robyn.

One of the pieces of business I had to do in New York was check on a Honolulu-based company, Alexander and Baldwin, which owned the Matson Steamship Line and a lot of land in the islands. A friend of mine from San Jose State, Dick Benfer, was the editor and publisher of *The Journal of Commerce*, a shipping publication, which had its offices on the twenty-seventh floor of Tower No. 2 in the World Trade Center. Benfer had recently been in Honolulu visiting with Alexander and Baldwin executives and had written about the company's prospects. I was looking at putting a number of my clients into Alexander and Baldwin shares but thought, considering that I was in New York, I'd meet Dick and see what else I could find out about the company first.

When I telephoned, Dick invited me to lunch at Windows on the World but suggested I drop by his office first. The *Journal of Commerce* offices occupied most of the twenty-seventh floor, and Dick came out to the receptionist's desk to greet me. His office was huge and was located on the corner with nine or ten windows. The view was spectacular and included the Statue of Liberty, the harbor, New Jersey, and the Verrazano Bridge, plus the surrounding buildings. The date was February 26, 1993. Dick and I talked about old times and old friends and what a great party school San Jose State was. Suddenly, there was a sharp explosive sound and I felt a vibration go through my chair. Dick and I looked at each other in mutual surprise.

"Sounds like an electrical generator just blew up," said Dick.

"All the phones are out," said Dick's secretary, rushing into the room with a startled look on her face.

"Editorial has some cell phones; tell them to find out what's going on," said Dick.

Moments later, the managing editor came into the room.

"Apparently, there was an explosion in the garage," he reported. "Building management says we should stay put for the time being."

I looked down on the street and could see nothing out of the ordinary. But after about five minutes, the smell of smoke began to fill the office. I suddenly thought, *What if the building is catching on fire? How will we get out?* But those were just rhetorical questions. After that one moment of wondering, I really was not worried. I assumed the building was virtually fireproof with elaborate sprinkler systems. I stuck by Dick's side as he moved from office to office, talking with his people, urging them to stay calm. Some of the elevators had continued to work on emergency power, but then that went out. We were standing at the bank of elevators when we heard an urgent pounding on the door of one elevator. Dick and a couple of people managed to pry it open. Out came three well-dressed men who rushed past us into the smoky stairwell just across the lobby. I looked out into the stairwell. It was not only smoky, but also packed with people, and there was no lighting. People were groping their way downward one step at a time.

"What floor is this?" one man asked. When told, he said to a friend, "We're almost halfway down." Obviously, they had started somewhere in the fifties.

It was more than thirty minutes after the blast that the word came that everyone should evacuate by the stairwells. Dick and I were the last to leave our floor, and it took us an hour to reach the ground floor. We were fortunate that there was a man with a flashlight just ahead of us when we entered the stairwell. And the smoke was not that bad—sort of like an Irish Pub, or at least, so it seemed. As we slowly descended, several firemen passed us coming up, carrying an enormous amount of gear. (The memory of those duty-bound firemen came back to me in vivid detail when the twin towers were destroyed on 9/11). Nobody panicked, and the crowd was mostly good natured and polite, sometimes even erupting in laughter over someone's wisecrack.

"You picked a helluva day to visit," said Dick.

"What do you think of Alexander and Baldwin?" I asked.

"I like them a lot," said Dick.

It was a lot less detail than I had hoped for, but I guess you could say I got what I came for.

On the ground floor, Dick and I chatted for only a moment. His people were waiting for him to give them instructions on what to do. It was clear the World Trade Center would not be operational for several weeks.

"Your nose is black, and you have smudges all over your face," he laughed.

"So do you," I said. In fact, I was picking black goop out of my nose for the next six hours. The smoke in the stairwell had obviously been much thicker than I thought.

I called Robyn that evening and told her about my experience. I was feeling a bit groggy, and because I was leaving early the next morning, we decided to pass on our dinner that night.

"It was wonderful being with you, and thanks for everything, Uncle Dan," she said. "You're like a second father to me, and I love you very much."

"If I had a daughter, I'd wish for her to be exactly like you," I said.

Six people were killed in the 1993 WTC terrorist bombing, and more than 1,000 were injured. The explosives, weighing 1,500 pounds, were brought into the underground public garage in a rental truck. The crater left by the explosion was 200 feet by 100 feet. The terrorists had hoped to bring both towers down. But I never really thought I was in serious danger—mostly because the towers seemed impregnable. Years later, following the 9/11 destruction of the twin towers by two hijacked commercial jets, I came to view my experience quite differently. I recalled going down that smoky stairwell and imagined how much worse and how much more terrifying it was for the people who fled the buildings on 9/11. The amazing thing to me was how many actually escaped. Dick Benfer's strategy of being the last out would likely have been a deadly one on 9/11.

CHAPTER 96

We celebrated my mother's eightieth birthday on March 21, 1994, and the party was attended, appropriately enough, by eighty people, all family or close friends. Richard Hamblen and Claire organized the event, and it was held in a private room at the Fairmont Hotel. The gathering was a total surprise for Constance, who had insisted to Richard that there not be any celebration.

"I don't feel eighty, and I don't want to remind people that I am," she had said when members of the family asked her about a party, which was all part of the setup orchestrated by Richard and

Claire. Mother thought that she was having a private dinner with Richard on her birthday and that the family would have a small party the next weekend.

"I was totally surprised, one reason being that I don't think Richard has ever lied to me before," my mother said afterward. "I did not want a party, but it turned out to be one of the nicest things that has ever happened to me."

A five-piece orchestra played "Happy Birthday" as Constance walked into the room full of smiling faces singing heartily. When they finished, a kind of spontaneous laughter broke out, because everyone could see my mother was so totally surprised. Champagne flowed, and the band played a medley of songs from 1914, including such chestnuts as "Alexander's Ragtime Band," "On the Beach at Waikiki," and "A Little Bit of Heaven."

Richard, being Richard, had insisted that during the cocktail reception everyone informally line up to personally greet Constance, a process that took more than an hour, because everyone wanted to tell her something that then prompted a reply and more conversation. The band, which in the course of the night played songs from each of Mom's eighty years, provided a warm festive atmosphere, as did the waiters dispensing the champagne.

Watching my mother, dressed elegantly in a navy blue silk dress with one bare shoulder and a hem line just below the knees, standing erect and still tall at almost five feet seven inches, and slim at 123 pounds, reminded me of how beautiful she had always been. Her hair was now a natural white, and her skin was clear, though pleasantly wrinkled. Her eyes were not as wide and lively as they once had been, but they still twinkled when she talked. Age had been kind to her, and she radiated inner beauty and love. She was clearly at peace with herself. Her focus was outward rather than inward, and she projected a keen and sincere interest in whomever she was talking to. Richard hovered around her like an attentive and highly dignified servant. It was clear he worshipped her and she him.

Caviar was served during the reception, along with pâté, tiny crab cakes, and a special guacamole mix. Dinner consisted of stone crab flown in from Miami, Alaskan king crab, clam chowder, grapefruit and spinach salad, and a choice of abalone caught that day in Monterey Bay or Kobe beef, flown in from Japan. I chose the steak. It was the best I have ever eaten, so tender it almost melted in my mouth. The red wine was a 1982 Chateau Margaux, as spectacular as everything else on the menu. Mother had arrived at seven o'clock and it was ten o'clock before the three-tiered birthday cake was brought into the room, accompanied by an even more rousing "Happy Birthday."

The crowd was happy, but I did not notice anyone consuming too much alcohol. I learned later from Richard that he had instructed the waiters to slow down the wine service during dinner, especially to those who might appear to have an appetite for drinking more than they should. Leave it to Richard to think of everything!

Richard served as toastmaster, and he heaped praise on Claire for organizing the wonderful food and orchestra and for seeing to it that just the right eighty people were in attendance. He asked Claire to stand, and everyone else stood up too to give her a loud and lengthy ovation.

"We are here tonight to honor a lady who holds a special place in all of our lives, a lady whose loving nature and warmth are a gift, a very rare gift, that each of us is fortunate to share ..."

Richard's three-minute tribute was a hard act to follow, but it seemed everyone wanted to try. About half of those present stood up to say something. At 11:00 PM, Richard said it was growing late and time to hear from Constance.

"Thank you, Richard, and thank you, beloved family and beloved friends," my mother said. "And a special thanks to Claire. What a wonderful fuss."

Despite the late hour, Constance went around the room and said something warm and personal about everyone present. She began by saying how proud she was of her three sons.

"I can remember when they were all very little, taking that ferry boat from Oakland in 1938 after traveling by train from Fort Riley, Kansas," she said. "We all stood at the bow of the ferry, and I'll never forget how excited we all were to see the San Francisco skyline and the Bay Bridge. If you have ever been to Fort Riley, you can imagine how happy we were about living in such a beautiful place as San Francisco, and the Presidio was probably as comfortable an assignment as an army officer could have. It is funny how fate sometimes intervenes. We were supposed to be assigned to the Philippines the following year, but my late husband Joe's arthritis forced him to retire from military service. That's how we became permanent San Franciscans.

"When Joe went back into the service after Japan attacked my birth home in Honolulu, Joe Jr., Danny, and Jim were the bravest boys you'd ever see with their dad away. Then, at the end of the war, when Joe was killed in Germany, we were all so grief stricken that I wondered how we would ever survive. But Joe Jr. rallied us all, even though he was only ten or eleven. It took me years before I could reconcile myself to the loss of Joe. He was a man of the greatest integrity, thoughtful, loving, and sensitive and a great father and wonderful husband.

"Frankly, I thought I would never marry again, and I did not until many years later, after my boys were grown up, and Conrad Sutro came along. But we were very lucky in the meantime, because after the war was over, Richard Hamblen came into our lives. Richard served with Joe in Germany, and they were good friends who dreamed together about what life would be like after the war. Unfortunately, my Joe never made it, but Richard and his late beloved wife, Claudia, became our little family's best friends, and we spent many wonderful times together over nearly fifty years. Richard was so helpful with the boys and in helping with our financial planning, and Claudia and I became as close as two friends can be. Oh, how I wish she could be with us tonight, together with my late loving husband, Conrad, who was about the nicest and sweetest man who ever lived."

Constance had everyone's rapt attention as she recounted key moments in her life, speaking in a cheerful upbeat tone that made her seem much younger than her eighty years.

"One of the great things that has happened to our family in the last year has been the establishment of an adoption agency by Jim and his lovely wife, Pamela," she said. "In just over a year's time, they have found homes for ninety-three orphans from China. It makes me so proud to hear Jim say he is no longer interested in making money, that he really wants to spend the rest of his life helping others.

"Of course, my son Danny is still trying to make money for some of the people in this room with his ability to pick winning stocks. I think Danny always saw himself as the turtle in a family of hares, but I think he always underestimated his ability to focus and to succeed in whatever he attempted, whether it was being a radio producer, a sports executive, or a stockbroker. Danny is not only reliable; he is steady as a rock.

"One of the things my three sons have done for me is to enrich my life with three wonderful daughters-in-law. I first met Joe's wife, Claire, when she was only in high school. In all of those years since, she has been the loving daughter I never had. And Karen and Pamela are so lovely and optimistic and fun to be around, I can't imagine my life without them."

My mother proceeded to mention each of her grandchildren, what they were doing, and how proud she was of each of them.

"I have only one fault with the younger generation," said Constance. "I don't have any great-grandchildren. Robyn, you and Kare are two of the most beautiful girls in San Francisco. I know you can find the right man if you just put your minds to it. And Big Joe, I know that you and Adam Sutro are very successful in business, so I think it is time for you to find a wife. You possess some pretty fine genes, and as I see it, your number-one assignment in life is to keep those genes alive."

The comments about Robyn, Kare, and Big Joe drew a lot of laughs and cheers from the crowd. The confidence of the three grandchildren was evident as they smiled and nodded their heads in agreement that they would heed their grandmother's advice.

Afterward, Karen said she could not believe how successful the evening had been.

"It was perfect from start to finish," she said. Turning to Jonathan, she said, "I bet you won't forget tonight for as long as you live. I was very proud of you; you were a perfect gentleman, and you listened to every word."

"I thought it was quite interesting," said Jonathan. "It is too bad Grandmother wasn't born sixty years later; she could have had a life expectancy of 125 to 150."

"Where did you get that, Jonathan?" I asked.

"It is a very common expectation among scientists who know about such things," said Jonathan. "The life expectancy of the average person was fifty at the start of this century, and it will be eighty at the end. I don't think that it is unreasonable to expect even longer lives based on accelerating medical breakthroughs and the ability to replace worn-out or deteriorating body parts."

"Have you ever talked to your grandmother about this?" Karen asked.

"Once, but she said she did not want to live that long," Jonathan said. "She said she doubted the assertion that man could have everlasting life on earth by means of science. She said God programmed mankind for a set life span. I said God programmed mankind to do whatever was possible and that amazing things were happening all over the world."

Jonathan's precocity was an unending source of amazement to me. When I was twelve, all I cared about was sports. To hear Jonathan talk about the potential of nanotechnology, robotics, cloning, and genetic engineering was a reminder that he clearly was a breed apart. I always assumed Jonathan's brains came from Karen's side of the family. Karen's dad had a master's degree in engineering and was definitely the brainy type. She also had an uncle who had been Phi Beta Kappa somewhere, and several other men in the family had achieved scientific accomplishments as well, dating from the nineteenth century.

"It's too bad we can't have Grandmother cloned," said Jonathan.

CHAPTER 97

Early in 1995, Adam Sutro and Joseph Booker III asked me if I wanted to help develop a master limited partnership for the purchase of a sprawling eight-story office building, constructed in the early 1930s, in downtown San Francisco. Big Joe asked me if I would like to check it out with him. My role would be to sell units of the limited partnership to my clients at $50,000 apiece. Sutro and Booker Development would serve as the managing general partner. Adam and Joe saw the project as a test case, which, if successful, they would repeat in still-larger ventures, such as the purchase of hotels and possibly even start-up office buildings. Previously, their projects had all been achieved through bank loans.

I thought Joe and I would be touring the place alone at 8:00 AM the Tuesday morning we met, but in fact there were four other people, including two building engineers from Joe's company, an electrician who was a private contractor, and the current superintendent of the building.

"Let's start in the subbasement and work our way to the roof," said Joe, who added he wanted to inspect every nook and crevice in the building. The previous week, Joe had studied the original construction drawings plus the plans for several remodeling jobs that had taken place over the years. For openers, he said, he read that there had been some cracks in the foundation during the 1989 earthquake, and he wanted to examine the repair work.

Joe's attention to detail was interesting to observe. He didn't like the condition of the sixty-year-old wiring and agreed with his electrical engineer that it would have to be replaced. The same was true of the water boilers and the heating and air-conditioning systems. Joe's two engineers agreed that the foundation needed further buttressing. By noon, we were only on the fourth floor!

"We want to make this an absolutely, like-new, first-class building," Joe said over lunch. "If we put the Sutro-Booker name on this, it has to be a class triple-A building. In sixty years, even the best buildings, and this is a good one, wear out and require all new fittings."

"That's why I think it is for sale," said the superintendent. "The present owner does not want to spend the money to make the fixes. Anyhow, he's in his seventies, and he wants to have his holdings in a more liquid state."

We finished our inspection tour at just after five o'clock. I was exhausted and suggested, as we said our good-byes and thanks to the others, that Joe and I have a drink. He said it would be a good chance to talk about the deal.

"I'm glad you came along today, because I think it is imperative that you understand just what we plan to do before you start selling to your clients," said Joe. "Tell me, Uncle Dan, what was your overall opinion?"

I said that I liked the location and the art deco look and that with enough money for the redo, it looked like a great project that could command top rental dollars in excess of $30 to $35 a square foot.

"So you think you are going to be comfortable in this?" asked Joe.

"Well, it is a given for me that you and Adam are going to do what you say, so yes, I feel very comfortable."

"I think we can do better than $35 a square foot," said Joe, "especially if the economy keeps moving ahead. The Clinton administration seems to have consumer confidence in good shape. That is key. Fortunately, most of the leases in the building are up in the next three years, and two of the large tenants are working on month-to-month arrangements. They have been told the building is being upgraded, and at least one has indicated that he is willing to pay more given the promised improvements."

Joe said the idea was to hold onto the building for four or five years and then sell it for a nice capital gain for the investors, which would be in addition to the estimated 6 percent annual dividend.

"We get 20 percent of the capital gain, even though we put up only 5 percent of the capital," said Joe. "We also get a management fee. Of course, we are the ones who put it all together, and that counts for a lot."

"Joe, it seems very fair to me, and I am really looking forward to dealing with you," I said.

The conversation moved on to family matters. Joe said he was concerned about his dad, who he said seemed depressed; he was looking pale, was not doing his exercises, and was drinking more than he should.

I asked Joe if he was following up on his grandmother's admonition to find a wife.

"Funny you should ask," said Joe. "Robyn introduced me to a lady I have been seeing for the last couple of months. She's a looker, sort of retro, and I think we hit it off on that score. I really haven't done a lot of serious dating since Ashley Robinson dumped me.

Kathleen, her name is Kathleen Spillane, told me that if she were Ashley, she would have dumped me too. That's the way she is."

"Then why is she still going out with you?" I asked.

"She says that she will stop if I take her for granted and continue working what she calls insane hours," he replied. "I said I would cut back, and in fact, I have. I told Adam I was no longer going to be working weekends unless it was life or death. Adam said I was obviously taking to heart what my grandmother had said and that it was okay with him."

Joe said he wanted me to meet Kathleen and suggested we have dinner the next week.

"She knows Robyn, but I want to introduce her to the family slowly, starting with you and Aunt Karen," said Joe, an invitation I took as a compliment. Of course, I could understand it was a "three-fer" for Joe; he could talk a little business with me, take Kathleen out to dinner, and introduce Kathleen to his aunt and uncle. It was no wonder that Adam Sutro had given Joe 20 percent of the business. Joe was clearly worth that and more. In fact, by the turn of the century, Joe would own 49 percent of the business.

At thirty years old, Kathleen Spillane had clearly been very selective about finding Mr. Right. She was a vice president at Bank of America and a streaky blonde with great features, long legs, slim hips, and a large bust. But her best characteristic was her energy level and outgoing nature. Twenty minutes after we met, sipping drinks at a small and quiet Italian restaurant in North Beach, I knew Kathleen had found her man and vice versa. Mostly it was the way they looked at each other.

I could not stop myself from asking Kathleen why she hadn't gotten married before, adding that surely she must have had many proposals.

"I've had a lot of propositions," she smiled, "but only one real proposal and that was so premature I had to laugh, like, I think it was after the second date. But the guy was serious. He cried when I told him there was no chance. Actually, I guess I hadn't met the person I was looking for, so I never encouraged anyone. I was caught up in my work and wanted to get ahead, a lot like Joe's sister Robyn. Maybe that is why Robyn and I have become good friends."

"Kathleen has met her man," laughed Joe. "The trouble is she wants to change him."

"Joe," said Karen, "what a woman wants is a man's respect and attention. Without that, all of the love just goes down the drain."

"That's why it is important to find someone you are really compatible with," I said.

"We have that," said Joe. "I like to look at Kathleen and take her places and talk to her, because she always gives some fresh perspective that I have not thought about."

"Well, you make a beautiful couple," said Karen.

"We've decided to get married, but we haven't told anyone yet," said Joe.

"Oh my goodness!" said Karen, letting out a squeal of delight. She gave Kathleen a hug and a kiss on the cheek. "I'm so happy for you both. You are getting a good man in Joe, and from what I can see, you two are perfectly matched."

"The family is going to be very happy about this," I said. "Kathleen, welcome to the Booker family."

Kathleen told us she had been born and raised in Chicago and that her father was a pediatrician still practicing. She was the second of three sisters and had graduated from the University of Michigan at Ann Arbor. She had moved to San Francisco five years earlier and was currently sharing a house on Lyon Street near California with two other single women, one of whom was engaged. She said she had to oversee all the details of managing the house, neither of her roommates having any interest in such mundane chores. She was working in marketing for the Bank of America, and her chief responsibility was making sure her accounts were happy.

"I spend most of my time out of the office, and I've had to go to Asia twice to meet with customers in Tokyo and Hong Kong as well as Taiwan," said Kathleen. I thought to myself that even the Japanese, who had a reputation for not liking to do business with women, would make an exception for someone as young and lovely as Kathleen.

"Did they insist you get drunk with them in Tokyo?" I asked.

"They tried, and I had my share, but I did not get drunk," Kathleen said. "One told me I was a good man for a woman. I enjoyed myself both trips and did some good for the company, but I don't think I would like to make fifteen to twenty trips across the Pacific every year as some people do. Even when you are young and healthy, the jet lag is very difficult to overcome."

Kathleen said that she intended to keep working after her marriage but that she and Joe had talked it over and decided that three children was the right number.

"I have two sisters, and so does Joe, and we agree that three children is just the right size for a family," said Kathleen.

"I wish we had three children," said Karen.

"Maybe we are lucky to have Jonathan," I said. "Jim and Pamela can't have children."

"Oh, I hear Jonathan is some kind of genius," said Kathleen.

"He thinks he is," Karen smiled. "Have you set the date yet?"

"That's going to depend on Joe," said Kathleen. "We want a three-week honeymoon in Italy, and we have to figure the best time for him to get away.

"My parents are going to want to have the wedding in Chicago, so they have to be involved in the date setting. We are going to give everyone at least three months notice, and I want the reception to be at the Drake Hotel, which we have to reserve well in advance. My family is Protestant, not Catholic, and I would like to be married in an Episcopal church, and so would Joe, though neither of us is a regular churchgoer—not that we aren't believers."

As Kathleen talked, Joe just watched her with a big smile on his face.

"What are you smiling about?" Kathleen asked.

"I was just thinking how nice it is to like the woman you love," he said.

"Wow," said Karen, "what a nice thing to say."

Afterward, Karen said she liked Kathleen because she was so open and straightforward.

"She'll never be a shrinking violet," I said. "I think she will make a great wife and mother if Joe doesn't screw things up, which I don't think he will."

"The poor girl is going to find out how hard it is," smiled Karen, "especially being married to a Booker! Seriously, darling, I think Kathleen is just the sort of competent and beautiful woman Joe is looking for. They should produce wonderful children."

CHAPTER 98

The wedding of Kathleen Spillane and Joseph Booker III was scheduled for September 14, 1995. Kathleen wanted a big wedding with five hundred guests, saying she was only going to be married once in her life and wanted to do it right. She had eight bridesmaids, and that meant Big Joe had to recruit seven ushers, plus his best man, who turned out to be Adam Sutro. Months of planning had gone into the wedding, and Kathleen immersed herself in every detail, including the coordination of dresses to be worn by Claire Booker and Mary Spillane, Kathleen's mother. It would be a great wedding, one of the biggest of the year in Chicago. Dr. Michael Spillane, Kathleen's father, was highly respected and well known, having involved himself in civic affairs, particularly in Chicago's large Irish community.

My mother calculated that about 150 would be attending the wedding from San Francisco, and she and Claire worked on the details for hotel accommodations and other aspects, including theater tickets and restaurant reservations for those who wanted to do more than just attend the wedding and reception. A plan to charter a jet was examined and discarded. Mom and Claire also planned, along with Joe and Kathleen, the rehearsal dinner, to be attended by about 120 people, mostly family from the two sides and the wedding party.

In early August of 1995, Karen and I had dinner with Joe Jr. and Claire, ostensibly to talk about the wedding. We had invited them to come to our place, but Joe insisted we come to theirs, saying it was a lot easier on everyone if he did not need to leave the house. Joe was sixty-one, but the years and his stroke had taken their toll.

We had a couple of drinks before dinner, and I noticed that Joe had switched from his usual Dewar's and water to Dewar's on the rocks, filling the glass to the top. When he took his first long sip, he exhaled with unmistakable joy. "Well, that's better," he said.

By the time Joe had finished his second drink, he was slightly slurring his words but was in a jovial mood.

"I think the wedding is going to be a blast," said Joe. "You know, Kathleen's mom and dad were out here last week, and they are what Mom used to call 'lace curtain Irish'—you know, money and class. I think Mary Spillane was a helluva a looker in her day, and she still has a tight ass, none of that Mrs. O'Leary fat look for her. I told Big Joe that if you want to know what Kathleen is going to look like in twenty-five years, just look at her mother; she sure as hell passes the test."

Claire said Joe had gotten more and more "earthy" in recent months.

"I call 'em the way I see 'em," he smiled. "I can still spot a great ass."

I asked Joe what he thought of Big Joe's success working with Adam Sutro.

"Adam is damned lucky to have Joe, don't you think?" said Joe.

"I think they are a great team, and they both appreciate each other, how they complement each other," I said.

"I am losing interest in my stamp collection," Joe told me later as we sat alone on his balcony drinking coffee after dinner. Claire had told Joe he could not have any brandy, because he had already had enough. Joe had not argued.

"You know," he continued, "I'm losing interest in just about everything. If it wasn't for this wedding and the nightly cocktail hour, I could just as easily pack it in. Claire wanted me to go back and read all my books, and I tried, but I kept getting lost. I can't believe I ever wrote them. That damned stroke did it. I hardly even remember working as a correspondent in Asia. But it is funny, I remember growing up, and I can see Dad clearly in my mind, as clearly as I can remember Claire the first day I saw her at Lowell. But I watch movies on television, and I get two-thirds of the way through before I remember I have already seen it."

Listening to Joe talk was pretty depressing, to say the least. A couple of times, I could feel tears welling up in my eyes. I put on my glasses so that Joe wouldn't notice. I had read that stroke victims continued to develop those areas of the mind where the brain cells had not been destroyed. But that did not seem to be the case with Joe, who, if anything, was getting worse. Maybe it was the drinking, the lack of exercise, and the dreary moods. I tried to interest Joe in an after-dinner walk, but he said walking with two canes was too much trouble.

"Joe, I am beginning to think you have a death wish," I finally blurted out. "I think you have lost sight of all of your blessings. You have a wonderful wife, two delightful daughters, and a great son, a family most men dream about."

"Yeah, I have all that, but what use am I?" he said. "It is a pretty awful feeling to feel useless."

"When did you start to feel this way?" I asked.

"I don't know, maybe early this year," he said.

"Did I ever tell you how much Jim and I loved you and respected you growing up?" I said. "You were our idol, the boss, the perfect big brother, the greatest basketball player ever to come out of the Sunset District. I would have changed places with you in a minute."

"I bet you wouldn't change places today," he said.

"What I am trying to say is that all of us in the family love you, and we'll take you in whatever condition," I said. "What I really want to do is cheer you up, lift you out of this depression I'm seeing."

"Thanks, Danny; that's nice," he said. "I'll feel better in the morning."

Karen and Claire also spent time talking that night about the changes in Joe Jr. Karen told me after we left that night that Joe's doctor had told Claire that he was worried about Joe's blood pressure and his cholesterol, both of which were up, mainly, it was thought, because of a lack of exercise. I mentioned Joe's depression, and Karen said that tied into his inactivity.

"The solution seems pretty simple, the way you describe it," I said. "All we have to do is get Joe to exercise." I called Joe the next day and said that I was coming over after work and that we were going for a walk, canes and all. He laughed and said he would go only if I joined him for the cocktail hour afterward.

"One drink," I said.

I called Big Joe and briefed him on my feelings about his father and suggested that if he could get away, he could join us for the walk and the drink afterward. I said I thought there was a sense of urgency if we were going to halt Joe's decline. Big Joe said he would be there at a five o'clock.

It was a warm summer evening, and the sun was still high in the sky when we began what turned out to be a one-hour walk. We only covered six long blocks, because Joe moved so slowly.

"I feel pretty good," said Joe, huffing and puffing when we got back to the house.

"You should do this every day, Dad," said Big Joe. I chimed in my agreement and said I would be back at the same time tomorrow.

"Wait a minute—you promised you would stay for a drink, both of you," said Joe. We all went upstairs and sat on the balcony overlooking the deep blue bay with the sun shining brightly on the Bay Bridge and Alcatraz. Joe insisted on making the drinks, presumably to make sure he got his full allotment of scotch in his ice-only glass.

Big Joe delivered the drinks and said he was glad he had left work early.

"We don't get a chance to see each other as much as I would like," said Big Joe to his dad. "That was fun being with you on the walk with Uncle Dan. I bet you two were hell on wheels when you were growing up."

I said you had to put Jimmy into the equation, adding, "The Booker brothers were pretty well known all over the city."

"The only problem was Danny couldn't play basketball worth a damn, so he spent all of his time playing baseball, as a catcher, because he ran like he had a refrigerator on this back," said Joe.

"That's not true," said Big Joe.

"No, it is," I said. "I had lousy wheels, but I had a pretty good arm, and I hit pretty well. I just didn't get any infield hits."

"Hell, if Danny could have run, he would have batted .400 everywhere he played," said Joe.

Big Joe wanted to hear more stories about the three Booker brothers growing up in San Francisco. One drink turned into three, and we talked until past ten o'clock. Claire served us all dinner after checking with Karen, who said she could not join us, because Jonathan was eating at a friend's house and would be getting back at nine o'clock. It was a totally serendipitous evening, the kind I love but which happen much too infrequently.

"Dad, thanks for a great evening," said Big Joe, giving his father a full hug as we got up to leave.

"Son, I couldn't be more proud of you," said Joe.

Big Joe and I walked out together, and we were both upbeat about Joe.

"I think that walk did him a lot of good," said Big Joe. "We just need to force him out on a regular basis."

"I agree, but the walk should not always be followed by three drinks, especially the kind that your dad pours for himself."

"Tonight was kind of special," said Big Joe. "I can't remember when just the three of us spent that kind of time together."

"You are right, Joe; it has been a special night, a night to remember," I said. "By the way, how are you feeling about your wedding? No cold feet, I hope."

"Ha, that's a laugh," he said. "I'm so in love with Kathleen I can hardly wait. She doesn't believe in sex before marriage, or at least two months before marriage."

Three days later, on August 15, 1995, at about 12:25 AM, Joe suffered a severe stroke and was in a coma by the time he arrived at UC Hospital shortly after 1:30 AM. Claire called me from the hospital and asked if I could call everyone and let them know that Joe was in critical condition. I said that maybe we should hold the calls until morning and that Karen and I would be there in less than an hour.

Claire was waiting outside the intensive care ward. Inside, doctors were doing their best to keep Joe alive.

"We had gone to bed about eleven," Claire told us. "I usually sleep right through, but tonight, I woke up just after midnight, and I heard Joe cry out 'No.' I put on the light, and he was white as a sheet with a contorted look on his face. It wasn't like the first time, when he was gurgling. He was totally out. The ambulance got there in less than twenty minutes. They said his heart was beating fine, but they put an oxygen mask on him and got him into the ambulance right away. I rode with him, and I could hear him breathing. He hardly moved."

Claire said the doctors told her that they would call her the minute he awoke and that she could see him in a few hours. Karen and I stayed through the night with Claire, who had steeled herself with the thought that God was in charge. At eight o'clock, I started making all of the necessary phone calls, the toughest of which were the ones to Joe's three children, Big Joe, Robyn, and Kare. I told everyone that Joe was expected to recover.

Unfortunately, he never did. Joe remained in a coma for a month before he blessedly slipped away on September 13, 1995.

On September 1, Kathleen and Joe III had announced they were postponing their September 14 wedding. Neither wanted to celebrate anything with Joe clinging to life in a San Francisco hospital. Instead, in early October, two weeks after Joe's well-attended and well-publicized funeral, the couple flew to Reno, where they were married by a justice of the peace, and from there, they flew to Italy for a three-week honeymoon.

My mother was a wreck for the first week after Joe's second stroke. Then, when she understood that the brain damage was so severe that he would be like a vegetable if he did manage to wake from his coma, she told me she believed the best thing would be for him to die as soon as possible.

"Joe had everything, including some bad luck," my mother said. "I can only imagine what his life would have been like if he hadn't been in that accident on Bayshore Highway when he was a senior in college."

"You are right, Mom—that accident changed him from a highly trained athlete into a partial cripple who, by the end, never really got any exercise. But he raised three wonderful children, and he had the love of everyone who knew him, even when his personality changed after his stroke. And his books are going to outlive us all."

"Danny, you and I are a lot alike," said my mother. "We're both born optimists!"

CHAPTER 99

The merciful passing of my brother, like the death of Conrad, drew the family closer. Jim and Pamela got Constance more involved with the work of the P&J Adoption Agency, particularly with the periodic home visitations where children had been placed. Although Constance was eighty-two years old in 1996, she seemed much younger, was in remarkable physical shape, and somehow managed the good posture that always characterized her impressive presence. Dr. Bonita Everest, the executive director of P&J, took my mother on her first house tour two months after Joe's death, and the result was that Mom came out of the six-hour day looking happy and animated.

"Oh, what happiness Jim and Pamela have created," my mother told me over dinner with Karen and Jonathan. "The children look so healthy and so loved. To think there have been three hundred adoptions completed in the last three years is so wonderful and so amazing."

I had always felt slightly less close to Jim than I had to Joe, possibly because things had come so easily to him. It was hard not to envy his good looks and his prodigious memory. Of course, I loved Jim, but early on in our teen years and adult lives, I hadn't always liked the way he treated women. I thought he was insensitive and believed women were fair game to be used and discarded. For much of his life, Jim was the master of seduction—until he met Pamela, whose delightful personality and fun-loving nature by all accounts kept him on the straight and narrow.

The P&J Adoption Agency had been Pamela's idea, and Jim became engrossed in its creation to please Pamela. Once the children started getting placed into homes, Jim seemed to take more delight in his work than he had at any time in his life. Jim realized that he had been given a lot, had taken a lot, and was happiest to be giving back. Mom said it was tragic that Pamela and Jim didn't have any children because they would have been superstars. Though Jim and Pamela considered adopting after P&J was launched, Jim felt that he was too old and that it was better to channel his energies into matching children from Asia to northern California families.

"I love the work," Jim told me one day. "In our first three years, we have only had to take back for readoption two children, in one case because of a divorce and another because of the death of the mother. I hope I live long enough to see some of these children in college."

Others were impressed by Jim and Pamela's work as well. "Jim and Pamela are making a huge and selfless contribution that will be felt for centuries," said Richard Hamblen, ordinarily not a man given to hyperbole.

Twelve months after the marriage of Joseph Booker III and Kathleen Spillane, Joe telephoned shortly before 9:00 PM one night to say that Kathleen was in labor, and he was taking her to the UC Hospital. Karen and I immediately left for the hospital, telling Jonathan where we were going. Joe met us there, along with Kathleen's parents, Dr. Michael, and Mary Spillane, who had flown out from Chicago the day before. Shortly thereafter, Claire, the prospective grandmother, arrived with her daughter, Robyn, followed by the prospective great-grandmother, Constance, who, of course, was accompanied by Richard Hamblen. All of us were excited to see a new Booker coming into world. Jim and Pamela were in Asia.

While we were waiting, Robyn told me privately and in a low whisper that she had finally met her man and that she soon expected to announce her engagement. She said the prospective bridegroom was Arthur Butler, a financial analyst for Smith Barney. Robyn, now thirty, said Arthur was fantastically smart with a great sense of humor and two years older than she. He had graduated from the University of Southern California and had a master's degree in business administration from Stanford.

"You are going to love him, Uncle Dan, even though he doesn't play golf," said Robyn. "He has the best sense of humor of anyone I have ever met, and I think he is very handsome, though I did not think so when we first met. He has the kind of looks that grow on you."

"Has Arthur met your brother Joe?" I asked.

"Yes, and he loved him," said Robyn, motioning for Joe to come over to join us.

"He's the first guy Robyn has dated who is her equal, maybe even more than equal," smiled Joe, once we told him what we were discussing.

"Oh, he is much smarter," said Robyn. "You have to read his reports on the Silicon Valley technology sector. He writes quarterly thirty- to forty-page reports full of facts and analysis on the top ten major technology companies, and he has had a great track record in picking the biggest winners."

"Oh, he is that Arthur Butler," I said, rather lamely. "In fact, I have read some of his reports; he is quite well respected."

"I thought you would know of him, Uncle Dan," said Robyn. "You know, he was on the swimming team at Southern Cal, and he still swims three days a week."

I gave Robyn a hug and a kiss and said I was very happy for her, adding I was eager to meet Arthur.

"Both Arthur and I want to have at least three children," said Robyn, "just like Mom and Dad."

"You had better tell your grandmother about this," I said.

"I will, but not now," said Robyn. "I don't want to distract from Kathleen's baby."

Robyn was looking more beautiful than I had ever seen her. Her younger sister Kare, by contrast, although her usual bubbly self, seemed to me to have lost some of her youthful freshness. She was perhaps ten pounds overweight, though it was the lack of wholesomeness that concerned me. I knew she liked to party and probably drank too much. In fact, she was the last of the family to arrive at the hospital, saying she had been out to a late dinner party and had not arrived home until after eleven. She looked tired and rough around the edges, but her bouncy spirit and infectious laugh still combined to make her attractive and fun to be around.

Richard Hamblen sat quietly through most of the evening. He was eighty-six and moved slowly. It was past his bedtime. I noticed he kept his eyes on Mom as she chatted excitedly around the hospital waiting room. Mom seemed to have developed an excellent rapport with the distinguished-looking Spillanes, who appeared quite comfortable with their new San Francisco family.

Big Joe grew tenser as the night progressed. Kathleen had gone into labor just after 8:00 PM. By midnight, Joe said he was kicking himself that he had not taken the training so that he could be with Kathleen during the birth.

"I made my work too high a priority, Uncle Dan," he said. "I am going to change and put my family first."

"That's something I don't think you will ever regret," I said, with the knowledge that Big Joe had no financial worries, given his successful real estate ventures with Adam Sutro.

At 2:00 AM, the doctor came into the waiting room to say that although there were no problems, the birth was taking longer than expected and could last another four or five hours. He suggested we all come back in the morning. Constance questioned the doctor about the delay, wondering if something was perhaps wrong. The doctor assured her everything was fine and that nature sometimes operated on its own clock. With that, all of us agreed to come back as soon as we got the call from Joe. Robyn said she would stay and keep Joe company while the rest of us left. I had to get up in three hours, and Richard appeared exhausted, so the break was well received.

Somehow, no one seemed worried about the outcome. And we were all right! Joseph Booker IV was born at 7:14 AM on October 21, 1996. He weighed nine pounds and one ounce. He had a long, angular body, seemingly a sign of Booker genes.

When Karen and I returned just before noon, Kathleen was radiant sitting up in her hospital bed, holding her baby with a giddy look on her impish though swollen face. Joe III was sitting on the bed with his arm around his wife, proudly saying he had ordered a box of Cohiba (Cuban) cigars that he would be passing out later in the day, and in fact, he planned to have one himself. Big Joe would be thirty-two in December, and he had it all, a beautiful loving wife and a baby son who his mother, Claire, said looked just like he had when he was born. Importantly, he had a job that he loved and that had already made him a millionaire. He appeared to be on the road to becoming the most successful of all the Bookers. And Kathleen said she wanted to keep having babies.

I could not have felt better for Big Joe, whom I loved like a son and who treated me warmly and with great respect. Claire was ecstatic and looked better than she had in years. She and Mom had been spending a lot of time with Kathleen and had come to love her and were especially happy over the way she treated Joe.

"Kathleen knows how to handle a man," observed Richard Hamblen, adding, "So do all the other women around here."

"I guess that is why we break our backs to make them happy," I said.

The women all laughed.

"I am going to call for a doctor," said Karen. "Maybe Dan needs to be put in traction."

"Poor Uncle Dan is breaking his back, poor baby," said Robyn.

My mother laughed the hardest.

It suddenly dawned on me that the Booker family was now dominated by women!

CHAPTER 100

I could not bring myself to vote for Bob Dole, the Republican candidate selected to oppose Bill Clinton in the 1996 presidential election. Of course, I could not vote for Clinton either or, for that matter, for Ross Perot, whose candidacy had given Clinton the victory in the 1992 election.

Clinton received 49.2 percent of the votes cast in 1996 to 40.7 percent for Dole and 8.4 percent for Perot. I was not alone in my apathy. There were 9 million fewer votes cast in 1996 than in 1992. My reasoning was that I did not like the sometimes nasty, crusty persona displayed by Dole, who also seemed old and infirm next to the youthful and energetic Clinton. Moreover, Dole was a lousy speaker, whereas Clinton could be both eloquent and charming while speaking from either a script or extemporaneously. Dole disliked scripts but seldom came across as a clear thinker without one.

Anther factor in the voter apathy was that everyone thought Clinton was going to win by a large margin. Another four years of Clinton did not seem like a disaster. Both houses of congress were controlled by the Republicans, and there was little Clinton could do without Republican approval. Importantly, Clinton had moved politically to the center after the Democrats were crushed in the 1994 midterm elections, in which the House came under control of the Republicans. This turnabout was in large measure a reaction to

Clinton's highly liberal agenda during his first two years in office, which included using his wife Hillary to lead a failed battle to create a greatly expanded government health care program. Wall Street roared ahead during the Clinton years, the federal budget was balanced, and inflation and unemployment were nonissues. I was making more money than I ever thought possible, as was almost everyone else as the rising tide on Wall Street lifted all boats.

In early 1997, Constance invited "the girls" to spend the weekend at the Pebble Beach cottage, ostensibly to plan for Robyn's wedding, which was scheduled for April 23. Present, in addition to Constance and Robyn, were Robyn's mother, Claire, Kare, Karen, Pamela, and Kathleen. It was the first tribal council of Booker women!

The group of seven arrived late Friday afternoon and had dinner at a cozy restaurant in Carmel, where they consumed several bottles of wine with their meal. I learned afterward from Karen that everyone had a good time, especially Kare, who became a bit loud and boisterous, increasingly so in direct correlation to her wine consumption. When Kare tried to order another bottle of wine, Constance said the restaurant was closing, and she could have another glass at home. Back at the cottage, Constance and Pamela went to bed, but the others stayed up to talk. Kare had another glass of wine while the others had tea or water, and they talked until 2:00 AM.

"I have something I have to tell you all," Kare told the group about an hour into the conversation. "But maybe I shouldn't tell. Well, I will. I am quitting my job at Southwest. I mean, they asked me to resign, so I am going to quit."

Robyn jumped to Kare's side and put her arm around her younger sister.

"What happened? I thought you loved your job?" asked Robyn.

"They said in the last year I had failed to make three flights and that it was unacceptable, even though I told them the reason why, which is that I have been suffering from insomnia and can't go to sleep—and then can't wake up when I do fall asleep."

"Since when do you have insomnia, darling?" asked Claire. "You have always been the best sleeper in the family."

"After I had to break up with Ned Ridder," said Kare.

"Who is Ned Ridder? I've never heard you talk about him," asked Claire.

"He's a pilot for Southwest who I was seeing for I guess about six months," said Kare.

"Why do you say you had to break up?" asked Robyn.

"Because he told me we had to," said Kare.

"I don't get it—did you love him?" asked Robyn.

"Very much, and he loved me," said Kare.

"So why did you have to break up?" asked Claire.

"Because he was married, and someone told Southwest that he was seeing me, and they told him if he continued to see me, a fellow employee, he would be fired."

"Oh my goodness, Kare, darling, you could have any man you wanted; why did you have to pick a married man?" said Claire.

Kare began sobbing. "Because I loved him. It started out as friendship. I knew he was married with two children, but we just fell in love. It was so stupid."

"So since you broke up with Ned, you have been having insomnia," said Karen.

"When I missed my second flight, the human resources department said they were going to fire me, but the union supported me, and I got sent to a psychiatrist to cure my insomnia," Karen said. "The doctor told me—I saw him about ten times—that I had a tendency to make poor decisions, that I had bad judgment, and that I drank too much, because I lacked self-esteem and self-confidence. He also said I had established a pattern of drinking that had caused me to crave alcohol. He said the answer to my problem was to stop thinking about Ned, to stop drinking, and to start thinking about the implications of my actions."

"But you haven't stopped drinking, darling," said Claire.

"I am going to. So far, I have tried, but can't," she said. "The doctor was right, saying I have developed a craving for alcohol. Right now, I would like another glass of wine."

"Honey, you don't need it. It's very late. I think we should all go to bed, and we can talk some more in the morning," said Claire, putting her arm around Kare. "Would you do that for your mom, honey?"

"Sure, Mom," said Kare, once again beginning to sob as she pressed her face into Claire's shoulder. "I am sorry to be the only mess in the family."

Kare did not get up until nearly noon the next day.

When she walked into the kitchen and saw Robyn there, she asked, "Why didn't you wake me up, Robyn?"

"We figured you needed the sleep," said Robyn. "The others have gone into town, and we are supposed to meet them for lunch at one o'clock."

The rest of the weekend was spent planning Robyn's wedding. The subject of Kare being fired did not come up again. No one wanted Constance to learn about it just yet, and Kare limited herself to two glasses of wine at each of the three subsequent meals that the group of seven had together.

I later learned that Constance had overheard part of Kare's confession but had decided not to broach the subject until she could talk it over with Richard Hamblen.

"She obviously needs a lot of love and support," said Richard, upon hearing the news. "Poor Kare is surrounded by some very intelligent and wise women, and I can see how she could feel insecure. She has always been loveable, and she's quite lovely, though I can see the strain of her situation starting to show in her face."

Constance and Richard talked for hours about Kare, and in the end, they decided to get me involved.

"Danny, Richard thinks that you are the one to take the lead in trying to help Kare," said my mother. "We know she is comfortable around you and that she loves you very much and that you are like a dad to her."

I was intrigued to learn that the psychiatrist had said Kare suffered from bad judgment. I thought he was right on. And he was right that Kare felt inferior to her mature and disciplined brother Joe and her judicious and intelligent sister Robyn. Kare liked to say that she lived one day at a time and that the name of the game was having fun. But part of that devil-may-care attitude was a cover for what she perceived as her inadequacies, her failure to find anything important to do in life. Kare had never appeared to be very serious about anything, and I suspect her allegedly poor judgment included more than just falling in love with a married man.

I said to my mother and Richard that I would do anything they suggested but that I had no confidence I could succeed where a professional had already failed.

"I wouldn't say the psychiatrist failed," said Richard. "Remember, Kare was able to report—by all accounts, quite objectively—on his conclusions. That tells me she is not in denial, which is so often the case in alcoholics. So I think that is a positive."

"I guess you heard all about it," Kare said when I telephoned.

"I think we have a lot in common," I replied, suggesting we meet for breakfast.

"Can we make it lunch?" she asked. "My insomnia is so unpredictable that I hate to have any meetings before noon."

It took nearly two weeks before we could finally get together. There was no question that Karen was stalling and did not really want to discuss her problems.

We met at a trendy new restaurant south of Market, taking a corner table where we could talk.

"How old were you when your dad had his stroke?" I asked as we were eating our salads. Kare had ordered a glass of red wine and had almost finished it. I could see in her face that she had not stopped drinking. In fact, she looked as if she had been drinking a lot. The wine caused her fair skin to flush, and it clearly relaxed her.

"That was 1981," said Kare. "I guess I was thirteen."

"What were you feeling when that happened?"

"Gosh, I'm not sure. I loved my dad. He was such a wonderful father—home most of the time, always ready to do things with us. Then suddenly he wasn't the same person anymore. It was like he was a stranger. Funny, what I really guess I was thinking was how awful it was for my mother, to at first have to take care of Dad as if he was mentally retarded. That changed, and he got better, but thinking back, I felt really bad for my mother, like she had been cheated and did not have much to look forward to, even though she was only forty-five or so. I said to myself, 'I hope that never happens to me.' I mean, the only man she had ever known, had ever loved, was my dad."

"Do you think your dad's stroke changed you in any way?" I asked.

"In one sense it made me closer to Mom, but in another, it made me want to have more of my life outside the home, with friends. I guess, thinking back, I did not always pick the best friends. Not like Joe and Robyn, whose friends were good students and more serious than average, people who had ambitions about what they wanted to do in life. I sort of gravitated to the party crowd, kids who drank even in high school, kids who had experience in sex. I went out with a lot of different guys, fell in love several times, and thought life was pretty great. Then I would come home, and my mother would be sweet and cheerful and upbeat, even though I knew she wasn't having any fun."

Kare and I talked for two hours that first lunch. It seemed to me that if Kare was going to get her life together, she was going to have to find something about which she was passionately interested. Clearly, her father's stroke and death had scarred her, especially as those events related to her mother. I assumed that Kare had done some things that she on one level regretted, but on another level did not. I knew she had a spiritual center, but the problem was bringing it to life. I wasn't sure I was the one who could really help. But Kare said that she thought our lunch was helpful and that she would like to do it again.

CHAPTER 101

Two weeks after my lunch with Kare, my wife called me at the office, saying that Claire had just telephoned to say that she had found Kare in a drunken state in her apartment the previous evening. She was apparently so intoxicated that Claire thought about calling an ambulance, but in the end, she decided to spend the night with her daughter while she slept it off. Karen told me Kare had apparently consumed two bottles of wine after an unsuccessful job interview with United Airlines that morning. The United personnel person had told her that her dismissal by Southwest would probably make it difficult to get a job with any airline.

When Kare woke up early the next morning and found her mother sleeping next to her, she began crying uncontrollably. She told her mom she was a complete failure and was beginning to think she would be better off dead. Claire talked with Kare for several hours, fed her, and by afternoon talked her into taking some mild sleeping pills that would help her get some much-needed rest.

While Kare was sleeping, Claire called all of the members of the family and told them what had happened. At a meeting of the family the next night, we agreed to confront Kare and get her into a rehab center for at least thirty days so that she could dry out and get some urgently needed counseling. Richard said that he had done some research on rehab centers and that one of the best was located in San Francisco, halfway up Twin Peaks.

It took hours of conversation to convince Kare that it was a necessary step, but she ultimately agreed, and on March 2, 1997, she was admitted to the Self-Help Resolution Center. The premise of Self-Help was that patients had to be the prime mover in solving their own problems. But first, Kare had to cleanse her system, a process that involved angry fits of temper and despondency, all of which the staff expected and handled in a quiet and assured way. By the end of two weeks, Kare had perked up, but was still unconvinced that she could change her life. However, by the end of the Kare's month of rehab, which included a strict diet, colonics, massage, exercise classes, motivational talks, and training in meditation, she seemed to be her old self and said she was sleeping well and hadn't felt better in years. Her former spark was still not quite there, but she was vastly improved.

Kare moved in with her mother when she was released, and Claire was on duty twenty-four hours a day, involving her daughter in exercise classes, long walks, health foods, trips to movies and museums, and talks that lasted often past midnight. Meanwhile, Robyn and Arthur Butler decided to postpone their wedding until August so that all of the family could focus on getting Kare back on her feet.

My wonderful wife, Karen, proved to be a critical element in Kare's hoped-for turnaround. It happened at Pebble Beach. Karen and I had gone there for a weekend in late April with Kare and Claire. Karen told Kare during a private conversation that she had been in a similar situation when she was in her twenties.

"I was married at twenty-one and divorced at twenty-two, and even though I had a good job starting out in advertising, I did not feel good about myself, though I did not really understand that at the time," said Karen. "I worked hard, but I liked parties. I got involved over the years with a number of men, none of whom ever asked me to marry them. You know the old saying, "why buy the cow when the milk is free"? It got to the point where men would call and just ask if they could come over—and didn't even bother to ask me out for dinner. I was drinking a lot, I gained some weight, and I began to look older. When I was twenty-seven, people thought I was thirty, at least. My mother had been married four times, and I seldom saw her, but I was doing worse than following in her footsteps."

"Wow," said Kare. "Knowing you as I do, that is almost hard to believe. How did you change?"

"I don't think there was any one thing, but I remember reading an article in a magazine that was entitled "Self-Respect Is Everything." The thrust of the argument was that the best way to happiness was through self-respect and that the most important thing to know was that self-respect came from within. In other words, all of us have the power to control how we feel about ourselves. And the way to get positive feedback from yourself is to do things that make you feel proud of yourself."

"But what if deep down you really don't respect yourself and hate what you have done with your life and in your life?" said Kare.

"That was my reaction, too," said Karen. "But the writer—I wish I could remember his name; he was a doctor of something—he said you had to abandon all your regrets, because there was nothing you could do about them. He said that you had to find little things to start a pattern of success, like making your bed in the morning, showering, flossing, having a healthy breakfast, exercising, saying a prayer, thinking about a way to help someone who needs help. He said if you do and act in that manner, you will get your day off to a positive start, and you will feel good about yourself.

"I decided to start reading the Bible, and I began reading self-improvement books, stopped drinking, and stopped seeing any of my former boyfriends. I know it sounds contradictory, but I decided to hide my looks, purposely making myself unattractive to men while at the same time I was trying to make my soul beautiful. I forget where I got that idea, but instead of worrying about the way I looked to people, I tried to project a pure and considerate and loving soul. I enjoyed dressing down, wearing glasses, letting my hair hide my face. People began reacting to what I said and not to what I looked like.

"Gradually, over time, I began to regain my self-respect. I dated, but I did not go to bed with anyone. At work, after about six months, my boss said I was a changed person, much more creative, more energetic, more sensitive, more mature. He gave me several new large accounts to handle, and I got a substantial raise. Because I was seldom thinking about myself, I had a lot more energy, and it showed not only in my work, but also in the things I did outside of work. I joined the Young Republicans and became active in the Advertising Club and subsequently was elected to the board.

"For the first time since high school, I felt genuinely good about myself, and I had just turned twenty-nine. I bought my own apartment and even tried to heal my relationship with my mother. I also started to see my father and his family in Southern California. It is funny that when you feel good about yourself, you want to do more things. But I have to tell you, Kare, it is never a straight and easy course. There were lots of times when I was tempted to resume my old ways. It was a daily battle, but over time, it got a little easier. It takes discipline, and you have to learn to do it one step at a time—make your bed, floss, exercise, and on and on."

"That is a wonderful story, Karen. It sounds like an approach I could take," said Kare.

"If it was easy, a lot more people would straighten out their lives," Karen said. "But once you get in the habit of respecting yourself, doing all the little things that you know you will respect yourself for doing, it becomes a habit that is hard to break. One thing I did not tell you is that I also used to smoke. That was harder to give up than drinking, and it took me a year of trying to finally break free of what is truly a filthy habit."

Later that day, Kare told me about her conversation with Karen and said that she was going to try the approach Karen had taken when she was her age.

"I need to reinvent myself," said Kare.

I told Kare that I thought she could succeed but that it was not easy, that I had gone through a similar change in lifestyle when I was in my early forties.

"The changes I made in my life were the hardest things I have ever done," I said. "I was never a really disciplined person, and I had developed a lot of bad habits, like you, like Karen years ago. But I stuck with it, and the good Lord rewarded me by bringing Karen into my life."

"Oh, Uncle Dan, tell me all about how you met Karen and how you fell in love," said Kare.

When I had finished a possibly romanticized version that took an hour, Kare said that it was a fabulous story and that I had helped her to understand what she wanted most in life.

"I want to find a really good man," said Kare. "He doesn't have to be Prince Charming. Karen said marrying the Prince Charming types often turns out to be a mistake. She says I should look for character, someone with similar values. I want to believe in God, and I want to be around someone who does. I want to have someone with a good soul, who loves me and is going to make our children proud. Someone who puts his family first."

"That sounds like criteria ready to be posted on the Internet," I joked.

Kare laughed and said she had a lot of work to do on herself before she was ready to start looking for a man.

"Your wife told me if I can get my act together, everything will take care of itself, eventually," said Kare.

"Well, just remember that what you are talking about is akin to a New Year's resolution, most of which are doomed to failure," I said. "I don't say that to be negative, but to emphasize that you can't relent."

"Thanks, Uncle Dan. I am really going to give it my best."

CHAPTER 102

Even though Kare said all of the right things, I was not altogether certain that she would be able to keep her resolve. Most people didn't. Kare did not want to join Alcoholics Anonymous, but gave no reason. Once again, it was Richard Hamblen who came up with the critical suggestion. He said it might be good for Kare to do some volunteer work at Alonso Washington's center for the homeless, which Alonso had established with the help of Constance and Richard. Washington's rehabilitation after the ordeal with Conrad and Mom, in which he had tried to rob them, had made him a poster boy in San Francisco, and the establishment of the Washington Center, with most of the funding coming from the efforts of Constance and Richard, was the crowning achievement of his life.

Alonso had wanted to name the center after Mom, but she declined, saying it was Alonso's idea and his effort that had made it all possible. Richard had arranged for the purchase of a dilapidated three-story building on Ellis Street near Taylor in the heart of San Francisco's tenderloin district, where homeless people dominated the scene. Washington organized street people to do the refurbishing of the building, which took six months and cost more than $900,000.

The goal of the Washington Center was to provide free lunch and dinner for homeless people seven days a week. In addition, a huge bathroom and shower facility was available under the supervision of Alonso's "orderlies," one of whom was Abraham Washington, a six-foot-nine-inch black man who presided over the cleanup station. Alonso said he wanted to run a tight ship with no hanky panky, no disrespect, and no rowdiness.

The cafeteria was designed to seat 150 people and provided good basic food, purchased fresh at wholesale prices and prepared by two paid cooks, who were assisted by volunteers. Lunch was served in two sittings between eleven and one o'clock, and dinner was also served in two sittings, between five and seven o'clock. Alonso, who had turned out to be as good an administrator and manager as he was a motivational speaker, oversaw every detail of the operation. My mother said the fund-raising was the easiest part, particularly when the would-be donors actually visited the Washington Center and saw firsthand the cleanliness, the efficiency, and the orderliness of the operation, together with the obvious appreciation of the homeless.

The center included a popular wardrobe room where men could pick up clean clothes that were obtained via an agreement with the

Salvation Army. There was also a theater-style room that could accommodate up to one hundred people for motivational talks by Alonso and others he designated. These were surprisingly well attended. The room also served as a reading room when not otherwise in use.

It was here that Kare was induced to become a volunteer while she concurrently looked for permanent employment. The Washington Center took care of men only, who constituted the vast majority of San Francisco's homeless. Washington had said it would be too complicated to have to provide facilities for both sexes, and furthermore, there were already shelters and eating places for homeless females in the area. Mom had agreed with the decision.

Kare began working as a volunteer, serving food cafeteria-style to each of the men. Although other women also worked on the serving line, most were forty and older, and although they probably had beautiful souls, their physical attractiveness, if it had ever existed, had long since faded. Kare, on the other hand, was beautiful, cheerful, and full of fun. Her six weeks of healthy living and abstinence from alcohol had put the bloom back in her face. So even though she wore virtually no makeup and dressed conservatively under her large white apron, the men seemed delighted to be in proximity to such a creature. Alonso told Mom that Kare seemed to love the interaction with the men and had learned many of their names, and it was not long before most of San Francisco's homeless had heard about the beauty serving food at the Washington Center. Meals soon were filled to capacity. Kare was known to all as "Miss Booker," and she seemed to bring out the best in the men, some of whom planned elaborate and polite greetings to her. Alonso said most of the men spent more time cleaning up before eating than they used to.

Claire said that when Kare came home at night she was full of stories and excited about what she was doing. After about a month, Alonso asked Kare if she would like to become the official receptionist for the Washington Center. The job entailed signing in each visitor, keeping track of the issuance of plastic disposable razors, and recording all clothing gifts. Kare accepted and soon became conversant with every aspect of the center's operation and began assisting in the acceptance of deliveries, in taking people on off-hour tours, and in a thousand other things that invariably seemed to come up. Alonso assigned William Stevens Brown, one of his most trusted orderlies, to remain near Kare at all times when she was in the center. William was a three hundred-pound, six-foot-three-inch black man, and his mere presence seemed to preclude anything but the most civil behavior around Miss Booker.

Kare loved the job much more than she had enjoyed being an airline stewardess.

"I really feel that I am doing something that brings happiness to people, and I don't think there is any better feeling," Kare told Karen and me over dinner after she had been at the center for two months. "These men all have a story, and it is amazing how smart some of them are. One of them who calls himself 'Ashley' says I remind him of Scarlet O'Hara and that I have to look out for dreadful people like Rhett Butler. I said I had read *Gone with the Wind* and asked if he had been named after the Ashley Wilkes character. He said indeed he had been and that hence it was ordained that I would fall in love with him. I laughed, and he really smiled even though he was missing some teeth.

"These men are so lonely, so starved for love, so abandoned by themselves and others, that they really appreciate human interaction with people from the normal world," Kare added.

"Kare, you are looking so beautiful now, you must be driving the men crazy," said Karen.

"No, it's not like that, I don't think. It's more that I am like a daughter or a sister who cares about them," said Kare.

"Well, I think Alonso is very wise in having William Brown at your side at all times," I said.

"William is wonderful. He smiles at all of my jokes, and all of the men hold him in awe. Apparently, he is one of the strongest men in San Francisco, and he works nights as a bouncer at a nightclub in North Beach. Alonso says William has been fully rehabilitated from drugs and alcohol and was supposed to stop working at the center next month. But William says he doesn't trust anyone else protecting me and that he is staying on."

Karen and I both laughed heartily at the picture of William, the 300-pounder, protecting the 120-pound Kare.

"You two must be quite a sight," I said.

"Kare, do you miss drinking?" Karen asked.

"Funny you should ask. I think I have forgotten all about drinking. And I don't think about any of my former boyfriends. I feel I have more love in my life than ever. I love my life and think I am doing some good. Of course, I can't keep living off Mom. I have to get a full-time job and earn a living. But I don't want to stop working at the Washington Center. You know, I think Alonso Washington is a truly great man. And he says he owes everything he has in life to Grandmother Constance."

Talking with Kare was an absolute delight. I could not believe how much she had changed in so short a time. She looked to be in her early twenties rather than almost twenty-nine.

In early July of 1997, Kare received a telephone call from a man who identified himself as Professor Ellsworth Boswell from the sociology department at the University of California at Berkeley. He said Alonso Washington had given him her number and had said that Kare might want to help him on a study he was undertaking on the homeless. He asked if she could meet him for lunch, and Kare suggested he come to the Washington Center after she learned he had never been there.

"My, this is quite an extraordinary setup," said Professor Boswell, a wispy, thin-haired man in his late thirties, after eating lunch and going on a tour of the facilities with Alonso Washington. "Miss Booker, you seem to have a remarkable relationship with these men. I say that based on the way they look at you and how they smile. Frankly, I am quite used to being around the homeless, and I am quite unaccustomed to smiles."

"That's because the men seem to recognize in Miss Booker that what is on the outside is matched by what is on the inside," said Alonso.

"Oh, I quite agree," said Professor Boswell, flashing a big smile at "Miss Booker."

Alonso excused himself, saying that he had already been briefed on the professor's project and that he supported it 100 percent.

"I have been given a substantial and generous grant to study homeless people in the Bay Area," Boswell began. "The purpose is simply to try to find out how these people have gotten where they are and hopefully to gain some insights as to how they might be helped in a longer-term sense. Would you be interested in assisting in such a project?"

"I would, but how much time would it take?" Kare asked.

"Probably six months to a year, because we want to do at least five hundred fairly in-depth interviews," he answered. "We have already started work in Oakland, but one of the things we are finding is that many people don't want to be interviewed, even if we offer them money. And some of those who do agree tell us tall tales that are of no use. I am glad you suggested that I come here because I strongly sense, based on what I see, that you would be able to overcome the obstacles we have found in Oakland. We would be able to pay you $4,000 a month for your efforts and possibly more if we find ourselves having to go into overtime mode."

"That is very generous, and I like the idea, because what you want to learn is exactly what I have been dying to find out," Kare responded. "I have had lots of superficial conversations, but time and circumstances have prevented anything deeper."

"So you will accept?"

"I am almost 100 percent, but I want to consult with my family first," Kare said. "Did you know that I spent thirty days in a rehab center for alcoholism earlier this year?"

"Yes, I did, and I have also been told you have come through quite splendidly."

CHAPTER 103

Constance wrote one of her longer diary entries on June 18, 1998. Although she was eighty-four years old, her handwriting was still strong and clear.

I write this on a lovely morning at Pebble Beach. Richard and I have come to relax, walk on the beach, read, and talk. I've had so many wonderful times here, I can't help but feel nostalgic. Oh, how I love this house and Carmel and the rocky and rugged shoreline. Of course, my beloved Conrad died here. But, as Danny has said, he had the kind of death most men dream about. Conrad and I had 19 happy years together. I can't believe that it has been 14 years since his death. Thinking of death is a reminder that most likely I have only a little time left. I thank God I still have my health and "all my marbles" as the grandchildren like to say. That in itself is a blessing, because I have so many fond and vivid memories of my life and my family. I can remember as if it were yesterday when I first met 2nd Lt. Joseph Booker, as handsome and polite a man as I have ever seen. Thank God for what happened on the beach that night when Joe Jr. was conceived. I don't know what came over me to cave in to my carnal self, or Joe, for that matter. But it happened. If it hadn't we probably never would have gotten married, because Joe was soon to be reassigned to Fort Riley, and I was so young. Our marriage was wonderful, with three loveable and very different sons, even though it lasted only just short of a dozen years, the last three of which Joe was away from home and the last 14 months of which we did not see him at all.

The mind turns to all of the things I am grateful for, even though the deaths of my two Joes are scar tissue on my soul, like so much in life, the result of God's will. My two Joes shared one thing: each of them fathered three wonderful children. Joe III is so much like his grandfather and father, so serious, so intelligent, so handsome. And he has found a wonderful wife in Kathleen Spillane. Robyn's marriage to Arthur Butler is just what she wanted and just what she deserved. And I am so happy we have Joe IV, and I know it won't be long before another great-grandchild is on the way. I think Kare is going to end up marrying Dr. Richard Stein. He is such a talented and lovely man, so charming, and I love that he is half Italian and half Jewish. We need some non-Nordic genes to spice up the family tree.

I continue to be so proud of Danny and Jimmy. Though Jimmy and Pamela have not had any children of their own, they have more than made up for it with their adoption agency. Danny and Karen have only Jonathan, but he is so brilliant, so interesting, and so nice. I know he is going to be a great scientist. One of the things I am most grateful for is that I have three loving daughters-in-law. I have so many friends tell me what problems they have with their daughters-in-law, how disrespectful and unpleasant they can be. Some are totally estranged. I have never known a moment of that. Claire has replaced Claudia as my closest friend, and I could not love Pamela and Karen more. Jimmy and Danny are lucky to have them and thankfully they both know it, especially because their first marriages failed.

I am so blessed to have Richard. It was more than 50 years ago that he came into our lives. He is still handsome but he is slowing down. His mind is sharp though it is not quite as energetic as before. As we age, it is nature's way that we slow down. Actually, I enjoy the slower pace. No matter what we do, our bodies are wearing out. I remember my father when he retired—he was tall and dignified and was still very thoughtful, though he moved very slowly. My mother said he died a graceful death. My time will end sometime in the next few years. And Richard will go too. What is important is to appreciate all that we have, to make a contribution to others, to enjoy our families as one generation gives way and another and yet another come to the fore. I wonder if there is really a heaven. What would the purpose be for life in Heaven? Can it be better than I have been given on this earth?

Some women who are blessed with plenty take it all for granted as if it was their just due. Not my mother. She genuinely appreciated everything she was given in life, and she took the sorrows and tragedies in stride, seeing them as part of God's design. In the process, she set an example for us all, though, clearly, none of us could rise to her level. But it was her example and loving nature, her sense of fun and humor, her interest in everyone, that held the Booker family so closely together. Christmases, Thanksgivings, and birthday celebrations were all opportunities for Mom to demonstrate family love and togetherness. Mom not only pulled us together—she made us want to be together. In every way, she taught us the importance of family and giving. Frankly, I have never been exposed to any family as close as we Bookers are. Families like the Bookers are sadly a fast-disappearing phenomena in modern America. Being born a Booker was easily the most fortunate thing that ever happened to me.

CHAPTER 104

Kare had met Dr. Richard Stein at a party to which she was taken by Professor Ellsworth Boswell. A few months earlier, when her research work interviewing homeless men had been completed, Professor Boswell had made her his administrative assistant. Kare told me that Professor Boswell seemed very fond of her, and she guessed he wanted to marry her, but she was not in love with him, though he was a man of the highest character.

Dr. Stein was a practicing surgeon who also taught at the University of California Hospital in San Francisco. With Dr. Stein, Kare said, it was almost a case of love at first sight. She said he was very handsome with dark hair and an athletic build that he kept in shape by running five miles in Golden Gate Park three or four days a week. Kare said that Dr. Stein took her aside at that first meeting and asked her if she was engaged to Professor Boswell or otherwise involved. When he found out she was free of any ties, he asked if she would have dinner with him the following Friday night. She was delighted, and it took only three more dates for the couple to realize they had both fallen madly in love.

Richard Stein's father was a retired executive who had spent most of his career with K-Mart. His mother was a onetime opera singer who had ended her career upon marrying David Stein, with whom she began a family of four children, of which Richard was the oldest. Richard's parents were both living in New York when they met, but after their marriage, the young family moved to Bloomfield Hills in Michigan, where David went to work for K-Mart.

Richard studied premed at the University of Michigan at Ann Arbor and knew from the start that he wanted to be a surgeon, following in the footsteps of one of his uncles, Dr. Stephen Stein. After medical school at Northwestern, Richard Stein completed his internship at the UC Hospital, a move partly brought about by his father's retirement and subsequent purchase of a small vineyard about an hour north of the city. Another factor was that Richard had just broken up with his girlfriend of six years, who had fallen in love with another man. Richard said the breakup was his fault; he had taken her for granted while devoting himself to the grind of medical school.

Richard said that after the breakup, he dated sporadically, but had never found anyone who captured his fancy—until he met Kare. He told her that she was the loveliest, most wholesome person he had ever met and that he loved her sense of humor and sense of fun. After they had known each other for a month, Kare told Richard about her past and alcohol rehab.

"My God, Kare, they should put you on a poster," Richard had said.

"All I did was regain my self-respect, thanks to a lot of homeless people and my very supportive family," Kare replied.

Richard, thirty-seven, and Kare, thirty, were married at Grace Cathedral in San Francisco on December 11, 1998. Difference of religion was not a problem. Richard's mother, who was born a Catholic, had not attended church since her marriage. The same was true of his father, who had no official ties to the Jewish faith of his family. Both Richard and Kare fit into the Booker family mode of believing in God, but not in organized religion.

Kare often said that Richard was like a saint, because he performed many operations for which he received no money and, unlike many surgeons, made a point of meeting and getting to know everyone he operated upon. "Richard is a rare modern surgeon with an empathic bedside manner," Kare liked to say.

More than three hundred people attended the wedding and reception afterward at the Fairmont Hotel.

"Surgeon Marries Angel of the Homeless," ran a headline in the *San Francisco Chronicle*. The article quoted Alonso Washington, who had told the reporter about Kare's work for him. The article also went into the Booker family history. Constance was quoted as saying she was delighted to have some Mediterranean blood in the family.

Jonathan Conrad Booker, my brainy son who would turn seventeen on December 29 and who was scheduled to enroll at the

University of California at Berkeley starting in the spring semester, got a bit tipsy at the reception and danced the whole evening, showing a side of his personality not seen before. Jonathan had grown to just over six feet but carried only 150 pounds on his slender and graceful frame. Jonathan had been offered a physics scholarship to Berkeley based on his perfect academic record at Lowell High School, but I turned the money down, saying it would be better spent on a student who could not otherwise pay.

"I think Richard Stein is brilliant," was Jonathan's summary judgment of Kare's new husband at the wedding reception "Not only that, but he is also quite charming with everyone he meets. It is going to be genetically fascinating to see what kind of offspring evolve."

Constance overheard Jonathan's remark and laughed heartily.

"Jonathan, darling, I always knew you had a way with words, but I never realized you danced so well," she said.

"That was really the first time I have done much dancing, but I have watched those old Fred Astaire movies," Jonathan smiled. "It was a lot of fun, more fun than I supposed, and several of the girls said I was very good."

Jonathan had not been involved with any one girl in high school, though many of his friends were girls. Watching him on the dance floor made me realize I needn't worry about Jonathan attracting girls and eventually a wife, but that was a long time down the road. Jonathan had his heart set on a doctorate in physics.

The Steins, the Bookers, and the Sutros all got on famously during what turned out to be a three-day celebration involving visits to the various family homes and including a lovely dinner at the Stein Vineyards, given the night before the rehearsal dinner.

Constance said she was so proud of the younger generation—Robyn and Arthur Butler, Joe III and Kathleen and their beautiful son, Joe IV; the wonderfully precocious Jonathan; and the newly married Kare and Richard.

"It is all so much more than I could ever have reasonably hoped for," Constance said to Richard Hamblen as they sat holding hands at the reception. "With Robyn pregnant and Kare married, I think everything is in place. We can just sit back and enjoy life; our job is done. The next important stop is to meet our maker."

"I think you are going to live to be one hundred," said Richard Hamblen.

"Only if you promise to keep me company," said Constance.

CHAPTER 105

The year 1999 was Bill Clinton's seventh in the White House. The federal budget deficit had disappeared, and the stock market, led by the Silicon Valley dot-coms, soared to new heights. But all the news was not good. In early February, Richard Hamblen, age eighty-eight, was diagnosed with an inoperable brain tumor. His death did not come until September, and it was an agonizing period during which Richard deteriorated to a point where he could no longer speak and his body became like a skeleton. His death was slow and agonizing and extremely painful to us all. My mother was by his side the whole time, fulfilling his wish to not die in a hospital. During this time, my mother began to look her age. During the last five months, Richard was attended to by a twenty-four-hour nursing service, but Mother was still virtually always there with him. Despite numerous invitations to stay overnight with family members, the hope being that getting away from Richard's depressing circumstances would do her good, Constance steadfastly refused.

"I wish I could understand why God allows these things to happen," my mother said to Karen one day. "There has been no more saintly person than Richard; why should he suffer so?"

Karen said that the Bible was full of stories about the sufferings of the just but that it was a side of God's provenance that was beyond her ability to comprehend.

"Maybe we will find out the answer when we leave this earth," Constance said.

The *Chronicle* published a 1,500-word obituary on Richard, and his funeral attracted more than a thousand people, including most of the city's legal community, plus leading politicians, including Mayor Willie Brown.

By Thanksgiving Day in 1999, my mother had returned to a semblance of her former self, thanks in part to a two-week trip in early November that she made to New York with her daughter-in-law, Claire Booker. The two widows stayed at the Plaza and attended nine different Broadway performances. Jim and Pamela insisted on hosting the Thanksgiving dinner that year, and all of the members of the immediate family attended, plus Adam and Lillian Sutro and their twin sons, Alan and Richard, eighteen, both in the midst of their freshman year at Stanford. The Sutro twins were on the smallish side, about five feet nine inches, but lean and confident, as befits heirs to serious money. They also had a ready sense of humor that they worked into most of their conversation, being a lot like their jovial late grandfather in that sense, and quite unlike their serious parents.

"Every other generation," Alan explained to Constance when she remarked on the personality resemblance to Conrad. "Dad is so serious he makes us want to change the subject."

"We have to try to be funny to keep Big Joe happy; he's almost a foot taller than we are," said Richard Sutro. "And it looks like Joe IV is going to be seven feet tall."

"Uncle Joe, is it true you have Junior enrolled in a basketball school for three-year-olds?" asked Alan, smiling.

"What do you boys want to be if you grow up?" Big Joe responded, putting his big hands on the twins' shoulders, towering a full head above them.

"Eight inches taller," laughed Richard.

The big news that Thanksgiving was that Kare was pregnant, with the baby expected in June. And just one month earlier, Kathleen had announced that she and Joe III were expecting their third child in May of 2000, thus fulfilling their plan to have three children. Joe IV was now three, and his sister, Kimberly, was fourteen months.

Robyn, who had given birth to Audrey Constance Butler on February 1, 1999, said that she hoped to have her second child sometime in late 2000; if it was a boy, she was going to name him after me, and if it was a girl, she planned to name her Claire, after her mother.

"Well, that certainly gives me something to live for," said Constance. "Imagine three great-grandchildren all born in the first year of the new century."

"I think it is wonderful," said Claire to Constance. "That will give you six great-grandchildren."

"It will also give you six grandchildren, Claire, and look at you—you don't look a day over fifty," smiled Constance.

The twins spent a lot of time talking with Jim about our father's World War II experiences and about brother Joe's fabulous basketball career at Stanford and his work as a foreign correspondent. Alan said he would like to be a writer like Joe Jr. Richard Sutro said he probably would go into the family business with Adam and Joe III.

"I'm glad to see boys have your serious side," said Jim.

"Did you know, Uncle Jim, that our cousin Jonathan over there is considered by some girls we know as the handsomest geek at Berkeley?"

Jim laughed. "Is that true, Jonathan?"

"I prefer to be known for scholastic achievement, which is something I am responsible for at this stage of my life," Jonathan said.

"Brains and looks are both gifts that people may or may not be born with," said Karen. "We all need to be grateful for whatever we are given and certainly not lord it over people who have less."

"Mother," said Jonathan, "all of us are created by virtue of a random selection of the gene pool, over which we have no control. But we do control what we do with our gifts, which can sometimes be a curse. I can tell you that it takes a lot of discipline to resist the kinds of temptations that are available on today's college campuses, even for geeks. I am fortunate that I love studying physics and that I have a friend who feels the same way."

"Who is she?" asked Jim.

"I didn't say it was a she, although it is: Thelma Rossiter," said Jonathan.

"Oh, you should have brought her," said Constance.

"Her family lives in Texas, and she is home for the holiday," Jonathan said, adding that Mr. Rossiter was a nuclear fuels expert who worked for NASA.

Jim told me late in the day that he would love to be around in 2050 to see how the Bookers had evolved by then. I said that would be the same as going back to 1949 and trying to figure out what was going to happen to us.

"We've been pretty lucky," said Jim. "I have a wife I am still deeply in love with, I am part of a great family, the adoption agency is flourishing, and thanks to you, I have been making much more off my investments than we are spending."

"We've been lucky, all right," I said.

Karen and I decided to visit a friend in Los Cabos, Mexico, during the first week of the year 2000. There had been numerous speculative reports that the turn of the century was going to create havoc with the world's computer systems and that the chaos would cause shutdowns of, among other things, the airline industry. Fortunately, it did not happen.

Jim Wiles, my longtime friend from San Jose State, together with his third and much younger wife, Jean, had purchased a huge house in Palmilla Norte, which was part of the Palmilla hotel and golf complex. The house overlooked a wide beach and the Sea of Cortez and totaled 7,800 square feet of enclosed space and another 5,000 feet of terraces and open patios. The furniture, the art, the views, and the gardens were all spectacular, the best that money could buy, which was no problem for Jim Wiles, who had just sold his twenty-one new-car dealerships in the San Francisco—San Jose area while retaining the real estate.

We had never been to Cabo before. Jim explained that the term Los Cabos referred to the southern cape of the Baja peninsula. He said that there were two towns twenty miles apart that served as bookends to the tourist area, connected by a four-lane highway off of which most of the beachfront hotels were located.

"Cabo has the best weather in the world," Jim said as he drove us from the San Jose del Cabo Airport, where we had flown nonstop from San Francisco. "Average rainfall is about three inches, and this time of year, the temperature is in the mid-seventies in the daytime and cools to the high fifties at night. We never use our air-conditioning, though if we came in the summer, we would have to. But between December and May, it is like this every day."

We watched the sunset while sipping drinks on a large terrace overlooking the water. The glow of the setting sun was well off to our right, which put me off a bit, because I was used to seeing the sun drop into the water.

"We are actually facing more eastward, toward the Sea of Cortez, but we still have the sunset from the mountains, which puts some dazzling colors in the sky, in the water, and on the hotel," said Jim.

Jim said he had bought the house three years earlier in what he described as a distress sale. His wife, Jean, an interior decorator, had spent a year furnishing the house and making some significant structural changes, including the removal of walls, which created a giant living and dining room that opened to a magnificent kitchen.

"This house feels so airy and open," said Karen.

"I hope the sound of the waves doesn't keep you awake at night," said Jim. Our bedroom was located on the first floor of the three-level house and had a lovely balcony. Slightly below it was a swimming pool. The beach was about fifty feet further down, and it was reachable by a wooden stairway that had a lockable gate at sand level.

We had dinner that night at the Palmilla Hotel, which was landscaped with thousands of well-watered palm trees and flowering plants. The hotel had been built in the 1950s on a spectacular point of rocky sea-front land.

"I had no idea this place even existed," I said to Jim over a dinner of freshly caught red snapper and lobster.

"More people are beginning to find out about it, especially with the building of the golf courses during the early 1990s," said Jim. "It was always known for its fishing. They catch more billfish here than anyplace else in the world. I caught and released a 145-pound marlin just last week, though I prefer to go after yellowtail and dolphin—not the mammals, the fish."

We spent a week with Jim and Jean, playing golf and fishing on alternate days. Karen and I liked the little town of San Jose del Cabo, only ten minutes away from Palmilla, where there were several good restaurants, art galleries, a lovely church, and the atmosphere of old Mexico. We liked much less the town of Cabo San Lucas, located twenty minutes away in the other direction, which dated from the 1950s and centered on a large marina; it was known for its bawdy nightlife and spring-break atmosphere. On the plus side, it did have a good movie complex and some excellent restaurants.

Jim anchored his forty-two-foot Bertram Sport Fisherman about a hundred yards offshore in front of his house. On days we went fishing, his mate would pick us up on the beach in a motorized dinghy and take us to the larger vessel, where the captain stood ready to begin the quest for fish. The Palmilla golf course, designed by Jack Nicklaus, was located a mile from Jim's house, on land that rose from the sea so that the water was visible on every hole. I enjoyed the fishing, but liked the golf even more. Jim said he was planning to join a new private club called Querencia, which was scheduled to open the next year on land adjacent to the Palmilla course. Jim said he and Jean spent about sixteen weeks a year in Cabo.

"Jean and I are about to buy a small art gallery, which will keep us busy when we are not fishing and playing golf or entertaining friends and family," said Jim. "I have four grown children from my first marriage, and they love to come here, and Jean has two teenaged boys who are in boarding school, and they come down at Christmas and Easter. Naturally, they love going to San Lucas. I hire a driver for them when they go—I want them to have fun, but I don't want to be worried about them."

"Jim, I have to salute you," I said. "It seems as though you have your life magnificently organized. But there is something I want to propose to you when you come back in April. I would tell you now what I am thinking about, but I have a lot of work to do first. I am planning to retire next month, and I am going to have the time to work out details of a project that I think you will find interesting."

"I'll be glad to listen to anything you have to say, Danny, my friend," Jim replied. "And I am going to be on the lookout for a house in this neighborhood for you and Karen. At our age, who needs those rainy San Francisco winters when there is perfect weather every day right here in Los Cabos?"

CHAPTER 106

I, Daniel Booker, age sixty-four, officially retired on February 28, 2000. There were several reasons. One, I did not like the outlook for the stock market and thought a significant correction was looming. Second, I was tired of getting up at 5:00 AM every working day and wanted to play more golf, travel, and just enjoy myself without having to worry about the stock portfolios of more than two hundred mostly serious investors. Third, I had all of the money I could ever possibly need, in all about $15 million. I know baseball players can make that much in a year, but the reality is that it is an insanely large amount of money for a person like me who does not indulge in lavish living or spending, though I live quite well. Fourth, I wanted to pursue some "giving back" the way my brother Jim and his wife had done with their adoption agency.

My idea for helping others stemmed from my own experience in life. I was a lousy student in school, but I still got into college and ultimately learned that most people succeed through hard work and focus rather than innate brilliance. I knew a lot of people at San Jose State who ultimately became hugely successful, though you never would have guessed it when they were students.

What I proposed to do was establish a foundation that would grant scholarships to junior college students who were seeking either a four-year university degree or a graduate diploma. Youngsters in California went to junior college for two basic reasons: they did not have the grades to get into a four-year college, or they did not have the money—and oftentimes they had neither. Basically, I wanted to help the late bloomers who needed financial assistance and who could demonstrate the kind of resolve necessary to succeed.

I bounced my idea off of the registrars at both San Jose State and the University of San Francisco. Each said they had scores of applicants from junior colleges, many of whom were financially needy. I asked if they would be interested in submitting the names of applicants for a scholarship, and they replied that they would prefer to just notify the students that scholarship money was available and give them application forms. I will spare the readers further details, but it took me six months to put the program together and grant ten scholarships for the fall semester of 2000. The Late Bloomers Foundation was initially funded with $3 million of my money plus another $11 million that Karen and I raised from our family and friends. My friend Jim Wiles matched my $3 million, and my mother gave $2 million. Interestingly, I sold shares in several dot-com stocks to make my donation, shares that were worth less than $1 million by the start of 2001 following the dot-com market crash. The bottom line was that I in effect made a profit in giving the money away because of the tax deduction gained from the gift. Go figure!

For the 2001 fall semester, the Late Bloomers Foundation received 348 applications from junior college graduates who were seeking entrance to the San Francisco Bay Area's major four-year colleges, including Stanford University and the University of California. In all, forty full scholarships were awarded at a cost of just over $1 million. Of those forty students, six were black, six were Hispanic, eight were Asian, and twenty were white. Thirty-two were males, and I can't explain that other than to say that 74 percent of the applicants were males. Maybe women don't regard themselves as late bloomers! I met most of the successful candidates and tried to see them again after their first year. Jim Wiles was a hugely energetic participant in the interview process, and I must say I found it stimulating to work with him and could easily see how he had amassed his millions in the car business. My wife, Karen, also became deeply involved, and she was quite vociferous about the need to give more scholarships to females. Of course, one of the key functions was to invest the foundation's money so that further funding would not be necessary to maintain the program. That was my job.

Timothy Johnson from Burlingame was one of the first to be awarded a Late Bloomer scholarship. Tim had been a football star at Burlingame High during his sophomore and junior years and had been considered a shoo-in for a football scholarship to a Pacific Coast Conference university, most likely one of the schools in Oregon or Washington, because his grades in school were less than sparkling. But Johnson's football career ended when he suffered a knee injury that surgery only marginally improved. Johnson, an only child who was raised by his mother and who had never met his father, was devastated that he could no longer play football. After graduation, Johnson enrolled at San Mateo Junior College and continued to live at home while working part-time at a McDonald's restaurant where he flipped hamburgers on weekends. Johnson's mother worked as a ticketing agent for United Airlines at nearby San Francisco International Airport. She wanted Timothy to get a four-year-college diploma but did not have the means to finance it. Johnson, who had been at best a C student in high school, began to take his studies more seriously in junior college, where he became a manager of the football team, whose coach, Bob Kilmer, took a liking to Johnson and became a mentor to the once-promising football player.

Kilmer was impressed by Johnson's work ethic and resiliency and suggested he try to get into the University of California upon completing his two years at San Mateo JC. Johnson said there was no way he could afford Berkeley and no way he could get a scholarship, because he was not an A student. Kilmer said he had read a story in the *San Francisco Chronicle* about the newly started Late Bloomers Foundation, which he said seemed to be created for people like Timothy Johnson. Kilmer urged Johnson to apply for admission to Berkeley and three other four-year colleges and said that he would seek more information on the Late Bloomers Foundation.

At that point, the foundation consisted of just my secretary and me, so when Kilmer telephoned, he spoke with me. I was impressed that Kilmer would be going to such trouble to help his team manager, who he said had a talent for management and dealing with people and who wanted to get a degree in business. I agreed to interview Johnson and came away tremendously impressed with his maturity and seriousness about seeking to become an executive in a large corporation. He said he had wasted his first twelve years in school and only began to understand what life was really all about after his football career ended.

"I was a big easygoing dude who had it made and who suddenly became just another washed-up black athlete," Johnson told me. "Thanks to my mother and Coach Kilmer, I realized I had the intelligence to make something of myself if I worked at it. I was a somebody once, and I want to be a somebody again."

After meeting Johnson, I called the registrar at Berkeley and told her that the Late Bloomers Foundation had voted to give Timothy Johnson a scholarship for any of the four-year schools that would accept him but that his first choice was the University of California. Two weeks later, I was elated to hear from Johnson that he had just received his letter of acceptance from Berkeley. Karen and I could not have been happier for Timothy if he was our own son. We had a lovely dinner with Timothy and his mom, and I came away feeling that launching the Late Bloomers Foundation was perhaps the best thing Karen and I had ever done.

George W. Bush narrowly defeated Al Gore in the 2000 presidential election. Like most of my family, I voted for Bush, though I can't say that any of us particularly liked him. His Texas twang and strange facial expressions caused me discomfort. When the attack on the World Trade Center took place on September 11, 2001, Bush displayed some impressive leadership, and his popularity soared for a time. There were two things about him that I respected. First and foremost was his wife Laura, who would have made a great daughter-in-law in the Booker family. Second, I was tremendously impressed by Bush's decision to quit drinking. Had he not made that decision, by all accounts his marriage would have failed, and he never would have been elected president. Of course, some might argue it was too bad George gave up the booze. If he hadn't, his brother Jeb might have been elected instead!

I have said several times in these pages that I seriously doubt I ever would have won Karen if I hadn't given up alcohol the year before we met. I was forty-four when we married, and she was thirty, though at that time I was in better shape for my age than she was for hers. Alas, as I celebrated by sixty-sixth birthday in June of 2001, that was no longer the case. In our twenty-two years of marriage, Karen had aged only about fifteen years in her appearance, and people often said she appeared to be in her mid-forties rather than her early fifties. In my case, I seldom heard anyone guess that I was younger than my age, and most people did not bring up the subject. I think all those mornings getting up before dawn had taken their toll. Clearly, I had sacrificed my beauty sleep in quest of the mighty dollar.

After my retirement, I easily fell into the habit of sleeping until 7:00 AM, often getting more than eight hours of sleep. What surprised me about retirement was how little I missed my work. I found that I transitioned smoothly into doing exactly what I wanted and was seldom at a loss for something to do, whether it was reading, playing a golf game, or working for the Late Bloomers Foundation. I also was able to spend a lot more time with Karen, Jonathan, my mother, and other family members.

It was nice to have leisurely lunches at Fisherman's Wharf or the Cliff House, followed by long walks along the water. San Francisco is a great walking city, and Karen and I systematically attempted to cover every corner, including all of the hills and neighborhoods. Those walks, plus my three or so rounds of golf per week, constituted my exercise program. When Jim and I met for lunch in Palo Alto, as we usually did about once a month, we would follow the meal with a long walk on the Stanford campus or in downtown Palo Alto along University Avenue. When we spent the weekend at the family cottage at Pebble Beach, we walked a minimum of two hours a day, not counting golf.

Usually, the walks were accompanied by some spirited conversation, and I considered myself pretty well informed by virtue of the availability of cable news, which really came into its own starting in the 1990s. I loved Fox News but dutifully watched the more liberal CNN and CNBC as well to make sure I had all points of view. The attack on the World Trade Center and the subsequent invasions of Afghanistan and Iraq provided alternately horrifying and riveting news coverage that kept me and millions of others glued to our screens.

The advent of the Internet and its many refinements also had life-changing impact. I managed all of my stock market investments on my laptop computer, which I also used to do company research that gave me the information I needed to decide whether to buy or sell stocks. E-mail had replaced about half my phone conversations, and it was a marvelously efficient way to keep in contact with literally scores of friends. I also used a cell phone, but mostly to receive phone calls from my mother or other relatives. I was not a big cell phone fan, but I could appreciate its usefulness, particularly for those still in life's fast lane, which I was definitely not.

My mother was spending most of her time with Claire and the grandchildren in the first years of this new century and was attuned to the events of the world. She remained an avid San Francisco Giants fan and was in love with PacBell Park, where Barry Bonds was putting on the greatest home-run display ever, ending the 2001 season with an all-time record of seventy-three. Karen and I took Mother and Claire to at least five games in 2001, and it was easily the most exciting season in San Francisco history. We did not know for sure (though we guessed it) that Barry was loading up on a medley of steroids and hormones that had transformed him into an incredible hulk. That my mother, at eighty-seven, could be excited about the outcome of all 162 regular-season Giant games was an inspiration that made me feel she would easily make it to one hundred, which gave hope to my goal of achieving four score and ten.

Alas, it was not to be. In December of 2001, my mother told me that an X-ray had revealed a tiny but suspicious spot on her lung. A biopsy revealed the spot to be malignant, but not immediately life-threatening. Doctors recommended radiation therapy rather than surgery because of the belief it would be a lot easier considering her age.

Meanwhile, I began to feel oddly fatigued starting in January of 2002 and was amazed when my doctor told me I was suffering from second-degree heart block, for which he recommended an artificial pacemaker. He said the problem was that the electronic signal from the upper chamber of my heart to the lower chamber was not getting through on a regular basis. This was resulting in a delayed heartbeat. If the situation exacerbated to a complete heart block, my doctor said one of the possible consequences would be a heart stoppage and death.

On that cheery note, I agreed to have an artificial pacemaker implanted just below my left collarbone, a procedure that required one hour to perform plus two days of hospitalization. What had caused my heart block? The doctor said there was no way of knowing, though he did say that it was fairly common among trained athletes. I liked that explanation. I learned that pacemakers last five years and longer, and over time, I became scarcely aware that I had one. There is no certainty that my second-degree heart block would have led to a heart stoppage, but putting in a pacemaker seemed like a sensible move that, as I write this in 2006, I now know was indeed the right move.

Life is nothing if it is not ironic. Not long after I had started thinking that Mom would live to be one hundred and that I could reach ninety, we both came down with conditions that were life-threatening. In my case, the situation became more complicated when a biopsy revealed that I had prostate cancer. Unfortunately, there is no easy quick fix for prostate cancer as there was for my heart block. My urologist recommended that I either have a radioactive seed implantation that would kill the prostate and the cancer therein, or take external beam radiation over eight weeks, which would produce the same results. Some of the possible side effects to these two treatments included incontinence, impotence, and fecal incontinence (though rare), plus a number of other nasty consequences.

I spent months searching the Internet and reading about prostate cancer and in the end decided to try to deal with it through diet and exercise plus the power of positive thinking. Thus, I opted for what is known as "watchful waiting." In other words, I would not seek any treatment until my prostate cancer had clearly gotten worse, evidence of which would be a rising Prostate Specific Antigen test score or physical evidence determined by my doctor during a quarterly digital rectal examination of my prostate.

Karen thought I should opt for the treatment and get it over with.

"Honey," she said, "you could be like the guy jumping from the top of a ninety-floor building who was asked how he felt as he passed the fortieth floor. 'I don't feel a thing,' he answered." She later admitted she had not made that up but had read it on the Web in an article citing the dangers of putting off prostate cancer treatment.

"Look," I said, "about 230,000 Americans are diagnosed with prostate cancer every year, and only about 30,000 die. Most people with prostate cancer die of something else, and there are a lot of people who believe that a lot of the treatments for prostate cancer are not only unnecessary, but even harmful."

"I think you are in denial," said Karen. "There are a lot of people out there who are alive today because they were smart enough to get treatment."

CHAPTER 107

Learning to live in the present is a great suggestion but sometimes hard to do. I always loved a particular line from the *Gone with the Wind* heroine, Scarlet O'Hara: "I'll worry about that tomorrow." Scarlet was not one to let looming problems ruin her day. My mother was like that.

"The doctor says I have a very small tumor on my lung and that he is going to zap it right out of existence, so I am not going to even think about it," she told me the day before her radiation treatments were about to begin. "I'm going to savor every moment."

Mom's zapping program called for treatments five days a week for six weeks. Her attitude was such that she viewed her painless fifteen- to twenty-minute treatment sessions as a pleasant part of the day, getting her out of the house so that she could chat with the nurses and the technicians, spreading her special brand of charm. Karen or Claire usually accompanied Constance on her daily visit, and they all agreed that I should be getting similar treatment for my prostate cancer.

"I feel a bit tired most afternoons," my mother told me three weeks after the start of her treatment. "But other than that, I feel completely normal. Danny, you should really do something."

I replied that there was a big difference between lung cancer and prostate cancer, the former being much more deadly. Second, I said, the side effects from treatments were pretty unpleasant, whether it was internal beam radiation or implanting radioactive seeds.

"I guess I know better than to argue with you, Danny, but you could spend more time listening to your wife," my mother replied.

"I've talked to a number of people who had seed implants and external beam radiation, and they have told me that if they had to do it over again, they might be more prone to consider watchful waiting. I took that to mean that they were suffering from side effects, namely incontinence and impotence. My rationalization is that since prostate cancer kills only about 15 percent of the people who get it, there is an 85 percent chance it won't kill me. Even so, if my PSA score goes up, if it doubles, then I am going to do something. My last three PSA scores have been up only a little bit."

"Well, if a positive attitude counts, I am sure you are going to do just fine, Danny," said my mother.

Jim Wiles telephoned me in late April of 2002 to say that there was a house on the water near his own home in Palmilla Norte that could be bought for $1.1 million, because the owner had suffered severe losses in the stock market and needed the money immediately. Real estate sales in Cabo had softened considerably in the wake of the World Trade Center destruction. The seller, who had listed the house with a broker, had retained the right to sell the house himself if he found a buyer. Jim said if I bought directly from the owner, there would be no real estate commission. So Karen and I flew to Los Cabos the next week.

The beautifully furnished house was on direct waterfront, about fifty feet above the beach. It had five bedrooms, was about 4,500 square feet under roof, and had the same airy feeling we loved in Jim Wiles's house, though it was not nearly so grand. Jim said he thought that the house in normal times would be worth $1.8 million and that it represented a fabulous long-term investment that we could rent out when we were not using it. Jim's enthusiasm was contagious. We bought. I jestingly told my wife that we were now Karen and Dan Booker of San Francisco, Pebble Beach, and Los Cabos, Mexico—just like old money! Actually, Mother was the sole owner of the house at Pebble Beach, but we used it more than anyone else, and her will stipulated it would go to Jim and me. I should note that most of Mom's money was to be put into trust funds for her grandchildren and great-grandchildren, which was fine with both Jim and me. We had all of the money we needed. Mother was giving her Pacific Heights flat to Claire, who had been sharing that opulent space with Mom since Richard Hamblen's death.

As I reflected on the financial condition of the Bookers, I realized how fortunate we were in comparison with average people who struggle to make house payments, pay credit card bills with their outrageous interest rates, and pay taxes and then deal too with the rising cost of living. When we were kids during the war, average people seemed to live much better than today. Of course, our expectations were no doubt lower. Money has never been a problem for any members of the Booker family in my lifetime. I don't think many families can say that. I think all of us have used our money wisely. Mom has given millions to the homeless and other charities, and Jim and Pamela have done the same with their adoption agency. Karen and I both feel good about our Late Bloomers Foundation. I can only hope that the next generation of Bookers will be as fortunate, that they will be responsible with their trust funds, that they will adopt the notion of giving back as a key part of their lives. I know that research shows that third-generation offspring tend to squander family wealth, but our son Jonathan is definitely not in that mode. He cares only about his studies and is openly disdainful of excessive spending, though he loves Pebble Beach and our flat on Telegraph Hill. He knows that I bought it for under $40,000 and that by 2002 it was worth more than $2 million.

"It helps being lucky, Dad," Jonathan commented when we were discussing the tremendous appreciation in the value of northern California real estate. "I don't think young people today will be so fortunate as you and Uncle Jim."

"I'll take luck over skill anytime," I smiled.

"Well, if you want to deal in clichés, a rising tide lifts all boats, but it also lowers them when it recedes," Jonathan said. "Wasn't the depression of the 1930s an example of what could happen again?"

"Ever since I was a kid, Jonathan, what I have heard is that economists learned from that experience, so another depression with the same severity of the 1930s is highly unlikely," I said. "And so far, that prediction has been right; we have not had another depression in more than sixty years."

"Well, it could happen, just as Earth almost certainly will have another ice age," Jonathan replied. "At the same time, the problem with global warming is even more serious than a lot of people believe. If all of Earth's polar ice were to melt, the level of water in the oceans would rise by almost two hundred feet. That would put a lot of San Francisco underwater.

"Most people don't properly appreciate the present era of tranquility we are enjoying here on Earth," Jonathan continued. "The earth is more than four billion years old, and much of that time, it has been completely frozen over or else so hot and dry that it was an arid wasteland uninhabitable for creatures like man. Earth and its climate are constantly changing, and sometimes these changes happen almost overnight. One of my professors thinks that global warming could cause the oceans to rise up to twenty feet in just a matter of a few years."

"I just hope you and your generation are as fortunate as mine has been," I said. "I have believed all of my adult life that those of us born in the 1930s have been the most fortunate in American history."

"The only guarantee for my generation is that there will be surprises and challenges that will have incredible significance we can't even imagine today," said Jonathan.

"The only certainties are death and taxes," I smiled.

"You and your clichés, Dad. I can give some scenarios in which neither would be inevitable," said Jonathan. "Man could learn to live forever, or the earth could be completely destroyed, meaning no more taxes. Both scenarios are entirely possible, and I can show you why."

"Jonathan, I am sure you are right, but just for now, I want to be in the now and not worry about the future," I said.

I love talking with Jonathan. He might jump all over the lot with his vast knowledge of so many subjects, but his conversation is never mundane and always challenging. By the way, he really believes that man will learn to live forever, and he thinks the subject is worthy of his first book. He also believes that at some point in the future, maybe many millions of years hence, the earth would be destroyed.

"That is why God has given us so much room out there—so we will have someplace to go when man has to leave this earth," Jonathan said. "By that time, man will have developed and evolved to the point where each individual has a mental capacity millions of times greater than we have today. Granted, it will take thousands and thousands of years to develop, but we are already moving in that direction."

"You make it sound as if man will be as powerful as God," I said.

"That is a good analogy, but I think you probably underestimate the power of our creator," Jonathan replied.

"Do you still think there is life after death?" I asked.

"Grandmother will know the answer to that sooner than any of us," he answered.

I told my mother about my conversation with Jonathan and about his views on life and where mankind was heading.

"He certainly is a remarkable young man," Constance said. "I wonder what he will be like when he is my age? For that matter, I wonder what the world will be like by the year 2075. People then may look upon our times as a golden era, a simpler time, much the way we look back at the start of the twentieth century. But, you know, Danny, I really have never given much serious thought to the future. I don't think many of my contemporaries have either. We have spent our lives raising families, dealing with life one day at a time, trying to do our best, helping, and trying to spread a little happiness."

"What would you change in your life if you had a chance to live it over again?" I asked.

My mother paused. Her wrinkled face had a pleasant expression as she turned her mind to the question. There was a full minute of silence before she said, "I don't think I would change a minute of it, in spite of my many mistakes. I have been blessed from the start, and what happened in my life, good and bad, was God's will, and I will always be grateful."

In the last year of her life, Mom found her greatest joy was being with her great-grandchildren. They instinctively loved her for her happy spirit and the special surprises that she planned for every visit, sometimes just an inexpensive toy, an article of clothing, a game, or a book that she would read to them.

"Oh, I have so much fun with those kids," she told me time and again.

My mother lived until June 12, 2003. She died at age eighty-nine from complications of a staph infection that she had contracted in a hospital where she was being treated for pneumonia.

Only Claire was with her when she died at 4:15 AM. Doctors had fully expected she would pull through, and hence there was no bedside vigil, as would have been the case if any of us thought the end was near. Karen and I had visited her the previous evening, and she had seemed in good spirits, though she looked tired and spoke slowly. She wanted to know how many scholarships we expected to grant through the Late Bloomers Foundation for the upcoming school year. She was pleased when I told her more than 120.

"That is wonderful," she said. "You know, I am leaving some money for your foundation in my will."

"Can't you give it to us now? We don't want to wait that long," I smiled.

My mother laughed. "What if I agree to a five-year limitation?"

"That would be better than waiting until you are 105," I smiled.

"I suppose that could happen, but sometimes I feel I could drop off at any time," my mother said. "I am ready. I think I have finished everything."

Claire said that she had been dozing in a chair next to my mother's bed when she was awakened by the sounds of Mother talking in her sleep. She said she could not at first make out what Mother was saying. Claire looked at her watch. It was almost 4:15 AM.

Claire said my mother had a peaceful look on her pale face. Her eyes were closed when suddenly she broke into a smile. Her last words were "Dad, it is so beautiful."

CHAPTER 108

There was considerable discussion among the family about the last words of Constance Elizabeth Connors Booker Sutro. What was she seeing when she said, "Dad, it is so beautiful"?

I said the obvious interpretation was that she had seen her father, who was welcoming her to the Promised Land. Jonathan said that although that may have been the case, the vision could also have been an automatic chemical reaction in the brain.

"There have been thousands of instances of people near death who upon recovery report having seen a heaven-like environment that they felt they were floating into," said Jonathan. "Many said that it was so beautiful they wanted to stay and that death was indeed a very pleasant experience. They also often mention being greeted by deceased loved ones. Although some say these experiences constitute proof of an afterlife, most scientists believe these visions are caused by the brain, in effect, a built-in soft landing to death."

Claire said regardless of what was right, there was no debating that mother had had a pleasant death and that she had been ready to go on to the next experience, whatever that may be.

"Constance died as she lived, a very happy person," said Claire. "She was easily the most remarkable person I have ever met."

Had Mom died twenty years sooner, no doubt a thousand people would have come to her funeral. But she had outlived most of her friends and contemporaries. As it was, more than four hundred came to Grace Cathedral for her final rites. Jim and I gave eulogies to our mother, both of which were upbeat, stressing the positive and celebrating her long and productive life. Jim recounted the time in 1947 when Mother and her dog had saved a young woman in Golden Gate Park from two rapists, attacking them with one of Dad's old swagger sticks, which combined with a fearless assault by Skippy the dog to drive them off.

"Although our mom was always a gentle person, she was fearless when it came to doing the right thing," said Jim.

"I'll vouch for that," said a voice from the back of the church. Everyone turned around and noticed a gray-haired elderly woman standing with a quite serious look on her face.

"I was the young woman your mother saved that day," said the woman, who identified herself as Linda Wright. "Your mother risked her life for me. I don't think there are many women who would be brave enough to do what she did."

Someone started clapping, and everyone in the church stood up, seemingly to salute Linda Wright, but in reality, I think they were applauding my mom's heroism.

Jim thanked Linda and said he hoped to talk with her afterward.

"I once made a serious mistake in high school," said Jim. "My mother was so angry with me that I can still feel her wrath almost fifty years later," Jim said. "My mom hadn't only physical courage, but also the courage of her convictions and a keen sense of right and wrong. I did not naturally or immediately come to accept all that she believed, but I do today, and I think she provided a moral compass that regrettably has fallen out of fashion in today's world. To be around my mother was always an uplifting experience. She always appeared to be in a good mood, and she was always optimistic, and she always wanted to know how you were feeling, what you were doing. She was always full of praise and appreciation. She was that way with everyone, not just her family and close friends."

When I took the podium to speak, I said I could feel my mother's presence.

"I can almost hear her saying, 'Danny, stand up straight; you are slouching.' The reason I can hear her saying that is she told me that all of my life. My posture was one of her few failures: 'Why can't you stand up straight like your brothers? They have perfect posture.' Of course, Mom knew that I always had self-esteem problems—who wouldn't with two perfect brothers—and I have to say that she did her best, whenever I saw her, to make me feel good about myself. Mom, how is my posture now?" I jested, stretching into my best upright position. Everyone laughed.

I said the best evidence of my mother's success in life was what she had left behind. I then mentioned by name her four grandchildren, the three spouses, and the six great-grandchildren. I asked them all to rise from their front-row seats. The crowd applauded enthusiastically.

"The genes of Constance Booker Sutro are alive and well in the twenty-first century," I said. "May she never be forgotten."

By far the most powerful eulogy came from Alonso Washington, the onetime street bum who had become the founder of the Washington Center, famous for feeding the homeless and providing them inspiration.

"It is wonderful to hear Jim and Danny talk so lovingly and so respectfully about their beloved mother," he began, speaking in a soft, clear voice that belied his tall and bulky frame. "I am honored to be here in this fine church to speak about a person who changed my life and also the lives of thousands of others.

"It was twenty-seven years ago that I encountered Constance Sutro. She and her husband were climbing up Nob Hill. You have all heard the famous Martin Luther King speech, when he said he had been to the mountain. Well, in 1976, I was deep in the valley, so close to the bottom that the next stop was hell. Because of alcohol, I had lost my job. I was in and out of jail in Atlanta, and I thought I would turn over a new leaf by moving to San Francisco. The only trouble was that I brought me with me. I was still the same drunk in San Francisco that I had been in Atlanta. I was bitter and nasty, and I hated people who were well-off and hated people who were white, and above all, though I did not really know it then, I hated myself. I tried to rob Mr. and Mrs. Sutro, smashing a bottle over Mr. Sutro's head when he fought back thinking I was going to attack his wife. I was bending over his body to take his wallet when Mrs. Sutro caught me by surprise and pushed me sideways on the steep hill over her husband's body. My head hit the pavement, and I was dazed for a moment. Mrs. Sutro rushed into the street and stopped a car. Two men were getting out. I ran down the hill.

"Two weeks later, I was put into a police lineup, and the Sutros identified me as their attacker. Then a funny thing happened. To this day, I don't know what caused me to do it. It was at the preliminary hearing on the robbery and assault charges against me. I saw Mrs. Sutro sitting in the front row of the courtroom. She looked at me, and for a second, I felt our souls were communicating. I can't believe what I did. I mouthed 'I'm sorry.' She sort of nodded back with a faint smile on her face.

"I ended up being sentenced to six months in the county jail after a plea bargain. There was no trial. In my first week in jail, Mrs. Sutro came to visit me. She said that she was touched that I had apologized and that it seemed to her that anyone who would do that probably had a lot of good in him. She wanted to know all about me, and I told her that I had begun drinking out of control when my wife took up with other men while I was away driving long-haul truck routes. I told her about my drunk-driving arrests. About drunk and disorderly conduct arrests. About losing my job. About being in jail. About what I was thinking when I tried to rob her and her husband. I told her what I was like as a kid. She listened to every word I said.

"She visited me a second time and a third time, and then just before I was going to be released, she asked me if I would be interested in doing some part-time maintenance work on homes in Pacific Heights, for herself and for people who were friends of hers.

She said the only stipulation was that I had to join Alcoholics Anonymous. She said she felt we had become friends, and she trusted me. She said she wanted me to regain my life. She said I was still young and that she believed God had something He wanted me to do. Can you imagine what I felt like? I felt like I had met my guardian angel in the form of a beautiful white-haired lady. Someone who cared for me, who had love for all mankind in her heart, and who was not like anyone I had ever met.

"Today, thanks to Mrs. Sutro, I can say I have not had a drink in twenty-seven years. I have a wife and four children. Mr. and Mrs. Sutro came to my wedding. Ten years ago, thanks for the moral and financial support from Mrs. Sutro, I founded the Washington Center to care for the homeless. I wanted to call it the Sutro Center, but Mrs. Sutro said I had come up with the idea and had done all of the work, so it should be named after me.

"I consider Mrs. Sutro the best friend I ever had. I truly think that if God has angels on earth, Mrs. Sutro was one of them. I am sure as we gather here to celebrate her life, God has a smile on his face, because Mrs. Sutro is back home."

Alonso Washington's stirring remarks brought down the house, the applause lasting more than three minutes.

After the funeral, about one hundred people were invited to the Sutro mansion for a reception hosted by Adam and Lillian Sutro. It was the only place big enough, and truth be known, we all regarded Adam as one of the family, just as he regarded Mom as more than just his onetime stepmother. Oddly, though I felt a great sadness that Mother was gone, the occasion itself was not inherently sad; in fact, most people were smiling, saying what a spectacular person mother had been and what a worthy life she had lived. As I looked at the grandchildren and the great-grandchildren, it struck me that the torch had indeed been passed. I suddenly realized that it was the first Booker family event that I had ever attended where I was the oldest person there. Of course, I quickly reminded myself that if I lived as long as Mother, I had another twenty years to go!

"Danny, your family has been a matriarchy for a very long time," said Karen. "Now you are the patriarch, and Jimmy is your first deputy."

"What does that mean in your eyes?" I asked her.

"I think it means that we have to do the things your mother did to keep the family close, just the way we have been, getting everyone together on holidays, remembering birthdays, talking on the phone, e-mailing—really, I think we have to work at it. I think what makes the Bookers special is that family and character do matter. Having good role models is critical for the younger ones."

"I never looked at it as work; it was just what we always did," I said.

"Well, I had many conversations with your mother about this, and she regarded maintaining a close-knit family a necessary function of being a mother," said Karen. "She said if you don't work at it, it doesn't happen."

Just then, Linda Wright came over.

"I liked your remarks about your mother," she said. "May I add that I have met most of the younger members of your family, and they certainly are an impressive lot. You are quite lucky, but I guess you know that. I was never able to have children, but I worked forty years counseling rape victims, and I got a lot of satisfaction out of that."

Alonso Washington joined the conversation.

"That was quite dramatic the way you stood up during the services," Alonso said to Linda. "Mrs. Sutro was a guardian angel for a lot of people."

Adam Sutro came by and pulled Alonso aside.

"Here's my card—let me know if you ever need anything," Adam said. "Can you come with me? I want to introduce you to my wife and twin sons. I think it would be good for them to meet you."

Alonso waved back at us as he was led away.

"He is a man of formidable character," said our son, Jonathan, who had his girlfriend, Thelma Rossiter, on his arm.

"I think it is wonderful that your mother agreed to let Jonathan take a tissue sample for her DNA," Thelma said to me.

I looked surprised.

"Dad, it is for down the road," Jonathan explained. "Maybe someday they can use it to replicate Grandmother Constance."

Karen and I looked at each other and laughed. We were both delighted that Jonathan had found a brainy and highly compatible soul mate, perhaps a lifetime keeper!

"Stand up straight, Uncle Danny; you are slouching," said Kare, pinching my waist from behind with both hands. She let out a big laugh, much the way my mother used to do.

"You not only need to stand up straighter; you also need to lose some weight," said Robyn, patting me on the stomach. Kare and Robyn, both at the height of their beauty, stood together laughing and smiling sweetly.

Karen put her arm around me and said, "I'm going to start getting him back into shape, starting tomorrow. He's promised me he is going to write a book about the Booker family."

ACKNOWLEDGMENTS

Although I always hoped I would one day get around to writing a fictionalized version of my experiences in life, real and imagined, it never would have happened were it not for the encouragement and support I have received from family and friends. I began this book in January of 2005 with the notion that I would produce two or three chapters a week, each averaging 1,500 to 2,000 words.

After the third week, I realized that I could not work in a vacuum and that I needed some feedback. I enlisted Maureen Becker, my wife of forty-five years and an avid fan of Edith Wharton, to read each chapter as it came out of my computer and let me know what she thought. I also added to the list of instant reviewers my former administrative assistant, Estelle Baron, and a Greenwich neighbor and close family friend, Maureen Blum.

Over the next fourteen months, these three lovely ladies read and reacted to every chapter. If I lagged in my production, Estelle might query as to whether I had run out of energy, the answer to which was an "of course not" followed by a fresh chapter. Being inherently lazy, I had unwittingly overcome that weakness by setting up for myself the kind of deadline pressure I knew from the news business! Having bragged that I would start and finish a book, I could not relent.

Maureen Blum also provided critical computer expertise that greatly aided in the book's production. So did Ed Keith, a genius and a golfing pal of mine who winters in Los Cabos, Mexico.

Once the first draft was finished, an old friend and retired professor of English at Dartmouth, William Spengemann, volunteered to do a critique. I was elated when he said he had read the book in three sittings and did so avidly and "with pleasure." He also gave me twenty handwritten pages of suggestions, many of which were implemented and for which I am most grateful, not only to Bill, but also to his wife, Sycha, who said she loved reading the book.

Albert Kaff, one of my former bosses at United Press International and a veteran foreign correspondent, now retired, also read the completed manuscript, catching a few errors and generally encouraging me to seek a publisher. Enthusiastic support also came from my sister, Gayle Becker, and Susan Edmonds, a longtime friend. I am also grateful to three college pals—Dick Bender, Martin Connelly, and Douglas Walker—who provided a variety of input. Others whose help and encouragement kept me going included my two sons, Jim and Brian; my brother, Bob; and Tony Carpenter, another golfing buddy. Don Wade, a successful author, was helpful in my finding a publisher. I am also grateful to Google and the World Wide Web, which make research today a piece of cake. And I thank the San Francisco Public Library for coming through where the Internet failed. Finally I wish to commend my editor at iUniverse for a thoroughly splendid job in polishing the final manuscript.

Writing a book is great fun. I recommend it to all!

Don C. Becker, January 2007

978-0-595-41267-9
0-595-41267-X

Printed in the United States
79363LV00001B/1-42

9 780595 412679